Stanley Lane-Poole

The Life of the Right Honourable Stratford Canning

Stanley Lane-Poole

The Life of the Right Honourable Stratford Canning

ISBN/EAN: 9783337403966

Printed in Europe, USA, Canada, Australia, Japan

Cover: Foto ©Raphael Reischuk / pixelio.de

More available books at **www.hansebooks.com**

VISCOUNT

STRATFORD DE REDCLIFFE

VOL. II.

THE LIFE

OF THE RIGHT HONOURABLE

STRATFORD CANNING

VISCOUNT STRATFORD DE REDCLIFFE

K.G. G.C.B. D.C.L. LL.D. &c.

FROM HIS MEMOIRS AND PRIVATE AND OFFICIAL PAPERS

BY

STANLEY LANE-POOLE

With Three Portraits

IN TWO VOLUMES : VOL. II.

CONTENTS

OF

THE SECOND VOLUME.

———•◦•———

CHAPTER XV.

CHAPTER XVI.

CHAPTER XVII.

CHAPTER XVIII.

CHAPTER XIX.

CHAPTER XXII.

CHAPTER XXIII.

CHAPTER XXVI.

CHAPTER XXVII.

CHAPTER XXVIII.

CHAPTER XXIX.

CHAPTER XXX.

CHAPTER XXXI.

CHAPTER XXXII.

PORTRAIT.

LIFE

OF

STRATFORD CANNING,

VISCOUNT STRATFORD DE REDCLIFFE

———•◦•———

CHAPTER XV.

THE HOUSE OF COMMONS.

1828 32.

THE official life of Stratford Canning falls into two well-marked divisions. From the age of twenty to forty-two he was with but one considerable respite almost continuously engaged in diplomatic service. Then from the early part of 1829 to the close of 1841, with the exception of two brief special missions, he disappeared from the world of embassies and despatches. Then again from the beginning of 1842 to 1858 he was seldom absent for many months from the Porte. The first diplomatic period, 1807 to 1828, (with an appendix in 1832,) comprised miscellaneous missions in different parts of the globe, unconnected by any fixed purpose, unless it were that of being quit of diplomacy at the first honourable opportunity. During this period Canning felt no special tie, no compelling sense of duty, towards any one Court or State. It was different with the second period, when he returned again and again to the city he liked so little, drawn almost against his will by the feeling that he might perchance be able to save Turkey from herself. This feeling gradually grew upon him, however, and there is no reason to suppose that he felt any

D

peculiar link with the country with which his name is inseparably connected, during the interval of work and rest in England which divided the first half of his career from the second. He had not yet discovered that his presence was essential to the Porte: it may be questioned whether he ever fully realized his own power in the East.

For rather more than twelve years his chief public interest was centred in the House of Commons. Whilst still ambassador he was elected member for Old Sarum in the spring of 1828.

"I was indebted for the seat to my father-in-law, Mr. Alexander, who jointly with his brother, the East India director, possessed the nomination at Old Sarum. I cannot say that I was much attracted by the honour of representing the rottenest borough on the list. But several considerations pleaded in its favour. The seat was free of expense ; it had been occupied by the best of patriots, Lord Chatham ; it bound me to no party ; and, whether I was the member or not, it would still be a close borough. Moreover, it gave me the true constitutional position as I understand it, of a member free to act on his own judgment, though, what is not so constitutional, it also relieved me from all responsibility to the constituent body. My constituents were eleven in number. They voted in obedience to their landlord. Not one of them did I ever see. Their votes however served to gratify a long-cherished wish of my heart. But did they enable me to attain the object of that wish ? No : I cannot say that they did. I was kept back by something under the name of shyness or timidity, and penury, I fear, of spirit 'repressed my noble rage and froze the genial current of my soul.' It cost me a good deal to walk up the House. To go above the gangway was for some time simply impossible. I screwed up my courage to the point of speaking once in my first session ; but the sentiment which inspired left my judgment to shift for itself, and the few sentences I pronounced in favour of a pension to Mr. Canning's widow had little to recommend them but a certain proud earnestness and warm devotion to his memory. At later periods I overcame this weakness in part ; but to this hour the remains of it hang like a wet swab round my thoughts, and smother in speaking the better half of my natural faculties.

"By way of consolation I know that many of the most effective orators have never been able to free themselves entirely from this detestable nightmare. The late Lord Derby chaffed me one day on this subject. I said, ' Come, come, my lord, in spite of your great ability and success, how is it with you ? ' ' Well,' he replied, ' I'll tell you honestly. When I have a statement to make in the House I don't feel at all comfortable. But in debate, when I have to deal with some antagonist, the case is quite different,' and a flash from his eye confirmed the truth of what he said. Canning once told me that he never rose without the fear of not succeeding. Peel shewed strong symptoms of nervousness in the beginning of a speech. I was in the gallery when Orator Milnes attempted a second speech. He broke down at the end of the first sentence and never tried again. I saw Mr. Hawkins, who, like Mr. Milnes, had gained a high position by his first speech in Parliament, lose himself in a second, not indeed so as to sit down at once, but ultimately in such a manner as to feel that his hold upon the House was gone. Robert Smith, known familiarly by the name of Bobus, a man of proved ability, a wit, a scholar, a lawyer, underwent a similar fate. To use a naval phrase, he ' missed stays ' in passing from one branch of argument to another, and was obliged to sit down."

This frank admission of his want of oratorical powers does not wholly account for Canning's failure to achieve a prominent place in the House of Commons. Bad speakers may make excellent ministers. But there was a second and more formidable obstacle to his success. His honest and straightforward mind was not suited for party warfare : he was, what was then the most hopeless thing in politics, a Liberal-Tory or a Constitutional Liberal, according to the side of the House from which the phenomenon is regarded. He was not even strictly what was known as a " Canningite." He belonged to what George Canning himself told him was "your favourite sect of the independents," and an independent member, unless he possesses peculiar gifts both of oratory and self-propulsion, is seldom a popular character with ministries. The result was that the man who knew more about foreign policy than any other member of the House of Commons saw others his inferiors in knowledge and experience walk into high office, while he remained a private member, respected indeed, and consulted by many of the most distinguished leaders, such as Stanley, Graham, and Sir Robert Peel, but with no more hope of office than if he were still at Stambol.

He describes his taking the oaths, and his maiden speech (13 May), on the pension to Viscountess Canning, in letters to his old friend Richard Wellesley :—

To R.
Wellesley,
3 April

I have just been taking the oaths and a seat in the House of Commons, in consequence of having been yesterday returned (of course after a severe contest) for the venerable and constitutional borough of Old Sarum. Your first question will be, whether this appearance on another stage involves a total change of character, or only a partial change of costume. I rest my claim to consistency on the latter clause of this sentence. In going into Parliament at this moment I mean only to occupy a vacant spot, without making any alteration in my diplomatic station ; and what is of more consequence than my meaning, I have taken care that a clear understanding exists on this point in the proper quarters. I am sorry to add to this communication that I can hold out no hopes to you of witnessing the immediate failure of an old friend ; as I think it exceedingly improbable that anything should occur to induce me to shorten that novitiate of silent observation, which is allowed even to the indiscretion of youth and to the candour of the most unbridled patriotism. You will agree with me that I act wisely in this determination.

Fazakerley will tell you, if you ask him and if he has not already told you, that he does not approve of my going into the House just at this time. I respect every opinion proceeding from that sage and loyal Jacobin ; but in the present instance I have weighed his objections against my own replies and fancy that the scale preponderates on the side of the latter. This may very probably be an *hallucination* ; but all that a poor devil can do is to listen to the advice of friends, and to decide according to the best of his judgment.

I never before felt the full force of what is called " breaking the

1828

———

ÆT. 41

To R.
Wellesley,
17 May

ice." A young gentleman taking a Sunday walk in fine frosty weather along the banks of the Serpentine is ambitious to shew off his skating among the graceful evolutions of the season. Away he goes in full confidence, when in the middle of the first figure of three the treacherous flooring gives way, and in he souses amidst the fragments of ice, splashes about for a few minutes, and finally succeeds in scrambling to land very much frightened and not quite drowned. If this simile agrees as well with your recollection as with my more recent sensations, you will readily conceive with what satisfaction I perused the *humane* congratulations which the Brighton post brought to me yesterday morning. Seriously, I am glad to find that what I said in the debate on Tuesday met with your approbation. It was no occasion for a speech, properly so called. A relation was not the person to make a panegyric, but I felt that my place, if any, was to be the first in resisting the opposition to the grant. Madame de Staël has said somewhere that in speaking a foreign language one says "ce qu'on peut et pas ce qu'on veut." A beginner in Parliament is very much in the same predicament. I could have wished to throw in a parenthesis in favour of economy in general, and a second in recognition of Lord Althorp's respectability ; but the fear of losing sight of my road threw me into a hurry, and utterly incapacitated me for stopping to pick up flowers by the way. Be it observed too that I spoke on an empty stomach. The consequence of which was that Lord Althorp's decided tone of rejection, his expression that the proposal was *an insult on the nation*, got into my head like the first glass of wine that one drinks after a long fast. My position was really a very difficult one, for I had had no previous communication either with the Government or with Lady Canning's friends, and meant on no account to speak unless roused by a strong opposition. On the whole—as you ask for and deserve the truth at my hands—I suspect—though I know very little about the matter—that I have gained more credit for spirit than for tact, for enterprize than for eloquence. My own feeling is that I was just as frightened as I expected to be, that with practice I may in time perhaps be able to do a something, and that meanwhile I have done my duty as well as I could, and I trust without more forwardness than a very natural and pardonable excitement of feeling may account for, towards the man whom of all others I most admired and whom I was most disposed to love. In short, I think myself lucky in having given my first words to him, as in having given my first vote to the Catholics. If I have had the misfortune to give offence to any of Lord Althorp's friends, it is a sacrifice which I make cheerfully to the occasion. Some people seem to apprehend still further opposition on the second reading. I confess I think it unfortunate for Canning's memory that the grant has been brought forward at all, and if those who are nearer to him than I am had my feelings on the subject, I do not think that it would have been brought forward. Bankes made an odious speech in opposition to it. A friend and great admirer of Canning's amused me by saying that he had left the House rather than trust his feelings with an answer. D—n such feelings !

The papers will tell you that the Lords have agreed to a conference on Burdett's resolution about the Catholics. All sensible people agree in thinking that it will be best for the question that it should not be stirred again this year. But I fear that the House of Lords will be brought to a vote upon it.

We catch a glimpse of his life in London, during the few months which elapsed between his return after Navarino and his departure for the Conference at Poros, in a letter to his wife. Lady Davy (widow of Sir Humphry), Sir Henry Holland, and Sir R. Inglis were friends at whose houses he was always welcome.

To his
Wife,
10 April

A famous dinner at Lord Dudley's. I left home at *ten minutes after eight* in great trepidation, but was in the drawing-room before my lord. There I found the reverend beauties of Tighe, Davy, and Beauclerk, with Mrs. Orde. Among the males were Charles Grant and Sir Francis Burdett. The latter I never met before, but found him what I had heard, a gentlemanly, pleasing, unassuming guest. I was amused with his English love of small-beer and apple-pie. Our host was more lively and good-humoured, without being a bit less absent than usual. He attacked me before his whole party about the quantity of papers which I had sent him from Windsor. Charles Grant goes to Tunbridge Wells I believe to-day. I am always sorry not to see more of him.—Dined to-day with Sir Robert Inglis at Battersea ; a horrid bore and expensive in the way of coach hire.— The fair Beauclerk brought me home last night !—Holland came in, by the way, and gave a most comfortable account of L.—The women all asked most kindly after you. The Davy reckons upon you for Tuesday. The Berry is publishing—gone to Petersham to be confined of a volume !

On his return to England, after his disagreement with Lord Aberdeen about the Greek frontier in the spring of 1829, he divided his time between close attendance in Parliament and quiet country life at Mr. Alexander's house at Somerhill.

" Even in our ungenial climate," he remarked, " there is a mild and cheerful zone of life between the extremes of fox-hunting and place-hunting, where one may re-enact the dreamy enjoyments of the Roman poet :—

> Nunc veterum libris, nunc somno et inertibus horis,
> Ducere sollicitae jucunda oblivia vitae."

After his many years of hard work the relaxation and enjoyment of the peculiarly English scenery of Kent—

> With books and sleep the dreamy hours to share,
> And quaff the sweet forgetfulness of care, —

were peculiarly soothing, and he wrote very happily to Planta :—

As for me, I am so well pleased with the rural and domestic objects which surround me, that I cannot find fault even with the weather. It is an old remark that England, in spite of its weeping climate, is peculiarly favourable to out-of-doors exercise ; and, in fact, notwithstanding the drenchings we have had, there has been no difficulty in riding, driving, or walking every day. Much of the delight I take in this country life is, no doubt, owing to the cares and fatigues which it has been my lot to experience abroad ; but, without meaning to set up a hermitage, I am persuaded that a third or a half of the year may be far better employed among the fields and green lanes of Kent than in town, where there are no fields but at Lincoln's Inn, and nothing green save turtle-fat. This is a confession which I should not have dared to confide to you at the Treasury, and I am not sure that it will meet with an echo even at Fairlight.

In the midst of his rural pleasures he was summoned to London to receive the Grand Cross of the Bath,—the least honour that Government could recommend after his long services and the singular manner in which they had, for the time, been terminated. By some oversight, however, the chapter was not held till December. He announced the promise of the distinction as early as July in a letter to his mother,—" You will be glad to know that the King has graciously consented to make me a *fifteenth* Knight of the Bath, and I am now only waiting his Majesty's pleasure for the

1829

—

ÆT. 42

To his
Mother,
17 July

formation of a chapter to assume our new honours : "—he repaired to town for the purpose of institution ; but King George had happened to forget all about the chapter. " I had the honour of kissing his Majesty's hand yesterday at St. James's. He was very gracious, and confirmed his intention of giving me the red riband ; he even mentioned most kindly that he had not thought of doing it yesterday ; but he will contrive to have it at the earliest opportunity at Windsor. This may answer very well."

The earliest opportunity turned out to be somewhat tardy ; but meanwhile Canning was absorbed in the American boundary papers already referred to in Vol. i. p. 337, *note*.

Finally the deed was done. He was invested with the red riband and paid some £400 in fees, and then returned to his hotel with the feeling of a man burdened with a troublesome load.

To his
Wife,
11 Dec.

I quite agree with you my dear E. [he wrote to his wife] it *is* a horrid bore, and I am sometimes half tempted to blaze out against the waiters and cooks who seem to have an understanding together for the trial of my patience. Yes; Sir Stratford ! No; Sir Stratford! You must not be surprized if I go back to Windsor and beg his Majesty to unknight and unriband me. . .

The North American papers have half killed me. I worked at them yesterday, by tongue and pen, from breakfast-time till two at night.

1830
MEMOIRS.

" I ceased to be representative of Old Sarum[1] on the accession of William IV., and was not immediately returned to Parliament for any other place. In the autumn of 1830 I made an attempt at Leominster in the character of what is called a ' third man,' that is, a candidate who stands for the independence of a town in opposition to private interests. I acted under the advice of my attorney, but with so little confidence of success, that I took every conceivable precaution to avoid being made a dupe. Among the friends who accompanied me was the late Lord Cranworth, then Mr. Rolfe, and also Colonel Barnett, who was subsequently consul at Cairo and Warsaw. I sent a legal agent the day before to

---

[1] Two of the Alexander family represented the borough in the new Parliament.

1830

ÆT. 43

see the leaders of the independent party at Leominster, and to ascertain in what temper and in what numbers they were prepared to go to the hustings. The agent was to meet us at the last stage of our journey. He did so, and having heard his report in company with my friends, I declared my readiness to go on, or to turn back according to their advice. They were for proceeding, and on reaching Leominster I had to harangue some forty or fifty people by moonlight from the box of the carriage. Next morning the election came on, and I went to meet my competitors at the Town Hall. Lord Hotham and Mr. Marshall had good reasons for not fearing my assault, and it soon became evident that my supporters were more remarkable for zeal than for numerical forces. Preparations were indeed already made for chairing the two favourites of a large majority, and I could see the banners of their party procession through the windows of the Hall. Making a merit of necessity, and having all but exhausted the votes in my favour, I addressed my opponents and their friends, saying that I had come to afford the independent electors and their friends the opportunity of vindicating the rights of an ancient and honoured borough, but finding their numbers unequal to the object, I had no wish to give unnecessary trouble, and should therefore retire at once from the contest with a just sense of the fair treatment I had experienced. My speech was received with cheers, which were repeated from the street, and although a defeated stranger, I passed though the hostile ranks with every demonstration of respect, and was on my way back to London before the procession could set out.

" I have to record another unsuccessful attempt of mine to get into Parliament. Southampton was the scene of action, and I went with letters of introduction from Lord Palmerston. A lawyer was to obtain a footing on the hustings, and subsequently to make room for me if I chose to stand. On reaching Southampton, and hearing that the candidates were already engaged in addressing the public, I went at once to the place of meeting and listened to the speeches as one of the crowd assembled in the street for that purpose. I was not long without discovering that my friend the lawyer meant to make room for me only when he had reason to despair of getting the seat for himself, and that the appearances afforded no prospect of success. I took my resolution accordingly, and returned to the hotel where I had alighted on my arrival. I had not been long there when I received a message from the lawyer inviting me to come forward and take his place. I told the messenger in reply that I was not ignorant of what had passed at the meeting, having been one among a crowd of listeners, and that with due sense of his friend's civility I had no mind to take the ostensible position of a candidate with so little prospect of making a successful poll. I left the town forthwith and heard no more of the matter.

"Stockbridge was the next place I canvassed, and there the result was more satisfactory. My return [April 1831] was secured by the payment of a thousand pounds to Mr. Vizard, the attorney. Considering that the borough figured in Schedule No. 1 of Lord John Russell's Reform Bill, and consequently that my seat was not likely to be good for more than one or two sessions, the price was sufficiently high. The canvass was a mere form. The constituents were few, and most of them, if not all, had been long in the habit of selling their votes. The candidates, whatever they might have guessed, took no immediate part in this corruption, and in my particular instance I had nothing to do but to shake hands with a portion of the electors, submit to the process of chairing, and give a cheque for the sum originally settled. The chairing was a very primitive operation. The bearers might or might not be sober. At all events they were anything but steady, and the member hoisted on their shoulders had little reason to enjoy his elevation. My colleague was Mr. Barham, the first husband of Lady Clarendon. We called one day together on a shoemaker or cobbler, whose vote, however saleable, was to be solicited. The man was at dinner with his family. On seeing us, he exclaimed, without rising from his seat, ' I know what you are come for, and do you see this knife, I advise you to clear out, that is all.' I replied that we were much obliged to him for his hint, and wished him a pleasant afternoon. To his mind we were evidently robbers, and he would have fought to the knife for what he considered a fair source of profit."

One or two extracts from his letters during the period of
inactivity preceding his election may come here :—

1830

ÆT. 43

I should perhaps be better pleased to have some occupation of
deeper interest. But that is not very probable just now. I have endeavoured without success to get into Parliament again ; and the votes
which I have already given are not likely to recommend me for employment, while the administration remains as it is. I will not fatigue
you with an explanation of all this. Suffice it to say that I know not
how it could have been otherwise unless I had made a sacrifice of
principles and feelings to which I am deeply and inseparably attached.
If these feelings are, as I trust, honourable, and those principles correct, I shall have my reward in due season. If I am under an error,
I must be content to pay the penalty. For company meanwhile I
have reflection and hope, which is patience with wings. . .

The only *great* people by whom I have been entertained of late
are Prince Leopold and the Lansdownes. My plan is to seek no one,
to be wanting to no one, and to let matters take their course. My
only exception to this rule was walking some days ago to the Regent's
Park (which, by the way, is a beautiful thing) to leave a card on the renowned Sir Walter Scott, to whom I had been introduced in something rather more than a common way. In leaving my card without
an address, I thought to make a most respectful visit to the Prince of
Romancers. I met him since, and he was all but uncivil—as much
so, at least, as the rule of suavity which he has prescribed to himself
would admit. I sometimes suspect that poets were more in their
places a hundred years ago than now. They were then kept in tolerable order, though not so well as another century back.

To his
Mother,
Somer-
hill,
23 Aug.

One talks so much in this horrid town that there is really no time
for anything else. And would that our conversation were of an agreeable
kind ; but everything alas ! that one sees and hears inspires alarm for
the state of the country. The agitation of people's minds is quite fearful. The Government is far from strong ; their adversaries quite as
weak. But little prospect of an understanding between the best on
both sides, which might form the salvation of the country ; and the
awful question of Reform coming on like a fire-engine, not to ex-
tinquish the combustion, I fear, but to increase our perplexity and
alarm. The King had his carriage windows smashed in going to the
theatre on Tuesday ; though there was no riot and his reception in the
theatre itself was good. The French Government is partially changed
and the Chamber of Deputies is to be forthwith dissolved, with
the probable effect of increasing the force of the Republican party.
Nothing else appears to move towards a settlement, and to crown all,

To his
Wife,
Travellers'
13 Feb.
1831

the *Courier*, as you will see, presents us with an actual rebellion in one if not two parts of Ireland. I trust that these circumstances when put together thus rapidly have a more dismal appearance than the reality warrants ; but without being a very determined croaker, it is impossible to divest one's mind of many a painful and alarming impression.

It was in this mood that he stood for Stockbridge upon the Reform Bill dissolution as " a very moderate reformer indeed,"—so said the Government of Earl Grey,—and he admitted to his friends that he dreaded " a flood of reforming opinion that will sweep everything before it." Yet he saw that opposition was useless, and his address to " the worthy and independent electors of Stockbridge " (who were about to pocket his thousand pounds) stated that he was " not unfriendly " to the principle of " safe and necessary reform ; " and in due course he voted for the Bill when the division was called. His letters during this stormy time are peculiarly interesting. He was an eager attendant at the debates, though obliged sometimes to go to the House very early to secure a place. On 4 July he found 150 seats taken at 7 A.M. The crowd that thronged to hear the King's speech on 21 June was dense :—

A line to you, dearest E., if I die for it, though it is within five minutes of the time when I must be in the House. *There* I have been already and was nearly squeezed to a mummy. Such a crowd ! and such a rush ! Seriously, it was quite frightful, and would have been tragical, if Sir Tommy Tyrrhwitt had not made us laugh in the midst of our agony. The little man, you know, is Usher of the Black Rod, and it is his business to summon the Commons to hear the King's Speech in the House of Lords. The House of Lords itself was as full as it could hold ; and in a forest of feathers I was just able to distinguish your Mama. My chief object in passing through so many dangers was to see, what is nowhere else to be seen but on a signpost—a king with his crown on. Alas ! I failed in my attempt. I heard every word, or nearly every word, that his Majesty uttered ; but hearing was the only sense that was gratified. The Speech, too, sounded most dolorous,—a series of disagreeable subjects, though the King pronounced it exceedingly well. How he was received by the populace I know not ; but when I went out, after his departure, to thread the long string of carriages and passengers, I saw nothing but good-humoured faces, glowing under a sun which would have done honour to Stambol. I just learn that there is to be no amendment in so far as the *Speech* is concerned, though perhaps the ministers may say a something to render the proposal necessary.

I got home soon after 12 last night, having sat out the greater part of the debate. There was no amendment ; but plenty of indifferent speaking. Stanley, I rejoice to say, was the one who spoke most to my satisfaction : manly, and decided, and explanatory, without diffusion or personality. I have strong hopes of him ; and there is patriotism even in the hope at such a time as this. Sheil made an harangue about Ireland, which did not answer. Dawson and Lord Stormont were violent and overstepped themselves. There were several *Irish figurants*, who displayed all the eloquence and not a little of the accent of their country. Peel's speech was very moderate, but rather too easy and jocose for a man who considers the institutions of his country in danger.

To his
Wife,
22 June

In truth I have done nothing and seen nobody since the debate last night, which went on over a variety of topics till 3 in the morning. I took the liberty of retiring about 1, and it was well that I did, for I was down here at 9 to secure a seat. This early arrival is the only chance of getting a convenient place in the House. The debate last night was greatly to the credit of the Government. Sir J. Graham and Stanley were the heroes of it. O'Connell was fairly taken advantage of by the latter, and in the course of the evening even Hunt's impudence was abashed.

To the
same,
1 July

From what I wrote yesterday you will conclude that no division took place, and your curiosity will keep quietly till to-morrow morning. But the division, sweetest, did take place at 4 this morning, and the second reading was carried by a single unit. I was at the House from after the opera till half-past 1, but no possibility of squeezing in. I left them under the impression that there would be another day's talk ; but Peel said no more, and Sir F. Burdett said nothing at all. The opera, by the way, was dulness itself. Lablache as usual to be seen, and David—but the women very indifferent, and the house thin in consequence of the disappointment about their Majesties. The Ballet of Kenilworth is a beautiful thing in point of scenery, and there was some fair dancing. The most remarkable object was a hat and feathers of gigantic dimensions. I can compare it to nothing but the plumes in the Castle of Otranto. Russian, they say, is the lady who wore them. If so, she did her best to keep a due proportion with the empire. But to return to politics. I am

To the
same,
Wednesday
[6 July]

anxious to know what is likely to happen about dissolution. I rather think there must still be one, and that it is a mere question as to time, and that within a short interval. But the wiseacres say the new Parliament will be as short-lived as the present one. This is one of the hundred considerations which I shall have to weigh as to my own fate. . . . In some shape or other depend upon it that Reform will now be carried—there may be modifications, perhaps even considerable ones, of the Bill, but a great substantive measure will pass ere long, be sure.

If you will look into your *Courier*, you will find a most *eloquent speech* by a person who shall be, and I dare say is, nameless, if indeed his voice reached the Reporters' Gallery at all. The fact is that I was so thoroughly ashamed of my weakness in not daring to get up on the subject of consuls, that I was determined to say a something upon the very first question that came afterwards. I succeeded in saying what I wanted to say—but I felt that I expressed myself in a *hurried* and *naked* manner. On such occasions indeed I always feel like a boy who after hesitating long on the brink of a cold stream plunges in and bustles away, half swimming and half struggling to the opposite bank. I wish I had not a nerve in my body, or that they were all made of cart-ropes. *Vive l'impudence !*

Sir J. Malcolm and Inglis said something civil to me this moment about speaking yesterday. They kindly wanted to encourage me; and what gave me pleasure was that the former evidently thought I had been very well listened to. I thought so too, to say the truth, but felt no confidence in my own impression. I really was too nervous about it, and begin seriously to fear that, in spite of my hustings efforts, it will not easily wear off. At all events you see by the efforts I made yesterday I was not disposed to sit down quietly under so very painful and humiliating a feeling. We have decided against presenting a petition for Stockbridge. All parties agree that it has no ground of its own to stand upon, and what is more, I find on referring to the old records of the H. of Commons that it has been accused and once, I think, convicted of bribery, and narrowly escaped disfranchisement. Under these circumstances we should really do the poor *trout-catchers* more harm than good by putting them forward.

The month of July brought an event which to Canning was of even more moment than the passing of Lord John's Reform Bill by the Commons. His mother, his earliest and always constant friend, died on the 12th. His letters have shewn how deep was his love and reverence for her, and during the long correspondence which they maintained for a quarter of a century not a single word of discord can be traced. Mrs. Canning had seen much happiness since her early years of trouble were over. In her sons, one of whom she had often near her in the cloisters at Windsor, she had good reason to feel pride and satisfaction. The boys who had been left to her, with but doubtful prospects, had answered to her spirited call, and if one had died, it was on the most glorious of England's battle-fields. Her daughter-in-law Lady Canning, to whom she was tenderly attached, was happily present to soothe her last moments. In spite of her advanced age— she was past 80—she retained her faculties to the last, and her loss was deeply mourned by all her children, but by none more than by her youngest and perhaps most beloved son Stratford :—

To his
Wife,
21 July

[Putney
Church-
yard]

It was indeed a sad sight to see the remains of one I had so much loved and respected placed in that dark vault, but I felt consoled by the idea that they were placed by the side of my father's coffin, and I felt that we performed a duty in placing them there. It was impossible at the same time to listen to that affecting and solemn service for the dead without feeling that the tribute we were paying to mortality had nothing in common with the glorious hope of resurrection and future happiness in which my mother, no doubt, resigned her breath. God be with her now and ever more ! and may the memory of her many virtues, dearest E., attend us through the remainder of our lives, to save us from the world in prosperity and to raise us above pain and sorrow in the hour of trial.

Some lines written long afterwards may come here, not because they display the writer's poetic powers at their best, but because they were written when the son was himself an old man of 90, and shew that nearly half a century of separation had not weakened his tender memory of his mother :—

> Dear saint, whose image, though long years have fled
> Since thou wast numbered with the viewless dead,
> Still with my heart's best treasures holds a place,
> Time fondly hallows, nor can e'er efface.

I hail thee now, ere life quite ebbs away,
And this last tribute to thy virtues pay.

.   .   .   .   .

For many a year one desolating trace
Dimm'd the clear eye and marr'd the genial face ;
For many a year the weeds of mourning told
How love by sorrow harden'd grows not old.
But soon the tears not Heav'n itself could chide
And all foreboding cares were dash'd aside ;
Thoughts nursed by hope thy bosom nobly stirr'd ;
What purpose flagg'd when Duty's call was heard ?

.   .   .   .   .

Oh ! loved and honour'd ! to life's latest beat,
Dwell, e'en as now, in memory's faithful seat !
Oh ! type of those who most by worth excel,—
In one dear word, my Mother, fare thee well !

Another loss in the same year was deeply felt by Canning. His old school friend, Richard Wellesley, ended a life of great promise at Brighton.

At the beginning of winter Sir Stratford set forth on his Special Mission to Constantinople (Vol. i. Ch. XIV.). On his departure he wrote thus to Lady Canning :—

To his
Wife,
London,
2 Nov.

Yes, I do *trust* and *hope* that the present trial will end well, and will conduce to our future happiness. These sentiments will carry me through the enterprize far better than post-horses, or sails, or steam-engines, and I pray that the beneficent Being to whom I commend myself, as a most weak and sinning nature will allow, may protect us both and keep us steady to Him and to each other under all vicissitudes. I say this and I mean it most cordially, but in the hurry of preparation, in the anxieties of business, I am but too apt to swerve aside from the course which in calmer moments I shape out. Your nature—your woman's nature and your own dear individual nature—is steadier than mine; and as you are half of me, I hope that the excellence of *that* self will atone for the imperfections of the other, and then, somehow or other, both moieties, the one gently and evenly, the other limpingly and now and then a little *swearingly*, may at last reach the good port.

On his return in 1832 he settled for awhile at St. Leonards, where he was near his old friend Planta, who lived at Fairlight Place.

Your letter has just found me at this *rising* place of flies and bathing-machines, and I cannot better employ the calm interval between the payment of the bill and the arrival of the post-horses than by making you my acknowledgments for the favour. . . As Plenipo. you will enter into my joy at being received with perfect approbation (I believe that is the phrase) by his Majesty and his Majesty's Government. You ask by what necromancy I have contrived to deserve all this, and I am sadly puzzled to answer your question. All I know is that I went to Constantinople, as I married, to wit, with a lively faith in God's mercies; and both enterprizes have succeeded marvellously well. You also appear to be sensible of much good fortune in having effected your translation from Paris to Berne, and I need not assure you that I am delighted at your happiness. I could only wish that the poor country in which your lot is cast for the present were equally favoured by fortune. . . . I voted for Parliamentary Reform last year in the conviction that the Monarchy could not go on without it. I did my best at Stambol to persuade the Sultan that his only chance of safety lay in reform, political, municipal, and military. But in spite of all this there is no doubt that the tree of Jacobinism has put forth new shoots, and that there is a powerful active party with agents almost in every part of Europe busily engaged in sapping the foundations of government, property, and religious establishment. How to stop them is the rub. *Here* I trust that the ministers mean at least to make the attempt, though in order to succeed there must be something more positive than a good intention.

1832
—
Æт. 45

To D. Morier, St. Leonards, 19 Oct.

While the member for Stockbridge was absent at Constantinople his borough sank beneath his feet—in Schedule A of the Reform Bill. He had only spoken once in the House during his tenure of the seat, and its loss did not affect him much. Planta wrote to him :—

I entirely agree in what you say of the happiness of being out of the way of politics. They have become wicked and discouraging things since, in the person of your cousin, a great mind, high feelings and most exalted views were defeated by selfishness and through narrowness of mind—when a short-sighted obstinacy took the name of consistency, and private dislike that of public principle—and thus one of the best hearts and the greatest of minds was broken, and driven from this world long before its time.

From, Planta, Fairlight, 21 Sept.

At the general election of December 1832 Canning found himself without a seat, and consoled himself with the pleasure

1832
———
ÆT. 46

of spending a Christmas at home, for the first time since he had left Eton, save only twice when he kept the feast at Windsor with his mother. Four times had Yule-tide overtaken him while tossing about on the element least conducive to a due appreciation of the good things of the season. A very important event however had happened to him on his return from Constantinople : he was gazetted ambassador to the Emperor of All the Russias. The appointment gave the greatest pleasure to all who knew anything about foreign policy, whose opinion was summed up by Captain Chesney when he wrote (2 November), " I am glad of what is in the Gazette for your sake, and I may add John Bull's, who will (if I mistake not) know *what the Bear is about,* and be a match for his course amidst the rocks and lairs of northern politics ; and I am only sorry that your Excellency cannot be, like Sir Boyle Roche's bird, in two places at once—Stambol as well as Petersburg." To the Court and Government of Russia, however, the choice was exceedingly distasteful, and the Emperor took the unusual course of refusing to receive Sir Stratford. Various reasons were suggested for this embarrassing decision. It was said that Madame Lieven, the wife of the Russian ambassador in London, had taken some offence, and had revenged herself by intriguing against Sir Stratford's reception at Petersburg. We know that Canning's quick feelings and outspoken frankness were apt to make him enemies, and he was not a favourite of the lady who endeavoured to manage Russian affairs in England. Another ground was discovered in some alleged disrespect shewn by the ambassador to the Grand Duke Nicholas when at Petersburg in 1825, and this excuse was alleged by Count Nesselrode in an interview with Mr. Bligh, the English chargé d'affaires. There was only one objection to the plea, and that was the fact that the Grand Duke and the ambassador never met in 1825. As has already been pointed out, the only occasion on which the two men who were destined to be rivals in a great contest found themselves face to face was at a fête given by Schwarzenberg at St. Cloud in 1814, just forty years before the Crimean war. If there had been an affront in 1825, it must have been a negative one, such as not leaving his card upon Nicholas ;

Vol. i.
p. 374

but so far as the documents go there is nothing to justify even
this assumption, and even if true it would be a curious ground
for refusing to receive the chosen representative of the King
of England. The following extracts from a report of Mr.
Bligh shew that the Czar retreated from this position, and,
whilst denying the supposed affront, would give no other
reason for his rejection of the King's ambassador.

1832
—
ÆT. 46

" I asked if my suspicions were well founded. Upon his replying
in the affirmative, and stating that something unpleasant had taken
place, in the quarter I supposed, upon Sir Stratford Canning's leaving St. Petersburg, after his special mission, I read from your letter
enough to shew that the supposed want of respect on the part of Sir
S. Canning towards the Emperor when Grand Duke arose entirely
from a mistake ; but Count Nesselrode would not entirely agree
to this, saying that it had proceeded from one of those ebullitions
of temper and *touchiness*, of which, he added, we should have
to witness instances every day in case of Sir Stratford Canning's
coming here again, which he sincerely hoped would not be the case ;
and upon taking my leave, he begged that I would report to you
faithfully, and without extenuation, all that he had said on the
subject."

St. Peters-
burg,
17 Nov.

(This report was accordingly written, and read over (apparently
on a subsequent day) to Count Nesselrode. After which Mr. Bligh
proceeds :)

"When I finished reading, his Excellency acknowledged the
correctness of my report of what had passed between us ; and then
begged me to add, that the Emperor had since declared to him that
he had no recollection of the circumstances which occurred upon
Sir Stratford Canning's leaving St. Petersburg, and that his (the
Emperor's) objections to seeing him here as his Majesty's representative did not arise from the circumstance alluded to, but were such
as would place his Imperial Majesty under the disagreeable necessity
of formally objecting to his nomination in case of its being pressed
by your lordship."

In a subsequent report, of 23 November, Mr. Bligh says that
Count Orlov "gave him to understand that the Emperor had expressed himself very warmly on the subject, but had never alluded
to the supposed affront, for which you imagined he might harbour
resentment."

There was naturally considerable indignation, not only
among Canning's friends, but in all who appreciated the depth

1832
—
ÆT. 46

and meaning of the insult offered to England. It meant, first, that Russia thought fit to dictate to England what sort of ambassador she should send to Petersburg ; and, second, that the sort she would accept must not be one who knew too much about her proceedings in the East. The truth was that Sir Stratford's eye was much too keen to be suffered to explore the mysteries of the Russian Foreign Office at head-quarters : they were afraid of him, and with good reason. Still that was no argument for England to submit, and Palmerston stood to his guns for some time, declaring to Count Lieven that the Czar's conduct was " an outrageous piece of arrogance." Planta, as an old Foreign Office servant, and late Under-Secretary, felt his official as well as his personal wrath stirred within him, and was greatly annoyed when it was decided to compromise the dispute by appointing no ambassador whatever, and thus to leave Russia in the humiliating position of receiving no more exalted representative of England than a chargé d'affaires (until 1835). This step of course compelled the Czar to adopt a similar course in London, and to recall the Lievens. Some of the correspondence must be published here :—

From Lord Palmerston, 7 March, 1833

The question between us and Nesselrode about your appointment remains where it was. I have repeatedly been told by Lieven and Bligh that the Emperor persisted in declining to receive you, though no reason could be assigned except the old one, " I do not like you, Doctor Fell," and I have as often replied that we looked upon this refusal as a piece of intolerable arrogance, and as an interference with the right of the King of England to choose his own servants, which we never can submit to ; and that therefore they must receive you or have a chargé d'affaires, and Lieven the other day said that Nesselrode had no objection to our having a chargé d'affaires.

I have written Nesselrode some most useful letters, and told him many wholesome truths, hitherto strangers to his ears, by means of private letters to Bligh, sent to him by the common post, and which of course Nesselrode has had the advantage of reading : but it is still possible that the Tartar may be stiff-necked, and in that case we cannot send you to be affronted by an offensive reception, or by a refusal to receive you at all.

The anticipation proved correct, and on 18 July Canning

was definitely informed that his Majesty had resolved not to
send an ambassador to St. Petersburg. It is unnecessary to
say that he was exceedingly angry with this decision.

He wrote to Planta :—

We do *not* go to Russia ; nor is anyone else to go instead of us,
but it remains to be seen whether the Lievens will have to make a
back somersault over the Baltic.   I am indignant, and so, I understand, are the King and the Government; but the affair is still a
mystery, if you please, and not to be talked about.   Seriously, the
less it is known the better, until the course to be adopted is actually
decided upon.   Palmerston is ready to do anything for the protection of my *character* and *interests*, which are no doubt exposed in an
unpleasant manner.   The conduct of Russia throughout the business is as offensive as possible, and only just not worth quarrelling
about.

To Planta,
London,
20 July

Planta's comments are just and come from a man of long
official experience :—

The decision which has been come to on the Russian business,
though it implies the very good consequence, to me highly gratifying,
of keeping you in England, does not altogether satisfy me.   I cannot
understand any foreign Power being allowed to take such a course
as this, or that things should not be so managed by our Foreign
Office as to prevent it. . . . I have often heard of soundings and confidential communications, and inquiries "would this or that man be
agreeable or fitting," but then these always preceded the public declaration of an embassy, and its formal announcement in the Gazette.
I have no hesitation in saying, that if I were in my old post in the
F. O. and were asked my advice as G. C. would have asked it, in
this matter, I should, as far as I am at present informed, have said
that nothing should prevent me, after your name appeared in the
Gazette, from sending you to your post.   To St. Petersburg you
should go, and then a private understanding should be had with you,
as to your not remaining longer than you yourself might like, say a
year. . . . After much reflection, I cannot conceive a reason why
the E. of R. should take this line—except this : that having now his
chief attention turned on Turkey, he does not wish to have as ambassador with him from this country one who is thoroughly acquainted
with the whole policy of Russia towards Turkey, who best knows the
remaining resources of the Porte, if she have any, and who has already
dealt with and thwarted Russia in her earlier transactions with Turkey.

From
Planta,
Fairlight,
23 July

1833
——
ÆT. 46

Now these are the qualities which make you the fittest man in England now to fill the embassy to Russia, and is it not somewhat too bad then that *they* should be permitted to *prevent* your going there? . . . As to this producing the recall of the Lievens, Gioia, gioia ! if it does. We shall be the better for it, and have Masuchevitz, a clever English-liking man, in their place, perhaps.

Canning had throughout refused to retire voluntarily from the embassy, because he thought such deference to an unreasonable objection was a "dangerous and discreditable" precedent in our relations with Russia. He submitted of course to the decision of the Foreign Minister, but he demanded at the same time that his name and character should be vindicated, and that he should not be allowed to appear in the light of a discarded servant. The world must be taught the truth of the matter, and the only way of teaching it was of course to confer some fresh distinction upon Sir Stratford Canning. The natural reward of long services would have been a peerage : but the threat of creating a majority in the Lords for passing the Reform Bill a year before had brought such a flood of claims upon the Government that they were very chary of looking at the subject. Lord Palmerston indeed recommended that a peerage should be conferred, but the Premier's reply printed below shews the difficulty of carrying out the plan :—

31 Aug.

My dear Palmerston,—I return Sir Stratford Canning's letter. You know my opinion of him, derived chiefly from what I have heard from you and others, but entirely confirmed by the communications which I have had with him personally since I have been in office. You know also what my feelings have been with respect to the treatment he has met with from the Court of St. Petersburg.

I must therefore necessarily be anxious for any opportunity of shewing not only that the Government appreciates his talents and his services as they deserve, but would repair, as far as it may be in its power to do so, the injustice which he has suffered. If a Mission, suited to his rank, should be opened, he has evidently the first claim to it ; and this would, I think, be the best way in which the object so feelingly and so justly described in his letter could be effected. I know of no distinction which could be offered to him except a Peerage, and with respect to this you are fully aware of my difficul-

ties, on account of the numerous and powerful claims which are
pressed upon me.   Ever most sincerely yours,

GREY.

Sir Stratford Canning was the last person one would expect to sit down under an injury ; yet he took the submission
of the Government to the Czar's prejudices with marvellous
patience, and so far from holding Palmerston to the promise
contained in Lord Grey's letter, he formally released him from
that engagement when the Grey ministry broke up in 1834.
He felt that he could not accept patronage from any member
of Lord Melbourne's administration, from which he was satisfied that " nothing but evil could result." Accordingly in the
spring of 1835 he declined Lord Aberdeen's offer of the
governor-generalship of Canada, which was afterwards accepted
by Lord Amherst. Canning was then again in Parliament,
and too much interested in the struggle waging over " the
decline and fall of the Whig administration " to desire employment abroad.

TOWARDS the close of 1832 Lord Palmerston proposed that Canning should go to Madrid, and endeavour there or at Lisbon to make peace between the brothers Dom Pedro and Dom Miguel, who were then contending for the crown of Portugal, the former on behalf of his daughter Donna Maria. The mission was intended to be, as Palmerston phrased it, merely "an episode to Russia," and in Canning's letters of credence to the King and Queen of Spain he was styled "Ambassador to the Emperor of All the Russias." It was to occupy only a few months, and he started, with some hope of success. The Prime Minister, Lord Grey, founded his belief in the possibility of a reconciliation between the two brothers upon the recent change in the government of Spain, where a more moderate party had replaced the "Apostolicals" in the seat of power. He thought that the new ministry would be eager to get rid of Dom Miguel, whose Court would naturally be a rallying point for the "Apostolicals," and that they would coöperate with him in inducing the elder brother to retire to Brazil, while his daughter reigned in Portugal under the control of a regency. In the instructions which the special ambassador received from Lord Palmerston it was urged that the analogy between the situations of Spain and Portugal might furnish an argument in favour of this policy. The Infanta Isabella stood towards her uncle Don Carlos in very much the same relation as Donna Maria to Dom Miguel. The King of Spain was apparently ready to suspend the Salic law in order to secure the succession for his daughter :

would he not sympathize with the efforts of Dom Pedro to place *his* daughter on the throne to which she was constitutionally entitled? And would not Donna Maria's success strengthen the cause of the Infanta? There was a rumour that both parties in Portugal were willing to listen to overtures of peace. The war had so far been unfruitful in decisive events. Dom Pedro at Oporto dared not advance to the Tagus; Dom Miguel at Lisbon did not venture to lay siege to Oporto. The people were suffering severely and there seemed every chance of a favourable reception to suitable proposals for a settlement of the dispute. Palmerston's proposals were "the establishment of Donna Maria on the throne as queen; the relinquishment by Dom Pedro of his claim to the regency during the minority of his daughter; the appointment of a regency, consisting of men of moderate opinions and connected with each of the parties; the grant of a full and complete amnesty, without any exception whatever, for all past political offences; the restitution of all confiscated property; the suspension of the Constitution of 1826, with a view to taking steps, at a proper time, and as soon as the state of the country will admit of it, for reconsidering the laws of Portugal, and for introducing therein such changes and amendments as the wants and wishes of the nation may require; a provision for Dom Miguel suited to his birth; and a corresponding arrangement for Dom Pedro, it being stipulated that neither of the brothers shall hereafter reside within the Portuguese territory."

With these proposals Canning journeyed to Paris with his wife and children, "like diplomatic gipsies wandering from Court to Court with our children at our backs." He was graciously received by the King, and submitted his instructions for the consideration of the Duc de Broglie. It was eminently desirable to have the support of France in the negotiation. All the Northern and Eastern Powers were of course on the side of Miguel, who was identified with the autocratic and reactionary principle. France, however, sympathized with Donna Maria, and agreed to support Canning's proposals, with certain limitations: the interference was to be purely pacific and the French Government declined to enter into the suggested argument as to the analogy between the two princesses of Spain and Portugal, inasmuch as the Salic law was a fixed principle in France, and the question of its suspension was disagreeable to the Bourbons. At the same time the Duc de Broglie did not conceal his misgivings as to the success of the mission. He considered Dom Pedro's cause to be decidedly unpopular in Portugal, and he believed that the Spanish ministry depended largely for support upon Dom Miguel's party. A conversation with Pozzo di Borgo, the Russian ambassador at Paris, brought out a further discouraging fact. It appeared that Zea Bermudez, who had been recalled from the Spanish Mission in London to preside over the Foreign Office at Madrid, had before leaving England made no secret of his intention to reject Lord Grey's proposals. This discovery naturally excited Canning's indignation. Without Spain it was hopeless to influence the struggle in Portugal. He could not imagine why Lord Palmerston had concealed the Spanish decisions, and he was not the man to enjoy being sent on a fool's errand. He might have been justified in suspending his journey till he had again communicated with the Foreign Secretary: but he reflected that Palmerston had sent him in full knowledge of Señor Zea's views, and that it was not the place of the ambassador to question the minister's judgment. Pozzo di Borgo, moreover, as the representative of a dissentient Power, might have exaggerated Zea's language. He therefore resolved to go on, though he did not conceal from Palmerston the unfavourable ideas he had formed at Paris :—

To Lord
Palmerston,
17 Dec.

I little thought a year ago that there was anything in negotiation more impossible than the Greek question, but the enigma of the two Doms beats it hollow. The little glimmering of hope with which I allowed myself to be seduced in London is extinguished here, and the only difference I find between friends and adversaries is that the former are prepared to lament the failure which the latter are bent upon producing.

With Pozzo di Borgo, who is an old acquaintance of mine, I had a long conversation this morning. I need not tell you that he is all for Dom Miguel. What he seems most to dread is our leading France into a situation which may commit her beyond our intentions.

I told him that he could not hit upon a better method of realizing this fear than by getting up an opposition to the present overture. It is possible that the dread of a joint proposal from France and England may reconcile him to my negotiating with the support of the French minister at Madrid. But the prevailing impression here is that nothing but counteraction is to be expected from the Northern Powers, and Zea's Circular [of 3 Dec.] and Ofalia's language are little calculated to remove it.

1833
———
ÆT. 46

These forebodings proved only too accurate. Canning found himself unable to effect any good at Madrid. "Zea" he wrote " is the great stumbling-block. He is a bundle of prejudices on the subject of Portugal. I am nothing against such fearful odds;" and again, " Your Spaniard is as hard a negotiator as your Turk." His official reception, indeed, was courteous enough, but it was clear that nothing was going to be done.

To Planta,
10 Feb.

" My first interview with the Spanish minister was far from encouraging. No want of courtesy in his manner or language—the usual cant of friendly sentiments—but a polite hint that it might prove impossible for the Spanish Government to accept my proposals, ' without an abandonment,' as I reported to Lord Palmerston, ' of those principles and resolutions which, during his late mission to London, he had himself stated to your lordship in several official notes by the express orders of his Court.' As the name of Portugal was not pronounced, though the allusion could not be mistaken, I thought it best to take a tone of general goodwill, accompanied with suitable assurances and the expression of a cordial hope that when my overtures were duly brought forward and considered in a right spirit, whatever difficulties might be apprehended at a distance would ultimately disappear and give place to the desired understanding.

MEMOIRS

" On presenting my credentials two or three days later to the King and Queen I found the same appearances, whether for good or for bad. The reception was gracious, but nothing more. It was indispensable that I should not let the audience close without expressing the desire of my Government that the Spanish minister should be empowered to join with me in a serious endeavour to re-establish the tranquillity of

Portugal. The King, who was still so weak in consequence of his recent illness as to receive my letters sitting, referred me on that subject to his ministers ; and the Queen, however gracious in manner, observed a complete silence on political topics, no doubt bearing in mind what was due to her husband's usurpation of the royal authority."

Ferdinand did not believe a word of Lord Palmerston's assurances, and Canning, as he read out his credentials, could see the King's cunning little eyes twinkling up at him, as much as to say, "What an actor you would make, when you can mouth those lies so gravely !" His Majesty was pleased to regard the mission as an elaborate farce, and there is reason to believe that he was, no doubt unintentionally, encouraged in his scepticism by Canning's old friend and secretary Henry Addington, who was then minister at Madrid, and was known to be at variance with his Government on the Portuguese question. It soon appeared that King Ferdinand was in sympathy with Dom Miguel, while Queen Christina, inspired by more liberal views and moved by a feeling of interest for the young Portuguese princess whose situation bore so strange a resemblance to that of her own daughter, was all for Dom Pedro. The consequence was a vacillating policy.

" My chances of success fluctuated with the King's health. Whenever his Majesty was too ill to attend to business, the reins of government fell into the Queen's hand, and my prospects wore a less gloomy colouring ; but no sooner did her royal husband reappear in person on the stage than a deeper shade was cast upon my communications with the Premier. Zea Bermudez was not an agreeable person to deal with. His talents were little above the ordinary level ; his manners were those of a promoted clerk ; and in fact he had passed, I know not why, from a commercial house at Petersburg into the State-service of his Catholic Majesty. He was very deaf, and, if not obstinate, uncommonly tenacious of any purpose he had once adopted. His official room was in the palace. It was partitioned off from a spacious apartment, and the partition was constructed of such slender materials as to give an easy passage to any sounds from within. I had to raise my voice in talking to dull ears, and of course whatever I said was audible to anyone outside. I was not long without having a decided proof of this peculiarity. The *Morning Herald* to my great surprize contained in one of its numbers a full account of a conversation I had held with Monsieur Zea, and I found on inquiry that a person whom I had remarked on the same day on passing into the minister's cabinet was 'our own correspondent' to that defunct newspaper. Whether chance or choice, manœuvre or accident, the fact was enough to make me understand that I was walking on slippery ground."

1833
——
ÆT. 46

We gather from Canning's letters that he was not favourably impressed with Madrid :—

I will not presume to inquire whether you deserve a line from me, but proceed at once to tell you that we are as quietly settled at Madrid as if we had been here since the beginning of the century. We have a huge ground-floor, looking into the Prado, to expatiate in, and with the help of three fireplaces and a host of braziers we manage to keep out the cold. . . . The town is not lively, but there are interests and novelties enough to amuse us. Above all there is a glorious collection of pictures close at hand. Such Murillos ! Such Velasquezes ! Such Riberas as are only to be seen in the capital of Spain. Our journey proved less appalling than we had apprehended, though we were obliged to travel twenty-two hours the last day. This was trying for the children. But they are none the worse for it now. Heaven only knows when we shall be able to turn our horses back towards England !

To W. Canning, Madrid, 25 Jan.

Your friends are quite right in not viewing the Catholic question— I mean the *new* one—through party spectacles. It is emphatically *national*. If the maintenance of the union be incompatible with Church reform, there is an end of the matter, for I am satisfied that the Church Establishment in Ireland cannot be maintained as it is. But surely the two questions have no alliance except in the over-heated heads of some Catholic demagogues. As for the authority of Government, it *must* be upheld, and never in my mind so well as when recognized abuses are in a course of judicious amendment. At the same time there is no denying that it is a difficult country to deal with that same Paddyland ! No wonder 'gainst reason and order he pulls,

To Planta, Madrid, 10 Feb.

with his head of potaty and mouth full of bulls ! Apropos of bulls, I have seen a bull-fight, and I have no fancy for seeing another, except it be a very super-excellent one indeed. It is a disgusting sight—the horses are cruelly used, and the men are not killed half often enough. My only consolation was in seeing a Picador carried several yards round the ring on a bull's horn.

Society : We never dine out except about once a fortnight with Addington. Soon after our arrival we were dined diplomatically and splendidly by the Russian, Austrian, Sardinian and Prussian Missions. No Spaniard has ever shewn us a silver fork. Our own exploits in this way are very limited from want of suitable means. We contrive however to collect now and then as many as a dozen people about our round table, and as we sit down at 6 and break up at 8 the sacrifice of time is not very formidable. If we chose to open our house for evening parties, there would be no lack of guests, but that does not suit our habits. Out of doors, the French ambassadress and the Russian have each a night for being at home ; but Spaniards seldom appear, and the party consists of half or three-quarters of the Diplomatic Body assembled round a tea or a card table. On *Sundays* we have the only Spanish party to which foreigners can go with certainty of being welcome. There is a certain old Duchess of B—— who has done the honours of Madrid during the last half-century, and whose great delight it is still, "though now her eightieth year be nigh," to collect a crowd of people in her apartment.

Public amusements : An indifferent theatre, a worse opera, some masked balls before Lent, and Sunday oratorios since. An occasional bull-fight on Sundays, and the King's Picture Gallery as often as we please. Now and then a gala, or as it is called here a *Besamanos,* at Court. The public walks are excellent for dryness and air, but they are sufficiently monotonous, and there is not space enough either for driving or riding agreeably.

Whilst at Madrid, Canning received an offer from Palmerston to make him permanent ambassador to the Court of Spain, by way of compensation for St. Petersburg : his reply is contained in the following letter :—

I do indeed rejoice at your magnificent majority on the Irish Coercion Bill. It was a splendid triumph not only for the Government, but for the country itself, and I trust it will be duly appreciated throughout the civilized world, including Ireland. I mean to make the most of it here. Next to the pleasure of seeing you heartily opposed to the Radicals, I am delighted at the forced support which

you levy upon the Tories ; and have only to wish, in terms of Spanish
courtesy, that it may last a thousand years.

I will not affront you by extending this wish to your Belgian controversy.

With respect to our Turkish friends, I fear we have been a little
too late.   The Sultan's army appears to have been even more rotten
than I had supposed.   As matters now stand, it would be something
if Syria were at least detached from Egypt, and placed under the
separate command of Ibrahim Pasha.—The Sultan's acceptance of
Russian aid is surely a terrible step towards his dependence upon
that Power.   Let me entreat of you to adopt a regular system at
Constantinople in order to counteract that influence, ere it be quite
too late.   Austria may say what she will, but the object of the Czar
is neither more nor less than to take the Porte and Persia into keeping.   What we do in that way is modestly concealed between the
Indus and the Ganges.

I fancied that you might have done something with Austria, but
perhaps it is not possible, while Metternich and his Emperor are
pleased to go on living.   The Austrian envoy here, Count Bonnetti,
has told me of a conversation between you and Neumann about
Portugal and Donna Maria.   He has politely offered his services to
obtain *correct information* on the whole subject, and to get us a renewal of our treaty and other good things, if we will but make up our
minds to Dom Miguel.   Your instructions do not exactly square with
this obliging offer ; but I cannot help fearing that, if Zea carries the
day, as he probably will (God bless the King!), you may be compelled
in the end to put up with any tolerable arrangement.

After thanking you for the key to Pozzo's reception in London,
of which he has contrived to make rather a handsome thing in the
newspapers, I come to the point at issue between the Czar his
master and your humble servant.   I have but little to say upon the
subject.   It is not for me to decide what the public interests may
require, but as my good fame is at stake, excuse my saying that I will
not voluntarily recede from that embassy.   With respect to an embassy here, I am willing to go through with what I undertook in
coming, but I beg you will not ask me to do more.   Exclusive of every
other objection, I cannot consent to expose myself to the suspicion
of having supplanted an old friend in the person of Addington.   I
should be sorry if this sounded too peremptory to your ears, but I
really think it a duty to leave no doubt as to my intentions.

Anything of much interest to be done here turns upon Portugal
and the succession.   With respect to Portugal, the chances are
sadly against us, and as for the succession, the King is so much
better that he is sleeping again with the Queen, so that not only may
his Majesty's life be preserved to the world for twenty years to come,

but he may yet have a prince to succeed him and to settle the point now at issue between Don Carlos and Donna Isabella.

The Spanish mission soon came to an end. Had Ferdinand died in March instead of September Canning might have secured his object. But with a convalescent King and a time-serving minister, the odds were all against him. On 5 May the British proposals were definitely rejected, and the ambassador hastened to take leave. Lord Palmerston, however, expressed himself as wholly satisfied with the able manner in which a very difficult negotiation had been conducted, and Canning proceeded in due course to wait upon the King on his return. William IV. was then at Brighton.

To his
Wife,
Brighton,
20 Dec.

It was well that I disengaged myself from Fazakerley, for the "Age," in spite of its promise, did not get here till nearly 7. A fly conveyed me to the Norfolk Hotel, where a blazing fire and a cheerful waiter, followed up by a hot mutton chop and a pint of *ardent* sherry, soon made me happier than I ought to be at a distance from you and the chicks. The hotel is quietness itself, and old Phipps, who good-naturedly came downstairs soon after breakfast to ask me to dine with him, speaks in high terms of its cleanliness and cookery. The remaining third of the house is occupied by Mrs. Sullivan, Palmerston's sister. I wish you were here to tell me whether I know her or not. If I do and leave no card I am a lost man, and to leave a card without being introduced would be wrong. I am just come in from my first round of duties. I have inscribed myself at the Pavilion ; I have called on the Fazakerleys, I have seen the Godfrey, I have inquired for Rogers, I have opened a communication with the post-office, and I have taken a place in the "Age" for Tuesday. But such a hurricane of wind ! It was as much as I could do not to *run* along the Marine Parade in going, and in coming back it was like walking in a treadmill. The sea is in a perfect passion. . . . You would have laughed to see the ambassador unpacking his bags last night. I never felt so thoroughly independent. This morning the waiter called me to a moment, and supplied me with salt water. No mistake, for I knew where everything was to be found ; clothes brushed, and boots cleaned to perfection. Then the quiet bachelor breakfast,—but I beg pardon, you will not understand this kind of comfort. In short, I feel like having just alighted *from heaven* ; and marvel much at my virtue in securing a place in Tuesday's coach. An absurd thing happened as I was leaving town yesterday. We picked up an old lady at Charing Cross and both of us wanted to set our watches at the Horse Guards.

Conceive us both watch in hand, straining our eyes to look at the clock, and, on finding it *without hands*, staring at each other a moment in utter astonishment, and then bursting into a hearty laugh. . . .

The Queen did not make her appearance nor the Duchess of Gloucester till the evening. Her Majesty returned from her morning drive with an attack of lumbago. The Duchess looks thin but not ill. She dreads damp, and means to stay on at Brighton. The Duke, her *sposo*, comes to-morrow. There is a gathering for Christmas, and diplomacy is expected. No official visitors, I find, sleep in the Pavilion, except Lord Grey, and the members of the family. The party at dinner was large, but not so large as the table. The King looked in health, but fagged a little and at times drowsy. He called me to his round table after dinner, and asked questions in the style royal ; but no politics. The Duchess of Gloucester asked kindly for you and the children. I wish with all my heart you were here. I shall make a point of calling on Sir Herbert Taylor and others before I go. Barnard (Sir A.) was there yesterday. I revived acquaintance with the Duke of Argyll, who is Lord Steward. He good-naturedly took me home— *in a fly*.

Canning was not sorry to find himself back in England, but his position was singularly embarrassing. He had no seat in Parliament, and his professional duties as ambassador to Russia were somewhat contracted by the circumstance that he was not permitted to proceed to St. Petersburg. In the absence of foreign employment, home politics engrossed a large part of his thoughts.

I care very little [he wrote] whether the late change of ministry was owing to an intrigue of Lord Brougham's, or to the honest blundering of Althorp and Littleton. One thing is clear, O'Connell in Ireland, and the Radicals in England, have gained all that the Government has lost in talent and character. We look back upon indiscretion and inconsistency ; we look forward to more innovation and increased danger of collision between the two Houses of Parliament. You ask what Palmerston and Charles Grant can be about. The latter I presume is a purist. With the Tories he was always going out ; with the Whigs he is always staying in ; and hence I infer that his views of reform lengthen as he goes ; the stopping point receding like the north to a man who travels northwards. Palmerston, I fancy, confines himself pretty much to his foreign affairs. But as Lord Melbourne stayed in to support the King, he probably stayed in to support Lord Melbourne. There is no denying that

1833
—
ÆT. 46

what justifies the one justifies the other, and if it be true that Peel was unwilling to coalesce with them, and Stanley unprepared to join Peel, the complete dispersion of Lord Grey's Cabinet might have thrown everything into confusion. You may, perhaps, think that Peel might have found a government of his own friends ; but could he in that case have managed the House of Commons ? My favourite dream, as you know, is a junction of the Moderates to the exclusion of the *Impracticables* on the one side, and the *Precipitates* on the other. But so great are the difficulties of such a combination without the master mind to consolidate and direct it, that there is little chance of its ever being realized. But the next session will probably tell us what can and what cannot be done. Meanwhile to judge from the language of the *Globe*, the present ministers are the true men of the *milieu* ; and if they can succeed in maintaining that character, while they slide on in their course of accelerated reform, they may continue to govern us for many days to come. The flattering unction which they seem to lay to their consciences is the necessity of more reform, and a persuasion that, Peel and Stanley not combining to any efficient purpose, they will be tolerated through fear of the ultras, be they Whig, or be they Tory, or be they Radical. Yet surely the light cannot long be kept out from this mystery. If they intend no changes of an unsafe character, the Radicals will soon grumble and the country will ask to what purpose it has exchanged the men who have gone out for the men who have gone in. If on the other hand they exhibit an essential difference between their measures and those of the late Cabinet, their opponents in Parliament must be singularly dull if they cannot expose the danger and shew how abuses can be remedied without incurring it. I am mistaken if we are not still at that point where the friends of order predominate. But the current still sets in favour of change on some important matters ; but not, perhaps, on many ; for after all much has been done. To say nothing of Parliamentary reform and reduction of expenses, think of the West and East Indies, the Poor-Laws, the Bank Charter, the Irish bishoprics, and the several new legal arrangements, in all of which the prevailing popular opinion has been fairly consulted. To be sure, there is the debt, and the pensions, and the tithes, and the Dissenters, with a small list of etceteras : but I speak only of those questions on which alone a government, not avowedly Radical, would hear of any alteration, and surely on those it ought not to be difficult for men such as Peel or Stanley to rally the better part of the country in defence of what they esteem essential to the principles of morality and property. In cases where these principles are not visibly and positively concerned, I confess that in times like these I should be inclined to make considerable sacrifices for the sake of conciliation and peace. But

my firm conviction is that concession is useless and dangerous the
moment those foundations of the monarchy, and indeed of all social
order, are successfully invaded.

When these lines were written he saw no opening for a
seat in Parliament, and it was a curious incident that turned
the current of his quiet life that winter.

"The change of ministry which took place in the autumn
of 1834 was followed by a dissolution of Parliament. Lord
Althorp's elevation to the House of Peers on the decease of
his father, Earl Spencer, had afforded the King an opportunity
of substituting a Conservative for a Liberal Government.
The Duke of Wellington was first sent for, but subsequently
Sir Robert Peel was charged with the construction of a new
cabinet, and, until he could return from Italy, where he was
travelling at the time, the seals of sundry chief departments
were entrusted to the Duke, who paid a daily visit to the
several offices, and exercised his judgment on the affairs
which in each required immediate attention. Some little
time before, Lord Melbourne's Cabinet had been weakened
by the secession of four of its members, namely, the Duke of
Richmond, the Earl of Ripon, Lord Stanley, and Sir James
Graham. A question affecting Church property was the
ostensible cause of their retirement from office. Their watchword and that of their friends at the election was *A fair trial
for Peel.* I wished to obtain a seat in Parliament, but could
hear of no suitable opening. My father-in-law, moreover, and,
in consequence, his daughter, were adverse to my wish, being
of opinion that its accomplishment would carry with it too
great a sacrifice of income. There was but too much truth
in their objection, and I could only meet it by declaring the
grounds of my readiness to make that sacrifice. Judging
from what passed at the famous Lichfield House meeting, I
could anticipate no good from a government reconstructed
by Lord Melbourne. I thought it would rest upon an unconstitutional basis, and that if I took part with an opposition
capable of excluding it from power on principles of Liberal-
Conservatism I should but perform my duty towards the public.

As parties were likely to be almost balanced, an unusual value would necessarily attach to a single vote, and, oddly enough, though Peel on the meeting of Parliament was obliged to give way to superior numbers, Lord Melbourne in the end was in his turn upset by a majority of *one*. I have now to relate a curious circumstance. Perceiving that my desire to obtain a seat in the new House of Commons gave no little anxiety to my wife, I endeavoured to set her mind at ease by assuring her that, whatever I might wish, I should take no active steps for that purpose. I told her that if an offer came to me, I should not accept it unless it coincided entirely with my own opinions, and that the extreme improbability of any such occurrence was equivalent to a resolution on my part in her sense. We were then at Somerhill, and in less than three hours after this declaration of mine, we were roused by a smart ring at the house-door bell, which in the country is often an exciting, if not an alarming, sound. After a brief pause Lord George Bentinck was announced, and being wholly unexpected, his arrival was a fresh cause of surprize. The visit, I soon learnt, was to me ; and when we were together alone, he told me that a seat was open at Lynn Regis, in Norfolk, which he had himself represented, and proposed that I should stand in concert with him as a candidate for that borough. We might have a contest, but he thought his friends were strong enough to carry my election as well as his own. There would be no bribery, the legal expenses would be small, I should be expected to support Lord Stanley, who was to act on the idea of giving Peel a fair trial, but in every other respect my votes would be free. The case was so clearly in accordance with my own views that I should

have been justified in starting with him at once. I took, nevertheless, a few hours for consideration, and then, my first impression being fully confirmed, I set out with Lord George for Lynn. There we found a cordial welcome, and also an opponent in the person of Sir John Scott Lillie, a Middlesex magistrate of Radical politics. We had therefore to go through a regular canvass, calling personally on every one of our constituents, whose number amounted to more than eight hundred. Our party was a mixed combination of Liberal

Tories and frightened Whigs. The most powerful interests opposed to us were those of Holkham, Lord Albemarle, and Sir William Fowkes. Our return was finally secured, and we were drawn triumphantly through the town with the usual display of flags and ribands.

"When the session began I took my seat in the House near Lord Stanley below the gangway on the right of the Speaker's chair. On the first trial of strength, which was not long deferred, the new minister found himself in a minority, and was obliged to pass over to the Opposition benches. Lord Stanley and his friends retained their position, without making any nearer approach to the ministerial policy. As the debates proceeded it became more and more evident that there was no real difference between Lord Stanley's opinions and those of Sir Robert Peel, and it seemed to me that much and more than awkwardness would eventually arise from so marked a want of agreement between the appearance and the reality. Under this impression I wrote privately to Lord Stanley suggesting the advantages which he might derive from quitting an equivocal position and presenting to the public eye a party of Liberal constitutionists unmistakably united. He wrote me a friendly answer, but was not prepared to adopt my suggestion. It happened not long after, that in consequence of a taunting speech from O'Connell, he had to cross over to Peel's side while the House was sitting, and take his place among the Conservatives. The two distinguished statesmen had been brought together more by accident than by sympathy from opposite points of the political compass, and I have some reason to believe that they met for the first time in society at a dinner in my house in Grosvenor Square. With respect to Lord Stanley, I take this opportunity to remark that although he gave offence now and then by a sort of schoolboy recklessness of expression, sometimes even of conduct, his cheerful temper bore him out, and made him more popular than others who were always considerate but less frank. From the time when he made one with the Conservatives, Sir Robert took the lead at all their meetings, whether general or select. I was rarely absent from those of either kind, but I must in candour admit that

I might as well have kept away. Though I took a lively interest in all that passed, and did not fail to form my own opinions, I never could overcome a certain diffidence as to taking part in any discussion, and consequently from first to last maintained an unbroken silence."

For seven years, 1835–42, Canning represented Lynn in the House of Commons. He was re-elected in 1837 after a close contest with Major Keppel, and for a third time in 1841, when he was unopposed. Now and then, rather against the grain, he was obliged to journey into Norfolk to take part in a loyal and constitutional dinner at which the members were expected to speak. As Lord George always spoke first there was not much for his colleague to add, and this was a relief to one who announced to his family that "the delivery of a speech is a most awful piece of business—depend upon it." This feeling too often prevailed in the House, where Canning would sometimes arrive armed with careful notes, and then retire without making the intended speech. He forced himself to speak now and then, however ; asked questions, after the fashion of diffident members ; and had the great satisfaction of calling O'Connell and Hume to order. Only four or five times in these seven years did he make any considerable oration. Twice he spoke at length (in 1836 and 1841) on the subject of the lawless occupation of Cracow, and his indignant protest brought a letter from Prince Czartoryski to thank him for the "noble zèle et l'habilité avec lesquels vous avez plaidé la cause de Cracovie." He attacked the Government roundly for their foreign policy, not only as regarded Cracow, but (in 1837) on the affairs of Spain. In 1838 he moved for a select committee on the seizure of the *Vixen* off the Circassian coast, and on a division was defeated by only sixteen votes (184 : 200). But if he was not a shining light in debate, he could always be trusted to appear at a division. Four days in the week he refused all evening invitations in order to devote himself wholly to the business of the House.

It is evident that his object in this constant application to parliamentary work was to fit himself for that employment at home which we have seen was his earliest desire and most constant ambition.   Society on a large scale had never any special attraction for him, though the conversation of clever men and women was a real enjoyment.

When Parliament rose he went into the country like the rest of the world.   We find him at one time living at Sutton Place, a quaint old-fashioned house near Guildford :—

To Planta,
27 Aug.
1834

Think of a great pile of brick with college windows just three centuries old, in the middle of a park ; and then to counterbalance this external magnificence, imagine all that is old-fashioned and queer in the shape of rooms and furniture.   Be that as it may, we have air, and space, and quiet, and whenever you come this way, we shall be delighted to shew you our lions and our ghosts.—

at another at Oxonhoth, a place belonging to Sir William Geary, which besides its own special merit of overlooking the Weald of Kent, had the advantage of being only six miles distant from Somerhill.

A more lengthy expedition was made in 1836, when, accompanied by his wife, Canning paid his first visit to Scotland.   This was before the days of railways, and three months were easily spent in moving leisurely from one country house to another, sowing the seeds of many friendships which, lasting through all the agitations and absences of the next twenty years, blossomed again with renewed vigour when Lord Stratford returned in his old age to settle at home. Inverness was the farthest point reached, but Taymouth, Inverary, Kilgraston, Wishaw, and many other places were visited, while on the return journey some days were spent at Netherby Hall with Sir James Graham, for whom he entertained a high admiration.   He was delighted with this tour. " I rejoice to have seen Scotland " he wrote ; " we have experienced great kindness and hospitality."

In 1839 he took his family abroad.   He had now four children, and the loss of his diplomatic pension, which was the necessary consequence of holding a seat in Parliament, made it necessary to economize ; but there was another and a sadder reason which led to this breaking up of the English home.   Soon after the return from Spain in 1834, while staying at Bognor, the boy whose birth had so crowned his happiness two years before was taken suddenly ill, and, after struggling for many days between life and death, recovered indeed, but only to be a constant source of anxiety and care. The baths of Wildbad in the Black Forest were recommended by the doctors, as well as a subsequent residence in Italy ; but though for a time the change seemed to have a beneficial effect, gradually the hope of a permanent recovery faded away.

To have a son who, trained and modelled on his own ideal of an English statesman, should in the future succeed where he had failed and perpetuate the name of the man he honoured most—for in his boy he proudly hoped to see a second George Canning—had always been his great ambition ; the prize seemed placed within his reach only to be snatched away, for no other son came to fill the vacant place, and none but the wife whose patient faith helped him to bear the burden knew how heavy it was or how nobly it was borne. Henceforth every fresh step in his career brought painfully to his mind that he stood alone, and each time that he turned from the busy public life to the quiet of private life it was to miss more and more the son in whom all his chief interests would naturally have centred.

It was characteristic of Canning's energy of character that no sooner had he shaken off the trammels of Parliamentary life and found himself in the solitude of the Black Forest than he set to work to study German, and to such good purpose that he was soon able to enjoy the writings of Goethe and Schiller. The latter was perhaps the special favourite, and he attempted with some success the difficult task of translating the *Glocke* into English verse while following with scrupulous exactness all the changes and varieties of the German metre.

The beginning of winter, 1839, saw them settled at Genoa in the pretty villa Salicetti, overlooking the Mediterranean ; here the best part of the next two years was spent by Lady Canning, who found in the constant kindness of her many Italian friends some compensation for her loneliness while her husband was absent in London for the session.

There she remained until the summer of 1841, when she

rejoined her husband preparatory to his departure for the fourth time as ambassador to the Porte. His letters during this period, when his parliamentary duties kept him in London, are full of interest, but only a few can be quoted. We may begin with an extract from a letter to Lord Ripon written at the time of the election at Lynn Regis :—

Although I decided against trying my fortune at Paisley, I hope you understand that I am fully sensible of your kindness in thinking of me. At Lynn I have not only been a candidate, but a successful one. I did not indeed go down with the expectation of a contest ; but the struggle, which has ended in keeping out such a Radical as Sir John Scott Lillie, leaves no room for regret. The enemy accused me of being a *Tory*. I said that I was no more a Tory than a Radical ; that I was no friend to party nicknames ; that I thought the ministers ought to be supported, if they fulfilled their promises of Reform in a right spirit ; and that wherever I found a Liberal-Conservative or a Conservative Whig, to that man I was ready to give my hand. To express all this in much better language than either my colleague or I could pretend to do, we reprinted Lord Stanley's address to his Lancastrians. In writing as well as in speaking, his tone (Lord S.'s) and manner are perhaps not always quite so statesmanlike as those of Sir R. Peel or William Pitt. But there is an honest clearness of purpose and a noble alacrity of spirit in him which are well suited to the times, and I trust that in common with the D. of Richmond, yourself, and others, he will be instrumental in saving the country. High character is so essential to the usefulness of a public man that I am unwilling to think him wrong in having declined Peel's tender of office. His refusal has, however, had the effect of rendering the composition of the ministry less Liberal and by consequence more unpopular and unsteady than if you had all joined it at once.

We had an excellent *Grillion* yesterday, the largest and best within the memory of man—that is of our secretary, Sir R. H. Inglis —twenty-one in number, and 100,000 strong in spirits. There was Stanley—the cock of the day- and our poor friend Sp. Rice and the Littleton—with their feathers not quite so clean and glossy—but making the best of it. I am going to dine with Stanley after the debate—a Cabinet dinner, *entre nous*. I am curious to know who and what will be there. I observed that several of the young nobility, aspiring like himself, watched their occasion and gave him a little touch when they could. Morpeth said a sly word, while he

(S.) was displaying his comic powers, which brought up a comparison between him and that "respectable actor Mr. Cowper." The muscles of the young hero relaxed for an instant, and then he got over it. Lord R. Grosvenor told him that he thought he would make an admirable bishop, apropos of something else, and Lord Mahon twitted him for his chancellor-of-the-exchequer-like skill in figures, of which he was then giving a specimen. Stanley in each instance winced, but went on without noticing the hit.

Well ! and what is to come next ? The strong like to exercise their strength, the interested like to grasp their object. So I suppose we shall have plenty to do and perhaps to lament next week. Peel will not think of budging, I presume, upon yesterday's defeat ; but his prospects are not flattering. His countenance when the numbers were announced expressed mortification ; but that it is prone to do on similar occasions. The argument was entirely on the side of our last Speaker. Perhaps he allowed the stories to his discredit to go too long unanswered. I glory in my vote, and only lament that I have not the power to give it more effect ; but Stanley spoke very well and said all that was to be said on our side. Think of Burdett keeping out of the way !

What shall I tell you ? Everyone looks blank. The beaten because they are beaten ; the victorious because they find themselves pledged to many dangerous steps. Some people are eager to defend themselves for supporting Abercromby, and throw dirt in the prosecution of that purpose. There is a rising cry for Lord Stanley ; but somehow or other he has not got the following that his talents, character, rank, and principles would seem to challenge for him. I have passed an hour with Ld. Ripon, more in lamentation than in the discovery of remedies. I have also had a conversation with Hallam. I shall cultivate him ; he is learned in our history, very liberal of his information, and very candid in his opinion, though having an inclination towards the constitution party. Everyone expects that an amendment will be carried to the Address. I only hope that it may be made so gentle as to admit of Peel's accepting it. He must not be too nice. All is at stake. To shew you the difference of people's opinions, Faz. told me to-day with his most honest look that he never heard anything so conclusive as Lord J. Russell's speech. Heaven help him ! say I.

The position of his friends the Stanleyites, who continued to sit on the right of the Speaker after the change of government, was anomalous, and Canning was anxious to cross over

to Peel's side.   His old schoolfellow Gally Knight, who sat
beside him, was of the same opinion.

My impressions as to the expediency of *crossing* agree with
yours.   I should be glad to better myself in point of hearing.   The
old seats are detestable in that respect.   Then, I am inclined to
think that our "whereabout," though a mere formality, should har-
monize with our principle.   We supported Peel in the persuasion
that he would fairly redeem his pledges.   The present ministers are
pledged to what we oppose, and they owe their power to Radicals
and Repealers.   Our relation, therefore, to them is the very reverse
of that in which we stood towards their predecessors.   Is it likely to
improve?   I doubt it.   The Whigs cannot afford to lose the support
of the Radicals.   If Stanley and his friends were numerous enough
to make up for the defection of the latter, there are jealousies and
dislikes which would operate as barriers to a coalition.   At all events,
as matters now stand, we are nearer to the Liberal-Conservatives than
to the Whig-Radicals—to Peel than to Ld. John.   Why then should
we mystify the public by taking up a false position in the House?
Why should we encourage the tendency of waverers towards power
by acting timidly?

But, perhaps, the question is not merely as to *seats*.   It may be
thought better to retain the character of a third party, and in that
view to neutralize our real identity with Peel by an apparent approximation to his opponents.   My humble conviction is that all third
parties are in their nature temporary, and that they cease to be
respectable the moment they lose that degree of weight by which
they may occasionally turn the scale, or that distinctness of colour
without which the country sees only a difference of names and not of
principles.   A deficiency in either of these respects is rarely supplied
by the force or brilliancy of individual talent ; and, in point of
personal attainments, who is there now in the H. of Commons to
compete with Peel?

Let us consider what it is that we really have at heart.   Is it not,
to keep down the dangerous influence of Radical counsels? or, in
other words, to support those whose principles and measures are best
calculated to unite the effective improvement of our established institutions with their continued maintenance in peace and safety?   Apply
this test to the two great parties of the State.   Immediately at issue
between them is the question of the Irish Church.   Is there any
ground left for us to take up broadly and decidedly distinguished
from that which they respectively occupy on this question?   Is it not,
on the contrary, notorious that Stanley and Graham in arguing the
question started from a higher point of conservatism than Peel him-

self? With him they must virtually coöperate throughout the approaching debates on that subject. With respect to other pending questions English tithe, English Church, Dissenters, Corporation, may we not fairly apprehend, after what we have witnessed during the last three, or rather ten, months, that the Radical leaders will not be wanting in any measures now to be brought forward for their settlement? On three of them we have proofs of the liberal spirit in which Peel is prepared to act. His views as to the fourth admit of greater doubt ; but Stanley would of course have explanations on so important a point before he consented to join forces with him.

A letter to Sir Robert Peel and the reply are worth quoting:—

Under other circumstances I might want the courage to intrude, even for a few moments, on your invaluable time. But I see you, though possessed of every enjoyment that private life can afford, engaging yet more deeply in the great political struggle of the day, and at every personal sacrifice nobly planting the standard of high constitutional principles as a rallying point for all who stop short of revolution. This conduct accords so entirely with my expectation— it forms so natural a sequel, in this more onward stage of the contest, to your declarations and measures when Prime Minister, that, for one, I feel it a duty to offer you thus directly the pledge of my assent to the principles you have proclaimed. Taking your speech at Glasgow in connexion with those which you delivered at Tamworth and Merchant Taylors' Hall, I am satisfied that you are not adverse to any measures of sound practical reform consistent with that paramount object —the maintenance of our fundamental establishments in Church and State.

In the H. of Commons it has given me the liveliest satisfaction to see Lord Stanley and Sir James Graham acting constantly from the same benches with yourself, and lending to your preëminent exertions the aid of their distinguished abilities and high parliamentary character. My humble support is almost wholly confined, as you know, to voting. Such as it is, I shall never shrink from giving it to those great principles which engage my conviction, happy when, in spite of adverse majorities, I find them, as they now are, so clearly laid down, so ably and fearlessly maintained.

Every man of reflection and good feeling must view with regret the deepening array of parties throughout the country. But the spirit of coöperation in which all sorts of unconstitutional and anti-constitutional reformers move together, if not for one evil purpose, at least in the prospect of one evil result, would seem to leave their opponents without a choice. My persuasion is that in joining to counteract their league, and to recruit from the ranks of the new constituency, Conservatives only discharge a duty required for their own defence and for that of our free Constitution. In the place which I represent this course, I am happy to say, has been pursued with every appearance of success.

Dear Sir Stratford Canning,—I am much gratified by your letter. All my habits and feelings and wishes are for Reform, but I am confident that the time is come when the broad line of distinction must be drawn between Reform and Revolution.

The immediate practical questions are, I conceive, the maintenance of the House of Lords and of the Protestant Establishment. It is clear that both are aimed at by the more reckless agitators, and that those in authority are so indifferent and lukewarm in their defence, that the influence of authority in their favour is little or nothing in the scale.

I will not say more, than that I think you do very great injustice to your own powers of aiding in the struggle for their maintenance.

I took up my night's quarters at Netherby both in going to Glasgow and returning, and was glad to find such a very agreeable resting place on my hurried journey.

Believe me, My dear Sir Stratford,
With sincere esteem, most faithfully yours,
ROBERT PEEL.

Canning was one of the privy councillors who met on the eventful 20 June, 1837, and, like all who were present, was charmed with the young Queen's manner at her first Council.

I cannot better express my thanks for your bulletins about the health of our good old departed King than by telling you that nothing could be more satisfactory than the demeanour of our young Queen at the Council this morning. She has really gained everyone's good word by her modest self-possession, and the excellent manner in which she delivered her declaration. I was present and can honestly bear witness to the truth.

A letter to Sir James Graham, who lost his seat at this election, will serve to shew how sincerely Canning felt the loss of this able member of his party :—

1837
———
ÆT. 50

To Sir J.
Graham,
Radford,
13 Aug.

Neither to condole with you, nor to express my concern, do I write, but in search of consolation for the blow which has been struck, through you, at our friends and principles. Surely, there must be some arrangement in view for your return to Parliament. Your absence from the House for any length of time would be a serious misfortune to the party, It appears that we have gained considerably in numbers, but numbers alone can never supply the place of distinguished parliamentary talents. I have no right to put questions to you, but it would be a great satisfaction to me to find that there is some opening for you in prospect, though I am well aware that in these times such openings are not easily commanded. At all events, your example in fighting so gallant a battle is not lost to the cause, and many of those who deserted you will live to repent their folly. It requires no inspiration to foresee this. But it does require, if not the spirit of prophecy, more of sagacity, at least, than I possess, to divine the result of the present equilibrium in parties. One thing indeed is tolerably clear. Our adversaries have no chance of carrying the great pending questions in their own way. So far we have obtained a signal triumph. But will they be able to carry on the government with a bare majority? If they resign, will their successors be strong enough, with or without a fresh election, to maintain themselves in power? Come what will, as to these points, it strikes me that another session can hardly terminate without the settlement of the Church-rate and Irish questions. The party in power, whichever it may be, must bring them forward in a shape so moderate as greatly to diminish the means of resistance, and even the motives to it. What I see most reason to apprehend, in a comprehensive national sense, is the depreciation of official character in the one case, and a further expansion of ultra-Liberal feelings in the other. This is my guess, but in presence of your penetration I am fearful of its shallowness.

Since I wrote to you on Monday I have been prodigiously busy. Never were so many nothings crowded into the same space. Visits, purchases, debates, sights, dinners, &c. &c. have succeeded each other in rapid whirl. The pity is that so many good things should be thrown away upon a *single* gentleman of my years. The only consolation I can think of is a hurried description of the magic lantern. Our dinner at the Granvilles was at once most Whiggish and most fashionable. D. of Devonshire, looking marvellously young—an effect, I presume, of deafness—the Dawson Damers, none the worse for a twenty days' journey over the desert—Bear Ellice, Lord Douglas, the Fullertons, and a fry of Howards. In the evening came Princess Lieven, Madam Durazzo and Brignolle, the Russian ambassador, with a few others. The Princess was gracious, the ladies of Genoa good-natured, though I was amused to find that they knew little or nothing of us except from the Bowyers. Of this I shall probably learn more, as I am to dine with the Brignolles to-morrow. Madam de L. seems to be in correspondence with Lady Clanricarde. She is to visit the Duchess of Sutherland this year. . . . I tried to look as if I had forgotten everything, meaning to smooth the way to another and more interesting conversation. We shall see. On Pozzo I have left my card, but I did not ask to go in. Lord Granville went some weeks ago, and after being kept in the ante-room for twenty minutes was obliged to leave the house without seeing its owner. His intellect is sadly overthrown, but he is well enough to move about, and *at times* to talk with coherency. In general the old people seem to wear wonderfully well. The ambassador himself looks good for another ten years of diplomacy. . . .

I went last night to the Français. *Mithridate* (Racine) was acted, and Mlle. Rachel, the young and celebrated Jewess, played the part of the Queen. Her acting was like the play, much to admire, but something unsatisfactory. What pity that such genius and taste as Racine's should have been pinned down to such rules and subjects as those of the French drama! The Jewess has defects both of countenance and shape; but on the whole she is pretty, her complexion very fair, with small eyes and nothing very distinguished in the voice. Her style is natural—an immense advantage, particularly in contrast with the male ranters.

Our *crisis* here is more urgent than ever; and the votes of Friday next will probably decide it. The Cabinet is beaten black and blue, but life is not extinct, and Sandon, as Matador, is to give the *coup de grâce*. Having been forced to give up their Irish Bill, the Ministers presented their Budget, which we know they reckoned upon as presenting something of a popular and saving character. Out it came, and such a Budget was never yet seen! Perhaps it owes its singularity in part to the extraordinary circumstance of its having been produced by a Chancellor of the Exchequer in the middle of his honeymoon. There is a large *deficit*, and in order to get the money to fill it up, Mr. Baring proposes a great change in the duties on sugar, timber, and corn—the latter announced as if leading to a total abolition of the Corn Laws. This desperate proposal has lit up a famous conflagration here, and it is meant to throw the whole country into a blaze, though I very much doubt its having that effect. The whole Conservative party is opposed to it; some of the Whigs themselves dislike it and several important interests and active classes of people are stirred up against it. Mr. Gordon, the Secretary of the Treasury, resigns his place. One of the Whig members for Lincolnshire declared in the House last night that if it depended on his vote the Government should never have an *opportunity* of bringing on their measure. I met Bear Ellice in the street just now. He evidently gives the game up, and in truth nothing short of a miracle can save the party now. The best of it is that they have so timed the matter that they *cannot* dissolve Parliament at present, even if they dare. The language held by some of their friends conveys, nevertheless, a suspicion that some expedient is still in reserve, yet it is difficult to imagine what it can be. At all events, we cannot, I think, be far from the end of this long party struggle. If the Ministers were, contrary to all present appearance, to recover themselves and to get through the Session, there is nothing to prevent their going on for another ten years. But the odds are decidedly against them, and the prevailing impression is that they will all be out of office before the end of next week.

These detestable Ministers, though killed in power and character, still survive in place, and much do I grieve to say that one, who ought by this time to have learnt better, is the principal cause of their tenacity. Yet do not think that they can escape. At least, if they do, the country is doomed and they are immortal. My belief is that they will be in a minority of from ten to twenty on the next division—I mean the pending one relative to the sugar duties, part of their Budget ; and that they must then go, or dissolve, and that the latter alternative, though they still hesitate, they will not venture upon. I may be deceived, but this is what I expect. Their friends give them up. On Friday Dr. Lushington and Mr. Handley, the member for Lincolnshire, condemned them in set speeches and without sparing. The language of our old friend Faz is that the battle has been fairly fought and fairly won. He retires at the next election. The Whigs of the old school—Lord Grey in particular—are unmeasured in their condemnation. Lord J. R. did his best in a very gallant and in some respects a masterly speech ; but so many feelings are shocked and so many interests alarmed that talent and ingenuity come too late into the field.

Think of Rogers and Tommy Moore being seen at the opera on Saturday in two adjoining stalls. If what I have heard be true, the latter must be going down fast. I am assured that he literally went abruptly away from a party the other evening, in consequence of having failed in drawing attention to a story which he had told—or rather which he had repeated after some one else had told it the moment before in his presence, but probably unheard by him. He ran downstairs, and disappeared into the street, before he could be caught up by those who ran after him.

1841

ÆT. 54

Politically, all is right. The Ministers have resigned gracefully, though late, and Peel has been to Windsor this morning. From all that I can learn, there is every appearance of his acting judiciously, and being able to justify the turn of public opinion in his favour. There is a good working majority of 80 ; and I really believe that the Queen, though regretting the chief at least of her late advisers, has made up her mind to act with fairness and sincerity towards their successors.

London,
30 Aug.
1841

Personally, all is in the dark. I do indeed know some few of the forthcoming appointments ; but in general Peel has kept his word of reserving himself till after his first interview with the Queen. I have been twitted with the tardiness of my arrival ; but everyone admits that the diminution of such a majority by a single unit was of no consequence either to the State or to the party ; and as for myself, I must have toiled and sacrificed to little purpose for the last six years if the present omission were to affect my interests. . . .

His hopes of a place in the Conservative Government were doomed to disappointment. He had been passed over in 1834-5, when Peel formed his first short-lived administration, in which Canning had expected to find office. Probably Lord Stanley's refusal to join the Government had something to do with this : but Sir Stratford's deficiency in debate might account for the omission. When Sir Robert came into power again in 1841 Canning's name did not appear in the list of ministerial appointments. They again offered him Canada, See p. 23 which he did not want, and the Treasurership of the Queen's Household, which was not suited to his tastes and feelings of independence. He did not feel attracted by the routine of a Court appointment, and he did not wish to leave England. On the other hand, he was making no useful progress in the House of Commons, and his seat deprived him of his diplomatic pension. A revival of his old disagreement with Lord Aberdeen, now Peel's Foreign Secretary, suddenly brought this undecided state of things to an end. A warm dialogue ended in a hasty demand for an embassy, and Sir Robert acceded to the just claim.

"Lord Aberdeen then sent for me, and his first words were, 'I have now an embassy to offer you, but one, I fear, which you will not like.' 'Perhaps your lordship will tell me what it is,' I replied. 'Constantinople,' was his answer. 'With your lordship's permission I will take forty-eight hours to consider it.' He assented, and I took my leave with a resolution to give his offer a calm unprejudiced consideration. There was no positive duty, no imperious necessity to fix me. I had only to determine which course would be the most reasonable in my situation. I consulted no one, and on a careful review of all the circumstances concluded by accepting. Then only did I acquaint my wife with the resolution I had formed, and I gave her the choice of sharing my new banishment, or staying at home. She preferred the former course, and it was finally agreed that I should set out as soon as the necessary arrangements could be made, and that I should precede my family, who would follow in a few months. My sole companion on the journey was Mr. Curzon, afterwards Lord Zouche. It caused me no small regret to turn my back on Parliament, and particularly on my constituents at Lynn, who had stood firmly by me during three elections, two of them contested, although I had no opportunities of promoting the local interests. I should have liked to retain my seat, but that could not be, and after a short interval the present Lord Derby became my successor.

"November was well advanced before I started for my foreign destination. I took the route of Paris, Strassburg, Vienna, Gratz and Trieste, at which last place the *Devastation*, a large steamer, was to meet me. At Paris I found M. Guizot in power. There was no business to transact between us. My conversation with him was limited to such occasions as a morning visit and a private dinner at his house afforded. His manner was friendly, his tone serious. An amiable trait of character appeared in the affectionate respect he shewed to his mother, an old lady of homely demeanour, who shared his table and resided under his roof. I had hoped to meet Reshid Pasha, but he was absent, and did not return till after I had left. Princess Lieven was living at Paris. I called and saw her. She gave me an affable reception, and

expressed her regret at my exclusion from the embassy to
Russia.   Having strong reason to believe that she had been
at the bottom of that intrigue, I replied that my only regret
had been the premature loss of her society in England, re-
minding her thereby that the Prince her husband had been
recalled because Lord Palmerston could not be induced to
make another appointment in my place."

From Vienna he wrote to Lady Canning :—

Athens will be a good breathing place.   It is curious, but everyone seems to wish that I should go there, even the Russian.   Sir
Edmund Lyons has written a most pressing invitation.   I wish it was
in my power to justify this confidence.   God will perhaps put some
useful ideas into my head when on the spot.   The poor country
wants help.   At Munich I made a point of seeing both the King
and the Prince Royal on purpose to give me an additional chance of
making some impression on their Royal relation's mind.   In Syria
there have been bloody conflicts, and everyone augurs ill of our
episcopal appointment there.   At Constantinople there are movements that seem to imply a change of parties and of counsels.   I
find the prevailing opinion to be that little can be done to improve
the Turks, though they may go on for some years without breaking
up.   I reserve my opinion till I am amongst them ; but I have no
mind to watch a bedridden patient who will neither die nor take
medicine.   I have had some long talks with Prince Metternich.   He
is still a clever man, with habitual powers of thought, and much
experience ; but age and recent illness have shaken his strong constitution, and he is living, like a bear in winter, on his fat.   A greater
change cannot be far distant.   You may judge of its importance
when I tell you that there is no one to replace him, that he is
emperor here, and together with Louis Philippe the mainstay of
peace in Europe.   The Princess is more than thirty years his junior.
She is rather handsome, lively, and very decided.   They receive
company every evening after the play. . . .

The ancient dulness of Munich is enlivened by his Majesty's
taste for the fine arts.   Wonders have been done by him, and in
general the buildings are in admirably good taste.   When I saw the
King it was natural to compliment him on what he had done in
that way.   He made a modest bow of acknowledgment, and added
quickly, with his broad German accent, " And my *finances*, Sar !
are all in varry goot order."   Both he and his son the Prince Royal
talk English—the latter very well.   The King made a great stretch in

1841
——
Æ.T. 55

Vienna,
4 Dec.

receiving me without a uniform. He was himself dressed in an old green chasseur's dress with a *couteau de chasse* at his side.

And so in a doubting and not very hopeful frame of mind Sir Stratford Canning returned to Turkey, there to make for himself a position, an influence, and a name, unparalleled in the annals of diplomacy.

CHAPTER XVII.

THE REFORMER OF TURKEY.

1842–58.

IN the earlier half of the present work I have been dealing with what may almost be called ancient history. The Treaty of Bucharest was signed three-quarters of a century ago, and the actors in it are long since dead. Of the brilliant group of sovereigns, statesmen, and soldiers who were gathered together at the Congress of Vienna in the winter of 1814, Lord Stratford de Redcliffe was the last survivor. Even of those later proceedings which culminated in the revised frontier between Greece and Turkey in 1832, it would be hard to find a solitary witness of official authority. Those that survive, if such there be, are not of the chosen few who are admitted into the *arcana* of diplomacy, and their evidence must necessarily be that of mere spectators. Hence in the earlier part of the *Life* I have been compelled to rely wholly on documentary evidence.

In the period which we now enter the case is different. From 1842 to 1858, with brief intervals of absence, Sir Stratford Canning held sway at the British palace at Constantinople. Turkey was then no longer the unexplored country which she had appeared during his former residences within her borders. The stream of travellers had increased year by year as the means of transit became more rapid and as the influence of the ambassador himself assured more and more the safety of Christian wanderers in the provinces of Islam. Finally the war in the Crimea brought a flood of curious and critical strangers to the Bosphorus and made the Elchi's name a household word. Contemporary witnesses, friendly and hostile, abounded during this later period, and I am thus able to clothe the dry outline of documentary evidence with the many-coloured raiment spun from various minds. Many indeed of the chief actors in those times have passed away in silence ; others have left their impressions in books, and in articles in the periodical prints : but many still survive, in full possession of rare mental faculties, who have generously placed at my disposal the recollections which live in their memories. I have listened to the enthusiastic praise of Lord Stratford's admirers, and also to the detraction of his most violent opponents ; I have honestly tried to judge every issue without prejudice, and to place the result before my readers without concealment ; and after weighing scrupulously the detractions of adversaries and the exaggerations of friends, I am surprized at the agreement which prevails among all classes of my informants. On two or three controversial points I found, as was natural, strongly contrasted opinions ; but on the main qualities of Lord Stratford's character and policy there was but one view. The minor differences could not obliterate the striking unanimity of the general verdict ; and what I had conceived the Elchi to have been in the climax of his life,—from the study of his earlier career and his written testimony,—that conception I found reflected in almost every word, every characteristic trait or anecdote, every weighed judgment, which issued from the well-stored memories of my varied informants. On the grand outline of the character all were agreed, and it depended to a great extent on the intellectual and moral calibre of the witness whether he laid more or less stress upon those surface faults which were visible to those who came within the more immediate influence of the great ambassador.

It was during his long reign at the Porte in the fifth and sixth decades of this century that Canning displayed those qualities and acquired that influence which have gained him the title of "the Great Elchi." Every Turkish scholar knows that the title is founded on a misconception. It is only in England that the words bear the special signification which Mr. Kinglake has made immortal. In Turkey every full ambassador is styled *Buyuk Elchi* or "Great Envoy," to distinguish him from the mere *Elchi*, which is the term

applied to an ordinary minister plenipotentiary. The ambassadors of France and Russia were as much Great Elchis
at Constantinople as Canning himself. The Christians who
dwelt under his protection used a much higher title when
they spoke of their deliverer : they called him " the Padishah
of the Padishah," the sultan of the sultan. But the term is
nothing ; for the meaning is undisputed. What we understand in England by " the Great Elchi," what the Armenians
and Nestorians and Maronites and other downtrodden sects
meant by " the Padishah of the Padishah," what every victim
of wrong or persecution in the most distant province of
the Ottoman Empire appealed to when he used almost the
only English name he had ever heard,—in this there is no
ambiguity. The various words were but synonyms to denote
that unparalleled influence for right and even-handed justice
which was exercised throughout every part of Turkey, in Asia
as in Europe, by the Great Ambassador. An English noble-
man who was journeying in the wildest parts of Asiatic
Turkey in 1853 told me how touching was the trustfulness
with which people of all races and religions looked to the
British palace at Pera for protection. Nestorians, Yezidis,
Maronites, Druses, " and the dwellers in Mesopotamia, and in
Judaea, Jews and proselytes, Cretes and Arabians," Christians
and Musulmans, one and all turned for succour to the far-
reaching arm of the British ambassador. From end to end
of the Turkish dominions his power was felt ; and it is significant of the supreme position which he held, that when Lord
Raglan arrived at the Bosphorus as commander-in-chief of the
English expedition to the Crimea, one of his earliest charges
to an officer was : " Lord Stratford wishes this ; and I would
have you remember that *Lord Stratford's wishes are a law to
me.*"

Years of patient labour were needed before this supreme
influence was attained. In former pages we have seen something of the nature of Turkish government and the obstacles
which the slow crafty dilatoriness of the Ottoman ministers
was able to throw in the path of the ambassador. To the last,
even his authority was unequal to overcome this procrasti-
nating quality, the *vis inertiae* of the Porte ; and though he

often won his point it was not without contesting it inch by inch.

No greater mistake can be made than to conceive of Stratford Canning as a simple ambassador—a mere mouthpiece of the decisions of the British Government. He belonged to a time when the foreign representatives of England were much more independent of the home authorities than they are now ; and though he gradually passed into the new order of things, he never entirely submitted to it. When he began his diplomatic career his communications with the Secretary of State were slow and occasional. To receive an answer to a request for instructions involved a delay of four months, and by the time the instructions came, the crisis for which they were required would in all probability be past. The minister was thus compelled to act upon his own responsibility, and partly in consequence of the distance from home, partly because the Foreign Office chose to leave him unnoticed for nearly the whole of his earliest mission, when he was but a boy-minister, he acquired the habit of acting on his own responsibility to a degree which no modern ambassador could realize. To be hampered by frequent instructions from home was intolerable to one who had so long borne the weight of personal responsibility, and a study of the later correspondence shews that there was sometimes a touch of jealousy between the ambassador who had been accustomed to steer by his own chart and the Foreign Secretary who sought to bind him with the complicated knottings of official red tape. The latter did not always recognize the important fact that, while Canning, like other envoys, owed his official dignity to his government, he added thereto a personal ascendancy which no Cabinet could command and which raised him into a peculiar and authoritative position wholly distinct from that of other ambassadors. On his side, Canning knew too much of departments, and could barely conceal his contempt for them. He made too little allowance for the difficulties of a Cabinet minister, and ascribed the timidity of one or the caution of another to mere weakness, when the cause should have been traced to considerations of expediency—for which, it may be added, he had no respect whatever : right and

wrong he knew, but the expedient was a middle course which
he refused to recognize.

In support of these independent views came a peculiarly
exalted conception of the character of ambassador. A
minister may be nothing more than the spokesman of his
government, but an ambassador is the personal representative
of his sovereign.   To Canning this was a very real doctrine,
and one that affected his conduct in many ways, both in
relation to his government and in his bearing towards foreign
powers.   He felt that it belonged to him to sustain the
dignity of his Queen by his every act ; that he was the
embodiment of the English Crown in the eyes of the Court
to which he was accredited ; that a slight offered to him was
an insult to his sovereign.   This high and noble feeling had
nothing personal in it.   Those who knew him best at the
epoch of his greatest renown agree in describing him as
singularly unassuming, almost humble, in his private capacity ;
diffident as to his personal qualifications and glad to avail himself of others' knowledge.   Self-absorbed he was, in a degree,
—it was the natural result of his career, of his long solitudes,
and his official supremacy ; but he was far from over-rating
his personal attainments, and would converse as frankly and
modestly on great matters of State with a youth fresh from
the university as with a grey-headed statesman.   To young
men who came in contact with him during the critical
period of the Crimean war his frank graciousness was capti-
vating.   Somehow, when engaged in intimate converse with
the many strangers whom his lavish hospitality welcomed at
the Embassy, he contrived to lay aside the awful majesty which
made the Great Elchi a name of terror, and shewed only the
aspect of the cultivated scholar of Eton and Cambridge, the
simple-hearted gentleman, the poetic idealist, the man of high
thoughts and glowing imagination.   His conversation was
brilliant.   Persigny said that to talk with him on such things
as literature or history was delightful ; but once let a contested
point of politics be raised and " immediately you heard the
roar of the British lion."   Canning the man, with his perfect
grace, his manners of the old school of courtesy, his tone of
preux chevalier, possessed a charm which was felt by all who

were capable of appreciating so refined and exalted a nature : but Canning the image of the Queen of England—the embodiment of the country he loved—was a majestic personage. The thought of the Sovereignty which he had to impress upon an ignorant nation—full of its own conceit and incredulous of the might of England—inspired him to an almost heroic ideal of conduct. He was the sort of man to have defended the divine right of kings in the seventeenth century ; and in the nineteenth, his enthusiastic loyalty and patriotism, and his own responsibility for the worthy maintenance of English honour, led him to a line of action which seemed almost to embody a doctrine of the divine right of ambassadors.

Perhaps he carried this high view of the dignity of an ambassador too far. He certainly earned the reputation of arrogance and even of vanity by such pretensions. His stately manner and proud look were pointed to as proofs of personal conceit. But it may well be doubted whether he could ever have acquired that transcendent authority over the Turks which is inseparably associated with his memory if he had been less majestic, less tenacious of his dignity. The Oriental takes you as you would be taken, and to acquire his respect you must *impose* yourself upon him ; and it is impossible even now (and how much more forty years ago) to compel the Turkish mind to action without the aid of such outward machinery. We have seen many ambassadors at Constantinople since Lord Stratford de Redcliffe turned his back for the last time upon the Porte, and exactly in proportion as they followed his proud steps, or yielded up their dignity in the fancied hope of conciliation, has their success been real or vain.

A writer in the *Augsburg Gazette* in 1845—a German and therefore the more impartial, though obviously not the less enthusiastic—describes the impression produced by Canning's manner in words that are worth recalling :—

Among the European diplomatists who reside at Constantinople Sir Stratford Canning is the only one so far who by his imposing presence inspires respect among the grandees of Turkey. In the

East where a fine bearing and a noble stature have more weight than in any other country of the world, a dignified carriage is of more use, even in diplomatic relations, to the representative of a foreign power than can easily be believed in Europe. Orientals are apt to estimate a nation by the presence and stature of its ambassador. A cultivated Turk, himself a man of fine manners, told me once that there was a great difference between the impression produced upon the Sultan and the pashas of the Divàn when a minister like Sir Stratford, with his noble aspect, imposing carriage, and air replete with dignity, opened his lips at an audience or conference, and that made when a man of mediocre appearance, of timid air, and forced reverences came bowing before the Grand Signior. At every diplomatic dinner, ball, or soirée, I noticed the national pride which the English visibly felt as they saw how their ambassador's presence dominated all his colleagues. It is true that in all the lands that I have traversed I have never in my life encountered a countenance so noble and also so *spirituel* as his. . . . There stands the character of Sir Stratford Canning fully portrayed : the masculine energy, the courage, the majestic calm, the gravity, the unquenchable determination,—and with all these an expression of benevolence, sweetness, and kindness. . . . . In conversation Sir Stratford exerts great influence precisely because he is extremely simple, because he despises the false elegance of affected speech, because everyone knows by his grave and quiet words that what he speaks is reflected from the mirror of his heart, because one never finds in him those suave mannerisms, that feigned and affected friendliness, or even that condescending affability which in my opinion is a thousand times more intolerable than rudeness. . . . But if one engages Sir Stratford in a serious conversation on any subject one is surprized by a depth of thought which has nothing in common with the diplomatic salons of Pera ; and he who has need of the protection, the intervention and the sympathy of the British ambassador for himself or for others, he who would excite his compassion for the oppressed, the persecuted, the wronged,—in a word for the unhappy,—will find in the character of Sir Stratford such feelings of humanity, so lively, so real and so warm, as no other diplomatist can pretend to.

The German writer's estimate of the character of Sir Stratford Canning, despite its exaggerated air, is substantially correct. The plain directness of his conversation was the effect of the perfect simplicity of his nature. In such a hotbed of intrigue and trickery as Pera, it was natural to imagine that the ways of all diplomatists were alike ; yet

Canning was no diplomatist in the common sense, of manœuvre;—statesman is his true title, and his successes were
gained by the simple expedient of being so straightforward
that everyone suspected a plot of more than Machiavellian
craft. To say that he did not meet mine by countermine, and
that he never had recourse to secret interviews and private
sources of information, would be to acknowledge that he was
incompetent for his post ; but in no single instance did these
confidential transactions approach the character which we
reprobate in the term " plot." To outwit an antagonist is one
thing, to trick him is another ; and while Canning was a master
with the foils, and could turn his opponent's guard with consummate skill, he never condescended to an unworthy expedient. Above all he never fought for himself: his country
alone commanded his sword. This honourable straightforwardness was perhaps the most striking feature in his conduct
as a statesman, and especially in such a place as Constantinople. The Turks were slow to perceive it ; but even they
came by degrees to believe that what Canning told them was
true, and that he honestly meant them well ; and that was a
novel and reassuring thought in a land of diplomatic mirage.

Yet there was one part of his statesmanship which impressed them even more than his veracity : they never felt
sure that he had come to his last cartridge ; they could never
tell what weapon he held in reserve. There is hardly an
instance, in his long career, of his exhausting his resources.
The retirement from Constantinople after Navarino may be
an exception, but in that instance others had interfered with his
plans. When he won his first and greatest diplomatic triumph
in the signature of the Treaty of Bucharest, he retained
unexchanged a secret article which would have cost England
a third of a million of money ; that *ultima ratio* was held in
reserve. In his later missions to Turkey he acquired such a
thorough confidence in a skilful use of peaceful methods that
he was content with very limited credit. When he drew up
his own instructions in 1853, at the critical time of the Menshikov negotiation, he gave himself no extraordinary powers :
he merely assumed the discretion of requesting the English
admiral to hold himself in readiness for sea,—he did not take

authority to call up the fleet ; and had he been left without 1842-58
interference from home the fleet might never have appeared
in the Dardanelles. High words he spoke and often to the ÆT. 55-71
Porte ; deep and ominous was his menace ; but there was
always something behind to be used in the last extremity ;
and above all other qualities, it was this suspicion of latent
power that impressed the Turkish imagination.

A sincere friend is seldom a popular character. Canning
found himself no exception to this rule. The Turks might
respect his honest truthfulness, but when it took the form of
plain-spoken, and sometimes very hotly-spoken, reprimand, they
began to wish for a little polite insincerity. The British ambassador was a good doctor, the best of them allowed, but his
physic was exceedingly disagreeable. Wholesome truths do
not fit in well with Ottoman notions of government, and most
of the pashas were out of sympathy with their physician's
theories of Turkish reform. They had not forgotten the prominent part he had taken in the emancipation of Greece, the
first serious step towards that partition of the Ottoman Empire
into Christian States which has since taken so large a development ; they knew that he had come to protect the despised
rayas, and this was no title to their regard ; they had no faith
whatever in his scheme of equal citizenship for the Christians.
Moreover if they were obliged to endure a mentor, they would
at least prefer one who was a trifle less dictatorial. "They Kinglake,
felt that he humbled them by making his dictation too clearly i. 121
apparent, and they were often very conscious that the motive
which made them succumb to him was dread." The ministers,
except Reshid, (and not always excepting him,) lived in terror
of a personal visit from the ambassador. When Pisani or even
Alison made his appearance at the Porte, it was possible to
shuffle and evade :—*Bakalum* "We will see," *Bukra* "To-
morrow," and such like expressions, might be usefully em -
ployed with perhaps temporary success. But when the set
face of the Elchi himself penetrated the Sublime Porte, panic
seized upon every official, and the Grand Vezir himself would
condescend to hasten in a tremor of anxiety to meet his inexorable visitor and learn his behests.

Personal interviews of this kind were rare and always

1842-58

Æт. 55-71

meant serious business. When Sir Lintorn Simmons, then a young officer, was about to leave Constantinople on a boundary commission, he found himself hindered by all kinds of delays on the part of the Ottoman grandee who was to act as his colleague. The Englishman was ready, but the Turk was still peacefully engaged with his *chibuk*. At last Colonel Simmons, in despair of ever getting off, ventured to apply to the ambassador. "Why did you not come before?" asked Canning, and forthwith ordered his horse. But even the time needed for saddling was too much for his patience, and he dashed off on foot, and breathlessly mounted the narrow streets of Stambol till he reached the Porte. In a moment the news had spread through every office in the building —"the *Buyuk Elchi* is here," and every man's heart dived into his slippers. The Grand Vezir received his visitors with precipitate politeness, and offered the customary pipes and coffee. "I have not come here to smoke pipes but to do business," said the Elchi; "and I think it would be well if the Sultan's servants smoked less and worked more.—Why is not the Turkish commissioner ready?" In a few minutes the matter was settled, and by the following morning the dilatory official was on his way to the scene of negotiation.

The clubs were once full of similar tales, often much exaggerated; but that the Elchi had a quick temper is a matter upon which there has never been the smallest controversy. Indeed Mr. Kinglake has rightly discovered something of a virtue in this natural irascibility. "His fierce temper," he writes, "being always under control when purposes of State so required, was far from being an infirmity, and was rather a weapon of exceeding sharpness, for it was so wielded by him as to have more tendency to cause dread and surrender than to generate resistance." In private his wrath was less vigilantly guarded, but it is only fair to say that in most cases it was rather the fiery indignation against wrong and falsehood, the fierce scorn of baseness, than the petty irritability of small men. He hated what was mean and dishonourable with a living personal hatred, and could not suffer deceit or insincerity.

Invasion,
i. 119

Yet it were vain to pretend that the Elchi always "did

well to be angry." Little things would irritate his nervous and overtaxed brain to fits of unnecessary passion, to which his natural quickness of temper made him especially prone. The many letters that have been quoted in earlier chapters of this work reveal clearly enough that his nature was impatient ; a small thing would " put him out," especially when the pressure of work was severe and matters were not going well at the Porte. Sometimes he would come in after a long and exasperating conference with a dilatory minister, and then nothing would satisfy him, and woe betide the attaché or servant whom he first encountered. Absolute meekness and silence were the only policy : opposition was out of the question. On one such occasion his *chef* sought vainly to please him ; dish after dish was sent away in disgust, and finally down came the Elchi's fist on the too fragile table, and plates and glasses went crashing on the floor with the *disjecta membra* of the unoffending article of furniture. Battiste, an old courier of the first Napoleon, was in attendance when this happened, and of course came in for his share of the storm : but next morning the ancient servant had some kind words from his master, who was never above tendering an apology to his subordinates, and would sometimes explain regretfully that " something at the Porte had upset him." His servants knew that there was a reason for his impatience, and the best proof of his essential kindness is that they remained with him year after year. One of them was with him nearly forty years, and death alone severed the connexion. In spite of his hasty temper, they knew how to appreciate him ; and one reason of this was the brief endurance of his wrath. He did not bear malice, and his anger seldom lasted till the sun went down.

It is true that Canning seldom made friends of his attachés. In general he treated them with something of the stern discipline of a military commander. The young gentlemen stood in considerable awe of the terrible Elchi, and it is said, though probably fictitiously, that one of them never held converse with his Excellency without keeping a grasp on the doorhandle, ready for instant escape. An ambassador, after all, holds an exceptionally dignified position, and his relations with the young fellows who execute his orders resemble those of a field officer with subalterns ; and strict discipline is the more necessary because an attaché is not a subaltern, and has to be taught what obedience means. The great difference of age had much to do with this over-emphasis in Canning's authority. It was otherwise when he was a young man, and David Morier or Henry Addington was near his own age. At the time of the Crimean war he was nearly seventy, and could hardly be expected to form many new friendships with the young men of his staff. There was a further obstacle in the morals of some of the attachés. To a man of Lord Stratford's tone their conduct and habits were often intensely distasteful. And, apart from such contrasts of character, he too often found in his staff a lack of sympathy in the objects which he had set before himself as most worthy of ambition. They took no interest in Turkish reforms ; they only cared to live their frivolous self-indulgent lives as freely and carelessly as if they had been placed in her Majesty's Embassy for the mere purpose of amusing themselves, frequently at the expense of the natives; and they thought the ambassador was absurdly particular and anxious about things which they considered of no possible consequence.

Lord Stratford was not beloved by such as these ; but as a rule the better sort of attachés, the men who did not shirk work, not only respected—few could help that—but liked him. It was known that, hard as the ambassador worked his men, he worked harder himself. If Mr. Hay had to copy despatches for thirty hours, Sir Stratford was writing the drafts all the time. If on Mr. Odo Russell's arrival at Constantinople, the ambassador, delighted to get a fresh vigorous young hand, kept him imprisoned and hard at the grindstone for six weeks before he allowed him to satisfy his curiosity about the mosques and bazars of Stambol, he at least shared the imprisonment and worked unflinchingly at his side. It was no uncommon thing for an attaché to enter his Excellency's room in the early morning and find him still in his evening dress. No doubt the ambassador forgot that even young men might not possess his iron endurance and marvellous power of work. Few could toil as he did.

Rising at five or six every morning, Canning sat down to
the long file of petitions which always lay on his table for
immediate attention: petitions from persons of all kinds,
—merchants who had claims against the Porte, Ionian
scoundrels who used the protection of England to cover
their crimes, Christians of every race and form of creed
who sought his protection against injustice and persecution.
These being duly docketed with instructions to the consuls
or other officials, the correspondence began, and often lasted
through a great part of the day, varied by much pacing
to and fro, as is the habit of thoughtful men. Sometimes
the stress of business compelled him to postpone luncheon
till it was almost time for dinner. At ten he retired,—but
retiring seldom meant immediate rest. Far into the night his
light was burning, and in times of great pressure, when the
courier was at the door, waiting for despatches, it was often
morning before the last signature was subscribed. Six o'clock
nevertheless saw him again at his work.

He was essentially a desk-negotiator. He reserved
personal conferences for the last resource, and preferred to
transact all business by the pen. We have seen examples of
the memoranda he wrote for the dragomans to read to the
Turkish ministers and of the detailed plans of negotiation
which he drew up for his own guidance. All these involved
considerable manual labour, and the usual rule confining each
despatch to the Foreign Office to one subject greatly increased
the bulk of his official correspondence. Besides this, at the
time of the Crimean War, there was correspondence with three
generals, with heads of all the army departments, hospitals,
transports, foreign colleagues, ambassadors at other courts,
besides the routine business with consuls, pashas, merchants,
and in short with everybody who had something to do or
of whom something had to be obtained. His power of continuous work was the more remarkable because Lord Stratford led a sedentary life. Since he left school he had never
attempted athletic amusements. He rode, it is true, whenever
he could; but he was not much of a sportsman, and though
he made an annual expedition to the forest of Belgrade to
shoot boars, he took care to keep a good marksman by his

side. In short he spent most of his day at his desk, and a by no means regular walk, ride, or drive, was his principal form of exercise.

He disliked the climate of Pera, and Therapia was his breathing place ; but even there, with incessant work and little exercise, it needed great care and abstemiousness to ward off illness. In 1844 gout laid its hand upon him, and from that time forwards he was liable to its onslaughts. When the attack was sharp, and the heat was trying, and the business of the Embassy weighed heavily, Canning might vent his irritation in good honest Saxon, but he never slacked speed at his desk, though it had to be placed on his bed. When the courier had departed, the ambassador alone appeared unmoved : there was " a general occultation of the minor luminaries." He was often surprized to observe how easily he bore fatigues which disabled the young men of his staff. On one occasion when he made his annual excursion to the forest of Belgrade accompanied by the attachés, the ambassador was the sole survivor at the dinner-table. The day had been long and fatiguing, and they had ridden from the early morning to 9 at night, when they returned to the palace to find some guests awaiting dinner. Lord Stratford was dressed and at table in ten minutes ; but not a single attaché appeared.

Naturally a man who at the age of seventy could endure fatigue such as this was not likely to be an easy taskmaster. The attachés complained that he worked them to death. Sir John Hay told me that he was once very nearly killed by overwork ; and as Canning, immersed in business, had little time for studying the complexions of his staff, the Embassy doctor took upon himself to warn him that Mr. Hay must have rest. The Elchi was the last man to overlook such a hint : he put the attaché on board a man-of-war then lying in the Golden Horn and sent the vessel with despatches to Malta. The staff knew that if once a man found favour in the ambassador's eyes and did his work well, Canning would be staunch and loyal to him to the end. No one under his orders ever suffered for lack of his support. Whatever error there might be, Canning took the responsibility of his subordinate ; and each man, be he attaché or consul, knew that he could depend on his chief's support even against the Foreign Office itself. While thus just and staunch to all subordinates, he had his preferences. He was quick to form his impressions, and his first likings seldom changed. The ambassador's eye saw deeply into a man ; people used to say that he looked them through ; and Titov the Russian minister remarked that this eye was its owner's chief enemy. Instead of the easy frank unsuspicious air which a diplomatist should employ when he wishes to lure his antagonist on to compromising revelations, Canning, said Titov, appeared to be gazing right into your soul, where he evidently expected to find something very disagreeable. This is the criticism of a friend and there is some truth in it. The Great Elchi was by nature or by force of circumstances over-apt to suspect insincerity and double-dealing, and his eye would sometimes betray him ; but that he could suppress the penetration of his glance when occasion demanded was frequently shewn, and notably at the famous conferences with Prince Menshikov. When circumstances required it he could become blind ; and when the Russian plenipotentiary once insulted him, he turned the matter over in his mind a moment, and, seeing that a quarrel was inexpedient, immediately *became deaf.*

This watchful air undoubtedly did him injury not only with opponents but with his official "family ;" yet in the midst of the intrigues of Constantinople nothing was more natural. So much treachery had encircled him there from his youth up, that he needed a wary eye ; and it is not always easy to change one's mental attitude to match one's surroundings. On his arrival in 1842 he took a step dictated partly by this feeling which brought him at once into disfavour with the staff. He had learnt before leaving England that one of the secretaries of the Embassy, when at another Court, had been guilty of some official indiscretion : it was said that he had disclosed information which ought never to have escaped from the archives. Determined that this should not occur under his rule, one of the first questions which he addressed to the staff, when they came to pay him their respects on board the man-of-war which brought him out, was "Gentlemen, who has charge of the archives?" The reply was unsatisfactory. It appeared that all the attachés had access to the papers and went to consult them whenever they pleased. Lord Ponsonby's indulgent government had in fact allowed the staff to get into somewhat irregular habits. Canning did not hesitate at the risk of unpopularity to put a stop to this laxness. Singling out one among the staff, he informed him that he alone was to open the despatches and hold the key of the archive presses ; no one else on any pretext was to have access to them. The cause of the restriction made an attempt to override the rule ; but the offence was not repeated.

The whole staff felt not unnaturally aggrieved at what they regarded as want of confidence in their honour ; yet there can be no doubt that the ambassador was right in the interests of the public service in restricting access to the archives. It seems highly dangerous to allow any young man who happens to be an attaché, with or without discretion, to run loose among state secrets. But it must be allowed that the restriction might have been managed with more tact. Young English gentlemen do not like to fancy themselves distrusted ; a question of honour is very delicate and brittle to handle ; and Canning, sensitive as he was himself on such a point, was perhaps hardly indulgent enough towards the same feeling in others. He lacked address in managing his subordinates ; his own temper was too impatient and fiery, and his standard of work too high for their desultory diligence. Moreover he had been accustomed to the old order of things when an ambassador selected his own staff from among his friends and most of the *personnel* of an embassy changed with each succession in the command. It was new and unpleasant to him to have unknown youngsters thrust upon him by the Foreign Office, some of whom may have had no other recommendation than being the relatives of noblemen who were useful to the government.

If Canning was sometimes over-severe with his staff, he had often only too good cause. On the other hand, whatever the eccentricities of some of his assistants, few ambassadors have been served by an abler, one may even say a more brilliant circle of men. The Oriental secretary, Charles Alison, with many peculiarities, was not only a marvellous linguist, but a man of subtle and penetrating mind, and his services proved invaluable to his chief. He it was to whom Canning entrusted the most difficult negotiations, where a knowledge of Turkish was essential; he was more at home in Turkish families than the ambassador could possibly be, and if there were an intrigue on foot Alison was tolerably sure to hear of it from his extensive Turkish and Greek acquaintance. The despatches are full of praises of his achievements, and however little sympathy on most great questions there might be between the ambassador and his Voltairean *laissez-aller* secretary, the latter was a zealous and efficient instrument of his chief's designs, and Canning never failed to give him full credit for his success. A staff that included from time to time men of such varied attainments as Percy Smythe (afterwards Lord Strangford), Lord Stanley of Alderley, Lord Napier and Ettrick, Robert Curzon (Lord Zouche), Lord Cowley, Odo Russell (Lord Ampthill), Sir John Drummond Hay, and such outside assistants as Layard, Rawlinson, and Newton, can hardly be described as less than highly distinguished in many brilliant qualities of mind and learning. To their abilities much of the success that marked Canning's reign at Constantinople was undoubtedly due; but it may well be questioned whether without his firm hand and stern resolution, which some of them found hard to bear, all their combined intellects would have brought about the diplomatic triumphs which he attained. His success at the Porte was mainly one of character; and though he needed clever supple minds to work out his measures, the ideas originated with him alone, and owed their effect mainly to his rigid resolve and unflinching perseverance. His brain conceived the scheme, the heat of his enthusiasm forged and welded the scattered links of Turkish reform, he alone dreamed of a regenerated Turkey where Christian and Musulman alike should resist in firm unity, shoulder to shoulder, the insidious approach of Russia. Alison and others might help him, and did help him with infinite skill; but Alison, who liked the Turks very well as they were, would have shrugged his shoulders at reforms, and let them alone, had not the fiery zeal of his chief set him to work. Whatever was great, whatever made for even justice and the protection of the oppressed, whatever, a cynic may add, was Quixotic and impracticably ideal, in the statesmanship of the British Palace at Pera, was due to Canning alone. Others might trim the sails of his vessel of state, others might load her guns and stand ready with the match, but so long as he was captain of the ship no hand but his touched the helm, no other voice rang out when the broadside was to be fired.

Yet it is above all things noteworthy that with this immense influence, with an authority which was as nearly despotic as that of a Christian and a foreigner can ever be in Turkey, he was not arbitrary. He used his power, not for power's sake, but to attain a definite end. He entered upon his dominion at Constantinople with a fixed purpose—to make the continuance of the Ottoman Empire possible by making it European. His policy was open, avowed, straightforward. Private motives he had none. He would save Turkey in spite of herself if she could be saved at all. Whatever made for this goal found a firm advocate in Canning. An equitable pasha, a wise minister, a just law, a single-minded colleague, need fear no opposition from him ; his voice was always ready to be raised in their behalf. But let all take heed how they thwart him in his *grande idée*. Should the French ambassador seek to increase the prestige of his king or president or emperor by supporting the Turks in their opposition to reform, or by any policy hostile to his great scheme, that ambassador would probably be recalled. A Turkish minister who attempted to return to the old Ottoman ways was doomed to fall. A pasha who refused to execute the humane laws passed at Canning's instigation lost his post. But all this was in pursuance of a fixed policy, a policy that never once wavered during sixteen years of sore trials and many reverses. He had laid out his road before him, and in that road he and the Sultan were to walk. If any man uprose in the way, he must be made to stand aside ; if another would come and join in the procession, he was heartily welcome. But whether they stood in the road or followed in his train, one thing was plain :

—he was going straight on. In spite of obstacles, and with or without assistance, he would pursue the path he had marked out for himself and for the empire over which he dominated. To the Turks, this immovable resolution carried with it something of the air of destiny. " If what he directed was inconsistent with the nature of things, then possibly the nature of things would be changed by the decree of Heaven, for there was no hope that the Great Elchi would relax his will. In the meantime, however, and by the blessing of God, the actual execution of the ambassador's painful mandates might perhaps be suffered to encounter a little delay." Delay indeed was the one form of opposition which Canning found hardest to bear and to overcome. How he overcame it step by step ; how he sought to impose upon the Sultan and his ministers his idea of a New Turkey, an empire worthy to take a place in the councils of European States ; what he achieved, and where he failed ; this is what we must survey in the chapters to come. As the story wears on we shall often see a strong man in adversity, but we shall never be tempted to forget for a moment that the man is strong.

It is time, however, to consider the conditions in which the Great Elchi began his work of reformation and the change which had taken place in Turkey since his former residences.

When for the fourth time Sir Stratford Canning went to take charge of the English Embassy at Constantinople in 1842, he found himself in almost a new Turkey. Outwardly, at least, everything appeared changed. Stambol, as he remembered it in 1810, or even in 1826, was a different place from Constantinople in 1842. The mosques still crowned the Seven Hills, the narrow crowded streets and bazars climbed upwards from the Golden Horn, the " Bab-i-Humayun " itself —the Sublime Porte—was still to be dutifully visited hard by the ruined vestiges of Eski Serai : but the character of the place, of the people, of the Porte itself, was altered and transformed. The day when Sultan Mahmud II. struck the resolute blow which put an end at once and for ever to the baneful tyranny of the Janissaries was the birthday of modern Turkey. On that day an old system passed away and a new one came into being. The paralysing panic of

1842-58

ÆT. 55-71

Kinglake,
i. 120

military despotism was removed ; the royal power was restored ; and in the hands of Mahmud that power might be exerted for great ends. He was the one ruler who in happier conditions could have saved Turkey. He it was who saw the needs of his country, formed his purpose, pursued it secretly for twenty years, then dealt his sudden blow, and at once inaugurated his reforms. Such resolution, such immovable firmness, such patience, are rare among princes ; and though strength of will in Mahmud carried with it an unpleasing rigidity and in religious matters a quality of fanaticism, there is no doubt that he had the ability as well as the desire to revive the ancient lustre of his house by bringing to it some glimmer of the light of Western civilization.

It is easy to look back now with a pitying smile over the failures, the broken vows, the paper constitutions, of half a century of Ottoman history, and to wonder why people expected so much of Mahmud's reforms, why men hoped for the regeneration of " the unspeakable Turk,"—aye and continued to hope for many years after the reforming Sultan had been laid in his grave : but at the time there was something touching in the strong ignorant man's struggle against the corruptions of his empire—his blind feeling after the best means to raise his country to the level of a European State. We picture to ourselves the Sultan casting aside the fond traditions of the past, unlearning what he had been taught in his youth, and groping blunderingly among new principles and new customs. We do not imagine him an ideal reformer, a man of broad views and the wisdom that comes from ripe study : his mind was built in a narrow and unbending mould, and he did not dream of such a regeneration of Turkey as Canning afterwards attempted. But he saw the first obvious necessities of government and he made unhesitatingly in their direction. He knew that a strong ruler upheld by a loyal and disciplined army alone could rescue the empire and stem the tide of corruption and foreign aggrandizement, and he knew that an army such as he needed could only be formed on a European model. Hence we see him immersed in a French drill book ; hence he unlearns his old Turkish riding, and fearlessly mounts a barebacked horse till his long legs acquire the seat of an English dragoon ; hence he casts away the turban and kaftan, and assumes the European coat, trousers, and boots, and retains as a distinguishing mark only the red fez.

It was a brave effort, and the more astonishing since it was made in solitude and isolation. No one prompted Mahmud, no one man can be pointed out as having prominently and voluntarily assisted him : what help he had he commanded and he rewarded. It was his misfortune as well as his glory to be before his age, to attempt reform, however crude and elementary, at a time when no one understood the necessity or believed in the policy. He began single-handed, and his greatest difficulty was to find a single capable instrument to carry out his designs. He failed to realize his ambition, not from lack of force or resolution, but because his countrymen were not prepared and because foreign powers left him unaided. England, France, and Russia were the foes that crushed Mahmud's wise projects. Russia perceived that her prey was escaping her, and determined to strike at once. Filled with a half-Christian half-antiquarian enthusiasm, England and France joined in the Czar's designs and outraged the national feelings of the Ottoman Sultan by demanding the dismemberment of his empire for the sake of the Greeks. They allowed Russia to make a wanton war upon him just at the moment when they had so tied their hands by treaty that they could not defend him, and when they had seriously injured his chance of success by sending his fleet to the bottom of the bay of Navarino.

The loss of Greece and the humiliation of the Treaty of Adrianople destroyed much of the Sultan's spirit and prestige ; and when, with an incredible lack of political capacity, and in disregard of the solemn warnings which Canning addressed to them, the English Government had succumbed to French ascendancy and allowed Mohammed Ali to carry his triumphant standards across Syria and well-nigh to threaten the sacred city of Constantine itself,—then broke the proud spirit of Mahmud ; and the man, who had so resolutely and so carefully planned a new era for his country, just lived to see his every hope extinguished, and closed his eyes in welcome death that he might not witness the dissolution of his empire.

Yet the end of Mahmud's reforms was not all failure. The improvements of Abdu-l-Mejid and his advisers were the fruit of his father's sowing. Above all it was Mahmud who first awoke Canning's interest in Turkish reform. During his earlier residences at the British palace at Pera it is not too much to say that the ambassador had hardly given a thought to the separate and independent interests of the Ottoman Empire. To Turkey as the barrier against Russia, the door-keeper of the Dardanelles, he ever gave his hearty support : she was necessary to England, and that was enough. But to improve, to Europeanize, the vast disjointed empire of the Grand Signior, seems hardly to have occurred to him as a possibility in those early days. From 1810 to 1812 he was busy night and day in defending England's rights and resisting French influence. In 1826–27 his attention was again diverted from Turkey to an extraneous object. His mission was directed almost exclusively to mediation on behalf of the Greeks, and this alone was sufficient to extinguish every hope of sympathy between him and the Turkish Government. In Mahmud he saw chiefly the relentless despot of Hellas : he had no time to view the other side of his character.

It was not much before 1832 that the ambassador whose name is now identified with the cause of reform in Turkey began to see clearly the necessity of radical changes in the administration of the empire. His intercourse in that year with the Sultan became suddenly more intimate and confidential. Mahmud perhaps began to perceive that if foreign aid were needed to realize his hopes, there was no man more fitted by nature to help him than the resolute ambassador who had so often defied him. Canning on his side felt more kindly and respectfully towards the Sultan ; and with the growing esteem came a corresponding interest in the policy of internal reform. He had witnessed the destruction of the Janissaries, and his despatches shew that he was not blind to the critical nature of the revolution, though as yet he did not feel himself called upon to sympathize or coöperate in it. Since that momentous event, circumstances had come by degrees to his knowledge which led him to bestow more attention on the new policy. The following letter from one of the attachés to Sir R. Gordon's embassy formed part of the information which now came to him with increasing force :—

1832
———
ÆT. 45

What engrosses everybody here [is] the extraordinary change which is daily taking place in the manners of this people. You yourself witnessed the commencement of the change, but, if I am to believe . . . every person who has been absent and has now returned, the change since your departure has been still more extraordinary. Very few years more, and not a turban will exist. Grand Vezir, Reis Efendi, Ulema, employés of every description, now wear the red cap, cossack trousers, black boots, and a plain red or blue cloak buttoned under the chin. No gold embroidery, no jewels, no pelisses. The Sultan wears a blue jacket, cossack trousers, black boots, and the red cap like the others, and he now contemplates adding a shade to the latter. He has paid a visit to Madame Hübsch, has been boar-shooting at Belgrade, on which occasion he borrowed Black's house, and in fact behaving so unaccountably that . . . Cartwright [the consul] cannot account for it in any other way than by believing him cracked, and he supposes that it is to be attributed to drinking. Chabert assures me that all the old Turks are outrageous and that several have lamented to him that they were becoming infidels ; the young ones are however all decidedly in favour of the new system, and of such his officers and armies are composed. I have not seen an officer of regulars who was apparently above thirty ; some of the soldiers appear scarce fourteen : they go through the evolutions with great precision, and have entirely the appearance of regular troops. The Sultan himself occasionally appears incognito at the capital, with scarce any attendant, goes to the mosque in the dress I have described, and although some of the populace have occasionally betrayed their discontent by abuse, he has apparently taken not the slightest notice of it . . . Black on the contrary conceives that the Sultan knows extremely well what he is about ; that he has got rid of the old Turks and is certain of the young ones ; that he will conciliate the good opinion of the whole world by the course which he is pursuing, and that let him but get peace on honourable terms and recruit the exhausted resources of the country, he will confer permanent blessings upon this country. . . .

In the camp every officer, every private, loaded us with civilities, shewed us their tents and arms, went through their manœuvres, offered us pipes and coffee, &c. Several officers have already dined us, and conduct themselves quite like Christians, particularly in

Fr. R. C.
Mellish,
Constanti-
nople,
28 June,
1829

1832
———
ÆT. 45

drinking. That there is something not quite right about the Sultan's mind I almost feel convinced of : but whether Providence is not working a change in this extraordinary people by means of a mad-man is a matter of curious speculation. I can scarcely doubt his personal bravery now. He heard the other day that the Topjis [artillery] were determined not to adopt the red cap and new dis-cipline and that they were violent in their abuse of his measures. He immediately went *quite alone* to their barracks, visited their mosque, and walking through every part of the building seemed to defy them. Not one word of abuse was heard.

Information such as this prepared Canning in some degree for the astonishing alterations which he observed in Turkish manners in 1832. The Sultan and his ministers for the first time appeared to treat "infidels" as though they were equals. It was possible to transact business with some of the officials without either humiliation or threats. The younger genera-tion of Turks were becoming positively civilized. Canning began to approach nearer to confidential relations with them, and with this came a more accurate insight into the position of affairs. He grasped the vital importance of the crisis ; the time had come to choose between two courses : to leave the Turkish Empire to its inevitable fate, or to try to save it by "an approach to the civilization of Christendom." He announced this conclusion in a memorable despatch to Lord Palmerston—almost the first hint of the policy to which he devoted the rest of his official career.

To Lord
Palmer-
ston, XII.
7 March,
1832

The Sultan as your lordship is doubtless aware has long sought to render his authority independent of the restraints to which his more immediate predecessors, though equally absolute in principle, were obliged practically to submit. In the prosecution of this favourite scheme during a reign of twenty-five years he has been eminently successful. The pashas of Baghdad and Scutari, the famous Ali of Janina, the Derébeys or feudal lords of Asia Minor, the Janissaries, and finally the Albanian chiefs, have all in succession sunk beneath the weight of his sceptre. To these may be added the Mamluks who were treacherously butchered in cold blood by the present Viceroy of Egypt, acting under the sanction if not at the instigation of the Sultan, and the Wahhabis who were subsequently reduced to insignificance by the forces of the same pasha. . . .

The Sultan's habit, and it may be essential to his safety, is to

look into every department of the State and to manage all its concerns himself. He goes about at all hours, and in all weathers,
residing even at this season in a small country palace on the
Bosphorus, where he is in a great measure free from the restraints,
the expenses, and the dangers, of the Seraglio. But neither his
activity nor his resolution has hitherto made him independent of
favourites. . . .

The great end and aim of the Sultan's exertions is the formation
of a military force capable of maintaining his authority at home and
enabling him to recover the station which he has lost for the present
with respect to foreign countries. For these purposes he has it in
view to establish a sort of national guard throughout the empire, and
he no doubt hopes that after a few years his military orphan school at
Constantinople will furnish a sufficient number of native officers to
command it. Muskets and cloth for the use of the army are already
in part manufactured at home, and the government would not perhaps
refuse to receive a certain number of Christian officers into its service,
although their habits and the high pay they would expect are felt to
be drawbacks to the advantage of employing them.

The main and perhaps insuperable obstacle to the establishment
of a large national army in this country consists in the necessity of
adopting at the same time a totally new system of administration.
Without a basis of this kind the Sultan will labour in vain to erect a
military structure of any real strength and utility, and hampered as
he is by the vices of a worn-out system founded on religious faith,
and by the incongruous elements of which his empire is composed,
to say nothing of his commercial treaties with foreign powers and
more particularly of his various entanglements with Russia, it is difficult to conceive by what means so great and perilous a task can be
achieved. It may be true that nothing is impossible to genius ; and
the natural resources of the Turkish Empire are infinitely greater than
those of Russia when Peter the Great undertook to transform his
barbarous hordes into a civilized and powerful nation. But although
the character of the reigning Sultan is in some respects worthy of
praise and even of admiration, it may well be doubted whether he
possesses knowledge and capacity equal to the crisis ; and bountiful as
nature has been to this empire in every capital point, yet such is the
ruinous tendency of institutions raised on false principles that the
greatest natural advantages would seem to be unavailable now that
the circumstances which once gave an extraordinary impulse to the
Turkish people have ceased to operate. With the exception of the
Ulema, and the border chieftains of Bosnia, whose strength lies in
their castles, there is no longer any constituted body or class of
hereditary proprietors in Turkey ; life and property are still unpro-
tected by an adequate system of laws ; and the despotism of the

Koran is evidently yielding to the influences of Christianity, the religion of civilization. The Turks of all ranks have lost in a great measure that pride and confidence in themselves which at times supplied the place of real strength, and though it is not impossible that some flashes of their ancient spirit may yet on a favourable occasion break forth, there is little prospect of its revival proving in any case more than partial or temporary.

The great question to be resolved is this : *How far is it possible to introduce into the present system of administration those improvements without which the army and finances of the country must be equally inefficient?* Pertev Efendi I know has said within the last few days that as soon as the Greek and Egyptian questions are disposed of, a regular plan of improvement will be commenced. But it is to be feared that other urgent questions originating in the decayed state of this empire will occasion fresh delay even when those which now occupy the government shall have been settled. More than five years have elapsed since the Janissaries were destroyed, and although some regulations of a better kind have been adopted, and the Sultan's policy is in general of a milder and more protecting character, no beneficial results, except that of a diminished animosity between Turks and Christians, are yet visible. The regular army is not more numerous now and scarcely better disciplined than it was before the war with Russia. The financial embarrassments increase, and commerce is still depressed by a pernicious system of monopoly. . . .

Such my lord is the substance of the information which has lately come to my knowledge, and I am anxious to bring it under notice, even at the risk of wearying your lordship's patience, because *I think the time is near at hand, or perhaps already come, when it is necessary that a decided line of policy should be adopted and steadily pursued with respect to this country. The Turkish Empire is evidently hastening to its dissolution, and an approach to the civilization of Christendom affords the only chance of keeping it together for any length of time.* That chance is a very precarious one at best, and should it unfortunately not be realized the dismemberment which would ensue could hardly fail of disturbing the peace of Europe through a long series of years.

In the words which I have italicized we find the germ of that policy of reform for which Canning laboured during sixteen years. He was not yet sure of Mahmud, as the tone of the despatch indicates : but his opinion of him improved as the year 1832 wore on, and the final audience of leave—the last occasion on which he saw the Sultan—made a deep impression upon him.

Then he returned to England and the House of Commons, and for almost ten years he had no voice in Turkish affairs, till at last in the fulness of time he went forth again to the Bosphorus, and now—not to hold the fort against the French, nor to mediate for insurrectionary Greeks—but to work for the Turkish Empire itself, to carry out that policy of reform, that approach to the civilization of Christendom, which he had foreseen in 1832.

This was the keynote of his mission. The first "instruction" which he received from Lord Aberdeen, after the usual command to support the Sultan's authority and the integrity of his empire, proceeds forthwith to the burning question : he was to "impart stability to the Sultan's government by promoting judicious and well-considered reforms." He was not indeed to meddle busily in the internal affairs of Turkey —that was not within the province of an ambassador— but he was to support and even to suggest such measures of reform as were manifestly and imperatively called for. In the list of pressing questions the reform of the army held the first place : the Turkish forces required to be limited and subjected to better discipline. The whole administration and police were to be improved for the better tranquillity of the empire. Public officers were to be chosen with more care. Christians were to be treated with humanity. The trade and resources of Turkey, her mines and forests, should be developed by an enlarged system of roads and increased steam communications. The chief cause of provincial discontent was to be removed by a better system of collecting the taxes. Such were the leading points in the outline of reform presented in the instruction of her Majesty's Government. In addition Canning was to promote a good understanding between the Porte and the Pasha of Egypt, to endeavour to settle the outstanding pecuniary and commercial difficulties with Greece, to press upon the Porte the utmost indulgence towards the Christians and Druses of the Lebanon, to soften the animosities and allay the frontier disputes between Turkey and Persia, and, in short, generally to use his every effort for peace abroad and tranquillity and good government within the borders of the Ottoman Empire.

1842
———
ÆT. 55

Despite many outward changes the state of affairs on his arrival was by no means encouraging to the hopes of improvement with which he had left England. A strong reaction against Western influence had set in. Fortunately we are not here concerned with the management of diplomacy in Turkey during Canning's absence ; otherwise it might be necessary to inquire whether a firm steady policy such as his might not have saved the Porte from the many troubles which encompassed and well-nigh overwhelmed her between 1833 and 1841. At least we may be sure that the Treaty of Hunkiar Iskelesi would never have been signed had he been at the British Embassy. The tardy though eventually signal intervention of England between the Sultan and Mohammed Ali might also have been accelerated by a strong · ambassador. Lord Ponsonby, however, did his best, and the settlement of the Egyptian question owed much to his exertions. But he left the Porte in very evil plight, and in no very grateful mood towards her lethargic Allies. The war with Egypt, the temporary loss of Syria, numerous insurrections and defections, had seriously impaired her strength and finances. Syria had indeed been restored to her by the Allies, whose army and fleet had just been withdrawn ; Mohammed Ali had been reduced to what England considered his proper place ; the Turkish fleet had been surrendered by the Pasha of Egypt ; and the most dangerous article of the Treaty of Hunkiar Iskelesi had been repealed by the Treaty of 1841 whereby the Bosphorus and Dardanelles were once more made Turkish and not Russian waters. But Turkey had been alarmingly weakened by the attacks of the past fourteen years. Russia and Egypt between them had refused Mahmud that period of peace which alone could have rendered his reforming policy triumphant. Moreover the great Sultan was dead, and an

1839

amiable but irresolute youth reigned in his stead. How far the well-intentioned weakness of Abdu-l-Mejid was on the whole an advantage in the hands of such a tutor as Sir Stratford Canning we shall see as we go on : but in the absence of some such controlling influence the change from a mind— narrow perhaps, but resolute, indefatigable, and commanding —like Mahmud's, to the mild intelligence of his son, must

appear an incalculable calamity. Canning indeed presaged
good results. He preferred a pupil to a rival, and wrote, after
his first audience of the new sovereign, that "the graciousness
of his manner, and the intelligent, though gentle and even
melancholy, expression of his countenance, warrant a hope,
perhaps a sanguine one, that with riper years and a more experienced judgment he may prove a real blessing and source
of strength to his country."

Subsequent intercourse with the young Sultan confirmed
this favourable opinion. On one occasion when the ambassador had a private audience of his Majesty, with no one
present but Riza the grand chamberlain, and the interpreter,
the Sultan was unusually affable and encouraging. He
spoke openly of his personal views, and said that "the great
object of his policy was the happiness of his subjects; he intended and had ordered the execution of those humane laws
which had been promulgated at Gulhané and consigned to
the reformed code; he wished to maintain relations of peace
with every European Power and those of confidence and intimacy with Great Britain." Reform, he protested, was dear to
him, and could he but find ten pashas to coöperate he would
feel sure of success: the difficulty was to find willing instruments. Swayed as the young prince might be, to and fro, by
divergent counsels, at heart he was always true to reform and
staunch to its chief European advocate. "He possessed"
wrote Canning in later years "a kindly disposition, a sound
understanding, a clear sense of duty, proper feelings of dignity
without pride, and a degree of humanity seldom, if ever, exhibited by the best of his ancestors. The full development
of these qualities found a check in the want of vigour which
dated from his birth and which his early accession to the
throne and consequent indulgence in youthful passions served
to increase. The bent of his mind inclined him to reform
conducted on mild and liberal principles. He had not energy
enough to originate measures of that kind, but he was glad
to sanction and promote their operation." What fitter qualities
could be desired in the royal pupil of the Great Elchi? The
intimacy which gradually sprang up between them was something unprecedented in the Turkish State, and assumed by

1842
——
Æt. 55
To Lord
Aberdeen,
IX.
28 Jan.

6 June

cxxv.
7 June

1842
——
ÆT. 55

degrees the character of personal affection. At a private audience one day Canning ventured to say that the first time he had been presented to his Majesty his heart had gone forth towards him. " And mine towards you," was the Sultan's response. Without this intimate understanding the ambassador's task would perhaps have been hopeless. His intercourse with Abdu-l-Mejid, whether by audience public and private, or by means of the secret agent who went between them, was his final weapon when diplomacy had exhausted its resources upon the Porte.

1839

With the Turkish ministry he had far less cause to be satisfied. Reshid Pasha, by his too rapid and sweeping reforms, outlined in the famous Tanzimat or Hatti-Sherif of Gulhané,[1] had not only procured his own fall, but had created a dangerous reaction. The government manifested a petulant impatience of European interference. Its policy was reactionary, fanatical, and anti-Christian. It was mainly composed of the old Turkish party and aimed at a return to the system overturned by Mahmud. Redress of any sort, if granted at all, would be granted in its minimum. Least of all would the government listen to the advice of one who had so often offended its prejudices before. Canning was aware of this disfavour :—

MEMOIRS.
21 Jan.
1842

" On reaching Constantinople I soon learnt that several of the Turks in power, and those the most influential, disliked my appointment, some on account of my former transactions with Greece, and some, perhaps, from the apprehension of having their interested intrigues detected and shewn up. The Grand Vezir [Mohammed Izzet Pasha, a gallant soldier, but over-severe and fanatical, who shortly made room for Raüf

[1] This document, the Magna Charta of Turkey, provided for the security of all subjects, without distinction of creed, in life, honour, and property ; for the equitable distribution and collection of the taxes ; and for the systematic recruiting of the army. It confirmed Mahmud's ordinance by which no one could be executed without regular trial and sentence, and established the principle of public trial for all accused parties ; it asserted the right of all persons, criminals included, to hold and devise property without let or hindrance ; and appointed a council to elaborate the details of administrative reform. See Sir E. Hertslet, *Map of Europe by Treaty*, ii. 1002.

Pasha], had little to distinguish him beyond his high official position. The Minister for Foreign Affairs was Sarim Efendi, a shrewd and rather ill-favoured person, who had figured as the Sultan's representative in Persia, with the reputation of surpassing the natives in their art of drawing the long bow to perfection. Others of the Ministry by no means wanting in talent were supposed to be more alive to their interests than those of the State. One very old man, not actually in office at that time, continued to enjoy a certain amount of credit, not so much in virtue of his achievements, as of his moderate and judicious sentiments. He lived in retirement without having given up his claims to public employment. This respectable veteran was Khusruf Pasha, who had been governor of Egypt, when the famous Mohammed Ali got possession of that province. The man of greatest importance, if not by talent and character, at least by official position, was Riza Pasha. He owed his elevation to Sultan Mahmud, whose boon companion he had been in the latter years of that Caliph's reign. He was in 1843–4 at one and the same time chief intendant of the palace and commander-in-chief of the army, which he had himself constructed and supplied for the most part with officers. I had not been long at my post before I learnt on good authority that between this formidable pluralist and the minister of finance, a man of distinguished ability, there existed an understanding, which, aided by two Christian capitalists, had for its secret object the enrichment of the four confederates at the expense of the public treasury. The youth and inexperience of Sultan Abdu-l-Mejid rendered their machinations at once more feasible and more dangerous. A sense of duty and the interest I could not but feel for a young sovereign exposed to a thousand hazards induced me to keep a strict watch on their proceedings. At one time indeed I thought it might be necessary to warn the Sultan of his imprudence in leaving power, so obviously susceptible of abuse, in the hands of a single individual. On further reflection, however, I satisfied myself that the danger was one of appearance only, and that the Sultan's authority, though of late somewhat limited, was still sufficient to control any minister who might be tempted to raise the banner of revolt.

This conviction was eventually justified by the facility with which Riza Pasha was deprived at a later period of his two-fold command. He had scarcely returned one evening from the discharge of his official functions, when he received an order of dismissal, with which he humbly and dutifully complied, nor did the public evince the slightest interest in his disgrace."

The downfall of Riza (in August 1845) was largely Canning's work ; but it took more than three years to make his influence tell against so formidable an adversary, who had detected an opponent the moment he saw the ambassador. Any approach to reforms in favour of the rayas was impossible with ministers who carried their hatred of Christianity to the length of excluding from the public service even Turks who could speak Christian languages. " It would be a great mistake," he wrote to Lord Aberdeen, "to suppose that the Porte is the best judge of her own interests. She possesses no such advantage. Her ministers . . . have neither the capacity nor the knowledge to grapple with the difficulty of the times. They have not even the sagacity to recognize their real friends. History and recent experience are lost upon them." And again, "information and suggestions for improvement are at present thrown away. A change must first be made in the minds of those who govern. The consuls are complained of for complaining, and a foreign representative is esteemed in proportion to his tolerance of abuses."

To Lord
Aberdeen,
LXVII.
27 March,
1842

CCLXIX.
17 Dec.
1843

The general state of the empire was such as might be expected after the late troubles, and under the existing rulers. Disorder reigned in the provinces. The misgovernment of Wallachia offered an opportunity for Russian intrigues ; Bulgaria had caught the fever of disquiet, Albania soon broke into revolt, and in 1843 Servia rose against her prince. The local pashas did as they pleased. At Scutari three Christian peasants were executed without trial ; at Trebizond the pasha cut the throats of two criminals in the public street ; the governor of Mosil rushed out one night, mad with drink, to murder at pleasure ; two towns were razed to the ground by the troops in Albania ; the soldiers mutinied for their pay at

CCXLV.
4 Nov.
1844

1842

ÆT. 55

Salonica, tried to kill their colonel, and then burnt the stores in a caravanserai, while the pasha looked on ; unequal and cruel taxation was driving the people to despair ; the ministers of the Porte used their official authority in favour of their private trading, and invited presents of hush-money from offending pashas.   Fanaticism against Christians was increasing, and Pera was placarded with threats of burning the Frank quarter.   " There is no such thing as system in Turkey: Every *Ibid.* man according to his means and opportunities gets what he can, commands when he dares, and submits when he must." Financial embarrassment, public and individual, prevailed to an alarming extent.   The only active trade was the traffic in lucrative posts in the public service ; but salaries were in arrears ; commerce languished ; the currency was ruinously debased ; forests and mines and other resources were neglected ; communications were bad—no roads or mere tracks ; good land on the coast within fifty miles of Constantinople was to be bought for two shillings an acre, while Russian grain was sold at a comfortable profit hard by.   Ignorance and corruption prevailed in every department of the state ; brutal violence and torture were employed in the law courts ; Christian evidence was not accepted against Muslims ; Christians were annoyed if they entered the Turkish quarters of the capital ; constant cases occurred of fraud and outrage against them : yet in spite of these disabilities the rayas were slowly advancing in wealth, education, and independence, whilst the Turks were losing ground.   There were exceptions to this sweeping indictment.   Omar Pasha of Salonica and Black Huseyn the Janissary of Vidin bore the reputation of mild and upright governors.   Namik and Ya'kub in the Divan were said to be enlightened men.   But as a whole no attempt was being made to carry on Mahmud's policy, and the humane provisions of Gulhané remained a dead letter.

A drastic remedy was necessary : but how was it to be applied in face of the opposition displayed by the government to all foreign interference ?   The intervention in Syria, though in the interests of Turkey, had left a sore feeling at the Porte, and foreign representatives, indeed foreigners of all grades, barely maintained their positions.   If Lord Aberdeen wished *Ibid.*

merely to stand well with the Turks, wrote Canning, he had better not meddle at all, but let matters drift. On the other hand the rising importance of the rayas might end in revolution, and it would be impossible to uphold the Porte against its progressive Christian subjects. Popular sympathy, secret societies, the power of the press, all would urge England in the opposite direction. What then could be done? He advised "an active but friendly interference," in the interests of Turkey and Europe, with real united action among all the Great Powers, so that the Porte might have no opportunity, as heretofore, of playing off one Power against another. The only alternative was "tacit acquiescence" in the reactionary policy now pursued by the Turkish ministers: to keep on good terms, and "never mind the credit." He perceived no middle course.

With such an envoy, it is needless to say that the former alternative was adopted. The Foreign Office indeed cautioned the ambassador repeatedly to proceed gently; but to proceed, not to stand still, was the policy he was to choose. Yet "active but friendly intervention" was more easily conceived than executed. Canning was hampered by countless obstacles. The relations of the Porte with Greece and Syria were a source of obstruction: the Turkish ministers, while accepting his good offices in bringing the Greeks to reason, could not forget the share he had taken in setting them free; and Syria, though restored to the Sultan mainly through the exertions and arms of England, was a constant cause of suspicion and jealousy. And apart from these outside disturbances, there were serious difficulties to overcome in his own relations with the Turkish Government. As ambassador, his first duty was the protection of English interests. Just as in 1812 he would not move a step to help the Porte in its negotiations with Russia until the commercial claims of England had been admitted; so in 1842 it was impossible to stand forward as the friendly adviser of the Sultan in Turkish interests until the grievances of British subjects had been redressed. Unfortunately there was a heavy crop of English claims to be reaped. The previous ambassador had left a disagreeable inheritance behind him. The wars and disturbances in Syria had involved British subjects in losses which the Porte was bound to make good. An Englishman had been dismissed the Turkish navy without cause, and compensation was demanded. The Commercial Treaty of 1838 required revision. There was a monetary claim on the part of her Majesty's Government itself. Some of these demands were not disposed of till 1846.

Besides purely English claims, a large class of " protected " subjects appealed to the British ambassador. These were natives of Malta and the Ionian Islands, who could claim the privileges of British citizens, though not subject to English laws ; and these formed by far the most troublesome branch of Canning's clients. They were clever enough to absorb a large amount of the British trade in the Levant, and unprincipled enough to constitute the most conspicuous class of criminals. Constantinople itself was flooded with miscreants, who fought in the streets, or stabbed in the dark, and then fled to the Embassy for protection. Canning sent them back to their native lands in 1844, but they returned in the following year, and he found he had no legal means of banishing them. The position of guardian to such wards was so embarrassing that he appealed to the home Government to relieve him of the responsibility by effecting some change in the consular jurisdiction. There was no English prison, and no English police : consequently it was difficult to arrest " protected " criminals, and necessary, if an arrest were effected, to consign them to the horrors of the Turkish bagnio, or to release them on very doubtful recognizances. Some important changes were made by Act of Parliament and Orders in Council in 1843–44, whereby the consular jurisdiction was securely established as part of the statute law and consuls were empowered to call in assessors from among the British residents to assist them in their labours. The consuls were at the same time made fully responsible for verdicts in their courts, and a considerable burden was thus removed from the British Embassy. Much however was left undone, and the consular system remained in an unsatisfactory state for many years.

Moreover, whatever might have been the legal bounds of

British protection, Canning took a very elastic view of his responsibility. In places where there was no American consul he took upon himself to afford protection to citizens of the United States. Dutch Jews in Syria looked to him for satisfaction for their wrongs. Greek artisans in Pera owed their safety to his intervention. The long-continued persecution of the Armenians, which had burst forth with relentless severity after the battle of Navarino, was ended at his instance ; and the Nestorians in Mesopotamia, victims of a cruel and bloody oppression, found an untiring advocate in the British ambassador.

CHAPTER XVIII.

THE CHRISTIAN RENEGADES

1843-46.

THE many subjects of complaint and remonstrance referred to in the preceding chapter naturally tended to exasperate rather than soften the reactionary ministers of the Porte, and for some years Canning found the position of adviser to the Sultan a trying and irksome one. Finally an incident occurred which tested to the full his power of enforcing reforms. If he failed, the future was perhaps desperate : if he succeeded, he might feel some confidence in his authority. The case involved much more than ordinary principles of justice and humanity : it required a reversal of a criminal law presumed to be based upon the Koran. A Christian who had embraced Islam had recanted, and by the law of Mohammed was executed. Could this law be repealed ? This was the problem to be solved, and Lord Stratford shall tell the solution in his own words.

1843-6

ÆT. 56-9

" A painful incident, the execution of an individual on religious grounds, brought on a most important change in the practice, if not in the principles, of the Sultan's government. A young Armenian, subject of the Porte, adopted the Musulman faith, or, to use a vulgar expression, 'turned Turk.' He soon repented of his apostasy, and returned to the Church of Christ. A relapse of this kind drew down upon him the vengeance of Turkish authority. He was imprisoned, tried and condemned to death."

MEMOIRS.

Aug. 1843

1843-6

—

Æт. 56-9

Corr. rel.
to Execu-
tions in
Turkey,
pp. 1, 3

In spite of threats, promises, and blows, he maintained his resolution, refused to save his life by a fresh disavowal of Christianity, and was finally decapitated in one of the most frequented parts of the city with circumstances of great barbarity. The first intelligence received in Pera of this occurrence was the appearance in the streets of the unfortunate lad's mother, tearing her grey hair and rushing distractedly from the scene of bloodshed. The poor old woman, when assured of her boy's fate, returned and sat in grief by the corpse, from which she was afterwards removed. A petition of the Armenians for the corpse was rejected, and it was after three days' exposure cast into the sea.

MEMOIRS.

"The case was brought to my attention by some of his nearest relatives, who intercepted my carriage one day on the road from Pera to Buyukderé, and throwing themselves before the wheels implored my interference on his behalf. A friendly intercession was all I could undertake, and my efforts at the Porte in that sense were unhappily attended with no success. The unfortunate renegade was executed. But his blood did not sink into the ground unfruitfully. My report to the Foreign Office and that of my French colleague to his government were followed by pregnant effects. I was armed with decided instructions by Lord Aberdeen. Baron Bourqueney was directed by M. Guizot, at that time Louis Philippe's chief minister, to act in concert with me. We were both authorized to require of the Porte that punishment should no longer be inflicted on persons who seceded from the Mohammedan religion. No precise form or limit was given by our instructions to what would be the consequence of refusal. It became our business to produce the strongest possible apprehension of eventual consequences in the minds of the Turkish ministers. My official note to the Porte was framed with that view. When I placed it in the hands of Mr. Frederick Pisani, our principal interpreter, he remarked with his habitual bluntness that it never would succeed. I looked him in the face with fixed determination, and said, ' Mr. Pisani! *it shall.*' To say the truth, in using this curt phrase, I rather expressed my will than my conviction, and I felt moreover the necessity of conveying my own intense earnestness to the mind and manner of my agent and through him to the Turkish minister. Rif'at Pasha, who

4 Oct.
Ibid. p. 9

held the Foreign Office, received my missive with his natural courtesy, and a long negotiation, not of the most promising kind, ensued."

The details may be read in the *Correspondence relating to Executions in Turkey for Apostasy from Islamism*, laid before the House of Commons in 1844. It was clear from the first that the better minds among the Turkish ministers revolted from such sanguinary acts. Raūf, the Grand Vezir, said that personally he had not the heart to kill a fowl, and that his sentiments were entirely in accord with the ambassador's: but the law of the Koran was inexorable, and the execution was "a misfortune for which there was no remedy." The Foreign Minister expressed equally humane and equally discouraging opinions. It appeared however that there were bigots in the Divan, notably the President of the Council, who insisted on enforcing the law. The Grand Mufti was not one of these; for when consulted on a similar case he had advised the ministers "not to bring it under his Holiness's notice, as he had no choice but to declare the law; and a charitable intimation was added that, where a State necessity existed, the Porte would herself be found the most competent judge." No one however doubted that the law was distinct and final; and all that Rifat Pasha could suggest was to issue instructions by which future apostasies might be hushed up without capital punishment. The Porte, he said, not only could not alter a divine law, but could not risk her character as a Musulman Power even by a written reply to the remonstrances of the five Powers led by the British ambassador. A very deep and serious impression had indeed been made by the general feeling of indignation aroused in Europe; but no repeal of the law was so far considered possible. Meanwhile another religious execution took place at Brusa, this time of a Greek, Dec. 1843 followed by similar protests from the five ambassadors. Lord Aberdeen supported Canning by an unusually vigorous despatch (No. 15), which, when communicated with due solemnity by the ambassador, produced such an effect on Rifat Pasha that he jumped up and left the room for some minutes. Still the Turkish minister maintained that "a law prescribed by God

1843-6
———
ÆT. 56-9

himself was not to be set aside by any human power." The Sultan, he said, might risk his throne in the attempt. Canning perceived that the only course that remained to be tried was to "search the scripture," the Koran itself.

MEMOIRS.

Incl. in
XXXVI.
1844

" It so happened that on leaving my bed one morning I remembered that some one had given me a French translation of the Koran. Where to find it was the question. My search was amply rewarded, not only by finding the book, but on opening it to fall at once upon a passage which made me think that Mohammed in condemning renegades to punishment had in view their sufferings in a future state and not their decapitation here. I took measures without loss of time to ascertain whether the passage in question, as translated, was in strict accordance with the original text. The report in answer to my reference confirmed the truth of my impression. Thereupon I sent the reporter, Mr. Alison, to Rifat Pasha, with whom he was personally well acquainted, for the purpose of drawing that minister's attention to what appeared to be the true meaning of the Koran with respect to the punishment of renegades. A close and animated discussion took place between the parties. Rifat was sore pressed, and in his embarrassment sent for the Imam of his district to continue the discussion. Neither the priest nor the pasha could make any head against Mr. Alison's arguments, and I had the satisfaction of thinking that, although the opposition to our demand would be still sustained, the authority, on which it principally rested, was so far shaken as to invalidate its motives, and give more weight to considerations of policy and humanity. Such, however, was the obstinacy of the Porte that doubts arose as to the justice or expediency of further proceedings."

Canning was perfectly right in holding that the Koran did not warrant the law. As a matter of fact no passage in the Koran is explicit on the subject of punishment for apostasy. A possible hint may be detected by the over-curious in the 5th Sura, verse 35 : " He who slayeth a soul, unless it be for another soul, or for *wickedness* in the land,

1843-6

ÆT. 56-9

is as though he had slain all mankind ; and he who saveth a soul alive is as though he had saved the lives of all mankind." The italicized word is no doubt capable of a liberal interpretation, but it has never been cited as a special authority for killing apostates : it has rather been held to refer to flagrant offenders in general, and idolaters and highway robbers have been mentioned by commentators as examples of its application. Apostates might come under the description, but the sense is too vague for a foundation of criminal law. The special passage to which Canning referred was, I imagine,[1] that contained in Sura XLVII. vv. 27-9, the substance of which is here subjoined in translation :—

" Verily they who turn their backs after the Guidance hath been manifested to them, Satan hath deceived them and emboldened them : . . . How [will it be] when the angels shall cause them to die, smiting their faces and their backs ! "

The context shews that the warning refers to certain half-hearted Muslims who were seeking pretexts to avoid following the Prophet's standard in the early battles of Islam. It has been the custom, however, of Mohammedan jurists to accord general applications to temporary and limited judgments, such as this, and the fate of those who turned their backs, physically or dogmatically, at the time of the field of Bedr, might be extended to all who deserted Islam in later days. But in the passage just quoted there is nothing about human punishment : the angels kill and flagellate the renegade. Probably those twin terrors of an evil conscience, Munkar and Nekir, are intended :—the angels of the grave, who come to the tomb and make the defunct sit up in his narrow bed and subject him to a tedious and searching examination on the sins of his earthly career. At all events no Mohammedan lawyer would venture to claim this passage as a precedent for decapitation.

[1] Canning did not keep a copy of Alison's report, and the rules of the Foreign Office forbid an examination of the original. I am informed, however, that upwards of sixty passages in the Koran were cited, and an opinion was expressed that none of them countenanced the law of execution for apostasy.

1843-6
—
ÆT. 56-9

The truth is that Mohammedan law rests mainly upon other authority than the Koran. That sacred volume contains a modicum of legal definitions.[1] The main source of the jurisprudence is the body of Traditions (*Sunna*), or unofficial conversations of the Prophet, and the long chain of judgments analogically founded thereon, delivered by eminent jurists. The law of apostasy is perfectly explicit in the Traditions : those who changed their religion were to be killed. This was modified by the lawyers in respect to women, who were to be imprisoned ; and compulsory conversion and the apostasy of lunatics and drunkards were excepted.[2] But the main law, founded on a Tradition of the Prophet Mohammed's own words, remained unchanged : a voluntary male convert to Islam who afterwards apostatized must be killed. The Muslim makes no distinction between the various sources of his law : whether based on a clear statement in the Koran, or on a private remark of Mohammed, or on the deductions and explanations of commentators and doctors, it is all one to him—the ordinance of God himself. In the lips of a Turk, " the law of the Koran " means the law whether traced distinctly to the Koran or not : it is equally holy and irrevocable.

Nevertheless, the fact of the ambassador's venturing to carry the war into the sacred boundaries of Koranic hermeneutics brought dismay to the Turkish ministers. Council after council was held, with no result. The Divan perceived that it was transfixed on the horns of a dilemma : " If we refuse, we lose the friendship of Europe ; if we consent, we hazard the peace of the empire." Rif'at Pasha begged Canning to come and settle the dispute "amicably and confidentially " with him, but the Elchi saw clearly that no promise to " avoid as far as it might be practicable occasions of enforcing the law " would be adequate. Lord Aberdeen would have accepted such a promise : but Canning stood firm. " There is, in truth," he wrote to the Foreign Secretary, in his despatch of 29 February, " no lasting security against the recurrence

To Lord
Aberdeen,
XXXVI.
29 Feb.
1844

---

[1] See *Speeches and Table-talk of the Prophet Mohammed*, by S. Lane-Poole p. 140.

[2] See Hamilton's *Hidaya*, ii. 227, &c.

of the barbarous practice except in a real surrender of the principle.   Together with that principle," he sanguinely added, " the main barrier between Turkey and Christendom would be removed."   Apart from grounds of humanity there was always the possibility that apostasy might occur in the person of a British subject ; and it was important to clear away the difficulty in a case where no English interests were involved, rather than to wait for an instance which might jeopardize international relations.   Therefore he persisted steadily in his demands, even when the home Government began to feel frightened at its own boldness.   The crossing of despatches allowed him grace for this, and he persevered, alone and unaided.   The northern Courts had discontinued their representations, and at last even France, after much steady coöperation, gave up the struggle.

" The French broke off : I was left to carry out the exist- MEMOIRS. ing instructions as I best could.   Monsieur de Bourqueney behaved with much candour and personal good-will.   He told me that he could go no further with me officially, but that he would persist in giving me what support he could without compromising his government.   At the same time he tried to dissuade me from going beyond the length of his tether.   Too much was at stake for me to be held back.   I was resolved to carry the point in hand, and I thought it could be done without prejudice to our peaceful relations with the Porte.   So it turned out ; but the final agreement was something of the Mosaic kind.   The answer to my note, though virtually a surrender to our demand, required a supplement to make it permanently effective.   The Sultan was to complete the engagement by an oral declaration to me ; . but a form so fugitive required some addition to fix it, and therefore I addressed another note to Rif'at Pasha expressing in distinct terms the construction to be put upon the whole concession.   His silent reception of the note would be sufficient for my purpose.   He had wit enough to perceive this consequence and struggled hard to escape.   It was not till we met for my audience at the Imperial palace that I succeeded in forcing the note upon him, and even then he only yielded

1843-6
———
ÆT. 56-9

to a threat of my demanding his dismissal if he continued to resist. My audience followed, and Abdu-l-Mejid performed his promise to the letter. He added that he was the first Sultan who had ever made such a concession, and was glad that the lot of receiving it had fallen to me. I replied that I hoped he would allow me to be the first Christian ambassador to kiss a Sultan's hand. 'No—no—' he exclaimed, and at the same time shook me by the hand most cordially. Thus ended this redoubtable negotiation."

It was on occasions like this that Canning's fierce zeal bore all before it. Nothing less than violence could have taken that kingdom by storm. His indignation had been worked up to a white heat by reports which reached him early in March. Christian children were being seized in various parts of Turkey, forcibly made Mohammedans, and confined in harems. His energetic protest hastened the slow steps of Ottoman diplomacy ; and the direct but secret communications he was then holding with the Sultan clinched the matter.[1]

[1] The following details are required to complete the sketch given in the *Memoirs*. On 14 March, 1844, Rifat Pasha presented a note containing the following promise :—

"As the law does not admit of any change being made in the enactments regarding the punishment of apostates, the Sublime Porte will take efficacious measures, the measures which are possible, in order that the executions of Christians who, having become Musulmans, return to Christianity, shall not take place."

This was refused, as inadequate, and as reasserting a bad principle ; and on the 21st, after other essays, which were contested word by word, the Pasha despatched the final assurance referred to in the preceding extract from the *Memoirs* :—

Corr.
P. 37

"The Sublime Porte engages to take effectual measures to prevent henceforward the execution and putting to death of the Christian who is an apostate "

Canning accepted it in these words—the "addition to fix it " mentioned above —

"The official declaration communicated by his Excellency the Minister for Foreign Affairs shall be transmitted to the British Government, who will understand with satisfaction that the Sublime Porte, in taking effectual measures to prevent henceforward the execution and putting to death of any Christian, an apostate from Islamism, relinquishes for ever a principle inconsistent with its friendly professions ; and the further assurances to be given at the ambassador's audience of the Sultan, in the sense of the instruction presented in copy to the Porte on the 9th ultimo, will fully satisfy the British Government that Christianity is not to be

Canning announced his triumph to his government in the following despatch :—

1843-6

Æ.T. 56-9

I have the honour and satisfaction to inform your lordship that the question of religious executions is happily and, to all appearance, conclusively settled. The concession has been obtained with great difficulty ; and, even to the last moment, it required the firmness of resolution inspired by your lordship's instruction to overcome the obstacles which were raised against us, and to keep the Turkish ministers steady to their professions. I felt it to be my duty to accept nothing short of your lordship's requisition in its full extent, notwithstanding the risk of being incompletely supported by the French minister, whose instructions, modified after the communications with Austria, were not on a level with mine. But this obligation did not preclude me either from adopting such means of success as were best calculated to hasten a favourable result, or from accepting that result in a conciliatory though effective shape. By availing myself of an overture to communicate directly with the Sultan, I succeeded in obtaining all that was necessary, and in receiving his Highness's acknowledgments for the consideration I had shewn to his wishes.

To Lord Aberdeen, XLIX. 23 Mar. 1844

These transactions have so little interest now, that it would be a waste of your lordship's time to enter upon a narration of them. It may suffice for me to state that, after several unacceptable propositions, the Porte's definitive reply was communicated to me and to the French minister in suitable terms, and also in writing, which had been long obstinately refused ; that, to leave no doubt of what I understand to be the meaning of the Porte, I sent in an acknowledgment, of which a copy is herewith inclosed, together with a translated copy of the Porte's declaration ; and that to-day, at my audience of the Sultan, his Highness not only confirmed what the Porte had declared, but added, in frank and explicit language, the assurances

insulted in his Highness' empire, nor anyone professing it to be treated as a criminal, or persecuted on that account."

The acceptance of course vastly extended the meaning of the original assurance, as the ambassador intended it should, and Rifat Pasha definitely refused to receive it. But Canning was not to be denied. Before his audience of the Sultan on the following day he encountered the Foreign Minister, and presented the note to him once more. Rifat put his hands behind his back. Then the Great Elchi, advancing in his wrath, literally thrust the paper upon the pasha. The Audience set the seal to the whole, and a revolution in Islam was thus peacefully accomplished : though it must be admitted that in later years the Turks endeavoured to minimize the concession.

Report of F. Pisani 22 March

which I had previously required as to the general good treatment of the Christians throughout his dominions. He, in fact, gave me his royal word that henceforward neither should Christianity be insulted in his dominions, nor should Christians be in any way persecuted for their religion.

Important as it was to obtain this assurance from the lips of the sovereign himself, I should have thought it right to demand an audience for the mere purpose of removing false impressions from his Highness' mind respecting the motives and objects of her Majesty's Government. In this respect, also, I had every reason to be satisfied. The Sultan expressed the strongest reliance on the friendly intentions of Great Britain ; he fully appreciated the motives which had actuated her on the present occasion ; he acknowledged more than once the signal and frequent services rendered to his empire by British arms and counsels ; he declared that the great concession which he had now confirmed, though entirely consonant with his own feelings, but opposed to the prejudices of his people, had been made to his sense of obligation towards the British Government ; he called upon me to convey his thanks to her Majesty for the good treatment experienced by the millions of Musulman subjects living under British sway in India, and his anxious desire that the engagements which he had taken to protect from violence and undue interference the Christians established in his empire should be appreciated by her Majesty's Government, and prove a source of increased good-will between the two nations, and an occasion of eliciting fresh proofs of friendly interest on the part of Great Britain towards his dominions.

What passed at this audience is the more important and binding, as it was one of a formal character, applied for on public grounds ; and, to give it still greater value, the Sultan, after I had retired from his presence, called back the dragoman of the Porte, and desired him to assure me that what he had said in public proceeded from his real conviction, and was, in fact, the sincere expression of his personal sentiments.

I have only to add that I am thankful to your lordship, under Providence, for having made me the humble instrument of contributing, not only to the abolition of a barbarous practice, but to the establishment of a great and beneficent principle, without which it may be safely affirmed that the preservation of this empire for any length of time is impossible. This is the truth which I have to-day endeavoured to impress upon the Sultan's mind, as pointing out the line of policy which it is essential for him to pursue in the present state of his empire, brought as it is daily more and more into contact with Christendom, and exposed to dangers from within even greater than those which threaten it eventually from without.

He naturally received the Queen's approbation of his success in bringing the question to a close : but Lord Aberdeen was not a little alarmed by the manner in which this had been accomplished. Indeed in reading this minister's despatches one is perpetually reminded of old Mr. John Gladstone's remark that Lord Aberdeen might become Prime Minister if it were necessary to put the British Cabinet under jury masts. In an amusing despatch—if the term be not self-contradictory—Canning lets us behind the scenes. It is evident that the British Government, having no previous idea of the extent to which the ambassador had pushed his demands, was afraid that his triumph would inspire him to seek other laurels in the same field. In reply to some such hint, Canning writes, in all humility, that he must of course "keep steadily in view the terms and spirit of your lordship's instructions" ; and then continues :—

I am forbidden by them to "stand forth as the avowed protector of the Christian subjects of the Sultan," and I am to avoid being "considered as the organ through which complaints of hardships or persecution should be conveyed to the knowledge of the Porte." At the same time I am authorized by another of your lordship's instructions to offer in such cases to the Turkish Government "the earnest exhortation and advice of her Majesty's Government founded on the evident interests of the Porte ; " and further I presume that whenever the rights or interests of her Majesty's subjects are immediately concerned, I am at liberty to assume a more decided tone, and, in pleading their cause, to afford any Christian subjects of the Sultan, whose case may be similar, the benefits of my arguments and official representations, as in the recent instance of torture. With these landmarks to guide my course I have endeavoured to befriend the persecuted without committing her Majesty's Government or causing any inconvenient results which it was the object of your lordship's instructions to avoid.

Her Majesty's Government might try to curb their mettlesome representative, but while Canning was at Constantinople it was of no avail to endeavour to shirk responsibility. He had made up his mind that Turkey was to be saved only by assimilation to Western principles of liberty, toleration, and good government. One of the chief points in his programme

Margin notes: 1843-6 ÆT. 56 9 ; CXII. 1 June 1844

was the removal of all the distinctive disabilities which oppressed the Christians : he meant to make the rayas the best,
the most free and progressive, part of the Sultan's subjects. To
that end he was resolved to stand forth as their protector—
not because he would not protect Muslims, towards whom he
never failed in his duty—but because the Christians, after
centuries of practical outlawry, required more protection to
bring them up to a political level with their Musulman fellow-
subjects. This was his view, and he never swerved from it,
let the home Government "instruct" him never so wisely. The
abolition of religious executions was his first great step in this
direction, and it was completely successful. Of course instances occurred where popular fanaticism brought lynch law
into operation, but the provincial governors, acting under
strict orders from the Porte, exerted themselves to save the
lives of renegades, and several instances of successful intervention occurred in the autumn of 1844.

Fortified by the "bloodless victory" which he had won
over the Porte, he proceeded to advocate reform after reform,
and to remove one disability after another. Two months had
not elapsed when he obtained a notable firman by which the
use of torture was formally abolished throughout the empire.
In September 1845 he gained a long-contested point, the right
to establish a Protestant church at Jerusalem for British and
Prussian subjects—a success for which he received the cordial
thanks of the King of Prussia in an autograph letter, in which
his Majesty expressed his gratitude for the ambassador's able
and indefatigable efforts, and assured him of his personal
high esteem. In 1846 he mediated on behalf of the newly-
declared Protestant sect of Armenians, which was exposed at
once to the persecution of the Porte and the enmity of the
Armenian Patriarch, and his efforts resulted in the complete
restoration of the sufferers to civil rights and religious toleration. He even removed so trifling a disability as a distinguishing flag by which the Christian ships of Turkey were
branded, and obtained a common mercantile ensign for all
vessels of the Porte irrespective of their owners' creeds. His
vigilant eye searched every corner of the empire, and when
persecution was discovered the offender was instantly reported.

To Lord
Aberdeen,
XC.
17 May,
1844

LXXXV.
17 May,
1846

In 1846 the Pasha of Salonica was removed for inhumanity to Christians. The consuls were instructed, whatever Lord Aberdeen might say, to report to the ambassador any cases of oppression, and Canning took so liberal a view of his duties that he encouraged his agents to inform him of the wrongs of Greeks, Armenians, and others over whom he had no authority, as well as of British subjects. The consuls obeyed, well knowing that the Elchi would take all the responsibility. A case occurred where a Greek monk was righted and saved from a false charge by the mere presence of a British vice-consul, who had no claim to interfere, but who remembered the ambassador's instructions, and threatened to send a report to the Embassy. Had he not been present, it was admitted, the monk would have been sacrificed. Canning was extremely careful to support his consuls in this and every just cause. Once the Foreign Office sent out a "circular" calling the attention of the consuls in the Levant to certain reports which prevailed to the effect that they were overstepping their duties, and meddling in the internal affairs of the empire. The ambassador of course forwarded a copy to every consul : but he appended a private note in which he stated to each that he had no reason to believe that it referred to any fault in that particular consulate.

"The measures of reform, which were subsequently obtained in slow succession, and not without much discussion, may be now briefly enumerated, with what little order my recollection can supply after so long an interval. One of the earliest was the complete abolition of torture by means of a special decree applied to the whole empire. The Turks, even when I first went among them, were not addicted to cruelty in their inflictions. This may at least be truly said of the Imperial Government ; although in the provinces there was here and there a pasha, like Ali of Janina, who ruled by inspiring fear of pain as well as of death. Impalement, as far as I know, had ceased. The bastinado for minor offences, and decapitation for those of higher degree, were the usual modes of punishment, often applied unjustly, and with corrupt views, but more blamable on those accounts than for any extreme severity. Imprisonment in many cases was of course a necessary consequence of accusation as well as of conviction, and the Turkish prisons even in the capital are still, I fear, very much what ours were two or three centuries ago.

" A decree is one thing, its execution is another. A striking instance of this came under my own observation. It so happened that an English traveller was murdered on the high road somewhere in Asia Minor, and it became my duty to send down a Turkish agent for the discovery of the murderer. On his return my emissary reported what he had done, and he did not hesitate to describe the kinds of torture which he had permitted in order to enforce confession. One of the means employed for that purpose was the application of a metal basin, awfully heated, to the crown of the head. The sufferer, moreover, was a respectable woman who endured the pain rather than expose her youthful niece to a similar infliction.

"An onerous excise tax may not come under the head of torture, but it approaches so near in its pressure on some classes that I may take credit here for obtaining the abolition of the *iktisab*, which produced a revenue of forty millions of piastres.

" In Turkey the political and social system being founded on what passes among its Mohammedan inhabitants for Divine inspiration, the difficulty of removing abuses or introducing reforms must obviously be in proportion to the degree in which they affect any religious prejudice. This remark does not apply exclusively to the votaries of Islam. Jews and Christians are alike jealous of their respective forms, and unwilling to admit the rights of conscience in spiritual matters. The relation in which they stand towards the Porte enables them, moreover, to call in the arm of Turkish authority in support of their bigoted pretensions. The Protestants having no such appeal to make were constantly exposed to obstruction and persecution directed against them as occasion offered from every side. No member of church or synagogue, who migrated to another religious body, could hope to effect his purpose with impunity. It was therefore with great satisfaction that I succeeded[1] after much trouble in securing a recognized position for the Protestants, as such, and the right of converts to be protected by the civil authorities from vexation on the part of their relinquished churches. The promulgation of an Imperial firman to establish a Protestant church at Jerusalem was also a subject of rejoicing. Prussia took a joint interest with us in carrying that point ; but the exertion of British influence was, no doubt, the preponderating cause of success. Whether from religious or political motives, the opposition to it was very strong. Neither to the French nor to the Russians could the establishment of a Protestant church and the recognition of an Anglican bishop at Jerusalem be agreeable. There can be little doubt that the latter looked upon those measures with a jealous eye, and it may therefore be presumed that they laboured in secret to obstruct them. Be that as it may, the local authorities retarded as much as they could the execution of the Porte's instructions. It became necessary to demand fresh orders of a more peremptory kind from Constantinople, and even then it required all the address and resolution of an able agent despatched for that special purpose to enforce their execution at Jerusalem.

"Suleyman the Magnificent is said to have been the first to grant privileges by treaty to a Christian power, and more than three centuries have elapsed since that pregnant transaction took place. Selim III.'s innovations towards the end of the last century were cut up by the Janissaries and had left very slight traces of their brief existence when Sultan Mahmud came to the throne. It was not till the suppression of the Janissaries eighteen years later that the ground was cleared for reform, as an adopted system of policy. The Greek war of independence, which followed, and the example of Egypt, together with its dangerous growth of power, to say nothing of Navarino and the Russian invasion, may fairly be supposed to have opened Mahmud's eyes to the necessity of moving on more rapidly and with less contracted limits. At length the Charter of Gulhané was promulgated, and

1843-6
——
ÆT. 56 9

Nov. 1850

Sept. 1845

1839

---

[1] See *Correspondence respecting the Condition of Protestants in Turkey*, laid before the House of Commons in 1851.

the measures, to which the Sultan then gave his solemn
pledge, could always be appealed to, either when their enforcement was to be urged or their extension to be recommended. Progress in these respects was still retarded by
numerous obstacles. Jealousy of foreign interference, fear of
responsibility, popular prejudices, the ignorance, the corruption, the incapacity of individuals intrusted with authority,
and the spirit of ambitious intrigue had in turns or all at once
to be resisted. The social condition and the political atmosphere in Turkey were enough of themselves to repress hope
and to paralyze exertion. But as time rolled on, it became
more and more evident that the Turkish Empire suffered by
its estrangement from Christendom, and a perception of this
truth by its ministers made them more open to my suggestions and remonstrances. England moreover had the advantage of standing towards Turkey in the light of a real friend,
troublesome at times from the pressure of its counsels, but
believed, nevertheless, to have the Sultan's best interests at
heart. It was, no doubt, under this persuasion that Abdu-l-
Mejid pledged his honour at my instance to maintain the
adopted policy of reform. To complete this useful impression I made it my object to convince his Majesty that my
personal inclinations rather went before than followed those
of my government.

"Among the ministers, whether in office or expectant,
Reshid Pasha was the one who in sentiment and policy
sympathized most with me. The Sultan seemed to be jealous
of our intimacy. Some intriguer had probably turned his
mind that way. 'You are too fond of Reshid,' he said to me
one day. 'Fond, and not without reason,' I replied, 'for I find
him the most able and faithful of your Majesty's servants.'
By birth and education a gentleman, by nature of a kind
and liberal disposition, Reshid had more to engage my sympathies than any other of his race and class. He was bred, if
not born, in the Morea. He lived for a time, I believe, in the
family of Veli Pasha, son of the famous Ali of Janina, and
governor, either in whole or in part, of that country. At
an early age he began his official career at Constantinople.
When he first drew my attention he was one of the under-

secretaries of state at the Porte, and in that capacity assisted 1843-6
at Therapia in giving the form of a convention to the points
of agreement settled in the summer of 1832 between the   ÆT. 56-9
Turkish Government and the representatives of the three
Allied Powers, with a view to the territorial enlargement of
Greece.   His features were cast in the Circassian mould, their
expression was lively and intelligent.   In point of stature he
was below the middle height, and his general appearance
conveyed the idea of a cheerful, inquiring, sympathetic character.   I saw but little of him at that time.   Subsequently
he arrived in London as the Sultan's ambassador, and our acquaintance was then renewed.   I remember that he opened
himself to me on the subject of reforms in Turkey.   It
was evident that he looked to taking an active part in the
new policy inaugurated by the overthrow of the Janissaries,
and stimulated by the example of Mohammed Ali in
Egypt.   He asked me when and how the promoters of the
system ought to begin.   I replied, ' *At the beginning.*'   'What
do you mean by *the beginning*?' he said.   'Security of
life and property, of course,' I rejoined.   'Would not you
add the protection of honour?' he asked.   'No doubt,' I said.
But in truth I wondered what he meant by honour among
Turks, until I recollected their practice of applying the
bastinado without discrimination to persons of any class or
rank whatever.   He was right, I thought, and so I told him.
Nor did the intention stop short of performance.   Summary
inflictions of corporal punishment are excluded from the new
code of law in Turkey.   In the days of M. Guizot's administration Reshid was ambassador at Paris.   [He returned to
Constantinople in March 1843 and was appointed governor
of Adrianople—a favour which he regarded as a sign of
political ruin ; and it was finally arranged that he should
return to his embassy in France in November.   Thence he
was suddenly recalled towards the close of 1845 to assume
the command of the Turkish Foreign Office.]   A weak constitution, the education of the Seraglio, and a total inexperience of State affairs consigned the young Sultan to a condition of helpless dependence on his ministers, whose titles
to his Majesty's confidence were none of the best.   It was

very desirable that he should be in better hands, and I thought that Reshid restored to office would prove a suitable keeper of the Imperial conscience. When he was at Balta Liman on the Bosphorus in 1843, we wished mutually to meet ; but in Turkey an unemployed minister has to be constantly on his guard, as intercourse with a foreign ambassador lays him open to suspicion, and therefore we had to meet in a third house and quite secretly. A change of ministers in due season was the consequence of these meetings, and I found in Reshid Pasha on many occasions a friendly and powerful auxiliary. We agreed in principle on most questions of reform, but in point of execution he was timid and tardy, not indeed so much from any unwillingness to act as from the difficulty of bringing his colleagues into accordance with his views.

"In truth if the Pasha had some distinguished qualities, he had also his failings, and if he had many warm friends, he had an equal number of insidious rivals. In three respects he differed remarkably from most of his race and creed. He was tender-hearted, extremely susceptible of blame, and beyond measure apprehensive of death. The love of life is more or less natural to all of us ; to him the very idea of death was so painful that the perception of his feeling even in conversation distressed me. A grandchild of his scarcely emerging from infancy died at his house in town, and he would never sleep again under that roof.

"He had learnt from some quarter that I did not entirely exempt him from the charge of building up his private fortune at the public expense, and to remove the impression from my mind he sent me a detailed statement of the sources of his income and the modes of his expenditure. His temperament in short was highly impressionable, and in talking of the Sultan, he would sometimes, when displeased, employ the most disrespectful expressions. Such imprudences were atoned for at other times by extreme demonstrations of a contrary kind. One day when he was present at an audience I had of Abdu-l-Mejid, his Majesty paid him a compliment in my hearing. He ducked so low and so suddenly in testimony of his satisfaction that I literally lost sight of him, and could not

imagine for several seconds what had become of him. The
Sultan looked at me as if he would have said ' What unnecessary degradation !' It happened not unfrequently that his
fear of being compromised obliged me to use strong language,
or at least a very decided tone, but on the whole and to the
last I found him greatly superior as a statesman and a philan-
thropist to his Ottoman contemporaries. Our parting was
that of friends, and I grieved to hear of his decease."

1843-6
———
Æʏ. 56-9

While it is true that the ambassador's most signal victory
over Turkish prejudices, the abolition of capital punishment
for apostasy, was achieved without Reshid's help, it is not
less certain that Canning owed much to the support and
friendship of the most enlightened minister of modern Turkey.
Before his accession to power the two men had been on
unusually friendly terms. Reshid used to come to dine at
the embassy and bring his children with him. When he
scented a plot, on his appointment to the government of
Adrianople, it was to the English ambassador that he applied
for advice and protection. In 1845, when Lady Canning
passed through Paris, Reshid told her that he knew her
husband to be " the most loyal conscientious and upright of
men and the truest friend to his sovereign and the Turkish
Empire," and hoped he would not leave Constantinople too
soon or for too long. Hardly had this conversation been reported when Reshid returned to the Ottoman Foreign Office.
Canning had been aiming at this ever since his arrival in
1842. He had set to work systematically to remove minister
after minister. They on their side fought hard. Rif'at secretly consulted A'li Pasha, then ambassador in London,
as to the best mode of procuring the recall of the troublesome envoy, and Sarim Pasha, A'li's successor in London,
was to try to bring this about. Yet Rif'at was among the
more enlightened of the ministers and was sorely puzzled
how to reconcile his own views with the reactionary policy
of his superiors. Before we take leave of the old system
it may be interesting to read a calm and moderate statement of that policy as reported by Mr. Alison in November
1843 :—

I had a long conversation with Rif'at Pasha this morning on the actual policy of the Porte. It consists, as avowed by the Pasha himself, of three essential points. 1st, a retrograde from the liberal policy adopted by Reshid Pasha, as unadapted to the moral condition of the Muslims and dangerous with regard to the Christians. 2nd, a desire to conciliate the evil, as far as it has gone, with the religious code of the Mohammedans ; and 3rd, to act in a manner, while guarding these points, so as not to incur any severe censure on the part of the Christian Powers. The Pasha said, with regard to the first of these points, that it was a dangerous experiment to introduce among the Mohammedan population principles which, while in direct opposition to the precepts of the Koran, were beneficial in their effect to Christians alone. That notwithstanding that a great many improvements had gradually introduced themselves into the empire without meeting any opposition, it could not be denied that the great scarcity of men of talent and integrity among the ministers of the Sultan, connected with the total absence of education among the Turks, rendered any avowed measures of reform of the nature alluded to a matter of very dangerous experiment. The party in power, therefore, had directed their attention to the achievement of that which was most consonant to their own feelings and easiest in the execution. That the Sultan was fully cognizant of these views and sanctioned them, and that Riza Pasha advocated them with the readiness of one who felt their expediency under the circumstances of his position. He said that the ministry were so wholly engrossed at present with the scheme of placing the army on a thoroughly efficient footing, that they had no time to give attention to anything else. . . . He said it was likely that Reshid Pasha would be sent to Paris to relieve the Turkish minister there, who was not content to remain, but that the post he was best qualified to fulfil was that of *Grand Vezir.* I told the Pasha that it was a most desirable thing that Reshid Pasha should be employed in the ministry were it only for the confidence which his name inspired in Europe, while he might be assured that no acts of a government formed upon a system of retrograde would ever have the merit of being appreciated. It is evident from the Pasha's language that while he has but little power himself to alter the state of affairs he would be very willing to take office under a reform administration —he confesses himself to be very much embarrassed at present, for although his own principles would serve as a check upon the more liberal tendencies of Reshid Pasha, they do not permit of his lending a cordial support to all the measures of the present clique.

The policy thus enunciated by Rif'at Pasha was doomed, but for a time it appeared to be triumphant, and at the close of 1843 its bigoted rigour increased with a change in the ministry. Riza Pasha, the intimate of the Valida, was made seraskier as well as high chamberlain in September 1843, and the Divan was soon filled with his creatures. Shekib Efendi, who followed Rif'at at the Foreign Office in November 1844, did his best to oppose Canning, and openly spoke of his "violence," till forced to apologize.

The apostasy question and the hold which Canning had obtained over the Sultan himself at last gave him the upper hand. Riza was dismissed in August 1845, and this promising event was followed by the compulsory retirement of the Finance Minister, Safti Pasha, whose peculations had left the Treasury in debt to the amount of 820,000*l.* The new ministry, though under the same mild and inoffensive Grand Vezir, Raûf Pasha, was an improvement : but there was still much to desire, and the necessary change came very soon. On 23 October Reshid Pasha had been reinstated in his post of Foreign Minister. He fully perceived the importance of the change, which was no result of caprice or Court intrigue, but of general conviction. Reshid's opponents had had a fair trial, and they had by their maladministration reduced the empire to the lowest pitch of anarchy and corruption. The provinces were in revolt : the public service was openly venal. People agreed in condemning the reactionaries, and when they were replaced by a more moderate government affairs were but slightly bettered. There was a general cry for Reshid, as "the man of the crisis," and Reshid came. Canning had worked hard in private to induce the Sultan to recall him, and at last Rif'at Pasha, who had become president of the council, joined in the entreaty. One of the most satisfactory circumstances in the manner of his recall was a message which the Sultan simultaneously sent to the English ambassador, in which he assured him that the appointment was not due to any wish to be agreeable to France, but that "his sole motive was to give to all an undeniable pledge of the policy which he had sincerely adopted and which was to be invariably directed to the improvement of his empire, the relief of his people, and the cultivation of friendly intercourse with the States of Christendom." And

1843-6
——
ÆT. 56 9

To Lord
Aberdeen,
CCLXXXIX
21 Dec.
1844

CCXLVIII.
30 Oct.
1845

what surer pledge could he give than by restoring to power the author of the Constitution of Gulhané? Canning regarded Reshid as the last hope of salvation for the Ottoman Empire, and his anxiety as to the future was proportionately intense. "If the chosen instrument," he wrote, "of the Sultan's policy were to fail in realizing the hopes which he has inspired, either by introducing a wanton spirit of innovation, or through inability to cope with the difficulties of his station, I know not where it would be possible to find another rallying point. The various parts of this vast empire are too ill assorted and ill balanced to preserve a state of repose by mere cohesion. The old system of administration has caused that exhaustion for which a remedy is wanted. If the principles now in requisition are found unequal to the process of restoration, what but despair can ensue, what but indifference to all within the empire and a mistrustful apprehension of all without?"

Reshid did not disappoint these high expectations, though the difficulties which encompassed him retarded and sometimes prevented their entire realization. He did not rush excitedly into innovations—or as Henry Addington said "lay on too much steam and blow up the engines." On the other hand he steadily persevered in the course of reform which he and Canning had marked out for the future. His coöperation was invaluable if not essential to the ambassador's plans, and though when we look upon Turkey as she is now we must lament how much remains to be done, we must remember that these reforms, however much they may be in abeyance, have not been repealed, and that such internal improvement as may be discovered in the Turkish Empire was mainly their work. What Canning once hoped to accomplish may be read with interest in his own review of the subject. It was too large a scheme, as he knew, to be hurriedly attempted: but a succession of Reshids and of Cannings might have carried it at last.

"Years have passed since I left Constantinople, and at that time, in spite of all previous concessions, and much real progress in important respects, far greater than the improve-

ment was the mass of evil which still renders Turkey a
byword of weakness and an example of bad government.
Among the national statesmen were several who perceived
and some who lamented the defects or abuses so prevalent in
their administrative system.   But the one who more particularly recognized and sought to remove them was Reshid Pasha.
To him I could at least submit my suggestions without fear
of cavil or dislike.   I must confess that at my hands his
patriotism underwent some rude trials.   How could it be
otherwise? Wide was the field on which I had to sow European principles, and every part of that field cried loudly,
more or less for amendment.   Finance, justice, commerce,
education, the laws of property, the recruitment of the army,
the means of internal communication, and the whole administrative machinery, were so distraught as to sap the very life
of the State.   It was necessary to watch for opportunities,
—the *mollia tempora fandi*,—to deal cautiously with deep-
rooted prejudices, and not to overstrain the springs of action
and advancement.   Interesting as these matters may prove to
every reader who comprehends the full meaning and compass
of what is popularly called 'the Eastern Question,' I cannot
venture to increase their natural weight with a heavy load of
detail. A light sketch, or mere outline of the several plans I
suggested at various times, may suffice by way of record. The
first may be taken as an envelope for the rest.   It was intended
to secure an effective execution throughout the provinces of
such new measures as were adopted at the seat of government.
For this purpose it was essential to have a trustworthy
governor in each of the provincial districts, and as men of
that class are few, to diminish the number of pashaliks by
throwing here and there the smaller into one. I think they
were reducible in Europe and Asia to sixteen, and I gave in
a list of functionaries, who by character and experience
might be deemed equal to the discharge of their respective
duties. They could be well paid without any increase of
expense to the State, and with the assistance in each case of
a Mohammedan and a Christian secretary, appointed by the
Porte, and authorized to have constant knowledge of their
chief's decisions and official reports, they might be found

to merit a full measure of confidence. This scheme was founded in the main on precedents, occasional indeed and limited, but sufficient to meet the objection of radical change or untried innovation. In appearance it was favourably received, but never really adopted, except in one partial and successful instance, required by local occurrences, and ceasing with their pressure. Akin to it was the idea of admitting a Christian element into the Council of State, and dividing the Council into committees each of which might take cognizance of some great question, and submit it, with or without modification, to the judgment of the who le body.

"I kept carefully in view the expediency, indeed the necessity, of leaving Ottoman authority at the apex of every proposed measure. That authority, much as Christendom may deplore it, is the keystone of the empire. In the present state of things a substitute could only be found in foreign conquest, for whose benefit I need not specify. Thus, on the acknowledged ground of a signal falling off in the numbers in the Turkish population, I advised the recruitment of the army from all classes, without reference to religion, accompanied with the permanent abolition of the Kharaj (*haratch*), or raya capitation tax, and the formation of regiments subject to Ottoman command, though officered from among themselves. So with respect to the police in town and country my desire was to see a force of mingled classes headed by a Turkish director. For education of a general kind I wanted to have colleges established in the principal cities of the empire, similar to one at Pera, which under Turkish direction admitted scholars of all persuasions, and which, though founded on the study of medicine, opened its arms to the humanities at large. In the department of justice it was a great step to obtain a level position for Christian and Mohammedan evidence. In cases before the higher tribunal the recognized presence of a consul or other Christian representative was a kind of security, valuable though imperfect, against prejudice and corruption. The department of finance was a dunghill of corruption, abuse and ignorance. Farmed taxes, a debased coinage, extortion, malversation and private loans at ruinous interest were its

principal features. Piecemeal improvements were introduced
from time to time, but I could never persuade the Porte to
raise by public loan a sufficient sum to meet the cost of
establishing a sound system, without which there could be
no complete or effective cure. The wretched state of the
roads was, and I believe still is, another evil of great prejudice to Turkey. The facilities of water-carriage owing to
the intermixture of land and sea have, no doubt, partly
remedied, as well as partly caused, that serious check on
produce and trade. The mischief however still operates to
a degree which may yield in time to rail and steam, and probably to nothing short of those gigantic powers. I strove in
vain to open the Sultan's eyes on this subject. Once at my
suggestion he sent one of his ministers to open a carriage-
road from Trebizond to the Persian frontier. The work had
scarcely begun when it was abandoned, and its only results
were a job of some profit to the agent and the leaving a
wide field of lucrative commerce open to Russian enterprize.
Another important object of my endeavours fared no better.
The long frontier between Turkey and Greece lay constantly
open to the inroads of sympathizers from the latter country
and of brigands from both. Nothing was more easy than to
have formed a chain of military posts on the Turkish sides,
backed by a strong station of reserve and a small force of
cavalry for communication. If I had to docket this little plan,
the words would be ' virtually accepted, effectually limboed ' !
In contrast with these abortive efforts it is pleasant to state
that freedom of conscience in religious matters, and (more
recently) the admission of foreigners to the possession of
landed property, have formally and really become the law of
the land, and to the credit of my predecessors the trade of
Turkey with foreign countries, as regulated by treaty, has
been made to rest on principles of better effect, and brighter
promise than before. Upon the whole it may be fairly said
that if there is much to deplore in the administrative condition of Turkey, there is also reason to rejoice, and room for
hope as to its further improvement.

   " In principle all that could be reasonably required was
finally obtained, publicly proclaimed, and formally recorded

in the Treaty of 1856. Measures, I doubt not, have been retained or adapted in harmony with a part at least of the
principles thus avowed, but how far they are realities in practice, how far they have been followed up by others of similar
tendency, and in what degree the Christian governments, each
or all, have continued to urge the progressive movement, I
cannot say. Their friendly stimulant, though of course to be
applied with judgment, can rarely be found superfluous, and
at times they may be reasonably and justly employed for
purposes useful to Turkey itself and recognized as such by
the Turkish Government with that degree of authority which
ensures compliance. At one period by the influence of mere
persuasion I obtained from the existing Grand Vezir a promise that domestic slavery should be abolished throughout
his sovereign's dominions, and his reservation of Arabia from
the immediate operation of the measure encouraged me to
believe that his intention was sincere. Not that the policy
was as clear as the justice of such a change in the manners of
the nation, and, setting aside the broad principle of right, important considerations not excluding those of humanity might
perhaps be pleaded in favour of a practice no longer tolerated
in any part of Christendom. Far is it from my notions to
recommend any system of bullying, when we have to press
reforms required by its own interests on any foreign country
in friendly connexion with ours. But Turkey stands in a very
exceptional position towards us. Her independence is constantly threatened ; her means of resistance are weak ; and we
have not only spent our treasure, and shed the blood of our
soldiers in her defence, but we have pledged our faith to repeat the sacrifice whenever her independence is vitally im-
perilled. Surely in these circumstances there dwells not only
a right but a duty entitling and impelling our government to
see that the pledges given by the Sultan be fully redeemed,
and that all reforms accepted by him, and deemed essential
to the recovery of his empire's strength, be faithfully, continuously, and practically, carried out.'

CHAPTER XIX.

GREECE, SYRIA, AND PERSIA.

1842-45.

THE "high o'ertopping interest," to use Canning's words, of his mission from 1842 to 1846 was the question of internal reform. This was the subject that engrossed his attention and commanded his energies day and night during those years. But it was far from being the only troublesome problem to be solved. Never was the ambassador confronted with a larger or more bewildering forest of difficulties and complications. His letters to friends commonly begin with some such phrase as "I have but a moment to tell you," &c., and the state of his handwriting renders the study of his hurried *brouillons* or draft despatches a fit problem for a palaeographer. It was often beyond the skill of his attachés, and even of himself. On one occasion, in order to save time, he proposed to read a draft despatch aloud for an attaché to copy at dictation. The Elchi had not proceeded very far when he stopped, and after holding an illegible word in various lights in the hope of deciphering it, finally exclaimed in desperation, "Zounds! I can't make it out.—Here, *you* read it."

I may perhaps be excused for reproducing here a well-known story which I heard from Sir John Drummond Hay, till lately minister at the Court of Morocco. There had been a very busy time at the Embassy, where Mr. Hay was then acting as the Elchi's private secretary. It was the time of the Apostasy question and the disturbances at Mount Lebanon, and many despatches had to be drawn up and copied for home For more than thirty hours the ambassador and his assistant sat at their desks, with but brief intermissions for hurried meals.

At last the bag was sealed up for the messenger, and Canning observed that it might be as well to go to bed. It was an hour or two after noon. As they were leaving the room, the ambassador turned round and remarked that he expected a special courier presently, and Mr. Hay would have to receive and prepare the papers for his chief. Mr. Hay made no reply but inwardly resolved that after thirty hours' strain he would *not* be baulked of his sleep. Accordingly on reaching his bedroom he summoned his Greek servant and shewing him a pistol informed him that if anybody opened his door before six P.M. he would infallibly put a bullet into him, no matter who he was. The servant retired in consternation, and in due course the special messenger arrived with despatches. "Where is Mr. Hay?" was his first question. "In bed." "Go and call him." "If you please, sir, he has a pistol at his pillow and swears he will shoot the first person who opens his door before six." Mr. Hay was naturally allowed to repose in tranquillity. At six he dressed, and very soon a message came that his Excellency commanded his presence. He found Sir Stratford in no very amiable mood. "What is the meaning of this, Mr. Hay?"—and the ambassador indignantly recounted the messenger's story. The attaché explained that after thirty hours of unremitting work he really could not keep his eyes open. "D——n your eyes!" burst from the Elchi's lips before he could control himself. Mr. Hay was not the man to be backward at such an invitation. Gracefully combining respect with the expletive, he replied "D——n your Excellency's eyes!" Upon this Sir Stratford became suddenly very grave and stately. "I am sending off despatches this evening, Mr. Hay," he remarked with studied politeness, "and you shall convey them to England. I shall inform the Foreign Secretary that I have no further need of your services." "I shall be ready to start, sir," replied the attaché, and left the room. While he was hastily packing up for his journey, Lady Canning, who ever acted the part of peacemaker, came and besought him to apologize, or at least to go and say good-bye to the ambassador. After much persuading, he consented to bid his Excellency farewell. Hardly had he entered the room when Sir Stratford had him by the hand, saying "My dear Hay, this sort of thing will never do : what a very bad temper you have!" The two were firmer friends than ever after this, and Sir John Hay now looks back with pride and gratitude to the training he received at the hands of the kind if passionate ambassador.

Troubles with Greece, disputes with Persia, disturbances in Syria, such was the staple of the reports which poured in daily upon the Embassy. To relate a tenth of the negotiations, proposals and counter-proposals, intrigues, disputes, promises and retractations, that came at this time under supervision, would demand a separate volume. The correspondence about Greece alone is enough to dismay the stoutest heart that even a biographer of diplomacy can boast. Canning and Sir Edmund Lyons, then Minister at Athens, exchanged reams upon reams of closely-written manuscript on this provoking subject, and never seem to have approached a step nearer to a satisfactory solution. In those days Greece was the *bête noire* of politicians. Nothing could be made of her, and all the aspirations of the great and good men who had devoted their lives to her regeneration had crumbled to dust. King Otho and his German following seemed to invite deposition, and persisted in refusing the constitution which formed one of the conditions of the monarchy. Foreign despotism had reduced the country to a state of suppressed revolt little better than the anarchy which had preceded it, and such order as existed was only obtained by severe repression. Nothing appeared to grow towards settlement. This anarchic condition was a perpetual thorn in Canning's side. He felt a degree of responsibility towards the country which he had largely contributed to free ; he knew that his influence there was considerable ; and he resolved to use every endeavour to heal the wounds which an unwise government had rent in her polity.

On his way out he had stopped at Athens, and given very outspoken counsel to King Otho. A few sentences in a letter to Lady Canning refer to this :—

One more line to you, dearest E., from this classic spot, and then away for Stambol. My long and unfinished letter must take its flight, if ever, from the shores of the Bosphorus. This, like its predecessor of last week, must be short, a mere certificate that I am

1842-5
————
ÆT. 55-8
still, thank God ! alive ; and still yours. I have been and still am
in that sort of bustle to which I seem to be doomed. The reception
I have met with is enough to turn my head—not grey,—that it is
already,—but giddy. All classes have vied with each other to do
honour to your poor strolling husband, and with the honour comes
the expectation that I am to do wonders for the country, and
in my bosom springs an anxious desire to meet and to satisfy that
expectation. It has been hard work, and there is more of it in store ;
yet acting upon *your* great principle of kindness and confidence,
united to mine of energy and straightforwardness, I have succeeded
in much, and laid, I trust, the foundation of further success hereafter. What I have effected is the removal of all immediate causes
of quarrel between the Greeks and the Turks, and the commissions
which I take with me to Constantinople will probably be of use
in opening my communications with the Porte.—I have just been
to take leave of the King and the Queen. They were both very
gracious, and I am the more pleased that the latter [*sic*] was so,
because I have been obliged to tell him many unpleasant truths.
He concluded the audience by offering me the *grand cordon* of his
order, St. Sauveur, in a very respectable red morocco case, but I
declined it, until the permission of the Queen—our own Queen—
be obtained, which I shall leave him to ask for or not as he
pleases.

He wrote in a similar strain to Sir Robert Gordon :—

To Sir R
Gordon,
17 Jan.
1842
What I have wrung from King Otho is the fruit of much
hard labour, how hard you may guess when I say that amongst
other unpleasant things I was obliged to tell him that his royal word
was greatly at a discount. I have acted upon the principle of giving
him a last chance of setting himself right with his allies and with his
people, but though I have trusted, I have been careful to take the
best securities within reach, and I feel confident that Mavrocordatos'
appointment will be duly appreciated by the Allied Cabinets. He
expects to start in ten days or a fortnight.

My success in domestic matters has not, as you perceive, been
very extensive. I think however that a foundation for future improvement is laid in the King's mind, and it is absolutely [necessary]
that the superstructure should be raised, by him, if possible, or if not,
by others.

My last act in taking leave of the King this morning was an
endeavour to make him feel the importance of acting more frankly
and cordially with the representatives of the Allied Powers. My own
relations with them have been all that I could expect, and if my
conduct and language have only had the effect of abating the spirit

of party, which is one of the scourges of this country, I shall think
myself well paid for the enormous trouble I have had. Sir Edmund
Lyons has done everything in his power to make things easy to me,
but there are difficulties that even his talent and generous character
cannot overcome.

Whatever the effect of his advice, Lord Aberdeen did
not stint his praise of the ambassador's conduct. Canning's
despatch on Greek affairs written after his arrival at Con- To Lord
stantinople draws a gloomy picture of the state of parties at Aberdeen,
                  24 March
Athens. The royal authority was degenerating into despot- 1842
ism ; the better classes and working people were disgusted
with their Bavarian Court ; the country had not justice done
to it, its resources remained undeveloped ; and some constitutional check upon the crown, and some responsible form of
administration, and above all a tribunal of public opinion,
were needed to appease the popular discontent and to give
character and soundness to the Government. Any king of
Greece, he admitted, must have a difficult part to play ; but
Otho was personally despised, lacked the qualities of mind
and character which were essential to his position, and had
no sufficiently capable council or minister to make up for
royal deficiencies. Canning went so far as to tell King Otho
that he must beware of the course he was pursuing ; that "the
throne of Greece had not been set up as an idle pageant, but
for purposes which Europe had a right to expect that he
should realize." Advice however sound was of small avail,
and the ambassador foresaw that an internal explosion or
interference from without would probably be necessary before
a thorough change of system could be introduced. The
former came in a calm and prudent form in the revolution of
September, 1843.

Of that event he wrote in some relief to Sir Edmund
Lyons :—

It must be allowed that there never was a neater revolution, or To Sir E.
one attended with less popular outrage or of personal suffering. I Lyons,
                       2 Oct.
had long been apprehensive of worse and felt inexpressible relief 1843
on reaching the end of your narration. Unfortunately the best of
revolutions is a fearful experiment. Even when the first dangers are

avoided and the first difficulties surmounted, a wide unknown sea opens before the vessel of the state, and if water and provisions are on board, it is a chance but the compass has been left ashore. In the present instance there may be plenty of moral justification, though not exactly that overt act of the Government which strikes at the fundamental laws, and in free States, like that of modern France, has been held to justify resistance. What most jars on a conservative mind is the voice of the army overpowering the King before the civil authorities had declared themselves. What I look forward to with most apprehension is the National Assembly, the theatre which will there be opened for foreign intrigue and private ambition, and the formidable question of the *succession*, which it will be next to impossible to suppress. My hopes are that the present tranquillity, or rather freedom from popular excesses, may continue ; that the Powers will take what has been done, after the consent of the King, as a *fait accompli*, and lend their united counsels for the construction of a more national and at the same time a more stable order of things :—that the King will find it his interest to conform sincerely to the spirit of a constitutional monarchy ; and that our friend Mavrocordatos will acquire an ascendancy worthy of his talents, his European experience, and his honest sensible views.

So strong was Canning's faith in Mavrocordatos, whom he had managed to secure early in 1842 as Greek minister at the Porte, that he took the unusual step of sending him straight off to Athens at this crisis in an English man-of-war. The Greeks at Pera were enthusiastic over the new constitution, and when they met in the street, instead of using the usual " How d'ye do " and " Good morning," or their Hellenic equivalents, one would say Ζήτω, and the other reply Σύνταγμα : " Long live "—" the Constitution !" The hopes of the English party were soon doomed to disappointment and none deplored the fall of Mavrocordatos and the accession of Colettes more grievously than Canning. His correspondence with Lyons and Church shews how keen was his interest in the shifting scene of Greek politics : but he could do little at Constantinople to steer the ship, and while he never quite despaired of Greece his forebodings were at times far from cheerful. He often appealed to Addington, the under-secretary, to use more vigour, but the Foreign Office dared not risk war. " You ask how long we mean to allow King Otho to play his

antics with Colettes and Piscatory," replied Addington ;
" What can we do except by force ? but force is not lightly to
be resorted to—besides, two can play at it . . . Is Greece
worth such a stake ? A knife will walk into Otho and Colettes
too one day if they don't take care. But a vacant throne
would not suit us more than a perverse sovereign and minister."
As ambassador at the Porte Canning had to consider the
Turkish aspect of the Greek question, and that there was
danger to the Sultan in the rash and unscrupulous policy of
the Greeks was beyond doubt. The *grande idée*, which consisted in the foundation of a Greek Empire on the ruins of
Ottoman domination, was especially objectionable to him, and
he did his best to repress it. Border disputes moreover were
constantly occurring, and the Porte found it necessary to keep
a considerable force on the frontier to guard against marauders.
The violent language of the Greek press and Colettes' government encouraged systematic brigandage, and it needed all
Canning's influence to soothe the irritation of the Porte, especially as the French representative strenuously defended the
arbitrary and foolhardy action of the Greeks. The expro-
priation of the Turkish inhabitants, also, under the provisions
of the Treaty of 1832, involved claims for compensation which
were not honoured without vexatious contention and which
opened the door to more serious disagreements.

The Persian Frontier Commission was another constant
source of anxiety. The two Mohammedan States were in
imminent danger of war in June 1842, when the Persian
Foreign Minister requested Canning to use his good offices
in obtaining a reasonable settlement of the various matters
in dispute.

" The case had not been foreseen when I left England ;
but my instructions were urgent as to the maintenance of
peace in the East, and the difference between those Powers
required immediate attention. It was necessary for me to
act at once. Russia was the acknowledged mediator in
Turco-Persian affairs, and therefore my first step towards
the prevention of war was the establishment of a concurrent
action with the Russian envoy, M. Buteniev. I found but little

difficulty in persuading him to accept my coöperation, and together we went to Sarim Efendi [the Foreign Secretary] for the purpose of diverting him from the adoption of any precipitate measure, and of engaging him rather to look to us for a joint and friendly mediation. Whatever dislike the Turkish minister may have had to my interference, he did not offer any firm resistance to it. But he shewed no favour to the proposed mediation, and it was only by little and little that M. Buteniev and myself succeeded in giving a decided character of that kind to our proceedings. Enough for a beginning was, however, gained by the admission of negotiation, as the principle on which to act, instead of defiance and preparation for hostilities. We lost no time in communicating with our respective colleagues at Teheran, and they were not backward in seconding our plan of procedure.

"In this manner the cloud which had so imminently threatened the tranquillity of the East was so far dispersed as to admit of mutual arrangements for settling the differences by a regular treaty. Erzerum was to be the seat of negotiation. The Persian and Turkish plenipotentiaries were to meet there, and, in order to ensure a favourable progress, they were to carry on their discussions with the knowledge and, in case of disagreement, with the advice of English and Russian intermediaries appointed for that purpose. It so happened that two or three of our military officers were then at Constantinople. They had been sent out from England under an impression that their services would be acceptable to the Porte for instructing its new levies ; but they were in competition with the Prussians, to whom more confidence was apparently given by the Turkish authorities, and finally our Government determined to recall them. The first among them was Major Williams, who afterwards rose to distinction on the surrender of Kars, and it occurred to me that he might perform the functions of British intermediary. Unfortunately he fell ill while preparing to set out, and, although his brief illness was not of a nature to unfit him for his work, I thought it prudent to give him an associate, the journey being arduous and its terminus distant. The colleague I proposed was [one of the attachés] Mr. Robert Curzon, afterwards Lord Zouche. He had

travelled with me as a friend from England, and his qualities   1842-5
were such as fully to warrant the appointment.[1]   The Commission started in January 1843.   ÆT. 55-8

"The points of difference to be settled were numerous
enough to give plenty of employment to those concerned.
The principals had much national jealousy and traditional
grievance to keep them asunder. The chief bone of contention
was the boundary, in several parts disputed, extending from
the mountains of Armenia to the head of the Persian Gulf, a
distance of more than seven hundred miles, and occupied in
a great measure by nomadic tribes, who often shifted their
residence, and were consequently claimed as subjects by both
the contending Governments. A frontier line clearly laid
down by mutual agreement, and maintained by a series of
forts, presented the only chance of effecting a durable settlement and removing a constant provocative to war between
the two countries on whose pacific relations the general tranquillity of the East so much depended. Views so extensive
increased, no doubt, the difficulties of regulation, but the prospective results, in respect both of policy and of humanity,
promised an ample return for the additional labour. The
work, in truth, was slow, and its success at times endangered ;
but finally a treaty was concluded [apparently] to the satisfac-   Oct. 1847
tion of all parties."

How slow and wearisome was the progress of the negotiation may be understood from the following extract from a
letter of Mr. Curzon's to Sir Stratford :—

It has occurred to me that both the Plenipotentiaries are desi-   From R.
rous of getting any one of the Commissioners into a scrape and   Curzon,
particularly of sowing dissensions between the English and Russian   Erzerum,
Commissioners. Every time that I have seen Enveri Efendi alone,   30 July
he has begun a tirade against Russia ; I have always without one   1843

---

[1] Mr. A. H. Layard arrived at Constantinople in July 1842, and his knowledge
of the Turco-Persian frontier proved very useful to the ambassador, who employed
him in various confidential services, and endeavoured to reward him by a post at
the Embassy, but was opposed by the Foreign Office. A good account of the
Turco-Persian dispute is found in Sir A. H. Layard's *Early Adventures*, vol. ii.
ch. xix. (1887).

exception answered that whatever the policy of Russia may be in other respects she is of the same opinion with the British Government on this subject ; and when he has said he feared the two Governments would not always be of the same mind, I have replied that that should be an additional reason for his taking advantage of their present cordiality with each other. . . . Both Plenipotentiaries seem to consider it an axiom that they should give evasive answers to every question which we put to them ; they go off invariably into all sorts of discussions which are nothing to the purpose ; hours are wasted in this way ; they do not puzzle us, for when we are transacting business, I never swerve from the main point, and repeat my question again and again, till I have got an answer ; but they puzzle themselves most grievously sometimes, I am sure. Poor Mirza Tekel, whom I believe to be a well-meaning man in his way, looks considerably perplexed occasionally, and Enveri Efendi swings about and grunts in a peculiar manner, till he has routed out some new subtilty, or some other little quibble, which he desires the Commissioners to refute, if they can.

I really hope that your Excellency will be able to do something for us this time, for we are now in a disagreeable position. We are accused and misrepresented by both parties ; they pay but little respect to our mediation ; we are constantly trotting about in the sun, smoking pipes, and listening to all this garbage, without any good coming of it ; and as much thought, and caution, and trouble is expended in this way as would enable us to settle the really grave questions of international dispute.

I hope that you have got better of the gout. I fear you have been in great pain with it lately, though I must say that I think an ambassador with the gout at Constantinople is any way in a much more agreeable position than a commissioner with two plenipotentiaries at Erzerum.

The obstacles were indeed formidable. To draw a boundary line through migratory tribes is an almost insoluble problem, as our Afghan frontier commissioners have more than once discovered. In the case of the Persian boundary there were also serious religious jealousies to be overcome. A massacre at Kerbela in 1843 had rekindled the old animosity of Shi'ite against Sunnite to a dangerous heat ; protection for Persian pilgrims to holy shrines in Turkish territory was hard to ensure ; there were difficulties about Persian marriages, judicial trials, and other matters, on Turkish soil ; and there was a claim on the side of the Porte to the town of Moham-

mara, which the Persians, supported by Russia, stoutly resisted.   Colonel Williams deluged the Embassy with long
rambling letters and despatches ; the other agents in Persia,
Colonels Sheil, Farrant, and Rawlinson, sent frequent communications ; and endless interviews took place between the
ambassador and his Russian colleague, who was now (1843)
M. Titov.   The home Government supported Canning with
some vigour, thanks to a great extent to his old friend
Addington, who became Under-Secretary of Foreign Affairs
early in 1842, and endeavoured to put a backbone into Lord
Aberdeen's policy.   The latter was in perpetual dread that
Sir Stratford would commit the Government by some too
decided act and frequently rejected Addington's draft-
despatches as being too vigorous.   Referring to an opportunity
for putting additional pressure on the Porte the Under-
Secretary wrote :—

1842-5
—
AT. 55-8

> This incident has furnished us with the means of instructing you
> with some vigour *de omnibus rebus*.   But do not use more vigour
> than the *res* requires.   Lord Aberdeen was not altogether agreeable
> to the *stoutness* of the instruction, and particularly wishes that you
> should do as much as you can with the least practicable amount of
> menace or compulsion ; resorting, however, in case of clear necessity
> to the full extent of the authority given you.

Fr. Ad-
dington,
20 Nov.
1844

It was often hard to induce the Office to support Canning's
firm policy at the Porte, and such a message as the following
was not unusual :—

> I hope your chief will understand that I have done my best to
> settle them [certain difficulties] here, and that I now reckon upon
> his vigour and public spirit to enable me to put a finishing stroke to
> the whole nest of corruption and injustice.   Depend upon it that
> what I have consigned to my long public despatch is the truth : the
> Embassy, with all its interests of every description, is dished if you
> do not allow me to carry the business through in a decisive manner.

To Ad-
dington,
2 Oct.

The harmonious co-operation of Canning and his friend
Titov effected an arrangement to which Turkey assented in
1846 : but Persia threw it out, and the whole negotiation had
to be recommenced *de novo*.   At length, the Treaty of Erzerum was concluded, as has been said, in October 1847, but

To Lord
Aberdeen,
cxxv.
20 June,
1846

was concluded in name alone. It soon appeared that the settlement was purely formal.

MEMOIRS.   " When the terms of the treaty came to be applied to the actual delimitation, fresh disputes, of a local character, arose between the two Musulman negotiators, and all the exertions of the mediating parties failed to reconcile their conflicting pretensions.   An appeal to the respective Governments became necessary, and at my suggestion it was eventually agreed that a map of the whole frontier country should be made on scientific principles, and that the positions thus indisputably ascertained should regulate the application of the treaty.   Year upon year passed during these operations, and after a term which sufficed for the siege of Troy, the Crimean war came on, and the mediation was suspended. I proposed that the joint action involved in that idea should continue in spite of the war, as a matter of science directed to benevolent results, and hitherto agreeable to both parties. Lord Clarendon submitted the proposal to Russia, but the Russian authorities declined it.   In the year 1856 the conclusion of peace brought all the Powers into a state of friendly relations, and measures were subsequently taken to submit the proposed map, and to make it the instrument of realizing the treaty which it had cost so much to bring about between Turkey and Persia.   Another long period elapsed, and at last the combined process of astronomical, trigonometrical, and topographical measurements resulted in a paper fac-simile of the frontier country on a breadth of fifty miles along its whole extent.   It still remains for me to learn whether the means of adjustment thus fully obtained at no small cost of time, money and labour, have yet been used to effect their intended purpose."

MEMOIRS.   Another subject involving infinite trouble was the unhappy condition of the Lebanon.   " Syria, after the expulsion of Ibrahim Pasha and his Egyptian troops, had remained in a very unsettled state, and the Allied Powers deemed it their vocation to take a leading part in restoring some kind of order amongst its discordant elements.   The Porte had owed to all of them, except to France, who favoured Mohammed

Ali, the restitution of that interesting province to its own immediate authority. It was natural, therefore, not to say necessary, for the Turkish Government to acquiesce in their interference. Their five respective representatives, the French ambassador being one of them, were charged with the task in question. We had numerous meetings, much correspondence with our consuls in Syria, much discussion among ourselves, and occasional communications with the Porte. We found no end of obstructions in the way. The Turkish ministers were averse to every limitation of the Porte's authority. The old Sheykh of Mount Lebanon wished to recover and fortify the former condition of approximative independence which he had contrived to maintain before the war. The Druses, half heathen and half Mohammedan, were ready to draw the sword at any moment upon their Christian neighbours. The respective populations, including patches of Greek, Armenian, and other races, were so intermingled as to make their political separation next to impossible, and the French had no mind to give up a tittle of their ancient pretensions, warranted in some degree by treaty, to the protection of the Roman Catholic mountaineers. The manner in which this complicated skein was finally unravelled has little interest now. The cordial desire of the Powers to deal fairly by all parties, and the influence of such of them as had no immediate interest in the country, enabled us in the end to form a plan which placed the whole province under the paramount authority of the Sultan, but secured a separate administration, more or less independent, to each of the tribes distinct in race and religion. That all the parties under such circumstances should be completely satisfied was not to be expected, but we had reason to believe that our arrangement on the whole was generally acceptable, and in particular both M. Guizot and the French ambassador in London expressed to me their approval of it, though in truth the old pretensions of France with respect to Mount Lebanon were neither confirmed nor even recognized." [1]

To Lord Aberdeen, xci. 27 May, 1846

[1] The current French view of these negotiations, which is not favourable to "perfide Albion," and is especially antagonistic to the brusque proceedings of Col. Rose, may be read in the Vicomte A. de la Jonquière's *Histoire de l'Empire Ottoman* (1881).

1842-5
—
Æt. 55-8

The foregoing brief outline gives but a faint idea of the perplexities and intrigues in which the pacification of the Lebanon was involved. Those who care to pursue the subject further will find abundant material in the four Bluebooks of *Correspondence relative to the Affairs of Syria* presented to Parliament in 1843 and 1845, and comprising together 760 folio pages. The Great Powers were at first by no means disposed to cordial coöperation. They had indeed agreed in 1842 to a scheme of pacification proposed by Prince Metternich, but they seem to have agreed in order to differ, and it needed all Canning's diplomatic skill to bring the five ambassadors together in a common policy in 1844; and when this had been accomplished, fresh difficulties sprang up from the discord which reigned between the Turkish governors in Syria and the foreign consuls, and between the consuls themselves, especially Colonel Rose, of whose indiscretion and overbearing pretensions very disparaging reports reached the ambassador at Constantinople. Even so late as 1846, when affairs seemed really on the point of settlement, M. Guizot and Prince Metternich suddenly and publicly announced as a fact that a Catholic emir was to be appointed governor of the whole of Mount Lebanon, in defiance of all previous understandings. The announcement was entirely baseless: but it demanded great firmness on the part both of Canning and the Foreign Office, as well as of Reshid Pasha, to resist the influence brought to bear upon the Porte. It was in reference to this new obstacle that Addington wrote these lines :—

XXII.
4 Feb.
1846

XLVIII.
19 March

20 Jan.

We send you a fresh Syrian instruction to-day, to stick to Metternich's original plan of 1842 *versus* his plan of 1846. Jarnac has been pegging at Lord Aberdeen to place a Shihab on the Lebanon *throne*, and to throw overboard the scheme of 1842. But he did not prevail, and the draft which I had made already of your present instruction carried the day. Jarnac takes his Bible that Reshid has declared himself in favour of the Christian Head for the Mountain : a sheer lie, I apprehend, such as diplomacy permits and rather glories in.

In the end the original scheme was carried : but "Some

1842-5

.ET. 55-8

MEMOIRS.

modifications of the terms took place at a later period, our
consul at Beyrout, Colonel Hugh Rose, having availed himself of a visit to England to impress Lord Palmerston favourably as to certain opinions of his own which were not to my
taste. The instructions I received in consequence were by
no means agreeable to me. I was bound however to attend
to them, though I could not but feel a sore regret at the want
of reliance on my judgment and representations which the
minister's conduct, unreflectingly perhaps, displayed. I have
no sympathy with proceedings of this kind, and I still wonder
that a man of Palmerston's straightforward character should
even for once have made such a slip. In my judgment no
public servant employed abroad in a high responsible position should ever be called upon to act upon instructions
varying from his own recorded opinions and suggested privately by a subordinate in the same department of service.
I have since had more reason to complain of this kind of injustice from others, and, giving myself credit for some experience and local knowledge, am still persuaded that the public
interests have suffered on that account."

The progress of these various negotiations and the general
character of the work accomplished in 1842–46 will best be
seen in extracts from Canning's private letters. This source
of information is, however, very irregular, and there are long
intervals of silence. His most frequent correspondent, his
mother, had ended her long and honourable life in 1831, and
had been followed a few years later by his sister and eldest
brother; Richard Wellesley was dead; Gally Knight and
Planta were both in bad health; the former died in 1846, the
latter a year later; Fazakerley lived in strict retirement. A
few letters to Planta and Addington form almost the sum
of Canning's private correspondence with old friends. The
usually invaluable source of unofficial letters to the Foreign
Secretary fail us at this period, either because the ambassador
was not on very friendly terms with Lord Aberdeen, who
held the post, or because he did not keep copies of his correspondence. The two chief aids to our knowledge of his daily
life and work are several long letters to his only surviving

brother William, then a canon of St. George's Chapel, Windsor, and the ample correspondence which he kept up with Lady Canning during the months of their separation, in the early part of 1842, when he preceded her to Constantinople, and again in the summer of 1845 when she and her children returned to England, in the expectation that she would speedily be followed by her husband. Pressure of work, however, and the dilatory habits of Turkish ministers, kept him at the Porte till June of the following year, and his letters during the year of separation were frequent and full of interest. We can trace in them the gradual growth of hope and confidence as one measure of improvement after another was carried into effect, and we shall never again have so good an opportunity of witnessing his daily round of work and pleasure—much of the first and a little of the second—at Constantinople. The earliest extract, from a letter written to his wife before she joined him at Pera, shews his astonishment at the change which had taken place in the attitude of the Porte towards foreigners, while it also proves that he had instantly detected the retrograde movement which marched behind this outward improvement.

To his
Wife,
26 Jan.
1842

This morning I had my visit of the Grand Vezir, [Izzet Mohammed] who received me with remarkable politeness and attention. In appearance the old pretensions are gone, and I was treated as an equal, or rather more than an equal. We went in an open carriage sent by the Vezir and crossed to Constantinople over the new bridge erected by the late Sultan. It was an awful journey, but we broke down only once, and there was much to amuse as well as to edify. To-morrow I have my audience of the Sultan, whom I have already seen, for I went to the procession of the Corban Bairam, incog., the morning of my arrival. He has a gentle expression of countenance, expressing sensitiveness rather than firmness or energy. . . . Think of my driving last night through the streets of *Constantinople* [i.e. Stambol, not Pera] after dark in a phaeton. I was with the Reis Efendi, and he asked me to dine and sent me home in his carriage. There's a change for you—but a deal remains to be done, and there is a party at work to go back again to the old system.

The Grand Vezir endeavoured to conciliate the ambassador's goodwill by a handsome present of horses: but these, in accordance with his invariable custom, Canning politely declined.

To his cousin, Lord Canning, he wrote more plainly :—

Symptoms of reaction are certainly strengthening ; and as the Grand Vezir, though he has cautiously abstained from any outbreak since his return to power, is at heart and in nature a thoroughly violent man, proved to be so by atrocities committed in former days, I shall never be surprised to hear of some astounding *capriccio* on his Highness' part. This and other probabilities of a similar kind will soon, if I be not mistaken, have to come under serious consideration. Every fresh communication with my colleagues draws out the latent shade of difference. "*Pèsez sur la Porte*" is Monsieur Guizot's doctrine : "*Status quo*" and "*point d'ingérence*" are the watchwords of the Russian.

Towards the end of June Lady Canning joined her husband. He sent her a few words of "welcome to old Stambol. You took rather a discourteous leave of it a few years ago [after Navarino], but we are on quite another footing now, and please God! all will go well." It was characteristic of his devotion to duty that he did not go to meet her after a separation of six months. The courier was waiting for despatches, and no private interest could be allowed to interfere with his public duties. Accordingly Lady Canning and her children proceeded alone to the country house at Buyukderé, where the ambassador joined them in the evening. Though political matters had improved since their former visit, in the comforts of life they had much to desire. The palace at Pera had been burnt down some years before, and for the present, pending the erection of the new embassy, they had to accommodate themselves in town to an inconvenient temporary house ; while the hired villa at Buyukderé, prettily situated on the water's edge, was hardly calculated to offer a firm resistance to the weather. Of society there was little to be enjoyed. Canning bewailed the change to his old friend Planta :—

You have written to me four times and alas ! I have not written to you once. In return for my gratitude you must give me your compassion. I have really no time to write to those of whom I most frequently think. My public duties absorb the whole of my day, and often cut deep into the night. This was always a busy place, but the labour which was formerly occasional is now become incessant. The worst of it is that, compared with former days, I have no house, less society, a diminished salary, and fifteen additional years. Yet somehow or other— I know not why, I know not how,—the struggle goes on with more spirit than of yore, and neither health nor cheerfulness is wanting. . . .

Here as elsewhere the events of Kabul and Nankin have given a great impulse to our credit. We have also had our fingers in the pie of Eastern pacification. The Syrian question is settled, as far as diplomacy can settle it, and the Turks and Persians, instead of cutting each other's throats, are going to negotiate, with fair prospect of success, under the joint mediation of England and Russia. Old Turkey and her young Sultan do not make a very good match : but the latter means well, and I hope that Reshid Pasha, who is recalled on his own request from Paris, will help in time to put him more completely in the right way. Great changes have certainly taken place here within the last twelve years. But they are rather on the surface than at the bottom. On arriving I found a system of reaction established in spite of Syrian laurels and the Quixote who preceded me. It has cost me months to upset the private influence of the Seraglio and to turn out a President of the Council and a Grand Vezir. These things being happily accomplished, it remains to look out for the fruits thereof ; but they are slow in coming.

I really believe there is some truth in the old maxim, "A busy man has not time to be ill." What surprizes me is that I am sometimes kept indoors for ten days, and still not the worse for it. Perhaps we require less exercise as we get older. We certainly do with less sleep, and might I suspect get on better with less food. I rarely go to bed before twelve or half-past, and I am called at six, though I will not answer for being up every morning quite so early. I generally shave, however, by candlelight. The business of the Embassy is certainly immense, and what is worse, it grows with success, and, what is still worse, buried affairs *walk*. A few weeks ago we flattered ourselves with having fairly and discreetly interred the *Syrian* question, and the King of France gave the world its epitaph in his last speech ; but it has since "burst its cerements" and promises to become a most troublesome ghost. . . . Last week I sent off commissioners with about three reams of instructions to patch up peace between Persia and Turkey, and I have since heard of an incident at Bagdad [the Kerbela massacre], which threatens to blow up the

whole negotiation.—Woe is me ! Alhama ! In spite of all this I
work on as well as I can, grumbling and swearing—with a *r* or a *t*
as you please. . . . The narrow, dark, close, muddy streets of this
miserable suburb are odious ; but we have fair views of the Bosphorus, and fine air on the hills.   We mean to rush back into the country
as soon as possible ; but the amusement costs some 600*l*. or 700*l*. a
year, Government not choosing to allow a country house, as France,
Russia, and Austria do.   Our opera, bad as it looks, is really very
tolerable.   But we do not go often, though we have a box, which is
the envy of all the diplomatic body.   We have boats, and carriages,
and saddle-horses in abundance ; but the difficulty is how to use
them.   When we do use our four greys and English postilions, half
the town assembles to stare, though our Excellencies may go out on
foot without drawing a look.   E. gave a children's ball some days
ago, and we succeeded in getting (for the first time in history) a
dozen of Turkish boys and girls of good family to dance with the
little Christians.   I was glad to hear that the Sultan's prime favourite,
who was present, regretted that he had not sent his children too.   It
is a small matter, dearest William, to read of in this scrawl of mine,
but a great and a good deed was done in that hour, and the seed
there sown shall be a tree, when I am in my grave.   You have now
reached the truth at the bottom of the well.   It is this hope that
sustains me through trouble, fatigues, and privations, not omitting
the bitter feeling of disappointment under which I came here for the
fourth time in my autumnal days.—God's will be done !   I have
obeyed and hope it may not be in vain. —But you need not be told it is
uphill work.   Such roguery, corruption, and falsehood and deep anti-
social selfishness.   Still, my influence strikes deep root, and I hope
against hope.

1842-5
—·—
ÆT. 55-8

We are not rich in society.   Yet E. continues to get up an occasional party, and to please those who come to us.   Turks, Greeks,
and Armenians will occasionally make their appearance, and though
we cannot always converse with our guests, the novelty of their appearance, and the prospect which it offers, amuse and interest us.
Thank God !   we are free from the plague, and though " fire " is calling at this moment, I trust we shall escape, the whole quarter having
been burnt down about four years ago. . . .

To the
same,
30 March

The "rascally Pasha," about whom you have been reading in
the papers, has nearly well nigh thrown the whole of Persia into a
blaze, as well as your indignant brother.   With infinite trouble I
have got up the negotiation to which her Majesty was pleased to
allude in the speech, and that rascal has taken the opportunity to
cut the throats of several thousand Persians at a frontier place called

Kerbela. I do not despair of living to give a good account of him. He is a long way off, though—to wit, at Bagdad.

An extract from a despatch of the previous autumn, though of little apparent importance at the time, is interesting now : " On Thursday, 22 September [1842] one of the ladies of the Sultan's harem gave birth to a prince who has received the name of *Abdu-l-Hamid.*"

Letters from his few remaining old friends were among his consolations, especially when such events as the Servian revolution and Russia's menacing interference endangered his influence at the Porte :—

To Planta,
29 April,
1843

The sight of the well-known hand afforded me the sincerest pleasure and I am particularly obliged to you for making the effort so soon after the commencement of your recovery. Every such mark of friendly kindness is a bright spot in my circle of daily labour. It grieves me to think that you have suffered so much from ill-health. It may comfort you to know that at times I almost wish for an illness to give me an interval of repose from business and anxiety.

What you tell me of Parliament and Sir Robert's position therein is very satisfactory. Peace too, I trust, will be maintained, though *our* horizon here has been rather overcast by the Servian discussion [1] between Padishah and the Czar, nor is the danger quite gone by, if the reports from Belgrade be true, notwithstanding the perfect submission which, under the advice of your old friend Doctor Metternich, the Porte has made to Russia.

Between ourselves enough has taken place to startle those who remember the spirit and decision of ancient days, and I fear that we have purchased a precarious lease of quiet in these latitudes at the cost of our own influence and of our friend's independence.

To his
Brother,
25 July

As for me, did you ever hear of the gout ? I also have more than heard of it, and if you were here you might see the five gentlemen of my left foot looking through the slashes of a lacerated shoe, like so many debtors in prison. I begin, however, to get out again, and hope soon to be on horseback, with the firm intention of leading the most anti-arthritic life I can think of. . . . You are right in supposing that I have plenty to do. Your old friends the Persians are not the least troublesome of my neighbours. The present tendency however is towards a calm, as far at least as the *nervous contractions*

---

[1] See Sir A. H. Layard, *Early Adventures,* vol. ii. ch. xix.

of this vast and half-exhausted empire, feeling about for its lost
strength, and shaken by every exertion, will allow. Here as elsewhere,
a great man is wanted—the master-mind, the gigantic hands, that
grasp and press and mould at will the scattered elements of empire
Alas! that such things should be so rare! I am much concerned at
what you tell me of the Government. Your language, I presume,
expresses more thoughts than your own. The *Times*, I see, makes
no concealment, and that paper is always a formidable assailant.
These are days of compromise, often well meant, and vastly Christian,
but at times neither fortunate, nor *common-sensible*. Still I love to
think that the native constitutional vigour of our system will sur-
mount its trials; and the frequent exhibition of danger will probably
in the end convince the most self-willed that the inconveniences and
sacrifices necessary for a cure must be endured. In politics, as in
morals, the true principle can never long be relinquished without
a foreiture. This might be the preface to a very long croak—but I
spare you.

In 1844 the renegade question, Syria, Persia, and a revolt
in Albania, fully occupied the Elchi's time, and when he wrote
to friends he confined himself to the briefest possible bulletins.
At the opening of the new year he made amends to his
brother in a long epistle, which contains some interesting
retrospections :—

In politics too I have had very uphill work,—that is uphill for
me, but down hill for this country. . . . At this moment the position
is so far improved that I am fighting with all the weight of Government at my back. It is a last deadly struggle with corruption, and
here on the spot I am alone, though in the light of a clear and resolute conscience. To you at a distance this may sound a little ro-
mantic, but there is in reality no exaggeration in it. Luckily for
yourself you are too far off to provoke me to an explanation, and
the newspapers will probably in due season give you the result *in
shorts*. Our *last* result belongs to the deceased year. It was a great
one but little understood beyond the veil. It reads innocently,—
" Renegades from Islamism to be no more put to death."—Yet was
it the first dagger thrust into the side of the false prophet and his
creed. Such wounds may widen, but they never close,—Which grave
remark is not the worse For being, as you see, a verse. Whenever
we meet again, if it please God that we should do so, and you rather
like to be bored to death, I will tell you how marvellously and provi-
dentially the whole affair was carried through. In the meantime you
may bear being told that we go to town in two or three days, having

already weathered half a winter of cold winds and snow in the country. . . . Our large wooden house on the river's edge with a large
marble hall and a saloon to match it overhead is so little suited to
the season that we had much difficulty in uniting our few half-frozen
neighbours under a magnificent bunch of *mistletoe* on Christmas Eve,
which, on looking *afterwards* into the rubric, I blushed to find appro-
priated by our Church to seriousness and not to revelry. Visitors,
with one rather peculiar exception, have long since left us, and we
have been obliged to make the most of our own resources. They,
as you may imagine, are rather monotonous, and at this season not
a little interrupted by the badness of the roads, which break up regularly in autumn, as boys in England do for the holidays. As for me,
during a great part of most days and occasionally of the night also, I
am glued down to my writing-table, which is often a thankless task
separating me from those I love, and putting me in contradiction with
the younger and more careless spirits around me. Not that I mean
to complain. I took the cup deliberately, I am content to drink it,
and rather look forward with hope than backward with regret. There
are, nevertheless, weak as well as trying moments, and, not having
the constitutional placidity of my Uncle Toby, I fear that I have been
caught swearing more than once. It might be some comfort to a less
benevolent ambassador that his young and reckless *attachés* have not
a sound constitution among them. Not one of them is equal to half
the fatigue which I endure, and often after the departure of a messenger there is a general occultation of the minor luminaries. Lord
Napier left us two days ago with views of marriage for the benefit of
a prettyish and clever daughter of Lady Julia Lockwood's. It was to
relieve the dulness of copying a long despatch that he laid down his
pen and stepped across the street to propose.

CHAPTER XX.

1845-46.

EVERYONE has heard of the discoveries of Layard and Newton, of the palace of Nimrud and the colossal tomb of Mausolus ; but few are aware that but for the liberality and public spirit of Sir Stratford Canning these discoveries might never have borne fruit and the British Museum might have been deprived of some of its chief treasures. I do not mean merely that without the ambassador's influence the *firmans* or necessary permits, by which alone excavations, purchases of land, and exportations of antiquities, could take place, might not have been obtained : I mean that it was Canning's enterprize and money that rescued the first fruits of the Mausoleum and enabled Layard to begin his famous work at Nineveh. Without being an archaeologist, the Elchi was an ardent classical scholar of a good old type which we miss now-a-days, and everything connected with ancient history excited his keenest interest. In the midst of pressing political duties, we shall see how his mind wandered away with enthusiasm to the labours of his agents at Mosil and Halicarnassus.

Mr. Austen Henry Layard had arrived at Constantinople in 1842, after a rough experience of travel in the frontier lands between Turkey and Persia. Canning was not slow to perceive the abilities of the explorer, and employed him in more than one tour of observation in the disturbed provinces of the Ottoman Empire, and Layard's reports on the state of affairs in Servia and Albania were scarcely less useful to his employer than his knowledge of the provinces in which the labours of the Turco-Persian Boundary Commission were centred.   The ambassador would have willingly seen so intelligent and industrious an assistant enrolled among his attachés ; indeed so earnest were his recommendations that the Foreign Office went near to reproaching him with importunity ; and it was certainly no fault of his that Layard did not obtain his first step in diplomacy at the Embassy at the Porte in 1845.   Failing in this, and deeply interested in the traveller's reports of promising mounds, suggestive of buried cities, in Mesopotamia, Canning resolved to attempt an exploration of the sites thus indicated, and despatched him in October 1845 with such funds as he could afford to risk.   He gave him a salary at the rate of £200 a year, and £120 to begin his digging.   It was not much, but the expenses of the Embassy left little margin for a speculation of this kind, and the sum was enough to enable Layard to establish the truth of his conjectures and to draw the attention of the Government to the importance of his discoveries.   The explorer was "to inform Sir Stratford Canning of his operations and to give him a full account of any objects worthy of curiosity which he might see or discover ; to abstain carefully from meddling with anything of a political or religious character ; to avoid confidential or frequent intercourse with missionaries, whatever might be their country or religion ; to shew respect and deference to the Turkish authorities and to lose no opportunity of cultivating their goodwill ; to maintain the character of a traveller fond of antiquities, of picturesque scenery, and of Asiatic manners ; not to leave without communication ; and to do his best to obtain permission on the spot for the removal of the objects discovered," &c.   He was furnished with letters of recommendation, and in May 1846 he was sent a firman or Grand Vezirial letter authorizing him to excavate and export sculptures. Lord Stratford's Memoirs contain a few sentences on this subject :—

MEMOIRS.   " With respect to the spoils of Nineveh, its sculptures, inscriptions, and human-headed bulls, there seemed to be a kind of fate in our acquisition of them. Mr. Layard, to whom the country is so much indebted, arrived from Baghdad an utter stranger to me, with letters from our consul there. Employment was an object to him, and forming a good opinion of his abilities and activity, I favoured his wishes, and had no reason to regret my confidence. He gave his mind a good deal to the discovery of antiquities, and pointed out a spot not far from Mosil where he thought an excavation might be made with success, and where a tributary stream would facilitate the transport of any discovered objects worthy of being conveyed to England. It so happened that I remembered having read of the same place in Mr. Rich's narrative as likely to conceal important remains of antiquity. The coincidence struck me, and I made up my mind to inaugurate an excavation by means of Mr. Layard. He undertook the adventure at once, although I could only give it a private character, and engage his services on my own account. On reaching Mosil he met with a courteous reception from the Pasha, to whom I had given him letters of introduction, and much friendly counsel and liberal encouragement from M. Botta, the French consul, himself an earnest and successful explorer. Nothing could be more satisfactory than the manner in which Mr. Layard conducted the enterprize. His zeal, his judgment, his energy were alike conspicuous. He shewed much skill in managing the numerous labourers who worked under his direction, and I must add that in point of expenditure he never lost sight of the economy which prudence had obliged me to enjoin."

Such was the unambitious commencement of perhaps the most astonishing and important series of discoveries which any Englishman has conducted since the days when Belzoni explored the Tombs of the Kings at Thebes. In 1846, moved thereto by Canning's letters and Layard's reports, the Trustees of the British Museum took over the work which the ambassador had begun, and thenceforward Assyrian antiquities poured in an avalanche upon the astounded officials of Bloomsbury.

The excavations at Budrum, the ancient Halicarnassus,

1845
——
Æt. 58

were even more the special delight of the ambassador than those at Nimrud. It had long been known that the Castle of St. Peter at Budrum was built by the Knights of St. John with the stones of the Mausoleum which Queen Artemisia constructed in B.C. 353–1 in memory of her husband Mausolus with such loving magnificence that it was numbered among the Seven Wonders of the World. Portions of the ancient sculptures had been detected in the masonry of the fortress, and Canning resolved to rescue these noble remains of the school of Scopas from the risk of Turkish demolition. In June 1844 Charles Alison, the Oriental secretary, was sent on a mission to Syria, and was instructed to call on his way at Budrum and report on the extent and condition of the remains

To C.
Alison,
12 June
1844

of the Mausoleum which were visible in the walls of the fortress ; and the Elchi told him that he was prepared to find the necessary sum for transferring them to the protection of the British Museum. Alison's report, albeit not that of a specialist, was convincing as to the importance of the sculptures, and the ambassador redoubled his exertions to induce the Porte to grant him permission to remove them. It was not however till 1846 that he triumphed over Turkish procrastination and had the satisfaction of learning, not only that he had leave to extract the marbles from the walls in which they were embedded, but that the Sultan, in sign of his high regard, was graciously pleased to make them a personal gift to the ambassador himself. Any ordinary present would have been respectfully declined, but these monuments of Greek art were too precious to be lost for a scruple, and they would enrich, not the Elchi, but the British nation. The gift was accordingly accepted with gratitude, and Alison was again sent out to complete his task by superintending the removal of the antiquities. The work was successfully accomplished at a cost of three or four hundred pounds, and twelve out of the seventeen slabs of the frieze of the Order, representing combats of Greeks and Amazons, executed in the finest Parian marble, which now adorn the walls of the British Museum, are the fruits of these operations.

"The composition of this frieze," writes Sir Charles Newton, "is distinguished by the wonderful animation and

energy which pervade the whole. A happy boldness of invention is shewn in the incidents which represent the varied
fortunes of a combat in which neither side can claim a decisive victory. A consummate technical knowledge is applied
throughout to render the expression of each figure and group
as emphatic as possible, and proportions are boldly exaggerated to produce more telling effects."

1845

ÆT. 58

*A Guide
to the
Mauso-
leum
Room,*
British
Museum,
p. 7 (1886)

We read a great deal about the beginning of these discoveries in the very interesting correspondence which began
when Lady Canning left for England in the summer of 1845.

So far all goes well, and I have great hopes of getting through all
my labours soon, and having in prospect all that I can presume to
expect for so rotten an empire as this. I am working like a mole—a
beaver—an ant—a horse in a mill—a *devil*—to secure the good
within reach. The weather is still intensely hot, and we are as dry
as tinder. But never mind, please God we shall have rain as well as
other good things. You will be glad to know that the Sultan is
coming out handsomely. . . . We all jog on well together—Layard,
and Alison and all. You are never forgotten by any of us.

To his
Wife,
17 Aug.

P.S.—If this finds you at Paris contrive to let Reshid Pasha
know in confidence that, though silent, I have never lost sight of his
interests, and that I trust the present change will soon make an
opening for him. But he must be very quiet for the present, and
prepare to be very prudent in future. Find out what he now is, and
what he thinks, and let me know, but *not* by the French post.

I have got the *Church Firman* at last, and am to have the
Persian answer in a few days. The commission too is drawing to a
close, and old Shekib is to be off the same day for Syria, where things
are looking better, and where Rose is quite enchanted with the new
settlement, or rather the end of the old one. All this has a third-
volume air, and yet I have fears of being kept here till towards
Christmas. . . .

5 Sept.

I am preparing to send a couple of heads to England, of
heads from Nineveh, think of that! About 2,600 years old, and
they would no doubt talk if they had not left the language behind
them. They are deep reliefs, in good preservation, more than the
natural size—a warrior and a eunuch—well defined, and they are to
be the first arrivals of the kind in England, precursors of M. Botta's
treasures, which, though of the same description, having come from
the same place, are of course superior.

1845
———
ÆT. 58
To his
Wife,
9 Sept.
Woe is me! There are moments when I am sadly puzzled in speculating on what is to come out of so many steamers, and rail-roads, and printing-presses, and daguerreotypes. Its *first* effect is diffusion, and all diffusion is weakness ; but under the scattered materials there is, perhaps, a fertilizing principle, which may in time be the parent of a rich crop of social blessings, resulting in a vast extension of human happiness. But to realize this hope, there must be no premature disturbance of the heart's education ; the quiet domestic moralities interwoven with our earliest affections must not be frightened away, like Thames salmon, by the rush of steam and gas ; the Bible must go forth with the engine ; and every choice assortment of Manchester stuffs must have an honest John Bunyan to distribute them.

27 Oct.
The *beginning of April* must be the *extreme* limit of my patience, and this is more than a fair allowance for all that I have it at heart to do, or that can possibly be done at present. The nine points, which I have carefully written down on a small scrap of paper, may be accomplished sooner, and if so what is to keep me here ? I have already scratched out the one which seemed but a few days ago the most difficult of all. It stands thus on my memorandum : ~~Recall of Reshid~~. Who knows whether I may not be equally fortunate with the other eight, especially as two of them may be fairly united into one ? Already I think one may be considered as good as scratched out. I mean *Persia*. Pisani has just written on A'li Efendi's authority, " La décision sera satisfaisante ; je puis l'annoncer."—I have also strong reason to believe that *certain marbles*, to which you know I attach great interest, will be given me before ten days are out. That will erase another notch from my stick. . . . The change of policy is now complete, and the Sultan and his ministers vie with each other in shewing me confidence, and, as far as Turkish natures allow, making me amends for past vexations and disappointments. This is doubly gratifying as it confirms my *trust in principles*, and awakens in my heart that feeling of gratitude to Providence which is at once a source of the purest joy and an incentive to further exertion in the right path. Help me with your prayers and sweeten sweetness itself by making part of it your own work. It is now four days since the order for Reshid's return went to him. I wrote you a few lines on the same occasion and enclosed them with my despatch to Lord Aberdeen. I wrote also to Reshid himself, and you shall have a copy of my letter with this. I would not say more by such a conveyance, and indeed I almost said too much as it was, for the Turkish courier turned out to be an Austrian *estafette*, and all my effusions will no doubt pass under Metternich's eye. The *imbroglio* was a regular Turkish one, and

would have made me angry under other circumstances. I reckon
on Reshid being here about Christmas, and before he arrives I must
have a thorough understanding with him, the more easily as what you
said to him and caused him to say will serve as an excellent preface.
There is a little inclination in the public to connect his return with
the French and what they have lately been doing on Syrian affairs.
But it is only connected with them as the antipodes are connected
with us. I have the Sultan's own voluntary assurance, conveyed to
me by an express message, for this. The Russians do not quite like
this move towards positive improvement ; but I have recommended
communications which may reconcile them in some degree to what
can never be entirely to their taste. Supposing all to go right, a few
weeks after Reshid's return will enable me to lay a foundation which
may harden and consolidate during my visit to England and be fit
for a superstructure of worthy proportions afterwards. If God be so
pleased !

Candili, 21 *Nov.* 1845.—Think of that ! and such a morning of
brightness, and green sunny banks, strewed all over with daisies and
glittering yellow flowers! It would be spring, if I had not found the
turf, where we ate poor Layard's strawberries, sprinkled over with
autumnal leaves. Mounted on my fat donkey, with the tallest of the
two Slavonians at my side, I sauntered, if one can saunter on four legs,
over to the steep wood of firs beneath the signal house and thence, from
a thousand shady nooks, and as many sunbright knolls, I looked up
and down the deep-blue, boat-mottled Bosphorus at half the lovely
spots we have so often visited,—Shchidler crowning them all,—and
I felt more solitary than words can express—why I need not tell you.
Alas ! that there should be so many beautiful objects without, and so
much loneliness within ! Yet I am far more happy here than in town,
where I can neither breathe nor look about me, nor please myself
with gazing on the waters which look up at me from between the
Castles, and as they glide along seem willing to bear my thoughts to
those who are absent.

Is it possible, my dear William, that *you* can complain of *me* for
not writing? At all events you have written, and here am I coming
to write. But alas ! my will is puzzled by the rub of not knowing
what to say. You don't care a farthing—now do you?—about
Turkish reforms, and Pashas and Efendis and such kinds of things
and persons ? On the contrary, you have scarcely even pity for poor
Tom, whose food has been of such like gear for the greater part, off
and on, of half a century. Never mind : I am told you would like
to know a little more of my goings on and so you shall. I must

begin, however, by observing that my goings on are often very much like standings still. At this moment for instance, though I have long wished to be amongst you all once more, and to rejoin my more especial belongings, it is to no purpose that I spur with both heels, use horse language, and vip, and vip, and vip ; the old hack will have its own way, sometimes with a start, then with a kick, not always unaccompanied with a plunge that bespatters one with mud, and not unfrequently with a dead stop. Not so with the mails and steamers. On they go, whizzing and whisking their paddles, or rattling their legs, and snorting out loads of paper,—instructions, reports, remarks, notes, letters, journals, reviews, petitions, and Heaven knows what besides. In comes the never-ceasing drift, under the doors, through the windows, down the chimneys—there is no possibility of keeping it out. I shovel it, attachés shovel it, the dragomans shovel it, but the heap never disappears, and all we can do by shovelling together is to save ourselves from being choked by the accumulation. Where it all comes from and what it's all about is sometimes a puzzle to me as well as to you ; but you may be sure that it is more pleasant to read about it than to deal with. The humanity department is perhaps the most intelligible, but it is also the most troublesome. I assist in turning wicked functionaries into good ones, griping extortioners into pleasing collectors, bigoted Musulmans into easy latitudinarians, decapitated renegades into smiling churchgoers, highway robbers into domestic attendants, and the whole tribe of torturers and executioners into so many obliging sinecurists. Sometimes an ill-favoured Vezir, who growls and snarls at having the half-gnawed bone kicked from under his nose, might be taught by a sound bastinadoing to walk more steadily in the right path, but individuals are protected under the new constitution in their lives, fortunes and honour (which lies throughout the East in the soles of the feet). And if it were not for an occasional massacre by the troops and the wholesale system of plunder in the provinces, there would be nothing to remind us of the good old times, when Turks did as they liked, and Christians were grateful for the use of their skins. One great object I long had at heart was to get hold of the Sultan ; and, if appearances may be trusted, I *have* him ; another was to turn out a sort of old tory peculating suspicious deceitful junto, and that too is done. Then war was to be prevented and friendship established along 700 miles of Turco-Curdo-Persian frontier. I won't answer for the *friendship*, but war is prevented, and the foundations of a great work of peace and improvement among the barbarous tribes is laid in the mutual, though somewhat reluctant, consent of the growling parties. Allow me next to present to your reverence the Protestant Church established under the Sultan's firman

1845
—
Æт. 58
Vol. i. p. 10

on Sion's rock. Though it cost three years to get that firman, it will take three thousand to "rail off its seal," or at least as many as Shylock told you in the old school at Hackney that it would take to rail the seal off another bond. I will not trouble you with commercial matters, but we have had some tough questions to manage in that department, and I am happy to say that they are all either settled or on the eve of settlement, or so arranged as to give us all we require, till the conclusive agreements shall be made. Our new Embassy house, or palace as it is called here, is rising rapidly above the ashes of the old one, and I have extorted a few thousand pounds from the Porte for the purchase of a row of Turkish houses, the removal of which will open the garden on one entire side to a fine terrace-view of Constantinople and its Golden Horn. When you come to preach in our chapel, instead of the young person of 72 who now does duty there, you will be able to appreciate this acquisition. In the meantime it will interest you more to know—though it is still an awful secret— that I have obtained a promise of the famous Halicarnassus Marbles —the remnants of the Mausoleum—which have been for centuries encased in the walls of a Turkish fortress, and which I hope to have on their way to England in a very few weeks. More than this, I have an agent at work among the mounds of Nineveh, and a letter received from him this morning announces the discovery of a marble chamber full of cuneiform inscriptions—now by Major Rawlinson's ingenuity interpretable—and of an immense adjoining edifice, apparently a palace, which he is endeavouring to penetrate by cutting trenches through the mound, and which tradition assigns to Ashur the lieu- tenant, or more properly speaking, I suppose, the whipper-in, of Nimrod !!—I tremble, while I inform you of these incomplete acquisitions, lest any feeling or appearance of premature confidence should indispose the genii and set them at work to defeat me. One is never so inclined to superstition as when some favourite project is advancing gradually, and all but reaching its final accom- plishment. "'Twixt cup and lip The foot may slip ; And those who think They needs must win, When near the brink May tumble in."— Thus have I tried, like a good younger brother, to give you some idea of the butterflies which it is my vocation to hunt. They are the more important to me because we have not the social resources of Paris or London at our command. Yet in a party of ten who dined with me yesterday, there was a traveller from New South Wales, another well acquainted with America, and Sir William Harris, our ambassador to the Christian King of Ethiopia and the Nimrod of Southern Africa. After dinner we broke off into chess, whist, and music, to which two of the guests contributed on the piano, one on the violin, and a fourth on the flute, and all admirable players. The day before, I had dined with the Austrian minister, under whose hospitable roof the diplomatic body with a fair sprinkling of the more amiable sex was collected. In the morning I had been at a conference with the Russian minister and the Reis Efendi, mounted on my good horse *Gazil*, a brown wicked arched-necked beast with a magnificent black tail, preceded by two kavasses (what *can* they be ?) on white and skittish hacks, and followed by my faithful grooms Joseph and Henry. To-morrow, with the blessing of Heaven, I hope to get into the country once more for a few days. In order to do this I must change continents ; for my country house, which to speak the truth is but a box, looks down from the top of a steep Asiatic hill upon the Bosphorus. A ride of forty minutes takes me to the water's edge, where I find my pretty caïque with its three pair of oars, and the men, a Greek and two Turks, dressed in full white Dutchmanlike drawers, with gauze shirts, and naked breasts and arms, and red waistcoats picked out with delicate black embroidery. Ten minutes suffice to convey me, without the help of a bull, across the most lovely of riverlike waters, and at the landing-place opposite—a village market with an admirable *hummum* and the minaret of a mosque hard by—I bestride a punchy, serious, good-humoured, and not talkative donkey, with a glorious pair of long flexible hairy ears ; and step after step, picking his way, never looking behind him, or betraying the slightest disrespect, he finds his way to the top of the steep declivity, where fifty more of his tiny jogging paces on level ground take me to the rural door. If it be night, and clear, I have all the host of heaven for lamps and flambeaux ; if it be day, there is a noble view up the Bosphorus, and another rich and noble view down the Bosphorus. . . . These strange particulars, my dear William, may serve to bring me nearer to your mind's eye, and to afford you a glimpse of the sort of patched harlequin life that I am leading. But if in my ardour to meet your wishes I have allowed any diplomatic cat to escape from its bag, you must put a string round its neck and keep it close to you whether by your fireside or in the pulpit.

To his
Wife,
Constanti-
nople, 3
Jan. 1846

Well ! my dearest E., the corner is turned, and we are fairly embarked in the new year. We are no longer in the year of *separation*, but, if hopes and appearances may be trusted, in that of *meeting*. I still hold to my intention of starting early in April, and I reckon upon being able to do so with a safe conscience. The only public affairs of interest must be settled by that time at least virtually, if not formally, and it is most desirable in every way that I should refit, and help you to look a little after our private concerns. . . . The establishment wants repairing as much as I do, and we all require to dive awhile out of sight in order to appear again more becomingly on the surface. Even for Reshid and his improvements it is better that I should go home after understanding him thoroughly, and return with the advantage of a recent contact with the sources of power. We are thoroughly agreed as to principles, and to judge from appearances I am in full possession of his good will and confidence, and perhaps even in the same degree of his Imperial master's ! The French, however, have the *shine*, and provided I have the substance, it is better perhaps to leave them in their enjoyment. They have not only the tinsel, but the talk also on their side, for M. Deschamps and his colleagues of the press omit no opportunity of puffing them, and shewing off their supposed influence at the Porte. . . .

N.B. At the close of this sentence I crossed over from my writing-room towards the street to the little drawing-room backwards, where I love to breakfast in sight of Somerhill and two at least of the children. There I found hard by the teapot a letter from Smyrna announcing a complete change of ministry in England ! MacGuffog and the little Count were with me. I read the whole aloud to them, and made them laugh at the hilarity with which I received *such news*—Johnny Russell for Peel, and Palmerston for Aberdeen. True, or false—it may be either—what care I?—The plot thickens. Letters of the 16th are come in from London by way of Odessa, which has amicably kept itself open for the occasion. Peel has certainly resigned. Lord John has certainly been sent for. But the last letter talks of his difficulties in forming a government, and "*as you were*" may finally be the order of the day. In this state of our information, patience and silence are our only resources. There is nothing for it but to wait. At present I am too ignorant to make a guess, and still more so to form an opinion. Of course I shall be most anxious to have information, not only from newspapers, but from friends, and particularly from you, my best friend. Even if I am recalled there will be points as to which I may wish a finger-post for my guidance, and yet greater will be my need, if the main point is left to my own decision. What I most dread is a state of prolonged uncertainty, which may impose upon me the duty of not using my leave of absence without taking a decided position. Poor Reshid expressed himself with much kindness to Pisani when he heard of the news. Whig or Tory, he said, made little difference in the policy of England towards this country, but he could not say how deeply he should feel my departure, were such to be the consequence of a change in Downing Street, and the tears came into his eyes. No doubt this is a transient feeling, but I believe it to be sincere, and it is gratifying. 'Tide what will, I rejoice at being here, and I also rejoice that you and the children are out of the way. Still more do I rejoice to think that all we could reasonably expect from our return to Constantinople is more or less realized. Honours, indeed, if any were within my reach, will probably be lost, but what are they compared with the consciousness of having acted upon sound principles, and contributed to beneficial results? As I said before, all the leading questions, in which I have been engaged, are either completely or virtually settled, and the provisions are laid for much additional advantage in the fulness of time. The difficulties which have retarded and obstructed my progress were not of my creation. I found them here, and they are removed. It would indeed have been more satisfactory to give the last formal finish to each question —but if I am deprived of that gratification, I only partake of what has fallen to the lot of the greatest and the best of mankind. When the moment of decision comes I shall try to act *rightly* first, and then *prudently*. All else may may safely be left to that Wisdom which never fails. . . .

I see little of anyone out of the house, and the town is duller than ever. On Christmas day I collected all the English bachelors I could think of, and we had a merry party of fourteen. On New Year's day I collected all the employés of the Embassy from Cumberbatch down to the two students. Wellesley was too ill to make his appearance, and that reduced us to twenty-one. Old Bennet said grace, and we drank the Queen's health standing, both which ceremonies reminded one of earlier and better days. I have not yet undertaken the diplomats, but must soon, and I meditate a Turkish dinner to Reshid and some of his friends. . . .

I have at last surmounted all my difficulties about the marbles at Budrum. The letters are prepared, a Turkish engineer appointed, and Alison sets off with them and him and one of Smith's masons the day after to-morrow to secure the whole prize—thirteen inestimable blocks of marble, sculptured by the four greatest artists[1] of the best days of Greece, mentioned in Herodotus and immortalized by the sentiment to which they owed their creation no less than by the genius which shaped them into perfection. Oh ! if they should stick in the wall ! Oh ! if they should break in coming out of it ! Oh ! if they should founder on the way to England ! Think of my venturing all at my own expense ! Think of the Sultan saying that he won't hear of my paying a sou ! Indeed, my own Artemisia, I shall be much disappointed if the new Ministry and the Corn Laws be not thrown into the shade by these celebrated marbles, which it has cost me nearly three years of patient perseverance to obtain. But this is not all. Layard is making very important discoveries in Mesopotamia. He has sent me the outline of a most beautiful piece

[1] They were Scopas, Leochares, Bryaxis, and Timotheos, of the later Athenian school.

of sculpture representing warriors in active fight, and chariots and
horses with splendid trappings, all of great antiquity and superior in
workmanship to anything discovered by M. Botta. The French are
jealous to an extreme, and the wicked Pasha of Mosil under their
influence is trying to counteract us. But I have a scheme, which I
think will defeat them and secure us all we want for ourselves, and
much more for the benefit of the world at large. Major Rawlinson
writes me from Baghdad in high admiration and offers to send up a
steamer in the spring to secure whatever Layard may have succeeded
in getting out. I am quite proud of my public spirit in the cause
of antiquity and fine art. But I must not ruin either you or the
children ; and I propose to call in the aid of Government—whether
Whig or Tory—to accomplish what may easily prove beyond my
reach. Now you must be tired, dead tired of all this, and perhaps
you think me crazy for caring so much about such trifles, but they
are trifles for which colleges universities and nations would take each
other by the ears, and as Major Rawlinson tells me, the inscriptions
are likely to throw much light upon Scripture history, particularly on
our old friend *Tiglath-pileser*.

Part of Canning's letter to Sir Robert Peel in support of
Layard's excavations is here quoted. He perceived that the
enterprize was too important to be neglected, and that larger
means than his own would be needed to carry it out successfully, and he appealed without hesitation to the Prime
Minister :—

While you are providing at so great a personal sacrifice for the
ages to come, allow me to claim another of your moments on behalf
of those which have preceded us.

M. Botta's success at Nineveh has induced me to adventure in
the same lottery, and my ticket has turned up a prize. On the
banks of the Tigris not far from Mosil there is a gigantic mound
called *Nimrud*. My agent has succeeded in opening it here and there,
and his labours have been rewarded by the discovery of many
interesting sculptures, and a world of inscriptions. If the excavation
keeps its promise to the end there is much reason to hope that
Montagu House will beat the Louvre hollow.

Although the operations have hitherto proceeded at my personal
expense, and without any formal permission from this Government,
I look forward to the time when you will think it worth while to step
in and carry off the prize on behalf of the Museum. In cherishing
this hope I may not, perhaps, have the fear of Exchequer sufficiently

before my eyes, but however the Chancellor may demur I feel confident that the representative of a learned university will open his bosom largely to the claims of *Nimrud*. The expense would be small in comparison with the object, which promises results of the highest historical interest :—

tenuis non gloria, si quem
Numina laeva sinunt auditque vocatus Apollo.

The appeal was not made in vain, and the Trustees of the Museum recognized so fully and gratefully Canning's share in the great work that they consulted him in every step they took and submitted the instructions they were sending to Layard for the ambassador's advice. The Sultan having made him a personal gift of the antiquities, Canning generously presented all the results of his own excavation to the nation, and only consented to the repayment of his advances, (as also in the case of the Budrum sculptures,) from a sense of duty to his family. Of his agent he always wrote with the warmest appreciation, and Sir Henry Layard long afterwards enjoyed the advantage of his employer's friendship and support.

The Mausoleum frieze had been safely shipped for England at the beginning of the year. Canning announced his triumph to his old friend Sir R. H. Inglis, one of the Trustees of the Museum, in great exultation :—

Did you ever hear of one Stratford Canning formerly a member, if not of Grillion's, at least of Parliament ?

Did you ever, as member for the University of Oxford, hear of Queen Artemisia—not Artemisia the friend of Xerxes, but Artemisia the inconsolable widow of Mausolus ?

My reason for asking is simply this. The above-mentioned gentleman has lately broken into a Turkish fortress, and carried off some dozen blocks of marble exhibiting reliefs of men and horses fighting, not like Trojans, but true Greeks ; and these,—the remains of the original Mausoleum or seventh wonder of the world,—he proposes to present to the Museum, of which you are a venerable and honoured Trustee,—that is to the British nation. Observe that the marbles were stuck into the walls of the fortress of Budrum, the ancient Halicarnassus—three or four outside, the rest within—and that the latter, though known to exist, have been invisible to all but Turkish

jailors and artillerymen for ages. My *right* of possession was obtained
from the Sultan, who has made them a personal gift to me ; the *de facto*
possession derives from the studied and determined exertions of a
party of people, headed by Mr. Alison, an Oriental savant here, whom
I sent down to secure and embark them. The valuables are now on
their way to Malta in H.M. ship *Siren*. They occupy sixteen cases
in all, weighing about twenty tons. I have only seen very imperfect
sketches of them, but if you wish to know more of their merits, you
may look into Clarke and Anarcharsis, Pliny and Vitruvius. The
height of the figures cannot be more than two feet and a half, though
the depth of the marble is about three, and the length varies from about
the same to six. It took me three years of patience and occasional
exertions to get them, and the operation of extracting, lowering, and
embarking them occupied many days. The operation was completed without a single accident, either to the men or to the marbles.
Time however though slow has not been idle, and some of the figures
are consequently the worse for wear, though not so much so as the
artists who made them, or the originals whom they represent.

It need hardly be said that the Trustees tendered their
" best and warmest thanks " for the liberality with which
Canning had presented the Mausoleum frieze to the nation.
Mr. Forshall, the secretary of the Museum, wrote with enthusiasm of the " Canning Marbles ; " but it is characteristic of the
ambassador's loyalty to the Sultan that he requested that
Abdu-l-Mejid's name should have the post of honour in the
official description of the monument. Accordingly the visitor
to the Mausoleum room in the British Museum now reads
beneath the frieze :—" Given by Sultan Abdul Medjid to
Viscount Stratford de Redcliffe, by whom it was presented to
the Trustees of the British Museum, 1846."

Canning's connexion with Halicarnassus did not end
here. In 1852 Mr. C. T. Newton went to the Levant as vice-
consul at Mitylene, with a special view to further excavations
in Ionia and the Greek islands. His preliminary visit to
Constantinople was more than an act of official homage : he
knew both the zeal of the ambassador in the cause of archaeo-
logical research, and his unique power to obtain the needful
concessions from the Porte. The firmans were readily promised, and Mr. Newton began the series of tours of observation and excavation which he has described in his authorita-

tive *History of Discoveries at Halicarnassus, Cnidus, and Branchidae* (1862), and in his eminently graphic and interesting *Travels and Discoveries in the Levant* (1865). Throughout these journeys of exploration Lord Stratford's influence was at work to facilitate the labours of the archaeologist, and in 1854–5 Mr. Newton prosecuted an independent series of excavations at Calymnos, with funds advanced by the ambassador, which yielded very valuable results in inscriptions and other antiquities of an interesting period. It was during his researches in the Levant that Mr. Newton completed the work which had been begun at Budrum, by his discovery—not of fragments built into later masonry—but of the buried Mausoleum itself, with the colossal statue of the king whom it enshrined. Before, however, he had embarked on this gigantic work, he made a discovery at the fortress of Budrum itself. He observed, jutting out from the walls which Alison believed he had ransacked, but on the outside, some boldly carved lions which obviously belonged to the same period as the frieze which had been previously removed in 1846. How they had come to be overlooked when the frieze within the fortress was being removed is hard to understand ; but there was now but one course open—to write immediately to Lord Stratford and beg for a firman to extract them. The agonies of suspense through which Mr. Newton passed before the firman could arrive may be told in his own words :—

Travels in the Levant, ii. 100–104

While we were making these discoveries on the site of the Mausoleum, we were anxiously waiting for the firman empowering me to take possession of the lions which I had discovered in the Castle last year [but one]. Unavoidable delays prevented the granting of this document, and in the meantime the Commandant of the Castle suddenly received orders from the Turkish Minister of War to remove the lions from the walls and send them to Constantinople. He lost no time in putting this order in execution, and before many days had elapsed two of the finest lions were extracted from the walls. It was not a pleasant sight for us to see this operation performed under our very eyes, after we had brought spars for scaffolding and all manner of means and appliances for the express purpose ; however I gulped down my mortification as well as I could, and despatched two letters, one by sea, the other by a swift overland runner, to Smyrna, to apprise Lord Stratford that the Turkish Minister of War was trying to steal a march on us. My messenger sped on night and day, and the Commandant pushed on with his work no less expeditiously. Two more lions were soon dug out of the walls. The extraction of two of my eye-teeth could not have given me so great a pang. When the Commandant had removed four lions, he paid a formal visit to my diggings, accompanied by all the principal Turks in Budrum.

"You have found nothing but little fragments I see," he said, with an air of triumph. At that time we were digging up small fragments of lions' tails, with an occasional leg or hind-quarter, but no heads. I endured his civil impertinence for about a quarter of an hour, till at last my inward chafing found vent in a strong expression or two in English, addressed to Captain Towsey. The Turks did not understand what I had said ; but guessed from the expression of my countenance what was passing in my mind, and withdrew with many ironical compliments. That same day, the lions, having been duly swathed in raw sheepskins, were placed on board a caïque to be sent over to Cos, where they were to be transhipped by steamer to Constantinople. I had a photograph made of two of them, and took a last fond look at these gracious remains of the school of Scopas. The caïque, as the Commandant informed me, was to sail that night, and I went to bed sick at heart. It was the end of a great hope.

At 4 A.M. the next morning I was suddenly roused from my sleep by the voice of a midshipman from the *Gorgon*. "The *Swallow* is come in from Constantinople, and the officer of the watch thinks that the firman is on board." I had had so many disappointments about the firman, that I received this news with sceptical indifference, and doggedly fell asleep again. At 6 A.M. another messenger from the *Gorgon* woke me up. "The captain wants to see you immediately." I hurried on board, and found Towsey pacing the quarter-deck impatiently, his gig alongside, ready manned.

"Why have you been so long ?" he said ; "the firman is come."

"Of what use is the firman now ?" I answered, very sulkily ; "the lions are gone."

"The caïque is still in the harbour," he said, "waiting for a fair wind to come out, and we are yet in time."

I jumped into the boat without a word more : a few vigorous strokes brought us into the harbour. The captain of the caïque was drawing in his little mooring lines in a lazy, sleepy sort of way. On the pier-head stood the doctor of the Quarantine, an Italian, who took great interest in our diggings.

"Don't let that caïque go," I cried out ; "I have a firman for the lions."

"It is all right," he replied ; "I have his papers still, and he cannot leave without my signature."

We walked straight into the Castle, and asked to see the Commandant.   Very much astonished he was at so early a visit from the Captain of the ship of war and the Consul.   He had evidently just emerged from his *yorgan*, and his *narguileh* was hardly lit.   We had boarded him with that indecent haste with which mad Englishmen occasionally invade the *Kieff* of an Oriental when any real emergency occurs, without waiting for the due interchange of compliments. After hastily wishing him good morning, I put the firman into his hand with that air of cool satisfaction with which a whist-player trumps an ace on the first round.   Turks are seldom astonished ; but my friend the Commandant was really discomposed ; he read the firman through several times.   The document was duly signed and sealed ; the wording of this writ of *habeas corpus* was so precise that there was no evading it.   The lions were to be delivered to me whether still in the walls or already embarked.   Suddenly a bright thought struck the Commandant.

"The firman," quoth he, "makes mention of lions, *aslanlar* ; but the animals in the walls are leopards, *caplanlar.*"

"Come, come, *dostoum*, my friend," I said, "aslanlar or caplanlar, you know very well what are the beasts meant by the firman, and where to find them.   I claim those beasts, and no others." . . .

The lions were forthwith handed to me, and the Commandant reimbursed.

We have anticipated the course of events in relating the capture of the Budrum lions by Lord Stratford's lasso, because this was his last important service to archæology, and fitly concludes the subject.   In future, for some years, we have to do with wars and rumours of wars ; and though it was in the midst of the intricate negotiations which enveloped the Crimean expedition that the ambassador found time to interest himself in Mr. Newton's discoveries at Calymnos, and to despatch the firman to Budrum, readers are not always capable of such divided attention, and the calm victories of archæology would but interrupt a narrative which centres at Balaklava and Sevastopol.   It is well, however, that the world should understand how much it owes to Canning's zeal in the cause of art, and that when it commemorates the signal services of Sir Henry Layard and Sir Charles Newton it may also give due honour to the statesman who was in a large degree the cause of their success.

A few more extracts from the correspondence will com-

plete the narrative of work at the Porte in 1846. Canning
was labouring assiduously to bring his various negotiations
to a close, but the progress was slow, and one obstacle after
another delayed his departure.

I made a great exertion yesterday to get through the Persian
business for your sake, and indeed for my own too. We had a conference here—Reshid and Titov and the interpreters. I dined them
all. And what would you have said to see five pipes puffing away in
your drawing-room? What a profanation! But the public service,
you know, required it, and the consequence was that we got through
our task completely. We broke up at half-past ten, and I was in bed
at eleven. Now we have only to get all the papers put into their
respective phraseologies, to pack them up, and to send them off that
the Persians may do the same, and the Plenipos. sign and seal
merrily at Erzerum. By the way Reshid has promised me a *nishan*
for Curzon, and if I can get him a " *Lion and Sun* " from Persia, I do
not see what should keep him from being knighted and sporting
"Sir Robert" till he gets his peerage in the course of nature. . . . The
Turks have been much vexed by a speech of M. Guizot's about Syria.
It is indeed but too much of a piece with much that has come of late
from the same quarter. Everything is on the point of settling ; and
there is an evident determination to throw all into confusion for
French purposes. Heaven knows what instructions the next messenger may bring me. Meanwhile I stand firm, and I keep the Porte
steady.

As for my political affairs —they are all moving on towards their
conclusion, but their mode of progression is by *short hops* after long
intervals of repose or *sedentary* agitation. Even the incomparable
Reshid is either not perfect himself, or is embarrassed by stupid
colleagues. Between ourselves I suspect that *all* colleagues are so.
If I can but settle all handsomely, secure my antiquities, leave Reshid
to travel gently with his Sultan, and turn my back upon as quiet an
empire as we have at this moment, after two or three measures of
internal improvement shall have been adopted, I shall be satisfied,
and forget all past and present vexations in self-content and the prospect of seeing you once more. In the meantime we are passing
rather a dull existence, a long spell of wet bad weather, succeeded
by a spell of fine cold ditto, very changeable, as you know. But, to
be just, yesterday was a glorious exception, and I sallied forth with all
my cavalry, seven horses from the stable, without the coachies, to pay
visits to departing pashas who had called upon me. I made the
grand tour of Constantinople and passed in returning for the first

1846
—
ÆT. 59

time over the new bridge—a very creditable construction. Wellesley went with me to see Suleyman Pasha, who goes ambassador to Paris. I found his more than octogenarian predecessor—old Khusruf—closeted with him, and I had some capital sport with the two, the old bird being by far the most alive of the two.

Think of my having five Armenian women closeted with me this morning—relations of poor persecuted devils excommunicated by the patriarch for *Gospel* opinions, &c. You will recognize in this the work of the American missionaries. So it is, and my position is most embarrassing ; but I am doing my best to rescue the persecuted in their civil interests and domestic relations without giving too much offence and exciting disobedience to just authority. A young lady of seventeen was the spokesman, and she delivered her English first through a yashmak and then, in her zeal, with uncovered lips. It is lucky for ambassadors that they are husbands and papas as well as elderly gentlemen.

24 March

At six this morning, dearest E., I was in my arm-chair at work, and at seven this evening I left it to dress and go to dinner. This is hard work for quiet times. Yet I would not repine if I thought that my labours were appreciated. It is very well for people in England to say that he is doing wonders in the East, that he can't be spared from Constantinople. That only means, if it mean anything, that he is best where we see and hear least of him. You compliment me upon the gaiety of my letters, and I rejoice to have succeeded in lighting you up with the reflection of my phosphorus. But in good earnest I know not why I should be gay, and there are moments when I am angry with myself for seeming so. Here it is the constant drudgery which makes Jack a dull boy. The efforts that are required to make an inch of progress with these Turks are inconceivable. Even Persia is not yet out of hand, though I trust that to-morrow will at length see the back of my last messenger in that direction. Though I am far better off than before Reshid came, yet the entanglement is still vexatious to a degree, and when I shake my wings and spring upwards to the breeze, the bird-lime holds my legs and I flap the air to no purpose. . . . . It would seem that like a coin of the country I can only pass current *here*. In the West I am a counter, and nothing more. Nobody would take me even in change.—Well, scorn for scorn ! If they *don't* know me, I *do* know them, and the country knows, which is more to the purpose. My circle is a small one, but the opinions I began with, I still maintain, and they have proved to be the right ones, and they have triumphed. This is something for the moment ; but what does it lead to ? Before you answer this query you will ask what is become of "philosophy." To speak frankly, it was a very short-lived taper, and soon burnt out leaving the snuff in my fingers. Never mind, I will try to get a few more inches of it before I go, and please God! we will read our book by it, and laugh at the world outside.

The day before yesterday or rather yesterday I went over to Stambol and made a round of visits on horseback. I saw Rif'at, who embraced me *tenderly*, and sent a thousand messages to you. I went also to see old Huseyn Pasha, who put down the Janissaries, and he told me the whole story of that famous day. It was curious to hear it over again from such lips. The Turks continue to be very civil, but there is still a wilderness of corruption, cruelty, and misery.

I made a *tremendous* speech at the dinner given three days ago to a prince of Hesse Darmstadt who has been here. He is a general in the Russian service and brother-in-law to the Czar's eldest son. The Sultan dined us at Beylerbey, but did not appear himself. I did not mean to give a toast, but was egged on, and so made the best of it—and nothing could equal the joy and compliments of the Turks. Mark too that Titov shook me by the hand. . . . Sarim is here,—the beast—he came sneaking up, and I was barely civil. He is already trying to insinuate venom against Reshid.

The speech in question has been preserved and may be printed here :—

Altesse et Excellences!—J'avoue que j'ai hésité avant d'user de mon privilège comme doyen du Corps Diplomatique pour hasarder quelques paroles en son nom, devant tant d'illustres convives et dans ce salon Impérial. Mais le sentiment qui doit se trouver au fond de chaque cœur dans cette occasion m'engage à écarter toute autre considération pour en être l'interprète, regrettant toutefois que l'interprète ne soit pas plus digne de la circonstance. Il m'est impossible de ne pas contraster le magnifique spectacle que je vois ici aujourd'hui avec tout ce qui m'est tombé sous les yeux lors de ma première arrivée dans ce pays. Un intervalle de plusieurs années sépare les deux époques. A la première tout était préjugé, froideur, et plus qu'éloignement entre les différentes races rassemblées sans être rapprochées dans cette vaste capitale. Les Représentants des nations étrangères n'avaient d'autre relation avec les fonctionnaires du gouvernement que celles de la cérémonie et des affaires diplomatiques. Les nations elles-mêmes se regardaient avec méfiance, et trop souvent avec des sentiments de haine mutuelle. Dans ce moment je me trouve ici entouré de tout ce qu'il y a de plus noble dans l'Empire Ottoman, à côté de tous les chefs de mission sans exception quelconque, dans le palais du Souverain, en présence d'un illustre Voyageur, et la réunion de représentants, pour ainsi dire, de tant de diverses races autour de cette table hospitalière s'adresse à la vue avec une éloquence qui surpasse la parole. Honneur à la mémoire du Sultan Mahmoud sous les auspices de qui ce changement merveilleux a commencé son cours ! Honneur et prospérité au Sultan plein de bonté qui se voue aujourd'hui dans le même esprit à l'accomplissement du même ouvrage. Le résultat de leurs soins successifs est l'indice d'un véritable progrès dans la société, et, comme j'aime à le croire, dans l'ordre social aussi. C'est en substituant la paix pour la guerre, l'amitié pour la haine, et la bienveillance pour les préjugés méfiants que l'on parvient à rapprocher les cœurs, à redresser bien des malheurs, et à améliorer le sort de l'humanité. Le toast que j'ai l'honneur de vous proposer n'est que le résumé de ces idées : *L'entente cordiale partout, et surtout entre l'Orient et l'Occident.*

To his Wife, 4 May

Though I am not yet quite free I am dropping my shackles one after the other. . . . The Persian negotiation is still the main, if not the only, difficulty. I have, however, taken leave of the Sultan, who was graciousness itself. He thanked me for my services to his empire, was satisfied of my devotion to his interests, regretted my absence, and longed for my return. What more could the fondness of a lover have suggested? The audience was a private one, and Reshid, by accident, was my interpreter.

18 June

Why stay so long, you say? Because I am goose enough to aim at settling every possible question before I go, not only for my own credit, but because the position is a favourable one for acting with success. The Sultan came back two days before his time, and by sea in a steamer, as I had most strenuously advised. His journey has done him good, in health, self-confidence, and reputation. He seems to mean generosity as well as humanity. . . Reshid is in high content and desires his particular remembrances and those of his ladies to you. Mrs. Redhouse will tell you a good deal about the Sultan. I really seem to have a hold on his kindness, and he is doing or preparing to do as much as the wretched state of his people and empire will allow. Think of fatty Rifat fairly throwing his arms round my neck the other day, and half crying with affection. He *explained* by saying that he had always liked me, but now perceived I was a better friend to the empire than all his colleagues.

Canning did not escape from the Porte till the end of

July, and he left with an unpleasant feeling that a reaction might be expected. His old enemy Riza Pasha had been recalled to office. " I fear that I have stayed too long," he wrote to his wife, 20 July ; " Riza is in office again, not very high, but still in office—Minister of Commerce in place of Sarim. It looks as if Reshid had been very weak—or worse. I have had suspicions for some days, and wormed the thing out, but too late to prevent. It may be less disastrous than I apprehend in the first moment, and I have my assurances to hope so ; but I am sick of assurances, and believe nothing." In this disconsolate mood ended his fourth mission to the Porte—a mission fraught with great results and marked throughout by an earnest ambition to save Turkey for her own and England's sake and raise her to a worthy place among European powers.

1846

ÆT. 59

Arrived in England, 17 August

A YEAR of rest and well-employed idleness, if such an expression may be allowed, followed upon five years of arduous labour. After so much vexatious toil and so many disappointments in the progress of his Turkish pupils, Canning was well pleased for a while to do nothing. The interval of leisure was soon over, and in the autumn of 1847 he was preparing for his return to Stambol. The journey was not, however, to be hurried or direct. There were signs in the political condition of Europe which caused uneasiness to Lord John Russell's Cabinet: the first mutterings were already audible of the storm which was to burst in 1848; and it was considered desirable that a tried diplomatist should visit the principal Courts of Central Europe and sound their views upon the alarming prospect which lay before them. The envoy selected for this delicate and responsible task was Sir Stratford Canning.

In spite of the attractions of so stately a progress through Europe, the return to Constantinople was anything but agreeable. Unless there were a definite prospect of real reform in Turkey, Canning felt that the position of ambassador at the Porte would be intolerable; and he accordingly wrote to a trusted friend to sound Reshid Pasha on this subject.

To Dr
Mac-
Guffog,
21 June

It has cost me a hard struggle to return, far more than to take leave of the Sultan, which I would willingly have done at any rate. In consenting therefore to return, I act under a sense of public duty —partly towards the Queen's Government, who continue to wish it

and partly towards Reshid Pasha, our friend, the friend of his country
in the best sense, and his Sovereign's most useful and enlightened
servant. But the execution of this duty must have its limits, and its
objects. I cannot set aside every interest and feeling of my family.
I am naturally anxious that the fifth act of my Eastern drama should
bear some permanent and beneficial results, beneficial to all classes
of the Sultan's subjects, confirmatory of the present cordial agreement between the two countries, and creditable to the individuals
more immediately concerned. I look to the accomplishment of
objects which are in principle both Turkish and European by means
which I believe to be as satisfactory to Reshid as to myself. *Here* I
foresee no difficulty. There ought not to be any at *Constantinople.*
Lord Palmerston is well disposed. Reshid appears to be confirmed
in favour. The only question that can be reasonably apprehended is
one of time. It is agreed that I shall be free from the end of next
year, and much as I should be mortified in leaving Turkey for ever
without the fulfilment of my hopes, I could not be expected to make
a holocaust of all other views, and of the claims, as just as they are
natural, of my family. The point at issue, then, is this :—Will Reshid
feel himself at liberty so to press forward the desired measures as
to secure their adoption before the close of 1848? Does he value
my coöperation sufficiently to induce him to strain every nerve in
order to turn to full account the fifteen months that I am prepared to
place at his disposal? It is but fair that we should understand each
other upon this point clearly and definitively. I cannot expect, nor
should I wish him to postpone his own duties and interests to a consideration for me, much as my own conduct is grounded on consideration for him ; but he is too just and too kind to leave me unnecessarily
in doubt as to his intentions and views taken in connexion with the
requirements of his official position. He would not willingly expose
me to fruitless vexation and disappointment. The present occasion
does not admit of much explanation in detail, but enough may be
said in few words to shadow out my notion more distinctly, and to
enable you to submit to the Pasha a sufficient groundwork for him to
open himself on. He may remember the papers which I sent in
confidentially to the Sultan and to the Council some months before
I left Constantinople. My project is that he should give effect successively, but without delay, to measures—principally those which we
have already talked over, and to which I know he is well inclined,—
calculated to bring into operation the general system of improvement
to which these papers were addressed, and which received the approbation of the highest authority in the Empire. Some of the reforms
in question have already been adopted in principle, and only require
a more accelerated progress. Such, for instance, are those which

relate to a better collection of the revenue, and the extension of education. Others are known to be agreeable to the Pasha, nor need I
specify more of them than what regards the Kharaj and Christian
Evidence. Others, again, are essential to the removal of any motives
of alienation between Turkey and Christendom on the one side,
and between the Sultan and his Raya subjects on the other. It is
scarcely necessary to mention the question of premature conversion
in the case of Christian children, and the persecution of seceding
Armenians. Besides the advantage which would accrue to Turkey,
and also to Reshid's administration, from an early adoption of such
improvements, a further result would naturally be a confirmation of
England's friendly policy towards the Sultan's Empire, and perhaps
even a more explicit declaration of it with a view to contingencies.
I am inclined to think that after the settlement of the Turco-Persian
negotiation and of the dispute with King Otho- or rather with
Prince Colettes—an interval of quiet as to internal affairs will allow a
convenient term of leisure for carrying into effect the proposed improvements. Be that as it may, there are always sufficient elements
of intrigue in one quarter, of encroachment in another, and of disorder in all, to make it of the utmost importance for Turkey to improve her internal resources, to extend her connexions with Europe,
and to consolidate her political intimacy with Great Britain.

The answer to this letter has not been preserved ; but
Callimachi, the Turkish ambassador, told Lady Canning that

From
Lady
Canning,
17 Dec.

Reshid is dying for your arrival. The Sultan has persuaded him
to take in Riza. . . Bourquency furious at the Greek question not
advancing. He is doing his utmost to finish it before you reach
Athens. . . Callimachi asked Lord Palmerston how long you were
to be detained—it was hardly fair on them. Lord P. answered you
would not be detained above a fortnight ; no one knew Swiss affairs
so well, and they wanted a man of your weight to send there. Callimachi then asked if you were equally to go through Berlin and Vienna
and Athens. Oh yes, just the same : you were to try and force Otho's
hands through these places ; if anyone could you would, but he feared
Otho was impracticable.

On the eve of his departure for what he believed to be
" the last act of his Oriental drama " he was delayed by a new
complication. The scene of one of his early missions required
his presence. Switzerland was then torn in two by a religious
contest. For several years the Catholic question had been

assuming formidable proportions in some of the cantons, and after long and careful consideration the Federal Diet, for reasons which were recognized as sound by the majority of the Swiss, had resolved upon the expulsion of the Jesuits from the cantons. In some parts, however, the Catholics preponderated, and here a strenuous resistance was offered to the edict. In the autumn of 1846 this opposition took definite form in the Sonderbund, a league comprising the Seven Cantons of Lucerne, Uri, Schwyz, Unterwalden, Freiburg, Zug, and Valais. After several fruitless attempts at reconciliation, the Diet in July 1847 proclaimed the Sonderbund as an illegal combination,— an infraction of the Federal constitution of 1815,—and insisted on the expulsion of the Jesuits. Civil war ensued ; in September the Council at Bern authorized military preparations, and the troops were ordered to dissolve the league and occupy the disaffected cantons. The Five Powers who at Vienna had guaranteed the Federal Pact of 1815 hastened to concert plans of mediation. Some were inclined to translate their protective function into a right of marching troops into the disturbed districts: but against armed intervention Palmerston stood firm. Austria and France naturally favoured the Catholics, England the Protestants. All five at length agreed upon an identic note offering their collective mediation, to be presented both to the Diet and the Sonderbund by representatives of the several guaranteeing Powers.

Canning's old connexion with Switzerland, and the share he had taken in 1814-15 in drawing up the Federal constitution, naturally marked him out as the man for this mission. He had never lost his interest in the cantons which had once given him so much trouble ; and the circumstance that his old friend David Morier was minister at Bern from 1831 to 1846 had enabled the former to keep up his information and acquaintances. In spite of the difficulties of the task, and the inclement season of the year, he was glad to feel that he might be of use to a country for which he entertained a genuine affection. " It is a work of much trouble and difficulty," he wrote to his brother, " but it is also a work of peace, and therefore I do not hesitate to obey." The main object of the mission, however, was frustrated by the time he

1847
—
ÆT. 61

To
William
Canning,
22 Nov.

had reached Paris at the end of November. Mediation implies two parties to be reconciled : but the Five Powers, proceeding in their cautious diplomatic manner, had not reckoned upon the celerity and thoroughness which the Federal army displayed ; and by the time the identic note was ready there were no combatants wherewith to mediate. The troops of the Diet marched into. Freiburg, defeated the forces of the Sonderbund, entered Lucerne, and brought the whole of the Seven Cantons to submission in November 1847 ; and Lord Palmerston of course instructed Canning to hold back the Note, since mediation had now no ground whereon to stand.

Corresp. relative to the Affairs of Switz. 1847-8, p. 267

The ambassador was nevertheless to continue his journey to Bern, to "make himself acquainted with the general posture of affairs in Switzerland, and . . . the sentiments and intentions of the leading men of the various political parties," and also to urge moderation upon the Federals, to counsel the Diet "to use its victory with temperance," and to warn it of the risk of armed intervention on the part of those Powers which had already viewed its course with disfavour.

On arriving at Bern Canning found that Palmerston's forebodings were in a fair way to be realized. The Provisional Governments which had taken the place of the Sonderbund leaders in the subdued cantons had entered upon a course of wholesale imprisonment and confiscation. The Catholic establishments were naturally the victims of the conquerors. For instance, of the indemnity of a million francs which the Diet had required from the Seven Cantons, 200,000 were to come from the Valais ; and this was how it was raised by the Provisional Government :— 80,000 fr. from the Convent of the Great St. Bernard ; 50,000 from the Abbey of St. Maurice ;

Ibid. p. 298

Bishop and Chapter of Sion 40,000 ; Dean Derinacy 10,000 ; which left 20,000 for laymen to pay. It was almost useless to urge President Ochsenbein to stop the excesses of the cantonal authorities : the Diet, he said, had no jurisdiction. The counsels, however, of the English ambassador had some effect in moderating the vengeance of the successful party, and his voice had a considerable share in preventing the occupation of Neuchâtel by the Federal troops. This canton had asserted its neutrality during the war, and the King of

Prussia, who was its hereditary sovereign, had sanctioned its
policy. The Diet acted on the principle that he who was
not with it was against it, and would have marched its men
into Neuchâtel, at the risk of bringing Prussia into the field,
had not Canning succeeded in inducing both parties to agree
to a fine to be paid for over-scrupulous neutrality.

By the end of December things were becoming settled ;
the army was being disbanded ; the Provisional Governments,
which after all had in Canning's opinion not been so ex-
cessively severe in their confiscations as was reported, were
being replaced by permanent authorities ; and nothing remained to be done, unless one or other of the Powers chose
to make work by persisting in their proposal for a conference,
when there was nothing to confer about.   Sir Stratford remained at Bern till the latter part of January, and then
returned by way of Paris, where he reported that he found
the King and Guizot jubilantly confident of their hold on the
people :—yet only a fortnight elapsed before the royal family
had to fly to England from the Parisian mob !   The ambassador was satisfied with what he had accomplished ; and
indeed, considering the thinly-veiled antagonism of the four
other Powers, it was no light success to have left Switzerland
pacified on the lines laid down by the British Government—
the expulsion of the Jesuits, the dissolution of the Sonderbund, and the restoration of the Federal Pact.   Palmerston
wrote : " You have been able to do much good and to prevent
much mischief. . . I am glad you have been able to mitigate
the hostile intentions of the Diet towards Neuchâtel. . .
Bunsen is much pleased with the result."   Everybody in
short, even the newspapers, agreed that nothing could have
been better done.

Canning arrived in London on 8 February.   The close of
the month was full of gloomy forecasts of the coming storms.
On the 26th the news arrived of the flight of Louis Philippe.
That evening at Lady Palmerston's reception all faces were
troubled and melancholy.   No one knew what had become of
the fugitives, but as the days passed, one by one the French
princes and ministers appeared in England, and anxiety now
turned upon Germany, where the riots were becoming so

violent that it seemed doubtful whether the ambassador could take his family with him in his progress through Europe. Lady Canning, however, decided that her duty took her with her husband, especially as the Mission to the Porte was "only for a very short time," and on 17 March the whole party embarked for Brussels.

MEMOIRS.   "In March 1848 I set out from England on my return to Constantinople. It was the famous year of revolutions. The example given by France was followed by several countries of continental Europe. Political convulsions were the order of the day. A general inundation seemed to be coming on. The rising waters beat against our own cliffs, and the spray of their surge was driven inward even as far as London. The sounder and more numerous portion of the inhabitants were unwilling to put the peace of the country to hazard for the sake of speculative improvements. But demagogues were not wanting to the occasion, nor was the swarm of roughs wanting to them. There was one day of positive alarm. A vast procession was to be formed. Multitudes, who were thought to entertain very questionable intentions, prepared to march into London on a given day. The Duke of Wellington was furnished with the requisite authority and adequate means for repressing any illegal attempt on their part. The future Emperor of the French was in England at the time, and he figured with a *bâton* in his hand among the numbers who displayed their loyalty by serving as special constables. I also in my undistinguished capacity of a householder was armed with a similar instrument, but as I went abroad on duty before the impending day came on, no opportunity of using it occurred.

"My journey was not made alone. Wife and daughters were with me. We crossed the Channel at night, embarking at Dover, and steaming for Ostend. So long an exposure to the chance of equinoctial gales inspired little confidence, but we had the luck of a clear moon and a halcyon calm, nor did I ever make the passage on easier terms. It was quite early when we reached the offing of the Belgian coast, and we had to wait a considerable time on board, before the state of the tide would allow us to land.

"Lord Palmerston, who still presided at the Foreign Office, had directed me to communicate, on my way through Germany, with the principal governments of that country. I had no official business to transact with any of them. I was only commissioned to make known to each confidentially the impressions entertained by the Queen's Government respecting the unsettled and perilous state of affairs in Europe. It may be as well to mention here that before leaving England I had received from Prince Albert in private an ample explanation of his own particular views on the same subject. Appearances were such as to warrant the expectation of great changes in the constitution of Germany, and the relative position of its component States. He would have been glad to bring the influence of England to bear on the movement, and it would have gratified me beyond measure to be the instrument of promoting the welfare and power of Germany as a consolidated empire. But matters were not yet ripe for a work of such magnitude, difficulty, and peril   There was still too much equipoise in the leading antagonists, too much exaggeration in the popular party, nor had the master-agent yet reached his seat of power in the destinies of his country.

"My last act before I embarked was one of respect to the royal exiles at Claremont. The visit, I knew, would not be pleasing to Lord Palmerston, who had given way to a strong feeling of resentment against Louis Philippe ; but the King had always behaved very graciously to me, and I wished him not to think that his misfortune had clouded my memory. I was received first by Queen Amélie. Her manner and countenance were in keeping with her well-known character. She was grave, but not depressed ; resigned, but not regretful. In talking of the late occurrences she displayed an unassuming manliness of tone which made me think that in her husband's place she might perhaps have reversed the fortunes of her family. The King meanwhile was writing in a separate apartment. As soon as he had finished his letters I was admitted to his presence. He had every appearance of health—cheerful features and lively spirits. If any regret or anxiety weighed upon his mind, there was no trace of it on his face, or in his demeanour. One might have thought that together with his crown and robes he had thrown off all the cares of life. I took the liberty to remind him of the fortifications round Paris, which he had rather boastingly explained to me at the Tuileries, and also of the consultation, held by his order some time before, with the view of providing against any case of riots and barricades. How was it possible to think of such things at such a moment ? was his only reply. I said no more, but could not help thinking that the outbreak, which had dethroned him and sent his whole family adrift, was just the very moment for turning precaution to account. Both he and the Queen extolled in warm and affectionate terms the conduct of their son, the Duc de Nemours. I had previously seen M. Guizot and Madame Lieven after their arrival in London. They had travelled in the same train from Paris without knowing it. The former told me that late on the night preceding the King's departure in disguise, he had left the palace fully persuaded that on his return next morning he should find the insurrection quelled. Marshal Bugeaud was on horseback waiting for orders to attack the barricades. Molé, Odillon Barrot, and another, were with his Majesty. Before giving the decisive word one of them proposed that a parley should be first attempted, and Louis Philippe assented. The experiment was made ; the reply was a threat to fire, the consequence a loss of time irreparable and conclusive. Early next morning, probably after learning this unhappy *dénouement*, M. Guizot was on his way to the legislative hall, when he met M. Piscatory, not long before French minister at Athens. Persuaded by that gentleman that it would be useless, and indeed dangerous, for him to appear in the Assembly, he turned aside with much reluctance, and took refuge in his friend's house until the means of escape could be provided."

Looking back from a distance of forty years it is difficult to realize the consternation with which all Europe regarded the upheaval of society which marked the famous year of revolutions. One capital after another became a prey to bands of students, soldiers, or mere rabble, who paraded the streets, and extorted constitutions from trembling kings. It needed some courage to pursue a journey, accompanied moreover by ladies, from one disturbed centre to another, and the news which greeted the ambassador on his arrival at Brussels was calculated to arrest his further progress. Berlin, he learnt, was a scene of massacre and anarchy ; at Vienna the students had stormed the council chamber and bearded Metternich himself. " Forty years," said the old man, when he had listened to their demands, " forty years have I served my country ; I have never yielded to an insurrection, nor will I yield now." One of the archdukes sprang to his feet and said " But we *must.*" Metternich merely bowed and left the room : he was soon a disguised fugitive bound for England, the only country where such storms broke harmlessly. On the 21st the news from Berlin was more reassuring, and Canning resolved to proceed ; but at Aix-la-Chapelle tidings came of more bloodshed and the flight of the Prince of Prussia. At Hanover he dined with the old King, who seemed in great alarm, and nothing was thought or talked of but the revolutions. The blind Crown Prince was the most cheerful member of the royal family : when the storm was at its highest, he said, sunshine was sometimes nearest. At Brunswick the national flag was waving from every window ; but on arriving at Berlin the ambassador was surprized at the stillness of the city. It seemed almost deserted, save where a dozen burghers, enveloped in heavy cloaks, but shivering with cold, and heartily tired of carrying muskets and swords, relieved guard with white-gloved students, who seemed exceeding pleased to be released from their posts. The old Prussian Guard was invisible, and *Burschen* marched before the Schloss. On the 29th the ambassador had an audience of King Frederick William, who had not seen him for twenty years, but greeted him almost affectionately with the words "Oh, que je suis content de revoir ces traits que je connais si bien ! " Dining thrice with the King at Potsdam, Canning was as much impressed by his simple kindness as struck with his weakness and indecision. " Society," he wrote to a friend 11 April, " is shaken to its foundation. No balls, no parties, no dinners ; theatres deserted, and conversation carried on in sighs and whispers. . . . I have witnessed some outward signs of improvement as compared with what we found ; but the blindness of years little fits the sight for braving such a rush and whirl of strange pathetic painful interesting objects as now dance before our eyes and so bewilder the judgment that not one man in a million can distinguish good from evil or right from wrong. Never was there a more good-hearted man than he who wears the Prussian crown, with more talent and knowledge than fall to the lot of many gifted men : but alas ! that which gives weight to the sceptre and dignity to the robe, and potential authority sufficient to the language of royalty, is not in proportion."

The 22nd of April found them at Vienna, where Lord and Lady Ponsonby entertained them hospitably, and they saw for almost the last time the old Court etiquette, and the quaint livery of the footmen who ran beside the ambassador's carriage and stood behind his chair at dinner. On 2 May the English travellers witnessed an *émeute*. They had left the delight of Strauss's band in the Volksgarten to attend a reception at the Prime Minister's, Count Ficguelmont. The other guests regarded them coldly, for the news of the quiet manner in which the great Chartist meeting of 10 April had dispersed in London had excited the envy of those who were less happy in dealing with popular movements. The Prime Minister only arrived when the ambassador's party were on the staircase on the point of leaving ; but instead of pressing them to stay, he seemed only anxious to hasten their departure, and no sooner were they in their carriage than he ordered his great *porte cochère* to be instantly closed. They had not proceeded far down the street before the cause of this singular behaviour was revealed. A great crowd of students, National Guards, and idlers, marching eight or ten abreast, stopped the carriage. Sir Stratford immediately let down the windows, and beyond some rather impertinent remarks and cheers for "the Republic," and a spirited performance of the Katzenmusik, the party escaped without inconvenience. The mob went straight to Count Ficguelmont's house and compelled him to come on to the balcony and address them, after which they went quietly home. The next day the streets were again in the hands of the students, who stormed the Prime Minister's house and office, and Fieguelmont promised to resign. The National Guard made no movement and the Prime Minister and his family fled the city.

Early in May, Canning, accompanied only by Lord Augustus Loftus, who had travelled with him from England and acted as his private secretary, paid a visit to the King of Bavaria at Munich; but the 22nd found the whole party reunited at Trieste, and ready to embark on board the *Antelope* for Athens and Constantinople. Trieste was at that moment in consternation, for Lombardy and Venice had risen, the King of Sardinia had espoused the cause of the Italians, and on that very morning his fleet had come in sight. The ambassador could not leave until he had assured himself of the safety of British interests in the Adriatic. The Austrian fleet was in the harbour, and not at all anxious to sally out again, but fortunately three British men-of-war were drawn up outside, and the *Antelope* joined them. The people on shore were hard at work erecting earthworks, and preparing for attack, but the governor was in low spirits, and nobody seemed able to give orders. The *Antelope*, with the ambassador's party on board, was then despatched to communicate with the Sardinian fleet, which presented a handsome line of five frigates, five steamers, four brigs, and three schooners; and the sensations of the travellers may be imagined as they approached this formidable array and made the agreeable discovery that the guns were all manned and run out, and the tompions removed. No catastrophe, however, ensued; the English were assured that Trieste was in no danger, and nothing worse than a blockade was intended; so leaving the three British vessels as an additional security, Sir Stratford proceeded on his way to Patras and the Gulf of Lepanto, crossed the Isthmus of Corinth, and taking ship again at Callimachi, arrived at the Peiraeus.

Greece had from the first been a main object of Canning's mission. The King of the Hellenes was on very unpleasant terms with his subjects, and both the King and the Hellenes in general were in perpetual discord with their neighbours the Turks, who, to do them justice, deserved better treatment.

How to bring King Otho and his subjects to reason was the problem ; and the solution did not appear hopeful even to the most sanguine. Palmerston considered the Bavarian an impracticable prince, and only instructed Canning to try what he could do with him because, as he said, if anyone could bring about a change for the better it was the man who had always taken so warm an interest in the formation and maintenance of the Greek State. The ambassador himself expected little good to come out of the attempt. He wrote to Sir Richard Church on the subject before his departure for Switzerland :—

Be satisfied that my interest in Greece and its prosperity has undergone no decay. What embarrasses me in corresponding on the subject is the difficulty of finding a remedy for evils which it is painful to contemplate. I can only give echo to your lamentations, and that is distressing, when aid is wanted, and the heart craves in vain the means of giving it. All that I can do I have done. I have put your letter into the hands of one who unites with wishes like mine a powerful official influence and a far more extensive range of diplomatic knowledge.

You appear to have written on the very day of Colettes' death, an event which I agree with you in fearing has come too late to check the progress of evil . . . were any idea of directing me to look in at Athens on my way back to be thrown out, I should be sorely puzzled between the desire of rendering service and the fear of finding things too far gone for any diplomatic cookery.

Indeed it is only a sense of duty that takes me back to Constantinople. I am not only tired of such repeated labours in the East, but family considerations increase the inconvenience of another remote excursion.

The idea of visiting Athens was thrown out, as anticipated, and Canning's digression to Munich on the road from Vienna to Trieste had no doubt a bearing on the case. Unfortunately, whatever reports he may have sent home on the subject of his interviews with the rulers of Germany have not been preserved in duplicate. There may have been little time for copying them, or they may very probably have contained matter of so private and confidential a character that it was deemed advisable to destroy them. However this may be,

we are deprived of the means of ascertaining with what precise views and intentions Sir Stratford arrived at the Peiraeus.
One thing is clear : he came with a fixed determination to hear
both sides and deal impartially with the whole question. So
rigidly did he adhere to this line of conduct that he alienated
for awhile some of his best friends. Sir Richard Church, the
gallant and devoted friend of Greece, who had sacrificed
career, friends, fortune, all save life and honour, to the land of
his chivalrous adoption, could not appreciate the ambassador's policy, and was deeply hurt by his apparent coldness.
Church had been Canning's guest at Constantinople in 1810 ;
he had been visited by the Elchi at his ragged camp during
the War of Independence ; and he had returned the visit and
been received with affectionate hospitality at Pera but a few
years before ; and for at least a quarter of a century the two
had corresponded as friends and comrades : but now Sir
Stratford seemed bent on keeping him at a distance, and even
went so far as to shew a marked disinclination to be seen in
his company on his entrance into Athens. Sir Edmund Lyons,
the English minister, was equally annoyed. He and the Elchi
were acquaintances and correspondents of long standing, but
Canning declined to stay at his house, and though the two
met daily on business there was little openness in the ambassador's conversation.

The explanation was simple enough. Canning came out
with strong sympathies for the principles and policy which
were identified with the names of Lyons and Church. But
he came to adjudicate, not to sympathize ; and he felt that his
character for impartiality would be compromised if, on his
first arrival, he appeared to be on intimate terms with men
who, with all their merits as honest politicians, and all their
claims as private friends, were avowed partizans, hostile to
Otho and his followers,—and one of them a Senator of Greece
who had freely expressed his opinions in the Assembly. It
must have cost him much to put on the disguise and appear
cold when he felt the warm promptings of time-honoured
friendship ; but to Canning was given an uncompromising
sense of duty, and when he was convinced that the public
service demanded certain sacrifices, he would take the knife

and go unflinchingly to the altar. He had determined that
for reasons of state he ought not to appear as the ally of men
who were committed to a marked policy; and he was ready
to lose his friends rather than injure his chance of doing good.
He endeavoured to take the two into his confidence; he told
them his reasons for wishing to keep aloof: but whether from
want of tact on his part, or lack of perception on theirs, or
most probably from both causes, the misunderstanding grew
to serious proportions, and a total rupture of friendly relations
ensued. The correspondence which took place between Canning and Sir Richard Church shewed how much the latter
felt his old friend's coldness; and it was perhaps the accident
of a bad attack of the gout which prevented that meeting
and face to face explanation which would have smoothed
away all differences. As it was, years passed before the
breach was healed, and the old friendship flowed back into
its former course: but before the Crimean War the reconciliation took place, and General Church continued one of
Lord Stratford's constant correspondents till death came to
part them in 1873.

After all, it may be questioned whether Canning's line of
action, by separating him from the English party in Greece,
did him any good with the King. Otho was, as Lord Palmerston feared, impracticable, and the ambassador left Athens on
19 June with little or nothing accomplished in the way of good,
beyond presenting the King with a memorandum of warning
and advice couched in terms stronger than even Sir Edmund
Lyons could have devised. It took fourteen years more to
get rid of King Otho, and during the whole period Greece
was a thorn in the side of Europe.

CHAPTER XXII.

THE REFUGEES.

1848-50.

CANNING'S fifth residence at Constantinople was marked by
a new phase in his relations with foreign Powers. His first
mission had been a long struggle with France, in which at
the close he had Russia on his side. In the second and third,
England, France, and Russia were united on the main question, the pacification of Greece; and in the fourth, though
occasional points of divergence arose, the three Powers were
on the whole sufficiently friendly to one another to allow him to
devote his chief energies to the internal reform of the Ottoman
Empire. In the fifth period, 1848-52, we see the beginning of
that coalition of the Western Powers against Russia upon which
the seal was set in the Crimean War. He now found himself
for the first time in acute antagonism to Russia, and in his
defence of Turkey in the matters of the Danubian Principalities and of the Hungarian refugees we find a foretaste of the
resolute policy which ended at Sevastopol. In former years he,
like almost every English statesman, had watched the policy
of the Czars with suspicion, but it so chanced that he was
absent from Constantinople on the occasions when Russia made
her most dangerous advances, in the war which terminated in
the disastrous Treaty of Adrianople, and in the no less menacing alliance which was signalized by the compromising Treaty
of Hunkiar Iskelesi. Accident had hitherto placed him in the
position of coöperation with Russia rather than of opposition;
and only in 1848 did that new condition of compulsory hostility begin which marked the concluding years of his mission
at the Porte.

There was a moment of peace before the struggle began,

of which Canning took advantage to undo the evil which had been wrought during his brief absence in the West. The tranquillity of the empire indeed remained undisturbed. The settlement of the affairs of the Lebanon had suffered no check. The Persian boundary question was still in an unsatisfactory state, and the border provinces on the Euphrates and Tigris were subject to periodical fits of anarchy and bloodshed, but there was no sign of coming hostilities between the two Mohammedan Powers. Canning remarked that never before had he known the internal condition of Turkey so quiet and peaceable. But the subjects most dear to him, the progress of reform and the improvement of the rayas, had rather receded than advanced since his departure in 1846. Hardly had his back been turned when the intrigues against the Grand Vezir, which the ambassador had so often thwarted, were successfully renewed, and a reactionary ministry took the place of the cabinet of reform. The timidity of the Sultan was most to blame for this untoward change; but it was also clear that Reshid had not the firmness to stand alone when his English ally was away.

The first step was to reverse these proceedings. The Elchi had been but a few days installed in the British Embassy when Reshid and A'li Pashas were reinstated, though the former at his own request, and by special favour of the Sultan, was given a seat in the council without a portfolio. More than this, the Sultan expressed his regret at having been induced to depose Reshid, and admitted that he had been surprized by an unworthy intrigue. Two days later, at the official audience, his Majesty said he had long wished to see the ambassador back at his post, but never could his return be more agreeable than now when all Europe was seething with revolutionary combinations which might at any moment threaten to draw his empire into difficulties. In less than two months Reshid was once more Grand Vezir, A'li succeeded Rif'at at the Foreign Office, and the last became President of the Council.

What was thought of Canning's return and its immediate results may be seen from a letter of one of the shrewdest of the consular agents, the elder Blunt of Salonica :—

To Lord
Palmer-
ston, II.
1848

To the
same,
private,
27 June

29 June

August

My great and frequent intercourse with all classes in this town, and with numerous individuals from the interior, gives me much insight into the characters of the people, and enables my drawing from them the expression of their private opinions ; hence your Excellency will permit me to repeat what I stated to Lord Eastnor and Mr. Wilmot Horton, viz. that your arrival at Constantinople was looked for with the greatest anxiety, and that it was hailed with pleasure, by all the well disposed, in this part of Turkey, but dreaded by those few who still hold to the old system.   In a late despatch to your Excellency I reported the feelings of the people in this part of Turkey respecting the disgrace of Reshid Pasha ; you will therefore permit me to say that (as there was no enthusiastic exaggeration in that report) a people who are sufficiently reformed to feel the value of Reshid Pasha's services, how much more then must they feel the value of your Excellency's return, when it is their conviction that all acts for the good of the country are at your instigation ; and the reinstating of the Turkish ministry *immediately* after your arrival at Constantinople has, if it were required, strengthened that conviction.

1848
——
ÆT. 61
From Mr.
Blunt,
Salonica,
12 July

The ambassador had fortunately succeeded in restoring his friends to power just in time.   The revolutionary wave broke upon the Danubian provinces in the very month of his return. A popular rising took place at Bucharest on 23 June ; the troops refused to act ; and the Hospodar conceded to the insurgents their demands of universal suffrage and the eligibility of all Wallachians to the princely office.   Had this involved nothing more than an expedition of Turkish troops very little trouble would have ensued ; but Russia claimed under the Treaty of Adrianople the right to maintain order in the Danubian Principalities, and the immediate consequence of the Bucharest rising was a proposal for joint occupation by Russian and Turkish troops.   There was more in this than met the eye.   The differences between Austria and Hungary were watched by the Czar with anxiety, and there could be little doubt, as the event proved, that the entrance of Russian troops into the Principalities would be but the preliminary step to a vigorous support of Austria.   If Turkey were thus to be made a base for military operations in other countries, the Porte's neutrality would be compromised, and a dangerous precedent created.

To Lord
Palmer-
ston, XVII.
30 June

1848
——
Æt. 61

In this strait the Turkish ministers, according to their wont, appealed for advice to Canning. He urged them not to treat the Wallachians as rebels, but to regard them merely as constitutional reformers, and to inquire into their demands and grievances ; and while he recommended the despatch of a special commissioner, he counselled a careful avoidance of military occupation, lest an ominous example should be set

XXVI.
14 July

for Russia to follow. The Turks accepted half the advice, and rejected the rest. They sent Suleyman Pasha to investigate the Wallachian demands, but they also despatched an army across the Danube, though not immediately to Bucharest. The natural result was that 4,000 Russians entered Moldavia. As the protector of oppressed Christianity against the barba-

XXVII.
15 July

rous Mohammedan, the Czar had no intention of allowing Turkey to act by herself in the Danube provinces, which he regarded as a close preserve, over which he and the Sultan had alone the right of shooting, with the proviso that the latter must never enjoy his sport without the accompaniment of the Russian gun. Turkey had already admitted far too much, though not the whole, of this doctrine in the Treaty of Adrianople and in the very preamble to the firman which accorded the Principalities their privileges. The Russian occupation evidently had the Porte's consent. The difficulty of the situation was aggravated by the totally divergent views of the two occupying Powers. Turkey, moved by the strenuous counsels of the British ambassador, was for mild measures, amnesty to the "reformers," liberal amendments in the constitution, and the speedy removal of the Russian troops. The Czar, on the other hand, imperiously demanded a severe repression of the "revolution," punishment of the "rebels," repudiation of free institutions, and a prolonged joint occupation in the interests of order. It was the old contest between the principles of the Holy Alliance and the liberal policy of George Canning.

Sir Stratford, true to his ancient views, strove to keep the Porte steady on the lines of moderation and reform. At first indeed he was disposed to hope for some internal improvement as the result of the Wallachian insurrection ; but rumours of a widespread reconstruction of the Christian provinces reached him, which were little likely to smooth the way to a settlement of the disturbed districts.

1848

Æт. 61

I had scarcely finished the last of my despatches, when a respectable neighbour called to inform me, on the authority of a member of the Greek Patriarchal Synod, that an immense combination of Slavonians is working together for the construction of an independent State of very large dimensions united by language and religion and having a national prince at its head. Wallachians, Moldavians, Croatians and Transylvanians, to say nothing of Servians, Bulgarians, and Illyrians, would figure in the combination, and what particularly interested the Synodian was, that a large class of religionists called *Unites*, remarkable for adhering to the forms and creed of the Greek Church, while they acknowledge the Pope alone, and scattered over districts extending towards Offen and Pesth, had renounced the Pope and adopted the Patriach in order to fraternize more completely with their fellow-labourers in the vineyard of revolution. I cannot dare to vouch for the reality of this mountain in labour, but nothing is improbable in times like these ; the incipient struggles between Croatia and Hungary shew to what a pitch the feeling of race is worked up, and sundry rumours and partial indications seem to announce a convulsion to which this empire may not prove entirely inaccessible.

I hope you will not be alarmed at my taking the field on Turkish reform. Whatever I may be in London or Germany, I always told you that I was a Radical, though I trust a prudent one, in Turkey. Our own affairs will at all events probably gain by the experiment, and if the Grand Vezir, who when he is occasionally sober has the appearance, with about the same degree of shrewdness, of Sancho Panza, should in the course of proceedings chance to topple over, I hope you will not call me to a very severe account.

To Lord Palmerston, 4 August

Russia was daily becoming more dictatorial. The interference of England, in a matter which the Czar regarded as one that concerned nobody but himself and the Sultan, tended to embitter his naturally despotic tone. Some extracts from the correspondence will explain Canning's attitude in this situation :—

Our principal affair here is the state of things in Wallachia. The Porte is very reasonable towards Russia and very benevolent towards the Wallachians. Unfortunately however, Russia is very dictatorial, requiring the exemplary punishment of the reformers, and holding out

To Lord Ponsonby, 4 Sept.

no prospect of improvement in the Principality. This may lead, though I hope it will not, to a coldness and renewal of old animosities. The Wallachians also are extremely exaggerated in their ideas, vapouring about Parisian theories of reform without applying themselves to the removal of practical abuses.

To Lord
Palmer-
ston,
4 Sept.
I find it not a little puzzling to keep a steady line of march between the Porte and Russia, to keep the peace and to respect the treaties on one side, and on the other to sustain the Porte's courage and to lay a foundation for real improvement in Wallachia.

At present Russia seems more disposed to force the Porte into measures of severity than to join with her in adopting those of improvement. If the Porte be pressed too hard, it is not impossible that she may appeal to the spectators. I would not put myself forward without necessity, but were the necessity to arise I could hardly err in trying by discreet and sensible means to rescue her from the humiliation of being forced to turn tail on her principles of benevolence and improvement. I am authorized to rely upon the concurrence of the Internuncio and of the French minister in such a contingency.

To the
same,
14 Oct.
I find that General Aupick [the French minister] agrees entirely with my foreboding of what may probably result from the present increasing state of tension between the Porte and Russia. Neither party, I presume, intends any mischief bordering on hostility ; but the determination of one, the awkwardness of the other, and the antagonism of both, may at any moment lead as heretofore to sudden and incalculable results.

To
the same,
4 Nov.
I have learnt by a message from A'li Pasha this evening, that a long and angry despatch from Count Nesselrode has been communicated to him by the Russian Legation to-day. In substance it accuses the Porte of playing booty with the Wallachian revolutionists ; complains in particular of Fuad Efendi [the new commissioner], because he objected to the entrance of the Russian army into Wallachia ; and insists upon his being ordered to act in concert with General Duchamel and to institute proceedings against the leaders and abettors of the late revolution. Reshid appears to be as much disconcerted by this despatch as A'li was by Titov's note. One would think that they are too much committed to give way now. Yet they have no reliance on the Sultan's firmness, and Callimachi's reports of a conversation with you appear to have taken the wind out of the sails with which your last messenger supplied me in the shape of an instruction approving and supporting my language about the Princi-

palities with a hint, if necessary, to appeal eventually to the Powers of Europe. The Sultan is evidently afraid of a collision, and would be glad to have the promise of a visit from Sir W. Parker and his fleet against the contingency of a Russian aggression. The Captain Pasha told me the other day that he did not know what might happen in the spring. In diplomacy they want to have some positive assurance of support, in the event of Russia persisting without compromise in its present plan of persecution, punishment, continued occupation, depletion of the inhabitants, and denial of reform. If you could act more powerfully on the Russian conscience itself, I think it would be taken kindly in the Seraglio. My advice to the Porte is always the same :—" Do not risk a quarrel with Russia as long as you can avoid it without serious loss or dishonour. Be faithful to your treaties, maintain your moral position quietly and firmly, and even when coöccupying keep your troops separate and if possible at some distance from the Russian."

As winter approached, the situation in Wallachia did not improve. The second Turkish commissioner was bodily threatened, and was forced to disperse the people by a charge of horse ; 12,000 Turks, marching into Bucharest, against Canning's advice, were fired upon, and retaliated with customary brutality. Russia talked of at least two years' occupation and had fully 30,000 men in the provinces. The Czar's attitude had been materially stiffened by a series of repulses at the Porte. He had proposed a close alliance with the Sultan, and had been put off with civil phrases. He had recommended a formal joint occupation of the Principalities, and the Turks had objected : civil measures not military, and a programme of reforms, had their preference. Russia urged vigorous concerted action ; Turkey replied that she could manage her own subjects unaided, and intended to manage them gently. Russia insisted on the Wallachians being punished as rebels : Turkey stoutly refused. In all this the Czar perceived rightly the influence of one man, and it was then that the personal dread of the British ambassador, which afterwards formed so prominent a motive in his conduct, first took strong hold of him.

If he knew what was passing between the Porte and its chief adviser at the time, he must have felt indeed that it had come to a personal duel. The Turks, in mortal fear of the

cxxxiii.
2 Oct.

xlvi.
2 Aug.

lvi.
4 Aug.

xcviii.
4 Sept.

Russian advance, were pressing for a defensive alliance with England at the very moment when Russia was seeking to bind the Porte to herself in the same way. Reshid and Rif'at Pasha had several interviews with Canning on this subject, and though the ambassador could not commit his Government to a definite opinion, and was bound to state objections, it is clear that the project met with his personal approval. The following confidential letter to Lord Palmerston shews how anxious the Porte had grown :—

My Lord,—Rif'at Pasha has requested me with much earnestness to inform your lordship how anxiously the Porte desires to *draw more closely than ever those ties of confidence* and cordiality which subsist between the Sultan's Government and that of her Majesty. He had recently seen the Sultan when he expressed himself to me in this manner, and it is therefore most probable that his language was sanctioned, if not suggested, by the Sovereign himself. His Excellency remarked that in these times the Porte was exposed to much danger, and that he trusted the British Government would be *prepared to countenance, uphold, and assist* her in the hour of need. He had previously tried to elicit my opinions as to the turn which European affairs were likely to take with respect to Turkey, and when I replied that in the midst of darkness and uncertainty there were three sources of danger more or less visible, and explained myself by adding that they were the eventual eruptions from France, the popular notion of races, and the prospective necessity of new political combinations, he fastened more especially upon the last contingency as a subject of anxiety and alarm to the Porte. In the Wallachian insurrection he perceives the approach of both the latter causes of uneasiness. With respect to France the Pasha said that he wished to be made acquainted with your lordship's views as to the acknowledgment of the French Republic, now that some progress had been made, and that two or three of the minor Courts had given in their recognition. England, he said, was the Porte's example on that subject, and he was therefore *anxious to be prepared for any more pressing application which might, perhaps, issue before long from the French Government* or from its representative at Constantinople.

It is evident that in the present unsettled state of Europe the Sultan looks upon England as his sheet anchor in the event of the storm extending to his dominions, and, giving me credit for friendly sentiments towards the empire, that he considers the opportunity a good one for improving and drawing closer the ties of sympathy which unite the two countries and their respective Governments. Your lordship will, I hope, think it *worth while to consider this overture*, vague as it is in terms, and to make me acquainted with your sentiments respecting it.

Lord Palmerston's reply to this overture was friendly but inconclusive. It was not advisable to rouse the jealousy of the Eastern Powers by a decided step of this nature. At the same time no pains were to be spared to keep Turkey firm in the English interest.

From Lord Palmer-ston, cv. 11 Sept.

Discouraged by the response of the British Government, it was only natural that the Porte should seek by all reasonable concessions to conciliate the Czar. The Sultan was ever prone to temporize, and now a yielding policy seemed almost his only resource. Fortunately he had behind him the strong will of the English ambassador, and the representative of France was not slow to support his colleague. Canning's suspicions at the moment were not so much directed against any scheme of aggrandizement on the part of Russia as against her obvious aim of acquiring an exclusive influence in the Principalities, to which her recent loan of 300,000 roubles, for the provisioning of her own troops, to be repaid by the unfortunate Wallachians, gave a fresh colour. To counteract the encroachments of the Czar upon the Sultan's sovereign rights, it was essential to give some definite sign of England's eventual support.

To Lord Palmer-ston, CLXXI. 3 Nov.

To keep them [the Turkish ministers, he wrote to Palmerston,] steady upon the lines of their just rights and interests, firm at the same time and prudent, avoiding to give offence, yet guarding their independence, has been the constant object of my efforts. . . . In order to secure any permanent advantage from the counsels hitherto given to the Porte, and more or less acted upon, a greater confidence must be established in the determination of friendly Powers and particularly of Great Britain to throw their moral weight into the scale, and to place an effectual restraint on the undue pretensions of Russia, striving, for objects exclusively its own, and by a forced interpretation of its treaties with the Porte, to substitute *the rights of protection for the obligations of a guarantee.*

cxcvi. 4 Dec.

During the winter of 1848-9 the relations between Russia and Turkey became still more strained. The Czar took upon

Instruc-
tions to
Drago-
man,
3 Feb.
1 March

himself to disarm the Wallachians without the Sultan's leave, and in all his acts and communications Nicholas assumed a perfect equality with the sovereign of Turkey in all that concerned the Danubian provinces. In January, when Wallachia was completely restored to tranquillity, Russia proposed a seven years' occupation of the Principalities and the signature of a Convention reviving those exclusive pretensions which it was the special object of the Treaty of 1841 to destroy. A further complication arose when the Porte was required to permit the Russian troops to pass into Transylvania for the purpose of crushing the Hungarian insurgents, and when Russia furnished Servia with 10,000 muskets for no other purpose than to stir up fresh strife. It is needless to say that all these proposals and proceedings were met by Canning's energetic resistance. The Convention was eluded and the entrance into Transylvania prohibited : yet the Russians marched against the Hungarians in defiance of the Porte, and were punished by a severe defeat at the hands of General Bem. The situation became daily more critical. The Turks, said Canning, must be " prepared for the worst," and England must finally make up her mind : "the time has come for adopting a definite and decisive course of policy with respect to this country viewed as to its relations with Russia. . . . A timely and effective demonstration of support, especially if it were concerted with France, might be expected to deter the Russian Cabinet from proceeding to extreme measures, or, should it fall short in that respect, to save the Porte from being overwhelmed in a single and unequal struggle." He evidently anticipated war, and hoped to enlist the forces of England and France on the Turkish side. For some time his eyes had been fixed on the Mediterranean squadron. Reshid, in evident anxiety, had asked about its actual position in November, and in February, when the Turks were arming for the expected struggle, and Russia was imperiously insisting on the proposed Convention, the ambassador went so far as to give the Grand Vezir a hint as to the possible approach of the fleet. He supported this in a vigorous despatch to Lord Palmerston, in which, whilst urging that no further concessions could possibly be granted to the overweening arrogance of Russia, he said :—

1849

ÆT. 62

It requires no spirit of prophecy to foresee whither an unchecked excursion over a field so fertile in pretexts and opportunities for aggression will ultimately lead—no effort of intelligence to perceive that if the independence and integrity of this empire have any value in the eyes of Europe for the sake of European interests, any weight in the scale of British policy, . . . the moment is arrived when general understandings, general representations, and general assurances, must be followed up with distinct agreements, positive declarations, and pledges, not to be mistaken, of sympathy and eventual support.

To Lord
Palmer-
ston,
XLVIII.
19 Feb.

Lord Palmerston did not feel that the time had actually come for a naval demonstration ; but he powerfully supported Canning's policy in a communication to Baron Brunov, and the Porte derived some additional strength from the Foreign Secretary's decided language. The Russians were given to understand that in the opinion of the Sultan there was no further necessity for their occupation of Wallachia. Reshid, who took no step without consulting his English adviser, declared he would resign sooner than give way to Russia, and firmly stood out against the convention. The Czar, temporarily repulsed by the Hungarians, and therefore unable to evacuate his base of operations in the Principalities, decided on a fresh effort. He despatched General Grabbe with an autograph letter to the Sultan and instructions to bring the Porte to terms.

CII.
24 March

The special envoy arrived in April and was received with unusual honours. In a conversation on the 17th he told Canning how honest and honourable were the Czar's views, how wholly ingenuous his aims, and how grateful the Porte should be to Russia for her benevolent pacification of the Principalities. At the same time the Russian agents repeated their old doctrine that no one had a right to interfere between the Czar and the Sultan in the affairs of the Danubian provinces, and the General did not scruple to style England and France, who acted loyally together throughout these negotiations,

CXXII.
CXXIV.

1849
——
ÆT. 62

CXXV.
28 April

CXL.
30 April

" les ingérens."　Draft after draft of an agreement between the disputants had been drawn up and amended by the English ambassador ; but finally, though the Russian "Convention" was again declined in consequence of an energetic note (22 April) from the British Palace, an " Act " was adopted (1 May) by which Russia gained most of her demands, and a Hatti-Sherif promulgating this result was duly issued. The Hospodars were to be nominated for seven years, the assemblies of Boyards were suspended, commissions for organic reform were to be appointed, and a temporary joint occupation was sanctioned.

Canning had striven against the Act in vain. Without material support from the fleet, his influence could not avail against the heavy pressure of the Czar.　He consoled himself with the reflection that the end " might have been worse," and took care that the Turks should not be deluded into a sense of security by the apparent termination of the dispute.　The armies and fleets of the Porte continued their preparations for defence.　In urging these precautions Canning shewed his usual foresight : but even he can scarcely have anticipated the eventful crisis which was about to occur.　The following memorandum, however, shews that he was anxiously forecasting the chances of fresh complications on the Danube :—

The special engagements subsisting between Turkey and Russia with respect to the military occupation of Wallachia and Moldavia are regulated by the official Act recently concluded at Constantinople. The objects for which it was therein expressly agreed that the armies of both parties should continue for a time in those Principalities were the maintenance of internal tranquillity and the protection of the frontier.　It was, no doubt, understood, on the part at least of Turkey, that the stipulations of the Act referred exclusively to the provinces themselves, and that after, as before, its conclusion the Porte intended to abstain from taking any part whatever in the quarrels of a neighbouring empire.　The local authorities were to be supported in keeping down every attempt at internal disorder, and the establishment of tranquillity along the frontier was to be the signal of a large reduction of the occupying armies.

Now, the whole character of this arrangement has undergone a notable change.　The Principalities, instead of being left to enjoy tranquillity and protection, have been used by Russia as the base of military offensive operations against one of the contending parties in Hungary. Notwithstanding that they constitute a part of the Turkish Empire, they have been made a place of retreat, whence the discomfited troops of one party have issued with recruited strength to assail their adversaries again, and where those of the other have been disarmed and dispersed ; with this additional disadvantage, that their arms have been given up to the foreign invaders of their country. More than this, the provinces are turned into a place of depôt for the Russian army invading Transylvania, reinforcements are brought in from Russia at the pleasure of the Russian authorities, and Moldavia is made the principal highway for their advance against the Hungarians.

The consequences of this perversion of the plain meaning of the Act are natural and were to be expected. The Hungarians have not indeed retaliated, as they might have done, on the inhabitants of the provinces : but they have disregarded the Porte's territorial rights, they have spread dismay throughout the country, and they have given a rough lesson to the Russian reserve in Moldavia. The tranquillity of the frontier and the peace of the interior, far from being secured, are seriously disturbed, and this disturbance, with its attendant prospect of danger, is entirely due to the unfair use which has been made of the military occupation of the Principalities.

An effectual remedy is manifestly required for so much evil, present and future, nor can it be obtained, independently of the operations in Transylvania, without either increasing the armies of occupation, and consequently the burdens already pressing too heavily on the Sultan's tributary subjects, or recurring to the declared purposes of the Act, and abstaining henceforward from any measure inconsistent with that neutral attitude which it is no less for the interest than for the honour of the Porte to maintain.

Those Powers which have combined to trample out the last spark of independence in a nation enthusiastically attached to its constitutional rights would naturally seize every opportunity to engage the Ottoman Government and Empire in the same scheme of policy with themselves. In proportion as the difficulties of their enterprize become sensibly felt, and the efforts of an heroic resistance attract the sympathies of Western Europe, their motives for securing the alliance and coöperation of Turkey will necessarily increase. But exactly in the same proportion will also increase those notions of self-regard and true national policy which must deter the Ottoman Government from embarking in a course so well calculated to entangle it in endless perplexities and to alienate the confidence of its most strenuous supporters.

Fatal indeed would be the illusion that should induce the Porte to plunge deeper into a connexion which has already proved so abundant a source of embarrassment, vexation, and anxiety. To throw away the experience of recent circumstances, and to rush wantonly on danger when the door is opening for escape, might be justly qualified an act of unpardonable blindness. The Porte is too wise to incur any such reproach. Her course of proceeding with reference to the late irruption of General Bem into Moldavia is pointed out by the obvious interests and duties of her position. The Sovereign's army of occupation has maintained order in Wallachia without imposing any financial burden on its inhabitants, or exposing them to the perils of retaliation by carrying war across their frontier into a neighbouring country. It is surely reasonable to expect that the example thus given by the Porte should not be rejected by a Power who has no right of sovereignty in the Principalities. On behalf alike of the Sultan and of his people the Turkish Cabinet is fully entitled to claim this proof of justice and friendly consideration from the Court of St. Petersburg. If the time be not yet arrived when the occupying forces can with prudence be altogether withdrawn, it is at least incumbent on the Porte to shew that she no longer acquiesces spontaneously in a state of things which cannot continue without operating more and more to her discredit, and compromising not only the peace of her empire, but the consistency of her political relations.

At first Palmerston had foreseen no rôle for England in the Hungarian question. He had written in May :—

From Lord Palmerston, 7 May
I always thought that one of the main motives for the Russian occupation of the Danube provinces was a desire to be ready to assist Austria in Hungary in case of need, and this seems now to have been the case. How far it may be wise for Austria, or how far it may answer her ends in the long run, thus to have recourse to a Russian army to coerce her own subjects, time will shew : but certainly one should think that she would have done better to have tried all means of conciliation before she had recourse to such foreign aid. It is possible too that Russia may not find her account in this intervention to the extent that she imagines ; and when so many of her troops are gone abroad, she may find work start up for them at home. However we do not mean to meddle with the matter in the way of protest, or in any other manner. We of course attach great importance to the maintenance of the Austrian Empire as an essential element and a most valuable one in the balance of power, and we should deeply regret anything which should cripple Austria or impair her future independence. I suppose that this forward movement of the Russians will make them attach less importance to the arrangements which

they wished to drive the Porte to conclude with them ; but I am still of opinion that the Porte ought to decline trying any fresh engagement which should contain a renewal of the principle of the right of Russia to interfere in the internal affairs of the Danube provinces. Ponsonby says that Schwarzenberg is quite sensible of the importance of preventing Russia from obtaining a permanent footing in those provinces, but that alone is no great security that Austria would stoutly resist Russia there if hereafter she should press down upon those provinces in earnest ; for the policy of Austria has been too much to yield to the strong while she has bullied the weak, and I am not sure that Schwarzenberg is at all likely to be the man to depart from that line of conduct. It would however not be wise for the Porte to come to an open rupture with Russia ; but of that from your accounts there does not seem to be any likelihood.

1849
—
Ӕ T. 62

Events were at hand which forced the British Government into a totally different attitude from that indicated in the foregoing letter. Within five months England and France found themselves apparently on the verge of war with Russia, not for a matter of territorial aggrandizement, nor even for the balance of power, but for a cause far more generous than any national interest, the cause of humanity.

From the early spring there had been indications of a coming dispute between the Sultan and the two Imperial Governments of Vienna and St. Petersburg on the subject of insurgents who might take refuge in Turkish territory. By Article XVIII. of the Treaty of Belgrade the Porte was bound to " punish " such " evil-doers, and discontented and rebellious subjects [of Austria], as also robbers and brigands," as might seek an asylum in the Ottoman dominions. Under Article II. of the Treaty of Kaynarji Russia could demand the extradition or the expulsion of refugees from Turkey, and *vice versâ*. Russia however had in former times disregarded her part of the mutual obligation, and the dispute was likely to turn chiefly upon the stipulation in the Treaty of Belgrade, where, it must be noted, there was no mention of extradition but only of " punishment." The question was sure to arise : Did the Hungarian insurgents, a nation in arms, come under the terms of Article XVIII. ? The Porte and its English adviser, though somewhat doubtful of the literal interpretation,

To Lord Palmerston, XLIII. 14 Feb.

held that in spirit the "punishment of evil-doers" applied only to ordinary offenders in time of peace, and could not be so stretched as to comprise the Hungarian patriots. Canning saw sufficient reason to believe that this view of the article might be sustained, and felt sure that the general sense of England would be in its favour. He counselled the Porte at all hazards to adopt a humane and generous policy, and to refuse to surrender those who might throw themselves upon its compassion. The best course would be to let the refugees pass immediately through and out of its territory; but if this could not be effected, let the Sultan shield them from certain

death. They should be disarmed, and made to understand that their safety depended on their good conduct: but they should not be given up to their enemies.

The occasion for exercising this humane resolution soon arose. On 14 August seventy-six fugitive Hungarians and Poles landed at Constantinople: they were immediately scattered about in places where they were least likely to attract notice. The Hungarian agent applied to Canning for assistance in procuring passports for sending them home. This of course the ambassador of a neutral power could not do, nor would the Turks take the responsibility, so he advised that the fugitives should be suffered quietly to remain in Turkey. The Internuncio of Austria at once demanded their extradition, and

the Russian envoy followed suit. A week or so later occurred a fresh invasion of refugees, and these of the first rank. The short-lived triumph of the Hungarians, over which Canning and Reshid had secretly rejoiced, was over, and Görgei's forced surrender to the Russian commander was followed by

a general flight of the patriots. Kossuth, Bem, Dembinski, and some fourscore less renowned civilians and officers, had crossed the Turkish frontier and were now at Vidin. The presence of the leaders of the insurrectionary armies, and of Kossuth himself, the mainspring of the national movement, safe in Turkey, was intolerable to the two empires. The Internuncio and M. Titov urgently insisted on their extradition. Canning, supported by General Aupick, his French colleague, counselled unfaltering resistance. On 30 Aug. the Council of the Porte decided that they could not give up the fugitives without dishonour. A note, revised by the British ambassador, was sent to the Austrian and Russian representatives, and the Porte stood firm to its duty.

On 4 Sept. the residents in the embassy house at Therapia were spectators of an ominous scene. An Austrian steamer entered the Bosphorus, and, pausing before the Russian embassy at Buyukderé, saluted and hoisted Russian colours at the fore ; she then steamed on to the Golden Horn. Soon afterwards Sir Stratford Canning received a message and departed instantly for Pera. On the 17th the vessel was observed returning the way she had come. She had brought Prince Michael Radzivil with an ultimatum from the Czar, and she was carrying the Prince and his ultimatum, discomfited and rejected, back to his master.

CCLXX.
Corr. p.
5 Sept.

The Emperor had not minced words with his brother of Turkey. The war, he announced, was over, and the extradition of the rebels must imperatively ensue. He demanded a categorical answer, yes or no. The further relations of the two empires, he wrote, would depend on that answer ; and meanwhile the escape of a single Hungarian or Pole would be regarded as a declaration of war.

This was the news that had summoned Canning to the Porte. What passed between him and the Turkish ministers was not committed to writing, but its tenor may be guessed from the result. The ambassador, with all the impressive solemnity which he knew so well how to use, bade the Porte have courage, be true to the everlasting principles of honour and humanity, be true to its own independence and dignity,—and boldly refuse to obey the Czar's command. And when he counselled unqualified resistance, the Turkish ministers knew that he was prepared to support them in the right course with the whole strength of Great Britain. He ventured even in writing to assert, and General Aupick coincided, that in case of war resulting from this resistance, it was certainly to be presumed that England and France would not leave the Porte unassisted. He had no authority to pledge the arms of England, and of course he left the Government the opportunity of repudiation ; but the case was desperate, and he knew that Palmerston at the Foreign Office was not

Corr.
p. 11,
15 Sept.

1849
—
Æt. 62

To Lord
Palmer-
ston,
17 Sept.

the man to desert him or to flinch from a resolute policy. He justified his action thus [1] :—

If I had suspended my support for a moment, the Porte, I have no doubt, would have given way, and on almost any question but one involving such obvious considerations of humanity, honour, and permanent policy, I might have been inclined while left to myself to counsel a less dangerous course in spite of reason and right. As it is, I felt that there was no alternative unattended with loss of credit and character, to say nothing of the unfortunate and highly distinguished men awaiting their doom at Vidin—Zamoyski among others. The dishonour would have been *ours*, for everyone knows that even Reshid himself, with all his spirit and humanity, would not withstand the torrent without us. . . I am sure that you will feel the importance of coming to the rescue as far and as fast as you can.

Hence he counselled a firm resistance, and the Porte, emboldened by his fearlessness, and even to some degree inspired by his own high spirit, straightened itself up and defied the Czar.

Corr. p. 9

The Turkish defiance was not, of course, quite the masculine "no" which Canning would have uttered. The Council at its second meeting, 10 Sept., decided upon a middle course: the Sultan should say neither "yes" nor "no," but Fuad Efendi should go to Warsaw or Petersburg and discuss the matter deliberately with Nicholas himself. It was a thoroughly Ottoman decision, and may be summed up in the typical Turkish evasion *Bakalum*, "We will see." Nevertheless, though mild in form, it was a rejection of the Czar's ultimatum. The Sheykh-el-Islam himself, the lord chancellor and primate combined of the empire, solemnly declared that the refugees could not be given up without a breach of the law of hospitality ordained by Mohammed the Prophet.

CCLXXIX.
16 Sept.

The Russian and Austrian envoys would take no such evasion. "Yes" or "no" must the Sultan say, or diplomatic relations would be suspended. Prince Radzivil refused to

---

[1] The public despatches may be read, in a somewhat curtailed but substantially correct form, in the *Correspondence respecting Refugees from Hungary* laid before Parliament, pp. 9 ff. Whilst of course working from the original drafts of the despatches, I have generally preferred quoting from the private correspondence, as necessarily more frank and confidential.

receive the Sultan's letter or to attend a farewell audience. The Turks were sore perplexed and but for the Englishman's courage they must have yielded. " Fear is knocking loudly at their hearts," wrote Canning, " and they want to be sustained and encouraged. I shall be again at work quietly to-morrow." He went to work with a will. He supplemented his promise of support by a menace : You are *not* bound, he said, by any treaty to surrender these suppliants. You must " *not* give way if you set the slightest value on your honour and future interests in Europe ; " if you yield, you " will alienate your most cordial supporters." To conciliate Russia and Austria would be another word for quarrelling with England and France. General Aupick spoke to the same effect. Thus it came to pass that the Porte stood firm ; the two embassies pulled down their flags, 17 Sept., and Prince Radzivil retired in angry amazement.

So far the victory was with Canning and his French ally, but they both knew it was but the skirmish of outposts which precedes the general engagement. A terrible interval of six weeks' suspense must be endured before they could learn whether their bold policy would be countenanced by their respective Governments. Meanwhile Russian troops might cross the Balkan ; the Sevastopol fleet, which had long offered unpleasant possibilities to the Turkish imagination, might sail into the Bosphorus and bombard Constantinople ; the Ottoman Empire in Europe might be disabled before the Western Powers could interfere. All these thoughts passed through Canning's mind as he paced his room at Therapia and cast an anxious glance at the narrow gap between the bordering hills through which he could see the billows of the Euxine. To wait was ever painful to his energetic nature ; but to wait then, with such issues at stake, must have been torture. Some relief, however, came to him in the first week of October. Admiral Sir William Parker, who had been apprized by him (17 Sept.) of the possible need of his fleet at the Dardanelles, grasped the situation in a moment, and made all sail for the Archipelago. Like the ambassador, he acted on his own discretion ; but there was nothing very unusual in a cruise in the waters of the Levant, and the

Turks were not, of course, to take it as a demonstration on the part of the British Government. Nevertheless there was joy in Stambol when a frigate carrying the reassuring white ensign made its appearance in the Golden Horn on 3 Oct. It might mean nothing, but there was that in the face of the Great Elchi which boded victory. The frigate had brought him information that Sir William Parker was on the watch.

Still three interminable weeks had to be gone through before the decision of the English Cabinet could be known at Therapia. Not a day was lost by the vigorous mind that ruled the Foreign Office. The decision of the Cabinet was taken immediately, and hardly was it pronounced when a messenger was off with a note to Canning. Palmerston hoped to relieve him from his anxious position a day or two sooner by sending a Queen's Messenger overland by Vienna; and, in case the first should meet with an accident, he presently despatched a second officer, whose name was renowned wherever hounds were running. His orders were stringent: the messenger was "not to spare himself, nor others." How Lieut.-Colonel (then Captain) Charles Townley [1] interpreted this instruction may be seen by his own narrative, originally published anonymously in Major Byng Hall's *The Queen's Messenger*.

On Sunday afternoon, 20 October, this Royal Messenger, who had been despatched from London on the 11th, left Belgrade with the precious letter. The Austrian despatches, which might undo all that the letter was to accomplish, reached the Danube as Captain Townley was crossing, and passed him at Belgrade. Three special relays of Tartars were

---

[1] I have selected Captain Townley's journey because he has recorded it himself, and because it is a splendid example of the pluck and endurance of a Queen's Messenger. But it is only fair to state that he was not the only, or the earliest, bringer of the good news, though he brought it quicker than anyone else. Palmerston was so eager to relieve Canning from his anxious suspense that he sent off *three* separate messengers. Lieutenant Robbins left London 2 Oct., immediately after the decision of the Cabinet, went by way of Vienna, and reached Constantinople on the 18th, after a journey of great speed. Mr. Waring was despatched on 7 Oct., and arrived at Therapia on the 24th, travelling by steamer from Marseilles. Captain Townley was sent on 11 Oct., and arrived at his destination on the 26th. It is probable that all three carried duplicate despatches and letters, though I am unable to prove this supposition by the documents.

ready to speed the Austrian message ; England depended on Captain Townley, unrelieved throughout the long ride. The odds were heavily against him, but he had pluck, and he won the race by thirty-three hours. Crossing the Morava at daybreak, after a night journey through deep mud, and enlivened by the howling of wolves, he picked up Rhisto, a tried Tartar of the embassy, at Alexinitza, and together they pushed on to Nissa :—

The Queen's Messenger, pp. 74-80

The Balkan range was very grand, but even if the night had not been dark, I should have seen nothing of it, for this was the second I had passed in the saddle, and I was reeling backwards and forwards in a very odd and ridiculous manner. I have a confused recollection of riding near the brinks of precipices, and of passing through defiles where the rocks closed overhead, and again of fording torrents, but everything was dim and vague, and it was not until a muezzin from a minaret in the town of Chaiju shouted the early morning hour that I had the slightest idea we were so near the brink of another day. . . .

We reached Sophia about nine P.M., and were off again for Ichtiman, another long twelve hours stage, at half-past. I think it was during this night that the most overpowering sensations of weariness I ever experienced came over me. I very nearly fell out of my saddle twice, a dangerous practice where the road frequently ran on the brink of a precipice ; but the cavalry escort led the party, and the pace was so rapid, that, except when walking, these sensations never completely mastered me. At Ichtiman we changed horses about one in the morning, having before us the ascent of the Balkan ere we reached Tatar Bazarjik, a village in the plains on the other side of the mountain, and about forty-eight miles distant.

I cannot explain how this night was passed, for I know not myself. Although we crossed some magnificent scenery, a dogged resolution to go on, mixed with the determination that as long as I could sit upright in my saddle I never would get out of it, sustained me ; and Rhisto, whose pride in my success was now roused, encouraged me in every possible manner. Indeed he watched me as if I had been his own son, and I am thankful to say, never once talked of giving in ; for although I should not have acceded to his request, it would have discouraged me.

Just as the first tinge of dawn crossed the horizon we surmounted the topmast ridge of the Balkan, and, after resting our horses half an hour, clattered down the sides of the mountain to Tatar Bazarjik. Thence to Philippopolis is a level plain, and we reached the latter place

soon after two ; but not before Rhisto had taken to his own share of
refreshment a water-melon about the size of a moderate balloon.
Philippopolis is celebrated for its steam baths, and I required one.
Moreover, they are most refreshing after long-continued exertion.
So I dismounted from my saddle and walked with Rhisto to them,
ordering fresh horses to be ready in two hours. I had felt some
pain in the morning from an old musket wound, but nothing to
cause me any uneasiness, and as I had been three days and nights in
the saddle without cessation, I attributed it to the great exertion,
and thought it would go off after my bath. I found, however, on
undressing, that my linen was covered with blood. To make matters
worse Rhisto was at this moment taken violently ill, and his once
manly face turned quite livid. What to do I knew not. I suffered
comparatively little pain, so, hoping for the best, I hurried on my
clothes again, went back to the posthouse, mounted a fresh horse,
and in a torrent of rain and wind, started on a long sixteen hours'
stage to Eskew.

At first poor Rhisto reeled in his saddle like a drunken man ;
but the saddle is the Tartar's home, and after the first hour or two he
shook his illness off and became the same quiet, energetic, attentive
creature as before. The rain set in, a regular deluge ; the country
through which our horses struggled was a regular swamp, and they
were nearly knocked up before they had completed eight of the sixteen
hours. . . . We turned into a roadside khan, and telling Rhisto to call
me when the horses were restored, I threw myself on a wooden bench,
and was fast asleep in half a minute. Rhisto told me afterwards that
he had not the heart to wake me, and that I remained quite motion-
less for six hours ; but about three A.M. we were in the saddle again,
and although the rain fell in torrents the whole day, by dint of hard
riding we reached Adrianople at seven in the evening. . . The moon
lit us cheerily enough out of Adrianople, but soon after ten our old
luck returned ; the night was black and dark as ink, and again I
could neither distinguish Rhisto nor the suriji, although they were
only ten paces in advance. Whilst descending a hill rapidly my horse
fell heavily and lay upon my right leg, but the ground was so soft, that
beyond the shake I suffered no inconvenience, and I was in the
saddle again before Rhisto, who had heard although he could not see
the fall, could come to my assistance. . . . About eight on the following morning my horse again fell with me, and wonderful to say,
although in falling he twisted the steel spur on my right boot like a
piece of wire, my ankle was in no way injured.

That evening they caught a glimpse of the Sea of
Marmora, and it is easy to imagine what relief the sight must

1849
—
Æ.T. 62

have given to the weary horsemen. The night was once more spent in the saddle, though Colonel Townley could scarcely see out of his worn and bloodshot eyes: but he knew it was the last night, and that the morning sun would shine on the domes and minarets of Stambol.

Ibid.

26 Oct.

Thank God, we had no other trouble but tired and jaded horses to contend with, and at half-past five on Friday morning I entered the old ruined gateway of Constantinople, traversed its narrow and tortuous streets, and crossing the Golden Horn in a caïque, reached the English Embassy at Pera, having been just five days and eleven hours in traversing on horseback eight hundred and twenty miles, having the whole of that time to contend with wind, mud, and rain, besides two heavyish falls, which, if they broke no bones, certainly did me no good. I felt a certain pride in hearing that it was considered the quickest journey ever performed in the winter, and that the best Tartars in the service of the Porte took six days during fine summer weather. I can claim credit for obstinacy, at least, if for no higher quality.

As one reads this quiet business-like narrative one thinks of the legendary ride from Ghent to Aix :—

> Not a word to each other : we kept the great pace
> Neck by neck, stride by stride, never changing our place—

and of how the rider came in gallantly, but alone—

> And there was my Roland to bear the whole weight
> Of the news which alone could save Aix from her fate.

27 May, 1850

It was a brave deed, and the Foreign Office did not forget it. Lord Palmerston referred to it in the House of Commons, and Captain Townley's ride became famous.

This was the momentous letter :—

From Lord Palmerston, 2 Oct.

As it is of importance to relieve you as soon as possible from anxiety in regard to the responsibility which you may think you have incurred by the advice which in conjunction with Aupick you have given the Porte, and as it is also essential not to lose an hour unnecessarily in relieving the Porte from its doubts as to whether it will find aid and support from its friends, I send you this private letter by a special messenger to say that the Cabinet has to-day decided to give an affirmative answer to the application for moral and material support which the Turkish ambassador by order of his Government has presented to us. We are therefore going to enter immediately into communication with the Government of France in order to settle the course of proceeding, assuming what we cannot doubt, namely that the French Government is willing and prepared to coöperate with us. What we mean to propose is that the two Governments should make friendly and courteous representations at Vienna and Petersburg to induce the Imperial Governments to desist from their demands, urging that the Sultan is not bound by treaty to do what is asked of him, and that to do so would be dishonourable, and disgraceful. We mean to propose at the same time, that the two Mediterranean squadrons should proceed at once to the Dardanelles with orders to go up to the Bosphorus if invited to do so by the Sultan, either to defend Constantinople from attack, or to give him the moral support which their presence would afford. I think it possible however that the admirals may already have gone up to the neighbourhood of the Dardanelles in consequence of the letters they will have received from you and from Aupick. I think it however much better that the Porte should be advised *not* to send for the squadron to enter the Dardanelles without real necessity. The example might be turned to bad account by the Russians hereafter ; and it would be too much of an open menace, and the way to deal with the Emperor is not to put him on his mettle by open and public menace. The presence of the squadrons at the outside of the Dardanelles or in their neighbourhood would probably be quite sufficient to keep the Sevastopol squadron at anchor in port, and the French have besides some naval and military force at and about Constantinople sufficient to make a resistance till our squadrons could get up. We have steamers that could tow the line of battle ships ; we have I believe six or seven liners ; the French about the same number ; the Russians I believe twelve or fourteen.

I have seen Drouyn de Lhuys and the Turkish ambassador since the Cabinet, and have told them confidentially our decision, and the Turk said he would write by this messenger to A'li Pasha. What I wish you to impress upon the Turks is that this communication is confidential, to keep up their spirits and courage ; but that they must not swagger upon it, nor make it public till they hear it officially. From Brunov's language, and I have also seen him since the Cabinet, I should infer the matter will be amicably settled. He says the treaty gives the Emperor the right to demand surrender, and to the Sultan the right of choosing the other alternative of sending the refugees away. Railways won't wait, and I must finish. You will have official communications in a few days after you receive this.

The formal despatch (*Corr.* p. 26), which arrived soon after, confirmed these arrangements : Palmerston sent a private letter with it :—

1849

ÆT. 62

Here at length are our official instructions, which I have been unable to send you sooner, but I conclude that you received in due time my private letter of Tuesday last which I sent by messenger through Vienna to give you the earliest information of the decision of the Cabinet that day. We have to-day heard from Parker, who wrote on the 25th from Corfu and meant to wait between that and Athens for orders from the Admiralty. . . . In this affair we are trying to catch two great fish, and we must wind the reel very gently and dexterously not to break our line. The Government here have resolved to support the Sultan at all events ; but we must be able to shew to Parliament that we have used all civility and forbearance, and that if hostilities ensue they have not been brought on by any fault or mistake of ours. There never was such unanimity in England upon a question not directly affecting the immediate interests of England ; but that unanimity would cease if we did not play our game with great discretion. It is for this reason among others that we have tried to make our communications to Vienna and Petersburg as civil as is consistent with a firm statement of our opinion on the case, in order that there might be no pretence for saying that we held out a threat and had thereby made it impossible for the Emperors to recede. I have upon this ground some doubt whether it would be expedient that the squadrons should come up to Constantinople, but you will be the best judge. Whatever we say in our despatches as to what is to be done by the two squadrons would apply to our own squadron singly if the French were not to act with us, which however is a case not to be supposed.

Fr. Lord Palmer-ston, 6 Oct.

These communications reached Constantinople between 18 and 26 October, and it is easy to imagine the intense satisfaction with which they were received. "The cause of honour and humanity has been vindicated," wrote Canning in proud delight, and the Sultan and his ministers were not behindhand in their expressions of gratitude. Abdu-l-Mejid sent a special aide-de-camp to the Embassy to tender his Majesty's thanks to the Queen and to signify his unfeigned pleasure at the outburst of sympathy which had sprung from the whole British nation. Indeed it was this unanimous sentiment, which re-echoed in every quarter of England,

CCCXIV. 25 Oct.

1849
———
ÆT. 62
Corr. p. 61

cccxxx.

Corr. p. 71

that carried the day. At the end of October the British
fleet, soon to be followed by the French, appeared off the
Dardanelles, and on 1 Nov. it entered within the Outer
Castles ; but it may be doubted whether even this demonstration would have sufficed to shake the two Emperors'
resolve if they had not been aware that the feeling of
the nation was enthusiastically enlisted in the cause of the
refugees. That being known, there was nothing for it but
to fight or to retreat. On 7 Nov. Canning informed Lord
Palmerston that Russia and Austria had withdrawn their
demand for extradition, in deference, said M. Titov, to the
pronounced expression of public feeling in England. The two
Imperial Governments were disposed to throw the blame of
the crisis upon the zeal of their agents, and to back out of the
position at all hazards. The danger, however, was not entirely
over, though the main issue had been triumphantly decided.
There was still the question as to what was to be done with the
refugees, and diplomatic relations were not yet renewed by
the offended Powers. The Turks were anxious to keep the
British squadron within the Dardanelles in case of further
emergency ; but Canning was aware of the jealousy with which
the entrance of the fleet in time of peace,—though it had been
effected merely for the sake of a safe anchorage in stress of
weather, and had received the Sultan's ready consent,—was
regarded by the Eastern Powers. He instructed Sir W. Parker
to move outside at the first opportunity ; and when in the
middle of November the ambassador paid a visit to the
admiral, he was pleased to find him stationed where no treaty
stipulations could be raised in dispute.

Some extracts from Lord Palmerston's private correspondence will shew how the Government and people of England
viewed these momentous transactions :—

Fr. Lord
Palmer-
ston,
11 Oct.

I think the impression seems to be that Stürmer and Titov went
beyond their instructions, fancying they could carry their point by
a *coup de main* and bully the Turks into acquiescence ; and they
would evidently have succeeded if it had not been for you and Aupick.
I should not be surprized if Stürmer were removed to some other
post. In the meanwhile this shew of courage by the Porte, and the
manifestation by England and France of a readiness to support the

Sultan by arms if necessary, must have a beneficial effect upon the future conduct both of the Porte and the two Imperial Governments. The Porte will probably put a little more firmness into its conduct, and the others a little more moderation into theirs. The Porte however must take care to keep on the right side of the post, especially with regard to the passage of the Dardanelles, and the Turkish Government should most carefully abstain from calling our squadrons up through the Straits, "*in time of Peace,*" unless they had the certainty that war was imminent, and an attack likely to be made immediately. It is very important that the Sultan should not set the example of infringing the stipulation of the Treaty of July 1841 ; Russia would be too ready to follow the lead when it might suit her purpose to do so.

It is a great pity that the Porte did not take your advice and send out of Turkey the chief refugees whom the five Governments wanted to have. That done the dispute would have ceased to have a practical object, and I hope that the Sultan will not have taken any engagement which shall prevent him from letting them all go, at least as many as can and choose to do so. In fact he can have no right to keep them prisoners in Turkey? . . .

But now is the time for the Turks to make all possible improvements in their army, their navy, and their defences. Some foreign officers brought into their army would introduce instruction for officers, which is probably what they want most. If they wish for any British naval officers to improve their naval services, let them ask and they shall have. We have sent Captain Slade, a very good officer, and who has already been, I believe, employed in their service and knows a little of the language, and Parker has sent some lieutenants to be useful for the moment ; but if they would like a few officers to command ships let me know, and Sir F. Baring will look out for some and send them. The considerations which led me to think last year that it would be better for them not to make such a request no longer exist, and it might be well to strike the iron while it is hot. Upon the same principle they ought to set to work and to put the defences of the Bosphorus into good order without delay, and to arm them with heavy guns, not forgetting to render them secure on the land side from being carried by a small force landed and sweeping through the batteries one after the other. Would it not be possible also for them to erect some strong batteries to fire upon ships which having passed down the Bosphorus might anchor opposite the town and threaten to lay it in ashes ? . . .

There never was I think in this country so strong and unanimous a burst of generous feeling as this demand of the two Imperial and imperious Governments has called forth ; all men of all parties and opinions, politicians, soldiers, sailors, clergymen and Quakers ; all newspapers, Tory, Whig, and Radical, have joined in chorus ; and this outpouring of indignation must I think have a salutary effect at Petersburg and Vienna, and must raise our national character in the esteem of the world, and shew that we are not quite so incapable of being roused to manly action as some speeches in Parliament and at our peace meetings and congresses might have led people to suppose. A Quaker shopkeeper at a meeting last year said, " Well, and suppose the French were to conquer us, what great harm would that do us ? I suppose we should make and sell our goods all the same, and the French are not such savages as to put us to death in cold blood." Upon which a French National Guard, who was present and who spoke English, got on the table and assured the meeting that they, the Quaker shopkeepers, were capital good fellows. I believe that the firmness of the French President and his determination to go hand in hand with England overruled some little weaknesses or intrigue which for a couple of days delayed the forwarding of the messengers.

You must have been very anxious in these discussions between the Porte and the two Imperial Governments, and your position was very embarrassing. On the one hand you had to keep the Porte from making any premature submission, on the other hand you had to avoid committing your Government by expectations of support, which decisions to be made in Downing Street might not afterwards have made good. All things however have turned out well. The English Government and nation have shewn a spirit, a generosity, and a courage which does us all high honour. We have drawn France to follow in our wake, after much division and difference of opinion in the French Cabinet and public. We have forced the haughty autocrat to go back from his arrogant pretensions ; we have obliged Austria to forego another opportunity of quaffing her bowl of blood ; and we have saved Turkey from being humbled down to absolute prostration. All this will be seen and felt by Europe ; all this should be borne in mind by ourselves, and ought to be treasured up in grateful remembrance by Turkey ; but all this *we* ought not to boast of, and on the contrary we must let our baffled Emperors pass as quietly and as decently as possible over the bridge by which they are going to retreat.

The outstanding difference between the Porte and the two Imperial Governments related to the surveillance of the refugees. The greater number of the Hungarian rank and file, 3,300 in all, had already accepted the Austrian amnesty and returned to their homes ; but for the leaders there was no pardon, and the difficulty was how to dispose of them. The Porte removed them to Shumla, and thence to Brusa and Kutahia in Asia Minor ; but Austria insisted on a strict guard being kept over them, and even stipulated for a surveillance by Austrian officers. There were also, as has been stated, rumours of a plot to assassinate Kossuth and the other chiefs, and this was said to be countenanced at Vienna. It thus became necessary not only to guard the refugees in the interests of Austria—a precaution to which the Porte had weakly consented—but to protect them against possible mischief at the hands of their enemies. Their condition under these circumstances was not agreeable. Turkish restraint involved hardships, and Kossuth and his friends complained bitterly of their treatment, and seemed to have forgotten the generosity with which the Porte had exposed itself to imminent peril in order to save their necks. To Canning, however, as the real cause of their safety, they shewed a becoming spirit of gratitude. He had restored their wives and children to them, and the little Kossuths, among others, had been cared for at the embassy. Their father wrote in touching terms :—

I have my children again, and the happiness of seeing them out of the reach of my poor country's oppressors is still more heightened by the presence of my dearest sister, who so generously undertook to accompany them.

They all find not enough words to praise the benevolent kindness they met with at your Excellency's house. Myself and my wife we are entirely penetrated of gratitude, and we will never cease to pray to God that He may bless your noble lady, and you sir, for the consolation you afforded to our parental feelings.

From Kossuth, 28 June

Whatever consideration they received, whatever mitigation of the hard conditions demanded by Austria, and only too likely to be conceded by the timidity of the Porte, they owed to the Great Elchi. Russia had retired from the discussion, having less interest in the Hungarians. M. Titov resumed his diplomatic relations at the close of December, and the squadrons left the Archipelago ; but Austria was still intractable. On 5 Feb. 1850 she demanded that the refugees should

cccxci.
31 Dec.
1849

xxxix.
1850

be kept under surveillance for twelve years; the term was then reduced to five years; but Canning would not countenance any term at all. The Sultan, he said, must be trusted to decide the proper time for their release. Palmerston also felt strongly on this subject. The Austrian demand he wrote (30 Nov.) was "quite preposterous": it was bad enough to allow what the Sultan had offered—"to keep watch over these Hungarians for a time and at his own discretion";—but Austria required that he should do so until she released him from his duties as keeper. "It is scarcely less derogatory to the Sultan," wrote the Foreign Secretary, "to be jailor for Austria than to be purveyor to the Austrian executioners." At last the Emperor gave way and resumed diplomatic relations early in April. The next object of the British ambassador was to induce the Porte to liberate the captives, for such they were, as soon as possible. He was authorized to draw upon public funds for their assistance: the American minister volunteered to ship them to the United States; but still the Porte trembled lest she should offend the Viennese Court. In Jan. 1851, however, with Austria's permission, the embarkation began. The Porte was liberal in its provision for the exiles, and gave them money, which was supplemented by grants from the British Embassy and from public subscription: yet their future must have been a pitiful prospect, in a strange land, and with small means of earning a livelihood. All the summer the migration continued, till there remained only the leaders, against whom the Government at Vienna still hardened its heart. At last, after repeated efforts and a personal application to the Sultan, Canning obtained his royal word that Kossuth and the rest should be released on 1 Sept. The promise was redeemed, and the refugees who for two years had kept four empires in suspense finally disappeared from the political horizon.

Canning's conduct throughout these trying negotiations obtained the hearty admiration of his Government, and never was he so popular with the whole people of England. Palmerston wrote (5 Jan.):—

I can easily conceive that you must as you say be overwhelmed with work, but you are doing your work right well, and the consciousness of that must make the labour less oppressive than it otherwise would be. . . .

The two Imperial Governments have made a great mistake in all this affair, but we have saved them from adding "un crime" to "une faute." If however the Turkish Government makes a proper use of what has happened, the benefit to Turkey will be great and lasting.

And again, 23 March :—

I was very glad to have an opportunity in debate of doing justice to your management of the important matters you have had to deal with.

Many private friends wrote to the ambassador in enthusiastic praise of his bold defence of the refugees ; and while he was recognized as the true champion of the honourable principle he had successfully sustained, the Porte obtained its share of popular sympathy for the generosity and highmindedness it had displayed in the affair. They were indeed as Palmerston said "frightened at their own courage," but they were not frightened out of it.

CHAPTER XXIII.

ADMINISTRATIVE REFORM.

1849-52.

1849
——
ÆT. 62

AMIDST such pressing emergencies it would have been but natural that the internal improvements upon which Canning laid so much stress should be neglected. That was not his way, however; and, far from forgetting reform in the heat of conflict, his policy was to claim reform as the reward of his support. Whenever a Turkish minister came with an appeal for England's interference, Canning told him that aid would be given when aid was earned; Turkey must make herself worthy of encouragement if the Queen's influence was to be used in her favour. If a private audience took place with the Sultan, the ambassador did not shrink from speaking similar home-truths. His Majesty must deserve the friendship of England by acts of reform and toleration. The price of British intervention at the crisis of the refugee question was a forward step by Turkey towards European civilization.

On his arrival at Constantinople in 1848, as we have seen, the ambassador's first act was to restore Reshid and his friends to power. Promises of future reforms thereafter abounded; even Riza expressed his regret at having formerly opposed Canning's policy; Rif'at engaged to do his best to improve the condition of the Christian rayas; but the actual moment was always deemed unfavourable for any definite innovation, and so the months slipped by, and nothing was done. Nobody denied the validity of the argument, that the best way of preserving the integrity of the empire and gaining the respect and support of foreign Powers was to remove every grievance that might occasion rebellion among the Rayas, every injustice that might invite foreign intervention, every barbarity that hindered the cordial sympathy of the Porte's Western allies. The justice and reasonableness of all this was frankly granted :—but the time, said the Turks, was not propitious—perhaps presently something might be done. The Grand Vezir found himself thwarted in the Council ; and the Sultan, alternately terrified by Russia and alarmed at symptoms of discontent among his more fanatical Muslim subjects, had not the courage of his real convictions. In Sept. 1848 indeed Reshid despatched a circular to the provincial governors enjoining justice and mercy, and condemning oppression and extortion, and at the same time gave practical effect to his teaching by the release of some Nestorians who had been unjustly imprisoned. The circular and the release gave great satisfaction to the British ambassador ; but a larger measure was needed to heal the wounds of Turkey. In Dec. 1848 a Commission sat at the Porte to take into consideration the various proposals which Canning had brought forward for the improvement of the internal administration. The experiment was tried of purifying the local councils by placing them under an approved president sent from the capital. Little however was effected ; the Sultan was timorous ; and the troubles in Wallachia occupied every mind to the exclusion of constitutional changes. Moreover the plan of an alliance with England had not been encouraged by the British Government, and the Porte was the less disposed to gratify the wishes of the English ambassador.

Canning's steady statesmanship during the disputes with Russia gradually effaced this feeling of chagrin, and the Turks once more began to draw closer to England. After an official audience of the Sultan in the spring of 1849, the Elchi was summoned to his Majesty's apartment for a private conference. Reshid, the only other person present, acted as interpreter. In the same breath the ambassador counselled a sturdy resistance to the Russian demands in Wallachia, and an energetic persistence in reform, despite the cloudy aspect of external politics. The Sultan replied that the Porte would always look to England for sympathy and help in the time of trouble. As we know, the Porte did not look in vain, and

1849

ÆT. 62

CI. 1848

CCXIX.
18 Dec.
1848

LXXXIV.
14 Mar.
1849

1849
——
ÆT. 62

CCCLXIII.
26 Nov.

Ibid.

CLXIV.
30 Nov.

it was natural that the prompt support rendered by the Western Powers on the refugee question should revive the scheme of a defensive alliance, either with England and France, or with the former alone. At the close of 1849 definite proposals were made by the Turkish Government, and in order to win Palmerston over to their plan, they agreed that if the alliance were formed England should be the sole arbiter as to whether or not a case for joint action had at any time arisen. Canning did not conceal his approval of the idea : he thought " the principle and objects of the alliance unexceptionable " and believed it would " emancipate the Porte and its ministers from the pressure of that baneful influence which fascinates their spirits and cripples them in every attempt at progress and independence." In recommending the Turkish proposals to Lord Palmerston he urged warmly : " We are now called upon to choose between a more determined and systematic support of this empire, with its attendant inconveniences, risks, and sacrifices, or a tacit acquiescence in the Porte's habitual submission to the superior fortunes and calculating energies of a neighbour whose moral ascendancy would prove more injurious in its consequences to Europe than even its territorial aggrandizement at the expense of Turkey." The Porte, he said, must either sink or swim : she could no longer *float.*

Charmed with the ambassador's reception of the scheme, the Sultan held out an agreeable prospect of reform, without which, it was remarked, the alliance would be impossible. Internal improvements, a thorough revision of the defences of the empire, and a systematic encouragement of commerce, were the chief points to be pressed, and Abdu-l-Mejid agreed most graciously to the programme, only remarking that some changes might be effected at once, but others would require time and opportunity. The leading internal reforms advocated by the Elchi were (1) the abolition of the capitation tax levied on Christians, and their admission into the army ; (2) Christian evidence to be allowed in the law courts ; (3) more Christians to be elected to local councils ; (4) the revenue to be collected in a more equitable manner. There was also a hint, but no more, as to the suppression of the slave trade.

The whole programme was by order of the Sultan laid before the Council.

Here, apparently, this promising movement ended. The alliance was probably postponed in deference to Russia. The programme remained " before the Council." It is curious to note that the only " reform " of any sort which took place within six months of the audience and promises above recorded was that of a small, though annoying, matter of etiquette. Canning thus describes the transaction in a despatch to Lord Palmerston :—

Being out on horseback a few days ago, my road lay through a public street which runs immediately at the back of the Sultan's palace. On reaching the guardhouse I was stopped by one of the soldiers, who told me that I could only go by on foot. Not choosing to submit to this degradation I made a round to avoid any further question on the spot, and sent next day a private message to the Sultan, informing him of what had occurred, with some appropriate remarks on the inconvenience, not to say more, of a custom which had nothing but its antiquity to recommend it, and excusing the liberty which I had taken in applying immediately to his Majesty, on the ground of my disinclination to raise an official question at the Porte.

The Sultan replied that what had occurred to me gave him much regret, that he had conceived the idea some time before of abolishing a custom which, though it might have been proper in former times, had ceased to have any useful effect, that he gladly seized the occasion of acting on his own impressions in that respect, and would send forthwith a peremptory order to his ministers to put an end to the objectionable practice. His Majesty graciously added that he was pleased by my having made a direct application to himself.

The Sultan has since redeemed his pledge. His subjects as well as foreigners are now relieved from a degrading usage and I have offered my humble acknowledgments to his Majesty for so kind and considerate an application of his supreme authority.

Local tradition avers that even this trifling concession was not obtained without violent pressure, and the scene when the Elchi found himself ordered to dismount by a common soldier has been the theme of many anecdotes. To be permitted, however, the privilege of riding near the back of the palace was hardly a sufficient redemption of the promises of November. At an audience on 5 June, Canning taxed the Sultan with forgetting his engagements : the Russian panic was over, he observed, and nothing now hindered the tranquil and orderly execution of the reforms sketched at the earlier conference. "The truth is," explained the official despatch describing the audience, "that little or no practical advancement accompanies the repeated professions of the Government. The few very limited measures brought forward by Reshid Pasha in concurrence with me encounter the most vexatious difficulties either in the Council or elsewhere. Time of immense value is wasted in idle discussion or timid hesitation, and, in spite of flattering addresses and the panegyrics of hired newspapers, there is more danger of losing what has been gained than of realizing what is professed." There had already been a great improvement in trade under the more liberal administration, and a far more considerable revival of industries and commerce might be expected if reforms were "honestly and vigorously carried out." The dangers ahead were a deficit in the revenue, the corruption of the official classes, and the steady decline of the Muslim population as against the Christians, who as they gained strength would be able to menace their oppressors. "Not one of these evils is incurable," said Canning, but the Sultan must give "the full light of his countenance" to the cure. The ambassador spoke freely and candidly ; Reshid and A'li, who were present, concurred in his views ; and Abdu-l-Mejid said he appreciated the advice and would carefully consider it. The advice was accordingly considered.

In August Canning reported that "nothing had occurred to enliven the prospect." His advice had been uniform and consistent, but all the fruits were "delays and evasions, unnecessary compromises, and weak compliances ; " corrupt practices in office, a low revenue, high prices, a pernicious system of recruiting the army and a worse one of farming the taxes ; discontent in the frontier provinces, and a fanatical spirit towards the Christians, who were massacred in several of the more remote districts ; want of inland communications, and a weak state of the military defences ;—in short an alarming decrepitude in every department of the empire :—Reshid dejected, and alive to the danger ; Riza, despite his promises, doggedly antagonistic ; the Sultan vacillating and timorous as ever—happy to hear the ambassador's counsels and read his memoranda of reforms, anxious to improve his empire, but never plucking up courage for a bold measure.

Palmerston was more hopeful than the ambassador. He wrote :—

> I have received your despatch and letter of the 5th and 6th, and have just taken leave of the Turkish ambassador, who starts on Thursday for Constantinople. I took the opportunity of requesting him to impress upon his Government the necessity of improvement and reforms, and of putting an end to the present system of corruption and injustice, and I begged him to recommend strongly to the attention of his Government the memorandum which you had given to the Sultan. There is obviously a great deal wanting to be done in every way and in every branch of administration to bring Turkey into line with other powers, and to put her in a condition to defend herself. But much has already been accomplished, perhaps more than ever yet was done before in the same space of time in any country in which there was so much room for improvement, and I am not discouraged, therefore, by the apparent slowness of progress, but only encouraged to urge them on to further advance. It may be true that much of what has hitherto been done exists more in regulations and orders than in actual execution ; but one ought not to undervalue the worth of rules and laws and institutions, even when they are not practically acted upon to the extent of their letter and spirit. As long as forms remain they are a fixed point to refer to, and as men improve, and opinion grows more powerful, those forms become gradually more and more the guide for conduct and events ; and that which at first is only theory in course of time is converted into practice.

Again the English scheme of reform, strongly supported by Palmerston in London, was "considered ;" again the ministers were more or less favourable ; and this time they even appointed special commissioners to travel in Asia and Europe and report on the abuses they might discover and the best way of removing them, and to enforce such administrative reforms as were already sanctioned. Canning was sanguine as to the results of this new step : but it may reasonably be doubted whether it was not merely a fresh contrivance for procrastination. Such at least is the impression

1850

ÆT. 63

Fr. Lord Palmerston, 24 Sept.

CCCXXXIII. 16 Nov.

XL. 4 Feb. 1851

1850
———
ÆT. 63

produced by the report of a later audience of the Sultan in February, when in reply to the ambassador's urgent entreaties that his Majesty would rouse himself to a sense of the dangers that encompassed him, Abd-l-Mejid replied with his exasperating affability that he did not see his way to any "striking innovation." Canning, almost in despair, reported that the Padishah shewed no "grasp of mind or force of character equal to the requirements of a vast and decaying empire." Infirmity of purpose was the salient characteristic both of the Sultan and the Grand Vezir.

With such weakness at the head, it was almost impossible for the ambassador, with all his energy and perseverance, to carry his reforms. Yet something was accomplished before he departed on leave in 1852. In November 1850 a firman

CCCL.
26 Nov.
1850

was issued according the same privileges to Protestants as to Greeks and Catholics in Turkey. The Protestants, who previously had had no *locus standi* in the Turkish State, were now formally and distinctly recognized as a separate body, they were instructed to elect an agent to represent their interests, and their religious rites and temporal concerns were to be secure from molestation. Canning declared that the firman granted all the protection that the Protestant rayas could pretend to, and he looked forward to the steady development of the now legally recognized community as a valuable counterpoise to Graeco-Russ and Gallo-Catholic influences. Mixed courts of criminal judicature were to be established, and the state of the Turkish prisons came under review. Another important concession was the enactment that from August 1850 no negro slaves were to be embarked on Turkish vessels. The white slave traffic was still undisturbed; but the Sultan regarded it as "a shameful and barbarous practice," and "hoped before long to abolish the infamous trade within his dominions." All these reforms however were only extorted by continual pressure.

To Lord
Palmer-
ston,
3 Jan.
1851

I am glad [wrote Canning to Lord Palmerston] to learn from your Slave Trade Despatch No. 9 that you are pleased with the Grand Vezir's instruction prohibiting the embarkation of slaves in Ottoman Government ships. Allow me, however, to say that the

Porte is little deserving of the thanks of H. M. Government on the occasion. Its conduct was shuffling, and I found a great reluctance to make the required concession. It was finally by referring to the Sultan that I carried the point, and to him therefore I propose to make known your satisfaction. In general, notwithstanding the policy of Reshid's Government and his personal good qualities, I find the greatest difficulty in making any progress of consequence, whether the object be one of administrative improvement, of public works, or of commercial progress. The new plan of criminal judicature was won inch by inch. I owe the principles of the new tariff to Reshid's fear of my speaking out all I thought of his conduct in Grabbe's affair. I got the Protestant firman by interesting one of his confidants with the hope of being supported in a scheme of his own. The only chance of getting the memorandum carried into effect is the pressure of financial necessity, with the fear of my access to the Seraglio. It grieves me to add that our three-tailed friend's reputation for being superior to the temptations of money is fast melting away under the sunny influence of his magnificent buildings and still more magnificent investments. I see these weaknesses with pain as well on his own account as with respect to the great political interests at stake. I know not, however, where we could find any other Turkish minister as good as he is, and, therefore, I am fully inclined to make the most of him rather than " fly to others that we know not of." At the same time if one could be *sure* of having him back at a minute's notice, it is not quite clear that a six months' visit to his friends in the country,—to Lamartine's farm, for instance,—would not prove of considerable use both to himself and to the empire. Some promising steps have nevertheless been taken, and more I hope are getting into course, but in my humble judgment little of a solid or lasting character will be done for humanity, and nothing whatever for European policy, unless the finances be restored to order, and a real *practical system* of reform, in harmony with the principles so often proclaimed, be frankly adopted.

The following letter to Mr. Layard is worth quoting :—

I have been at close quarters for some time with the Sultan and his premier on the subject of reform. I want to have reality and a system of progressive measures instead of professions and appearances. It would be tedious to tell you all I have done during the last eight months to attain this object. Something has been gained, more is promised, and I do not despair of a positive result. But it is uphill work, requiring an immensity of patience, and what is done bears no proportion to what remains to be done. When I look back to the period of my return in 1848, I find our conquests few and far between.   The first step was to replace Reshid and Co. in office. That was soon effected, and might have been followed with earlier consequences if the occupation of Moldavia and Wallachia, the mission of General Grabbe and the affair of the refugees had not successively occupied the Porte's attention and furnished pretexts for postponing everything else.   In the midst of these embarrassments the successful resistance to Russia and Austria was certainly a harmonious point, but the only lasting internal improvements have been carried since.   They are but four in number, exclusive of the tariff, which contains a most beneficial principle, but one of a commercial rather than an administrative character.   The four internal measures are the equalization of Christian with Musulman evidence, the collection of the Kharaj by the respective communities and not from individuals, the commencement of macadamized roads on a large scale, and the establishment by firman of the Protestant rayas on the same footing as the other non-Musulman religious communities of the empire.   I may add retrospectively the abolition of the old humiliating custom of making people dismount in passing the Sultan's palace, and prospectively the cessation of the far more mischievous custom of farming out the public revenues which has been promised and confidentially announced to me.   The *per contra* list of corruption, peculation, insurrection, massacres, pillages and financial disorder, is a formidable drawback on these advantages.   The deficit in the revenue is serious, and much discredit must result from the comparative impunity with which so many revolting outrages have been committed at the expense of the Christian population in Syria and Bulgaria. You are an eyewitness of the deplorable state of things in Baghdad and Mosil, nor have we yet reached the end of the troubles in Bosnia.   The Porte will probably continue its successes in putting down rebellion and pacifying the belligerent tribes, but in the meantime the process of exhaustion goes on, and if the work of reform be not more difficult, its ultimate success becomes daily more problematical.

I would not lightly give up the task which Providence appears to have assigned to me.   It seems, however, that the time is approaching when I shall either have obtained all the concessions which can possibly be obtained for a certain period, or be called upon to throw down my cards in despair.

The reactionary party was strong both in the Council and in the country.   Too rapid and vigorous reforms would very probably bring about a revolution, and there were signs that the Sultan's bigoted brother Abdu-l-Aziz would be a formidable

candidate for the throne.   Russia was ever on the watch, lest 1851
Turkey should become too civilized to justify her interference.
Reshid, Canning's chief hope, was an object of jealousy both ÆT. 64
to the inferior ministers and to the Sultan.   Reforms cost
money, but the Turkish treasury was just then in sore straits,
and salaries were reduced in every department.   To make
roads, build batteries, remove venal officials, and reform the
taxation would necessitate a foreign loan, and usury is against
the Mohammedan law.   Canning perceived that to press
the Porte further would only lead to his own disfavour and
Reshid's retirement.   Even Palmerston had become hopeless,
and had warned Reshid (24 November, 1850) that he foresaw
that the Turkish Empire was " doomed to fall by the timidity
and weakness and irresolution of its sovereign and of his
ministers, and it is evident that we shall ere long have to consider what other arrangement can be set up in its place ; " and
Canning had at last admitted that " the *great* game of im- To Lord
provement is altogether up for the present, and though I shall Palmer-
ston,
do my best to promote the adoption of separate measures, it 5 April,
1851
is impossible for me to conceal that the main object of my
stay here is all but gone."   He therefore paused and resolved
to give the Government time to recover itself.   He noted as
a good sign the novel circumstance that the Sultan assisted
in person at a Greek wedding, standing throughout the service,
because " he had vowed never to sit when prayers were addressed to God," and positively eating Christian food cooked
by Christian hands.   No Sultan had never done so before, and
Canning hoped the best from so tolerant a precedent.   Before cxxxiv.
leaving Constantinople in June 1852, "perhaps never to 12 June,
1852
return," he once more essayed to rouse the Sultan to active
measures, and was assured in return that his Majesty would
bestir himself.   Nevertheless the Elchi left in sadness: he 22 June
had attempted so much, and had attained comparatively so
little, and he knew that his departure would be the signal
for a return to the old order of things against which he had
striven with all his might for ten laborious years.   Yet he left
Turkey the better for his work, his seed had not all fallen on
stony ground, and little harvests of good fruit were springing
up in more than one quarter of the Ottoman territory.   More-

over he had steered the vessel of state safely through a tempestuous voyage ; the storms of 1848 had threatened to break over Turkey, and it was mainly his own hand that had averted shipwreck. He left the country tranquil and at peace with her neighbours. No alarms from without menaced the State he had taken under his protection. There had been a dispute between France and Russia relating to the Holy Places at Jerusalem, but this appeared to have come to an amicable settlement. On the eve of his departure, which was believed to be final, he was entertained at a great dinner given in his honour by the British subjects, and nothing could exceed their enthusiasm at his achievements, or their regret at his loss. Addresses poured in from the Armenian Protestants, the Greeks, the American missionaries, the merchants of Smyrna and Constantinople, and the Elchi knew that his labours were appreciated.

Before concluding the account of four years of hard work we may pause for a moment to quote a narrative of the one brief holiday which the ambassador allowed himself to take :—

"In the autumn of 1850 Sir Stratford, accompanied by his family, made a short expedition to visit some of the islands in the Archipelago. It was thought that a personal visit from the Queen's representative might have a calming effect on the population, who were as usual in a state of chronic dispute with their Turkish masters, aided secretly but constantly by the subjects of King Otho. Moreover at this time the monasteries of Mount Athos were used as hiding-places for arms and ammunition on their way across the frontier, and some inspection was very desirable.

"We started in the Embassy steamer, the *Antelope*, and rapidly crossing the Sea of Marmora, paused for an hour or two at Rodosto on the European coast, then passing through the Dardanelles came to Mitylene, where the groves of orange trees formed a striking contrast to the desolation of our next halt at the island of Lemnos. Here a very severe and sudden storm forced us to weigh anchor and go out to sea, lest we should be driven ashore. The next morning found us in smooth water beneath an unclouded sky, nearing the goal of our long cherished desires, the far-famed Monte Santo of

the Greeks. As the wonderful outline of this beautiful promontory gradually unfolded itself, we perceived perched on
apparently inaccessible rocks the picturesque Monasteries of
Mount Athos.   On the side nearest to Thessaly, by which we
were approaching, the coast is exceedingly steep.   The rock
runs straight down into the sea, and there is no safe anchorage : it was therefore decided that the ambassador should go
ashore at once, lest the wind rising should make the landing
dangerous.   By this time we were close in, but not a vestige
of an inhabitant was to be seen.   The ladies petitioned to be
allowed to land, if only to be able to say they were the first
who had been there since the traditional visit of the Virgin
Mary ; for it was at least certain that no woman had been
allowed for centuries to contaminate the holy spot.   Permission
was given, and we were eagerly exploring the little landing
place when to our astonishment a procession of monks leading
several mules appeared suddenly and asked for the side-
saddles.   We pointed to the ship and said we had only landed
for a few moments and had no intention of invading their
sanctuary.   However, they insisted that the abbot up above
expected the ladies as well as the Elchi.   To refuse would be
discourteous, so to our intense delight we soon found ourselves
mounting the steep and rocky pathway which led to the
monastery.   As we passed under the gateway, the monks
turned aside, muttering ' It is forbidden.'   After this salve to
their conscience, they threw their scruples to the winds and
came forward most courteously to do honour to their ' forbidden ' guests.   We were regaled with coffee in the abbot's
own sanctum, and admired the glorious view from his window.

   " From this point our road ascending lay through groves
of magnificent Spanish chestnuts, changing, as we mounted
higher, into forests of oaks and pines.   On reaching the top
of the ridge which ends in the conical-shaped mountain from
which the whole district takes its name, we were able to look
down on the opposite side.   Here the character of the land-
scape is quite different : long undulating valleys and cultivated
meadows take the place of rocks and crags.   The utter
solitude was only once broken by a monk riding on a mule :
his countenance, when he perceived our party, was so expressive

of terror, and the energy with which he crossed himself so great, that we felt convinced that he took us for some apparition of the Evil One ; and his mule seemed to partake of the same feeling, for he crushed himself against the rock as he passed us by. We had not time to ascend the cone, but a lovely winding path brought us down just at sunset to one of the largest Ionian monasteries, Agios Paulos : the sound of the bells' ringing in the ambassador's honour reached our ears while still up in the mountains, and it was dark before we got back to the ship.

"Next morning, after laying to all night, for there was no anchorage, we landed again, and went all over this most picturesque building. The monks were in the refectory munching Indian corn by way of breakfast. The entire want of intellect in all the faces, young and old, struck one very painfully ; the monotony of daily toil, broken only by the still greater monotony of daily services, seemed to have crushed out all life and hope, and the beauties of nature which surrounded them had no power to raise them to a higher level.

"There are thirty monasteries on the promontory, and as we steamed slowly round, they appeared in every variety of unapproachable picturesqueness. We visited one other monastery, Vatopedi, which lies on the north side, and is very rich with the produce of its olive trees. Here too we were received with all courtesy. We went down into the huge cellars to see the vats full of oil. The dark mysteriousness of the place, lighted only by a single torch, which the old monk held above as he dipped his hand into the oil to shew us its beautiful clearness, was a scene worthy of Rembrandt.

"The next evening found us steaming back to the Dardanelles. Unfortunately a head wind delayed our speed and we arrived half an hour after sunset. As we had been clearly visible for some time with the ambassador's flag flying at the main, we thought of course that orders would have been given to let us pass ; but a sudden boom and a shot just in front of our bows forced us to alter our course, with the instant result of being imbedded in a sand bank. It took us two or three days to get over this mishap, for it was only by unshipping the guns and unloading the coal that the ship was at length set free. The delay, though provoking enough at the time, was utilized in a delightful expedition to the plains of Troy, which otherwise we should have missed. One more halt to enable us to visit the ruins of Cyzicus ; a lovely ride through luxuriant vineyards, where immense bunches of grapes were offered to us at each step ; a rapid sail across the Sea of Marmora ; and then in the early morning our eyes once again rested with admiration on the walls and minarets of Stambol and our first and only expedition became a thing of the past.

1852

ÆT. 65

" Not so the indignation which our admission to the sacred place excited in the minds of some of our friends of the Orthodox faith.   It was a long time before they could forget the fact that the permission we had received to land had been refused to a Russian archduchess. We could only suppose that our position as ' heretics ' rendered us harmless."

Another subject calls for remark. In 1851 the Earl of Derby (then Lord Stanley) invited Canning to join his cabinet, should he be summoned by the Queen to form one, as Secretary for Foreign Affairs.   In the following year the opportunity of carrying out this intention presented itself ; but to everyone's surprize Canning was left out of the ministry and Lord Malmesbury by some freak of fortune found himself dignified by the office which had been marked out by the popular voice for the Great Elchi.   It was rumoured that Russia objected to a strong man at the head of our Foreign Office, and Baron Brunov remarked openly that Canning's appointment if true was " une plaisanterie," and more, " une mauvaise plaisanterie."   The ambassador's share in the protection of the Hungarian and Polish refugees was certainly not calculated to recommend him to the autocratic Courts, and this circumstance, taken together with the arguments of those who dreaded the effects of Canning's imperious will both in the Cabinet and at the Office, may have induced the Premier to reconsider the offer.   It was a severe disappointment, and when Lord Derby thereupon offered him a peerage, he was on the point of refusing it, and only consented to become Viscount Stratford de Redcliffe on the understanding that the title was the reward of past services, and was in no degree a compensation for the Prime Minister's change of

1852
—
ÆT. 65

mind. The correspondence is here printed unreservedly, together with the comments of the ambassador's cousin, Lord Canning :—

From Lord
Stanley,
8 March,
1851

My dear Canning,—It is long since we have had any communication on public matters, but I am unwilling that you should learn by report, or indirectly, that which I have to communicate, and which it is very desirable that you should know, both with reference to the past and to the possible future. You will have heard, both by newspapers and by private channels, full details of our late, or I might almost call it our present, political crisis ; for, although the late government, after several failures, my own among the rest, to form an administration, have resumed their places, they are so intrinsically and externally weak, so little supported by Parliament and the country, and so divided among themselves, that I think it very doubtful whether they can stagger on through the present session, even with every forbearance exercised towards them on the part of their political opponents. It is therefore *possible*—I do not say probable—that before the end of the session I may again be called upon to try my hand ; and great as my difficulties would be, they would be far less at the close of a session, with a dissolution in hand, than at the beginning, with such a step, from the state of public business, impracticable. You will have seen that in my public statement I announced that one of my chief difficulties had been the administration of Foreign Affairs, in which in the first instance I had naturally been desirous of availing myself of Lord Aberdeen's long experience and general popularity with the corps diplomatique, and failing him, of your relation Lord Canning, Aberdeen's *alter ego*, and whom he (Aberdeen) strongly advised to accept the offer. But I could not state publicly that which I believe is hardly known to anyone ; that failing them, I had proposed to meet, and I hoped to overcome, this difficulty by making a temporary arrangement, until I should have had time to refer to you to ascertain whether you would have been disposed to give to the Government which I might have formed the advantage of your coöperation as Secretary of State for Foreign Affairs. I may say to you in strict confidence that I had named this intention on my part to the Queen, who spoke in terms of high praise of the ability which you had shewn in the diplomatic service, and of the great satisfaction you had given in your present post, which however it was understood you would not be sorry to leave ; so that I think I can promise that no difficulty would have been experienced in that quarter. Other difficulties prevented the formation of a government at that time, and it was therefore unnecessary to send off a special courier to you ; but it is due both to you and to

myself that you should not remain ignorant what had been my intentions, and that I had neither overlooked your fair claims nor been
unmindful of our old personal friendship. I could not but feel
however that the objection, always strong, to making a merely
temporary arrangement would have been much increased by my uncertainty whether, after all, the proposal which I had to make to you
would obtain your assent, and as I have already said that it is possible
I may again be called on within a few months, it would be very
satisfactory to me to be assured beforehand that if I were again in a
position to make you the offer, I should do so with the probability
of its being accepted. The Foreign Office is so much removed from the
consideration of questions of internal policy, and you have of late years
been so far separated from the turmoils of Parliament, that I should
not apprehend much difficulty in respect to general policy, even were
our opinions likely to differ more than I hope they would be found
to do ; but in truth parties are so much shattered and broken, and
there seems so general and growing a disposition towards fair and
moderate compromise on questions which have divided public men,
that I do not foresee any serious impediment in the way of the harmonious action of a cabinet, once launched, such as I should hope to
form : and every day's proof of the weakness of the present Government would tend to facilitate the formation of another. I believe it
would be necessary that in the first instance, at all events, you should
be in the House of Commons, where I am not, and where would be
our principal weakness ; but if it were an object to you, and the government went on, I might probably be enabled at no very distant period
to recommend your removal to another and a quieter sphere of action.
I need not say that the whole of this letter is written in the strictest
secrecy, and that I shall look anxiously for an early communication
from you in answer.

Believe me,
Yours very sincerely,
STANLEY.

My dear Stanley,—Your letter marked secret reached me yesterday
in original, and a few days before in duplicate. Be assured that I am
fully alive to all that it conveys of personal kindness and confidence,
to all that it implies of public responsibility and embarrassment.
The direction of the F. O., at any time serious, is in these times a
truly arduous undertaking, and I mistrust my own capacity too much
ever to have sought the charge. But neither would I shrink from it,
when offered by one like yourself in prospect of difficulties which
stimulate the sense of public duty. Your previous offer of it to
others, more worthy than I can presume to be, is a relief to my mind.

The character and experience of Aberdeen entitled him fully to the preference, and I should be sorry if any thought of me had cast a shadow on the path of my relation, who, besides his own claims to general esteem and private affection, is Canning's son. Looking to questions, it must be admitted that in the present state of parties and of opinions practical results are more considered than abstract principles. The country seems to require efficient rather than infallible ministers, a working reasonable cabinet rather than a strictly uncompromising one. If our foreign policy admits of any difference, it is rather in character and conduct than in principle ; and as to commercial matters, including their connexion with agriculture, no essential countermarch seems possible without a clear expression of the country's will in its favour. At all events the Government must in some way or other be carried on. If Lord John can neither maintain nor remodel his cabinet, and you continue unable to form a new one, it is evident into what hands we must fall, and what risk of confusion may ensue.

I have now said enough to convince you of my willingness to attend your summons. This, if I have entered into the spirit of your letter, is all you want to know from me at present. Your object is not to hasten the impending contingency, but to prepare for it. This is the view under which I propose to deal with my connexions here. They are purely diplomatic, admitting of my departure on reasonable notice, without breach of duty. More information will however be necessary for my guidance hereafter. It would be puzzling at this distance from home to take part in an election scramble, which, against your wishes, may possibly come on at any moment after Easter. Meanwhile the highest sanction in the realm, and your friendly reliance on my ability to justify it in a wider sphere than Turkey, are certainly great encouragements, though the turn of events in Parliament may or may not realize your flattering proposal. I can only say that with these inspirations I am prepared to do my best. The experiment will at least serve to declare my personal sentiments of old date towards you and in what degree I appreciate the Queen's difficulties and those of the country, together with your high-minded conduct in the midst of them.

Believe me, my dear Stanley,
Very sincerely yours,
STRATFORD CANNING.

My dear Sir Stratford,—I have not, I assure you, forgotten the handsome and friendly manner in which you responded last year to my call upon you for official coöperation, while engaged in an attempt, which proved abortive, to form a government ; and nothing would

have given me greater pleasure than to have been enabled, when
again summoned to attempt the same task, to avail myself of your
assistance, had you been still disposed to afford it. But the suddenness of the call made upon me, and the advantage, not to say the
necessity, of allowing neither hesitation nor delay, compelled me to
apply at once to those upon the spot ; and I may say that a favourable impression was produced upon the public mind by the fact that
the Cabinet was constituted and approved by the Queen within forty-
eight hours of my being first sent for. In addition to this, in the present
state of Europe, the Foreign Office was, of all others, that which could
least bear to be left in abeyance for a period of three or four weeks ;
and within that period, judging from last year, I could hardly have
hoped to have received your answer. I have not however been unmindful of your claims upon the country on the score of long and
able public service ; and in my first audience of her Majesty, I submitted to her the propriety of publicly recognizing them, by raising
you to the rank of a Viscount of the United Kingdom. The Queen
at once, and most readily, adopted the suggestion ; and it gives me
great pleasure, in offering this high honour to your acceptance, that
the first and only recommendation of the sort which I have made
(except of course the Lord Chancellor) should be one which meets at
once the claims of personal regard and of public service. As soon as I
learn your acceptance and the title you desire to take, I will give
directions for your patent to be prepared. I hear at the Foreign Office
that you have applied for, and obtained, leave of absence ; I hope
however that this letter may still find you at your post, that you may
quit it honoured by this mark of your Sovereign's high approbation.

Believe me,

My dear Sir Stratford,

Yours sincerely,

DERBY.

My dear Lord Derby,—The messenger, delayed at sea by bad
weather, did not bring me your letter till the day before yesterday.
I beg you will accept my warmest thanks for the kind and flattering
manner in which it is expressed. After our correspondence of last
year it was natural that I should expect to hear from you on the formation of a government by yourself ; and I will not profess an entire
freedom from disappointment on learning that my absence had
obliged you to relinquish your intention of naming me to the Queen
as Lord Granville's successor. But I am quite ready to acquiesce in
the soundness of your view. The immediate completion of a government was justly your paramount consideration under such critical
circumstances, and you would have paid me a poor compliment if

you had doubted my readiness to yield cheerfully to the public service any claim of mine. What little awkwardness has arisen from the general expectation of my appointment is much softened by the precarious state of power in England and the still prevailing idea of your arrangements being more or less *temporary*. Be that as it may, your very kind offer of a peerage, with the rank of Viscount of the United Kingdom, in respect of *past* services can be accepted only with mingled sentiments of pride and gratitude. Much, however, as I value so high a distinction, enhanced by the Queen's unhesitating assent as well as by your considerate attention to my credit in the time and manner of suggesting it, I could not with any satisfaction accept it as a substitute for effective office or as an honourable consignment to the shelf. So long as I am allowed to keep my health and faculties I hold it a duty to devote them to the public service whenever a proper occasion offers, and I feel assured that you will not lose sight of one who is honoured with your friendship and who has responded so frankly to your confidence.

I beg you will submit the expression of my humble and dutiful acknowledgments to the Queen. I cannot but entertain the deepest sense of her Majesty's generous condescension in publicly recognizing by so distinguished a mark of royal favour my past very imperfect endeavours in the service of the Crown.

To you, my dear Lord Derby, it would be idle for me to say more. I propose to stay here no longer than is necessary to receive the patent which you have kindly undertaken to order to be prepared on hearing affirmatively from me. Lord Malmesbury has met my wishes by sending me the leave of absence which I had asked of his predecessor.

Yours most devotedly,

S. C.

If you found a convenient opportunity to say a few words in parliament with reference to my elevation to the peerage, I should feel still further obliged by your taking advantage of it to place the matter before the public on its proper grounds.

During this last convulsion, I have had no communications with Lord Derby ;—and although I see Malmesbury frequently, our intercourse is confined to matters concerning the F. O., and has never extended to home politics or personal arrangements. So I can only guess at what may be the present condition of your relations with Lord D. I do indeed know that Malmesbury's position is permanent ; and I believe that Lord D. has written to you, offering the tardy justice of a peerage :—but beyond this I have no knowledge ; and as by this time you must have heard from Lord D. himself, I need not trouble you with my surmises. I only hope that the "heroic" Minister (I use your epithet and wish I could adopt it) has satisfactorily reconciled 1852 with 1851.

I cannot say how glad I am that you did not act upon your first impulse, and resign on Cowley's appointment. The stronger and more notorious your right to complain, the less the necessity of publishing it to the world by any act of your own. As it is, no one doubts that an injustice was done you ; whereas, if you had taken your cause into your own hands, I am sure that the act would have been severely criticized, and would have been viewed as one of pique and resentment and forgetfulness of public duty, and sympathy would, *pro tanto*, have ceased to be on your side. I make bold to say this unreservedly, because it appears to have been pretty nearly your own view of the matter when your final decision was taken. As regards Granville, I must in justice add that he said no more than was true when he spoke of the necessity of sending some one to Paris immediately. From what I have heard in other quarters, I believe it would have been quite impossible to leave —— in charge of the Embassy a single day longer than necessary.

The last paragraph refers to another instance of the indifference of the Government to Lord Stratford's claims ; but this time it was not the Tory administration but the Whig cabinet which preceded it. A pleasant letter from Lord Granville, who had replaced Palmerston at the Foreign Office, after the famous Normanby incident, opens the subject :—

If the freemasonry of Grillion's was not sufficient, the connexion between my father and your cousin, and the respect I have for one who has for so long a time held such a distinguished position among our diplomatists as yourself, makes me very happy in beginning a private correspondence with you. I am afraid our English political feelings are wide apart, but although this may, together with the necessity of choosing a man who could repair immediately to his post, have influenced H. M.'s Government in not offering the Paris Embassy to you, I hope it will be no bar to your writing to me most openly on all questions of foreign affairs and any points which affect your personal comfort.

From Lord
Granville,
5 Feb.

After forty-five years of diplomatic service, mainly spent at a spot peculiarly distasteful to him, Canning was entitled to the blue ribbon among embassies ; and as he was no party man, but had been appointed to various missions by both of the great political parties, Lord Granville's plea of diverging feelings upon home subjects was unavailing. It was a little galling to see one of his own assistants—the same Henry Wellesley, afterwards Lord Cowley, who had served under him at the Porte in 1846—raised to the dignity of ambassador at Paris, while his old chief remained buried at Stambol ; and according to the Dowager Lady Cowley no one was more surprized at the injustice than the fortunate diplomatist himself. Coming almost at the same moment as Lord Derby's retractation, the slight must have been irritating, but Canning, after a little reflection, submitted quietly to being passed over, and wrote in friendly terms to Lord Granville :—

To Lord Granville, 4 March
The kind remembrances with which you have opened a private correspondence with me must naturally influence the spirit of my reply. I trust indeed that a letter of mine which crossed yours on the way will have served to shew already that I am not insensible to such recollections. I should perhaps have been better pleased if circumstances had allowed you to give me the *option* of going to Paris, though rather in a diplomatic than a personal point of view. But I repress any tendency to act in that sense not only from consideration for you, but because I should be sorry to close my volume here with a semblance of *pique*, and more particularly because an abrupt step taken by me at this moment would place the public service as well as myself in a false position. Whatever may be the degree of difference between us on matters of home policy, I willingly accept your offer of confidence on foreign questions, and depend upon it that while we stand in our present relations towards each other I shall write to you respecting them, as I wrote in days of yore to your father's friend.

Events, however, were gradually forming into shape which must have made the Great Elchi feel that there were compensations for the loss of Paris and the Foreign Office, Had he been appointed to either, who was there in the whole roll of diplomacy that could take his place when the storm that was gathering burst in all its fury upon the Porte ? Hardly had he been away six months when there arose a universal cry for Lord Stratford to return and protect his ancient ward. Ministers bowed to the necessity. Probably neither Lord

Aberdeen nor the Foreign Secretary Lord John Russell was
personally eager to restore a man whom they could not understand and of whom they were half afraid : but no one else
could manage the Turks, and Lord Stratford, who had resigned
his embassy in January 1853, was begged to resume it and
start with as little delay as possible for the scene of action

1852

—

Æт. 65

CHAPTER XXIV.

THE RETURN OF THE GREAT ELCHI.

FEBRUARY—APRIL 1853.

1853
———
ÆT. 66

LORD STRATFORD'S conduct of the negotiations which preceded the Crimean war will probably stand as the cornerstone of his career. Seldom, indeed, has diplomacy enjoyed so wide and pregnant an occasion for the exercise of its powers as was then presented. From April to December 1853 the British Embassy at Constantinople was the depositary of a series of proposals, emanating from various sources, for the settlement of the dispute between Russia and the Porte. France, England, and Austria had each in turn its own special nostrum to heal the rupture. The four representatives at Vienna ran an eager race against the four ambassadors at Pera for the prize of solving the problem. Never, even in the history of diplomacy, was there such a bewildering succession of rival schemes, often crossing each other in the swift exchange of royal and imperial messengers; never was so much ink and paper lavished upon a simple issue,—never, said Lord Stratford, with happy disregard of Homeric conditions, since the Siege of Troy. Through all this tangled web, two men alone held the ends of the skein; two men knew exactly what they wanted, and resolutely kept to "the Question." Governments and ambassadors at St. James's, Paris, and Vienna might try their hands at notes, conventions, and declarations, which seemed to them to meet the exigencies of the case: but these two men instantly detected the flaw, and reverted to "the Question." One of them was the Emperor Nicholas, who, after a quarter of a century of moderation, had resolved to win for himself a predomi-

nating ascendancy over Turkey: the other was Viscount
Stratford de Redcliffe, who already possessed the very influence that was coveted by the Czar, and who had no intention
of allowing English prestige to be outshone by Russia.

It is essential to examine very jealously the whole course
of the intricate negotiations which centred round this main
issue. There are those who have laid to the charge of the
ambassador the blame, if blame it was, of bringing about the
Crimean war; and if it should appear from the documents
that he used his individual influence in such a manner as
to frustrate negotiations which, without sacrificing the main
Question, would have conduced to peace, then the blame must
be impartially awarded. If, on the other hand, the cumulative
evidence of his official and private papers proves that he
supported with all his great influence every proposal that
could possibly have brought about a reconciliation between
the two parties, without yielding the main Question, then let
there be no further talk of blame. "The Question," be it
understood, was *the Eastern Question*: in this case it took
the form of an attempt of Russia to obtain a recognized
ascendancy in Turkey by means of a new hold upon the
Greek subjects of the Ottoman Empire. That ascendancy,
in the opinion of every statesman in Europe, outside Russia,
was to be resisted at all costs. There was no divergence of
views upon this: Paris, London, Vienna, and even Berlin,
would have nothing to do with a Russian protectorate over the
Greek Church in Turkey, with all its obvious consequences.
The only debatable issue was how far this inadmissible protectorate or ascendancy was included in the original Russian
proposal, and how far it was eliminated in the various amendments thereto proposed at different times by the different
Powers. The point for Lord Stratford's biographer to ascertain is whether in resisting or suspending this or that proposal, and in supporting an alternative, the ambassador was
overstraining his suspicions of Russia and needlessly endangering the prospects of peace.

A few words must be said on the subject of authorities.
The official papers relating to this period have been published
in considerable detail. The volume of *Correspondence respect-*

ing the rights and privileges of the Greek and Latin Churches in Turkey (generally referred to under the title of *Eastern Papers*) for 1853 occupies nearly a thousand pages. Comparing the printed pages with the *brouillons* or drafts, I find that very few of Lord Stratford's despatches of any importance are omitted, and that in those that are published the excisions are trifling, and usually dictated by the well-known rule of the Foreign Office that sentences reflecting upon the sovereigns and ministers of friendly Powers must be cancelled. The ostensible despatches of an ambassador, however, are not necessarily the fullest commentaries on his conduct. Sometimes the really vital motive of a transaction is suppressed from prudential reasons. I have never found this to be the case with Lord Stratford's reports ; but, having a future Blue Book before his eyes, it was necessary that he should write more cautiously and reservedly in a paper intended to be laid before Parliament, than in private letters. His despatches contain the truth and nothing but the truth ; but sometimes one has to look further to be sure that it is the *whole* truth.   For this I have relied on his private correspondence with Lord Clarendon, the Foreign Minister. Writing confidentially to his chief, the ambassador was able to unbosom himself freely of all the doubts, difficulties, and suspicions that choked his progress.   Further, I have used the instructions given to, and the answering reports drawn up by, the dragoman who was the daily intermediary between the Embassy and the Porte.   In addition to these ample materials, the ambassador's private correspondence with Lady Stratford is a valuable guide.   Her letters during this eventful period shew that she worked hard in her own province as her husband's representative in London, and some of her interviews with Lord Clarendon and other ministers cast a vivid light upon the policy and proceedings of the Government.   The correspondence with Vice-Admiral Dundas, and with colleagues at other Courts, such as Lords Westmoreland and Cowley at Vienna and Paris, and Sir G. Hamilton Seymour at Petersburg, occasionally add something of importance to our information ; and some letters of Mr. Alison, the Oriental Secretary at Constantinople, furnish interesting details of the negotiations in which he was a prominent instrument. Few transactions can be cited which are exposed to a fiercer light than those which are recorded and reiterated in these various documents. Had Lord Stratford anything to conceal, it is hardly possible that he could have prevented its escaping through one or other of the many confidential channels to which his biographer has access, and of which he proposes to make a frank and unreserved use.

It has been suggested on the authority of the Russian Foreign Office,[1] with reference to a supposed understanding between Lords Stratford and Palmerston, that " if the private correspondence of these two statesmen could be known, it is probable that in it would be found the secret of all this Oriental crisis." The insinuation belongs to a long series of a similar character in the Russian official " history:" it is wholly false. Lord Stratford wrote twice to Lord Palmerston in 1853, on insignificant subjects, such as about a traveller who brought an introduction from the Home Secretary. There was no political correspondence between them. Indeed Lord Stratford had no leisure for anything beyond his official correspondence, and even his wife was often forced to be contented with a hurriedly written scrawl on a small half-sheet of note

---

[1] *Diplomatic Study on the Crimean War: Russian official publication* (Allen & Co., 1882), i. 211. This singular work, which is understood to represent the views of the Russian Foreign Office, is a most valuable contribution to the history of diplomacy, and the strongest testimony to Lord Stratford's penetration that could possibly be produced. In it the Russians stand condemned out of their own mouths. The astonishing frankness of the book, its bold confessions of error and deceit, are so startling that one is tempted to overlook its frequent and glaring misrepresentations. There is hardly one date to a dozen pages, and this omission in a history which to a great extent turns upon questions of exact dates is very convenient to the author's purpose. But the most curious feature in the work is the amazing ignorance it displays of documents which are within everyone's reach. It seems to have been written from imperfect recollections after an interval of years without any consultation of the authorities. Almost every page of the chapters on the negotiations at Constantinople and Vienna contains a serious misstatement —to use no harsher term—which a superficial study of the ordinary official papers is able to correct. If lie one must, it is a pity to lie in the face of established facts. Something may perhaps be allowed on the score of a bad translation. The English version abounds in blunders of spelling, and displays a very thorough ignorance of diplomatic names and acts; and the dates are given indifferently in Old and New Style to the confusion of an inexperienced reader. For a happy mixture of candour and misrecital of facts the book is perhaps unequalled; and it is not safe to trust a single paragraph of it unless supported by other evidence.

paper. Had Palmerston been Foreign Secretary, the Russian insinuation might have had some plausibility; but with Palmerston at the Home Office it would never have occurred to him to carry on a political correspondence. Though the two men held very similar views on foreign policy, the ambassador did not then entertain that full and friendly confidence in the "Firebrand" which would have led to private confidence.

The diplomatic transactions preceding the Crimean war fall naturally into three principal divisions. The first consists of the direct negotiation at Constantinople between Russia and Turkey through Prince Menshikov between March and May 1853, and concludes with the exchange of notes between Count Nesselrode and Reshid Pasha, and the consequent passage of the Pruth by the Russian troops. The second period is that of neither war nor peace, when Four Powers exhausted their ingenuity in devising remedies for the crisis; and it ends with the formal ultimatum of the Porte to the Russian general in the Principalities in October and the ensuing advance of the Allied squadrons into the Hellespont. The third includes the months during which Turkey waged war with Russia unaided, save by the mere presence of the fleets, and concludes when the affair of Sinope and the avenging entrance of the Allied squadrons into the Black Sea rendered all hopes of an accommodation futile. War was not declared till March 1854, but the advance into the Euxine at the beginning of January practically decided the question.

Everyone has read in the fascinating pages of Mr. Kinglake's first volume how the peace of Europe was disturbed on account of a door-key, a silver star, and the mending of a dilapidated dome. The historian of the British expedition to the Crimea has written with becoming gravity of the religious sentiment associated with these apparently trivial objects, but it requires all the impressive seriousness which he possesses to conceal the smile over the follies of poor humanity which lurks behind his narrative of the dispute about the Holy Places at Jerusalem. There was an old quarrel between the rival Greek and Latin Churches, as to which of them had certain, to us perhaps inappreciable, rights and privileges in the Sanctuaries of the Holy Land, and despite the impartial

police of the Turks many a sanguinary struggle had taken place
at Easter between the fanatics on the very site of the sacred
mysteries which both denominations revered.   France and
Russia espoused the rival causes of their respective Churches—
France from her policy of predominant influence in Syria,—
Russia partly from genuine religious fanaticism, partly because
she dreaded the weakening of her position as would-be protector of the Orthodox Church in the East, which it was her
constant ambition to establish.   In January 1842 the claims
of the two parties to repair the cupola of the Holy Sepulchre
came before the Porte, and Sir Stratford Canning, with his
usual good sense, advised the Turks to repair it themselves.
The question reappeared from time to time, and in 1850–2
attained alarming proportions.   M. de Lavalette, the French
ambassador, carried his remonstrances to the point of menace,
and a rupture seemed imminent.   The wise conciliation of the
Ottoman Government, however, calmed the hostile passions
of the claimants, and in March 1852 Canning was able to
report to Lord Malmesbury what he believed to be " the termination of the ill-advised and long-pending question of the
Syrian Sanctuaries." During his absence in England, however,
the dispute entered upon a new phase.   Russia, dissatisfied
with the arrangement proffered by Turkey, resolved to send
a special embassy to the Porte, and Prince Menshikov was
entrusted with the task of settling the pending difficulties as
to the Holy Places and obtaining satisfactory guarantees for
the future.   It was upon these guarantees that the problem of
peace or war turned.

There was seemingly little in this mission to rouse the
suspicions of the English Cabinet.   Russia had given explicit
assurances that Prince Menshikov was instructed merely to
obtain a satisfactory settlement of the Jerusalem dispute, that
he had no ulterior aims, and that his intentions were purely
pacific.   The question of a special convention, nominally to
guarantee the rights and privileges of the Greek Church
throughout the Ottoman dominion, really to establish Russian
ascendancy in Turkey, which formed part, and the essential
part, of the Prince's instructions, was not so much as hinted
at in the communications of the Czar's government with

1853

ÆT. 66

LVIII.
1852

England. There were rumours however of armed preparations in the south of Russia, and these, coupled with troubles
in Montenegro and the consequent despatch of Count
Leiningen to Constantinople with an Austrian ultimatum,
were enough to make the British Government anxious to have
Lord Stratford back at his post.   He had resigned his embassy
in January, and had fully made up his mind that he had seen
the last of the old place of exile : but under the circumstances,
with an Austrian and a Russian plenipotentiary on their ways
to Constantinople, a crisis in Montenegro, and an obscure
prospect in the religious dispute, he did not feel himself
justified in resisting the request of Lord Aberdeen and Lord
John Russell that he would resume his duties at the Porte.

Accordingly on 25 February 1853 he received his instructions.   It is an open secret that they were drawn up by his own
hand, or, as Lord Clarendon (who had just then taken
over the Foreign Office) put it, " largely borrowed " from the
ambassador's memorandum.   They are published in the
official *Correspondence concerning the rights and privileges of
the Greek and Latin Churches in Turkey* 1854 (No. 94, 8vo.
ed., pp. 83-6).   "At this critical period of the fate of the
Ottoman Empire " he was commanded by the Queen to return
to his embassy " for a special purpose and charged with special
instructions."   He was to counsel prudence to the Porte and
forbearance on the part of France and Russia.   He was to
neutralize by England's moral influence the alarming contingencies opened up by the demands of the two Powers and
the " dictatorial if not menacing attitude they had assumed."
On his way out he was to pause at Paris and Vienna.   At Paris
he was to dwell upon the identical interests of England and
France in the East, to further their " cordial coöperation in
maintaining the integrity and independence of the Turkish
Empire," and to point out the fatal embarrassment to which
that empire would be exposed if unduly pressed by the French
Government on the question of the Holy Places.   At Vienna
he was to express the pleasure of her Majesty's Government
at Austria's assurance that her friendly disposition towards
the Porte remained unchanged and her conservative policy
in the East would be strictly adhered to.   The Sultan was to

be assured of the friendly feelings of England, as proved by the return of an envoy so well disposed as Lord Stratford, and at the same time to be warned of the gravity of the situation which had compelled that return. He was left unfettered by special instructions for the settlement of the Holy Places' dispute : his own judgment and discretion might be trusted to guide him. The Porte was to be told that she had to thank her own maladministration and the accumulated grievances of foreign nations for the menacing tone now adopted towards her by certain Powers ; that a general revolt of her Christian subjects might ensue ; and the Sultan and his ministers were to be convinced "that the crisis is one which requires the utmost prudence on their part, and confidence in the sincerity and soundness of the advice they will receive from you, to resolve it favourably for their future peace and independence." He was to counsel reforms in the administration of Turkey, by which alone could the sympathy of the British nation be preserved.

" It remains " concluded the Foreign Secretary, " only for me to say that in the event, which her Majesty's Government earnestly hope may not arise, of imminent danger to the existence of the Turkish Government, your Excellency will in such case despatch a messenger to Malta, requesting the Admiral to hold himself in readiness, but you will not direct him to approach the Dardanelles without positive instructions from her Majesty's Government."

It has been insinuated that this final paragraph was worded so as to prevent the ambassador's impetuosity committing his Government by an indiscreet summons to the fleet : but there is ample reason to believe that the wording was his own ; and his whole conduct in reference to the squadron will be found to prove that he went behind his Government, rather than before it, in his desire for a naval demonstration. He had sufficient confidence in his method of pacific negotiation to be able to dispense with extraordinary powers for armed menace.

He started at once for Paris, accompanied by Mr. Alison, Mr. Layard (then Member for Aylesbury), Lord Pevensey (now Earl of Sheffield) and Count Pisani. They remained at

1853
—
Æt. 66

the French capital, intent upon gaining every possible insight into the policy of the Emperor, until the 17th, and during the interval some interesting communications from the ambassador reached his friends and the Foreign Office. It is clear that he had no suspicion of what was before him, that he anticipated an arrangement of the Holy Places' dispute, and dwelt most earnestly and also despairingly upon the prospects of reform in Turkey, which he believed the Russian ambassador would do his best to retard.   Thus he wrote to Lady Stratford :—

To his
Wife,
Paris,
March

The more I hear and the more I reflect on Turkish affairs the less reason do I see to reckon upon any success at Constantinople. France, I think, is inclined to move with us, and I question whether Russia even is ready to bring on a crisis, provided she be satisfied, which is by no means impossible, with respect to the Holy Places in Palestine.   But as to any real change in the Porte's system of administration, or the adoption of sound measures in a right spirit, I only don't despair because we live in miraculous times and because it would be too painful to go on without a glimmering of hope.

His impressions of Louis Napoléon and French policy are expressed in the following memorandum of a conversation which took place on 10 March :—

I had yesterday the honour of dining with the Emperor and Empress of the French. The dinner was served in the *Galerie de Diane* at the Tuileries. On returning to the drawing-room after dinner the Emperor took me into an adjoining apartment, and, when we were seated, entered into conversation at some length, though rather in a desultory manner, on political affairs.

He began by expressing his satisfaction at finding that there was nothing to prevent the two Governments from acting together in the East, and that both agreed in wishing to uphold the Ottoman Empire. He seemed to think that Austria had treated the Porte rather sharply in the late transactions at Constantinople, and he made some inquiries respecting what I understood to have been settled about the Turkish claims in the *Bocche di Cattaro*. He spoke of the Holy Places, and threw the blame of engaging in that question on the *parti prêtre* of the Montalembert school and the Legislative Assembly. He desired nothing better than to finish the affair. He was not disposed to make difficulties so long as his honour was uncompromised ; and he would not object to the maintenance of the

Sultan's firman, supposing France to retain what had been previously accorded. He talked of Egypt as having been an object of some difference between the two Governments. He understood that we only wanted the railway for our communications with India, and he had declared his mind to those who seemed to forget that England, not France, possessed extensive territories in that country. He said that he had no wish to make the Mediterranean a *French* lake,—to use a well-known expression,—but that he should like to see it made an *European* one. He did not explain the meaning of this phrase. If he meant that the shores of the Mediterranean should be exclusively in the hands of Christendom, the dream is rather colossal. Syria came next into consideration. I recommended a strict adherence to existing arrangements. He acquiesced, like a man who knew little of the subject. He shewed some curiosity respecting the Sultan's character, nothing that implied belief in the probability of Turkish regeneration. The Emperor then touched upon several topics unconnected with the East. He spoke of the refugees in England, more particularly of those in the Channel Islands, of the reproaches addressed to him by the English press, of the fears manifested in England of an invasion, of his position with respect to the Bourbons, and also of the famous *coup d'état*, by which he had cleared his way to the throne. In touching on these delicate subjects his language was moderate, his tone rather deprecatory than aggressive. In December 1851 he had acted from necessity. He was surprized at being suspected of hostility to England. His sentiments, on the contrary, were favourable to a country where he had received so many marks of hospitality and kindness. There was not, to be sure, much sentiment in politics, which generally turned on points of interest ; but if there were no differences, no grounds of quarrel, why should there be any hostile feeling ? The Press in England had treated him with much asperity, and the refugees, on account of their vicinity and malevolence, were naturally a cause of annoyance to him. He traced to them a recent design upon his life, which had been frustrated by the vigilance of the police. He remarked that the Comte de Chambord, though himself a quiet, inoffensive man, was pushed on by the more active spirits around him, and he added that the existence at former periods of a pretender to the British throne had for the time unsettled the friendly relations between France and England. He spoke contemptuously of orators, naming, by way of example, Berryer and Odillon Barrot, as men who, in the display of their talents, overlooked the real point in question. He talked with confidence of his hold on public opinion, especially in the provinces, saying that he required no guards, and could go alone into the most retired streets of Paris with safety.

1853
———
ÆT. 66

Reverting for a moment, as he rose and walked towards the Empress's drawing-room, to the affairs of Turkey, he declared his wishes to be in favour of Turkish independence and the progress of civilization.

Throughout our conversation it was my object rather to learn the Emperor's opinions than to hazard any of my own, especially on topics not relating immediately to the East. I endeavoured, nevertheless, as occasions offered, to impress on his mind the urgency of an effective reform in Turkey, and his obligation, in respect of the Holy Places, to be foremost in concession, as France had been the first to raise that embarrassing question. I ventured also to remind him of the means employed, however unavoidably, for the establishment of his power, and of the shock which the employment of such means had naturally given to the moral sentiments of England ; that in proportion as the resort to such extremities should be compensated by good results and by the prospect of better, public opinion would recognize its necessity and people would place more confidence in the principles of his government. Referring to the earnest assent which he had previously given to a remark of mine, purporting that every nation had a common interest in the general prosperity, I observed that, order being the basis of prosperity, we beheld its establishment under his auspices with satisfaction, and looked to the working of his government for the maintenance of that tranquillity in his empire, and of that peace throughout Europe, with which our best interests were indissolubly connected. With respect to the refugees I drew his attention to the late proceedings in Parliament, and brought them to his consideration in proof of our sincere intentions to do all that the institutions of the country permitted in order to give the full benefit of English law to those friendly Governments who were exposed to the machinations of the refugees. The sacredness of the right of asylum in a country like England, and the broad principle of humanity on which it rested, were not after all to be overlooked. Foreign States could hardly with justice complain of its exercise when the sovereign of the country enjoyed no better security than what was accorded by law to them and their rulers.

To Lord
Clarendon
II.
14 March

The impression left upon my mind by the conversation thus recorded is that Louis Napoléon, meaning to be well with us, at least for the present, is ready to act politically in concert with England at Constantinople ; but it remains to be seen whether he looks to the restoration of Turkish power, or merely to the consequences of its decay, preparing to avail himself of them hereafter in the interest of France. As it appears, moreover, that the maintenance of his own personal position is the mainspring of his policy, he is not likely to adopt without necessity any change of institutions calculated to give room for the play of influences adverse to his Government, nor can he be expected to abstain from any attempt required in his judgment by the circumstances of the time to consolidate his power or to avert any danger that may threaten its continuance. It may, therefore, be doubted whether his coöperation even in the East can be accepted by us without some shades of caution ; nor would it apparently be safe to rely upon his goodwill, unable as her Majesty's Government must be to remove all causes of difference with him, unless our means of defence be improved.

To Lord
Clarendon,
15 March

I or those with me have seen a number of celebrities belonging to the past or present day during our week of stay here. In general, as might have been expected, the Emperor is a blackamoor to the former and almost an angel of light to the latter. His adversaries say that his system has no basis and cannot last. His votaries ground their hope of its continuance on the difficulty of finding a substitute. All agree in thinking that he means it to last, and some are of opinion that he will stick at nothing to make it last.

It is an awful thing for a sovereign to be separated from all the talents and almost from all the moral principle of his country. In a highly civilized age and country the position is monstrous, except as a dictatorship required by special circumstances. It is so unnatural that it falsifies all the relations of the State in which it exists, and disturbs even the sympathy of national interests between one Power and another. Notwithstanding the present dispositions of this Government towards England, friendly as they seem to be, and probably are, you will find it difficult, I fear, in the long run to reckon with confidence on French connexion as a stable element of resistance to any dangerous combination of the anti-constitutional powers.

While at Paris, Lord Stratford received ominous news from Constantinople. Matters had apparently become so menacing that the chargé d'affaires, Colonel Rose, had taken the grave step of summoning the Mediterranean squadron to Vourla. Vice-Admiral Dundas refused to move without express orders from the Government, and his refusal was approved. The French, however, were more adventurous, and hastily despatched their fleet to the Gulf of Salamis : a movement which had considerable influence upon the question of peace or war. Lord Clarendon's opinion is given with sufficient clearness in the following letter to Lord Stratford :—

Lord Westmoreland will shew you the despatches containing the latest intelligence from Constantinople and the views of the Government upon it, as well as the communications we have had with the French Government. Rose acted hastily in sending for the fleet, and Admiral Dundas very discreetly in not quitting Malta without orders from home. The French Government have come to a precipitate decision in ordering their fleet to sail, but it will not go further than Salamis. Why it goes at all they are rather puzzled to say. After all the solemn and personal assurances given to us by the Emperor of Russia, it would have been utterly unjustifiable on our part to doubt his word, and we do therefore believe that the independence and integrity of the Turkish Empire are not endangered by the mission of Prince Menshikov.

It is certainly unfortunate that you should not have been on the spot when he arrived. Your experience and position might have kept matters in a right direction, and prevented both Russian and Turkish ebullitions, from which mischief is still to be apprehended. You know what importance Russians attach to rank, and that Prince Menshikov is therefore not likely to have paid much attention to the chargés d'affaires who represented England and France at this critical moment of Turkish affairs. I am sure under the grave circumstances of the case you will not lose an unnecessary moment in getting to Constantinople.

Admiral Dundas despatched a steamer immediately there to inform Colonel Rose that the fleet *would not come.*

Leaving Paris on 17 March, the Embassy entered upon a journey which was a series of mishaps :—

We are not fortunate, dearest E. We left Paris, as you know, at half-past 7 on Thursday evening, meaning by a strong exertion to reach Vienna to-morrow morning. Between Mannheim and Frankfort the train was accidentally—one could almost suspect designedly—delayed from want of water for the boiler, and we were obliged most reluctantly to pass the night of Friday at Frankfort. We have since struggled on night and day to overtake the night train, even at the expense of an express from Weimar to Leipzig. The difficulty of obtaining correct information in these small German States is great, and I fear that it will not be possible for us to reach Prague in time for the night train to Vienna. The consequence will be the loss of a whole day, and no chance of being able to do anything before Tuesday. How much in war must depend on fortune, when so slight an accident as this of ours can change the course of a journey ! . . .

As for me, when I am not reading or sleeping, and at times when

I am, my thoughts are divided between London and Paris, Vienna and Constantinople. The latter, as we move on, acquires the right to them, and I am very anxious to know more and to be on the spot. At Vienna we shall probably get some further intelligence. If the Menshikov act of the play continues till we reach the Bosphorus, there may be room for much. If not, it may, perchance, be as well for me to have been out of the way. *Bakalum !*

Brünn, Monday, 3 P.M.—We arrived here half an hour ago only to stick fast for an uncertain length of time at a distance of about ninety miles from Vienna. The weather is milder, but there is much snow, and the road is fairly blocked up ahead. They tell us that people are at work to make a passage, and we shall start as soon as they have succeeded in making one. Meanwhile we have patience for our only resource beside the *Restauration* in which I am writing. It is lucky that we did not take an express train from Prague. The result would have been an earlier stoppage here, and a heavy expense to no purpose. We have exhausted our meagre library, and there is no news to be had. Alison is better, but not right. The others, including the *Elchi,* owe their ill looks to want of shaving and washing. It must be allowed that there are serious drawbacks on the advantage of railway travelling. The hurry, the noise, the jostling, the confusion of tongues and persons, the dirty accommodations, the bad food, the ignorance of what one passes through, have all to find their compensation in the single advantage of speed. Accidents, however, are less frequent on the Continent than with us ; but we spare our lives and limbs at the sacrifice of a large proportion of that main object.

Tuesday morning.—Still at Brünn, but rumours of deliverance in four or five hours. We are lodged in a spacious hotel, accidentally full to the bewilderment of its *one* waiter. We are as warm as German stoves can make us, washed, shaved, and decently attired—fit, in short, for transfer to a civilized metropolis. Our rooms are uncommonly well supplied with bells, and each bell has an inscription over it. "Once for the waiter, twice for the chambermaid, three times for Boots," and so on. Unluckily every pull is not a ring, so that the most observant traveller may bring up the maid instead of the waiter, or Boots instead of the maid, quite innocently. The Count is for ever pulling, and somehow or other it is always the girl who appears. He has met with a friend from Paris three days older in detention than ourselves. This is a real consolation, and puts in a strong light the disadvantages and utter uselessness of despatch. No news of any kind : an old German newspaper, stewed to rags, has yielded a report that Menshikov's Ultimatum had been rejected. But the statement is immediately followed by a contradiction. *Que faire ? Que penser ?*

Vienna, Wednesday morning.—Here at last ! We got in between 8 and 9 yesterday morning. A tiresome journey from Brünn, by a monster train, and through avenues of snow which fully justified our delay. The fall of snow must have been great indeed, for even the streets are crowded with large heaps of it, and the road towards Trieste was not open yesterday. We expect despatches from Stambol to-day. A note of the 7th from Rose to Westmoreland rather puzzles than enlightens us. I had my talk with W. last night. He is just what he always is—slatternly in politics, infinitely good-natured, and 6 ft. 3 in. tall. He wants us all to dine with him to-morrow—a temptation, for our friend, the Herzog von Karl, where we are lodging, is not happy in his cookery. I am to see Count Buol, I suppose, to-day, and perhaps the Emperor to-morrow. H. I. M. is about again. It appears that he was all but given up for several hours. The blow was an awful one, and his escape quite providential. The stories of a popular movement against us are utterly groundless. The universal civility which we experienced on the road followed us to the very door of the hotel. There will be no *serious* refugee question. I have a few, but very few, private visits to make :— Metternich, Esterhazy, Von Hammer, and Lady William Russell, who is under this roof.

After interviews with the Emperor and Count Buol, the ambassador was able to report that the views of the Austrian Government in reference to Turkey appeared to coincide with those of her Majesty's Cabinet ; that the Emperor was not acquainted with any ulterior object for Prince Menshikov's mission beyond the settlement of the Holy Places' question ; and that, except in regard to the enthusiastic reception accorded to Kossuth and Mazzini and other " rebels " in England, the feelings of Austria to Great Britain were friendly. Writing to his wife on the 28th he said :—

I found it easier to leave Vienna than Paris, but not without using up a day or two more than I had intended. . . . In both capitals the functions of Government are so much concentered after a succession of singular incidents that I wished not to pass on without learning all I could of the real character and future prospect of those in power. The thing most evident is that in France and Austria, as in Russia, ministers and parliamentary institutions are completely in discredit. The one sovereign will is thought to be the best

1853
—
ÆT. 66

depositary of power, and those who think otherwise have mainly to thank themselves for the success of that opinion. In France the Emperor, in Austria the Empire, owes more to negative than to positive causes. Louis Napoleon keeps down the inconvenient and unpopular pretensions of several others. The different portions of the Austrian Empire are incapable of an independent existence.

This does not apply to the Italian parts of it ; but all the others find an interest in keeping them in submission and hate those who meddle in a contrary sense. . . . It is painful to note how the best hopes of improvement have been quenched by the follies and crimes of the democratic party—that is for the present—and Heaven knows for how long. The Emperors look to their armies, and nothing more costly or burthensome exists under the sun. I am half inclined to think that our business, as things now stand, is to look rather to international than to political sympathies—to the relations of material interest as between country and country, and not so much to forms of internal government. Our example does most, perhaps, for the cause of free institutions when we abstain from making proselytes or encouraging disaffections. We stand greatly in need of friends and are more likely to feel an increase than a diminution in the want. I have borne this in mind in all my communications with Vienna and Paris, I should hope not entirely without effect.

The journey to Trieste was not accomplished without difficulty.

We resumed our journey on Saturday. We crossed the Sommerang by moonlight. Four hours, bitter cold, over snow. The stars however were visible and the wind did not annoy us. Next day we railed it away through Gratz and Laibach : a slow process with frequent interruptions through a wilderness of snow. At Laibach warm rooms, dinner, and carriages awaited us, which made a pleasant though brief episode. At Gratz I could not stop to see the Archduke John, as I had intended. So I sent Acland's book to him with a highly respectful epistle of excuses for myself. It was a disappointment to me ; but it could not be otherwise. Railways are really good for nothing except to go blindfold from place to place with superior velocity, and here the latter advantage is not always to be had. We saw the town and village people going to their Easter church services, many of them in country costumes recalling the memories of a bygone age ; but the train hurried us along as a set of outcasts having naught to do with religion or with home. At 9 P.M. we mounted our carriages and entered upon the last portion of our journey. . . . Each carriage had four horses. The journey was to be

To his
Wife,
Prewald in
Carniola,
28 March

1853
—
Æt. 66

performed in ten hours, so that we reckoned on reaching the hotel at Trieste, prepared for our arrival, at 7 next morning. We soon found the snow much worse than we expected, fresh supplies falling to augment what was already on the ground. A strong north wind, a Borer, sprang up and save the clouded presence of the moon the night was most forbidding. On we toiled however, more slowly as we advanced until we overtook the post Eilwagen, drawn for *better speed* by oxen, which had at least the advantage of opening the road for us. After a long struggle of eleven hours we reached this place, 412 posts from Laibach, 212 posts from Trieste. Here we learnt that the mail from Trieste had been obliged to turn back, that our own post companion would go no further, and that we must stick here too. Our spirits rebelled, and King went forth to find a posse of peasants who would clear the snow away and help our carriages through. This fair appearance soon melted away. It was ascertained that two travellers from Trieste had been forced to return on horseback, leaving their carriages on the road, and that the carriages were fairly buried in the snow. Nothing remained but resignation to the will of Providence, and we are now waiting for the wind to go down and the road to be cleared.

To Lord
Clarendon,
29 March
-

Such a road from Vienna ! We were again snowed up in company with the mails, and travelled night and day with severe colds to no purpose. I am too old and tough to be the worse from this, but younger constitutions find it trying.

Meanwhile I cannot doubt your having judged rightly about the squadron. Russia, without meaning downright mischief just now, is probably seeking to restore her old prepotential influence, and unfortunately France has given her the opportunity. She has the vantage ground with respect to the Holy Places, and there would be little wisdom in tempting her further. She will, however, in my humble judgment, require to be closely looked after, especially as she has found so able an advocate in the *Times*.

I wonder that France should have sent her squadron upwards on a mere presumption of your doing the same. Alas ! the mischief done in politics by petty or oblique motives.

To his
Wife,
Sea of
Marmora,
4 April

We started from Trieste on Wednesday at 11 A.M., we entered the Archipelago on Saturday night, and we passed the Dardanelles this (Monday) morning at an early hour. Stephen Pisani is on board. He has been giving me all the news, and if things have remained at Constantinople as he left them more than a week ago there will be no lack of difficulty. The Russian demands and accompanying demonstrations seem to mean the acquirement once for all of a preponderating influence with all the Greeks in their train, or some act of territorial encroachment by way of substitute. The Turks are alarmed, the Greeks excited, the Sultan *as usual*, and his ministers fluctuating between their fears and better feelings. . . . I also learn that the Grand Vezir, though negotiating secretly with Prince Menshikov, intends to wait for my arrival before taking a decision. If he can stick to this resolution, I leave you to guess with what feelings of interest the appearance of H.M.S. *Fury* will be hailed to-morrow morning from both sides of the Golden Horn. The prospect is more than enough to make one nervous ; but there is hope to be derived from the best of books, and possibly a pebble from the brook by the wayside may be found once more the most effectual weapon against an armed colossus. My pebble is the simple truth, but I must stoop to pick it up where the heavens lie reflected on smooth flowing water. Do you understand my metaphors ?

Here is one of the reports, not remarkable for good English, which reached him from Constantinople :—

We seem positively threatened at this moment by a *grand coup de main* on the part of Russia, notwithstanding the *langage mielleux* held to this moment by the Russian *Dictator*, who, I understand, works first to form a Turkish Ministry of *his* choice and then put forward his frightful demands, such as, they say,

Revision of their treaties.

Cession of the disputed territory on the coast of Circassia.

Question of Jerusalem.

Question of Montenegro.

A sort of 'protectorat' over the Christian Raya population.

A sort of 'protectorat' over the Greek Patriarchate here.

Expulsion of the Hungarian and Pole emigrants, &c. &c. &c.

The Turks, to begin from the *highest*, seem seized with an extraordinary fright, and rumours are spread by the Russians of England and France being understood with Russia on the object of this Mission !!!

The arrival of your lordship is looked for with the *greatest* possible anxiety, and it will have to give to the Turks *le signe de vie ou de mort*. They seem to rely *entirely* upon that. The Sultan himself, I am assured, is getting very anxious about your arrival.

The *immediate* apparition of our fleet towards the Dardanelles would, no doubt, operate very favourably and efficiently in our sense ; and it would, perhaps, be the only means of checking the Russian torrent which, from all appearances, seems ready to overflow.

Finally, your Excellency will arrive at a *most critical and interest-*

1853
—
Æt. 66

ing time for Turkey and perhaps also for Europe ; and we all hope and trust that Divine Providence will inspire your lordship with whatever measures may be necessary for the general good.

Official accounts from Odessa report unusual military and naval preparations in those parts, and commercial advices state the same in regard to Bessarabia and the Azov.

It is very *remarkable* that the Prince Menshikov is accompanied by the commanders-in-chief of those forces.

It appears evident this time that the solution of the Gordian knot devolves on your Excellency. May it please the Almighty to do for the best.

To his
Wife.
Tuesday
evening,
my own
study in
the Palace

How strange ! and without you ? It cannot be, yet so it is. We got into port soon after daylight. A glorious morning—the domes and minarets towering above the mist and over each the crescent glittering in sunlit gold. I dressed and went on deck. Soon the old faces began to appear—Hardy, Black, Hanson, Skene, &c. &c. &c. Then came what would have brought your hands to your ears,—a row of saluting reverberated by a thousand echoes. The Colonel came on board, attachés also,—Hughes radiant, Smythe lambent,—a new uncouth cub. After a time old Duz Oghlu appeared, not a smile or a wrinkle the less. He kissed my hand, he inquired after you, he assured me of the Sultan's regard. . . . At 11 we landed under a salute from the *Tiger*, at Tophana on the place d'armes ; a crowd of English, Ionians, and Maltese were collected there. They received me with three shouts, which brought tears into my eyes, and made my horse very skittish ! The horse, richly caparisoned, had been sent to me by Rif'at with a dozen kavasses, and up the hill we went, followed by a long train and through ranks of people greeting the old ambassador. We reached the palace in due course ; I dismissed my friends with a speech, the pattern of brevity, and here I am, Heaven help me !

Invasion
of the
Crimea,
i. 128

"On the morning of the 5th of April, 1853" says Mr. Kinglake "the Sultan and all his ministers learned that a vessel of war was coming up the Propontis, and they knew who it was that was on board. Long before noon the voyage and the turmoil of the reception were over, and, except that a corvette under the English flag lay at anchor in the Golden Horn, there was no seeming change in the outward world. Yet all was changed. Lord Stratford de Redcliffe had entered once more the palace of the British Embassy. The event spread a sense of safety, but also a sense of awe. It seemed to bring with it confusion to the enemies of Turkey, but austere reproof for past errors at home, and punishment where punishment was due, and an enforcement of hard toils and painful sacrifices of many kinds, and a long farewell to repose. It was the angry return of a king whose realm had been suffered to fall into a danger."

CHAPTER XXV.

PRINCE MENSHIKOV'S MISSION.

APRIL–MAY, 1853.

1853
———
ÆT. 66

*Eastern
Papers,* I.
No. 136

THE ambassador had his suspicions of what had been going on in his absence. He was of course in possession of all the correspondence of the Embassy, and was aware from Colonel Rose's reports to the Government that Prince Menshikov had mooted much more serious matters than the custody of a key at a Sanctuary; that he had suggested a Turko-Russian defensive alliance, whereby a fleet and 400,000 of the Czar's troops would be at the service of the Porte to help her against any Western Power; and he had demanded secretly "an addition to the Treaty of Kaynarji, whereby the Greek Church should be placed entirely under Russian protection, without reference to Turkey, which was to be the equivalent for the proffered aid above mentioned. Prince Menshikov had stated that the greatest secrecy must be maintained relative to this proposition, and that, should Turkey allow it to be made known to England, he and his Mission would instantly quit Constantinople." So the Grand Vezir told Colonel Rose (1 April), and his Highness added that "nothing whatever should be added to the Treaty of Kaynarji; that he would ask to retire from office rather than agree to either of the two propositions made by Prince Menshikov, which would be fatal to Turkey." The statement is important as shewing that the dangerous character of Prince Menshikov's proposals was fully understood by the Turkish ministers before Lord Stratford's arrival, and that they said they were resolved to resist them before the Englishman had had a single conversation with them on the subject.

A peculiar inconvenience of the Russian demands was the mixture of the reasonable with the inadmissible. Russia was within her right in her claims about the Holy Places, but the granting of these just claims was to be comprised in a document having the force of a treaty and including certain guarantees for the future which, though introduced *à propos* of the Holy Places, had a much wider application than the Sanctuaries in Palestine : the trick was ingenious, and, as Lord Stratford remarked, " Jacob's voice and Esau's hand were never more skilfully combined." The issue of firmans according or confirming certain privileges in the Holy Places presented no special difficulty, if France could be induced to accept a compromise; but a general guarantee of the rights and privileges of the Greek Church in Turkey, conveyed *to Russia alone* among the Great Powers in a formal treaty, meant nothing less than endowing the Czar with the right to interfere in almost any matter relating to the twelve or thirteen thousand members of the Greek Church who were subjects of the Porte ; in other words it meant the surrender of the Eastern Question. Lord Stratford perceived the complication instantly, and cut the knot with characteristic sagacity. In the interview which he had with the Grand Vezir and Rif'at Pasha, the Foreign Secretary, on the day after his landing ,he said, " Endeavour to keep the affair of the Holy Places separate from the ulterior proposals, whatever they may be, of Russia. The course which you appear to have taken under the former head was probably the best ; and I am glad to find that there is a fair prospect of its success to the satisfaction of France as well as of Russia. Whenever Prince Menshikov comes forward with further propositions, you are at perfect liberty to decline entering into negotiation without a full statement of their nature, extent, and reasons. Should he ground them on any existing treaty, it would be equally incumbent on him to afford a full explanatory statement in the first instance. Should they be found on examination to carry with them that degree of influence over the Christian subjects of the Porte in favour of a foreign Power which might eventually prove dangerous or seriously inconvenient to the exercise of the Sultan's legitimate authority, his

1853

ÆT. 66

Majesty's ministers cannot be denied the right of declining them, which would not prevent the removal, by direct sovereign authority, of any existing abuse, or the more strict execution by the Porte 'itself of any treaty engagement affording to Russia a fair ground of remonstrance."

What Lord Stratford thus sketched out was precisely what happened. The Holy Places' dispute was satisfactorily arranged; the "ulterior proposals" were refused; and the privileges and rights of the Christians were guaranteed "by direct sovereign authority" and not by an instrument addressed exclusively to Russia.

We need not enter into the details of the negotiation respecting the Holy Places. This was not the critical part of the affair, and Russia acknowledged that the British ambassador had contributed to the happy termination of this misunderstanding. He had, in point of fact, brought the French and Russian representatives together, and a brief discussion face to face in the Elchi's presence had sufficed to remove all remaining points of difference. " I thought," he wrote, "it was time for me to adopt a more prominent part in reconciling the adverse parties." And as Mr. Kinglake says, he was more than equal to the task. " Being by nature so grave and stately as to be able to refrain from a smile without effort and even without design, he prevented the vain and presumptuous Russian from seeing the minuteness and inanity of the things which he was gaining by his violent attempt at diplomacy. For the Greek Patriarch to be authorized to watch the mending of a dilapidated roof—for the Greek votaries to have the first hour of the day at a tomb—and finally for the doorkeeper of a church to be always a Greek, though without any right of keeping out his opponents,—these things might be trifles, but awarded to All the Russias through the stately mediation of the English ambassador, they seemed to gain in size and majesty; and for the moment, perhaps, the sensations of the Prince were nearly the same as though he were receiving the surrender of a province or the engagements of a great alliance. On the other hand, Lord Stratford was unfailing in his deference to the motives of action which he had classed under the head of ' French feelings of honour;' and if M. de la Cour

E. P. I.
150

*Inv.
Crim.*
i. 144-5

was set on fire by the thought that at the Tomb of the Virgin, or anywhere else, the Greek priests were to perform their daily worship before the hour appointed for the services of the Church which looked to France for support, Lord Stratford was there to explain, in his grand quiet way, that the priority proposed to be given to the Greeks was a priority resulting from the habit of early prayer which obtained in Oriental Churches, and not from their claim to have precedence over the species of monk which was protected by Frenchmen. At length he addressed the two ambassadors ; he solemnly expressed his hope that they would come to an adjustment. His words brought calm. In obedience, as it were, to the order of Nature, the lesser minds gave way to the greater, and the contention between the Churches for the shrines of Palestine was closed. The manner in which the Sultan should guarantee this apportionment of the shrines was still left open, but in all other respects the question of the Holy Places was settled."

With the ulterior proposals however it was otherwise. At first the Turkish Foreign Secretary was afraid to reveal the full extent of Prince Menshikov's demands to the Elchi. No doubt Rifat stood in wholesome dread of the ambassador's lash, with which he had long been intimately acquainted ; but the chief reason for his reticence was the menacing tone adopted by the Russian envoy, as appears from the two following reports of Stephen Pisani, first dragoman to the British Embassy :—

All my endeavours to induce Rifat Pasha to let me have a copy of the *Note Verbale* given in by Prince Menshikov proved fruitless. He even refused to let me see it, and pretends that the Note in question was drawn up in Turkish ; whereas I can assure your lordship that it is not the case, because I have ascertained from good authority that the original of the Note containing the several demands of Russia was drawn up in French, and it is carefully kept by Rifat Pasha himself. Having pressed upon his Excellency to comply with my request, he finally told me very plainly that he was not authorized to communicate the papers presented by the Russian Embassy to anyone, and were he to do so, that would have for certain the effect of giving cause to a suspension of relations between the Russian Embassy and the Porte. I observed to his Excellency that his behaviour on this occasion was an unequivocal proof of his want of confidence in the British Embassy, and in that case he could not expect to be furnished with a correct opinion or advice upon the question at issue, as long as the papers were not communicated and properly examined.   Upon which Rifat Pasha repeated again his assurances of confidence and high consideration for your lordship, and told me that the matter at presents stands thus.   Mr. Argyropoulos called this afternoon to urge him on behalf of the Prince for an answer about the proposals of Russia and demanded an interview for Saturday.   Mr. Argyropoulos added that, as Prince Menshikov foresees that the question of the Holy Places will take some time before it could finally be settled, he wished at least to forward the other points at issue and bring them to a fair conclusion.   The demands upon which Prince Menshikov insists are the following :—

He demands to have the privileges formerly granted by the Porte to the Patriarchates and the Greek clergy confirmed in a treaty to be concluded between Russia and the Porte ; the right to Russia of interfering in matters connected with the Orthodox religion, and *an exclusive protectorate over those who profess it*, and the appointment of the Greek Patriarch of Constantinople for life, and independent of the Porte's sanction.   What they want, in fact, is a revision of the Treaty of Kaynarji, which they say is not explicit enough. . . .

Rifat Pasha pretends that he said to Mr. Argyropoulos, that if what Russia demands from the Porte was, as they contend, grounded upon some undoubted right, why do they so earnestly recommend secrecy ? This circumstance alone, added he, rouses suspicion and makes the Porte cautious of the line she is to follow.

While I was taking leave of Rifat Pasha, he entreated me most urgently to call again to-morrow and let him know what answer he was to give to Prince Menshikov when he calls on Saturday.   I replied to his Excellency that I thought your lordship could not give any correct opinion or advice upon a subject the bearings of which are not thoroughly known to you. . . .

8 April   The Grand Vezir informed me that the Council, after I left the Porte, had unanimously decided that the demands put forward by Russia were inadmissible and the grant of them would be tantamount to a distinct division of the empire, and they came to the conclusion that the answer to be given to the Russian ambassador at the interview which is to take place to-morrow at Rifat Pasha's house would be, that until the pending question of the Holy Places was definitively brought to a solution, the Porte could not enter into any new discussion respecting the other points which remain to be examined afterwards.

As regards the several papers presented to the Porte by the Russian Embassy, the Grand Vezir, having perceived Rifat Pasha's

1853
—
Æt. 66

marked reluctance to give copies or allow the papers to be seen by anyone, his Highness thought advisable to write to the Sultan and get his Majesty's sanction. I am requested by his Highness to assure your lordship that on Sunday, the latest on Monday, you will be furnished with copies of the papers in question.

Before concluding I think it incumbent upon me to tell your lordship confidentially that the great objection of Rifat Pasha to let you have those papers is, that Mr. Argyropoulos repeated to him over and over again that, were a single paper, communicated to the Porte by Prince Menshikov, to be given to any embassy, and especially to your lordship, such a proceeding would be considered as a breach of faith, and the consequence would be a suspension of relations.

By degrees, under the protecting influence which now emanated from the British Palace, the Turkish ministers revealed the full details of the Russian project. On 11 April Lord Stratford was able to transmit the substance of it to his Government. He was also in personal communication with Prince Menshikov, and, as Mr. Kinglake says, he "did not fail to deal with him tenderly: and for several days the Prince had the satisfaction of imagining that the imperious and overbearing Englishman of whom they were always talking at St. Petersburg was become very gentle in his presence. The two ambassadors, without being yet in negotiation, began to talk with one another of the matters which were bringing the peace of the world into danger. They spoke of the Holy Places. Far from seeming to be hard or scornful in regard to that matter, Lord Stratford was full of deference to a cause which, whether it was founded on error or on truth, was still the honest heart's desire of fifty millions of pious men. . . . Where he could do so with justice, he admitted the fairness of the Russian claims." Naturally the Prince's tone became "considerably softened" under this soothing influence; they even touched upon the "ulterior demands," and Menshikov "sought to attenuate their extent and effect; but I drew a clear line of distinction," reported the Englishman, "between the confirmation of special points already stipulated by treaty, and an extension of influence having the virtual force of a protectorate to be exercised exclusively by a single foreign Power over the most important

i. 133

F P. I.
155
16 April

and numerous class of the Sultan's tributary subjects. We both avoided entering into a discussion, which might have proved irritating, on this question : and I was glad to learn from Prince Menshikov that, notwithstanding the great importance attached to it by his Government, there was no danger of any hostile aggression as the result of its failure, but at most an estrangement between the two Courts, and perhaps, though it was not so said, an interruption of diplomatic relations."

E. P. I.
189, 195.
Dpl. Study
i. 163

This was the second falsehood uttered by Russia in the course of the negotiation. The first was Count Nesselrode's repeated assurance that Prince Menshikov's mission had no object beyond the settlement of the Holy Places' question ; of which concealment[1] the Russian official history with an amusing choice of words admits that " this *reserve* was very grave :" the second was Prince Menshikov's denial of any intention of hostile aggression, when two months later the Russian army was marching across the Pruth. Considering the reports which were constantly coming in of the massing of troops in Bessarabia, Lord Stratford must have listened to this denial with some scepticism, joined perhaps to amusement at the clumsy diplomacy that could commit itself to such a pledge. Throughout his intercourse with the Russian, the Elchi seems to have imposed upon himself a suave manner of conciliation which must have been exceedingly hard for one of his nature to maintain. The incapacity of his opponent perhaps helped him to keep calm, and the certainty of superiority in the science of diplomacy may have lent him consolation as he watched his adversary's false moves : but there is no doubt it was a stern work of self-repression when Lord Stratford preferred to seem deaf rather

XIII.
12 April

[1] On this subject Lord Stratford wrote to Lord Clarendon :—" It is remarkable that Count Nesselrode appears to have made no mention whatever of the ulterior and very important propositions brought forward by the Russian ambassador. This reserve corresponds with the endeavours made by Prince Menshikov to insulate the Porte in its eventual negotiation respecting them." But, according to Count Vitzthum's testimony, recorded in his memoirs, the cause of Nesselrode's " reserve " was not duplicity but ignorance. The Emperor Nicholas appears to have frequently kept his Minister in the dark concerning matters of the highest importance.

than hear an offensive remark, and the people in the embassy were so confident of a fiery altercation that a guard was posted outside the room in case the ambassadors came to blows.

The truth was that the matter was too important for temper, and Lord Stratford in matters of state always knew when he did well to be angry. He saw that to fight the domineering Prince Governor of Finland, aide-de-camp to the Emperor of All the Russias, with his coarse weapons of menace and abuse, would be to surrender his own advantages. So he conducted himself as a debonnair diplomatist, and with gentle tact drew the Prince on to his fate. As to the rumour that he *accepted* the Russian proposals subject to the omission of the clause about the Greek Patriarchs, there is not a word to support it in the numerous papers and reports of the period. That the Elchi was opposed to the evident sense of the Russian proposals may be seen from a memorandum which he drew up at the time, either for his own guidance or for that of the Porte:—

Additional demands of Russia, grounded partly on the vagueness of existing treaties, particularly of that of Kaynarji, and partly on the necessity of having a formal guarantee with respect to the Holy Places.

It is proposed to put these demands into the shape of a "Convention particulière qui doit avoir la force et l'effet d'un traité."

The treaties referred to are "le traité conclu en 1777," et les traités postérieurs, "ainsi que les articles 7, 8, 14, 16 du traité de Cainardjé" "confirmé par celui d'Andrianople."

The *projet* contains seven articles.

1. Protection of the Greek religion in all the Churches.

Right of the Russian representatives to give orders to the Churches and ecclesiastics which shall be "bien accueillis."

2. The four Patriarchs to be elected freely according to the laws, rules and customs of the *Oriental* Church, and to enjoy all the advantages, temporal and spiritual, secured to them by their *Berats*, as of old and now.

"Leurs attributions spirituelles" to be assigned separately, and exercised without hindrance.

3. The Patriarchs to be appointed for life, and not deposed,

except on proof of oppressing the Rayas, violating the laws of the Church, or being traitors to the Sultan.

4. Engagement *towards Russia* to maintain the Patriarch, Bishops, and Church of Jerusalem in the full enjoyment of their rights and privileges, which are to be confirmed, without prejudice to the rights of other Christian nations having access to the Holy Places.

5. That certain firmans, together with a new confirmatory Firman and Hatti-Sherif in favour of the Patriarchate of Jerusalem, and enumerating the Holy Places, with the rights of the Greeks respecting them, should be delivered formally to the Russian Government, literally enforced, and maintained hereafter with good faith.

6. That the Porte should grant permission to the Russians to build a church and hospital at or near Jerusalem, to be under the special inspection of the Russian Consul. Also that the Russian pilgrims should be protected on the footing of the most favoured nation.

7. Respecting the ratifications.

The effect of such a Convention would infallibly be the surrender to Russian influence, management, and authority, of the Greek Churches and clergy throughout Turkey, and eventually therefore of the whole Greek population dependent on the priests.

A declaratory act confirming in clear terms the various articles in favour of the Greek religion scattered through the treaties existing between Turkey and Russia, and collecting them, without increase or diminution, into one document, even perhaps in the form of a Sened, with the addition of articles, granting a church at Jerusalem, protecting the pilgrims, and enumerating the Holy Places, might be given without danger or serious inconvenience.

The danger will be in the *negotiation*, owing to the difficulty of keeping the Turkish ministers steady to principles and limitations after complying with the point of form.

There would, however, be an eventual danger in mortifying and irritating Russia by too complete a refusal. No hostilities would ensue, but a coldness and perhaps a suspension of diplomatic relations embarrassing and occasionally endangering the Porte.

One of these courses must be pursued—complete refusal, complete acceptance, or a consent to treat for certain specified and limited purposes, not comprising any *new* concession to Russia on the score of protection, direct or indirect.

In case of assent it would be desirable, and indeed necessary, for the Porte to confirm and make clear all the privileges which she has either left or granted, or is disposed to grant, as well to the Greeks and their religion as to other classes of Rayas, by a formal declaration

of her own, invested with the Sultan's sanction, and communicated,
not to Russia alone, but to all the Powers who recognized the independence and integrity of the Turkish Empire in 1841.

Such a declaration might even be combined with a *limited* agreement, as above, between Russia and the Porte.

It is meanwhile not to be doubted that the propositions contained
in the *Projet* of a Convention should be kept separate from those
which relate exclusively to the Holy Places, the latter being to be first
regulated.

If Russia complains of any breach of treaty, or abuse injurious
to the Greeks, let Prince Menshikov be called upon to specify it precisely, with the view of enabling the Porte to correct the one and to
remove the other.

In accordance with this advice the Turkish ministers
hurried the completion of the Holy Places' affair, whilst they
withstood all pressure to come to a decision on the larger
question. On 19 April Prince Menshikov addressed to Rif'at
Pasha a second Note, in which, after some offensive remarks
about the duplicity of his predecessors, the bad faith of the
Turkish ministers, and their want of respect towards the
Emperor of Russia, he proceeded to formulate the demands
of his Court, which culminated in the peremptory insistence
on a *Sened* or convention to guarantee the strict *status quo* of
the privileges of the Catholic Graeco-Russian Eastern Church.
" The Ottoman Cabinet," concluded this remarkable document,
" will be good enough also to weigh in its wisdom the gravity
of the offence that has been committed " in comparison with
the moderation of the demands now made for reparation and
guarantee ; and upon its response would depend the " devoirs
ultérieures " which the ambassador might have to fulfil.

On 21 April, Rif'at Pasha communicated the Note to the Drago-
man's
British ambassador, informing him at the same time that the Report
Russian had that morning sent to inquire whether the firmans
for the Holy Places were being drawn up, whether the Sened
was drafted, and also whether Rif'at Pasha was empowered to
enter into negotiation respecting the treaty to be concluded
between the two Powers. The same afternoon a messenger
again arrived at the Porte from Prince Menshikov and stated
to the Grand Vezir and the Foreign Secretary that he was *Ibid.*

directed by his master " to apprize them that the Prince was not at all satisfied with the answer brought to him by his dragoman that morning, and he conceived some suspicion that the Porte was doing a thing, very objectionable in his opinion, which is to consult and act upon the advice of the British ambassador, and that they had better abstain from doing so in future." The Grand Vezir was reported to have replied that the Porte had no occasion to ask advice of anyone, as the question was perfectly clear ; but at the same time he thought " no one could prevent their shewing regard and respect to one who on every occasion evinced so much good-will and friendly dispositions towards the Porte, and who takes so much interest in the promotion and welfare of this country."

In spite of his jealousy, however, the Russian allowed Lord Stratford on the following day to smooth away the remaining differences between the Czar and France, and thus to terminate the Holy Places' dispute, while the Porte was still uncommitted on the larger question. What the Elchi's views were at this point of the negotiation is seen in an instruction to the chief dragoman on 23 April, which was to be repeated to Rif'at Pasha :—

Pera,
23 April

Inform his Excellency of the happy result of my endeavours yesterday to effect a complete understanding between the French and Russian ambassadors respecting what remained of differences between them as to the Holy Places. " Préséance " on one side and "participation" on the other are both to be omitted. I hope the Porte will now complete and promulgate its firman without further delay, remembering, what I have so often urged, the importance of keeping the question of the *Holy Places* apart from that of the *Protectorate*. This latter question is, as the Porte well knows, a most serious and compromising one, notwithstanding that Prince Menshikov has now undoubtedly dropped what relates immediately to the *Patriarchs* and their *Berats*. I am not for irritating Russia *unnecessarily*. On the contrary, I should approve of any compliance with the wishes of that Power if *reasonable in themselves*, and entirely *free from serious inconvenience to the Porte*, *and, above all, from danger to its independence and honour*. But I greatly fear that the proposed Convention, though stated to have no object but that of confirming and explaining the Treaty of Kaynarji, has a strong tendency to acquire for Russia what she does not yet possess, namely, a formal right to interfere for the protection of the

Greek churches and clergy, that is to say, religion, throughout the Sultan's dominions, and, by virtual consequence, a vast increase of influence over the Greek population therein. It is essential that the Porte should avoid so dangerous a snare. Whether that may best be done by rejecting the proposed negotiation at once, or by entering into negotiation and subsequently rejecting whatever is found to be inadmissible, is now the question. My opinion is that the Porte has a clear right to say that the *Projet*-already given in by Prince Menshikov is too objectionable for the ground of a negotiation, and that if he persists in wishing for a Convention he must offer a *Projet* wholly different both in terms and spirit, the Porte reserving its liberty of consenting or. declining to negotiate thereon without offence.

Russia is entitled to no guarantee unless it be with respect to the Holy Places, and a sufficient guarantee in that respect may be given by the communication of the Sultan's firman to the Russian Embassy with an official Note couched in terms binding the Porte to its observance.

If want of confidence towards Russia on the Sultan's part be complained of, let an appeal be made to the intimidating position assumed by Russia, and to the nature of her demands.

If breach of treaty or the violation of Greek privileges be pleaded, let the case be specified by Russia and the remedy applied by the Porte itself.

There is no denying at the same time that, notwithstanding the general benevolence of the Sultan's Government and the imperial system of administration, the treatment of the Rayas continues in many instances to be very far from satisfactory.

The true remedy for this evil is in the Sultan's own hands. Now is the time for solemnly confirming by his own authority and proclamation all the privileges hitherto conferred upon the Rayas of every description, including the Greek, with such *precision* and *completeness* as may throw all foreign influence into the shade, and revive the sympathies of Europe, and most particularly of the English people, in favour of Turkey.

If this could be done in connexion with the publication of some benefits agreeable to the Musulman population also, there would be little left to desire.

Some passages from the ambassador's letters to Lady Stratford will illustrate this period. It is characteristic of his attention to details that in the midst of these urgent negotiations he tells his wife that he has "got the garden into order!" He was also planning excavations for Greek antiquities at Calymnos.

1853

Æ.T. 66

I am well, thank God ! but my brain is half on fire, and my fingers worn down to the quick. I get up at five ; I work the livelong day and I fall asleep before I reach my bed. . . . Affairs are getting on. The Holy Places' question is virtually settled and I had the good luck to bring the two ambassadors together in the nick of time. But we are not yet out of the wood. Russia wants what the Porte cannot give, and it remains to be seen whether Menshikov will be satisfied with what I may conscientiously advise the Turks to give him. You will be glad to know that I am so far on good terms with all the world. So at least it seems. I hope they will be satisfied in England.

Dundas was as right about the squadron as Rose was wrong. But Scotchmen you know are always right—except by the way when they tie me down about the use of the steamer here without necessity or propriety. . . . Well we have got over our Holy Places leisurely but surely. The Porte is thankful. I have also had the luck to receive from the Russian an assurance that he surrenders the worst feature of a very ugly sort of treaty which he wants the Sultan to adopt. Enough, however, remains, and there are strange contradictory appearances afloat, so that I can only say that, on the whole, there is less to fear than to hope. It seems certain that the Greeks are generally excited and sanguine, and also that the young men of the Russian Embassy are out of humour with their chief, who was yesterday unwell and in bed. Don't be alarmed, but people will have it that there is to be a rising or a massacre or both. Without believing a word of it, I have engaged the Porte to take quiet precautions, in the fashion of our poor lost Duke, to keep the peace at Easter, which takes place for the Greeks next Sunday. Massacres, like ends of the world, never happen when they are expected and talked of. . .

Though there has been much communication between the Porte and myself, I have only been out three times to any of them : once to the Padishah, once to the Grand Vezir, and once to the same personage and Rifat, the latter having called upon me. . . . Others, old friends, now out of office, send messages to me and information to me, but I keep personally at a distance, wishing not to excite suspicion at the Porte, and thinking it best for the moment to act fairly with the Sultan's ministers as persons enjoying his confidence, and reserving myself unpledged for future endeavours, to make a change if desirable. Reshid, I guess, is itching to recover his place ; but he has no right to be in a hurry, and I must have large explanations with him and strong pledges before I can even wish to see him restored to office.

The *grand* Russian question is getting about and exciting people's

1853
——
ÆT. 66

minds. I have had half a dozen lecturers this morning very anxious to electrify me, and I have held my tongue. The course I have to pursue lies straight before me. If the Russians are in the wrong, as I believe they are, my business is to make the wrong appear, and to stand by the Porte, or rather make the P. stand by me. If I can blot out the mischief and pacify them with a sop, I shall not fear the opinions of those who want a row.

A small thing, but very significant of the ambassador's position at Constantinople, occurred at this time. The Sultan's mother was dangerously ill, and Lord Stratford took the unprecedented course of addressing a letter of sympathy to a Turkish princess. Instead of resenting what might have been regarded as an intrusion from a misbeliever—and what was worse, a man—upon the privacy of the harem, the Valida was pleased with the attention, and, literally from her death-bed, replied in very gracious terms :—

I have received with great satisfaction the letter addressed to me by your Excellency, conveying the expression of your kind wishes and inquiries concerning my health. Your Excellency, a well-wisher of his Imperial Majesty, has for a long time given practical proofs of the friendly interest taken by you in the multifarious affairs of the Sublime Porte, and my appreciation also of the sincere sentiments expressed by your Excellency's illustrious spouse in the conversation which I lately had with her has increased the real friendship which I entertain towards your Excellency. The return of a friend like your lordship was thus a renewed source of pleasure to me, while I equally regretted that Lady Stratford should not have accompanied you. I trust, however, that she continues to enjoy good health.

The marks of continued friendly disposition afforded by her gracious Majesty the Queen of England towards my beloved son, his Imperial Majesty the Sultan, are manifest, and it is equally certain that your Excellency will also continue to evince your own friendly feelings. In thanking you, therefore, for your kind inquiries, I take the opportunity of offering to you the assurances of my perfect consideration and personal regard.

The Valida Sultan to Viscount Stratford de Redcliffe. Translation. 22 Rejeb, 1269 (1 May, 1853)

So unusual a correspondence had perhaps never before taken place at a Mohammedan Court.

About the same time, the Embassy suffered an appreciable loss in the departure of Mr. Layard, who had been invited to accompany the mission as a friend, and, being at the time a member of Parliament, felt that it was time to reassure his constituents about his absence from duty at the House of Commons. Writing to Lady Stratford, the Elchi regretted the decision, especially as Mr. Layard was going away with "nothing to shew for his excursion here" and "just as the serious conflict is coming on."

The next stage in the Menshikov crisis occurred on 5 May. The Note of 19 April had at least the merit of containing just demands for the redress of real grievances : for the Holy Places' affair was not settled till three days after its appearance. The Note and Project of 5 May had no such advantage. Lord Stratford had removed the grievances connected with the Sanctuaries out of the range of discussion, and the Czar's ambassador found himself obliged to create a grievance out of nothing. It was of course his own fault that he now found himself standing upon empty air : he had allowed the real ground of remonstrance, the Holy Places' dispute, to slip from under his feet, and now he had to find fresh ground, where none was, whereon to base his more serious requisitions. The Czar had probably by this time found out his mistake in sending a rude soldier to play with a master of fence ; he had hoped no doubt that the Prince would carry all before him in the absence of the ambassador, or that failing this happy end he would by his blundering menaces so outrage the dignity of the Porte and the British Embassy that both would lose their tempers. Instead of this the Turkish ministers and their English adviser maintained the same cool wary and courteous bearing towards the Prince Governor of Finland from first to last. They were never off their guard, but on the other hand they abstained from the slightest provocation. This prudent self-restraint, however, had an effect which might have been foreseen. There is such a thing as being too polite to a heated adversary, and the Turkish policy proved an example of this truth. The Czar, irritated beyond endurance by the unvarying reasonableness of his opponent,—for he saw but one hand and heard but one voice throughout the negotiations at Constantinople—lost his own self-control at the wrong moment.] Had he commanded violence at the beginning, Prince Menshikov might perhaps have carried the Turkish lines by a *coup de main* before the Elchi's arrival; and the peremptoriness of the measure might have been excused on the ground of the justice of several of the claims advanced by Russia, and by the precedent created by the very summary proceedings and success of Count Leiningen. But that moment was past: the real grievances had been repaired: nevertheless Nicholas selected this particular stage of the business to deliver more than usually peremptory orders to his representative, and Prince Menshikov, who must now have perceived clearly his blunder, was forced to send in the Note of 5 May. In this composition he acknowledges the receipt of the firmans granting all the original Russian demands concerning the Holy Places, but " having obtained so far no response to the third and most important point, which requires guarantees for the future, and having received the command to redouble his pressure in order to come to the immediate decision of the question which forms the chief object of the Emperor's solicitude, the ambassador finds himself under compulsion at once to address the Foreign Secretary and formulate his demands in the final limits of his instructions." He gave the Porte five days to decide, and threatened painful consequences in case of further delay. Enclosed with the Note was a *Projet de Convention*, which contained the old demand of Russia on behalf of the Greek Church, with the old effect of giving Russia the right of interference in the internal affairs of the Ottoman Empire. The Czar's ambassador changed the form of his requisition more than once, but from the first to the last Note the main point remained in all its unpleasant conspicuousness. What Lord Stratford thought of the Note of 5 May is expressed in the memorandum printed below. It should be explained that the bases referred to, as laid down by the Prince, were: (1) that the Orthodox religion, its clergy and property, should enjoy in future without diminution under the aegis of the Sultan the privileges and immunities which had been assured to them *ab antiquo*, and should share in any advantages granted to other Christian religions; (2) that the new Holy Places' Firman should have the force of a formal engagement with the Russian Government ; and (3) that the points thus summarized should form the subject of a *Sened* which should attest the mutual confidence of the two Governments.

In the demands of Russia there are some things which may be accepted without hesitation, there are others which might be acquiesced in rather than incur the risks of a rupture, there are others again which are inadmissible. With respect to the last, can they be so modified as to class with those of the second category? Let us take the *bases* as proposed in Prince Menshikov's official Note. There is nothing new in the *first* basis, except the application to those who profess the Orthodox religion of privileges enjoyed by other classes of Christians, and that which is new is not objectionable. The real difficulty consists in this : Russia requires the insertion of the aforementioned privileges in a *Sened* having the force of a treaty, and would thus make herself the arbitress of all that concerns the Russo-Greek religion and clergy. If another less binding form were given to the *Sened*, the proposed *basis* might be admitted in substance without danger of serious embarrassment, the Sultan, as before, protecting those privileges in virtue of his own promise, now to be renewed and repeated more explicitly than before in an Imperial firman, with a communication to the Four Powers by way of guarantee.

The second basis is already complied with in spirit and in reality by the official Note communicating the two firmans to the respective Embassies of France and Russia.

The *Sened* itself which forms the third basis may be admitted for objects divested of their objectionable qualities.

Thus it would appear that of the three *bases*, two might be accepted by the Porte, and the remaining one is shewn to be superfluous.

In answering Prince Menshikov's Note, care should be taken not to give too prominent a place to the grant of privileges, inasmuch as it is highly desirable for the Sultan to have the exclusive credit of the concessions confirmed or extended by him.

What relates to the bases ought also to be accompanied with or preceded by a temperate though firm vindication of the Porte's conduct in regard to such matters as admit of vindication in a frank and explicit manner.

The friendly assurances of Russia ought, moreover, to be responded to in a similar spirit, but not without notice being taken of the dictatorial proceedings which have characterized in some respects the embassy of Prince Menshikov.

Credit should at the same time be taken by the Porte for having met the wishes of Russia, in so far as existing obligations elsewhere admitted, in the question of the Holy Places. A readiness ought finally to be expressed by the Porte to remove any abuse and to redress any grievance clearly shewn to exist in anything connected with the Greek forms of worship and spiritual interests.

1853
—
ÆT. 66

This paper proves sufficiently that Lord Stratford, so far from urging the Turkish ministers to unnecessary resistance, went, as it might seem from subsequent evidence, almost too far in approving the Russian bases, especially the first. He may not immediately have perceived that the object of according to the Greek Church all privileges granted to other sects was to secure for it those advantages which were enjoyed by foreigners practising their rites within the Ottoman dominions, quite as much as to secure an equality between the Greek and the Catholic subjects of the Sultan. In fact, a good deal turned in the future upon the introduction of the apparently innocent words "sujettes Ottomanes." Lord Stratford's early objections to the Project were founded principally upon the creation by such an instrument of a special right of interference on the part of Russia whenever a Greek priest chose to assert a right or claim an immunity which might be just or not. This is clearly seen in the calm and temperate letter which the Elchi addressed to Prince Menshikov on 8 May, when that stormy negotiator had betaken himself into the country after discharging his Note. The transference to a foreign Power, and that the stronger, of authority hitherto reserved to the head of the weaker State, and the introduction of a foreign influence instead of the guardianship of the sovereign in internal affairs—these were his grounds for disliking the Project. M. de la Cour, the French ambassador, entirely concurred with his British colleague. The Prince however was not to be moved. He resented "the state of inferiority," *la position secondaire*, in which he said Russia was held ; he would go no further in the course of moderation ; he refused to meet the Grand Vezir in consultation ; and made it clear that he would enter upon no fresh discussions until the bases of his ultimatum were accepted by the Porte.

E.P. I.
184

At this stage of the proceedings, Lord Stratford visited the Grand Vezir at his country house on the Bosphorus. He

Ibid.

found Rif'at and the Seraskier already there in debate. The
Elchi urged them "to open a door for negotiation" in their
reply to the Prince, and strongly recommended that, if the
guarantee could not be granted, "a substitute for it should be
found in a frank and comprehensive exercise of the Sultan's
authority in the promulgation of a firman securing both the
spiritual and temporal privileges of all the Porte's tributary
subjects, and by way of further security communicated officially to the five Great Powers of Christendom." The Grand
Vezir asked whether the eventual approach of the English
squadron could be relied on. It was a pregnant question,
and shewed which way the Turkish mind was moving. "I
replied," said Lord Stratford, "that I considered the position in its present stage to be one of a moral character, and
consequently that its difficulties or hazards, whatever they
might be, should be rather met by acts of a similar description
than by demonstrations calculated to increase alarm and provoke resentment."

The ambassador was not to be drawn on faster than he
judged wise. He would communicate what he had to say
about the fleet in his own way and at his own time : not
at a hurried meeting by night at a minister's country house,
but at a solemn audience in the Sultan's palace. There on
9 May Lord Stratford in his most impressive tones informed
Abdu-l-Mejid that in case of danger he "was instructed to
request the commander of her Majesty's forces in the Mediterranean to hold his squadron in readiness." He had not
communicated this to the ministers, because he wished them to
make their decision without bias from without. They had
already made up their minds. They had adopted Lord Stratford's suggestions, and on 10 May Rif'at Pasha addressed
Prince Menshikov in a conciliatory Note, which, in substance,
was the work of the British ambassador. He agreed to negotiate
upon any points still left undetermined in regard to a church
and hospital in Jerusalem, assured the Russian envoy of the
Sultan's intention to maintain and confirm in perpetuity the
privileges of his Christian subjects, hinting at an Imperial document to this effect ; but he held it " contrary to international
rights that one government should conclude a treaty with an-

E.P. I.
203

E.P. I.
193

other on a dangerous matter affecting not only those things on which her independence is grounded, but, as is well known, her independence itself in its very foundations." On the following day the Prince replied. His letter expressed his painful surprize at the distrust of the Porte, and gave it three more days to reflect, before he considered his mission at an end and the diplomatic relations of the two Courts interrupted, with all the consequences. The Russian was not idle in the interval. He knocked at every door where the slightest chance existed of gaining a vote, he called upon old Khusruf, he wrote to Reshid, he employed secret agents to work upon Rif'at, he even waited on the Grand Vezir, and finally he forced his way into the presence of the Sultan himself, without previous consultation with the ministers. Abdu-l-Mejid, who ought not to have received him, had at least the wisdom to refer him back to his ministers; but the Grand Vezir, rightly indignant at this breach of official etiquette, resigned (13 May). A reconstruction of the Government ensued, in which the offices were shuffled rather in favour of the anti-Russian party. Mustafa Pasha, the late President of the Council, succeeded Mohammed Ali as Grand Vezir, and the latter became Seraskier. Rif'at Pasha took the presidency of the Council; and, most significant step of all, Lord Stratford's old ally Reshid went to the Foreign Office. The outlook for Prince Menshikov had certainly not brightened.

The term allowed by the Prince for the Porte's final reply to his demands expired on the day of the formation of the new ministry. That ambassador's last communication was not calculated to recommend his proposals either to the Turkish statesmen or their English adviser. Lord Stratford was fairly indignant with the tone of the letter, and wrote to Lord Clarendon " Can any degree of human indulgence reconcile the assurances given by Count Nesselrode with the demands now urged by Prince Menshikov with all the force of indignant virtue and unquestionable right ? Alas, my lord, these flaws of conduct cannot pass under notice without touching the springs of memory. They remind me but too painfully of the language ascribed to the Russian plenipotentiaries at Akkerman, and of the alleged duplicity of the

1853

Æ.T. 66

To Lord
Clarendon,
XLIV.
14 May

XLV.
14 May

Russian interpreter here during the triple Conferences of 1827." Nevertheless the Turkish Government prepared to meet the views of the Czar as far as was consistent with the sovereign rights of the Sultan. The new ministry could not be expected to take up the threads of so momentous a question in an hour, and Reshid requested a few days,—five or six,—in order to prepare the Porte's reply to the Prince's last Note. Without a moment's reflection the Russian ambassador declared his

official relations with the Porte to be broken (15 May). This precipitate step was of a piece with all his conduct. Like his Imperial master, he was always putting himself in the wrong. Just as Nicholas had gone out of his way to assure the world that he wanted nothing of the Porte but the settlement of the Palestine dispute, and then made a totally distinct and unwarrantable demand the ground of a quarrel with Turkey; just as his envoy had chosen, though perhaps not wholly of his own accord, the precise moment, when the Porte had removed every reasonable grievance, to put forth an Ultimatum based upon no recognized right or precedent ; so once more did the luckless would-be diplomatist break off his relations with the Porte at the very instant when every dictate of courtesy required a short period of delay to be accorded to a new ministry. And to make his position if possible more absurd than in nature it was, he coupled his declaration of the snapping of all diplomatic relations with a hint that he was still to be found at Constantinople for a brief while. He apparently expected the Sultan and his ministers to come to him on bended knees and tell him they were sorry. Reshid Pasha did indeed condescend so far as to overlook this ludicrous contradiction, and visited the Prince on 18 May, in the hope of favourably disposing him towards the Note then being prepared at the Porte, which granted everything that Russia demanded save only " the engagement with the force of treaty," which was held to be inconsistent with the Sultan's independence. To complete the maladroitness of his whole mission, at the moment when the Great Council had decided by a majority of forty-two to three to adhere to the Note thus described, the Prince sent in a final letter which left no further

alternative. He announced, in phrases which were to say the

least unusual as addressed to a free government, the termination of his mission ; threatened various consequences ; and
stated that the refusal of a guarantee would compel the
Russian Government " to seek one in its own might," and that
any injury to the *status quo* of the Orthodox Church would
be taken as an act of hostility to Russia and would " impose upon his Majesty the obligation of having recourse to
measures which, in his constant solicitude for the stability of
the Ottoman Empire and in his sincere friendship for the
Sultan, and that which he had professed for his august father,
the Emperor has always had it at heart to avoid." ^{.1.}

1853
——
.ET. 66

As soon as he heard of this " decisive Note " Lord Stratford
took an important step. He assembled the three other representatives of the Great Powers at his house and laid the
situation before them. By this act he placed the Eastern
Question on the sure and safe ground of European control,
and did all that lay in his power to prevent the possibility of
separate and interested interference. The four representatives
were entirely of one mind on the subject of the Prince's last
Note ; and M. Klezl, the Austrian chargé d'affaires, was requested to call upon the Russian ambassador, and, while
expressing the regret of the four at his decision, to discover whether he would consent to receive the as yet un-
delivered Note of the Porte through a private channel. To
this the Prince replied that he had no objection to receiving
the Note (which was accordingly sent) but that he was going
off that night (20 May) unless the Porte surrendered to his
demands in full. It then appeared that, like a bashful youth,
this extraordinary diplomatist did not know when to take his
leave. After having twice declared that there was no longer
a Russian Embassy at the Porte, he had sent a last Note to
be shewn to, but not left with, Reshid Pasha. What was to be
gained by this document, which reiterated the most objectionable parts of the preceding Notes, it is hard to see. The four
representatives, who met again at the British Embassy, could
not see any improvement, and communicated their opinion
to the Porte that " in a matter which touched so closely
upon the freedom of action and the sovereignty of the Sultan,
Reshid Pasha was the best judge of the line to be pursued : "

E.P. I.
196

E.P. I.
209, 239

E.P. I.
210

in other words, they supported the Turkish construction of the document. Lord Stratford's analysis of the Note of 20 May was sent to Reshid in the following memorandum :—

The *Projet* of an official Note or Declaration proposed by Pr. Menshikov to Reshid Pasha on 20 May should be examined with an earnest desire to make it an instrument of reconciliation.

We can hardly expect the Porte to give up what the Cabinet, the Council, and the Sultan have determined to be inadmissible. But if the essential objections be withdrawn in the proposed Note, or if the Note admits of such modification as would have the effect of withdrawing them, the Porte should doubtless be encouraged to close with the ambassador's offer, in spite of the rupture which has been declared by him.

Now, the main essential points on which Pr. Menshikov has hitherto insisted and which the Porte has determined to reject are the form of agreement having the force of a treaty, and the reference of the Sultan's confirmation of his Christian subjects' privileges to the requisition and protection of Russia. The first object of inquiry therefore is this : Does the Note in letter or spirit contain those two objections? Take each of them in succession. With respect to the first, we perceive that the phrase of "having the force of a treaty" does not appear in the Note. The words are expunged. Do their meaning and spirit remain? Now can anyone having the Note in his hand answer this question negatively? It has all the characteristics of an engagement binding solemnly the Porte for its strict execution in perpetuity to Russia, and giving that Power a distinct right to call the Porte to account for any remissness in that respect.

As to the second objection, the whole tenor of the preamble goes to make the Sultan's declaration in favour of his Christian subjects an immediate consequence of Prince Menshikov's embassy, and therefore no longer an act of grace on his part binding their affections to him and resting on his honour, as an independent sovereign pledged in the face of Europe, whose goodwill is essential to his safety, but as a deed of compliance with foreign dictation having for its immediate result the introduction of Russian influence, to be exercised with all the force of acknowledged right, into a department of internal administration affecting the religious sentiments and worldly interests of more than ten millions of the Sultan's subjects.

If this be a mistaken view of the subject, let the error be made clear. If it be a correct one, then the proposed amendment is a mere superficial change of forms and phrases, leaving the capital objects in reality as they were, and the Note would in spirit and practical effect be a *Sened* without the name, a treaty without its formalities.

Next comes the question of a possible modification. But it is self-evident that any modification calculated to remove the Porte's objections would be deemed inadmissible by Russia. The Porte's official Note prepared on 18 May under all the sanctions of the State was in truth the result of an earnest desire to make any concession to Russia short of surrendering the very points which it is the settled object of the Russian Ultimatum to secure to that Power.

What then is to be hoped from the new version ?

The paper may go before the Sultan and his Council. It may possibly be accepted by them, notwithstanding their previous decisions. Should such be the case, so flagrant an inconsistency would afford the Porte an escape from much inconvenience, some danger, and no small expense, but the responsibility of other consequences would rest with those who advised the measure, and more than a silent acquiescence could hardly be expected from one who, in concert with his colleagues, has hitherto approved the Porte's resistance, coupled, as it has been, with forbearance and conciliation.

R. P. might answer in the following sort of way : acknowledging the confidence shewn to him by the Prince in communicating a new plan of arrangement and manifesting a conciliatory spirit notwithstanding his official declaration ; stating the satisfaction he derived from the considerate omission of the form of a Convention or Sened, to which the Porte had reluctantly but unavoidably objected, and founding a hope upon this step towards accommodation of a complete adjustment if the Prince would suspend his departure and negotiate upon the joint basis of the Porte's Note and the ambassador's.

Reshid had already determined to resist the Russian demands in their last form. The claim to protect the Greek Church was obviously inadmissible : " it was not the amputation of a limb but the infusion of poison into the system " which had to be averted. The Prince had asked him to say a plain Yes or No : and No had been said.

Accordingly on 21 May Prince Menshikov's " untoward negotiations," to use Lord Stratford's words, came to an end ; the Russian arms were taken down from the palace of the embassy, and the Prince Governor of Finland steamed up the Bosphorus for Odessa. [On 31 May Count Nesselrode addressed an arrogant letter to Reshid Pasha, approving Prince

Menshikov's proceedings, and demanding the Porte's acceptance *sans variation* of the Prince's last Note, in default of which the Russian troops would cross the frontier, not to make war, but to obtain material guarantees for the satisfaction of the Czar's demands. To this Reshid, under Lord Stratford's guidance, made a temperate and reasonable reply on 16 June. Meanwhile, on 7 June, at the Elchi's instance, the Sultan had issued a Hatti-Sherif promulgating a new firman in confirmation of all the existing privileges of his Christian subjects, and thus taking the last breath of wind out of the Russian sails. So ended the first act of the drama which afterwards shifted its scene to the Crimea.

If any doubts remain as to the frankness of the Great Elchi's official statements,—doubts which could only be entertained by those who are unacquainted with his fearlessly open and straightforward nature,—some extracts from his private letters may be useful :—

To Lord
Clarendon,
5 May

I am sorry to throw so dark a shade upon the joy of having at last got through the question properly so called of the Holy Places : but in truth I fear that the worst chapter remains, and with every wish to let Prince Menshikov depart in honour and contentment, I find it difficult to imagine how, with the high pretensions of Russia, he is to be satisfied with the little which can alone be safely conceded to him. . . . The Turk is very much like a pig in a string ; you may get him to market at last, but his bolts and ziggings by the way are sadly puzzling and at times not a little provoking. The Russian also has a spice of the pig ; but where is the string by which to guide him ?

To the
same,
15 May

I have done everything short of advising an unqualified surrender to produce an arrangement, that is a second arrangement, for the *primative* question of the H. P. is arranged. I have the strongest reasons for believing that a treaty of alliance, offensive and defensive, was after all the real object in view. . . . Every opinion here except of sworn partisans is against Russia.

To the
same,
6 June

The film of religious bigotry is clearing away, and the Greek laity aspire to having a control over the temporalities of the Church and the selection of its dignitaries. The Synod itself has nose enough to smell out a rat in the new and remarkable phrase of *Orthodoxe*

Gréco-Russe. Its members would not like to be made dependent on the Slavonic hierarchy even for the purpose of hastening their return to the orthodox stalls of St. Sophia. . . .

What I most dread in looking forward is a continuance of the present menacing uncertainty. On the whole it is the most likely course for the Emperor to take, if he does not choose to place himself among the tame elephants. The danger, expense, and annoyance, would press sorely upon the Porte after a time, and in a moment of impatience and alarm the coveted object might be irrevocably surrendered. Most sincerely do I hope that you may be able to fence off this evil, and the Emperor appears to have given you a strong hold of him by his frequent declarations of peaceful and moderate views given in his Sunday character of a gentleman and man of honour.

1853
——
ÆT. 66

What is to happen Heaven only knows. *War* I think impossible if there be a grain of truth in the Emperor's assurances, but there may be an occupation of the Principalities.

To his Wife, 15 May

The Russians are still here, but they have declared the rupture of their diplomatic relations with the Porte and are preparing to be off in a day or two. There is still a bare possibility of better things, and I am engaged in making a last effort, but the prospects of success are gloomy enough. There will at all events be no *war* for the present, and that is something.

To the same, 19 May

These are stirring and anxious times. . . . There is much reason for alarm, and the Porte is preparing for the worst. I cannot make up my mind to believe in a declaration of war, but the Emperor Nic. may fly out in a rage and order some aggressive act just short of downright hostilities. Let the responsibility lie on the right shoulders. The Russians have played a double game, and it was impossible for the Porte to accept their Ultimatum. I have been writing and talking business since 6 this morning and it is now 6 in the evening. The same about every day.

To the same, 25 May

Exactly on this day four centuries ago did Mohammed II., Mohammed Ghazi, batter down the walls of Constantinople, turn St. Sophia into a mosque, and cut off one of the serpents' heads in the Hippodrome with his battle-axe. Twelve days more will bring us to the same anniversary, Old Style, and who can say what may happen between this and then? . . . The Turkish squadron is coming up to take position in advance of Buyukderé Bay, and all sorts of rumours and alarms are afloat. What a snug place one might have for seeing the battle behind Cowley's column in the garden, and then I should

To the same, 29 May

exclaim, how lucky that we did not throw it into the Bosphorus! Seriously all is in preparation for the worst, though no one I think can quite realize the idea of the danger. As for me, I think it logically out of, and accidentally in, the question. At all events we shall soon be able to judge better, and I think it best to keep my fears for the hour of peril, and though I cannot look about me without wishing you here, yet when I shut my eyes and meditate I am glad you are away.

I left Pera this morning impromptu to see Reshid, whom it was important I should see without delay. I found him in excellent spirits, and more like himself in better days than I have seen him for a long time. Little Melek was brought in, and she blushed and turned her little head aside, and then took my hand, and held and pressed it, and really seemed happy to see me, and she asked for you and for the children very prettily. It was really a pleasing sight and my affections were quite won over to her. . . . Reshid assured me that he does not wish to be Grand Vezir again—at least just now—and he speaks as if he were convinced that he had taken the right side in opposing the Russian demands. He has been working very hard for some days. The firmans renewing and confirming all the Christian and even Jewish religious privileges are prepared, and I put two good sentences into them this morning, having had the drafts of them communicated to me privately for that purpose. I hope other privileges will follow, and then I shall feel as if I was doing some good.

I rejoice to have been absent during the Leiningen triumph. Instinct told me to keep away. In settling the Jerusalem question I have been of some use. I would have settled the other, but it could not be. The Russians were determined to have the whole, and it was necessary to prevent them. The consequences of their defeat may certainly be very serious, but it was my duty to support the Turks in withstanding them, and *there* I have succeeded. On the point at issue there can hardly be two opinions ; but the fear of perturbation will cause many a sigh in England, and there are those who will be inclined to wish me at old Nic because I would not keep the peace by giving way to the *new* one. All now depends upon our Cabinet at home. Will they look the crisis fairly in the face and be wise enough as well as great enough, now that it has unavoidably occurred, to meet it fairly and settle it for ever ? *Shilly-shally* will spoil all. France it seems has come to a stout resolution : should Russia invade, the Emperor will come to the rescue. Such the private message conveyed yesterday to Reshid. We shall see. Even I who am behind the curtains, as it were, was half mystified at one time. How bad it must be when Austria and Prussia are with us ! So at least it would seem judging from the language of their repre-

1853

.T. 66

sentatives here. Even many of the better educated Greeks see through the Russian gauze. . . .

I found a letter from Calvert at the Dardanelles saying that the Russian merchants there had received official notice from here to wind up their affairs. This looks *very* bad. Yet there are contradictory symptoms too, and it is almost impossible to come to a steady conclusion. The Russians in the confidence of their power play with us. They mumble their prey to make easier eating of it. " Oh ! for one blast &c.," or rather, as I should say,

> Oh ! for one glance from Chatham's eye
> To make our vile misgivings fly ;
> Oh ! for one cheer like that which broke
> From English hearts when Canning spoke !

What had been accomplished in the six busy weeks which had elapsed between the arrival of the formidable Elchi and the day when Prince Menshikov was sent in confusion to Odessa may be summed up in few words. In seventeen days Lord Stratford had terminated the ostensible object of the Menshikov mission by inducing the Porte to grant the firmans about the Holy Places. For three weeks more he did everything in his power to keep the Porte in a conciliatory mood towards the Russian ambassador, and with the result that Turkey came out of the long conflict with an indisputable air of being in the right : while Russia had so mismanaged the weapons she possessed that she appeared solely in the light of a wanton aggressor. The one thing neither he nor the Turks would grant was a Russian protectorate over the Greek Church. The Turks had made up their minds upon that point before he came upon the scene : but even if they had been undecided, it would have been his duty, in view of what was, and, it is hoped, still is, the English policy on the Eastern Question, to bring them to the very decision at which they had arrived unaided.

CHAPTER XXVI.

THE TOILS OF DIPLOMACY.

JUNE—OCTOBER, 1853.

1853

ÆT. 66

WHEN Prince Menshikov had flown to Odessa to compose his ruffled plumage, the statesmen of Europe began to play what must have appeared to impartial spectators a curious and complicated game, whereof the exact name and rules were apparently not understood, at least by the players. There were four corners to this game: one was Paris, another London, a third Vienna, and the fourth Constantinople: indeed Berlin considered itself a fifth, but this was premature. The object was to throw a ball,—which they called by various names, as Note, Project, Declaration, Convention,—from Constantinople to the goal at St. Petersburg. But the most extraordinary accidents happened on the way. Sometimes the ball, after being thrown from corner to corner, got hopelessly lost. Sometimes, after much careful preparation, it never started on its way at all. But most often two balls were projected from opposite corners at the same instant, and meeting in mid-air broke each other in pieces. About a dozen of these missiles were flying about Europe in the summer of 1853, and the strangest part of the performance was that each was so timed as to arrive at its destination (if it did not burst on the way) exactly at the moment when another missile had been sent off. One only reached the Petersburg goal in safety, and that was found to contain some explosive matter, and was hastily dropped by the players.

It is not our wish to ridicule the efforts of the many wise and eminent men who devoted their anxious minds to the attempt to pacify the Czar of Russia. Their intentions, for the most part, were honest and right, and the reason they failed was perhaps chiefly because their aim was by nature unattainable : the Czar was not to be appeased. Nevertheless it cannot be denied that the old saying "in the multitude of counsellors there is wisdom " was hardly justified in this instance ; and it would be hard to discover in the history of diplomacy a more painful example of good intentions egregiously, we had almost said ludicrously, foiled by their own superabundance. Every Great Power, as represented by its Foreign Secretary, was laudably eager to have its share in the work of healing, and managed its contribution so skilfully that it was certain to be neutralized by some other prescription. A scheme is hatched at Vienna : nobody owns it, so it is fathered upon the French ambassador. All the Powers discuss it—and then it vanishes. No one can say what has happened to it, but it never is heard of again. But the incubation of Vienna is inexhaustible : a second chick is instantly produced, shewn round, approved, and sent to Turkey. It penetrates the Seraglio precincts, receives the Sultan's assent, and then, like its predecessor, is unaccountably mislaid. Seeing that Austrian broods do not thrive in Turkish air, other Powers set their wits to work, and, as though in order to insure failure, and oblivious of the space-destroying telegraph they elaborate their plans separately, unknown to each other, and with curious disregard of the real point at issue. So we find M. Drouyn de Lhuys full of his own scheme in June, while Lord Clarendon is simultaneously despatching his rival project to Constantinople, where it arrives just as Lord Stratford's own plan is leaving for Vienna, where this is received at the very moment when M Drouyn de Lhuys' Note, after emendation, has been formally adopted by the Great Powers. And this famous Franco-Austrian project, known as the Vienna Note,—which spoilt Lord Stratford's plan, which spoilt Lord Clarendon's Convention, which spoilt the first French draft, and so on, like the celebrated House that Jack built,—was found on examination to surrender the very point it was intended to guard !

So everything began over again, with very similar results. Austria strove to mend the breach without hurting the

1853

Æt. 66

1853
———
ÆT. 66

sensibility of Russia. France approved various pacific measures, and meanwhile pressed on the machinery of war. England agreed to everything that anybody proposed, and so anxiously strove for peace that she made war a certainty. Note, Convention, and Declaration, crossed and recrossed from London to Paris, from Constantinople to Vienna, and back again, to no purpose ; and meanwhile ships of war were doing their own work and rendering all the peaceful instruments of diplomacy vain and of no account. Eleven different solutions of the problem of peace with honour were exhibited between June and December, and all failed to avert war.[1]

E. P. I.
320

321,
24 June
330,
9 July

II. 63,
4 Aug.

I. 295,
27 June

II. 31,
2 Aug.

II. 18,
20 July

39,
23 July

[1] A concise list of these eleven plans is necessary to the understanding of the following pages. I. A plan, originating at Vienna, and proceeding, it was rumoured (but this was denied), from the mind of the French ambassador, M. de Bourqueney, consisted in sending a Turkish ambassador to St. Petersburg with the Porte's acceptance of the Menshikov Ultimatum, subject however to a declaration from the Czar clearly and satisfactorily defining the sense in which he understood the protecting powers claimed in that instrument. The Emperor Louis Napoléon considered, however, that the Czar should first submit the required definition to the Powers : and the so-called Bourqueney scheme was never formally presented to either of the estranged parties. II. The second was due to Austria, and recommended a *fusion* of the Menshikov Ultimatum of 20 May with the Turkish reply. The Internuncio laid it before the Porte in June, and in July it was forgotten. III. The *Clarendon Convention*, supported by France, was never tested, since it arrived at Constantinople (31 July) at a moment when the Turkish Government had already formulated a plan of its own. IV. Sir Hamilton Seymour suggested a new Hatti-Sherif embodying the Porte's guarantee of the privileges of the Greek Church to be duly notified to Russia. Count Nesselrode seemed to think that this would satisfy the Czar, but as it was never formally presented for his assent it would be rash to rely too much on this verbal assurance, especially as a Hatti-Sherif had already been issued (7 June) without effect. Lord Clarendon naturally shelved the suggestion, on the ground that at least two other proposals were already before the Porte. V. Meanwhile the French Government, ambitious to own a plan of its own, had elaborated at the close of June a draft, which, after some amendments on the part of Austria and of Great Britain, took the form of the famous *Vienna Note*, the *fifth* panacea which the wisdom of Europe prepared for the wounds of Russia. It was in effect that fusion between the Menshikov Ultimatum and Reshid's Note which Austria had originally recommended, and which the Turks had been unable to concoct. VI. But a project had been contemporaneously evolved at Constantinople ; it nominally emanated from Reshid Pasha, but was of course Lord Stratford's work. It had the advantage of the Porte's assent, besides that of the three other representatives of the Great Powers at Constantinople. This consisted in a letter from the Turkish Foreign Minister to Count Nesselrode, protesting against the occupation of the Principalities by Russia, but at the same time enclosing the firmans lately promulgated by the Sultan at Lord Stratford's suggestion, after Prince Menshikov's departure, in confirmation of all the existing privileges and rights of the Christian Churches in his dominions.

Of the eleven schemes of pacification eight came under Lord Stratford's official influence. These were Nos. 2 (the *Austrian*

Time was considered to be of so much consequence that the *Turkish Ultimatum* was despatched (20 July) direct to Vienna, instead of being first submitted to the Cabinets of London and Paris; and the representatives of the Powers at the Austrian capital were requested to forward it to St. Petersburg. But they had in the meantime adopted the Vienna Note, and the Turkish plan was accordingly arrested on its way; and the Vienna Note was simultaneously despatched to St. Petersburg and Constantinople. It was instantly accepted by the Czar; the Turkish Ministers however were shrewd enough to see the trap into which they were invited to fall, and on 20 August the Council declared that the Vienna Note could only be accepted with amendments, which were rejected by Russia (7 Sept.) for reasons—disclosed by mistake or by treachery—which induced the Powers hastily to drop the Note. VII. A *seventh* project was evolved between Counts Buol and Nesselrode at *Olmütz*, where the Czar and his brother of Austria met in friendly interview, and a Note was drawn up: but England declined to support it, as it could not neutralize the effect of the reasons alleged by Russia for rejecting the Turkish amendments. VIII. Lord Stratford suggested two plans:—either a new edition of the Vienna Note, introducing, *in substance*, the Turkish amendments; or else arbitration by the Powers. The former course was preferred, and an *eighth* solution of the difficulty was presented by Lord *Clarendon's Projet de Note*, which was forwarded to Constantinople with option for the British ambassador in concert with his colleagues to modify it if necessary. IX. But before the arrival of the Clarendon *Projet* Lord Stratford had succeeded with great difficulty in obtaining a brief delay in the commencement of hostilities, and had drawn up a "forlorn hope" (21 October) which Lord Clarendon strenuously supported instead of his own plan. This *ninth* suggestion consisted of a *Declaration* of the Four Powers, bearing something of the character of a guarantee, with an annexed Note in which all reasonable confirmation and warranty of the rights of the Greek Church were to be formally granted by the Sultan. England and France approved, and Prussia afterwards fell in, but it was now the turn of Austria to object. Lord Clarendon had refused to support Count Buol's Olmütz project; and now Count Buol would not entertain the new English suggestion. War having been declared (by Gorchakov's reply on 10 October to the Turkish Ultimatum), he remarked that something more than a Note was required to restore peace; and he was convinced that Russia would not accept the new device. The Austrian minister, armed with authority from Russia to mediate, was in favour of a Collective Note from the Four Powers. X. Always willing to fall in with any suggestion, and holding firmly to none, Lord Clarendon drafted a *Collective Note*, the *tenth* panacea, 29 November; the Four Powers agreed in recommending it to the consideration of Turkey (Protocol, 5 December); but before it arrived at Constantinople the Porte was carefully weighing a final—the *eleventh*—proposal, emanating from Lord Stratford, and supported by his colleagues (12 December), and including provisions for an armistice, the appointment of an Ottoman plenipotentiary to treat with Russia, and a renewal of existing treaties. The Collective Note was consequently held back with Lord Clarendon's approval until the Turks should have decided upon the eleventh scheme; and on 31 December the Porte unreservedly accepted *Lord Stratford's project*, and the approval of the four representatives at Vienna followed on 13 January. The acceptance however came too late. On 12 Jan. the Czar learnt the second decision of the British Cabinet on the

II. 54,
5 Aug.
71, 90, 91,
94

126, 5 Oct.
130, 7 Oct.

164,
24 Oct.

189, 190,
21 Oct.

15,
8 Nov.

236,
10 Nov.

282

370,
17 Dec.
369,
17 Dec.
380
396

1853

———

ÆT. 66

fusion plan), 3 (the *Clarendon Convention*), 5 (the *Vienna Note*), 5 (the *Turkish Ultimatum*), 8 (the *Clarendon Projet de Note*), 9 (the *Stratford Declaration* and Note), 10 (the *Collective Note* of the Four Powers), and 11 (the *Stratford Armistice and Treaty*). What were the ambassador's proceedings as each in turn came up for consideration will be seen from the contemporary letters and papers.

E. P. I.
321

The Austrian " fusion " plan was communicated to Reshid Pasha, the Turkish Secretary for Foreign Affairs, towards the end of June. The plan was an improvisation of Count Buol's, the Austrian Foreign Minister, and Lord Stratford had received no instructions from his Government how to deal with it. He anticipated little success from any attempt to unite views so divergent as those contained in the Menshikov and Reshid Notes of 20 May, especially since the former, and afterwards Count Nesselrode, had made it perfectly clear that they would not " hear of the slightest variation in the terms." Nevertheless, the Elchi saw the advantage of setting diplomacy to work to

29 June

gain time, if not to heal the breach ; " I think it right," he wrote to Lord Clarendon, " to catch at any chance of peace which is not attended with a sacrifice of principle' or a loss of time," and he forthwith assembled his colleagues of Austria, France, and Russia at his house. There the four agreed to a memorandum recommending Count Buol's plan to the Porte ; and by this simple expedient the exclusive mediation of Austria was skilfully quashed and the fusion scheme was offered to the Sultan with the joint weight and authority of the Four Powers. It is worth remembering that the idea of placing the Eastern Question of 1853 before a jury of the Great Powers was Lord Stratford's. He had called together the ambassadors in May to deal with Prince Menshikov's demands ; and now he repeated the measure. Baron Brück, the Internuncio, was not pleased to find the lead taken out of his hand, but the English ambassador was urgent, and from the meeting at his

---

affair at Sinope, and was forced to hear that his ships in the Euxine were to be ignominiously driven back into port by the Allied squadrons : this was too much for his scant patience ; Nesselrode despatched an ultimatum to England, 16 January ; and 4 February Russia broke off diplomatic relations with England and France. The Crimean war ensued.

house on 24 June dates the collective action of Europe which, properly directed, might have averted the misery and futility of the Crimean War. The Porte itself greatly preferred such collective action, and this preference was a weapon in the armoury of peace.

Writing privately to the Foreign Secretary at this stage of the negotiations, Lord Stratford said :—

1853

ÆT. 66

To Lord
Clarendon
CXXXI.
4 July
CXIX.
24 June

With respect to Menshikov's last alternative—I mean the Note which he drew up for Reshid to sign—he declared that he would hear of no alterations. Even the Austrian Klezl failed to soften him. In the pending attempt to make a fusion of the two drafts I firmly believe that we are trying to work out an impossible quantity. But there may be some germ of change in the Czar's mind, now that he knows how his best and most obliged Allies think of his proceeding, and at all events I have thought to act most agreeably to your wishes by trying to extract good from the most meagre proposition. I hope however at the same time that you will not hear of a *single* Austrian mediation, but approve my notion of treating Brück and Buol as we treated Klezl, namely make them the mouthpiece of the quadruple understanding, without exactly bringing the association into immediate contact with Russia. It seems to me that one of the great difficulties of the situation is that while Russia is bullying and intriguing, we are carrying our ménagements even to the point of concealing half of our thoughts, and appearing to admit much from the other side which ought not to be admitted.

Is not the time very near at hand when plain outspeaking will be best ? Might not something material be gained by giving form and substance to our understanding, which I hope is a cordial one, with France ? . . . Much as we are all bound to work for the continuance of peace, I cannot help thinking that we shall have reason to regret the close of these discussions and counter-preparations without some distinct settlement of the relations between Europe and Turkey, and a more improved one of those between the Sultan and his rayas.

To Lord
Clarendon
25 June

Baron Brück, discontented with his position as one of four, made a separate and more detailed proposal to Reshid Pasha at the end of June. In a confidential despatch on this subject Lord Stratford remarked that the new Austrian Note, " though it contains some secondary amendments, concedes the main point at issue," and Reshid, acting under his advice, refused to take the Note into the Porte's consideration

CXXXIV.
4 July

1853

Æт. 66

E.P. I.
No. 357

until, like the preceding " suggestion," it had been communicated to the three other representatives. This was not
done, and the original suggestion of a fusion of Notes was
accordingly laid before the Sultan and after some days
received his Majesty's sanction. At this time two circumstances occurred to delay negotiations. On 7 July news arrived
that the Russians had crossed the Pruth four days earlier.
Hardly was this known when Mustafa, the Grand Vezir, and
Reshid Pasha were suddenly dismissed from office. This
was believed to signalize the triumph of the war party in
the ministry. Lord Stratford went straight to the Sultan on
CXLIV.
9 July
the 9th, and, on being informed that purely personal causes
had led to the removal of the two leading ministers, advised
his Majesty to allow no secondary considerations to deprive
him of valuable counsellors at so critical a moment. Abdu-l-
Mejid restored the ministers on the spot. Extracts from the
ambassador's letters to Lady Stratford and to Lord Clarendon,
and a report from Stephen Pisani the dragoman, shew clearly
enough how the Turks relied upon their English adviser at
every step. Unprepared as they were, time was of urgent
consequence : he therefore bade them not resist the Czar's
armies, but to protest ; and they obeyed. Their Protest
against the Russian occupation, their answer to the Austrian
separate proposal, their abortive fusion Note, their circular
despatch to the ministers of the Porte abroad, were all submitted to his revision.

To his
Wife,
9 July
The Russians are actually in the Provinces, and we must try to
get them out without yielding the point in dispute. How is that to
be done without war, and war on a large scale ? I tremble to think
of it, and yet know not how, except by miracle, it is to be
avoided. At all events let people make up their minds, and equal
Russia in foresight and consistency. I have written oceans, public
and private—that is private to Lord Clarendon. Now is the time
for decision—one more attempt if possible at negotiation, and then
war.

We have had a sudden change of ministry again—the Grand
Vezir and Reshid out in a moment. I went bang down to the
Padishah and put them in again. But it is sad work at such a
crisis. The Sultan accuses his ministers of pestering him with their

petty jealousies and personal interests. They accuse him of weakness and duplicity.

1853
—
ÆT. 66

Brück asserts that he has no idea but that of securing the *principle at stake* ; yet his letter, as proposed to Reshid, contains a complete surrender of it. M. de la Cour is much inclined to run off the course in search of *expedients*, as he calls them, and, like all Frenchmen, he attaches too much importance to rumours and secondary incidents. But in the main I presume that he means the same thing that we do, and will act according to his instructions or rather according to your 81 to me, for he has not yet received, he says, a corresponding instruction from Drouyn de Lhuys. For my own part I bear that instruction fully in mind, and will do my best to act upon it, though I have no faith in its success, and find difficulty both as to fitting it for the Petersburg market and as to getting it there by any suitable means.

To Lord
Clarendon,
9 July

[No. 263,
10 June.]

M. de la Cour has lately talked to Reshid Pasha, without any previous intimation to me, of looking forward to the independence of the Danubian Principalities, and also of declaring all treaties respecting those provinces as abrogated by the occupation. The former idea I conceive to be premature ; the latter dangerous. Some of my informants here conceive the idea that France is wanting to get into a war, while we are wanting to keep out of it. I do not however find that the French ambassador's language to me corresponds with this notion. . . . Whatever may be hoped from negotiations ought, I submit, to be tried at once and brought to a point. Delay will prove most fatal to Turkey if prolonged beyond a very few weeks, and I confess my own impression to be that if the next attempt at negotiation fails, there will be no room for half measures. If the object be, as I presume, to get the Russians out of the Principalities without surrendering the main point in dispute, it is difficult to conceive how that object can have a chance of being accomplished without hard knocks on a large scale, or some counter-occupation which will be equivalent to a partial dismemberment of the Empire. . . . Surely it is time to come to a decision which may give consistency, *ensemble*, and energy to our proceedings. I am as much for peace as any man ; but if the object at stake is to be maintained, as I think it ought, there should be a limit to attempts which can only prove nugatory in the end and turn to the benefit of uncompromising Russia.

Reshid Pasha is much pleased with the Protest as amended by your lordship. It will be read in the Council which is to be held to-morrow at the Porte, and subsequently submitted to the Sultan's sanction. As soon as his Majesty's pleasure will be given to it,

From
Steph.
Pisani,
10 July

Reshid Pasha will lose no time in communicating it officially to the representatives of the Four Powers parties to the Treaty of 1841.

While I was with his Highness he received the Sultan's Iradé to the new proposal of Austria. The Iradé says in substance that the Porte cannot take into consideration the new proposal without communicating it, as the suggestion was communicated, to the other three representatives and waiting for their reply. This answer will be communicated in the most civil manner, to-morrow, to Baron Brück, who seems anxious to be acquainted with the Porte's opinion on the subject.

Reshid Pasha is preparing a Note to be addressed to the Russian Government, I mean a fusion of Prince Menshikov's last Note and that privately communicated by the Porte to the latter. He hopes to get it ready by to-morrow, when he will submit it to your Excellency's consideration.

I have the honour to enclose herewith for your lordship's approval a draft of a despatch drawn up by Reshid Pasha, intended to be addressed to the Porte's ministers abroad, on transmitting to them a copy of the Protest to be communicated to the four representatives here.

Although according to Pisani's report Reshid was busy with the proposed fusion Note, it was clear that something different was demanded now that the Russians had actually invaded Turkey. On 18 June Lord Clarendon had advised a protest against so unjustifiable an act, should the occupation of the Principalities really take place ; and on 9 July Lord Stratford reported that a union of the Austrian " fusion " with such a protest would probably be found the preferable course. " At the request of Reshid Pasha," he added, " I have endeavoured to adapt to that plan the draft of a protest which his Highness had originally prepared for the case which has since occurred."

CXLV.
9 July

Before dismissing the Austrian suggestion, it is important to inquire whether, supposing it to have been instantly accepted by the Porte without waiting for the coöperation of the three other ambassadors, there is any reason to believe that the Russians would have desisted from their advance into the Principalities. Two dates will determine this point. Baron Brück's communication took place on 22 June ; the Czar's Manifesto announcing that " we have found it needful to advance our armies into the Danubian Principalities " was dated 26 June. No communication from Constantinople could have reached St. Petersburg in time to arrest the Manifesto, and that document once published the Czar could not draw back.

Lord Stratford lost no time in carrying out the new plan of a Note combined with a Protest against the occupation. On 15 July the Protest was printed. It contained the principal ideas of Lord Clarendon's instruction of 18 June, and was agreed to by the four representatives assembled in council, 16 July, at the British Palace. The Internuncio acquiesced in the abandonment of his original fusion suggestion " on account of the delay and consequent change of circumstances." He and his French and Prussian colleagues seemed to believe in " a marked improvement in the disposition of the Russian Government." The four agreed in advising the Porte to send to Count Nesselrode, together with the Protest, copies of the firmans confirming the privileges of the non-Musulman subjects of Turkey, and they offered to transmit the Porte's communication to Russia by way of Vienna, and to write to their colleagues at St. Petersburg on the subject. On 20 July they met again, this time in conference with Reshid Pasha, and a letter was adopted to be addressed by the latter to Count Nesselrode, in company with the Protest and the firmans. They were all despatched post-haste to Vienna on the same day, and followed on the 23rd by a supplementary Note or *projet de convention* guaranteeing the enjoyment of the spiritual privileges confirmed by the firmans and promising to accord in future to the Greek Church " such other privileges and immunities as it may hereafter please his Majesty to grant to any other sect whatever of his Christian subjects." A General Council on the 24th approved the whole of this arrangement, which was declared to be of the nature of an Ultimatum on the part of Turkey. The most jealous scrutiny of these various documents can only elicit the fact that they contain all that the Porte could reasonably be expected to concede, and all that Russia had originally demanded in her communications with the Great Powers. The language of the Protest, whilst dignified, was eminently conciliatory.

1853

ÆT. 66

CL.
15 July

E.P. II.
18

II. 38, 39

I. 368

1853
———
ÆT. 66

Lord Stratford's letters to his colleagues, Sir Hamilton Seymour at St. Petersburg and Lord Westmoreland at Vienna, will shew the importance he attached to these proposals :—

To Sir
G. H.
Seymour,
20 July

I fear you will think me very troublesome, and perhaps a little presumptuous. I trust to your kind indulgence for excusing me on the score of our common anxiety to save two almost inconsistent things in the present state of Eastern affairs—I mean, *Peace* and *Turkish independence*.

I hope you will be able to keep up the character of *parti carré* which I have endeavoured to give to our proceedings here.

The evacuation is not less essential than the retreat [of the squadrons], as a nearly or quite simultaneous measure, is delicate.

I hope the Government at home will write to you without delay.

Reshid Pasha is to send by express to Vienna to-morrow or the day after—probably the latter day—a project of paragraph for insertion in the mutual peace-making Note about religious privileges. It has the suffrages of myself and my three colleagues. It remains to be seen what the Sultan in his Council will decide.

I hope Lord Westmoreland will lose no time in sending it on to you.

To Lord
West-
moreland,
23 July

The present batch is forwarded by an express, supplied by Reshid, and paid by "the Four." We are anxious that it should arrive without a moment's delay. If you really wish for peace, you must make the most of the present experiment. The Porte will hear of nothing else, and the war party is soon more likely to be in the ascendent than reduced to order. All the separate schemes have come to nought. Our own particular notion of a Convention was found no better than Buol's and Bourqueney's. We are now, I humbly conceive, on the right ground, and in the right direction. There must be firmness as well as conciliation.

To Sir
G. H.
Seymour,
23 July

I inclose the English original of the Note now offered by the Porte to Russia as warranting by its acceptance the appointment of a special ambassador to St. Petersburg. I beg to call your attention to it because it contains two or three words and turns of expression more agreeable, as I fancy, to Russian taste, and which might be replaced, I think, were it deemed *necessary*, whenever the Note comes to be made out fair for ultimate presentation. My hope, however, is that the Emperor will shew his sense of justice or, if you please, his magnanimity by accepting this last endeavour to avert the incalculable mischiefs of war, without a minute attention to the wording. An *ultimatum* and a condition may sound harsh to Russian ears, but I really do not see how the Porte can possibly, with justice to itself, take any other course after displaying so much unexpected moderation with respect to the Principalities, and being placed in so difficult a position with respect to its own subjects.

With ardent wishes for your success in the cause of peace, and repeated excuses for again writing my ostensible despatch in French for the reason already explained, I beg, &c.

P.S. I reckon upon much for the success of the Note derivable from its not requiring any kind of counter-declaration from Russia.

A few days after the forwarding of the Turkish Note, Lord Clarendon's Project of Convention reached Constantinople. As its author was ignorant of the plan which had already arrived at maturity at the Porte, the Elchi took upon himself to reserve the official presentation of the Convention, but placed it privately before Reshid Pasha, who consulted some of the leading Turkish statesmen. It soon appeared that Reshid and A'li considered it inadmissible: " the form of a Treaty, founded expressly on that of Kaynarji, involving an engagement in terms to Russia, and liable to be understood by that Power as extending over the Sultan's firman, could hardly fail of seeming dangerous " in their sight.] The other ambassadors agreed that it must be withheld for the present, and did not conceal their opinion that it was little less dangerous than Prince Menshikov's proposals. Lord Stratford wrote privately on the subject to the Foreign Secretary :—

To Lord Claren-don, cxcv. 4 Aug.

Though we are so far advanced in the plan adopted to-day that my project of a Note had passed the Council and I believe the Seraglio too, I did not hesitate to send your Convention privately to Reshid. 'It does not seem to have found favour in his sight and he expressed himself with much vehemence against its adoption. He apprehends danger from giving to the Treaty of Kaynarji even an air and appearance of value beyond its real meaning and intent, and I confess that, if the danger were avoided, I should imagine that the Russians would see the hook too clearly to swallow the bait.

To Lord Claren-don, 23 July

My French colleague seems to have had no information upon the subject, though you say that the Convention (an amended one I presume) had been approved at Paris ; at least he made no communication to me after the arrival of his packet yesterday, and he seemed to enter with zeal into the plan now on its way to Vienna and Peters-burg.

An idea originating at Paris, and taken in part from Bourqueney's suggestion so vaunted by M. Manteuffel, has been brought before Reshid Pasha, but he will have nothing to say to it, and it appears on the way to that limbo where the separate nostrums of Austria and Prussia are happily reposing. . . .

Perhaps by throwing all your weight and that of France after *our kite* promptly and vigorously you may give the best chance that can now be given to the adjustment of our unfortunate question. You are no doubt the best judge, but from this point of view I really do not see what else is to be done.

Meanwhile diplomacy at Vienna was becoming impatient as the weeks passed and no satisfactory news arrived from Constantinople. The last reports (of 14 July) shewed no pro-gress in the Austrian fusion-plan, and no information was to hand concerning any other scheme. Count Buol therefore proposed, on 24 July, a new fusion Note based on a draft drawn up at Paris, and Lord Clarendon assented by telegraph on the 25th. Three days later the Vienna Note was agreed to. This was 28 July. On that very evening or the following morning arrived the despatches of the 20th, bringing the Turkish Ultimatum from Constantinople. The London telegraph wire had spoilt all : for the Vienna Note being adopted, it was not to be supposed that the Turkish plan would be entertained. Count Buol said that, after taking the Emperor's commands, he considered that Reshid's letter was calculated " à aigrir les débats plus qu'à les concilier," and he declined the responsibility of transmitting it to St. Petersburg

F.P. II.
9, 10

The Constantinople despatches would be considered as " non-avenues." Lord Westmoreland telegraphed to the Foreign Office for instructions, and Lord Clarendon replied (30 July) that he was to suspend the Turkish Ultimatum.

Kinglake,
i. 370

It has been advanced on very high authority that the sup-pression of the Turkish Ultimatum at Vienna was justifiable on the ground that the diplomatists there rightly understood that the Czar would be more enraged than ever when he saw that the concessions therein announced had been peacefully obtained by the influence of his arch-enemy Lord Stratford ;

1853
———
Æt. 66

and no doubt it is more than likely that the Turkish Note would have been rejected. Subsequent events shewed that Russia had no intention of accepting any reasonable concession. But it cannot be denied that the representatives at Vienna took upon themselves a grave responsibility in detaining what was, after all, the Ultimatum of an independent Power to a State with which it was technically at war. Had the Note been sent on to Petersburg, whatever might have been the effect upon the excited mind of the Emperor Nicholas, at least this result would have been attained : Turkey would have appeared in the true light of offering the last olive-branch, and Russia would by her refusal have acknowledged that she wanted what no independent State could grant. Had the Four Powers, by their representatives at Vienna, been formally committed to this Note, its rejection by Russia would probably have been followed by a collective remonstrance and possibly a collective armed interference ; and the separate action of the Western Powers and their entrance into the Dardanelles in October would thus have been avoided. The whole position as against Russia would have been materially strengthened, and all Europe would have joined in united mediation on just grounds accepted by the aggrieved party. *Sed legatis aliter visum.* Austria and Prussia shrank from the prospect of extreme measures ; they wished nothing less than to be dragged into the approaching struggle. So the four representatives at Vienna threw away the opportunity for the collective action of Europe in deference to the selfish timidity of the German Powers. Pressed by Austria, they preferred to work upon a plan approved by Russia the aggressor than upon one recommended by Turkey the aggrieved ; and still more, with professional jealousy, they preferred their own plan to anyone else's. A hint of what was happening reached Lord Stratford on 4 August, and he wrote thus to Lord Westmoreland :—

I have this moment received your note of the 25th.

There is an old proverb well known to you as well as to me about broth suffering from the zeal of too many cooks, and I hope that we are not about to have a new proof of its truth.

To Lord Westmoreland, 4 Aug.

1853
——
ÆT. 66

Reshid Pasha told M. del Brück the day before yesterday, what indeed he had stated to us all officially and formally many days before, that the Porte will hear of nothing but the Ultimatum, which has probably been in your possession since Monday, and which goes on to St. Petersburg—if, as I trust, you send it on,—uniting all voices here and all chances in its favour with the advantage of springing, in so far as the Protest—its point of departure—is concerned, out of Clarendon's instructions to me.

There was some regrettable, though unavoidable, delay here, owing to Ramazan, Bayram, and our ministerial crisis ; but the earliest available moment was made use of to afford Russia one more generous opportunity for getting decently out of her scrape, and we all think here that if she rejects an offer, so little deserved by her previous conduct, she must mean worse than she has chosen to avow. The Porte has gone as far as it is possible for her to go without giving up the principle in standing up for which she has hitherto been backed by all the suffrages and sympathies of Europe—both Presses and Governments—even by the very herald of peace itself—the *Economist* (vide last number).

The delay, which you mention as causing the new proposal from Vienna, arose, in addition to the above-stated circumstances, out of the very general impression, especially prevailing at the Porte, that the idea of a fusion of Notes for any practicable purpose was, in reality, neither more nor less than moonshine. To say the truth, I lent myself to it, as a mere "suggestion," out of respect for the quarter from whence it came. . . .

The Convention, even if it had arrived in time, would not have been accepted by the Sultan's ministers. I am free to say, between ourselves, that even to my humble judgment, it does not seem to be a *safe* form of arrangement, if taken seriously, as Russia would necessarily understand it. Excuse all this and let me live in hope that the Porte's " Ultimatum " will be accepted with your assistance.

E. P. II.
47

On 9 August a despatch from Vienna informed him of the suppression of the Turkish Ultimatum and the simultaneous transmission of the Austrian Note to Constantinople and Petersburg. Telegraphing to the Foreign Secretary on 31 July, the British ambassador at Vienna said, " J'enverrai vos ordres à Lord Stratford." The " ordres " in question were dated 28 July, *before the Turkish Ultimatum was known to Lord Clarendon,* and they commanded Lord Westmoreland to " inform Lord Stratford that her Majesty's Government desire that this project [the Vienna Note] should be adopted by the Porte, *if no other arrangement has been already made*" (the italics are mine). As another arrangement *had* already been made, it is open to argument whether Lord Westmoreland ought not to have arrested the transmission of the Vienna Note. At all events Lord Stratford felt that it was necessary to wait for despatches from London before he could officially support this Note, of which, though he had seen it, he had not even a copy. Unfair use has been made of the consequent delay to shew that the ambassador did his best to counteract the instructions of his Government : but as those instructions were addressed through a third person subject to a condition which had not been realized, it was clearly his duty to wait till he should ascertain whether after being fully informed of the nature of the Turkish proposal Lord Clarendon still adhered to the Vienna Note. In his own polished language he "determined not to forego unnecessarily the prospect of acting with the advantage of your lordship's *deliberate* instructions." The word I have italicized marks the ambassador's sense of the hurried, one might say flurried, character of Lord Clarendon's telegraphic assent to the Vienna Note.

Two days later the *Caradoc* brought these "deliberate instructions," which were to the effect that while "entirely approving" Lord Stratford's proceedings, the Government agreed with Count Buol in setting them aside and substituting the Vienna Note, on the ground that Russia had adopted the mediation of Austria and that there was reason to believe that the Note in question would be acceptable to the Czar. Until the arrival of the *Caradoc* Lord Stratford had maintained complete silence on the subject of the new Note. Now he recommended it officially to the Porte, dwelt on "the strong and earnest manner" in which the Austrian project was supported by the British Government, and its similarity in general tenour to Reshid's original Note to Menshikov, and pressed the fact that the Emperor of Russia's acceptance of the Note had already been telegraphed. Reshid listened "with a very good grace," but took exception to certain portions of the document, which he considered would have the effect of creating a Russian protectorate over the Greek

1853
—
ÆT. 66

E.P. II. 5

To Lord Clarendon, ccv. 11 Aug.

E.P. II. 32

E.P. II. 67

1853
—
Æ.T. 66
To Lord
Claren-
don,
CCXIV.
13 Aug.

Church in Turkey: a danger, remarked the ambassador in his despatch, which "was carefully avoided in the *Projet de Note* [Ultimatum] drawn up here." In forwarding the Pasha's unofficial and personal comments Lord Stratford added : " My own impression is that the amendments do not cover his objections, but I have abstained from telling him so in order to incur no risk of encouraging an opposition to a Note so highly recommended."

On 14 August the Council of ministers held a stormy meeting, and the majority seemed determined to have nothing to say to the Vienna Note, with or without amendments. "They founded this determination on the preference they gave to
CCXVI.
14 Aug.
the draft of a Note which the Porte had decided on forwarding to St. Petersburg through the Austrian Cabinet, and the declaration which had been formally made by Reshid Pasha . . . that nothing beyond the terms of that draft would be accepted." This was the opinion of the President, the Sheykh-el-Islam, the Finance Minister, the Seraskier, the Kapudan Pasha, Mohammed Rushdi, and two others. The Grand Vezir, Reshid, and Kamil Pasha, were for modification. Five ministers kept silence. The Council adjourned without coming to a formal decision.

Meanwhile the French ambassador, M. de la Cour, was
CCXIX.
14 Aug.
following a very singular course. He advised the Porte to accept the Vienna Note, but he coupled with this advice a good-natured alacrity in helping Reshid Pasha to draw up amendments to it, and he indulged in many brave words about the ulterior and active measures which France was prepared to take in support of the Ottoman Empire. He made inquiries about landing troops on the coasts of Turkey, and even asked whether the Porte considered the Dardanelles as already open to the passage of the Allied squadrons. No doubt he had authority from his Government to adopt this peculiar mode of recommending submission to the terms arranged at Vienna ; but it looked as though the recommendation were not genuine. Lord Stratford, however, who was not authorized to pull both ways, discouraged the Turks in any present expectation of armed support.

On 15 August Reshid Pasha told the British ambassador

that there was no hope of obtaining a majority in the Council
for the acceptance of the Vienna Note, and that he could not
himself sign it without modification. He complained of the
inconsiderate manner in which the London Cabinet had
agreed to the compromising arrangement at Vienna. It would
have been better for Turkey, he said, to have yielded at
the first, than after so much support from the Powers to be
now unseasonably abandoned. In reply, the ambassador of
England "abstained from making any admissions calculated
to encourage the Porte in its resistance." But as soon as it
was certain that the Note would not be accepted as it stood,
Lord Stratford began to search for a middle course. "Not
being authorized to use intimidating language," he told Lord
Clarendon, "I felt myself free, indeed compelled by a sense
of duty, to suggest some form of decision which might present the character of an acceptance, and yet leave room for
such an adjustment of terms as would completely secure the
Porte." His plan was "simply that the Porte should signify
its acceptance of the Note under its own construction of the
objectionable passages, and for securities rely on the assent
and sanction of the Four Powers." Mr. Alison was at the
Porte while the adjourned Council was sitting on the 17th,
and as soon as he had ascertained that the Note was going
to be thrown out, he offered this suggestion. It was not accepted.] On the 18th Reshid shewed the Elchi the amendments and the arguments which he had drawn up and presented
to the Council, and Lord Stratford was obliged to conceal
his appreciation of the good grounds which the Turkish
minister had brought forward to justify resistance. The
Elchi himself had not anticipated so much sound reason to
distrust the Note. A painful scene ensued. The Pasha
kissed the ambassador's hand and implored him with tears
not to "forsake his country in the midst of such dangers
and distresses." Lord Stratford made one more attempt to
procure at least a conditional acceptance of the unmodified
Note: but on 20 August the Grand Council of sixty members
decided that it could only be adopted with certain specified
amendments.

There is no need to describe the Turkish modifications of

1853
___
_ÆT._ 66

ccxxii.
18 Aug.

E.P. II.
69

E.P. II.
71

1853
———
ÆT. 66

the Vienna Note. They were regretted by the Four Powers, (though the French Government, not unnaturally, admitted that they were improvements upon the original draft); but all united in urging the Czar to accept them, as being really too trivial to be worth a quarrel. There are times when fate seems to put folly in the minds of the wise: otherwise how could the statesmen of four Great Powers describe as trivial the very differences upon which the whole dispute rested? Lord Stratford told Lord Clarendon that, although he had

E.P. II.
73

"scrupulously abstained from expressing any private opinion on the merits of Count Buol's Note, while it was under the consideration of the Porte," he could not help confessing to his lordship that the amendments were in his opinion necessary, unless a full right of interference over twelve million subjects of Turkey were to be granted to Russia. The point in dispute was clear enough to him: and it was equally clear to the Court of St. Petersburg. The Four Governments however continued innocently blind, until the Czar rejected the Turkish

II. 91

amendments on 7 September, and soon afterwards the famous "Russian Analysis of the Three Modifications introduced by the Ottoman Porte into the Vienna Note" was let out of the diplomatic bag, and all the world was immediately aware that Lord Stratford and the Turks were right, and the Four Powers wrong, in their interpretation of that "highly recommended"

II. 117

document. Lord Clarendon hastily dropped the Note with as much the air of having burnt his fingers as a statesman can be expected to reveal.

What would have been the result of the acceptance of the Vienna Note by the Porte is thus summarized by the Russian

i. 211

Foreign Office in its ingenuous *Diplomatic Study*: "The triumph of Russia, who in fact was winning the day over the resistance of the maritime Powers, and saw her position in the East strengthened by a solemn covenant concluded with the participation of all Europe; the exhaustion of Turkey, forced to a gratuitous display of her military forces, which completed the ruin of her finances, to leave her after all at the same point; lastly, a complete check to the personal influence of the Ambassador, which in his patriotism he identified with that of his Government." Truly, a Daniel come to

judgment! We thank thee, Russian, for that sentence. Every 1853
act of Lord Stratford's finds its perfect justification in the
candid avowals of this remarkable work. There are, as it ÆT. 66
were, tears in its eyes as it laments the imprudence of Russia
in insisting upon precise definitions of her rights in Turkey:
" In face of the incurable mistrust of which we were the i. 218
object, it was better to leave a certain vagueness around these
delicate questions. It was always in our power to interpret
them in accordance with our views, which were perfectly
proper." Of course: but propriety varies according to latitude
and longitude.

That the Vienna Note was inadmissible was now evident;
and it seems scarcely worth while to ask whether Lord
Stratford did all in his official power to procure the acceptance
by the Turks of a proposal which was afterwards proved to
be delusive. That he saw the dangerous features of the Note,
at least in part, is obvious, and equally obvious that his private
influence could not be wielded in favour of a plan which he
could not approve. But the despatches shew that he used
his official power to the full in support of the instructions of
his Government, and that he " scrupulously abstained " from
letting his personal opinions transpire. More could not be
expected. It is absolutely false to insinuate that his private
converse with the Turkish ministers contradicted his official
acts; and on the strength of the papers before me I may be
permitted to give the lie direct to a statement on p. 210 of
the Russian *Study* (vol. i.) It has been surmised that in
such a case " silence gave consent; " but the papers of the
time shew clearly that the Turks required no consent, silent or
spoken, to make them resist the Note. The Elchi wrote to
Lord Clarendon (20 August) " I feel confident that you will
give me credit for having done my *official* best in support of
the Vienna Note. Reshid told me candidly that no personal
influence would have induced the Porte to give way." One of
the ambassador's letters to Lord Westmoreland will shew that
he was anxious that his conduct should not be misunderstood, and a note from Mr. Alison, who knew more about the
matter than anyone else in the Embassy staff, confirms what
has been said above.

1853
———
ÆT. 66

To Lord
West-
moreland,
20 Aug.

Under present circumstances it will be difficult for me to escape the suspicion of having rather hindered than promoted the acceptance of Count Buol's Note. Depend upon it, any such insinuation is wholly unfounded. Whatever my private opinions may be, I have done justice to Clarendon's instructions. The Porte is piqued at the cool way in which its Notes and Protests and Declamations were *pooh-poohed* at Vienna; it has also more confidence in its strength, and a stronger sense of the embarrassment of having to dismis sits army without *avoir gain de cause*. But the main thing is that it sees clearly and strongly the exceptionable parts of the Austrian Note, and is determined to have all its apprehensions removed, *coûte que coûte*. If you want peace, you must put up with its very natural and justifiable misgivings, and turn your diplomatic batteries upon the principal offender.

The Internuncio, after warning Reshid solemnly that no amendment would be admitted, has held a more comfortable language to-day, and he has obtained an addition to the Sultan's answer to the Emperor's letter, purporting that the Sultan hopes for his Imperial Majesty's favour for the proposed modifications.

The Turks have resolved to reject the Austrian Note in spite of everything that the united Elchis could say. Whatever Lord S.'s private opinion may be, you may rest assured that this has in no way added to their exultation by influencing them either one way or another. Considering the dogged attitude they have assumed, it is lucky that H.E. has a chance of preserving his well-earned influence. We have no idea of what impression these matters will produce at home ; so, indeed, with regard to the history of the cause of all this delay. But it is a most unlucky *contretemps*.

Lord S. is in very good health and pluck. . . .

'Tis a pity you can't see the Bosphorus about Therapia, swarming with ships of war, and the opposite heights crowned with the green tents of the Egyptian camp. Constantinople itself has gone back fifty years, and the strangest figures swarm in from the distant provinces to have a cut at the Moscov. Turbans, lances, maces, and battle-axes jostle each other in the narrow streets, and are bundled off immediately to the camp at Shumla for the sake of a quiet life.

It was natural that the ambassador should feel annoyed at the suppression of his own plan of pacification, and he wrote in some irritation to Lord Clarendon and to Lady Stratford :—

The last stage of the business has proved more irksome than any that preceded it. The formal approbation of my conduct does not make up for the rejection of the plan transmitted from here, which I had sent home in full reliance on its usefulness and with the conviction that within its circle everything was placed on its proper footing. I have not even the consolation of thinking that it gave way to a more successful invention.

1853
———
Æ T. 66
To Lord Clarendon,
20 Aug.

I was not aware, till after the arrival here of the latter, that a regular Conference was established at Vienna. My impression was that the occasional meetings of the Four were similar to those which have been held here, neither more formal nor more authorized. . . .

I hope you will feel yourself at liberty to approve and second the suggestions of the Porte. It is impossible not to fear that the Emperor of Russia's acceptance of the Note *telle quelle* may have raised an additional difficulty. The Porte is to all appearance ready for anything.

All that I had gained with much pains and some good fortune, as I thought, by the Porte's Ultimatum of last month, has been swamped, and I am reduced to the necessity of living on my credit. Reshid Pasha tells me frankly in the confidence of private intercourse that British influence is exposed to the danger of an eclipse, and that if the Porte be left to struggle by itself, a close connexion with Russia may be preferred as the only resource.

To the same,
25 Aug.

Excuse my repeating that I hold your paper *The Times* to be rather hard upon us with its insinuations of slowness and *fainéantise*. We have neither telegraphs nor railways, but in their places Ramazans, Bayrams, and now and then a ministerial crisis to boot. Every proposition has to go backwards and forwards more than once between the Sultan and the Council, to say nothing of the confusion of tongues, the distances, and the intrigues. These circumstances taken together may constitute or imply slowness, but they constitute also a necessity which relieves us from reproach. Then as to our unproductiveness : far from admitting the charge, I venture to assert, *con rispetto*, that the most effectively pacific steps have all originated here, and that our plan of the 20 and 23 ultimo taken in its *ensemble* and viewed with respect to right principles, legitimate claims to success, and to the preservation of British influence, left nothing to regret but the simultaneous production of another plan.

I am more than ever to be pitied. It is literally out of my power to write twenty lines to you. I wrote or otherwise laboured in public matters the whole of yesterday, and I have sat up writing all night. The subjects too are disagreeable and will give much annoyance in Downing Street and still more at Argyll House. The Porte will not

To his Wife,
Saturday night—
Sunday morning,
20-1 Aug.

accept the Vienna Note without amendments, and the Turks are altogether on their high horse. Who can wonder after all that has happened? Our joint labours were thrown overboard in the beginning of the month, and they think it hard to be so used. They have better motives, however, for following their present course. The Note proposed to them was not safe, and I think they have no less justly than courageously held their own. As the Emperor Nicholas had accepted, the shock may be *awful*, and it is difficult to say what will be the end of it.

26 Aug.　I have eased my mind by writing what I think to Clarendon privately. The whole state of things is infinitely disagreeable. But the accounts from the Turkish army are good, and the spirit of the Government is up. I hope they will be *prudent* and *just* at home. I look forward to the answers to my last despatches with anxiety. I feel confident of being right, but seeing the tone and temper of those who prevail in the Cabinet I scarcely know what to expect. If care be not taken our influence here will be cut up for many a day to come.

To Lord
Cowley,
28 Aug.
　I hope you will not infer from my irregularity in replying to your notes that I am indifferent to the advantage of receiving them. The fact is that one can never get leisure at the right time. Even wife and children sometimes go to the wall. My consolation with respect to you is that, seeing the despatches, you know all that is worth knowing. We are of course looking forward with anxiety to the result of the last batch. I always apprehended that extreme fear of a war would increase the danger of it. The uses and effects of protesting instead of trumpeting, when the occupation took place, have not perhaps been sufficiently appreciated. In advising the moderate course, I believed it to be the best road to a final triumph. Among the consequences to be expected was that of increased preparation for war on this side of the Danube, with a proportionate increase of confidence here, and of motive for requiring an effective and durable settlement. While this was working high, the Porte felt, not perhaps without reason, that it had been somewhat coolly treated at Vienna. Whatever proceeds from that quarter is as much suspected here as it is trusted at Petersburg. De la Cour is in a great fuss. He works secretly, and, as he fancies, without my knowledge. Fortunately I have still some means of control, and use them quietly to avoid disputes. Patience I conceive to be our best watchword for the present. I hope our next instructions may be such as to enable us to work together with a fair prospect of guiding the Porte to a *safe*, though peaceful, conclusion of this " eventful history."

　Buol's amended Note was recommended from London with so

much simplicity and good intention, that the surprize and disappointment will probably be greater there than elsewhere. I will not however allow myself to despair, and our Ottoman friends, though somewhat out of humour with us, still reckon upon the sterling qualities of John Bull.

I have read the Queen's Speech and I have skimmed over the speeches of her Majesty's lieges in the H. of C. They have both made a very uncomfortable impression upon me. Politically they make me fear that an abstract idea of peace has carried the day over every other consideration, that the Turks will be left to themselves, and that Russia will finally come back with a flood tide. Personally they seem to foreshadow an evil end to my embassy. . . . Alas! Alas! Such a triumph to be so thrown away! and why? Because the affairs of this country are not honestly looked in the face—because they are made subordinate to party politics and other interests elsewhere because people think small while they talk big—and finally because we make an idol of the aggressor and offer him incense when he ought to have smoke of another kind. Do not infer from this that your ancient is a chimaera breathing fire and flame. He is neither for peace nor for war. He is for the Question—for its settlement—its settlement on fair and durable grounds. If we are mistaken about the Question, if it has been exaggerated and has not the importance we have hitherto attached to it—let that be made clear—I will be the first to recant and to recommend the best piece of tinkering that diplomacy can offer. If on the contrary we are really in presence of the great Eastern Question, if it knocks at our door, stands on tiptoe and looks in at our window, it may be an ugly and frightful object, but we must look it in the face and deal with it as men and statesmen ought to do. Clarendon writes in private good-humouredly and kindly, and his despatches are all more or less approving: but our Constantinople plan of arrangement has been *overlaid*; my notions have not been followed up; and the Turks are treated with levity, not to say disrespect. The consequence of all this is that their pride is up and that they are so circumstanced with their army and subjects as to find it almost equally dangerous to give in or to resist. In short what I wrote to the Office several weeks ago may easily be realized: "The extreme desire of peace, if care be not taken, may bring on the danger of war." I know not what to think of it; but a very small slip in Downing Street, or rather at Argyll House, on the receipt of my last despatches may cause a world of mischief. The die is, however, probably cast by this time, and we shall see. . . . The Turks I think are bent on *war, unless their amendments are accepted*, and I fear they cannot help

1853
—
ÆT. 66

themselves with respect to their army and nation, now thoroughly roused though hitherto well behaved. The poor Sultan! I have much to say, but alas no time.

13 Sept.

You seem to have tumbled into the general mistake. You fancied that all was settled. You reckoned without your host. You thought that if the Eastern Question could linger beyond 12 August (grouse shooting) it could not by any possibility survive 1 September. The Turks are not sportsmen, as you know, and consequently enter little into such considerations. They have been thought *right* by all Europe—they have had much to swallow, and still have much to fear. They naturally therefore seek to make a good once-for-all job of it, and to secure themselves by a clear intelligible *finale* from future wrong. Unfortunately they have their own way of acting, even when they are right, and it is a way which is full of stumbling-blocks, pitfalls, and inconsistencies. I am doomed to share the blame with them, but I see little disposition to give me a share of anything else. During the last four days we have been to all appearance in imminent peril of a revolution. Guess how the ministers were frightened, when one of them asked me to take care of his jewels. Strong measures were proposed, but I resisted, not choosing to act blindly. Still I acted, though quietly and mostly by myself. This course seems to have succeeded and all danger seems to be appeased for the present. We are now expecting the Russian answer. It will probably arrive to-morrow. "No" may be war on the Danube; "Yes" may be tumult here. This is far from agreeable.

The Czar's total rejection of the Turkish amendments was, officially known at Constantinople on 25 September, and the

To Lord Claren-
don,
CCLXXVII.
25 Sept.

original Note was again recommended to the Porte. Lord Stratford himself joined anxiously in this step, and urged the Turkish ministers to accept the unmodified Note under a guarantee of the Four Powers. He implored Reshid to adopt this plan, but in vain: the popular spirit was roused, and neither Sultan nor minister dared stand against it. On the following day the Great Council of the Empire, mustering

E.P. II.
144

172 members, unanimously resolved that the unmodified Vienna Note could not be accepted on any terms, "even if accompanied by a guarantee of the Four Powers," and that

E.P. II.
149

war was inevitable.] On 4 Oct. a notification was despatched through Omar Pasha to Prince Gorchakov, summoning him

to evacuate the Principalities within fifteen days : a negative 1853
reply would be regarded as a declaration of war. The Russian
commander replied on 10 Oct. that he had " no authority to ÆT. 66
treat of peace or war or evacuation of the Principalities," and
this evasive but practically negative answer was accepted by
Reshid Pasha as the " beginning of war." Some importance
attaches to this date, as it has been contended that war did
not formally begin till the fifteen days after the receipt of the
notification had expired, *i.e.* till 24 Oct. But Omar Pasha's
letter to Prince Gorchakov distinctly stated that if, in the interval, a negative reply reached him, hostilities would be the
natural consequence. That negative reply reached him on
the 10th or 11th, and from that date, in theory at least, a
state of open war existed. Fearing that Russia might im- E. P. II.
mediately attack the capital with her fleet, they urged the 190
French and English ambassadors to bring up their squadrons
to protect the Sultan. But before we enter upon the naval
phase, a few extracts from the private correspondence may be
quoted in illustration of the period between the amending
of the Vienna Note and the summoning of the squadrons. A
letter from Mr. Alison to Lady Stratford gives an account of
the insurrection. :—

I hope that you were not very anxious about the conspiracy among C. Alison
the Ulema, and owing to which we brought up a squadron of to Lady
steamers. How the Russians must hate us for it ! It ended very Stratford,
Therapia,
quietly with those worthy doctors reciting the texts in the Koran 28 Sept.
according to which they ought to hold counsel with themselves and
go to war,—so far ; but it was a hint which the Sultan dared not
throw away, for they would have very shortly produced another text,
such as, for instance, "and when one of the rulers of the faithful
shall incline his ears unto the counsels of the ungodly, slay him, lest
he be thereby perverted, and save his soul to the Lord." It was for
this reason that the Sultan girded on his sword and swaggering about
as best he could sent for his ministers and made them a speech.
He said that he would have no more diplomatizing, and that he
would have nothing to say to the Vienna contrivances : that he was
determined, in short, to make an end, and he desired them to go and
take counsel together. The ministers lost no time. They assembled
a monster Council which lasted two days, and decided that they
ought to go to war. They will settle soon when they are to begin,

and we are all very curious to learn their projects. This great Council resembled very much a meeting of the Commons. The ministers were on one side and all the Pashas out of office on the other. At the bottom were the representatives of the Law, the Trades, the Army and the Navy. Then they have their parliamentary phraseology. Instead of saying " the hon. gent. got on his legs and said," they say " that Pillar of the State laid down his pipe and spake." Instead of "cheers "—" puffs of tobacco ; " and for " he sat down amidst general cheering," " he subsided into repose and was enveloped in clouds of incense." I have got one of their speeches but it is too long to transcribe, and too good to be mangled. Before this reaches you the telegraphic news will have already arrived, and I daresay that you will be all very much alarmed to no purpose. . . .

Lord S. is well satisfied with what has been done here hitherto, and they seem to be so at the F. O. also, as far as the Embassy is concerned. On this last occasion, also, everything possible has been done to damp the ardour of the Turks : more might explode the revolution, and we should have the blood of that weak good-natured Sultan on our hands.

To his
Wife,
1 Oct.

We have narrowly escaped a sanguinary revolution, and we have escaped it only to go *full tilt* into war. The Sultan and General Council have resolved upon war, and the Russians will soon be summoned to march out of the provinces, preparatory to hostilities if they don't, as they won't, comply.

This is an awful prospect—as near as it is awful. I have done what I could to avert it, but circumstances swollen by mismanagement have carried all before them. My only satisfaction is that I admonished in time and that I have kept the even march which I resolved on keeping from the commencement. Even now I am keeping the steamer in order to scribble this to you, and my feet are literally sore with standing at the upright desk for the last eight hours. I shall be asked to bring up the squadrons, and feel embarrassed beforehand. .

To Lord
Clarendon
4 Oct.

I fear that nothing can now prevent the declaration of war. There is just the possibility of something coming through Vienna in time to interpose a declaration or fresh overture more or less in the nature of what I have suggested before the formal declaration is published. But the better chance is that after the declaration no actual hostilities will take place during the present advancing season, and that a strenuous interposition of the *Four*, if that be possible, may produce a reconciliation while blood is still undrawn.

We have nothing to apprehend from disturbances *here*, and I regret that the French have shewn so little disposition to send away their extra force when the danger has passed away. I make no comments on M. de la Cour's telegraphic despatch. My correspondence, though I regret its tardy arrival in London, will have given you my estimation of the circumstances.

The French would seem to have some motive of *their own* for bringing up the squadrons. . . . I do my best to move in harmony with them, but they are jealous of our influence here, and are ever and anon endeavouring to carry out some by-object of their own under pretence of acting for the common cause.

I cannot see how the Emperor and the Sultan are both to be satisfied and avoid war ! The direct communication to Russia without having had the Sultan's consent is the real cause of mischief. England did this, and when Lord Clarendon told me he had done so, I ventured to say "What ! without the Turks knowing your proposition ?' He said what Carlo [Lord Canning] has since said : "Oh ! yes, we are to decide for them you know." My instinct made me fear this was not the same thing, but wiser heads saw it differently !

Fr. Lady
Stratford,
6 Sept.

Here is Sunday but no Sabbath. I wish you could see the litter of papers in my room. I am literally up to my neck in them and there are puzzling questions to be decided, and all on my own responsibility. Four months since Menshikov went away, and not only just as we were, but worse. In fact we are on the very verge of war, and only waiting for actual hostilities. Nobody, I suppose, is to blame on this side of the Danube, certainly not the poor Turks, who have done and are still doing, wonders, that is to say, in their way, and yet not quite in their way, for they have acted with singular prudence and good order. The head and front of the offence is that man who has been humbugging Europe, and perhaps at times even duping himself, for the last quarter of a century. He, and he alone, is the original cause—there have been accessories since—of a mischief which nothing short of a miracle can now prevent, and which sooner or later will probably drag within its vortex the greater part of the civilized world. I have done my best for peace—in *propria personâ* where I could with honour and conviction,—as *an agent* when I did not like the manner of proceeding :—but I have also stuck close to *the Question*, and we now have ample proof from Russia herself that the Turks were right in mistrusting the Vienna Note, and that there *is a question* worth contending for, as is admitted even by Mr. Reeve, the *Times* writer, who is now here and who dined with me yesterday. When I induced the Sultan not to declare war when the Russians entered the Principalities I did so not only for peace, but for the question also,—

To W.
Canning,
9 Oct.

meaning and thoroughly expecting that the "Allies" would coöperate with vigour to settle the dispute. On one side there was a strong man with a bad cause ; on the other a weak man with a good one. I leave others to say which of the two has been flattered and which repressed. If the quarrel had occurred in any street of London, it would probably have been otherwise. Be that as it may, the storm is coming on and it is more easy to see the beginning than the end of it.

If no serious hostilities take place during the winter, there may still be room for negotiation. But in the meantime all existing treaties between Russia and Turkey will have been smashed, and the Turks, if they entertain any hopes of a successful campaign next year, may be unwilling to revert to Notes and Embassies. War once begun, the *very least* that the belligerents can fight for is a thorough ascendancy on the one side and a decent emancipation on the other. My expectation is that both parties will be led by their natural desires and fears to a more comprehensive struggle, and that it will be found necessary not only to draw the sword but to throw away the scabbard.

CHAPTER XXVII.

THE SUMMONS TO THE FLEET.

October–December 1853.

THE question of bringing up the squadrons had long been a subject of anxious thought to Lord Stratford. He knew all the risks attending the appearance of the Allied fleets in the Bosphorus: so long as war was not declared, he was aware that the passage of the Dardanelles would be regarded as a violation of the Treaty of 1841, by which foreign ships of war are excluded from the Straits in time of peace, and he was therefore careful not to bring on the crisis by a precipitate appeal to the Admiral. It will be remembered that he left England for the East armed with no further powers than to request the Admiral at Malta to hold himself in readiness for sea. This power was augmented on 2 June when the Western Governments took the first united step towards war by ordering the fleets to Besika Bay, where they were to await the ambassadors' further instructions. It might be urged that the movement formed part of their ordinary cruising, but all Europe knew that they had gone to succour the Porte, and that their advance was a direct reply to the Ultimatum and departure of Prince Menshikov. Still, so long as the fleets remained outside the Castles of the Dardanelles Russia had no treaty-right to protest ; and Lord Stratford, whilst rejoicing in what he hoped was a sign of a manly policy, resolved that outside they should remain so long as he could keep them there.

There were two squadrons, however, and two ambassadors ; and the proceedings of the French at this time were more

1853

ÆT. 66

E.P. I.
198
2 June

1853

—

ÆT. 66

To Lord
Claren-
don,
CCXXXVIII
24 Aug.

than usually ambiguous. We have seen how, whilst urging the Turks to accept the Vienna Note, (admitting at the same time that he had no authority to "impose it" upon them,) M. de la Cour was continually throwing out hints that were apparently calculated to encourage them in resisting the very advice which he was ostensibly tendering. On 18 and again on 22 August he asked Reshid Pasha to give instructions to the Pasha of the Dardanelles to let the French fleet pass up, should Admiral Hamelin so desire, without reference to any corresponding movement on the part of Vice-Admiral Dundas. On the night following the day on which he had given the Porte a hint of the probable advance of the French fleet, M. de la Cour informed Reshid of a proposal for a new convention, which, while superseding the Treaty of 1841, should distinctly establish the integrity and independence of Turkey under the guarantee of the Four Powers. Lord Stratford had heard nothing officially of these plans, and lost no time in telling his colleague that he "was ignorant of any sufficient reason for bringing up the squadrons to Constantinople;" but he could not restrain M. de la Cour's zeal, and, as he wrote to Lord Clarendon, he began to suspect some "political escapade" on the part of France, who "seemed eager for war." Lord Clarendon himself told Lady Stratford that both he and Lord Aberdeen doubted Louis Napoleon extremely, and the conduct of the French ambassador was calculated to confirm their doubts.

The spirit of the Turks needed no rousing then. Even Lord Stratford found them "out of hand," and the Sheykh-el-Islam had declared that he would sooner break his seal than affix it to such a document as the Vienna Note. Reshid told M. de la Cour that the persistence of the Western Courts in recommending humiliating concessions to the Porte would end in throwing Turkey into the arms of Russia: to which the French ambassador replied that in such a case France would look to a close alliance with Austria and Prussia and would leave England and Turkey in the lurch. The high tone of the Porte found a ready echo in the voices of the theological students and professors, Softas and Ulema, who, as we have seen, rose in open mutiny, angrily protesting against

1853
———
ÆT. 66

concessions to the infidels.   Such movements are not unusual among the fanatical scholars of the East, and there is no reason to suppose that the insurrection was a device of the ministers to force the hands of the Western ambassadors. It had, however, that effect : for M. de la Cour, with all the Frenchman's vivacity, drew a harrowing picture to his Government of a coming massacre of his countrymen, and M. Drouyn de Lhuys hastened to the rescue.   It is amazing to read in his own words that Lord Clarendon, in concert of course with Lord Aberdeen, was induced by the representations of a foreign government, based upon a single telegraphic report, to take the serious step of ordering the advance of the squadron through the Dardanelles, without waiting for Lord Stratford's despatches.   A few days' delay would have shewn that there was no danger to foreigners at Constantinople and that Lord Stratford himself had quelled the disturbance and provided for the safety of the British colony without summoning the fleet.   He had only brought up a couple of steamers to protect English subjects, and the French had done the same : no more formidable preparations were needed.   An insurrection, the mere rumour of which had sufficed to frighten the Secretary of State into a panic, had been witnessed, met, and quelled, without discomposure, by the calm mind that watched over the Embassy at the Porte.   The strong man, loth to put forth his strength, imposes peace by the mere ascendancy of his dauntless will.   The weakling, in his dread of blows, cries out for weapons which he cannot sheathe.

E.P. II.
109

The immediate effect of Lord Clarendon's ill-starred despatch of 23 September was a remonstrance from Baron Brunov, the Russian ambassador, who declared that the instruction to the fleet was a breach of treaty.   To this the Foreign Minister replied that the Porte had "ceased to be at peace from the moment when the first Russian soldier entered the Danubian Principalities," and added that the whole fleet was to go up to Constantinople.   The sinister impression created at St. Petersburg by this correspondence forms an important link in the chain of circumstances that made towards war : but the singular part of the transaction is that

1853
———
ÆT. 66

at the place most concerned in the advance of the fleets Lord Clarendon's precipitate instruction had no effect at all. The mischief was done at St. Petersburg, but there was one at Constantinople who was determined that he would have no hand in it. Lord Stratford received the order to call up the fleet with characteristic coolness and sagacity. His reply shewed a delicate tinge of sarcasm. He was " deeply sensible " of the Government's " interest in the preservation of British lives and property at Constantinople, under the impressions derived from M. de la Cour's telegraphic despatch : " and especially of " that part of these instructions [of 23 September] which authorizes me to *consider the presence* of her Majesty's squadron here, *if I thought proper to require it,* as intended to embrace the protection of the Sultan also in case of need." Lord Clarendon had said nothing of the nature of the words which I have italicized: " Your Excellency is instructed to send for the British fleet to Constantinople " was his order. But Lord Stratford was determined not to understand it in its plain sense ; and his despatch very quietly went on— " Fortunately there is no necessity whatever for calling up the squadron on either account. . . . I am still of opinion that assistance thus limited [to two or three steamers] would have answered every purpose. . . . I wished to save her Majesty's Government from any embarrassments likely to accrue from a premature passage of the Dardanelles." The despatch from which these sentences are taken was written on 6 October, and for a fortnight longer Lord Stratford resisted every attempt to force on a hasty appeal to the Admirals. Had the order been obeyed, it might plausibly have been argued that the Treaty of 1841 had been violated : but it was not obeyed ; the situation at the Porte remained in the same state as it had been ever since Lord Clarendon's despatch of 2 June ; and the fleets were summoned, for a quite different reason, after the Turks had declared themselves to be at overt war with the Czar.

E.P. II.
183

II. 109

What was this reason ? Simply that the Porte, after giving Prince Gorchakov fifteen days to arrange for the evacuation of the Danubian provinces, feared that Russia would not wait the time, but would make a sudden descent, possibly upon the Bosphorus, and place the capital in jeopardy ; and the Sultan accordingly requested the protecting presence of the fleets, which he knew was provided for in the ambassador's instructions. The request was made on the 8th, but twelve days passed before Lord Stratford issued the momentous order to the Admiral. In the interval, Prince Gorchakov's reply to the Turkish notice to quit had removed the last doubt as to whether the two Powers were at war or peace, and the Treaty of 1841 formed, therefore, no-obstacle to the entrance of the squadrons. The Sevastopol fleet was also said to be under weigh. Accordingly on 20 October the ambassadors of England and France summoned the squadrons, and on the 22nd they entered the Hellespont.

In announcing this important step to his Government Lord Stratford made it clear that it was based upon his " original instructions "—*i.e.* to protect the Sultan. With reference to the order of 23 September he added, " The junc- ture for which the last ones were framed has long since ceased to have any existence in fact : " there was no longer any risk of a revolution. For nearly eight months he had held those original instructions ; for four months he had possessed complete authority over the fleet ; France had tried vainly to hurry him, and his own Government had rashly yielded to the imprudent counsels of Paris ; but Lord Stratford had stood unmoved till the time came when he could bring up the fleet with no breach of international engagements. He would have preferred to hold out yet a little longer, but the Turks were anxious, and the French ambassador was becoming unmanageable :[1] " I have almost risked

---

[1] " I might have preferred an additional delay of a few days in order to effect a complete coincidence between the passage of the Dardanelles by the squadrons and the actual or formal commencement of war [i.e. of actual hostilities] : but the instructions of my French colleague are, according to his assurance, so peremptory that by longer postponing my decision I should have incurred the risk of separating from him." This was written to Lord Aberdeen on 15 October, before Prince Gorchakov's reply to the Turkish notice had been received at Pera on the 18th : but the summons to the fleet was issued *after* that. It may justly be argued that the Turks did not act up to their theory that war began on 10 Oct., any more than they treated the entry of the Russians into the Principalities as a declaration of war. They did not begin fighting on the receipt of Gorchakov's letter. But this was because Lord Stratford, in his desire for peace, and anxiety to avoid

a quarrel," he wrote to Lord Clarendon, "by holding out so long.'

The entrance of the squadrons caused no break in the negotiations for peace. At the very moment when his summons was speeding to the Admiral, Lord Stratford was
communicating (21 October) to London and Vienna his " Note and Declaration," which he believed the Porte would accept, and which once more accorded to Russia all and more than all that she had any right to ask. At the same time he obtained with great difficulty the consent of the Turkish Government to a postponement of hostilities for ten days.

The message which procured this postponement is characteristic : it was addressed to Reshid Pasha through Stephen Pisani :—

Tell Reshid Pasha that I have fresh letters from London just come in, and he *must* prepare to stop hostilities for the moment. There is no avoiding it. He will lose all—France and England too —if war is precipitated. I also shall be materially injured. Steamers *must* go off *to-day*, *coûte que coûte*, with orders to Omar Pasha and to the commanders in Asia not to stir an inch without further orders. We —the four or the two—will bear the Porte out in this. Say all this to him *immediately*. I am waiting for the others, who are not come yet. As soon as we have talked, I will write again or go myself to the Pasha at Balta Liman, where you will stay for the present.

I sent my two drafts of Note and Declaration to Reshid Pasha *privately* this morning. He was only to read them for his personal information, and not to mention them to his colleagues in office. It was stated to him in explanation that the papers could not be previously submitted to either Government, because the principle was that of a simultaneous communication to both, and that all I wanted to know was his private impression, which I could not doubt would be like mine—namely, a conviction that the Note and Declaration together were all that the Porte could desire or expect in reason, and well worth acceptance when taken as an escape from the dangers of war. I am sorry to say that the Pasha's answer, as reported to me

causes of dispute, urgently restrained them. Technically they were certainly at war on the 10th, and the entry of the fleets could not be regarded as a breach of treaty.

by Mr. Pisani, was not as satisfactory as I had expected. He found no fault, but hesitated to express an opinion, and wanted to compare one Note with another before he could form a decision in his own mind. With respect to time his language was peremptory : he could not add a day to the term of suspension already granted with much difficulty, as he declared, and in this he differed from his language of yesterday, when he thought that something might still be gained if news favourable to the hope of peace came from Vienna. To account for this difference, it appears that the suspension has got wind, and occasions dissatisfaction among the people. It has also happened that a sudden order for the immediate departure of the Russian Chancery and remaining commercial functionaries arrived yesterday through the Austrian Legation, and it is under the Austrian flag that the Russians are to go partly to Odessa and partly to Galatz. The chief Russian interpreter Argyropoulos goes to the latter place, as if his destination was the army.

The upshot of all this is that Reshid cannot make head, even if he be so inclined, against his warlike colleagues, and that unless some proposal of a decidedly satisfactory kind should come in from Vienna very soon, there will be no chance whatever of avoiding hostilities.

To say the truth, I should hardly have ventured to launch my two expedients, even as possibilities and forlorn hopes, had the famous Russian explanations been known here at the time.

With respect to the term of fifteen days, I tried at the time to obtain thirty, but failed, though I succeeded in getting an extension from eight or ten to fifteen, with an underhand promise, which was kept, that a few days more would be gained by delay in preparing the summons and sending it off. I also obtained a promise that no act of hostility should take place on the Turkish side before the expiration of the fifteen days, even if Gorchakov answered sooner in a negative sense. After all, with the present addition we get a whole month, and Gorchakov had no mind to gain time. Alas ! I fear that war is the decree of the Fates and our wisest part will be to do what we can to bring it to a thoroughly good conclusion.

His Note was accepted at Paris and London. Lord Clarendon earnestly entreated that *anything* coming from Lord Stratford might be " favourably considered " at Vienna. But in spite of the arguments of the English and French Governments, the Note and Declaration were thrown over by Austria, on the ground that a Treaty of Peace, and not a Note, was required, now that war was declared. Thus for

1853
—
ÆT. 66

the second time Austria destroyed the chance of a collective pressure upon the Czar. The separate action of the Maritime Powers in entering the Dardanelles may be adduced as a reason for an offended feeling at Vienna, but can hardly avail as an excuse for repudiating a proposal which had no aim but that of attaining peace.

Lord Stratford, however, was not surprized at the failure. He wrote disconsolately to his wife :—

To his Wife, 22 Oct.

I have made another effort for peace—one which made three months ago might, I verily believe, have succeeded, in so far as anything tolerable for the Turks can succeed with the Czar. But it will only serve to figure in the Blue Book. War is a decree of the Fates and we shall surely have it. Therefore I have written urging the necessity of looking to the means of success at once on a large scale. Help the Turks we must, and the more decidedly we do it the better for ourselves in the end. . . .

I wrote my requisition to the Admiral to bring in the squadrons on the anniversary of the battle of Navarino.

25 Oct.

The squadrons have entered the Dardanelles, but our portion is not yet arrived. The winds have been and still are strong from the north.

You tell me to make another attempt for peace. I have done so, and with the greatest difficulty obtained a suspension of hostilities — the last—for ten days. My *forlorn hope* was accepted in London and at Paris,[1] and I put the whole into shape, so that the Porte most evidently could, and Russia ought to, accept it. But I am convinced that Russia never would accept it, and that Austria would not join in pressing it. On the whole I am satisfied that nothing can now avert the war, which in fact exists, though hostilities are not yet known to have begun.

To Lord Clarendon, 22 Oct.

If Austria had taken a favourable view of my *forlorn hope* surely we should have heard from Vienna by this time. I have concealed, and requested De la Cour to conceal, its having originated with me. Supposed to have been struck out between Paris and London it is more likely to succeed, if indeed there were any longer room for success in the way of peace. I took care to shew Reshid P. the strongest paragraph of your private letter about the Porte's tendencies to war *coûte que coûte*, and it had its effect upon *him*. Many, many

---

[1] He had sent a first draft of his project to London and Vienna on 3 October.

thanks for your numerous and very explicit private letters.   They are
a great source of comfort to me.

, Lord Clarendon's opinion upon these transactions was
cordially given to Lady Stratford :—

Think of my having had on 27 October one hour and a half's private
audience with the Minister of Foreign Affairs . . . Ld. Cl. explained
the whole position of the Eastern affairs to me, and gave me to
understand he *entirely* approved of your policy ; wished it had been
followed *at first* ; and declared he had now sent to the Porte, founded
on your *own* ideas from Constantinople, a paper for its approval (I
mean the Porte's) agreed on by France and Prussia with England, and
to be *seen* by the Austrian Government as the messenger passed
through Vienna, in case *they* might be disposed to agree to it, but
not subject to any *alteration* or *detention*, on *their* part, on its way to
you.   He expressed his great fear—as this paper was only sent on
the 25th, it might not reach you in time to save hostilities—or to be
listened to if they had begun.   Still, it was all he could do now, and
with the fleet to help you, he still *hoped* for peace, but dared not expect
it ; although if it could be gained it would be through *your* means,
and he should be the first to give you all the praise and credit ;
nothing could be more able or more wise than your conduct, as appeared to him, and the Government were entirely of the same opinion.
He talked of M. de la Cour's recall—did not like it ; mentioned a
report that *he* had complained of your being *reserved* with him.   I
said you had spoken always in high terms of him, but once mentioned,
"like his nation he required a little watching."   "Ah ! yes—well,
that is my feeling; we are perfectly satisfied with the part the French
have taken with us in the Eastern affairs, but we don't like a *military*
ambassador being *now* sent out, nor the military nor naval *readiness*
they always evince towards the East."

He seemed pleased and struck by the coincidence of *your* writing
to him of your surprize at the French admiral's flag being hoisted
up in the Golden Horn and their ships remaining so much longer
than necessary there, while *he* (Ld.C.) was writing to you about French
activity at Toulon and elsewhere.   He thought it most wise your
sending back the ships at once that you had called up when in fear
of the Bayram *insurrection*.   He rather complained that the Sultan did
not follow *your* advice as much as he ought to do or to have done,
particularly when you *wished* him to agree to the Austrian Convention
[Vienna Note] subject to the *trusteeship* of the Four Western Powers,
who would make themselves answerable for the Emperor's right under-

Fr. Lady
Stratford,
1 Nov.

1853

ÆT. 66

standing of it: "The Principalities would probably have been evacuated had this been done." I could not stand this, and ventured to say even to H.M.F.M. that the *direct* communication to Russia through her own vassal Austria and without any reference to the Sultan, and containing only the same demands that P. Menschikov had made so long ago, naturally, perhaps, exasperated the Sultan and the Turks, and made them believe they could not depend upon our assistance and must therefore satisfy their people's war cry, having no longer *any excuse* not to do so. Lord C. evidently did not like this and seemed to infer the Sultan was not in a position to help himself and should not therefore forget his situation.

I ventured to hope that Lord Aberdeen would now perceive that your impressions towards the E. were not so prejudiced as I feared he had always thought. I mentioned how often I had heard you say "you only wished to serve your country as well as the E. serves his," and perhaps no greater compliment could be paid to the E. He assented to this, and upon my asking whether he ever saw Brunov, he replied, " Oh no, never now ; he sees the scrape his master has got into and keeps aloof."

Fr. Lady
Stratford,
3 Nov.

Lord Clarendon is entirely with you in heart—if not in action. Lord Palmerston, I am told, has said " No harm will happen while you are at Constantinople ! " and I know you have the Sultan's ear. All this should give you courage to do what is right unflinchingly. Brunov says " he shall not sell his horses this year," which looks as if he still had too much of Lord Aberdeen's ear. Gladstone cries loudly for peace because he views the question on the narrow ground (in a political sense) of Christianity against Mohammedanism and because of his Legacy, Income, and no end of other taxes. But the world in general, though *against* war, are *not* for peace, unless to be gained with the honour of England. . .

Musurus has just been here. He says your proposal from Constantinople just received is *approved* of, but as Lord C. sent you one from himself on the 25th, I imagine, if it can hold good, you will make *it* do so, as losing less time than waiting for the consent to your own here.

8 Nov.

Lady Stratford found the Foreign Secretary in a less amiable mood a few days later. He was evidently frightened at the entrance of the squadrons, although a month earlier he had urgently commanded their advance :—

From the
same,
12 Nov.

You mention "*your forlorn hope*" having met with success. I rejoice at this. Can this be the proposition, so like his own, Lord Cl.

told me, that having crossed his (sent to you on 25 October) he had
determined to forward it, your note, (having the Turk's assent,) to
France and Prussia and finally Russia, not to lose time? "This proposal was excellent," he said, "and he could not pay it a higher compliment than sending it on." I bowed assent, but expressed distress
that your last despatches, on the whole, of 22 October did not
seem quite so satisfactory. He said "Why, he was sick of this Supreme
Council, which seemed to stop your endeavours at every moment ;
did not understand what it meant ; thought you were taken in ; that
Reshid promised to stop hostilities, but did not do so ; that Reshid's
letter was too ridiculously arrogant and exigeant ; that the idea of his
sending *our* fleet to the Baltic, the Black Sea, and declaring there
were too many ships at Constantinople, appeared to him monstrous ;
he doubted Reshid's being of the peace party more than the others.
He feared you were really seeing with too Turkish eyes ; that you
were calling for war on a monstrous scale. The Government
did not enter into your view on this question ; they did not believe
Russia was so much to be dreaded or intended such harm. *He* had
more hope of quieting the E. of R., whom he knew *now* desired
earnestly for peace, than quieting the Turks, whose head seemed so
turned that they no longer listened to *your* advice. He said an armistice must be declared. "Then will the Russians evacuate?" said I,
" and negotiations begin ? because till the Principalities are evacuated,
they cannot meet on equal grounds." "Oh no," he said, " how is that
possible ? No evacuation can take place till the preliminaries for a
treaty are begun, but as soon as the Turk sends his man to negotiate,
so soon will the Russians march out." " Are you quite convinced of
this—may I ask ? " "Quite: I will stake my existence that so it will
be." "We have waited long in great forbearance for this desired and
only just event." "That is true ; but the E. is in earnest *now* and these
stupid Turks are cutting their own throats, and every moment the war
lasts the case becomes more complicated." " They are fighting nobly
to regain their own country, unjustly taken from them—should not we
do the same?" "Oh yes ; but we have the power, they have not,
and we cannot bring Russia upon us, and produce a general war for
the Turks, who will not listen to our counsels." I said "France
seems much in earnest." He said "Yes ; but France would have
swallowed the Olmütz professions—it was I who would not listen to
them, and after consideration they agreed with me."

No sooner was one proposal rejected than another was
made. Indeed, as the correspondence has shewn, at the
moment that Lord Stratford's Note and Declaration were

1853
———
ÆT. 67

E.P. II.
164,
24 Oct.
travelling to Vienna, a new *Projet de Note,* based upon his
suggestion of a revised edition of the Vienna Note, was being
despatched from Downing Street. We must at least give
Lord Clarendon credit for industry if we are obliged to
regret his want of resolution. The Elchi and the Foreign
Secretary had been working at the same idea—Lord Stratford
had suggested it on 28 September—and the results took final
shape almost on the same day. Not to be behindhand with a
specific remedy, Count Buol was at the moment sketching and
the English Foreign Minister was amiable enough to aid him
E.P. II.
315,
6 Dec.
in preparing a Collective Note of the Four Powers, which,
together with a Protocol of an important explanatory meeting of the four representatives at Vienna, was despatched on
5 December to Constantinople.

But many things had happened at Stambol before the
Collective Note arrived on 17 December. The Austrian Internuncio, after endeavouring once more to obtain the acceptance
E.P. II.
185,
15 Oct.
of the original Vienna Note, was again ordered to approach the
Porte on peaceful aims intent. Russia had informed Austria of
her willingness to treat, and the Internuncio was accordingly to
assure the Turkish Government of the conciliatory desires of
the Emperor Nicholas, as explained at the meeting at Olmütz,
and the just and reasonable character of his demands on
behalf of the Greek Church. Lord Clarendon did not see the
E.P. II.
240,
16 Nov.
matter in this light. The recent manifesto of the Czar, the
appointment of a Russian governor in the Principalities, the
threats of Prince Gorchakov to the Sultan's subjects, did not,
in his opinion, breathe an air of conciliation. So thought the
Porte when the Note was laid before it on 24 November.
Moreover war was now briskly going on, and this did not
look conciliatory. Alison reported :—

C. Alison
to Lady
Stratford,
25 Nov.
H.E. himself is very well off, but we have nothing but our ardour
for peace to keep us warm. I suppose it will come about. The
Turks in the meantime are fighting like tigers. In the last engagement in Asia they threw away their muskets and attacked the Russians
with their knives, making no prisoners. They say that if we are not
expeditious there will be no Russians left to make peace with. The
great embarrassment is the number of peacemakers. Lord Cl. sends
a very reasonable project, and before we have half beaten it into the

heads of the Turks, the Frenchman abandons us to advocate an Austrian project newly arrived. With the greatest respect for Cabinets, all this is very foolish and playing into the hands of the Turks. When everyone else is dead I intend to write an Oriental romance, to be called " Les Mille et une Notes."

1853

.ET. 67

This was no exaggeration. When Austria failed, Prussia ventured to rush in with a proposal of her own. To make confusion worse confounded the French ambassador stepped forward with a new plan. And on the top of all this, with the Collective Note gradually being built up at Vienna, Lord Clarendon's Project of 24 October arrived at Constantinople with instructions that it should be submitted to the Porte with the concurrence of France, and if possible of Austria and Prussia. The despatch of course went on the supposition that hostilities had not yet broken out and that therefore no treaty of peace was requisite. The situation was embarrassing enough, but M. de la Cour did his best to simplify it by cordially consenting to act with Lord Stratford. The Note was laid before Reshid with little hope of success :—

F.P. II. 254; 5 Nov.

Your lordship [he wrote to the English Foreign Secretary] will have learnt. . . . how difficult, how all but impossible, is the successful execution of the instructions which I have now received, after the hostile occurrences which have taken place on the Danube as well as on the Asiatic frontier. By a strict interpretation of those instructions, I ought indeed to hold myself precluded from making the attempt under circumstances such as those in which I am placed ; but, knowing the immense importance attached by her Majesty's Government to the restoration of peaceable relations, on safe and honourable grounds, between the contending parties ; aware how deeply that feeling is partaken by all the governments of Europe ; and led by the information which has reached me, together with your lordship's despatches, to entertain a hope that the Cabinet of St. Petersburg is still disposed to a reconciliation with the Porte, I venture to confront the difficulties of the situation, and to exert all the means, contracted as they are, at my disposal, in order to obtain, if possible, a last chance for the cause of European peace. . . . I enter upon the execution of your instructions with a firm resolution to do justice, and if possible to have justice done, to them. But I cannot hope to carry them to a successful issue by my unassisted efforts, and the obstacles to

5 Nov.

1853
—
Æ.T. 67

success may be found insurmountable on their first communication to the Porte.

None of these misgivings, however, appeared in the urgent message which the ambassador now sent to Reshid :—

To S.
Pisani,
5 Nov.

Lose no time in calling upon Reshid Pasha and upon Ferik Efendi.

Say to the former that I have just received despatches of the utmost interest from London and Paris in ten days, and that I am under a strong impression that peace may be obtained with advantage and glory to the Porte, if Reshid's own wisdom and moderation can be made to prevail in the Council. He shall hear from me officially as soon as I can talk over matters with M. de la Cour. In the meantime I implore him to suspend any intended operation, by sea or by land, that may render a reconciliation on safe and honourable principles more difficult.

Say to Ferik Efendi the same thing, with this addition, that I have really strong, and I trust well-founded, hopes, that the Sultan's wisdom, if properly exerted now, will secure the honour and safety of his empire, with the advantage to himself of increased glory without further danger.

E.P. II.
287,
19 Nov.

2S8

304

M. de la Cour was recalled on 12 November,—it was said, because he was not warlike enough,—and his English colleague was reduced to exerting his "almost solitary efforts in favour of peace under every conceivable disadvantage, including even that which results, in Turkish estimation, from the presence of the Allied squadrons in these waters." Reshid Pasha admitted that two months earlier the Clarendon Note would have been accepted by the Porte with satisfaction, but it was different now that hostilities had broken out. Lord Stratford used every means to recommend the Note. He conscientiously approved it, as far as it went, as a tolerable compromise. He personally visited Reshid and urged its acceptance. He drew up a vigorous argument in favour of it. On 14 November, the evening when the Council was to meet to discuss the subject, he went to Reshid's house and remained with him till the very moment that he left to join his colleagues at the Council. "I omitted," he wrote, "nothing which my instructions, my recollections, or my reflection,

could support, in order to make an impression on his mind.
I lament to say that all my efforts were unavailing, and that
I could obtain nothing beyond a promise that my arguments
should be faithfully repeated to the Council before he expressed any opinion of his own.   I might accompany him, he
said, to the Council, and make my own statement to the
assembled ministers ; or, if I thought that he was an obstacle
to the acceptance of my proposals, he was ready to give in his
resignation."

It was idle to appeal from Reshid to his more warlike
colleagues : the Council did not approve the Note.   Yet once
more the Elchi reasoned with the Foreign Secretary :—

1853
——
ÆT. 67

I am beyond measure *distressed*.   The Pasha knows that without
a real conviction I would not have given the advice which I have
offered and still offer on this occasion.   He knows the sincere
interest which I take in the welfare of the empire, and he cannot
suppose me ignorant of European affairs and the views of my Government or the sentiments of my country.   With all these things in mind
I repeat that, if the Porte rejects the present proposition, she will throw
away a magnificent opportunity, and expose herself to the most perilous
chances.   I maintain that she has it now in her power to secure in
substance everything which she has *hitherto* claimed, and that, if her
acceptance were followed by a refusal on the part of Russia, she might
then go on to other more extensive objects with the goodwill of all
Europe, and the strenuous coöperation of her Allies.   Observe, that
when I speak of the present proposition, I mean the Note and the
Declaration *subject to amendment*, should the Porte require it on reasonable grounds, and I do not even exclude the adoption of the principles contained in them, *under some other form*—those principles
being a *safe* communication to Russia of the firmans and assurances
to remove doubt as to the religious privileges, and a confirmation on
the part of the Powers of the Treaty Declaration made in 1841 as to
the Sultan's rights, &c.   Of course there must be at the same time an
evacuation of the Principalities by Russia, and a renewal of the
treaties.

To S.
Pisani,
18 Nov.

Some extracts from the correspondence illustrate this
anxious November :—

I am still labouring for peace, but all alone—a thorough forlorn
hope.   Our present offer would undoubtedly have been accepted two

To his
Wife,
14 Nov.

1853
—
ÆT. 67

months ago. But now the case is altered wholly, at least to those who see and feel as Turks see and feel, not unnaturally too. I tell them that in all cases there is a wish and an opinion, passion and judgment. I sympathize with the wish, but judgment whispers that they had better accept. Still they have to answer to their army and nation—the former victorious, the latter enthusiastic to a degree. It is very difficult ; and the present offer, founded on my suggestion, but not carried out as I meant, yet tolerable, and enough for conscience. The fleets are at anchor in full [view] and others coming. We shall have a magnificent squadron. Thank Graham if you see him. Poor De la Cour is recalled. He does not like it, but bears it well.

To Lord
Clarendon,
15 Nov.

The evident desire, if not determination, is to get rid of every assurance respecting the religious privileges. To judge from the language held to me now even in a treaty of peace no article, however cautiously worded, would be admitted with reference to the spiritual privileges of the Greek Church. A note communicating the firmans to Russia might be obtained as an accessory, and that is all. But events may easily take a different turn, and even in anticipation of them a more favourable impression may possibly yet be elicited.

The change of French ambassadors has caused a delay with respect to sending out steamers to Varna. An expedition to the other side of the Black Sea on a larger scale is subject to serious consideration. While a pacific proposition is before the Porte, however unlikely to succeed at this time of day, everyone must hesitate to take a step in another direction, which may have the effect of changing our position toward Russia, and creating two, or rather three, wars in place of one. No language can express the embarrassment of the position ; and it is small consolation to say that I felt it by anticipation long ago, when I pointed to one definite and well-concerted effort for an arrangement, instead of a series of partial endeavours, catching at peace and beckoning to war.

To his
Wife,
19 Nov.

No peace as yet, and I grieve to say that Reshid is as hot upon war as the most military of his colleagues. There is much to excuse, to explain, and to justify this ; but I lament it in the conviction that all things considered peace is really best for the Porte on the terms which now appear to be within its reach. I have been exerting myself to the utmost under this conviction, but hitherto with no success. Reshid has declared however that two months ago the same propositions would have been accepted with satisfaction. Do not forget that they are founded on my suggestion.

1853
——
ÆT. 67

To Lord
Clarendon
19 Nov.

I should have preferred a *Declaration* to a Note, and such a Declaration, for instance, as I ventured to send you while the Note intended to speak for the Four Powers through their representatives was on its way hither. My notion was that Europe should speak out with dignity, not only for the present moment, but for times hereafter, without offence or injustice towards either party, but with protection for the Porte, and, by consequence, for all feeble States. I fancied that a tone and language of the kind would not only be European but eminently English. We have to confront the strong man with a bad cause as well as the weak man with a good one, and forgive me if I say that one longs to hear once more that diapason voice of arbitrament (something between Lablache and the Last Trumpet) which sounding high above the " gigantic intonations " of one Court and the querulous deprecations of another, might impose, without dictating, peace, and call forth the scales without the sword of Justice.

E.P. II.
307

How constant were his efforts in the cause of peace may be seen by the speech he made on 24 November on the occasion of presenting to the Sultan the Admiral and officers of the British fleet. " It was not without a feeling of national pride," he wrote to Lord Clarendon, " that I performed the duty of presenting to the Turkish Emperor so many gallant officers bearing her Majesty's commission, and called to Constantinople, under circumstances of unprecedented importance, for the protection of rights unjustly assailed, and in vindication of those great principles on which the tranquillity of Europe in a great measure reposes." If ever there was a moment for a little warlike enthusiasm it was then. But Lord Stratford's speech is full of peace and his old theme of reform, and closes with a warning to the war-party in the Council :—

In presenting to your Imperial Majesty the Admiral and Captains of the squadron which my gracious Sovereign has sent at your Majesty's request, and in concert with the Emperor of the French, her Majesty's powerful ally, to protect the rights and independence of this friendly empire, I perform a duty honourable and gratifying alike to them and to me. Their presence here at so extraordinary a juncture shews how wisely your Majesty and your Majesty's Government have appreciated the friendship and relied upon the sympathies of the British nation. Such binding and generous sentiments derive no small accession from the just and enlightened benevolence dis-

played in your Majesty's administrative policy.   It is not only to the
successful maintenance of a great European principle that the British
Government look for the reward of any sacrifice which they may have
to make in contributing to the protection of Turkey from unprovoked
aggression.   They look with equal steadiness to the prosperity and
strength which your Majesty could not fail to realize throughout
your extensive dominions by carrying into effect a system of improvement, complete though gradual, towards all classes and interests of
your Majesty's subjects.

Still their unrelinquished hope, and the more immediate aim of
their effective concurrence, is peace ; not indeed an illusive or precarious peace, but one which, by simple means, would fix on safe and
honourable grounds, without injustice to any other Power, the rights
of your Majesty's sovereignty and the independence of your Majesty's
empire.   To obtain such a peace at the earliest practicable moment
is always, I must presume, the anxious desire of your Majesty, as it
is the point most earnestly recommended by your Majesty's Allies.
I should be happy to learn that it is also an object duly appreciated
and strenuously promoted in a spirit of continued moderation by
your Majesty's ministers.

That the ambassador should have found it needful to
administer this public lecture—for such it was—to the Sultan
and his ministers shews how difficult it was becoming to
keep down the warlike spirit of the Turks.   For six months,
ever since Prince Menshikov's departure, he had pressed upon
the home Government the unfairness and danger of delaying
the settlement of the dispute.   Turkey could not bear the
financial strain of long-continued preparations for war ; and
the military zeal of her people, once kindled by the signs and
pomps of war, was not easily to be repressed.   Every week
had added to these dangers, and rendered the Porte less disposed to accept any proposal which seemed to carry the
smallest concession to Russia.   So far indeed they had had
the best of the campaign, and it must be remembered that
the idea that there can be only one end to a Russo-Turkish
war is quite a modern notion.   From the days when Peter
the Great was surrounded by the Ottomans on the banks of
the Pruth, and unfortunately let out, the superiority of the
Russian troops had never been proved.   The campaigns of
1809–12 were marked by no extraordinary successes on either

1853

Æт. 67

side, though Russia was probably winning, when peace was made at Bucharest. The triumph at Adrianople was a piece of daring impudence on the part of Diebitsch, and, had the smallness of his force been known, it would have ended in his total discomfiture. There are people now who argue, apparently with reason, that in the last war the Turks were really a match for their adversaries ; that Plevna would never have fallen but for bribes, and that then it fell to the attack of little Rumania, not to the onslaught of Russia. It is at all events certain that the Turks themselves in 1853 were by no means oppressed with a sense of inferiority. They were eager for war, and hopeful of success. Soldiers were pouring in from distant provinces ; Egypt was furnishing a contingent ; and there seemed every probability of an enthusiastic response to the Manifesto of the Khalif of the Mohammedan world. Besides, whatever the ambassadors might say, were not the armaments of the two greatest maritime Powers of the world now lying at anchor above the capital ? Was it to be believed that the fleets had come there for nothing, that they would not fight, and that England and France, in spite of big words, would fire no shot but paper notes, and projects instead of projectiles ? Is there any wonder that the Turks felt like fighting, and fighting in company ?

Lord Stratford had long seen this feeling growing, and was powerless to repress it. There might have been time had his July scheme been adopted at Vienna ; but now matters had reached such a pass that it was extremely doubtful whether any proposal for terms would be listened to by the Porte. Concession to Russia might mean revolution at Stambol. Yet it was essential if possible to place Turkey in the position of acquiescence in the wishes of the Powers, so that there should be no doubt that Russia was the real obstacle to peace. To effect this object, almost unattainable as it appeared, became Lord Stratford's intense desire. His calm and statesmanlike survey of the situation is nowhere better expressed than in the following despatch to Lord Clarendon :—

Moderation and firmness are the two principles of conduct which the Porte has been most assiduously advised to maintain in the course

E.P. II.
308,
24 Nov.

of her differences with Russia. She has exhibited the former to a striking degree from the time of Prince Menshikov's Ultimatum to the publication of her final manifesto. She has displayed the latter most particularly in rejecting the Note of Vienna, without modifications, and in collecting her means of defence with an amount of energy, good order, and perseverance, not easily surpassed.

The great test of her moderation was the course pursued by her Government when a Russian army crossed her frontier and insultingly occupied the Principalities. A respectful protest and a confiding appeal to Europe were her substitutes for a declaration of war. But half her duty would have been neglected if, while she gave time for negotiation, she had not provided for the contingency of its failure by preparing the means of an efficient armed resistance against Russia. The Allies might well have complained if the Sultan had betrayed a weak indifference to his own cause, and thrown the whole burden of its vindication on their shoulders.

The Ottoman ministers, in carrying out the policy prescribed to them alike by interest and by duty, roused of necessity a strong national feeling throughout the empire, and at the same time a general expectation that unusual sacrifices would be followed by an adequate return. Among the Mohammedans, as your lordship knows, patriotism is always more or less a religious sentiment, and the Porte could hardly be expected to restrain the fanaticism of its adherents without directing their zeal to some distinct object of national desire. It was no longer thought enough to resist any specific pretensions of Russia. The mortifying ascendancy of that Power was to be shaken off altogether, and the independence of the empire to be placed once for all on a level with that of its neighbour. A concurrence of circumstances originating in the presumption and duplicity of Russia appeared to favour this very natural ambition, and the united sympathies of the Government, the army, and the people, excited, no doubt, by the partisans of a war policy, had only to be acted upon with spirit in order to repress all dissensions in the Cabinet and to avert the danger, whatever may have been its degree, of a popular outbreak. The personal antagonism of Reshid Pasha and the Seraskier no longer disturbs the administration ; the former has gained a large accession of popularity, and also of the Sultan's favour, and his Majesty, to all appearance, has accepted frankly the decision of his people as expressed with unanimity by the General Council some two months ago.

If, then, it was true that circumstances for which the Porte is not answerable have naturally brought on a state of things imparting force, unity, and direction to a general sentiment laudable in itself, and offering, when adopted by the Government, much advantage and

convenience both to the Sultan and to his leading ministers, it is
hardly surprizing that with considerable armies on the frontier, the
squadrons of England and France on the Bosphorus, a pervading
enthusiasm in their favour, and some unexpected successes in battle,
the Sultan and his Cabinet should receive with reluctance and dislike any proposition invested with the badge of their old inferiority
towards Russia, and calculated to disappoint the hopes of the nation,
and, with the overthrow of their popularity, to expose them to the
most serious embarrassments.   It may be alleged with truth, and I
have striven to impress this truth in every form of language on their
minds, that, however natural such sentiments may be, their indulgence
on the present occasion is neither just, nor wise, nor humane, seeing
that the original difference can now be settled on safe and honourable
grounds, with every moral and political advantage on the Sultan's
side, while an unnecessary continuance of hostilities would invite
the most perilous hazards, the most exhausting sacrifices, a vast
effusion of blood, and, more than possibly, the horrors of a general
war.   Unfortunately the motives to forbearance are thrown into
shade by the dazzling illusions of hope, and passion is in league with
occasion to merge all fears of danger and all considerations o
prudence in a wild though attractive speculation, difficult at bes
to realize, and of which even the accomplishment would not be unattended with formidable drawbacks.

I question whether Reshid himself is at all times entirely free
from these delusive influences, though, to do justice both to him and
to his colleagues, they still profess a willingness to seek no further
advantage than a relinquishment of Russia's religious pretensions, and
of the notes prepared to embody them.   In their hearts they may
aspire to arrangements calculated to secure them from future disturbance, and they would gladly put forward claims to a new disposition in the Principalities, to the recognition of Circassian independence, and to the reimbursement of their military expenses.   But
deference to the counsels of their Allies would prevail with them to
forego such notions, and their cooler aspirations would, I think, be
satisfied with a renewal in clear comprehensive terms of the formal
declarations and treaties already existing in favour of the Porte.
What they never cease to insist upon is a clear and unquestionable
deliverance from Russian interference applied to spiritual matters.
They are persuaded that silence would be the best and safest form of
accomplishing that purpose ; and they are now bent upon excluding
every kind of note, however carefully expressed, as liable to offend
their own people and to afford a dangerous opening for what they
presume to be the real designs of Russia.

This apprehension is, I fear, but too well justified by the late proceedings of the Russian Cabinet, and, after so many sacrifices forced upon Turkey by that Power, it is but fair that the Porte should be secured from further molestation on the same score, not only virtually, but in a form and manner calculated to leave no room for mistakes upon the subject either here or elsewhere.

Should the Emperor of Russia, acting in the spirit of his new Manifesto, after giving the lie publicly to his neighbour, and supporting by force of arms his usurpation in the Principalities, decline a form of arrangement accepted by the Porte and recommended by her Allies, your lordship would probably agree with the Ottoman ministers in thinking that a wider region would then be opened for diplomatic views as well as for military operations. Most sincerely do I deprecate the occurrence of any such case, and no exertion will be wanting on my part, under the guidance of your lordship's instructions, to dissuade the Porte from wantonly bringing on a necessity of the kind. But should it so happen that Russia herself continues to be the obstacle to a pacific arrangement, the interests of international security, no less than those of Turkish independence, will probably be found to require exertions and remedies little short of those which the more sanguine Mohammedans already contemplate.

In accordance with these views the Great Elchi devoted his energies to winning the Porte's assent to a scheme of pacification, and at last he succeeded. Some of his arguments are well expressed in the following memoranda :—

Mem. I.   The Sultan's Government has acted on the late decision of the General Council.

War has been declared ; hostilities have commenced ; the Allied squadrons are here.

By land the Sultan's armies have obtained some successes. At sea the Porte has suffered loss, with no advantage but that of trying the loyalty and courage of its seamen.

Winter being now at hand, operations cannot be longer continued with effect ; nor has any lasting result attended those which have taken place.

Under such circumstances it is reasonable to think of peace,— the ultimate object of all lawful hostilities.

There are grounds for believing that it is still to be had on terms to which the Porte signified heretofore its willingness to assent.

An adherence to those terms may be adapted to present circumstances. The Porte need not now be expected to conciliate Russia

by an Embassy and a Note. Independent Powers at war with each
other are entitled to negotiate on equal terms.

But were the Porte to change her ground and to require advantages
heretofore unasked, she must calculate the means of success. This
is the more necessary because, if she were to meet with reverses, she
would not only lose what she can now secure, but she might even lose
all and have to submit to her enemy's dictation.

Can she reckon upon more assistance from her Allies than is
necessary to obtain peace on the old terms? Can she hope to drive
the Russians out of the Principalities single-handed? Can she reckon
upon gaining any other concession from Russia without repeated
victories on a large scale? Can she even make the necessary efforts
for those purposes without great sacrifices and risks?

Surely, then, it is the duty of the Government, as it is the interest
of the empire, not to let slip the present opportunity, but, weighing
with calm deliberation the counsels of its Allies, without further delay
to frame a distinct proposition, fit to be submitted to and accepted
by the General Council.

The Powers declaring that Russia is still ready to make peace,
why should not the Porte make a similar declaration to them?

Might not the Porte agree to negotiate on the joint basis of an
undelayed *evacuation of the Principalities,* of a *renewal of the treaties,*
and of a subsequent *communication, with assurances, to all the Powers,*
of the firmans concerning religious privileges, the agreement with
Russia as to Jerusalem remaining in force?

Let her then declare her consent to the *appointment of plenipo-*
tentiaries, to an *armistice,* and to a *negotiation on the above basis* in
some *neutral place,* with the *concurrence of representatives* from the Four
Powers.

It might be understood that the principles declared in 1840–1 should
be forthwith solemnly confirmed with adequate efficiency by all the
Powers concerned, the Porte on her side engaging to carry out an effective system of improvements calculated to insure by internal means
the independence of her empire and to satisfy the just expectations of
all classes of her subjects.

There was a singular fatality about the negotiations that
preceded the Crimean war : it seemed as though the best
conceived and all but executed plans were doomed to failure
just when all appeared to be going right. Diplomacy was on
the point of attaining its well-earned triumph, when a cata-

(margin notes) 1853 A.T. 67 Mem. II.

1853
—
ÆT. 67

strophe, for which it was not responsible, reduced its laurels to ashes.

To understand how this happened it is necessary to consider the position of the Allied squadrons. They were anchored in the Bosphorus and offered a complete bulwark between the Sevastopol fleet and Constantinople. But the coasts of Turkey are extensive, and the Allies proposed to defend them in all parts from Russian invasion. The most pressing danger was naturally on the Turkish shores of the Black Sea, and the obvious course was to send at least part of the squadrons out into the Euxine to reconnoitre. But here that disastrous duality, which England had afterwards such cause to rue, began to shew its baneful influence. Any movement of the Allied fleets required the assent of two ambassadors and two E.P. II. 310 admirals. The English and French ambassadors agreed, 11 November, in requesting the admirals to send out some vessels. The English commander, Dundas, did not relish a winter cruise in the Euxine, though, doubtless, ready to go ; but the French admiral, Hamelin, was positive against it. By ill luck the change of ambassadors happened exactly at this moment, and General Baraguay d'Hilliers succeeded M. de la Cour. The General found that he could not recommend the cruise : in fact, many of the French ships were not seaworthy in the sense which is required for a Black Sea trip. The British fleet could not issue out alone, lest the concert of the two Powers should be disturbed ; and Lord Stratford began to experience something of the embarrassment from which Lord E.P. II. 322 Raglan afterwards suffered so acutely. Lord Clarendon " regretted extremely " the refusal of the French admiral, and acknowledged that it was impossible to send out the English ships alone.[1]

E.P. II. 310

E.P. II. 322

---

[1] A curious illustration of the discordant opinions of the Aberdeen Cabinet is seen in the following extract from a letter of the First Lord, Sir James Graham, 24 November, to Vice-Admiral Dundas. What Lord Clarendon regretted, Graham approved : — '

" Austria is evidently becoming uneasy by the protracted warfare beginning to rage on her frontiers, and is more desirous to unite with France and England in strenuous endeavours to bring the hostilities to the close by holding firm language to both the belligerents and by insisting both on an armistice and on a peaceful settlement under the mediation of the Four Powers.

Meanwhile the Turks were longing to send out their own fleet. Lord Stratford perceived immediately the risks of being committed by a possible collision between the ships of Turkey and Russia almost under the guns, as it were, of the Allied squadrons, and by a threat of refusing to bring up the remainder of the British fleet to the Bosphorus, where only a portion had so far been stationed, he succeeded in arresting the despatch of any large vessels into the Euxine. "You must tell his highness," he wrote to the interpreter who carried his message to Reshid Pasha, "once for all that we *will not* be drawn in the *wake* of the Porte, and that if they want our assistance they must be content to respect our opinions."

Although the despatch of more ships was thus checked, it happened that towards the close of November eleven Turkish light vessels of war were lying at anchor in the harbour of Sinope. On the 30th six Russian ships of the line entered, anchored, destroyed the entire Turkish squadron, massacred 4,000 men, and presently sailed away. The importance of the action lay, not in its barbarity or wantonness, but in the fact that it was done in the face of the Allied fleets, and after Russia had been officially informed that they were there to protect Turkish territory from attack. The Turkish ships had been sunk, not on the high seas, or when engaged in any

E.P. II. 320, 331,

"A joint Note to this effect will most probably be signed in conference at Vienna and sent to Constantinople : and both the Divan and the Czar will be invited to send plenipotentiaries to treat at a neutral Court under the intervention of ambassadors of the Four Powers.

"The understanding between France and England is cordial, and the union of the Four Powers is daily becoming closer and more active.

"In these circumstances I am very glad that no detachment from the combined fleets on a large scale has entered the Black Sea. Indeed I hope that the necessity of sending any British man-of-war to the eastward of the Bosphorus has been avoided.

"Constantinople is safe, and this is the first object with Great Britain. Russia would be mortally offended by the presence of a British force in the Black Sea ; and I think the chance of peace would be diminished. The safety of Turkey does not require any exhibition of such naval coöperation, while France and England have twenty sail of the line at anchor in the Golden Horn ; and where our objects are the defence of Constantinople and the attainment of peace on terms not inconsistent with the honour of the Sultan, any measure which is irritating but not necessary should be carefully avoided."

Letters like this effectually neutralized all the efforts of the Foreign Office and the ambassador.

1853
— —
ÆT. 67
E.P. II.
345,
27 Dec.

330

hostile act, but when peaceably anchored in a Turkish port. Lord Clarendon could only look upon it as a challenge ; " it was not," he wrote to St. Petersburg, " the Turkish squadron alone that was deliberately attacked in the harbour of Sinope." To prevent the recurrence of such disasters, the admirals were ordered to take " complete command " of the Black Sea and to " require and if necessary compel " Russian ships of war to return to their ports. " We have undertaken to defend the territory of the Sultan from aggression, and that engagement must be fulfilled."

When matters had reached this point, Notes and Conventions cut but a sorry figure. The Collective Note from Vienna reached Constantinople on 16 December, one day after Reshid had received the final *projet* of Lord Stratford and the other three ambassadors at the Porte. They all agreed that it must be held back, as calculated to do more harm than good at the present juncture.

The private correspondence of December describes the strange state of affairs at Constantinople ;—the arrival of pacificatory Notes, side by side with the movements of ships of war, and another rising of the fanatical classes of the population, subdued, like the first, by the Elchi's presence of mind. Lord Stratford had infinite trouble to get the admirals out to sea, even after Sinope and Lord Clarendon's stringent instructions.

To Lord Clarendon, 5 Dec.

My belief is that we shall have to go into the Black Sea. I wish devoutly that it were otherwise, and I also wish that we had other friends than those of Islamism to support. But with a cause in hand which has sufficed to rouse Europe from one extremity to the other, we must not, I humbly think, be too nice, looking rather to the issue, as a matter of paramount European importance, than to the qualities of our companions and allies.

To the same, 17 Dec.

The Vienna Note arrived *yesterday*, and we all agree that its presentation must at least be suspended. It would mar all if presented *now* ; and should the plan adopted here and in the hands of Reshid Pasha since the *day before yesterday* fail of success, there will remain another string for our bow. Heaven grant that in some way or other we may get out of this mixed state of peace and war. It is far too painful and compromising in every way.

The admirals appear to be anything but pleased with the prospect of a Black Sea cruise, and I question whether my military colleague would not side with them if he were left to himself. I feel most severely how responsible my position is, but with God's help I will shrink from nothing which my judgment carefully exercised imposes upon me.

1853
—
ÆT. 67

The correspondence will shew how much I have been worried about the squadrons. . . Before the arrival of the messenger from Paris I had painful odds against me. . . Why are the squadrons here if they are not to be used? and what would be our position in the estimation of the whole Eastern world if we appeared to hesitate after the affair of Sinope, and when as a consequence of that massacre the whole Euxine was at the mercy of Russia?

To the same, 31 Dec.

There is no time to think of anything but the reigning question. I am still between peace and war—like Garrick between Tragedy and Comedy. The long continuance of such a state is very distressing to all concerned, and I long to get out of it,—peaceably if possible with honour,—but at all events anyhow. The Turks are beginning to listen once more to the voice of the charmer, and the General Council is clucking at this moment over an egg, out of which may come peace or war, though probably, I hope, the former. I have likewise laid an egg, with the assistance of the three, and the ministers will have to sit upon it as soon as they get permission, if they *do* get it, from the General Council. If this egg is not addled in the hatching, it will I trust be approved in Downing Street, and possibly in the end at St. Petersburg. The case stands thus. Turco has obtained some *credit by land* but no *durable advantage* as yet, and at sea he has been cruelly unfortunate. It appears as if he would have peace now with a settlement, safe and honourable for him, on the old principle, improved in *form* and *result*; but then he must forego his ulterior hopes, magnificent, natural, and seducing—but illusive, because he cannot carry them out by himself, and his two seconds are not prepared to back him *so far* at present. If he accepts our fair proposals and Russia also accepts, he gets a prize equal to his first pretension, though not quite equal to his outlay. If he accepts and Russia refuses, the whole game is before him, and I shall myself entertain a sanguine hope of seeing Russia put into her proper place. But we must *all* fight for *that*—and stoutly too. If the Porte refuses, there will be dudgeon at Paris and in London, and I fear the whole fabric of hope, pride and resistance will sink into the slough of despond, and the Czar will be triumphant, to the humiliation of this empire and the final disturbance

To his Wife, 17 Dec.

1853

Æт. 67

To his
Wife,
Christmas
Eve.

of every European interest.   Now you have the whole of it--that is
the cream.

Agamemnon, king of ships as well as of men, did not, with his
accustomed stateliness, arrive here till to-day.   The consequence was
that your "official report of a certain Conference," though dated the 12th
ultimo, did not reach me till an hour or two ago.   No harm, dearest,
as you had told me the essentials before, and I had the pleasure of
perusing with a return of appetite the same intellectual feast which I
had enjoyed so much on the first occasion.   You are not only a true
woman, as poor Rogers used to affirm, but a capital diplomatist, and
I have half a mind to think that if you had been here we should
have fared better in all respects.

I care very little about Cl.'s suspicions and fancies.   There is some
truth in his remarks as applied to the state of things two months ago,
but he overlooks the cause—to wit, his own vacillating conduct, and
the bit-by-bit endeavours to avert an evil which was only to be averted
by a firm and high-minded course from the beginning.   *My* expedient to which you allude, and which has been mixed up with one of
his, was thrown out in despair, and taken up too late.   I acted on the
plan erected upon it, not with any chance of succeeding then, but
for the purpose of laying a foundation for later success, —and in
that I have succeeded.   The proposal now before the Porte is
really all and more than all the Turks could presume to hope, unless
Russia were beaten to a mummy, and England and France took
a decided part in the operation.   Whether Russia will accept is
another question.   The Internuncio thinks she will, and he ought to
know best.   At all events his opinion is enough for me.   If Russia
refuses, woe be to her ;—if there be a spark of spirit and foresight in
the Western world.   The proposal is sent in by the Four, and it
was sent in thirty-six hours before the arrival of a Note from Vienna,
which would have spoilt all in fact, and which in *form* was an insult
to diplomacy here.   My ambition and hope was to have sent home
by one messenger a plan of negotiation accepted, a demonstration
of the squadrons in the Black Sea,--dreadfully wanted,—and an insurrection put down in execution of my suggestions.   Instead of all
this, the *Caradoc* starts in a gale of wind, with reams of accumulated
report—and not a single thing completed.   Is that old Strat.'s fault ?
No ; conscience says No !   It is the natural consequence of muddy
views and timid proceedings elsewhere.   Three days ago we were
threatened with an immediate insurrection, massacre, &c. &c.   Mac-
Guffog brought me the first account.   He was with the Grand Vezir,
who had just clapped on a host of blisters when he received news of
an approaching row from the Sheykh-el-Islam -- stripped off his blisters,

put on his clothes, got into his carriage, and started for the scene of disturbance. Soon after came note on note and messenger on messenger with tidings of horror. I was a little suspicious of exaggeration and consequent ridicule, but still I thought it right to be on the safer side, by taking precautions quietly in time. This I did, and if the rebellion had taken hold of the people I think we should have been tolerably prepared for anything. While the diplomatic body was assembled here, better news came in, and finally we dismissed our fears and became quite heroic. In the meantime two advantages were secured. The fire-engine was exercised, and I shewed my gallantry by inviting all the pretty women of my acquaintance to take refuge in the palace. A whole squadron of steamers, French and English, came smoking down from Baycos, and our poor friend Reshid took refuge at Beshiktash. He was the *bête noire*. The Softas and Muderris were the instruments,—Mohammed Ali was the instigator, the Sheykh-el-Islam the abettor.

Next morning at eight I sallied forth to see Reshid in his retirement. I found him looking dismal. He explained the whole history, as above, and lamented his inability to persuade the Sultan of the necessity for taking vigorous measures. While we were talking a messenger came in from Rif'at. Things are far from quiet, the Softas were still refractory—some were arming—the discharge of a pistol might fire a train of the most dangerous kind. This was enough. I took my line, and trotted off on foot to Padishah with Etienne at my heels. We were graciously received, and I told H. M. the true state of things and made him sympathize with his ministers by hinting that sovereigns who weakly gave up their supporters were sure to suffer in the end. After long talking he promised to give orders for everything I had advised, and he gallantly added of his own accord that he would go over to Constantinople himself and issue the necessary orders to his Council. All has since been done—the Seraskier was obliged to give orders against his own partisans—the Sheykh had to look on like a donkey,—the soldiers did their duty—and 170 Softas were shipped off for Candia before nightfall. When I told the French ambassador of all this—he having come full of his own notions—he confessed that I had done wonders and that he would give me a *brevet de général* on the spot. I did not tell him that I had seen the Sultan. Poor Reshid ventured back to his home last night, and though there were some soldiers still on foot this morning and a remnant of turbulent Softas, yet it was believed that by arresting half a dozen Hajjis known to be ringleaders the tranquillity of the capital would be confirmed. Then I trust will come a change of ministers, to the discomfiture of the war party and to the satisfaction of Reshid, who, though very far from a model, is perhaps the best of them and at all events the most reasonable *now*. I advised Paddi to maintain for the moment a complete union of himself and the ministers—compact against the mischievous—and then the necessary change at leisure afterwards. Riza is Captain Pasha, and means to be devoted to your *sposo*. What think you of that? If we can but have the proposals accepted in two or three days! Pisani seems confident,—and I feel so too. I wish you could see my despatch giving an account of how it was all brought about &c. . . . Then for the squadrons—I think it a horrid shame that they don't go out, but I have the French ambassador and the two admirals against me. Still I have fought the battle, though I feel confident that Government at home will be inclined to side against me. I would have *ordered* our squadron out alone—but there are reasons not to be explained here, and therefore our poor friend Turco must I fear undergo another humiliation. . . .

Here is Christmas Eve. We have had a dozen storms, winds from all quarters, thunders and lightnings, red, pink, and white. I am scribbling all alone in my dressing-gown in a room full of smoke; I dined alone in the little room,—scribble, scribble, scribble before and after. . .

My new colleague from Paris is queer: a thorough African soldier, a thorough man of the *coup d'état*, a thorough old French West-Indian of good family; saying everything that comes into his head, sometimes right, as often wrong; kind-hearted, courteous when humoured, very *sensible à bons procédés*, and not without a fund of dry quaint fun set off with the graces of a hearty laugh and loud tones. I try to meet him in all fair ways, and we differ amicably, discuss frankly, and agree cordially. Still there is danger in that sort of character, and I sometimes wish there could be less familiarity. Brück is the cleverest; he has obtained a sort of European reputation. I don't quite trust him, but he seems to like me, and he has the merit, and so has the General, of being an *individual*, and not a mere formality.

I never sent you a full account of the last great lesson the Turks got at Sinope. It was much too shocking, but you will see it all in the papers. There is one very rich passage. When the Russians manned yards and cheered for the victory, they perceived a number of wretches, crippled and burnt, clinging to the wrecks of the Turkish squadron. They sent off their boats and got all the able-bodied ones to lead in triumph at Sevastopol, and then cleared the wrecks with grapeshot. After this murderous work the ambassador was very anxious to send the fleets into the Black Sea to prevent any more of it; but there are so many objections to overrule. Our people say,—The time is not come—the weather is boisterous—there are fogs in the Black Sea ; if we keep snug now we'll be able to fight all the better by-and-bye.   The French say, — Ah—oh ! mais ! and, in short, *nous n'irons pas.*   The consequence is that neither of us goes.   Before that sad accident, which the Turks must have foreseen, they wanted to send their heavy ships into the Black Sea to protect the light ships which the Russians destroyed.   *Quels ignorants!* they would positively have gone out and might have succeeded if we had not dissuaded them on professional grounds.   But all that is past now, and we are all for peace.   The Turks cannot quarrel with their friends as well as their enemies.   In the course of pacification we had a little *émeute* the day before yesterday—the Softas, who would, they insisted, fight it out.   Above 160 of them are now on their way to Candia, and the rest of the opposition will soon follow.   It was, of course, a very exciting day, and everyone with his wife and daughters was in readiness to take refuge within at a moment's notice.   Poor Reshid was frightened out of his wits - no wonder—and slept away from his home that night. They would like to lay their hands on him.   Rif'at, on the contrary, behaved like a lion.   The troops are still patrolling the streets.

If it had not been for these unlucky movements of the Ulema and Softas we might have bagged by this time the Porte's acceptance of our quadruple proposals.   I flatter myself, however, with the persuasion that there is nothing worse than delay, and that in a very few days I shall have to forward a favourable decision.   There is, nevertheless, room for disapointment, and therefore I abstain from saying more, except that I feel the awkwardness of keeping back the Vienna post, but trust that a measure of such obvious usefulness and necessity will meet with approval.   I find so marked an improvement in Baron Brück's demeanour that I augur better of Austrian intentions than even your hopes have hitherto ever enabled me to do. He and my other colleagues are decidedly of opinion that we could not give in the Vienna Note—I mean the last one—without danger. What Russia will do is more than I can presume to anticipate. Austria ought to know best, and her representative here has so much appearance of feeling sure of the Emperor's acceptance that I resign my own misgivings and almost partake of his confidence.

My new French colleague is rather a strange bedfellow, and I should never be surprized to find that, like the man in Rabelais, he had turned in with his spurs on.   He is fond of asserting his opinion, disposed to aim at taking the lead, and it sometimes requires a stout expression of opinion to keep him within bounds.   But there is much to like in his character, though not all the frankness he supposes and loudly proclaims ; and, on the whole, I trust that we shall get on very tolerably well, in spite of occasional differences in a quiet

(right margin:)
1853
—
Æ.T. 67

To Lord
Clarendon,
24 Dec.

way. He is very pacific in language, and generally not otherwise in his proceedings ; but at times there is a casual outbreak, which seems to indicate a foresight of other courses when the fulness of time, if ever, shall chance to arrive. I am sure you will feel for my difficulties and embarrassments on the subject of the squadrons ; I venture even to hope that you will approve both of my *opinion* and of my *conduct*. Two more ships in addition to the ten now here under British colours and we might hazard all the chances of the Black Sea without a care but that of maintaining peace as long as possible . . .

Nothing will go well in this country till after the cessation of this amphibious state between peace and war; and if I may venture to recommend one thing more strongly than another, it is that your idea of the pending attempt being the last effort for peace under present circumstances should be realized. Most earnestly do I hope that peace may be obtained on the terms we suggested ; but supposing the plan to fail, we have no choice but either to coöperate vigorously with the Porte or to see her in all probability after a few convulsive struggles victimized by Russia.

The squadrons, about thirty sail in all, great and small, were under weigh for the Black Sea this morning, but a sudden change of wind has detained them for the moment. Their going out is making a huge noise. I have had much trouble and vexation upon the subject.

We send home the Porte's official acceptance of our terms. Heaven grant that it may succeed elsewhere. . . . I am well, but growing to my chair.

The last night of 1853, on which this letter was despatched, witnessed the consummation of the Elchi's diplomatic labours for peace. In the face of every difficulty Lord Stratford had induced the Porte to agree to terms of arrangement. In spite of Sinope, and in spite of the ominous rising among the theological students, who were burning for the

Holy War, his project was accepted on 31 December. Whatever might be the fate of this last plan, he remarked, " it will always be gratifying to remember that the injured and by no means unsuccessful party was the first to give proof of its pacific views, and to accede, with almost unlimited confidence, to the suggestion of its European Allies." [1]

---

[1] An interesting memorandum in Lord Stratford's hand shews what he intended and what he accomplished : —

So ended the work of diplomacy. There is no need to describe minutely the plan thus accepted both by Turkey and the Four Powers: its object was gained by the mere acceptance, and nothing could now stay the course of the European war which began in the harbour of Sinope. Lord Clarendon considered that the negotiation reflected "the highest credit on his Excellency," and he conveyed "the entire approbation of her Majesty's Government for the zeal and judgment" which he had displayed. The Foreign Secretary considered the Porte's reply "quite satisfactory." But the English and French squadrons entered the Black Sea, Lord Clarendon's stringent orders were put in force, the Czar's pride was irrevocably wounded, and diplomacy's work, at least at Constantinople, was at an end. For nine months many brains had striven, with varied powers, for a peaceful settlement. None had laboured harder than Lord Stratford to promote the cause of honourable peace. He had succeeded so far that he had placed the Turks in the right, and put Russia in the ignoble position of a wanton aggressor. He had so guided the Sultan that his Majesty had the sympathies of Europe. The just demands of Russia had been granted by Imperial firmans

Objects.

1. To bring France and Russia into an arrangement, proclaimed by the Porte for settling the question of the Holy Places. *Done.*

2. To prevent the proposed *protectorate* of Russia from being accepted by the Porte. *Done.*

3. To bring this about in such manner as may prevent a quarrel. *Not done.*

4. To secure the privileges of the Greek Church, and to remove its abuses by a national mode of proceeding under the Porte's independent sanction and approval. *First part done.*

5. To encourage Austria in the exercise of a legitimate influence independent of others. *Much progress made.*

6. To convince the Sultan and his ministers of the absolute necessity of adopting forthwith a more complete and effective system of administrative reform. *Some impression made.*

7. To recommend and obtain the adoption of certain measures adapted to that end.

8. To put the affairs of the Embassy on a better footing.

9. To guard the privileges granted to the Protestants from any danger of withdrawal or diminution, and to extend to all classes of Rayas such advantages as may be obtained for the Greeks. *Done.*

Query? Should a kind of general protectorate be recommended? *Recommended with limitations.*

Margin notes: 1853, ÆT. 67, E.P. II. 369, 396, E.P. II. 399

consolidating all the reasonable rights and privileges of the Christians of Turkey. The numerous proposals of the mediating Powers had been respectfully considered, and two projects of reconciliation had received the Porte's assent. The unjustifiable seizure of the Principalities had been met with exemplary moderation. From April to December the Turks had comported themselves with marvellous patience and judgment. The policy of patience had become more and more difficult to sustain as the warlike spirit of a people, whose name is famous in the annals of the battlefield, waxed fierce. Yet even in their zeal, in their bitter wrath when the news of Sinope came to their ears, the Turks still kept measure, and ended the memorable year with an acceptance of a peaceful settlement. During the long course of negotiation, of menace and of attack, there is no point where it can be said that the Turks provoked the war, or frustrated an honourable arrangement of the controversy. And this moderation and the righteousness of their cause had drawn to them the respect and sympathy of Europe, and had loosened the sword from the scabbard in the West. Let full credit be theirs for a display of rare wisdom and self-control : but the chief honour rests with the man who guided their steps, whose daily counsel ruled their acts, whose measures for peace were at once just and acceptable,—the man they called the Great Elchi.

CHAPTER XXVIII.

THE new year dawned in a wreath of stormy clouds. Turkey indeed stood four-square, and had committed no false move, save the error of sending part of her fleet to Sinope, and thus precipitating the crisis which everyone knew to be inevitable. The Porte, with this solitary exception, had done as Lord Stratford would have it do, and the very last day of the old year had witnessed its adhesion to the scheme of pacification which the Elchi had drawn up. Thus Turkey entered upon 1854 with a serene consciousness of being in the right, and the even serener conviction that all Europe, west of Russia, approved her conduct. But unfortunately that which was Turkey's right was Russia's wrong. "The Question" still remained unsolved, and would so remain as long as the two nations existed. The Emperor still insisted upon the protectorate which he had so long disguised from the eyes of the other Powers ; and the Sultan, whatever he might personally have been induced to concede, clearly perceived that to admit such a protectorate would cost him his throne : for he well knew that his brother Abdu-l-Aziz was ready to lead the war-party. It was impossible that this antagonism between Turkey and Russia could be allowed to end in an isolated struggle between the two. Whatever might have been the termination of such a conflict, the Western nations at all events were not sufficiently convinced of the strength and resources of Turkey to permit her to wage the war unaided. They had distinctly given the Sultan to understand that he

1854

Æ.T. 67

Z 2

would enjoy their support, and they had backed their promise by the presence of their fleets in the Bosphorus. Even if a reconciliation had been possible after so warlike a demonstration, the meaning which Lord Clarendon naturally put upon the action at Sinope excluded the smallest hope of peace. Whether that affair was a designed challenge to the maritime Powers or not, their subsequent action in taking the command of the Euxine and threatening to drive all Russian vessels back into port constituted something nearly resembling a declaration of war. It was obvious to everybody that Russia had no alternative but either to accept the terms of the Four Powers, or to break off diplomatic relations and wage war, at least with the two Western nations.

The fleets went forth into the Black Sea in the first week of January : but three months wore on before the declaration of war issued from the Queen in Council on 28 March. The interval was filled with abortive correspondence between the several Courts, with which Lord Stratford had nothing to do. He rested on his final scheme of pacification, accepted by Turkey and the Four Powers, and from a seat of perfect equity, and even of the maximum of concession, watched the progress of events as Europe gradually roused herself to action. Diplomacy had done its utmost ; the last possible effort had been made for peace, and all that remained was to wait and watch. The Great Elchi was in the position of the man who has wound up and regulated the clock, and now stands regarding the hands and listening to hear if it will strike the right hour. To all Europe he was the centre of the situation. Whether they blamed his policy or applauded it, there were not two opinions as to his influence. The late Speaker, Mr. Denison, afterwards Lord Ossington, only recorded the feeling of all the world when he wrote to Lady Stratford : " Probably in the history of diplomacy, such great events never hinged on one man as have lately hinged on Lord Stratford. If Turkey is called back to life, and set upon her legs, it will be mainly his doing, and if all the Great Powers are bound together in a confederacy to check the career of Russia, he will have had a chief part in weaving the band which ties them together. This will be a great work to have done, and will set up a mark to be for ever remembered in the history of the world."

But now the man at the wheel had made his last point, and stood by, while the steering gear swung idly to and fro and the rudder plashed uncertainly in the water. He had steered as long as steering was possible, and so far as his part lay he had avoided every rock and shoal in his course. His vessel, whose figure-head was the Sublime Porte, but whose flag was the Union Jack, still answered to her helm, but her course now depended upon other craft, and the steersman stood by, and waited for a signal. What he was thinking during this period of inaction may be seen from some of his letters to his wife :—

The importance of the work in hand goes on increasing. It is like the cloud on the horizon, no bigger than a man's hand at first, but destined to cover the whole vault of heaven. I thank God that it has been my lot to bring about the last offer of peace, and in such terms as to satisfy Government and to be thought acceptable by Russia. You may depend upon it that without me that offer never would have been made. My own impression is that the Emperor of Russia will *not* accept. Judging by my own notions, I do not see how it is possible for him to accept under the circumstances in which he has so wantonly placed himself. But our proposals are based on his own declarations. I took care to place them on that ground, and I consented to as many of Baron Brück's modifications as I could in order to have his testimony in proof of our plan being in harmony with the Emperor's own declarations as stated by Austria. In this manner the Turk is placed in the position of one who is sure of gaining a ten thousand pound prize in the lottery, and who may get a million. You must admit that this looks comfortable for the Porte, and most assuredly is satisfactory in every sense to your *worse* half, who has been thrown upon the Eastern Question like a fish upon a volcanic shore. But the "*million*" cannot be gained without much exertion, and strong reinforcements from the cardinal virtues. If we have war, as I expect, it will be a war of giants. We *must* not be losers. We cannot afford *that*; and we must make the sacrifices necessary for success, and obtain results equal to the sacrifices. For this we must gird up our loins, as they of old are recorded to have done, and the feeble hands must be held up when the battle fluctuates. I can fairly say that I have never seen the matter in any other light, and it was exactly because I foresaw the depth and extent of

To his Wife, 23 Jan.

the contest that I was against having out the squadrons in the first instance, that I was for peace if attainable with safety and honour to the Porte, and endeavouring to obtain peace by confronting the danger at once and imposing on Russia the necessity of either giving way to European principles, clearly and stoutly asserted, or of throwing off the mask and picking up the gauntlet without further prevarication.

What might and ought to have been done more than six months ago is now at last in operation, but under circumstances which make arrangement far more difficult, and a war, more or less general, far more probable. How wonderful is Providence in all its dealings! How strangely have things been brought to this pass! How inconceivable that such an atom as myself should be made the rallying point in such a chaos! I told you from the first that I would have no armour—nothing but a pebble from the brook: that when intrigues multiplied, their crookedness should be shewn by contrast with my straight line of conduct, and that I would see nothing in myself but a weak and humble instrument of Providence. Do me justice. I have never sought this distinction; my position here is an accident. I always thought that the great struggle of the East would not be in my time, and that I was destined only to fall in the ditch that others more fortunate in later times might pass over with less difficulty. It seems to be otherwise ordained, and with Heaven's grace I accept my lot, and will apply what little remains of me to reach the promised land. All generous hearts will be with me. . .

The Tritons came back yesterday, in spite of a steamer which I sent out four or five days before to keep them in the Black Sea. They are horribly afraid of losing their sails and their spars. I wish well to both, but I want full protection for the Turkish flag and territory, and not to risk, by sending out a small force, a dishonourable retreat before the Russians, many of whose ships we know *not* to be at Sevastopol. In the course of to-day or to-morrow I shall probably have to come to close quarters with them. I wish Lyons had the command. We quarrelled at Athens. I do not think we should quarrel here. His heart, if I mistake not, is in unison—as I trust one other heart is—with that mighty heart which throbs from John o' Groat's to the Land's End.

On 5 March the news reached Constantinople that the troops were ordered out to Malta, *en route* for Turkey. The order had been given on 16 February; eleven days later Lord Clarendon wrote to Count Nesselrode and required the evacuation of the Principalities by the Russian troops by

30 April on penalty of war; and on 18 March the Emperor Nicholas declined to make any reply to this communication. War was accordingly declared. In all these transactions France moved more or less shoulder to shoulder with England.

With *you* and the *country* on my side, I care, under Providence, for nothing else. The winds are beginning to pipe amongst the rigging of our heavy vessel; but the tempest is not yet fully upon us, and there is something awfully grand in the gathering of the elements before they burst. The Greek insurrection and the name less audacity of the Court of Greece are astounding circumstances in *degree* and *suddenness,* I confess, beyond my expectation. It is evident that the Emperor of Russia has a complete and direct understanding with the Queen [of the Hellenes]. I feel the importance of striking home at once, and no degree of responsibility shall stop me, if I can see my way to an effective interference. Meanwhile, the Turks are sending down more troops—ill spared from here. I completed my treaty for the reception of the Allied armies last night—twelve hours passed at Reshid Pasha's! I went out at 8, and returned after 9 this morning—no bed, no dressing, and I have scribbled ever since.

I have to thank you for several obliging letters. The last is dated 27 March.

You gave a very proper answer to Mr. Monckton Milnes. Everyone must look with pain and anxiety on war, its horrors, and its chances. But when the necessity of declaring it is manifest, there can be no regret. In the present instance all Europe unites with us in condemning the Emperor of Russia, and the published correspondence shews how entirely the failure of negotiation is attributable to him. We must now look forward, remembering that the most vigorous exertions in the commencement are likely to prove the most economical in the end, and that the final results must, if possible, with God's blessing, be in proportion to the sacrifices.

The stake at issue is not only the independence of Turkey—it is the very existence of the Empire, and together with it the future destiny of all this magnificent portion of the globe, involving a large part of our commercial prospects inseparable from those of civilization and humanity.

It is almost sunset, and the despatches are already sent to the messenger. Will you believe that I was up at half-past 4, and

1854
——
ÆT. 67

have toiled incessantly ever since? Yesterday arrived the first detachment of the army, 2,000 in the *Himalaya*, a magnificent steamer, a giant, which I would give the world to see, but cannot. I have housed them in the Scutari Barracks. The whole, as I learn to-day, are destined for Hunkiar Iskelesi, where they will soon be racked with all the pains which tormented poor Caliban. I have therefore made up my mind to keep the barracks open for all of them till Lord Raglan comes, when he may choose between the two stations. I hear that the troops at Gallipoli under Sir G. Brown are complaining. They are under canvas, and they find the mutton tough. The French arrived first and got the best of everything, they say. Everything that could be done by the Embassy was done, and done in good time. The Commissaries reported well, but you know this country and the innumerable difficulties thereof.

To the
same,
Easter
[16 April]

Who kill'd cock robin?
I, said the sparrow,
With my bow and arrow ;
I kill'd cock robin !

That's my answer to your wonderment about his Mohammedan Holiness, who seconded the ex-Seraskier in his factious dealings with the Softas. Rif'at made up the triumvirate—I mean of dismissal, not of faction,—for his faults were quite of another kind : weakness, to wit, incompetency in business, and, woe is me! corruption. Like Falstaff he was given to thieving, and like Falstaff he is fat and good-humoured. Getting him out was much like committing murder. He looked so innocent, and sent me such pretty *twists* from his own oven.

Pope,
*Essay on
Man*, i.
83

Pleased to the last, he cropp'd the flow'ry food,
And lick'd the hand just raised to shed his blood.

You may imagine that in our present *bulicame*, a united Government was very desirable. *That* we now have ; and old Shekib, who holds the scales of justice in Rif'at's place, rides over carcases like Juggernaut. The next thing was a council of war. The first suggestion was not mine, but I adopted it warmly, and forced the suggesters to make it a reality, and not, as they meant, a juggle. Since then we have had to deal with some tough questions. (1) Keeping Omar Pasha in order. He was for crossing the Danube, and risking all with a self-confident spirit fraught with danger to himself, the army, and the empire. I got Sir J. Burgoyne to visit him, thinking he was the man to influence him without his perceiving it. The plan *seems* to have answered, for the Pasha is quite an altered man. (2) The reform of the army in Asia. Immense mischief had already been done under Mohammed Ali's administration, and the wounds are still scarcely scarred over. Guyon has done marvels, I really believe, and I have obtained his appointment as Chief of the Staff, which is much as being second in command. I have also obtained the recall, and hope to obtain the signal, if not the condign, punishment of two most naughty pashas—one now here, the other expected. Ahmed Pasha is the type and personification of cruelty, falsehood, and cowardice. He committed horrors in Africa several years ago, and was appointed without my knowledge. If it depends upon me, he shall commit no more cruelties. Much remains to be done for the army in general, and particularly for that in Asia. But without money, knowledge, or roads, and an abundance of nothing but snow, what can be done ? (3) The irregulars, *Bashi-Bozuks*, as they are called ; miscreants, as they ought to be called. No pen can write the crimes they have committed. If they were paid by Russia they could not serve her cause better. In Greece they have burnt countless villages, in Asia they caused the defeat of the regular troops. I have at last obtained a right good firman for their control and chastisement. They will be tried for every crime by a court-martial, and executed, when guilty, on the spot. Their leaders and the regular generals are made responsible. (4) The Greek insurrection—all very bad—not even spontaneous, But stirred up from Athens. The scoundrels sent by Otho across the frontier are as murderous as the wildest Turks, and they force the Rayas to join them by burning the villages and plundering everything. I have got as many *regular* troops to be sent to Epirus and Thessaly as can be spared. But troops are still wanted in Bulgaria ; the garrison here is reduced ; and money and means of transport were deficient in the outset. I applied to the admiral for steam, and he found a plausible excuse, no doubt agreeable to our friend at the *telegraph*, if you know where that is. (5) The undescribable conduct at Athens ; for *Greece*? not a bit of it ; for Emperor Nic. and no one else. Is he not the Queen's uncle, or cousin, and has she not surrounded herself with Russians? If I had been free to act, that matter should have been settled six weeks ago. There is nothing for it but *force*, and the Allies must serve it out. They will in the end, but with speed and effect enough for the necessity, not. (6) The exclusion of the Greeks (Hellenic) from Turkey. The measure was not mine, but it is quite justifiable, I think, under such provocation, embarrassment, and danger. If the mischief be not stopped, it will compromise everything, and may prove fatal to our cause. I have done my best to soften the application of the excluding measure to *individuals*. I have saved all servants and people employed in British commercial establishments, and obtained more time generally for the settlement of affairs. My French colleague has set up a difference between the Greek subjects who are Roman Catholic and those who are Orthodox. The distinction is monstrous, and I have opposed it stoutly. Baraguay persists; appealing even, with complaint, from Reshid to the Sultan, who has referred privately to me, and adopted my opinion. Reshid would have resigned had it been otherwise. It remains to be seen whether his adversary will throw up, as he intimated to the Padishah. Never mind. I am satisfied that he is acting from his own, or, rather, other people's heads, without instructions, and that he has not a leg to stand on. Some of his own *ouailles* even condemn him. I have proofs of this. Among other motives for a blind foolishness; there is a rooted jealousy of *me*—and *us*. A Frenchman dining here the other day told me so, and urged the importance of soothing the vexation, not so much here, as at Paris. I asked him whether our influence was supposed to be exerted against French interests. "No," he said, "not that; but you are aware of our disposition—we don't like to be left out; if a pie is to be served, we like to have a finger in it, and your influence here is too entire and single." I fear there is truth in this, and I must write to Cowley about it. But there is danger in coupling too much with colleagues, who like to dictate as well as to share, and whose jealousy no degree of confidence can extinguish. (7) The organization of Poles and other emigrants into a legion, or other kind of military body. The question lies with me, but I think it better to wait for Lord Raglan. It involves military considerations as well as political and party ones. Meanwhile I am besieged by the Zamoyskis, the Wysovkis, and a host of others, agreeing more in name than in fact. (8) Plans for getting up Wallachian and Circassian resistance, which have introduced me to men of high spirit and persevering characters, laudable for military boldness and enduring patriotism All these things are to be done, but the difficulty lies in opportunity, mode of proceeding, and means of carrying out. Austrian hesitations and financial deficiency are sorely in the way. *Bakalum!* (9) Samos, where it has been necessary for me to take part in changing the governor, feeding the destitute, and providing against an attack from Greece. . . . There are lots of other questions in daily course respecting the fleet, the troops, the commissaries, the finances, &c. In short, my life is become an almost unbroken series of labours, vexations, and anxieties. But Providence is merciful—far more than I deserve—and, in spite of toils and privations, your venerable partner sleeps like a top, eats like an ogre, drinks like a fish, and walks and talks very considerably more than King Charles is reported to have done half an hour after the consummation of his martyrdom.

No news from the fleet. What can the Admiral be about?

Perhaps he is getting up a surprize. Who knows? Something grand
— the conflagration of Odessa; the scouring of the coasts of Circassia;
the explosion of Sevastopol? Well, Lyons is with him, and I don't
despair.

No news from Omar. He is getting strength at Shumla, and
will probably bide the grand attack there. Meanwhile I hear rumours
of a fresh encounter at Kalafat. If so, the Russians have probably
attempted another and more formidable passage of the Danube.
Paskievich is expected.

I am writing in *your* bedroom at a small table close by the fire-
place window. About an hour ago I was interrupted by a solemn
knock at the door. I had scarcely uttered "Come in," when Alison
appeared with an open letter in his hand. "What's the matter?"
"Read, and you'll see." I read and saw that 3,000 Greeks had
landed near Salonica and threatened to open insurrection on a new
scene. They have chosen their place of landing well, and may give
much trouble. I sent Etienne Pisani with the news in all haste to
Reshid, inquiring whether they could send troops and steamers at
once to the place of attack—close by our old friend Mount Athos. It
is of consequence, you know, to stop such things at once, if possible.
Before Pisani had left me, I learnt that an A.D.C. of the D. of Cambridge had arrived. Where was he to go to? What was to be done
with he horses?—thirty in all, though not the Duke's entirely. No
room here—so, off to the barracks at Scutari—and off they went.
Another knock. What now? Brigadier Adams with General Sir
De Lacy Evans! Shew them into the drawing-room and I'll come.
Anon, and I was smartened and appeared. Behold, not only the
brace of Generals, but their respective staffs—a room-full! To escape
bewilderment I flew straight at my General—Sir De Lacy—held out
my hand, and we were fast friends at once. The conference ended, I
made acquaintance with the junior red-coats, and found Percy Herbert
—looking very infirm—and Captain Gordon, a son, I believe, of the
Premier's. Squeezing of hands, rapid commonplaces, and mutual
attendrissement ensued. To-morrow I am to dine fourteen of them,
including the two Generals—and then to Brück's ball for the
Emperor's marriage. A fresh chasm. Since the last sentence I have
had some polite small talk with two officers—an interesting conversation with a French consul from Erzerum, a solemn conference
with two Commissaries, and a stand-up interview with the Captain of
the *Banshee*—my only naval officer—who has special orders not to
move to the *west*. I mention all these particulars that you may have
a notion of the life I lead, and cease to wonder at the *occasional*
shortness of my letters. Think too that only half the army is yet
arrived, and that the campaign is still to begin.

I have been out this morning to make a few calls. Not a soul at home, in compliment, I suppose, to the warm day—the first we have had. I found the streets very quiet, though full. Chabert has been to convey my compliments to the Greek Patriarch *àpropos* of Easter. He is of my own making, you know—but the old gentleman was too unwell to attend the service in church. I learn too from Chabert that the Duke's horses are all happily landed. He talks of their being so fine. He had never seen such before. The Turks too shewed a very good spirit. One said, "We must shew them every kindness. They are come so far for our sakes."

28 April

During the last three days my time has been taken up in a most unprofitable manner, thanks to my eccentric French colleague, the very quintessence of French vanity and recklessness. The day before yesterday he broke off his relations with the *Porte*, made preparations for going away, as yesterday, with his whole embassy, and took steps for preventing the arrival of Prince Napoleon and Marshal St. Arnaud. What for? you may well ask. Simply because he fancied himself *déconsidéré*, and thought the freak would set him up. The point in dispute was this. The Porte had ordered *all* the Hellenics to march off. Baraguay d'Hilliers would keep the *Catholics* and send the *Orthodox* packing by themselves. No! said Reshid, that would be playing Menshikov's game, introducing religion where we wish particularly to exclude it, justifying much of Russia's pretension, and setting all possible Greeks more than ever against us. Right, said I, there is neither justice nor sense in the pretension. Make exceptions, if you please; soften the blow whenever you can, but let the mitigations of your measure descend *alike on all.* Spare the servants, whether their creed be of Old or of New Rome; put all employés in commercial houses on the same footing; be indulgent to the poor and destitute, give more time to all, and still more in particular cases fairly made out, and nothing against the individuals. All these *improvements* were granted at my request and extended to the Catholics. Still B. d'H. would have his way. He gave in a list of nearly 1,100 Catholics—in fact *all here*, the servants *in this house* included—and going on from one thing to another, quarrelling with Reshid, appealing to the Sultan, complaining of me behind my back, ended, at last, in breaking off his relations, selling his horses, and preparing to march off after a few hours' notice. Think of such conduct at such a moment! The whole town resounds with it; the Change at Galata transacted no business the day before yesterday; there were goings and comings all day and night between the Porte and the French palace; in short, stir and noise enough to appease the most outrageous vanity. All this without a shadow of *right*, in the very teeth of common sense and sound policy and general opinion. The Porte and the Sultan alike referred to me, and I could not say "give way." Knowing my colleague's jealousy and irritability I kept clear of him, hoping that his passion would work itself out, and that he never would be mad enough to carry his threats into execution. In this respect I was out in my calculation. So, when things were rapidly surging to the worst, I went to him, talked over the whole subject, humoured him, laughed with him, reasoned with him, throwing in a home truth every now and then, and finally left him just as wise as when I sought him. He admitted all my statements and arguments, pretended to no right, disputed no reasoning, but stuck to his point. The sky might fall in, but he would have his way.' Reshid had broken his promise to him, he could not brook *déconsidération*. Reshid asserts that he broke no promise ; that from first to last he stood out on the *principle*, but tried to conciliate by soft language and partial concession, concealed from me till jerked out by force of collision. The fact is that by his habitual *ménagements* and *reticences* Reshid opened a door for mistake, which was increased by the trickery of the French go-between, and B. d'H., not being as much used to such pranks as I am, saw deception and falsehood where in truth there was nothing more than the usual proportion of *manœuvring*. It must be added that our colleague is thought to be vexed and *démoralisé* by the disappointment of finding that he is to have no command in the army, and that, on the contrary, St. Arnaud, who was formerly under him in Africa, is to be commander-in-chief. He is, moreover, suspected of intriguing to upset Reshid in favour of Mohammed Ali, and also to supersede my influence here. These charges may be exaggerated, but no doubt they have strong foundations in truth. But my story is getting very long and must now be cut short. Seeing the state of things, the mischief resulting from so much folly, the general tendency of opinions, blaming the madman but wishing the consequences of the madness to be avoided, I set about finding a remedy in good earnest. After twenty-four hours of rupture, and a delay of the time fixed for departure, yielded with difficulty to the importunities of Riza Pasha, whom I encouraged to go to the Frenchman, an arrangement has been made out and mutually accepted. The principle is saved, no right is admitted, but under a decorous and complimentary covering the Catholics with few exceptions will remain in Turkey until some new event takes place. The intrigue against Reshid has not succeeded, and it will soon be known that the French Embassy has been saved from a great scandal by that very influence which it sought to supplant. This was my point of difficulty. Determined to save the principle, but anxious to avoid the scandal at almost every sacrifice but *that*,

I could not hope to succeed by any open mediation. So, having failed in an attempt to get within the fortress by means of our present commander-in-chief, Sir De Lacy Evans, who had to call upon Baraguay, I got Zamoyski to go by night and work upon Benedetti, without making any direct overture ; and early next morning I went over alone to Reshid and suggested a plan of arrangement which he adopted, and then going to Baraguay under pretext of wishing him good-bye, as he probably would not have time to call on me, I tried to dispose him to acceptance without letting him know of my visit to Reshid. At a late hour last night, the Council sitting, after some verbal alterations of my plans, a final adjustment was agreed upon, and off went electric messages by telegraph with the news. Now we shall see how the public here will take it, and how it will be viewed at Paris and London. I have authority (between ourselves) from Cowley to say that the French Government does not approve of its representative's *pretensions* and *tone*. This I made known in a quiet way to my colleague yesterday. At home I am inclined to think that they will approve of my efforts for reconciliation, though in reality B. d'H. is allowed to do what ought not to be done. The Turkish ministers are very indignant at his conduct, and they will give me exactly what they have given him, if I choose to ask for it.

The French Government did not endorse the General's intemperate proceedings, and in May he was recalled.

When it was known in Constantinople that England and France had declared war against the Czar and were preparing an expedition for the succour of the Sultan, Lord Stratford discovered that he had suddenly changed his profession. For many months he was no longer to be the diplomatist, the statesman, the guide of the faltering Turks, and the no less hesitating English ministers. He was now apparently Commissary-General, head of the Intelligence Department, Quarter-Master-General, Director of Transports, and provider in chief of everything that the British war departments had forgotten to supply for the use of the expedition. He was even credited with the functions of Surgeon-General to the Forces. Such at least is the impression produced by a study of the various demands made upon him by officials of every rank and description. At one time it is the Duke of Newcastle, who wants

Lord Stratford to find boots to go over the trousers of 30,000 British soldiers, and who apparently expects that the bazars of Stambol will furnish an admirable supply of Wellingtons. Then it is Lord Raglan, who depends upon him, not only for reinforcements of Turkish infantry and artillery, but for planks for the hutting of the troops, and warm winter clothing for their comfort.   Or again it is the London newspapers, who angrily ask why the ambassador has not had the forethought to store up a sufficient quantity of lint and physic and bed-clothes for the sick and wounded at Scutari.   And finally there were those who reproached the diplomatist because he had not gone to the relief of the beleaguered fortress of Kars.

As one reads these multifarious demands, one wonders whether an ambassador is supposed to be a man or a god, that he should do all these things.   One who has served his country indefatigably with all his heart for nearly half a century, in the strict career of diplomacy, and whose labours have never led him into any kind of administrative activity, —who has guided nations with his pen, but has not once controlled a busy executive department,—is suddenly called upon to supply every deficiency that a notoriously defec-tive public service has overlooked.   The British army goes forth to the Crimea, practically in the clothes it stands up in, and when the men are shivering for want of blankets and huts, and the wounded are lying on bare floors for want of beds, and the investing lines before Sevastopol are exposed on their flank for want of reinforcements, a universal cry arises and resounds through the British Embassy, and Lord Stratford is to find the clothes and boots and blankets and huts and beds and reinforcements without a moment's delay.   And if it chance that the markets of Stambol and Brusa and Adrian-ople and Salonica do not possess the articles required, and some delay ensues, then there goes forth a general groan of indignation against the callous Elchi who has the misfortune to own but one brain and two hands with which to do the work of fifty experienced army officers, and who has to find in Turkey stores and materials that may not happen to be there.   It was of course to be assumed that with all these unexpected demands upon his activity, the Government would supply him with a large staff of temporary attachés or other assistants: but the assumption was unfounded. It was not till the middle of 1855, when the war was almost over, that Lord Stratford obtained the valuable assistance of General Mansfield as military adviser; and till then the same staff which hardly sufficed to carry on the ordinary work of the Embassy in time of peace, and which had now to bear the strain of an extraordinary correspondence—with generals, admirals, heads of transport, commissariat, and medical service, with special agents for special purposes in all parts of the Ottoman dominions,—was expected to add to their usual and unusual labours the work of saving the British army from the consequences of the blunders of an unprepared War Office and Horse Guards! The expectation was extravagant, and what we have to see is—not whether Lord Stratford did what fifty ambassadors could not have done, and what the Government had no possible title to ask him to do,—but how he achieved what no other man in his place could have accomplished; how he accepted without murmur the rôle of "general utility" in a company remarkable for its incapacity; and how whenever anything was wanted, let it be ever so difficult of attainment, and ever so remote from his own special department, he put his shoulder to the wheel and laboured unremittingly till the work was done.

No army perhaps ever went forth worse equipped for war than the expedition to the Crimea. For months Lord Stratford had warned the Government that if there should be war, they must be prepared for war on a grand scale; but they took no heed. It was not easy to move the torpidity of men who were under a spell of fifty years of peace. So the troops poured into Turkey, and depended upon Turkey for nearly all their wants. The difficulties began even before they arrived: barracks had to be found for them. Hardly had the first transport come in view when a universal cry for coal arose, and it was the English ambassador who had, if not to dig it, at least to arrange with the Porte, (and with the French chargé d'affaires, who was very punctilious as to who should have the *entrée* to the mine,) that some one should use the shovel. And so it went on. It was all very well for the

Government to express unbounded confidence in the ambassador, and for Lord Clarendon to give him *carte blanche* :—

You are kind enough to tell me that I may act on my own responsibility without fear of being called to account—but how can I act to any good purpose, if I have nothing to act upon? Things are now in a state requiring more than diplomatic action. There is an advancing and to all appearances a powerful enemy in Bulgaria, like that which ravaged the Palatinate in the last century. There is an insurrection in Epirus and Thessaly requiring to be put down with a prompt and vigorous hand. There is an unprincipled neighbour defying the Porte and its allies without a shadow of right and uncontrollable by aught but force. There is every prospect of a great increase of piracy in the Archipelago, and it would be difficult to say at what point of the coast or elsewhere something may not break out to call for immediate attention and means of repression or redress. As far as the Porte is concerned, my influence is not without effect, but the Porte's available resources, as I have often said before, are in every way inadequate, and the Allies alone can save this Empire, England from its superior steadiness and claim to confidence having principally to bear the brunt.

Such being the case, I naturally look to our fleets and armies for means of prompt action in emergencies. I have it in my power to draw the attention of their commanders to such and such objects, according as incidents occur. "But will they come when you do call?" That's the question ; and judging from the line taken by the admirals I must answer *no.*

The Government had indeed given him full powers, but the admirals apparently possessed the faculty of refusal, and it was in Lord Stratford's opinion largely owing to their unwillingness to convey the Turkish troops to Volo and Prevesa that the Greek rebellion was not immediately strangled. While the ambassador was pressing forward vigorous and effective measures, he was perpetually met by the irresolution of the naval commanders, and the evil did not disappear until the fleet was under the energetic control of Sir Edmund Lyons. With the home Government Lord Stratford experienced the same difficulty in making them understand the essential conditions of the struggle in which they were engaged. "My conviction," he wrote on 7 April to Lord

Clarendon, "is that, cost what it will, this awful contest must be carried through to a triumphant issue if it be in Hercules and the strong shoulder to keep the waggon moving ; and hence I conclude that the most decided, vigorous, and comprehensive measures in the outset are likely to prove the most economical in the end, and also—what I can never lose sight of—the most humane." But the Government never grasped this fact till the horrors of a Crimean winter taught them its truth, and meanwhile they trusted to their ambassador to do all those things which they ought to have done. Not only did they seem wholly unable to calculate the means required to attain the end in view, but they appeared to be groping in dim uncertainty as to the nature of the end itself. Lord Stratford was under no illusion as to this ; he knew well enough what the struggle was for, and how it ought to end ; and in a letter to Lord Clarendon, written some little time after the Allied forces had arrived in Turkey, he set forth his views with unmistakable precision. The letter is worth quoting in its entirety, and may be compared with advantage with the provisions ultimately established by the Treaty of Paris :—

To Lord
Clarendon,
12 June

I may venture to congratulate you on something like progress in our vast affair. Greece brought successfully to book—Austria all but in line with us, Prussia neutralized, if not enlisted, the Turks well prepared at Shumla, and shewing nobly at Silistria, the Allied armies taking up their ground on the scene of action, the conclusion of a loan in fair prospect, and no symptoms of mistrust between France and England—these, taken together, are surely just grounds of hope and confidence for the future. Not that I presume to expect an early termination of the war, even if Austria should coöperate heartily with us. Without her active assistance Turkey and its two allies may fairly reckon on driving the Russians back. But would that suffice to bring the Emperor to terms? His character, his position towards Europe and his people, the interests at stake, his great defensive resources, all seem to whisper, No ! Then, on our side, success must naturally bring with it an increase of expectation and demand. People, with a press and a parliament to plead for them, will not like to make sacrifices, going to the quick, and then sit down quietly under a canopy of laurels to heal their wounds and prepare for the chances of a fresh struggle. What says our greatest man upon this subject ? I think I

have read somewhere in the Duke of Wellington's Spanish correspondence a passage to this effect :—"Those who embark in plans of
this kind" (resistance to colossal power threatening the liberties of
Europe) "ought to understand that the sword, once drawn, cannot be
sheathed again, until their object is *completely attained*. They must
be prepared and even constrained to spare no sacrifice for the success
of their cause. In a struggle, where *everything is at stake*, there is
no comfort that must not be renounced, no risk that must not be
incurred."

If the words of our Cid were true in his day, are they less so in
ours? What signifies a *name*? We have to deal with a *thing*—that
most odious of things, the tyrannous will of one opposed to the
interests, the feelings, the convictions of millions. We have undertaken to curb that will ; but in order to curb it effectually, we must do
more than check its present outbreak, we must paralyze its spring of
action by bringing home to its inner sense a feeling of permanent
restraint—the "hither shalt thou come, and no further."

The Czar, in his agony, might exclaim—Well ! I am defeated by
a combination of all Europe against me, but the combination is
formed of elements which do not easily unite a second time, and the
power of Russia is a natural growth, instinctively encroaching and
necessarily united. Clip it, and it shoots out with greater vigour ;
stir the soil around it, and the very disturbance becomes in due season
a cause of its refreshment.

Now, what have we to do in answer to this very natural, but
dangerous, train of thought? The tree we have to deal with is of
the Upas kind : *Juniperi gravis umbra : nocent et frugibus umbrae.*
We cannot *girdle* it, if we would ; but we may stunt it by *pollarding*,
and that operation is a mere question of power and occasion, both,
perhaps, beyond our reach, and certainly not to be attained without
a skilful, vigorous, persevering application of means to the end. Our
best exertions, however, may fall short of their object, and in that
case we must submit to necessity, and be content with what we can
get. But if we wish to avoid reproach, we must be able to shew
that no means of success have been neglected ; that morally and
commercially, no less than materially, we have acted up to the opportunities afforded by Providence in so wonderful a manner.

Virg.
Eclog.
x. 76

Three mighty forces are those which I have named, and you know
better than I do how far they are already in play. Though more
despatch might possibly have been displayed, the fleets and armies
already called into action are admirable evidences of power, good
faith, and resolution. More, indeed, is likely to be wanted, and
judging from the "notes of preparation," *that* also will be forthcoming in due season. The wear and tear of cruising and campaigning

is itself a heavy charge.   Occasional reverses may occur, advantages already obtained may have to be followed up, and fresh enterprizes may be necessary to insure success.   Yet these contingencies must be foreseen, and, if possible, provided for.

Greece is still but a "scotch'd" snake ; Persia, with such a Shah, may forget her neutrality; the Slavic race, from Servia to Montenegro, requires to be watched ; the Sultan's Asiatic frontier is weakly defended ; the *Bashi-Bozuks* are not yet restrained.

Add to all this that Circassia remains to be cleared, the Crimea to be disarmed, and something worthy of our name to be achieved in the Baltic.

The list, I confess, is formidable ; but the object is great and beneficial.   With justice and necessity for our companions we have no room for groundless regrets or premature fears.   Back we cannot go.   Our duties are all ahead, and, with a timely preparation of *means* and a just estimate of *ends*, we may be masters of the future.

What ends and *what* means?   There's the rub.

To begin with the *ends*, what kind of Russia, what kind of Turkey, do we mean to have after the conclusion of peace?   Is it the Russia of Catharine, the Russia of Alexander, or the Russia of Nicholas ?   Is it Russia founded on the *status quo ante*, or Russia separated from Turkey by a *cordon* of principalities, or states, no longer dependent upon her ; or, finally, Russia, such as Russia was before she proclaimed without shame or disguise her appetite for territorial extension at the expense of every neighbour in turn, whether friend or foe?

There is little room for doubting which of these Russias would answer best to the interests of Europe, of commerce, and of humanity. The puzzle is not there, but in judging of the relation between means and end in each of the supposed cases.

The present combination vigorously carried out may suffice to procure not only diplomatic, but a certain degree of material, guarantee against further Russian aggression.   It is manifest, however, that the Emperor Nicholas will never voluntarily yield either the one or the other.   Position is to Russia what existence is to Turkey.   The Russia of this day is, more or less, a result of national tendencies and national traditions ably directed by a Government which, partly sympathizing and partly affecting to sympathize, employs them for the twofold purpose of dynastic despotism and political aggrandizement.   This, Heaven knows ! is formidable enough. But it is far from being all.   The power, thus raised on a million of soldiers trained to implicit obedience and selected from sixty millions of ignorant and fanatical slaves, is an ever-growing and ever-encroaching force—encroaching as much from inherent gravitation as from systematic policy. The strength of such a Power is the measure of our motives to resist it, multiplied by its character and the necessary consequences of its progress. Rome, of old, extended its sway by conquest. But wherever its eagles flew the arts of civilization followed, or the conquerors themselves were softened by the refinements of those whom they subdued. The Russian bird of prey has no such commission. It turns, indeed, towards the sun, but the shadow of its wings is blighting, and moral desolation closes on its flight. The Russian soldier is not contented with marching in a strait waistcoat. His knapsack is stuffed with spare ones for the accommodation of his foreign victims—partisans or opponents, as it may chance to be.

What have we then to choose? Where is our alternative? Look back! What says the past—the recent past? At Adrianople the Emperor seemed to be satisfied for life. He was satisfied before at Akkerman. But the Greek war was tempting; he stole a march on his friends, and took another meal, solitary like the boa's, and for a time tranquillizing. Then came the generous era. Forbearance, longanimity, protection, patronage, fraternal sympathy, and *Hunkiar Iskelesi.* The Sultan gradually discovered that hugging was pressure, and pressure coercion. He betrayed his alarm by an occasional struggle, and then came the era of loving remonstrances, imperious *aides-de-camp,* unpalatable Seneds, and smuggled occupations. The Porte was still feeble, and Russian influence continued to preponderate. The seeming moderation, which blinded Europe, might therefore yet go on without danger of escape. But the uneasiness excited at St. Petersburg by the Porte's independent conduct regarding the Hungarian and Polish refugees assumed a more alarming character when at one and the same time appeared the question of the Holy Places and a crisis intimating that Turkey must either sink into hopeless decrepitude or make a new start by the enforcement and expansion of its reforming policy. Russian susceptibility here found itself in presence of a danger and of a temptation—the danger of losing a paramount influence, the temptation of a dismemberment. Hence the secret overtures to Sir H. Seymour; hence, on their failure, the Menshikov requisition; hence a determination to rule the roast in Turkey, either by a concerted division of the empire, or through a recognized protection at Constantinople, by way of substitute during another turn of expectancy.

If this be true—and who can contradict it?—where, I repeat, is our alternative? The Emperor will fight as obstinately for his dictatorial position, his dominant influence here, as if the Turkish Empire were already in pieces, and he were scrambling for his share of the spoil. We cannot, then, hope to hasten peace and to staunch the wounds of

Europe by the moderation of our views. Take the object, for which we have entered the lists, in its narrowest proportions—reduce it to the principle, which we cannot without an overwhelming necessity surrender, and still we must see in Russia a determined adversary, pledged, as the Emperor Nicholas has himself declared, to stake his last soldier and his last rouble in a cause, as unjust and as idle as you please, but binding on all his sentiments, riveted by his prejudices, and sanctified by the workings of a mistaken religious zeal.

The prospect, I admit, is neither agreeable nor encouraging. But can we help it? Can we shrink from it? Does the responsibility rest with us? The answer must be negative. No other can be given without a sacrifice of truth and justice.

Our *ends*, therefore, resolve themselves into one,—an arrangement by which the integrity and independence of Turkey would be maintained under such material and diplomatic guarantees as are really indispensable for the purpose. Let a rigorous necessity be the limitation of our demands. Let a *minimum* of effective guarantee be the aim and goal of our exertions.

Now this must be measured with reference to our means. There is not so much difficulty in figuring the least that might suffice to bridle Russia, as in determining what aids are *required* and what *available* for reaching that minimum of security.

Take, for example, a settlement by which the course of the Danube would be free, the Principalities extended to the Black Sea, and released from Russian protection, Circassia restored to independence under the *suzeraineté* of the Porte, the Crimea established in a similar manner, the Black Sea opened to foreign ships of war, and Poland restored in the limits recognized by the Congress of Vienna. With these objects in view it would be most desirable, and indeed necessary, to have the material coöperation of Austria, and also to enrol a Polish Legion on national principles. But we may be sure that Austria would never look with favour on the latter measure, nor easily be led to contemplate conditions of peace so onerous to Russia.

Such being the case, if Austrian coöperation is indispensable, England and France would probably have to make up their minds to a guarantee such as Austria, consulting its own interests, would require. It may well be doubted whether Austria would extend its conditions of peace beyond the free navigation of the Danube, and possibly some improvement in the relations of the two Principalities with Russia and Turkey. The rest, according to her apprehension, would be mere *status quo* with the old diplomatic guarantees confirmed in clearer terms.

With this letter we must leave the statesman and turn to the man of action ; and we may begin this new phase in Lord Stratford's character with his first communication to Lord Raglan, to whom he despatched a comprehensive summary of the military situation, and of the various plans already on foot for the prosecution of the war in Turkey :—

1854

ÆT. 67

I learn from Lord Clarendon that you will be glad to hear from me at Gallipoli. It is little more than a year since I had the honour of sitting next to you at a dinner in Argyll Place, and you will find me as happy to meet your wishes now as I was then pleased with listening to your conversation.

No doubt you are already well acquainted with the general state of things in this country. I go, therefore, at once to the changeable points of more immediate interest. In matters of incident I am guided by our latest advices. The Russians on this side of the Danube have not made much progress. We only know of their being at *Babadagh*. Their Cossacks, however, are said to have been seen at or near *Karasu*. They seem rather to be engaged in strengthening their positions behind, near the river. Their numbers may vary from 20 to 40,000. Our Consul at Galatz stated them as something between 50 and 60,000 before they crossed. Having the river at their disposal, they can of course augment their numbers at pleasure. They have crossed heavy artillery, and there is some reason to presume that *Silistria* will be their next object.

Their whole force in the two Principalities and the *Dobrudsha* may be reckoned at something between 120 and 140,000 men of all arms. They may have 20,000 more in Bessarabia. Further reinforcements may be expected in June, or possibly at the close of May. They are strong in cavalry and artillery. Of their army in the Principalities at least 25,000 are in Lesser Wallachia.

The Turks have withdrawn from the Dobrudsha, leaving only a few hundreds, or it may be two or three thousand, of irregular cavalry. Omar Pasha is concentrating his army at Shumla. When last heard of he had about 40,000 men there. He had called in his cavalry from *Kalafat*, the position being still maintained, though with much loss from sickness, by the infantry. He is described as intending to bring in further reinforcements from some of the smaller garrisons on the Danube. He will not give battle without being attacked, and then only at or in front of *Shumla*.

At *Vidin*, *Rustchuk*, and *Silistria* there are strong garrisons. Varna is occupied by upwards of 8,000 men ; but Omar wants to have a third of them at *Shumla*.

To Lord Raglan, 17 April

The principal passes of the Balkan are defended by works, of what strength I cannot say. At *Pravadi*, between *Varna* and *Shumla*, there are three or four battalions and a thousand irregular horse. From *Sofia*, as well as from *Adrianople*, the reserves have already been absorbed by Omar Pasha. Scattered around are several thousands of irregular troops, or rather hordes—*Bashi-Bozuks*, as they are called, both horse and foot. They are, with few exceptions, a rabble of ferocious blackguards, ruinous to the country, dreaded by its inhabitants, addicted to every crime, and dangerous in battle to their friends, whom they abandon, discourage, and plunder when they can. . . .

Information has been received of a concerted plan between the Court of Athens and the Emperor of Russia for raising an insurrection in *Macedonia*, and passing a corps of 25,000 Russians above Kalafat by Sofia behind the Balkan, so as to open communications with the insurgents and perplex the operations of the Porte. Nothing can be worse than the apparent intentions of King Otho and his Russian Queen. I am assured that their infatuation goes to the point of putting themselves at the head of an armed force, and marching over the frontier into Turkey with an appeal to all of Hellenic race. . . .

Several auxiliary plans are in agitation. One is to scour to the coast of Circassia, to raise the natives by means of two or three of their chiefs now here, and to lay the groundwork of joint operations between them and Shamil Bey in Daghistan and the Turkish armies at Kars and Batum—the former about 40,000 strong, the latter about 10,000, but insufficiently provided in several respects.

The Russians have, I believe, a *corps d'armée* in the Caucasus, principally at Tiflis, and it is thought that considerable reinforcements are on the way thither.

Another plan in contemplation is to raise the inhabitants of Lesser Wallachia against the Russians, and it seems to be of a very plausible character.

A third is the formation of a Polish Legion, and the fourth the construction of a *corps étranger*, calculated to enrol the refugees from Hungary, Italy, and other countries. The principal military men who offer to take part in the organization or command of these auxiliaries are Count Zamoyski, with whom your lordship is probably acquainted, General Wysovki, who distinguished himself in Hungary, and General Klapka, well known for his defence of Komorn.

With all of these chiefs and officers I am in communication, and the Porte is prepared to follow my advice respecting them ; but, as you are so near, I think it better not to commit either myself or the Turkish Government till after I am made acquainted with your views.

At the end of April Lord Raglan took up his residence at the embassy while a house was being got ready for him at Scutari. The jealousies and intrigues which marked the greater part of the next two years began as soon as the French landed. An attempt was made to oust Omar Pasha from his post as commander-in-chief of the Turkish army, and it needed all the combined efforts of the English leaders to defeat the opposition of the Seraskier and Marshal St. Arnaud. A visit to Varna and Shumla, however, enabled Lord Raglan to convince Omar that the English were on his side, and this difficulty being overcome, the next question was the advance of the Allied forces to the support of the Turks on the Danube, and especially to the relief of Silistria. On 23 May Lord Raglan informed the Elchi of his intention of sending the troops to Varna, and intimated that the Turks would have to furnish "large supplies of horses and mules for the carriage of ammunition and provisions, as well as of waggons drawn by buffaloes or bullocks," all of which must be immediately afforded. Demands of this sort were coming in daily, and the worst was that there was no system about them. The General and his staff appeared quite unequal to drawing up a schedule of their wants, and request after request dropped in, often contradicting each other, and leading to nothing but confusion and delay. "I wish," wrote the ambassador, "your people would let me know *en bloc* whatever remains to be required or done for the service of your army by the Porte and its subalterns. I have asked for a conference with the whole Cabinet, and M. Benedetti will accompany me. Our object is to make them understand their duty with respect to the Allied forces and to facilitate by an appropriate arrangement the practical enforcement of their orders. By making the general demand in common, giving in a statement of requisitions, and appointing agents to see that they are really and properly complied with in the several departments, I should hope to obviate in a great degree the inconveniences and disappointments which seem to have been hitherto experienced by both armies, though not perhaps in equal proportions."

This was, of course, the right way to set to work, but the "general demand" was never furnished, and "what remained"

1854

ÆT. 67

31 May

to be required for the army proved to be incalculable. At the close of the letter which has just been quoted Lord Stratford expresses his uneasiness about Silistria, and says that he has urged that steps should be taken for its relief. The conference with the Cabinet took place on the following evening, and the Turkish ministers agreed to the suggestions of the two ambassadors ; they consented to employ Colonel Beatson in training a body of Bashi-Bozuks, to continue the employment of European officers in their army, to find supplies and money for the army at Kars, and to transfer the force at Batum to Bulgaria. Three weeks, however, passed before Lord Raglan left for Varna, and in the meanwhile the resources of the British Embassy were strained to the utmost. Here is an example of a day's work :—

To his
Wife,
7 May

It is now 7 P.M.—the Sabbath !—and I am still in my dressing-gown. I was, nevertheless, up at half-past 5, and working at half-past 6. Now, you shall have my day, and one will be as good as a score. Alone for two hours pen in hand, reading and writing. An officer with despatches from Varna and Shumla. The Count [Pisani] to "transact business." Breakfast in *your* bedroom, and MacGuffog. Etienne Pisani—instructions for the Porte. Another officer with despatches from the fleet off Sevastopol. Write to Lord Raglan ; write to the Admiral and to Captain Simmons with Omar Pasha. General Cannon announced from Bulgaria—conference with him. Prince Karaji—talk with him on Greek affairs. Bishop of Gibraltar— church matters. Chabert—instructions to him. The Persian chargé. Rothschild's confidential agent. "The Count" coming and going.— Borlase.—Aide-de-camp from Lord Raglan with despatches. General Wysovki—Polish affairs. Blondel, *en visite*. A sandwich, taken standing. A nap for half an hour, with a slight *touch of gout*, and you have papa's day !—But lo ! I am summoned to dinner, a lonely one in the "little cabinet," as King calls it. Now, I am back again, having turned over sundry pages of the *Quarterly*, and read despatches from Corfu, Prevesa, Scutari, and Samos and Smyrna. The Greek insurrection is going downhill, piracy is getting up, Samos and Montenegro are threatening. A few more sentences to you, dearest ! and an instruction to Pisani, then to bed, well disposed for sleeping. No Duke of Cambridge yet. He is expected in three or four days. The *Caradoc* was waiting for him at Corfu. Meanwhile Prince Napoleon has it all his own way. He is lionizing with imperial vigour, and, if my reports be true, jabbering in a slipslop way

about politics. Yesterday I made a round of Turkish visits to the 1854
—
ÆT. 67
Porte and other places with Lord Raglan. I was, more than ever,
struck with the poverty in manners, knowledge, and appearance.
All, however, was civility and attention. I never saw so many
people of all kinds in the streets of Constantinople. The weather was
fine, the trees coming into leaf, and altogether the scene was gay
and pleasing.

May 10.—A long interruption ! And here I am now, with the
Duke of Cambridge arrived, and unable to stir. A symptom of gout
on Saturday or Sunday has ripened into a regular attack on Monday
and Wednesday. I was unable to go to the Sultan's dinner to Prince
Napoléon, unable to receive Marshal St. Arnaud when he called, and
obliged to send Alison to meet the Duke. However, I have done
my best to write and to secure all attainable comforts for H.R.H.
Between ourselves, the French are riding roughshod over everything,
and I have it greatly at heart that our conduct should be in contrast.

The Duke of Cambridge stayed at the Embassy twice—on J. H.
Skene,
*With Lord
Stratford,*
p. 90.
going out, and on his return after Inkerman—and a characteristic story is told of the earlier visit. It was very early in
the morning, and the Duke's servant, who had just arrived,
was busily engaged in getting his Royal Highness's rooms
and baggage in order. Now the Ambassador had a strong
interest in seeing everything done with his own eyes, and the
interest became a duty while the Embassy was still without
a mistress. Inspired by loyal respect for his approaching guest, Lord Stratford personally visited the Duke's
rooms, attired in dressing-gown and slippers, and proceeded to instruct the valet in what he considered the best
method of arranging the various articles of baggage which
strewed the chambers. The man stared, and at last remarked :
" I'll tell you what it is. I know how his Royal Highness
likes to have his things arranged better than you do ;—so just
you shut up and be off, will you, old fellow ? " Lord Stratford
left the room in high wrath, and immediately sent an attaché
to tell the valet who it was that he had addressed in such im-
proper language. The messenger seemed amused when he
returned. " Well, what did you say to him ? " asked the Elchi.
" I said to him, my Lord, that the person to whom he addressed
such language was her Majesty's Representative in Turkey."

"Quite right. And what was his answer?"   "He answered,
my Lord, that he 'never said you warn't.'"   The reply tickled
the Ambassador's sense of the ludicrous, and a hearty laugh
banished all trace of anger.

The Duke's portmanteaux, however, were soon to be re-
packed by his independent servant; for all eyes were turned
towards Varna and the operations of the Russian army on the
Danube.   There is a passage in the following letter to Lord
Raglan which supplies at least a partial answer to the often-
asked question why the troops were not hurried up to the
relief of Silistria:—

To Lord
Raglan,
6 June

Having paid my intended visit to Marshal St. Arnaud this
morning, I fell in with Reshid Pasha and the Seraskier. The former
arrived soon after me; the latter was in the house when I arrived,
but was not produced till later.   There is evidently a private understanding between him and the Marshal, at which Reshid, I think, to
a certain degree connives.

We talked of Silistria. The Marshal is still indifferent to its
surrender. Relieving it, he says, would not do much for the war.
The season of Danube fevers approaching, it is better that the
Russians should be decimated by them than the Allies.   The loss of
Silistria would, moreover, hasten the movement of Austria in our
favour. Reshid did not acquiesce in this view of the matter, nor
did I. We had no *military* opinions to offer; but *morally* and
politically I ventured to object that the surrender of Silistria would
have a most discouraging effect throughout Europe, especially in
England; that the garrison, which displayed so much spirit and
resolution, deserved a better fate; that a retreat of the Russians
across the Danube would be a brilliant commencement; that, the
task accomplished, the Allied forces might resume more healthy
positions; that the Austrians would have the success of the Allies to
encourage them, with the evacuation of the Principalities as a motive
for coming forward; and after all, that to please a hesitating neutral
at the expense of those national feelings which were already engaged
in the cause would be at best a very questionable policy.

It may be added that the Allies having undertaken to protect
Turkey, it would seem to many strange if a fortress so important
as Silistria, and so well defended, were, without necessity, to be
abandoned almost in the presence of the Allied armies, without an
effort for its deliverance.

At last Lord Raglan set out for the scene of operations, but not without a severe struggle with the Turkish Divan, who happened to be celebrating the annual fast of Ramazan, and consequently were completely *hors de combat* for anything like vigorous action.

1854

ÆT. 67

Lord Raglan has just left me with his staff for Varna. He is very amiable, and very stout-hearted. He will do his duty on the field of battle, as he did it at the Horse Guards. He acknowledged with much kindness at parting my attentions to him, and the advantage which his health and spirits had derived from living here. I think the army will move on very soon after his arrival at head-quarters. The French also are on the move, but less forward. St. Arnaud leaves in a few days. I have had terrible work with the Turkish ministers and the Sultan to get the slightest result out of them in Ramazan. I must gather up all my forces and make a regular onslaught as soon as Bayram is over. Meanwhile I have helped to get a Turkish regiment 3,000 strong, with cavalry and twenty pieces of artillery, attached to Lord Raglan's army. The French will have an *annexe* of the same kind. You may expect to hear of important operations very soon. The Turks continue to fight like dragons at Silistria, which holds out, but rather precariously.

To his Wife, 20 June

The tide has rolled on. The slopes of Hayder Pasha are no longer mottled over with the tents of our army, and in place of old Neptune-Dundas and nineteen sail of the line, French and English— we have Admiral Boxer, two transports, and a steamer. Other troops have yet to pass, and when they are all together, there will be on battle-ground about 25,000 English, 50,000 French, and 70,000 Turks. making in all not far from 150,000 men. The Russians have, at the utmost, about 180,000, of whom half, it is supposed, on this side of the Danube, about 30,000 more immediately wi hin reach, and the remainder in reserve. Silistria makes a glorious stand. Some of our people have distinguished themselves favourably—above all, a young officer named Butler, who kept the Turks together in the most exposed battery when their officers left them. I had the good fortune to place a young engineer of great merit [Captain, now General, Sir Lintorn Simmons] at Shumla months ago, and he has rendered immense services. He was here three days ago fresh from Silistria, and described to me what he had seen and *heard*, for the minié rifle balls whistled about his ears wildly. Lord Raglan must be at Varna by this time. St. Arnaud follows in two days. I gave the latter a

To the same, 22 June

grand dinner *below*, with *music* last week. I question whether either of them will feel very well in Bulgaria. St. Arnaud will have the best of it, hereafter, in *verse*. Raglan is an awkward name for Helicon.

> Then rush'd St. Arnaud to the field of war,
> Then *Raglan* thunder'd from his British car.

Uncomfortable, is it not? His manners and character are the reverse of his name—attractive, gracious, tranquillizing. I am right glad to have seen so much of him. He left us with every appearance of being satisfied, and we are to be good correspondents in a quiet way. What is better, he had quite recruited his strength, and recovered his spirits, making me in that way the best possible return for hospitality and attention. The night before his departure I stayed with him and Napier till after midnight chatting of old times, comparing Spaniards with Turks, and ever placing the old hero of his youthful days in the foreground. He had seen the *king of men* at Busaco, stretched out in a furrow writing letters on finance, a few paces in front of his army arrayed in battle line against the French not 500 yards off! That is really great, thought I; not so much for the exposure to peril, as for the perfect command of thought under such circumstances.

My position, as chief of the Embassy I mean, is in sundry respects awkward and uncomfortable for the present. I am placed between Western energy and Eastern impassiveness, between British downrightness and local trickery, a red-hot horseshoe between the anvil and half a dozen sledge-hammers. I care not; such is my business just now; and I console myself by thinking of the illustrious Greek who served his native city as a scavenger, and of the modern general who has recorded that the fate of a campaign will sometimes turn upon a string of twenty mules. What I cannot brook is the slightest appearance of mistrust, or the foisting of consular opinions over the Embassy—both occasional results of the *clerkery* of the Foreign Office, and of a certain degree of incompleteness in its chief. Patience, which (you may dissent if you please) I possess at bottom under a very ruffled surface, is my anchoring ground.

CHAPTER XXIX.

THE INVASION OF THE CRIMEA.

1854.

ENGLAND and France had gone forth to aid the Sultan in driving the Russians out of the Principalities. Austria had taken the invaders in the rear with an army of observation, and had summoned the Czar to withdraw. But at this moment two events occurred which achieved the object of the three Powers without engaging any of their armies. The celebrated fortress of Silistria was the key of the situation ; until it had been reduced or masked no Russian army could venture upon an invasion of Turkey. General Paskievich accordingly laid siege to the fortress with extraordinary vigour in the middle of May. Perhaps with merely Ottoman commanders the garrison might have surrendered ; but it happened that two young English officers, Butler and Nasmyth, had thrown themselves into the beleaguered city and had inspired the defenders with a zeal and enthusiasm that no skill of Russian engineers could quench. Silistria was saved ; the Czar's army drew off ; and as if to shew that it was not only in siege works that the Turks were a match for their enemy, the Ottoman troops, headed by half a dozen British officers, followed the Russians, over the Danube at Giurgevo, and thus achieved the object for which two nations had sent forth their armies and a third had begun to advance. By the second week of July the cause of war had been removed ; the Russians were in retreat, and nothing remained but to make an honourable peace and ship the troops back to England and France.

It was hard for the Czar to be forced to hear that his

armies had been withstood, and even compelled to retreat, by
inferior bodies of Turks whose lack of numbers had been
counterbalanced by the skill and enthusiasm of a handful
of Englishmen.   Nicholas had made war out of jealousy of
England; he could not brook the supremacy of English
influence in Turkey, and this more than anything else had
prompted his reckless advance into the Principalities.   His
sensations may be imagined when he learnt that his troops
had been resisted and driven out of the provinces—not by the
Turks alone, for that to him was incredible—but by Turks
inspired to emulate their ancient warlike fame under the
guidance of a few young officers of that very England whose
position in Turkey was to him wormwood and gall.   It was
the last drop in a cup that was already filled to overflowing.

It was then that a new and perilous course was entered
upon.   The spirit of the English nation was roused, and
Louis Napoleon was ready to fan its zeal.   As early as
February the French ambassador had sounded the Porte
about an attack upon the Crimea, and the idea was soon
taken up in other quarters.   Indeed Lord Clarendon had con-
templated the step from the first.   On 28 June the Duke of
Newcastle, Secretary of War, wrote the famous letter, followed
by the still more celebrated soporific despatch, which in Lord
Raglan's opinion left him no alternative but to invade the
Crimea.   The opinion in England was that, until the fortifications of Sevastopol were destroyed, there would be no safe or
honourable termination to the quarrel.   What England did
not consider was whether the expedition was competent and
adequate for the task.   This consideration was nominally left
to the decision of Lord Raglan, but in reality was already
prejudged by the letter and despatch of the Duke of Newcastle.
In spite of his own better judgment, and influenced perhaps
by the more fiery spirits under his command, the General
gave way, and ordered, in concert with Marshal St. Arnaud,
that shifting of the scene of operations which was destined to
involve both countries in so many tribulations and to cause
the death of one of the most high-minded of England's commanders.   On 15 July Lord Raglan communicated the Duke's
letter to Lord Stratford, and three days later sent him the final

decision of the Allied commanders, which had not been arrived
at without sore misgivings, especially among the French
officers :—

Admiral Dundas and Sir Edmund Lyons, Admiral Hamelin and
Admiral Bruat, came from Buljik this morning, and Marshal St.
Arnaud and myself have had a conference with them, which lasted
four hours and half.

It has been determined to attempt a landing in the Crimea and
the attack of Sevastopol, and in order that our design should not be
immediately known, it has been suggested that Odessa should be reported as the object of the Allied armies.

In accordance with this determination the fleets eventually
set sail for the Crimea. Lord Stratford had of course no
voice in the decision, but there can be no manner of doubt
that he rejoiced in the thought of the destruction of Sevastopol.
The thing he dreaded most of all was a "shortcoming,"
inadequate peace. Two months, however, passed before the
Allies had landed at Old Fort, and the interval was rendered
all the more painful by the mortality from cholera at Varna,
and the daily more obvious insufficiency of the British arrangements for transport and commissariat. At last the expedition
was off, reports came in of a reconnaissance by the fleet, then
of a landing,[1] and finally one day near the end of September

---

[1] Lord Stratford's most direct information about the landing was brought by
Mr. Delane of the *Times*, who, together with Mr. Kinglake, had come out to
see the opening of the drama. "I cannot allow Mr. Delane to return," wrote the
ambassador, "without thanking you for the opportunity of making his acquaintance. His stay here was too short to allow of my shewing him as much attention
as I was inclined to do in the first instance on the strength of your regard for him
and subsequently for his own sake. I was able, however, to have some interesting
conversation with him in private, besides the share which I had in his society
during the few hours which he could afford to spare us. Whatever may have
been his published opinions in months of yore, he appears to be quite in the right
track now, and I was delighted to hear him express his conviction that if our
army were to perish before Sevastopol, the first thought of the nation at home
would be to raise a new one and go on. I say 'delighted' not from any particular taste for war, but because the experience of every day confirms my belief that
in the interest of the civilized world this great opportunity of giving a permanent
check to Russia must not be relinquished, cost what it may, and because Mr.
Delane knows better than anyone how to appreciate the character and feelings
of the country. It pleased me particularly to find that he is not the *flashy* man

From Lord
Raglan,
Camp on
the Alma,
21 Sept.

the ambassador came into the room where his family was assembled—and all who saw him say that the expression of his pale face can never be forgotten. He held a letter in his hand ; it told of deadly fighting on the Alma. " We attacked," wrote Lord Raglan, " we attacked and carried a most formidable position yesterday and we drove the enemy clean off it, notwithstanding the large force of infantry and artillery by which it was occupied. I never recollect to have been under so heavy a cannonade except at Waterloo, and many of the guns were of heavy calibre." This brief bulletin was followed by a more detailed letter from one of the officers engaged in the action, which is worth quoting :—

Alma
River,
22 Sept.

It is no use telling your lordship about the hail of cannon shot and shell and balls we have managed to get through, but there is a sad account of our loss. Two thousand and ninety-eight men and one hundred and twelve officers killed and wounded. Round shot were as plentiful as apples, and minié balls as thick as a shower-bath. If I ever have the luck to get clear off, I will tell your lordship, please God, some tales of the *French braves*, and how well they know how to take care of themselves. I had a wounded general and three officers lying at one time on stretchers in my tent, and some fifty or forty poor fellows outside. The information is startling. I have ascertained that there are 58,000 men, most of them in action the day before yesterday, besides cavalry. There are 12,000 cavalry to be here from Moscow on the *27th of this month* ; 4,000 Cossacks, 4,000 lancers, and 4,000 cuirassiers ; there are 8,000 coming from Anapa by the Straits of Kerch : they must pass by Balaklava, and we could if we had been in force cut them off. A week ago I

which at a distance might have been imagined. He is evidently a close observer, and his talent for description, though not flowing in expression, is vivid enough to impress the mind forcibly as well as agreeably with whatever he has to narrate. He is fresh from the spot which has the deepest interest for all of us at the present time, and his recital of what he has seen and heard there will be worth a score of despatches. The landing—when Lyons had only a few inches of water under his keel, and his men were up to their chins in surf, handing out regiments, squadrons of cavalry, and battering trains, with equal ease ; the 'first night' after landing, when 25,000 men stood without tents or fires on a muddy table-land in a storm of wind and rain ; Lord Cardigan's razzia on a grand sweep while the French cleared everything away by making an inner circle without his leave or knowledge ; and lastly, the horrors of a ship where hundreds died from its being overcrowded with invalids, are too real not to be related to you in his best manner."

1854
——
Æt. 67

entreated Lord R. to let me go to England, and in 28 days I would
have brought out all we could have swept from England, Gibraltar,
Corfu, and Malta, and France. I entreated him to let me come to
you. 10 or 15,000 Turks, any cavalry would have helped against
these 4,000 Cossacks ; but decision, decision is wanting. His lordship is a noble creature; he wanders amongst the shot and shell as
if he was on the banks of a trout stream, and no symptoms shewn of
anxiety but his poor stump going up and down.

The main body of the army we found has gone into Sevastopol,
but I believe this to be a feint. I do not think they will fight us at
the Kacha, because they now know our devilry. But they will
make a stand at the Belbek, which is the deepest of the two rivers ;
the place is honeycombed with mines, but I know their positions.
We shall then have to fight all our way over the high ground to a
great fort, which was commenced three weeks ago by 2,000 prisoners
and mined all over, and then we must fight every inch to their
entrenchments, and if we get any farther it will be a miracle. It was
a rash, rash expedition ; but there is no help for it now.

Two letters from Sir E. Lyons and Lord Raglan, relating
to the flank march, are interesting, not merely as shewing the
high spirit in which the leaders embarked upon the siege,
but especially because there is in them no trace of hesitation
about the much-disputed question of attacking Sevastopol
from the south side :—

A splendid flank march of Lord Raglan's, *steering by compass
thro' a dense wood*, has put us in possession of this convenient little
port, in which the *Agamemnon* looks like a Leviathan, but what is
more to the purpose is that it affords us the means of landing the
siege guns and all other wants of the army with safety and certainty.

From Sir
E. Lyons,
*Agamem-
non*,
Balaklava
Harbour,
28 Sept.

Lord Raglan is in high health and spirits, and we have a month's
fine weather before us, which will, I trust, be productive of events
that may make many a true and honest heart leap for joy.

Be assured of one thing. If ever a leader deserved success
Lord Raglan does. He has never thrown up his cap and cried
"Sevastopol for ever," as the poor Marshal has done, but never has he by
speech, or manner, or manner of acting, put it in the power of mortal
man to say that he has flinched from or regretted the *yes* he calmly
but decidedly enunciated at the Conference at Varna when St. Arnaud
put to the vote whether the expedition should take place or not. The
slightest symptom of vacillation on his part would have been seized

upon by the opponents of the expedition, who were always on the watch, and would have been wellnigh, if not altogether, fatal to it.

From Lord
Raglan,
Balaklava,
1 October

We arrived here and took possession of this place on 26 September, after having performed a flank march, for which the enemy were by no means prepared, with perfect success, and thereby secured a new base and a beautiful little harbour where the *Agamemnon* rides protected from every wind.   This is an immense advantage, particularly as it was found that the mouth of the Belbek was under the enemy's fire and could not be used as a place of disembarkation for our guns, stores, &c.

We shall now be enabled to attack the south side of Sevastopol. Our troops are investing it, and are barely without the range of the guns of the place.   Indeed some of them have fired over the heads of Sir George Cathcart's division.

We are busily occupied in landing our siege train, and have already got a good many heavy guns up the heights, and we shall open our attack at the earliest moment possible.

Lord Raglan had hardly settled down to the siege when he found himself in need of reinforcements.   He had already discovered that, if anything had to be done in Turkey, the Great Elchi alone could do it ; and in reference to the measures which had been taken to facilitate the transhipment of the troops to the Crimea, the Commander-in-Chief had listened to fervid eulogies from Sir George Brown on the

From Lord
Raglan,
5 August

ambassador's "zealous coöperation and the happy effect of his influence over the Turkish Government."   Accordingly to Lord Stratford he applied for more troops.   The result exceeded his highest expectations.   In two or three days, the reinforcements, to the number of some 4,000 men, were reported as ready, and though the usual delay, which disgraced all our transport arrangements during the early months of the Crimean war, kept the men in the Bosphorus a day or two longer than was necessary, they arrived at Balaklava in less than a week from the date on which Lord Raglan's application was received.   Two letters will shew the prompt and businesslike manner in which the ambassador made his arrangements, and the warm appreciation of his services by the Commander-in-Chief :—

I received your demand for Turkish reinforcements on the morning of the 7th and I have done my best to meet it. Six battalions, three of Regulars and three of the Imperial Guard, are to embark to-morrow morning in the three steamers sent to receive them.' I am assured that they amount to 4,000 men ; but 3,500 would suffice to fulfil my expectation. They are supplied with arms, ammunition, accoutrements, a month's provisions, and a million of piastres in money.

1854
—
ÆT. 67
To Lord
Raglan,
Therapia,
9 October

They are exclusively under your orders, and have a distinct commander, whom I have recommended to be carefully chosen. I inclose you herewith a copy and translation of his instructions.

All was announced to me as ready yesterday evening, but the coaling of the steamers cannot, Admiral Boxer assures me, be completed before to-morrow morning. I saw him myself yesterday, and send you now a copy of my subsequent notification to him.

I also inclose you an instruction for the commander at Batum, who will send you all the troops he can spare, not less, I trust, than 2,500, and as many, I *hope*, as nearly *four* thousand.

Admiral Boxer informs me that the coals on board the three steamers will suffice for their going to Batum and back, after completing their voyage hence to you.

Several battalions (seven) of infantry are also waiting in Thessaly for the means of their conveyance from Volo. I have applied for such means to the Seraskier and also to Admiral Boxer. The former cannot even hold out a hope of more than one steamer for that purpose. The latter is less hopeful, and only undertakes to let me know by-and-bye. Cannot you send down steamers for the purpose from Balaklava?

From here, from Varna, from the Dardanelles, not another Turk is to be got. Here we must use the Tunisians as garrison. The arrival of the Egyptians is uncertain.

When all is steamed together you will be lucky to get an effective of 12,000 men. I was not aware that the garrison of Constantinople was reduced so low. Recruits are coming in ; but they are too raw for service in the field.

The Seraskier appears to have acted in good earnest on this occasion, but it was necessary to get him out of bed for the purpose.

Your exertions have indeed been most prompt and successful, and I thank you most warmly for them.

F. m Lord
Raglan,
before Se-
vastopol,
13 Oct.

Thirteen hundred Turks landed this morning at Balaklava and the *Trent* has since arrived with at least as many more, and the third vessel is expected with equal or greater numbers. The *Himalaya* and *Simla* were despatched on the 11th as mentioned in my letter of that day, and the *Victoria* goes down to-night. I hope all these will return full. The more Turks we can get the better the chance of Balaklava not being attacked, and we shall give them every opportunity of entrenching themselves.

I shall always recollect with the most grateful feelings that we owe this timely reinforcement to you. You must have worked hard to have introduced so much activity into the Turkish authorities.

We have made good progress the last two days, with very little serious interruption from the enemy. In two or three days it is hoped that the Allied armies will be able to open a very powerful fire upon Sevastopol.

More Turkish troops arrived two days later, " a fine body of men," wrote Lord Raglan (15 October), " and in the most efficient state. . . . I must repeat my grateful acknowledgments to you for having so promptly and effectually provided me with so respectable a reinforcement : the six battalions amount to 4,400 men." And again (19 October) : " I cannot say how much I feel the exertions you have made for us. They have been eminently successful, which is a marvel, considering the sluggards you have to deal with. But you know them, and what would have been impossible for another was practicable with you. St. Arnaud used to say ' Le Sultan c'est Lord Stratford.' " Once more (24 October) : " I shall be delighted to receive the battalions from Volo. I am sure I am indebted to you for the despatch of the ships to fetch them as well as for the troops themselves." This was true enough : it was not sufficient to find troops ; the ambassador must also find ships to carry them, with little assistance from the transport service, and in spite of the interminable delays, obstructions, and jealousies of the Turkish officials.

The heavy losses of our troops at the Alma and Balaklava entailed fresh and onerous duties at Constantinople. It had been presumed that ample accommodation had been provided for the sick and wounded at the hospital at Scutari, on the Asiatic shore of the Bosphorus, immediately opposite Pera ; but when the transports laden with maimed and fevered soldiers began to arrive in an apparently interminable succession, it was soon discovered that there was neither accommodation, nor medical and nursing staff, nor furniture and stores, at all adequate to the sudden and severe strain. The worst sufferings of the wounded were endured on board the transports, where no sort of provision seems to have been made for the care of the sick ; but there was also mismanagement at Scutari. The long interval of peace had lulled the Medical Department into a torpor no less profound than that which in other branches of our military establishments benumbed every faculty save that of fighting ; and the situation was aggravated by the circumstance that, like persons in a state of intoxication, the sleepy officials refused to admit that anything was wrong. There is no jealousy like that of departments : and to have appealed to the Foreign Office for aid which should have come from the War Office would in the eyes of the medical and commissariat staff have been a worse crime than letting the patients die for want of such assistance. To the authorities at Scutari, the last person in the world to ask for help was the ambassador, not because he could not help, but because he belonged to a different department. The red tape was of the wrong sort.

Even the home departments seem to have been bound by the same official spell, for both the Admiralty and the Foreign Office, as appears from a despatch of Lord Stratford's, objected to his applying direct to Admiral Boxer when provisions had to be shipped for the Crimea, and requested him to apply always to the Commander-in-Chief. The ambassador had no choice but to submit : but he declined all responsibility for the consequences of the delay.

The moment it was known that 700 wounded were arriving from the Alma, their comfort became the special and most assiduous care of Lady Stratford, who had fortunately arrived with her daughters in September. Long before other help came from England, boats were daily going to and fro from Therapia to the hospitals, carrying food and wine and all that the Embassy could provide ; and, as Miss Stanley afterwards said, the ambassadress almost spent the winter " in a caïque between Europe and Asia."

Major Sillery, who was in command of the hospitals at Scutari, wrote on 30 September to thank Lord Stratford for " the articles sent for the use of the sick and wounded—many

1854

ÆT. 67

To Duke
of New-
castle,
21 Sept.

of whom have nothing but what they stood in at the time of their being wounded." The Elchi had already done all that lay in his power to prepare for the emergency. He had obtained from the Sultan the loan of the barracks and hospital at Scutari and Kulali, another small hospital at the entrance of the Bosphorus, and a Turkish hospital ship. On 24 September, being " tied to his ink-bottle " and immersed in despatches, he sent his first secretary, Lord Napier, to Scutari, to see what the Embassy could do for the wounded, who had just arrived from the battle of the Alma. On the 27th he sent Mr. Alison and the Embassy physician to help. On the 29th he went in person. The visit convinced him that a good deal was wanting, but he had no experience of hospital details, and the medical staff studiously kept him in the dark. Such obvious deficiencies, however, as could be seen Lord Stratford set himself to remedy, and the Turkish ministers were not slow (for Turks) to comply with his demands. From a letter written two days later to Dr. Menzies, the chief of the medical staff at Scutari, it appears that some of the hospital shortcomings were already in course of being remedied ; and we find the ambassador boldly recommending, what the army surgeon abhorred, the employment of women nurses, or at least, failing regular nurses, the soldiers' wives :—

To Dr.
Menzies,
1 Oct.

I beg to thank you for the return of sick, wounded, and prisoners which you have had the goodness to send me.

I hope you have more assistance by this time, not only in *persons*, but in *articles* of supply. I am assured that the Seraskier has sent you fifteen assistants, and I hope Dr. MacGuffog has been able to add to the number.

I saw enough on Friday to convince me that you must be taxed to the utmost to give even a fraction of relief to each of so many patients. There is the prospect too of more arrivals, for which you must have to make preparation.

I hear that the method adopted in the French military hospitals is very effective, but perhaps they have more hands at their disposal, and the *sœurs de charité*, I am told, are of great use.

I should have thought that the women—I mean the soldiers' wives—might be made available in your wards. But, I suppose, from their not being admitted, that experience has shewn the contrary.

I look forward to paying you another visit soon, and seeing the hospital as well as the barracks. But it is no easy matter to find a day for so long an excursion. In my profession, as in yours, we are obliged just now to work double tides.

1854

——

Æ.T. 67

Dr. Menzies seems to have entertained "a settled opinion that the admission of women, whether wives or not, was an unwise indulgence, unfavourable to medical discipline and the recovery of the patients." The doctor little knew what was in store for him.

To Duke of New-castle, 5 Nov.

At this early stage of the war the work of providing for the necessities of the hospitals depended almost wholly on the British Embassy, whence proceeded much active but quiet energy. We may be sure that whatever Lord Stratford was able to do was done; and, though it was manifestly impossible, with a small staff, and in face of the opposition of the medical authorities, to put matters in perfect trim, yet on 24 October the Elchi was able to record considerable progress. "Encouraged by your approval," he wrote to Lord Raglan, "I have made another visit to the hospitals and barracks at Scutari. According to my notions there is room for improvement: but things were in much better order than at first, though many new sufferers had just come in. I was assured that the medical attendance was no longer deficient; and that medicines were so abundant as to make the offers of a respectable chymist here superfluous. At the suggestion of the Duke of Newcastle, Lord Clarendon has authorized me to supply any additional wants, and I shall have much satisfaction in acting on the instruction." The wounded officers were even then, and much more later on, a special care of the Embassy, and, to quote but one among many, a young cousin of Mrs. Gladstone's, Grey Neville, who died at Scutari, bore eloquent testimony to the "wonders" that Lady Stratford was doing in the hospital: "and I do feel so grateful to you," wrote Mrs. Gladstone, "for I am sure your kindness and the sight of what you were doing comforted Grey, and we cherish the thought of this." On 29 October Lord Stratford sent to the Turkish ministers for a fresh supply of bedding, furniture, and stoves, which was immediately granted; and he provided

To Lord Raglan, 24 Oct.

fifty mattresses at his own charge. He found the utmost difficulty in inducing the Medical Department to admit a single deficiency, and repeatedly asked in vain for a list of requirements. "It is rather strange," he wrote to Lord Raglan, who was equally kept in the dark by the doctors, "that I have not received the list which you will perceive that I asked for. Without it I shall be working in the dark. It is to be inferred that in the opinion of Dr. Menzies the wants of the patients are either supplied already, or in a fair way of being so, without further interference on my part. However this may be, the arrival of Dr. Cumming, Dr. Spence, and Mr. Maxwell, is likely to clear up uncertainties, to say nothing of the valuable assistance to be afforded by Miss Nightingale and her assistants, who are already at work, and according to Lady Stratford's account, who visited both the barracks and the hospital this morning, likely to render very efficient services."

"I am persuaded," he told the Duke of Newcastle, "that any remissness in the beginning has been immensely exaggerated by newspaper clamours."

Miss Nightingale had indeed arrived with a brigade of forty nurses on 4 November, and thenceforward, so long as she continued her devoted work, it was almost impossible for anyone to be of use to the hospital unless at Miss Nightingale's initiative. Like many other admirable commanders, including Lord Stratford himself, she did not like colleagues. After she came he did his best to help her. He sent an attaché and chaplain to receive her, and begged that she would apply to the Embassy for everything that was required. In response to a prompt list of desiderata, for which he had vainly applied to Dr. Menzies, he wrote "I shall have much pleasure in procuring for the sick and wounded soldiers in hospital the articles which you mention as desirable for their comfort and progress towards recovery. Lady Stratford will give the necessary orders for that purpose and communicate further with you as circumstances may require. Pray do not hesitate to apply direct to me whenever any new occasion may arise.'

The ambassador of course could not personally visit the hospitals as often as he would have wished. All his influence was freely and powerfully given in behalf of the sufferers and those who came to help them, but it was given in vigorous strokes of the pen, while the personal superintendence was left, and safely left, in the hands of the ambassadress, aided by such men as Lord William Paulett, General Storks, Major Gordon, and Admiral Grey. That he spared no language to compel the Sultan to do his utmost for the sick and wounded may be judged from the following emphatic instruction to Stephen Pisani, written when the wounded were arriving from Inkerman :—

The Sultan and his Government must come to the relief of our hospitals without a moment's delay. I believe they are willing ; but they have still to understand the urgency of the case, and to give the requisite objects with becoming promptitude. Go to Ferik Efendi, to the Seraskier, and to Reshid Pasha, as soon as you can in the morning. Ask to see the Sultan himself. Our sick and wounded continue to come in so numerously that, notwithstanding the additional assistance and stores lately arrived, there is a deficiency in several important respects.

First of all, more accommodation is wanted. You must apply for the Kulali *hospital* again. You must insist upon having the *kiosk* on the cliff below the barracks at Scutari, if it is not already given up to us. Why should we not have the buildings at Hayder Pasha, where the Duke of Cambridge resided at one time ? Can we not have some houses in Scutari nearest to the Barracks ? The Seraskier was to send a person with one of our people to choose some of them ; but I have never heard the result. If these buildings cannot be granted, I must apply for the *Sultan's house at Seraglio point*. If necessity is good for one party, it is good for another. We sacrifice our hearts' blood—the best we have ; the Sultan must give us something more substantial than sweetmeats. If he cannot make his subjects turn out for our poor suffering martyrs, he must make room in his own palace. Don't hesitate to say so,—even to him,—though in respectful terms, if necessary.

The next thing is, that the buildings already occupied require some essential repairs. Application, as you know, has been made ; assurances have been given ; but the work remains to be done. Complain of this delay ; and insist upon the repairs being commenced immediately.

Then comes the want of stoves. The stoves themselves are in part to be procured from the Turks, and there is the fitting them with pipes, and putting them up. Look to this also.

Another urgent matter is the accommodation of the sick and wounded Russians. They have hitherto lived in the barracks, partaking of everything in common with our soldiers. Now, it appears,—as indeed I mentioned to you before,—that the apartments occupied by them are wanted for our own people, and, however reluctantly, we must think of providing for them elsewhere. Speak to the Seraskier of this also again, and ascertain without loss of time what is the best expedient to resort to. Remember that our honour, as well as humanity, is concerned in their good treatment. Remember too that they have a strong hold upon our feelings, as suffering from wounds and sickness.

On referring to a memorandum received from Major Sillery I perceive that I have omitted the *completion of the kitchen* in the barracks near Scutari, and the *erection of temporary barracks* "within the inner barrack square."

The *houses in Scutari* are wanted for 50 or 60 officers.

There is yet another serious want, namely, of a steamer to ply between Scutari and Pera every day at stated hours. This is most important. *Bread* was wanting yesterday. See Boxer—see the Captain Pasha—see Captain ——, or whoever may be the proper person, and in some way or other have the thing done, if possible.

It strikes me that the Kulali Barracks are a very long way off—arrangements nearer at hand would, I conceive, be preferable.

Perhaps the Russians might go there.

In one word proper accommodation and other necessaries must be supplied without delay, and I shall go in person to the Sultan and complain, if any difficulties are made.

We bear the brunt of the war, the Turks must bear the brunt of the hospitals.

I shall probably be at Scutari myself to-morrow—and afterwards perhaps at the Palace to see my lady.

Whatever difficulties were experienced in carrying out the constant demands for more accommodation and supplies were due mainly to the English authorities. The Sultan was ready enough to give up his palaces and barracks to the wounded, and to order his ministers to collect supplies and stores ; but it must be remembered that the Sultan and the Elchi and the markets were on one shore of the Bosphorus, and most of the hospitals were on the other side, whilst between them reigned one Admiral Boxer, in command of the transport service,—a gallant old seaman, by all accounts, but wholly incapable of

organizing the troublesome and intricate duties of his important department. Nor was this altogether his fault. He
was under-manned, and the supply of steam vessels under
his control was so inadequate that he could not furnish one
to ply across the Bosphorus for the service of the hospitals ;
as appears from the following letter :

In common with many others I have thought of little else but
the hospitals during the last five or six days. I made an effort to
get to Scutari myself on Sunday, but the weather, changing just as I
reached Pera, gave me a regular defeat, and I was obliged to return
in Boxer's steamer without effecting my purpose, or even seeing
General Bentinck and some of his wounded brother officers, whom I
sought in vain among the shipping. They went to sea in spite of
rain, wind, and mist.

What I could not have the pleasure of doing in person has been
done partly by correspondence and partly by deputy. The Sultan
and his ministers have listened to my supplications, and the wants of
the hospitals, in point of accommodation, furniture, and supplies of
various kinds, are either already relieved or in a fair way of being
so shortly. I should be a most unnatural husband if I did not tell
you that Lady Stratford has been actively employed for several days
in bringing the somewhat chaotic elements into order, and I really
believe that her exertions have contributed to the establishment of
an improved and still progressive state of things. The Sultan has
given up his reserved apartments and Kiosk ; he has ordered his
ministers to comply with all our demands, and the Captain Pasha
has provided a steamer to ply between Scutari and Tophana.

The great want was a competent head, who should be
able to give decisive orders without troubling himself as to
what particular schedule of what special department they
belonged to. If one applied to Admiral Boxer, it was as
likely as not that the reply was that the matter came under
the control of Major Sillery, or the Commissariat, or Dr.
Menzies ; and so the applicant was driven from pillar to post
without gaining his object. Someone was needed who should
be above all these, and so Lord Stratford reported to the
Commander-in-Chief :—

Lady Stratford is gratified by your kind message. She has
really worked hard at the hospitals, and I believe with good effect.

1854
——
ÆT. 68

I was there this morning and made acquaintance with Miss Nightingale, Mrs. Bracebridge, Mr. Sidney Osborne, and Dr. Cummings. The men are in a fair way to have everything which the liberality of the Government and the generous sympathy of individuals can give them. But the patients are numerous, the buildings are spacious, and many of the later arrivals stand in need even of proper bedding. Sillery, Boxer, and Menzies are excellent well-intentioned men, but they are not of the most clear-headed or energetic race, and the great obvious want is that of a Head—of some-one to represent you, to inspire respect, and to decide uncertain questions without hesitation as to responsibility. Cannot this be supplied?

We have got a Turkish steamer to ply between Scutari and Tophana every day at stated hours for the accommodation of those connected with the hospitals.

I have got the desired lists, and the articles which figure in them are applied for, and will, I hope, be speedily supplied.

Lord Raglan's reply was, as usual, satisfactory: he at once appointed Lord William Paulet to supersede Major Sillery and take entire command of the Bosphorus :—

From Lord
Raglan,
21 Nov.

I cannot say enough to you and Lady Stratford for all the interest you evince for the improvement of our hospital arrangements and for the trouble you take to secure that object, and I am sure that the poor sick and wounded and those concerned in the charge of them will feel your kindness as I do. I have taken advantage of the hint you gave me as to Major Sillery being hardly competent for so extensive and responsible a duty, though a most respectable man, and have appointed Lord William Paulet, with the rank of colonel on the staff, to the command of all the troops, sick or well, in the Bosphorus. I have advised him to communicate freely with you on all subjects, not I hope taking up more of your time than you can conveniently spare him, to look well after the officers and men on both sides of the water, to be very civil and attentive to Miss Nightingale and Mrs. Bracebridge, and to the commission, and in short to do everything that may be requisite to ensure comfort and produce regularity.

As regards Admiral Boxer I am powerless. No human power can make him a man of arrangement. He may be, and I believe is, a good officer afloat, and he is well intentioned ; but he has shewn no aptitude for the duties with which he is at present charged.

Even after this appointment, however, there remained difficulties with the worthy Admiral and the Medical Department. " It would really seem," wrote the Elchi, " that the professional people would sometimes rather look on in silence than accept aid from without." It must be admitted that Lord Stratford had a somewhat analogous feeling himself. He did not like private money being offered for Government purposes : in his eyes such subscriptions were a disgrace to his country's service. While he was furnished with large powers for providing whatever was needed, it displeased him to see private individuals unnecessarily coming forward to do things for which the public resources were properly responsible. So when a gentleman arrived from the *Times* with a large fund to disburse for the hospitals, Lord Stratford, in all sincerity, answered him that it was not needed, and that the money might more suitably be employed in building a much-wanted Protestant church at Pera. It should be added, however, that the ambassador had received a caution from Lord Clarendon in respect to the *Times'* representative, —a caution which, I am convinced, was wholly unjustified, but which amply explains the Elchi's reserve. In like manner, when private funds were offered for the repair of some hospital barracks, Lord Stratford hastened, at his own risk, to advance money from the Government to pay the workmen. He may have been over-sensitive, but there is something honourable in the feeling that the Queen's Government should provide for her soldiers' needs without having recourse to private charity.

Private charity and benevolence, however, were not to be baulked of their due satisfaction. The Bosphorus teemed with zealous helpers, and further supplies of nurses arrived, rather to Miss Nightingale's dismay. Indeed the lady-in-chief flatly refused to receive any more. She had left England, she told Lord Stratford, with a distinct understanding that none should be sent till she required them, and she was disagreeably surprized to find that the zeal of the War Office in this particular had overstepped her powers of arrangement for the best method of carrying out the duties of her

1854

*Æ*T. 68

To Lord
Raglan,
5 Dec.

7 Dec.

office. She considered indeed that it would be cruel, even were
it possible, to make the attempt to receive these females at
Scutari on their arrival ; and, she added, " I therefore must,
without further circumlocution, at once ask your Excellency to
provide for the reception, lodging, and maintenance of this
party, which may arrive without further notice." And so they
did : Miss Stanley, sister of the Dean, (then a canon of Canterbury, appeared at the end of December, accompanied by forty-
six nurses and sisters—a number, said Miss Nightingale,
" which exceeds my worst anticipations." It seems that there
was not accommodation at Scutari for more than six additional
nurses, and there was an imminent prospect of the new
arrivals being sent home discomfited. This appeared so
monstrous, at a moment when fifteen hundred sick were just
arriving from Balaklava, that the ambassador resolved to do
all in his power to utilize their services. The Turkish cavalry
barrack at Kulali, near Candili, on the Asiatic shore of the
Bosphorus, was obtained from the Sultan, and placed under
the sole authority of Lady Stratford ; and hither Miss Stanley
and her assistants were transported from the two houses
within the embassy grounds at Therapia which had been
placed at their disposal. Miss Stanley was appointed super-
intendent, and Lady Stratford spent a great part of her time
in attending to the necessities of the hospital, and among
her assistants none was more active than an engineer officer,
Major Gordon, who devoted his energies unceasingly to the
improvement of the accommodation and comforts of the sick
and wounded. In a very short time everything was in working order and managed not only on principles of benevolence
towards the patients but of economy towards the Government.
General Storks, who succeeded Lord William Paulet in command of the Bosphorus, and made himself very useful to the
hospitals, wrote that " the cheapest of the four hospitals is
Kulali," and Dr. Hall, the Surgeon-General to the Forces,
placed it on record that " both Lord and Lady Stratford de
Redcliffe have taken great interest in the military hospitals at
Scutari, and from all the accounts I receive her ladyship may
well be proud of the one at Kulali that is under her own
immediate protection." The hospital remained actively em-

To Lord
Clarendon,
DCCLX.

Dr. Hall
to Lord
Raglan,
24 Feb.
1855

1854.
—
Æt. 68

ployed till December, but Miss Stanley's delicate health compelled her to return to England in April, when her place was taken by Miss Hutton. A letter bearing a well-known signature may close the subject :—

Precincts, Canterbury, 5 Feb. 1855

My dear Lord,—I trust I may be excused for taking up a few moments of your time to express our deep gratitude for the kindness you have shewn to my sister. It is not for me to say anything of the public service which your Excellency has rendered in saving from utter wreck and failure the useful and benevolent scheme which my sister was sent out to assist. But I cannot forbear to tender the respectful thanks, which my father would have written had he been still living, for the support and help and sympathy which she has received from your lordship and Lady Stratford at a time when she most needed it.

Believe me, my dear Lord, to be
Yours most gratefully and respectfully,
A. P. Stanley.

The good work at Kulali was rivalled by the separate officers' hospital at Scutari, the requisites for which were entirely provided by friends in England. Lady Canning superintended all the details, in constant correspondence with Lady Stratford ; and the Queen took a special interest in this benevolent work.

Meanwhile, ignorant of much that was being done, and only too well informed of what had been left undone, the philanthropic soul of England was ablaze with indignation at the unprepared state of the hospitals. The newspapers had got hold of the subject, and in their hands it was not likely to grow less. The *Times* took the lead in the onslaught upon the authorities, and the country, following the *Times*, wept and gnashed its teeth at sufferings and cruelties which were half imaginary, and when strictly true were the consequence of an inexperience which was rapidly disappearing in face of actual duty. At first the *Times* correspondent cast no blame on the ambassador : it was suggested, on the contrary, that his willingness was checked by the ignorance of the real state of things in which the medical staff tried to keep him. The people to blame were the heads of the hospitals and commissariat : and these received but a short shrift from the leading journal.

Real good, however, came out of the excited tumult thus stirred up in England. Whether the hospitals were in as bad a state as was reported or not, it was a fine spirit of devotion that took so many English ladies out to the Bosphorus to face the horrors of a hospital at the seat of war ; and it was good to see men of fashion and indolence, natives rather of Bond Street than Aldershot, leaving their pleasures to go forth and minister to the wants of their wounded countrymen. Their task was not always smooth ; and at first they had to face a good deal of official prejudice. As an instance of this it may be useful to recal what happened to two zealous and devoted gentlemen who sought out Admiral Boxer in his office at Tophana, in order to beseech him to improve the steam communications between the city and the hospitals on the Asiatic side of the Bosphorus. The Admiral sat in an inner office, where he could hear the communications which the young men were holding with his clerk, and when they came suddenly face to face with the blunt old sailor, he was prepared for them. " I see who *you* are," said he ; " you're two d——d sympathizers. I'll tell you who *I* am—I'm ' Bloody Old Boxer' ! " The sturdy seaman who rejoiced in this *sobriquet*, however, had in the end to admit the necessity of improvement, and no one worked harder than he did afterwards in reorganizing the harbour of Balaklava, where he ended his life worthily, toiling for the good of the troops. The example of the ladies and men of fashion who came out to help the sick was not thrown away. A good principle was then established which has borne fruit ever since ; and a movement which began in what was little better than a " scare " has since expanded into an invaluable and well-organized branch of the service.

Later, when the newspapers attacked the Elchi for his supposed indifference, there were not wanting defenders. Every officer who knew the true state of things in the hospitals during the winter of 1854–5 was shocked at the recklessness of the charge. None knew more about the matter than Lord W. Paulet and General Storks, and their testimony was warmly decisive. The whole subject was conclusively digested in a pamphlet by Mr. P. Benson Maxwell, who had examined the evidence on the spot and who has since achieved a high reputation on the Indian bench, and his refutation of the charge brought against the Government and its agents gave Lord Stratford real pleasure. "Your lordship is probably aware," wrote Mr. Maxwell, "that in common with every other person directly or indirectly connected with the Eastern expedition, you have had an abundant share of abuse. Your name must therefore have found its way into the pages which dealt with that expedition ; but happily very few words suffice to shew the absurdity of the outcry which was raised against you by people who were in so excited a state as to cry out against everybody without the slightest discrimination." In acknowledging the letter and pamphlet Lord Stratford said, "I thought from the first that there was great exaggeration in the attacks directed with so much systematic virulence against the Government and its agents for the shortcomings and sufferings of our share in the war, and particularly that a large measure of injustice was dealt out against the Duke of Newcastle. It gives me a proportionate amount of pleasure to find that a man of your ability, character, and opportunities, actuated by a regard for truth and a spirit of fairness, has ventured even at the eleventh hour to unseal the eyes of the public and to expose its misleaders. As for the splinters which a discharge of so much vituperation has struck off to my disparagement, they have never given me any serious annoyance. . . . Your testimony on this occasion comes in aid of my creed [that the truth will always be established in time] and, however incomplete, is deserving of my gratitude. The rest will come, if it has not already come, in due season from other sources. But I am too little given to display and too much below my own standard to wonder at being sometimes wrongly or imperfectly understood." It is only fair to add that the *Times* came to see its error, and one who had the best authority for speaking in the name of the paper assured me of its absolute retractation of the charges which had been advanced in a period of popular excitement.

Lord Stratford's energies were soon required for repairing another branch of official incompetence. The surgeons' department was being put in order ; it was now the turn of the commissariat at the front. Lord Raglan had already told the Elchi that in his opinion it would be " impossible to winter in the Crimea ; " nevertheless, he was obliged to winter there, and this after the terrible hurricane which wrought havoc in the camps, and sent the *Prince*, full of stores, clothing, and food, to the bottom of the Black Sea. Letters from Sir T. Steele and Lord Raglan describe the battle of Inkerman on 5 November and the storm of the 14th :—

From Sir
T. Steele,
8 Nov.

The enemy attacked in overwhelming numbers the right of our position on the heights of Inkerman. The night was unfortunately very dark, and the morning so thick that little could be seen ; so much so that the outlying picquets were not aware of the extensive preparations for attack which must have been carried on all night. The outposts were quickly driven in by clouds of skirmishers, the columns of infantry advancing under cover of several large pieces of artillery which they had posted during the night immediately in front of the 2nd division. The Guards were on the right occupying a small redoubt, in course of construction, but not yet armed with guns : they had, however, only 1,100 men in the whole brigade. They were speedily attacked by four relays of infantry that advanced rapidly one after the other, but were steadily repulsed. After the fourth attack, the Guards were obliged to abandon the redoubt and retired slowly ; the 20th Regiment fortunately coming up in support, they cheered, charged and regained the redoubt, where a most obstinate conflict was carried on for some time. Sir G. Cathcart, who was sent to support the Guards, but who fancied that he could do better by endeavouring to descend the heights and get to the rear, found himself unfortunately opposed to a large number of the enemy who were above him, and it was with considerable difficulty and loss that his division regained the heights. Here he fell, shot right through the breast, and his adjutant-general, Charles Seymour, alongside of him. Both his brigadiers were badly wounded—Torrens and Goldie ; the latter died shortly afterwards. The Light Division and part of the 3rd were hotly engaged on the left. In the meantime the 2nd Division were heavily pressed, and were obliged with the guns to give way. At this critical moment two regiments of French arrived and opened a heavy fire, and enabled us to hold the ground until further reinforcements of General Bosquet's division of French came up, and with their assistance the enemy, after a severe contest which lasted from about 7 until half-past 2, were completely driven off the ground, and retired in great confusion over the Inkerman bridge to the ground they had previously occupied on the Belbek. Unfortunately, as at the Alma, we were not sufficiently strong to follow up our victory, which must inevitably have ended in the total destruction of their army. . . .

1854
—
Æт. 68

The 6th and 7th instant conferences were held between General Canrobert and the French generals of division with Lord Raglan, Sir J. Burgoyne, and Brigadier-General Airey. The result was, that in the present state of affairs, an assault would be too dangerous an experiment ; it was therefore decided that two large strong heavily-armed redoubts should be constructed on the right of our position, and a similar fort on the French left, in front of the bay in which their shipping is at anchor ; that the whole position of the Allied army is to be put in a strong state of defence ; and that the siege, without being raised, is not to continue until sufficient reinforcements arrive to enable us to cope with the army outside and carry the town.

When I wrote to you on the 12th instant I mentioned, I believe, that the weather was very bad and boisterous. It so continued the following day, but after nightfall on the 13th the rain ceased and the wind went down, and it remained fine until after 5 on the morning of the 14th, when suddenly a tempest arose such as I had never before witnessed.

From Lord Raglan, 16 Nov.

The tents in our several camps were blown down almost without exception. The sick and well were prostrate in the mud, and a scene of misery ensued of which the reality was perhaps beyond the power of description. The roads were rendered nearly impassable, and single horsemen in many cases found it impossible to make headway, and several horses were blown down with their riders on them. Fires could not be lighted, and the men were consequently unable to cook their food. . . .

You will see that our loss in shipping is immense ; it is equally great in provisions, forage, warm clothing, ammunition, and warlike stores.

The Commissary-General writes to Mr. Smith at Constantinople to send up without loss of time provisions, corn, and forage, and by the same opportunity I have directed Captain Wetherall, of the Quartermaster-General's Department, to proceed there for the purpose of purchasing warm clothing, and many other things that our soldiers want ; and I earnestly solicit your powerful assistance, which I am sure will be readily and cordially given, in the fulfilment of his instructions. If you could lend him one of your dragomans it would materially facilitate his operations, which at this inclement season are of vital importance to the efficiency, and I might say the very existence, of our troops.

When this news came in, the ambassador laid siege to the Porte and strove to hasten the despatch of supplies. It was hard work. He had written some time before to Sir E. Lyons (20 June) that his "solicitations to the Porte for necessary arrangements were sadly embarrassed by the never-ceasing slowness, ignorance, and prejudice of the Turks : there is no getting them out of the old ruts, and I lose my patience in fruitless efforts to make them worthy of our assistance." Still, the situation was urgent, and Captain Wetherall, aided by the 1st interpreter of the Embassy, attachés Doria and Moore, and a Greek gentleman, M. Revelaky, scoured the bazars for warm clothing for the destitute troops before Sevastopol ; the ambassador compelled the Turkish ministers, of whom Reshid Pasha was now once more the head, to help their utmost, and provided the necessary authority for levying requisitions upon the markets of Brusa, Smyrna, and other places. Whatever could be procured, we may be sure, "by hook or by crook," was sent off to the army as promptly as the transport service permitted : and an "urgent and peremptory" despatch to Admiral Boxer on the subject had some effect in hastening his usually deliberate move-ments : but as a matter of fact the Turks had generally to find the vessels as well as the stores. All the exertions of the ambassador and his small staff could not make amends for the short-sighted follies of the home authorities, the inadequacy of the transport and commissariat departments, and the criminal frauds of the contractors. Lord Stratford had tried to make the best of the confusion, but his patience gave way at last. "It is really time," he wrote to Lord Raglan, 14 December, "that some radical cure should be applied to the tendency which appears from some cause or other to exist towards getting things in a mess or a deadlock. I have been slow to admit much of what now presses irresistibly on my conviction as to the mischief arising from want of unity, fore-sight, and proper feeling—I grieve to say it—in some quarters where no such deficiency ought to be."

So the year 1854 came to an end amid troubles and calamities ; doubts and anxieties in the trenches, sickness and des-
titution in the tents. England was palpitating with sympathy
and indignation, but her hearty aid was long in reaching the
sufferers, and many of her gifts went astray and never served
the end to which they were so anxiously and lovingly destined.
A violent public feeling was rising against incompetent
officialism, and like most popular sentiments overshot its
mark. Everyone concerned in the war came in for his share
in the general vituperation, and the newspapers daily slew
reputations that had been won on hard-fought battlefields.
The inky Rhadamanthus spared none, weighed no evidence,
believed only its Special Correspondent. The Great Elchi
suffered like the rest, but the main cause for which he bore
most undeserved blame belongs chiefly to the next year.

Lord Stratford, despite his incessant toil, and not a little
disagreeable opposition and criticism, continued sanguine and
firm. The deeds of Alma, Balaklava, and Inkerman recalled,
he said, his young days, when Trafalgar and Waterloo were
the words in all men's mouths. He was proud of his country's
arms, and confident that, in spite of every obstacle from man
and the elements, the good cause would triumph in the end.

1854

Æ:T. 68

CHAPTER XXX.

THE SIEGE OF SEVASTOPOL.

THE first month of 1855 found every department of government, and not least the Embassy at Constantinople, absorbed
in the effort to remedy the effects of unpreparedness which
had plunged the army in the Crimea into that state of sickness
and depression and starvation that roused the indignation of
the whole people of England. The two chief difficulties
that hindered the proper provisioning and clothing of the
men were the crowded and disorganized state of the little
harbour of Balaklava, and the total effacement of all roads
by the frost, snow, rain, and consequent deluge of mud. On
6 January Lord Stratford wrote to the Commander-in-Chief,
apologizing for what might appear as an officious interference,
but strongly urging the employment of a body of labourers,
which he offered to send at once from Constantinople, to make
passable roads from the harbour to the camps, and also calling
his attention in urgent but very friendly terms to the disorder
that was still reigning at Balaklava. In the same letter he
remarked that every officer he had seen, both French and
English, believed that Sevastopol might be taken by assault
without further delay, and that reports were gaining ground
of the discontent of both armies at the hesitation of their
generals. A gloomy anticipation of failure had indeed begun
to take the place of that cheerful spirit which had hitherto
characterized the predictions of the soldiers, and there was a
general belief that a fatal mistake had been made in not
attacking the fortress from the north side immediately after
the victory of the Alma. A letter from the ambassador to

Lord Clarendon early in January conveys some of these impressions :—

1855

ÆT. 68

The opinion strengthens that a great mistake was made in not
attacking Sevastopol at first. We were next betrayed by our
generosity. We gave up to our allies the position assigned to us,
and undertook with smaller numbers to make approaches through a
rocky soil, at a greater distance from the sea and with a wider extent
of operations. Then came the natural consequences of excessive
fatigue, and exposure to wet and cold, in the unwelcome forms of
diarrhoea, fever, and cholera. Later again came the battles and the
hurricane, calling forth the noblest qualities of our army, but leaving
it thinned and harassed. Nor was this all. A suspicion awoke that
want of foresight and inattention to warnings had raised the price of
glory too high, sacrificing efficiency to renown. The siege is now to
all appearance languishing and the troops are suffering mainly from
two causes—want of practicable roads, and want of arrangement in
managing the supplies. The road from Balaklava to the camp and
trenches must be in an awful state, and I hear stories of neglect
and mismanagement which would be incredible, if they were not
so strongly averred. The elements unfortunately have continued to
increase our difficulties, and while our means of success become
more entangled, the object of our efforts would seem to be less
assailable. I had observed till quite lately that croakers invariably
ended by saying "Oh ! but we shall get into the place at last." No
such comforting conclusion now comes from their lips. The usual
finale is an ominous shake of the head. Two mails have gone by
without a cordial even from Rose !

To Lord
Clarendon,
3 Jan.
1855

It is possible at the same time that all this gloom may proceed
from impatient and disappointed individuals. The particulars of
difficulty may be true, and still at headquarters a way to final success
may be seen either through them or over them. *There* starlight and
sunshine may flourish, while all around is wrapped in mist and apprehension—*solemque suum sua sidera noscant.* If it be so, I wish the
secret were less diligently kept, that symptoms of progress were more
apparent, and the arrivals of sick less frequent.——

Æn. vi.
641

Here I was interrupted, and I may say agreeably so, by the
arrival of Mr. Beatty, the civil engineer. The idea of a railway being
laid down in a few weeks tinges every cloud with hope and operates
with the force of a cordial. There is still a perilous interval to be
traversed, and if it be true that the army sickens at the rate of nearly
a thousand a week, our present reduced force may be further reduced
by a third before the basis of operations is put into regular communication with the camp. For such a deplorable contingency a remedy

may, however, be found in those reinforcements which you continue to send out with such activity and perseverance. This is no triumph in itself ; but it is an escape from calamity, and, time thus gained, a brighter season may crown our exertions with success. At all events, the prospect may give us heart to stand firm to our principles, and to shun the temptations of a plausible arrangement recommended by expediency and the pressure of the moment.

Not that I mean to apply these terms to what you are doing. Your policy bears the stamp of a becoming resolution, and the interpretation which you have given to the Four Points[1] of departure for a negotiation is fairly adapted to European interests. I must have expressed myself awkwardly in former letters to have given you a different impression of my notions. The points only require to be *carried out*, and I conclude from your correspondence that the Cabinet is bent on performing that act of justice to the world, if cruel complications do not impede the freedom of its action.

It still remains to be seen whether Austria will march frankly along with us—that she can turn against us would seem to be impossible. If she only go so far as to neutralize Germany, Russia will surely find it difficult to hold out long against France and England.

The effects of a continuous and systematic blockade have still to be tried, and the Czar, without having to dread the fate of his grandfather, may be strangled as effectually through the medium of trade and finance.

I have already answered your appeal by stating in a former letter my very imperfect notions as to opening the Straits. I have now to add my desire that Sevastopol may, if possible, be turned into a free commercial port, and to repeat my conviction that no increase of territory could turn to the advantage of Turkey. With respect to the Principalities, making every allowance for situation and foreign influence, I should be sorry to see them deprived of their present fair prospects of internal improvement ; and if the war continues, notwithstanding the pacific possibilities which you have contributed to open in Vienna, I should not despair of having the barrier of Warsaw restored as the only effectual check to Russian encroachment on that side.

---

[1] The Four Points upon which the negotiations (which had never been entirely abandoned) for peace were founded were : 1. The abolition of the Russian Protectorate over the Danubian Principalities ; 2. The freedom of the Danube and its embouchures ; 3. The neutralization of the Black Sea and closing of the Straits to ships of war ; 4. The confirmation of the rights and immunities of the Christian subjects of the Porte without injury to the Sultan's dignity and independence.

1855
——
Æt. 68

In saying this I do not mean a Polish revival at the expense of Austria and Prussia, but a return to the principle of conservation recognized at the Congress of Vienna, which in my humble judgment we ought never to have seen overthrown without a far stronger remonstrance than the mildest of useless protests. The remnant of Polish independence connected with Russia by the Congress was a European Palladium which no inconvenience arising from rebellion could justify Russia in crushing.

The arrival of an engineer, soon followed by English navvies, for the construction of a railway from Balaklava to the camps, did not interfere with Lord Stratford's plan of sending labourers from Constantinople. Lord Raglan thankfully accepted the suggestion, and, though there was some delay in consequence of the men at first refusing to go to a place which by all accounts seemed to be little better than a pest-hole, a thousand navvies were soon despatched and did excellent service. Lord Raglan's reply to the ambassador's suggestions of the 6th may be quoted here :—

From Lord Raglan, before Sevastopol, 12 Jan.

I have received your letter of the 6th instant, and I am very much obliged to you for taking so warm an interest in our proceedings, and for your suggestion, which I consider most valuable, for the employment of labourers in the repair of the roads whom you can send us from Constantinople.

I most gratefully and readily accept your offer, and will thank you to send up the five or six hundred men you speak of, or, what I should prefer, double the larger number as soon as possible.

The greatest defects of Balaklava are the smallness of its harbour and the narrowness of the only road leading into the town. Men and beasts of burthen come there from all parts of the army for provisions, forage, and warm clothing, as well as for huts, and stores of every possible description. . . .

The great want of all, however, is that of *transport*, coupled with the insufficient establishment of the *Commissariat*. The Commissary-General is not only charged with the supply of provisions and forage, but likewise with the custody and issue of stores of every description other than warlike. With officers for the former he is not adequately supplied. For the latter duties not at all to any extent, and hence arises confusion, delay, and disappointment.

The means of transport are very limited, wholly insufficient, and since the roads have become impassable for the Malta mule-carts the men have frequently been obliged, despite their other duties, to fetch up their rations and warm clothing from Balaklava, a very positive grievance.

The parcels for officers have become a formidable item for care and attention. They come by all vessels, frequently without advice, and are sometimes got rid of by the masters of ships without previous intimation. I have established a party for the receipt of these parcels and for their delivery, and the arrangement works very satisfactorily.

The French army is very large, more than four times the size of ours, and the greater portion of it is either in reserve or placed as a corps of observation, with very limited duties to perform. Thus, therefore, the men have five nights out of the week to themselves, whilst our men are on duty every other night, or sometimes for several nights together. They are going to assist us, but the arrangement is one of great difficulty, and has already undergone much discussion. I hope we have nearly come to a settlement since I began this letter. The administration of the French army is excellent. The *intendance*, perfectly well understood, is complete in officers and men who are not combatants, and so is the hospital establishments. They have not made war in Africa since 1830 for nothing, and they have all these necessary adjuncts to an army upon a war footing before the war commenced. We had and still have ours to create.

All through January there was unabated activity at the Embassy on behalf of the troops. The correspondence about procuring, shipping, conveying, and unlading supplies of food and clothing was uninterrupted. The deficiencies of our transport service had to be supplied with such assistance as the Turks could render; the deficiency of stores, by what could be purchased in the markets of Turkey; and for both these purposes the authority and constant vigilance of the Elchi had to be unceasingly exerted. More houses had to be obtained for the wounded, and before the month was out, the Sultan had parted with every available accommodation, including several of his palaces and private apartments. Just when it seemed impossible to discover a single empty house or stable, a requisition came from the Duke of Newcastle for the ambassador to find accommodation for 2,000 horses; and somehow or other it was done. Hardly was this feat accomplished when the Sardinian contingent, which had gallantly come to the assistance of the Allies, required a depôt, and of course it was to Lord Stratford, and not to Baron Tecco, their own representative, that they looked for the satisfaction of their needs. Telegraphs were to be established, and the British ambassador was the only person to procure the necessary firmans and vezirial letters. Even the Turkish forces could not obtain the stores and other supplies of which they stood in great need without his mediation. Demand after demand was made from England and from headquarters for every conceivable kind of assistance ; and it is very noteworthy, in reading through the unpublished despatches, how frequently the requirements of Lord Clarendon or the Duke of Newcastle had already been successfully anticipated by the Queen's representative at Constantinople. But in spite of all the energy displayed by the Embassy, and also (when they awoke to the necessity) by the home authorities, such evils as had taken root at the seat of war were not to be speedily remedied. The report at the beginning of February was still far from encouraging, though not bad enough to justify the gloomy despair which marked every one of Lord Clarendon's letters to the ambassador at this period, and indeed almost throughout the war. Lord Stratford wrote on 5 February :—

I will not say that your letter of the 22nd communicated its gloom to me, for my spirits were already much depressed by the sad state of things in the Crimea, contrasting as it does with our undiminished requirements in policy and character, while harmonizing alas ! but too much with the official difficulties at home. I am sincerely grieved at what you tell me about the Duke of Newcastle. — I am convinced that he and Sidney Herbert are both as well-intentioned and zealous statesmen as ever embarked in a great and difficult political enterprize. But every whale must have a Jonah when the sea runs high, and, if the news from Bucharest be true, we shall soon learn that nothing short of a ministerial holocaust has satisfied the public wrath. Meanwhile I have no consolation to send you from the Crimea. In addition to our own shoals of sick, the French state that they have received 4,800 invalids within the last fortnight, and orders have been received to prepare for 3,000 or 4,000 more between sick and wounded. It is moreover stated on French authority that our effective does not exceed from 8,000 to 10,000 men, while the French themselves can boast no higher figure than 65,000, which, high as it is above ours, comes short of what was expected. I had ventured to hope that cold weather would check the spread of disease, but in this also we are disappointed. The strange thing is that many officers, both French and English, maintain that the assault might be made with every prospect of success. Remembering what you told me of Canrobert's opinions transmitted to Paris, I have tried to ascertain the language of French officers, and I am assured that it is generally sanguine as to the success of an assault. Among the painful apprehensions in prospect is the danger of our being too much reduced in numbers to share the triumph, if a triumph were achieved. These calamities make no difference in my unabated reliance on the spirit and resources of our countrymen, and if we can but tide over the breakers I firmly believe that the good old ship will find its way, as heretofore, with flying colours into a safe and glorious port. There is no denying, however, that the strain of the crisis may be too great even for her thick-ribbed sides, and that we may perish of hunger within sight of the land of plenty.

The tide of misfortune, however, was on the turn. The winter was drawing to a close, and with it the spirits of the troops and the hopes of the commanders were rising. Sir George Brown, who had been absent on leave, on his return reported the change to Lord Stratford in cheery tones :—

From Sir
G. Brown,
15 Feb.

I found Lord Raglan and all his staff looking extremely well and in good spirits, and I was better satisfied with the personal appearance of the troops than I was prepared to expect. But I could scarcely have seen them under less favourable circumstances, for a rapid thaw had commenced after the storm of the previous day, and it was impossible to move from one tent to another without being over the ankles in mud and half-melted snow.

Yet notwithstanding all this apparent discomfort the men seemed to be *cheery* and in good spirits, and the officers spoke hopefully of the future. They are now amply supplied with provisions and have fresh meat two or three days in the week, and the commanding officers and surgeons, one and all, assured me that the worst was passed, and that there was an evident change for the better as regarded the health and efficiency of the men. Dressed up in their furs, sheep's skins, and winter clothing, they look, to be sure, a motley set enough; but no one complains, and those that are left seem to be going on with their work with their accustomed good humour, and have all the appearance of vigorous health.

Most of the regiments have got up wooden huts for their hospitals, and some of them have nearly half of their men under a similar de-

1855
——
ÆT. 68

scription of cover; but the transport of the army has been so entirely broken up and destroyed, that this has been accomplished by means of the kit-horses and mules of the officers alone, and it is highly creditable to the public spirit of these gentlemen to observe that not a single officer in my division has as yet provided any other cover for himself than his tent, and that they all appear to have determined to provide for their men before thinking of themselves.

What now perplexed the onlookers was the marked hesitation of the French. Mr. Kinglake, the revelations of the French War Office, and the Russian *Diplomatic Study*, have since thrown a flood of light upon the designs of Louis Napoleon, but it is clear from Lord Stratford's letters that no suspicion of the Emperor's interference was at the time entertained either at the British headquarters or at the Embassy. The common explanation was that Canrobert was afraid of the responsibility of ordering an assault before his reinforcements arrived. A letter from Sir E. Lyons expresses this opinion :—

You will have heard from Lord Raglan, no doubt, that Canrobert, although he has nearly ninety thousand men here, talks of being "driven into the sea," and has been crying that Omar Pasha should come here with all of his troops who are not required for the defences of Eupatoria. Lord Raglan sees many objections to this, and so do I, and it is now arranged that when all is ready for the assault of Sevastopol, Omar is to come here with 20,000 or 25,000 men for a few days only, and then return to Eupatoria, whence with 50,000 men, including a considerable force in cavalry and a due proportion of artillery, he will materially contribute to the expulsion of the Russians from the Crimea.

From Sir E. Lyons, *Royal Albert*, off Sevastopol, 15 March

I much fear that Canrobert, though personally as full of courage as a forest full of lions, is too cautious for an enterprize of this kind.

Lord Raglan's equanimity is hardly disturbed by even this onslaught of the English press, and the simultaneous arrival of General Simpson and the approaching arrival of the Commission. I almost begin to doubt whether our institutions are compatible with vigorous warfare. As I *think* I said to you some months ago, I *know* that I said so to Sir James Graham, the success of this expedition must materially depend upon what Canrobert really is, and now more than ever, for his large force by the side of our small one naturally gives them preponderating weight in conferences ; the men we have are now, thank God, the picture of health and in high spirits,

1855
——
ÆT. 68 well fed and well clothed, the railroad progressing rapidly, and all that one sees looks *couleur de rose*, but I am told that we have still many sick. I believe that we have 23,000 capable of going into action.

We have no correct knowledge of the force of the enemy, but I believe they have on *paper* about 100,000. An Englishman who escaped yesterday from Sevastopol says that we might have walked into it after the battle of Alma.

Lord Stratford was soon able to test the soundness of these views with his own eyes. In one of the few autobiographical fragments which he wrote concerning the period of the Crimean War, he describes his first visit to the scene of operations :—

MEMOIRS. "I went twice to the Crimea, the first time at Lord Raglan's request, the second under instructions from home. If ever the characters of a thorough gentleman and gallant soldier were contained in one person Lord Raglan was the man. Companion in arms and friend of Wellington, heir of that great commander's military principles, he was naturally chosen to conduct the war against Russia in concert with our allies the French. More than a generation had passed away from the time of the battle of Waterloo to that in which he went forth at the head of our Crimean expedition. Vast changes had taken place in the interval. I will not say that England had declined from her warlike spirit, that, to use a well-known expression,

Lucan,
Civ. Bell.
i. 130

Longoque togae tranquillior usu
Dedidicit jam pace ducem ;

but certain it is that her habits of military practice had been entirely interrupted, except in India, and that new ideas, at least in degree, had sprung up with regard to the instruments of warfare, the comfort of the soldier, and the duty of the officer. These causes of increased difficulty in the conduct of a campaign were magnified by the critical activity of the press, the livelier sensibilities of the public, and other circumstances peculiar to the scene of operations.

" The spring was advancing in the second year of the war
when I received Lord Raglan's invitation. I embarked without
any unnecessary delay in the steamer *Caradoc*, commanded by
Captain Derriman, and landed after an easy passage in the
narrow but picturesque harbour of Balaklava, which was then
crowded with our shipping.   Lord Raglan paid us the compliment of a visit, and I rode up to headquarters, the ladies
remaining on board.   The wretched state of the roads, which
had been a principal source of suffering in winter, no longer
existed.   I had sent up a thousand hired labourers from
Constantinople as soon as I was at liberty to do so, and, what
was more to the purpose, a number of navvies had recently
arrived from England.   In other respects as well as in this
the pressure of unforeseen difficulties had ceased ; but the
operations against Sevastopol made no marked progress, and
plans of attack on other more distant points were suspended
by considerations which did not originate on our side.   Lord
Raglan proposed that I should take part in the councils which
were held between the respective commanders, but I thought
it prudent to decline an honour that would convey with it
a certain degree of responsibility and no adequate usefulness.
He told me that it had been agreed in council to send an
expedition to Kerch, but that his French colleague a few
hours later had receded from the agreement : during my
short visit Canrobert changed his mind about three times.[1]
A day or two after my arrival a review of the French army
took place.   It was a very pleasing sight.   The troops
appeared to be in excellent condition, and their gay well-
ordered step in marching was prettily set off by the vivan-
dières, who, in smart costumes at each end of the lines, kept
pace with the soldiers.   I was so near their general that we
could hold converse with each other while the march went on.
So good an opportunity of saying a word in Lord Raglan's
sense was not to be lost.   I expressed my admiration of the
gallant bearing and spirited movement of the troops, with
a hint in conclusion that it was a pity to delay their active
employment against the enemy.   The general replied in his

---

[1] It is only fair to add that recent publications have traced Canrobert's vacil-
lations to the direct interference of Louis Napoleon.

own language : ' Ah ! monsieur l'ambassadeur, les con-
séquences d'un insuccès dans la guerre sont très graves.'
' Sans doute, monsieur le général,' I rejoined, at some little
risk of causing displeasure ; ' mais il me parait que le plus
grand des insuccès c'est de ne rien faire.'

"No one seemed to apprehend an attack. The siege
operations continued, but they were directed against the
outward forts, particularly the Mamelon, and until they were
reduced Sevastopol could not be assailed with effect. Lord
Raglan and his staff occupied a house at no great distance
from the French headquarters, and a room was kindly
allotted to me within its precincts. One evening after dark
we heard firing on the French line. The moon was up,
horses were ordered, and I joined the party from mere
curiosity. We rode to a point known as the White House, and
a little beyond fell in with General Canrobert. We were on
high ground, and in a valley below an action was going on
between a portion of his troops and a Russian detachment.
We could not see them, but we were near enough to hear
their shouts and to perceive the flashes of their muskets.
Shells were at the same time careering in the air in our
direction, but from too great a distance to reach us. Messages
came in from time to time, and the general, taking me into a
little hut, allowed me to see them. I do not remember which
party got the better of the other. The engagement in fact
was of little consequence, except to those who were personally
concerned in it.

" On another occasion I rode out with Lord Raglan into
the valley, where the battle of Balaklava took place. It was
a striking scene, and the form of the ground made it easy
to understand with what disadvantages our cavalry had to
contend. Conceive a long shallow valley sloping gradually
to a gorge, with batteries on each side from one commanding
point to another and a crowning battery in front, that is, in
the gorge itself. It would seem probable that the charge of
our cavalry up this formidable pass—if pass be not too strong
a word—was a consequence of some misapprehension of the
orders, and it may be remembered that the officer, who
conveyed the order to Lord Lucan in a stimulating, if not

1855

ÆT. 68

insulting, manner, was killed by a shot from some battery just as the forward movement began. Lord Cardigan told me that he passed within the first battery while the nearest gun was going off, and I presume that the battery must have been taken, had it not been backed by a corps of Russian infantry. As it was, the enterprize had no result but that of displaying the gallantry of our troops and raising some question as to the conduct of their commander on the retreat.

"I had a fancy for going into the trenches under an impression, as in fairness I must add, that the chances were very much against my being personally the worse for a brief visit to their position. With this purpose in view I accompanied my host one afternoon, but, whether intentionally or not, he exhausted the time in making inquiries or giving directions, and we were finally obliged to gallop home for dinner without any adventurous experiment.

"All that I have related above took place in the months of April-May, 1855. I went at the beginning of May to Eupatoria with Sir Edmund Lyons, and on board the ship which carried his flag. Eupatoria was then in possession of a Turkish division commanded by Omar Pasha. I was received at the landing by the Pasha and his numerous party, dressed out in full uniform. Their finery made me feel ashamed of my plain clothes, which I had no means of changing, especially when I was called upon to mount a fidgetty charger accoutred in the Eastern fashion. Nor was the feeling of awkwardness diminished when I had to pass a saluting battery with my hat in hand, and an air of undisturbed serenity.

' The troops were drawn out in line along the ramparts of the town, and observing that their persons were considerably exposed to missiles in that position, I was told, in reply to my inquiry, that they were expected neither to duck nor to swerve however near the enemy's shot might come. This puts me in mind of what I had been told by a veteran admiral many years before. His story was that serving at a battery in Corsica, when the French were defending that island, he saw Lord Nelson come up and plant his telescope towards a redoubt from which the French were firing. His lordship, being asked what the enemy were about, replied, 'You will hardly believe it, but those fellows duck when the shot pass over their heads.' I knew, said my admiral, what he meant, for heads at our battery had gone down under fire just before. I kept silence, he added, till a fresh volley came, and Nelson had ducked in company with the rest of us. Then I thought my time had come, and I said, 'You see, my lord, the bravest are not exempt from the common instinct.' Whether the Turks, as fatalists, were or were not expected to be more than men, it is certain that they kept possession of Eupatoria to the end of the war.

"As for myself and party, we returned to Constantinople with the satisfaction of having witnessed a most interesting scene, and being entitled to entertain a reasonable hope of final success. There were other elements in this feeling of satisfaction. We left the army in health and relieved from all unusual privations, with an absence of any apparent differences between the respective commanders, and a most cordial understanding between the land and sea services in our own part of the expedition."

P. 92

Lord George Paget, in his interesting *Crimean Journal*, has recorded an amusing incident of the ambassador's visit. Lord Raglan, it appears, on riding down to welcome his Excellency, had ordered the Household troops to form a guard of honour. But here an unforeseen difficulty arose. By the "privileges of the Guards" those distinguished regiments could not present arms to anyone below the royal rank; and so Lord Stratford had to wait an hour or more on board ship till the Highlanders could be hurried up to do him honour! Lord George describes the sensation made by the ambassador and the party of ladies as they rode round the position at Balaklava up to the Crow's Nest; and again when the Elchi

3 May

and the Commander-in-Chief made a stately progress by water, followed by their staffs, round the vessels which were destined for the first expedition to Kerch. Lord George Paget had a special reason for remembering the occasion, for the visitors included his beautiful wife, who had been the guest of Lady Stratford ever since she had arrived in

Turkey. From a complete stranger Lady George soon became almost one of the family, and during those long months
of anxiety it was to her that the ambassador owed the chief
pleasure of his brief moments of relaxation. There was a
perpetual stream of people passing to and fro between Constantinople and the seat of war, and, whether they were
strangers or acquaintances, Lord and Lady Stratford considered them as their natural guests and shewed them every
possible kindness and boundless hospitality.

Extracts from two letters relating to this visit to the
Crimea may, at the risk of repetition, be introduced here :—

1855

—

ÆT. 68

Alas ! there is but one thing of which I can give you a positive
assurance—namely, that if Lord Raglan's opinion had prevailed, or
rather if his colleague had kept *to the agreement*, the assault would be
in progress at this very moment under my eyes. You will have from
better authority than mine an explanation of the circumstances to
which I allude. They present a melancholy picture of the difficulties
with which our noble army has to deal. It has the weakness of inadequate numbers, not always to be overcome even by heroic valour,
and it is condemned to witness a want of energy and steadiness of
purpose which might serve to paralyse the efficiency of any amount
of numbers. .

It is quite true that one ought to be on the spot in order to conceive the extent of the operations, and the difficulties of the ground.
Siege, there is none. Two parties are engaged in fighting with each
other by means of advanced trenches and earthwork batteries, one
of them having the advantage of a town and arsenal behind it with
stationary defences in aid of the advancing attack. I have read
enough in my small compass to know that an enemy under such circumstances must necessarily have the advantage. What I find most
general, as matter of opinion, is that the place might have been taken
at first, and would have been if common sense had not been overruled by the suggestions of science. All that I hear of Lord Raglan's
decision and firmness is greatly to his credit ; but with so many
delicate considerations, I will not say to warp his judgment, but to
arrest execution, the engineering on one side and French colleagues
on the other, there is little room for surprize that the " poor cat in the
adage " should come so often into play. Another general impression
is that the Russian outworks can be carried, though the success
would only, in the first instance, afford an opportunity, which, however, is indispensable, of knowing whether the possession of them
would enable the Allies to get into the fortress. . . .

To Lord
Clarendon,
British
Head-
quarters
before Se-
vastopol,
28 April

Canrobert, who has just been here to call on me, says that on the 10th of May the reinforcements will be here, amounting, as he declares, to 70,000 men, including the Sardinians, and that no time will then be lost in taking a decisive measure against the enemy's fortifications. He speaks in the highest terms of the English army. I told him in confidence, that almost all the officers I had seen were for an immediate attack. He said he was aware of it as to the inferior officers of both armies, but that fifteen out of twenty of the superior officers were for waiting for reinforcements.

· I observed that General Canrobert spoke in the course of conversation with great emphasis of Simpheropol as if he considered *that* the vital point of the Russians. It is possible that his thoughts were turned rather in that direction than to the attack of Sevastopol on the arrival of reinforcements.

I rejoice that you approved of my visit to the Crimea. To me it was a most interesting excursion ; and I agree with you in hoping that it may have been of some comfort, if not of any use, to Lord Raglan. In common with the generality of our officers he reckoned more upon Vienna than I have been accustomed to do. My language on that subject was not agreeable to him ; but he was glad to shew me over the ground, to perceive that I comprehended his difficulties, appreciated his improvements, and knew where the causes of inaction principally lay. His noble bearing, his cheerfulness, his courage and consideration for others, are the brilliant points of his character ; but time will tell upon the best, and his disposition does not inspire that energy which is so necessary to make all the departments draw well together. In Gordon Cumming's book of African field-sports there is a description of a Cape waggon with its span of twenty oxen stuck fast in the channel of a river, and extricated only when all the waggoners cracked their long whips at the same moment and kept them going. I thought of it when I was on the plateau, and wished that some one else had thought of it sooner. The effects of the first imbroglio have not entirely vanished; but the appearance of health and cheerfulness among the troops gratified me much, and all that related to their diet, clothing, and condition in the hospitals was either quite satisfactory or in a way to become so. Traces of pigheadedness and confusion still, I believe, linger about the Commissariat, and the fever, which has shaken sundry of its younger members, has spared with singular perverseness the grey veteran at its head. Old Boxer, who was out of his element here, has performed miracles at Balaklava, where, however, I understand that, since the arrival of the Sardinians, the shipping has become more crowded than ever. A fire or an attack there might be attended with awful consequences. Our three principal difficulties now may be referred to the over-caution of our mercurial colleagues, to the backwardness of our land-transport service, and the deficiencies of our steam conveyance. These drags upon our activity may occasion other difficulties by affording time for Russian reinforcements to arrive, by exposing our troops to the hot season, and by keeping such numbers together at a time and in a place where water may become scarce.

You are aware how much I have deplored from the beginning those hesitations and entanglements which have often damped the spirit and impeded the progress of our operations. They were difficult, perhaps even impossible, to avoid in the outset ; but I had hoped that, in proportion as the inconvenience was felt, and as the Western alliance gained confidence, they would be shaken off and that a more single-minded unfettered prosecution of the war would be obtained. Such, if I understand you right, was your own hope and view ; nor did you seem to be less disappointed than I was at the course of negotiation pursued under the shadow of Austria, and brought at length to a final stand, even in the estimation of Count Buol, at the thirteenth protocol, an ill-omened number, well suited to what may be fairly called a *Russian benefit*.

It is exactly because our difficulties are so great that we stand in need of a clear field and an unclogged use of our energies. We cannot afford to go on manœuvring for ever in a jungle. We ought by this time to know whether we can rely on France, whether Austria will go to war for us, whether our own people mean as much as they pretend. My creed as to these matters may be stated in few words : I believe in the spirit, resolution, and resources of the United Kingdom ; I believe that Austria is with us up to the verge of war and not beyond ; I believe that we may count upon the French Emperor ; I believe that, without the belligerent coöperation of Austria, the two great maritime Powers together may bring Russia to terms ; and I am furthermore persuaded that, if we do not accomplish that purpose, and put the seal on our success by obtaining material as well as diplomatic guarantees, we shall have to pass through years of bitter unavailing repentance.

No doubt we have hazards to incur as well as sacrifices to make. But would not a patched-up peace have also its hazards and its sacrifices ? Surely the answer is "yes,"—with this difference, that in one case even failure would leave us the resource of unstained, unquestioned honour, while in the other, success itself would consign us to the weakness of conscious shame.

Among the causes for dissatisfaction which weighed upon Lord Stratford's mind, none perhaps was more keenly felt than the excessive disparity between the two armies of the Allies. It galled his national pride to see the French out-numbering the British troops in the proportion of at least four to one. Not only was the disparity injurious to the success of the siege, inasmuch as our men were numerically incapable of working and holding the wide extent of front which was allotted to them, without undue and consequently injurious physical strain ; but the comparative insignificance of the British army brought the credit and prestige of England so low that her commanders found themselves compelled to give way to the superior influence of the French, even when there was no doubt that the latter were in the wrong. The effects of this disparity were felt as much in the Embassy as at headquarters. M. Benedetti, the French chargé d'affaires, who presided over the Legation pending the arrival of M. Baraguay d'Hilliers' successor, was unwearying in his efforts to counteract Lord Stratford's influence in every possible or impossible way. He intrigued with those of the Ottoman ministers who were known to be hostile to the Great Elchi in order to defeat every movement that was specially dear to England. He took advantage of Lord Stratford's absence for ten days in the Crimea to persuade the Sultan to recall his brother in law, Mohammed Ali, a notorious criminal, who had murdered one of his concubines, had been guilty of peculation and downright treason, and had at last been sent into exile. Freed from the control of Reshid, who immediately resigned on hearing of the recall of Mohammed Ali, and aided by this wretch and Riza the Seraskier, an old foe of the Elchi, M. Benedetti plotted to bring about the fall of Omar Pasha, the generalissimo of the Ottoman forces, partly because Riza personally disliked Omar, but more because the latter enjoyed to a certain extent the confidence of the British ambassador ; and it was largely owing to this sinister influence that Omar was not on his way to the relief of Kars long before he actually departed. Soon after Lord Stratford's return from the Crimea these plots bore fruit in the sudden resignation of the general-issimo. The ostensible ground was the decision of the Seraskier to withdraw five thousand men from the force under Omar's command, which was then usefully employed in holding the important position of Eupatoria. It was a very adroit move of the anti-English party, for it fell upon the Elchi as well as upon the general in whom he trusted. If Omar's resignation were accepted, his successor would of course be in the French interest, whereas if he were retained on condition of keeping his five thousand men, a favourite scheme of the ambassador would probably be wrecked.

This favourite scheme was the reinforcement of the small army of England in the Crimea by a Contingent of twenty thousand efficient Turkish troops, paid, clothed, and fed at the cost of England and officered by Englishmen. The plan, which went a good way towards reducing the disparity of the French and English armies, had taken firm root in Lord Stratford's mind as soon as the losses in the autumn battles and the subsequent sickness began to bring down the British force to so insignificant a figure as about ten thousand efficient troops. He took advantage of a private audience of the Sultan, at which his Majesty shewed an unusual amount of ill-humour, to counteract this display and turn Abdu-l-Mejid's thoughts on pleasanter subjects than the cause of irritation, by suggesting this plan of a Turkish Contingent, to be in the pay of England. The Sultan was evidently pleased, and Lord Stratford quickly wrote to sound Lord Clarendon privately on the subject. Instructions soon arrived authorizing an official proposal of the plan to the Porte; in December 1854 the Turkish ministers agreed to it without hesitation, and in February, 1855, a convention was duly signed. Steps were shortly taken to carry the scheme into effect. A somewhat similar plan had been already tried. An energetic, if somewhat hasty, officer had scoured both European and Asiatic Turkey in search of those irregulars (or Bashi-Bozuks—a term which means merely soldiers of no particular uniform, "rag-tag and bobtail "), who were known, from his name, as "Beatson's Horse :" he subsequently found a congenial chief of the staff, well acquainted with the habits of the Bashi-Bozuk, in Captain Richard Burton ; and Dr. Humphrey Sandwith, since famous also as a judge of atrocities, had shewn himself in 1854 active in recruiting the force of those irregulars whose proceedings in later days so justly roused his indignation.

"Beatson's Horse" however was not part of the Turkish Contingent ; it belonged to an earlier period, and was in the pay of the Turkish and not the English Government.　It was only in September 1855, after an unfortunate misunderstanding, which was followed by Beatson's retirement and a subsequent trial at law, that this body of cavalry was transferred to Shumla, where the Turkish Contingent, under the command of General Vivian, was stationed, under orders to proceed to Eupatoria.　The force had been raised without depriving Omar Pasha of the five thousand ; the Seraskier had been deposed ; the generalissimo had withdrawn his resignation ; and Lord Raglan had congratulated the ambassador on his success in appeasing the Pasha's wrath : " It is a wonderful achievement " he wrote, 5 June, only three weeks before his death, " and you certainly did not let the grass grow under your feet.

The Turkish Contingent, after being reviewed with no small feeling of pride and satisfaction by the ambassador who had prompted and carried out its formation, departed for the seat of war ; but its arrival, owing to the premature peace negotiations, was not destined to exercise any material effect upon the enemy.

" The war came to so early a close that the troops in our pay had no opportunity of shewing their prowess, but neither did they afford any grounds of complaint.　Even the irregulars submitted with good will to the command of Christian officers and to a degree of discipline which they had not previously undergone.　On returning to their respective provinces they expressed so much satisfaction with the good treatment they had experienced in our service that when the Indian Mutiny broke out it would have been easy to raise an auxiliary force from among the population of their creed.　I apprized the Sultan of the offers which had reached me to that effect, and probably with some expression of surprize, for he said in reply, ' You do not know my people ; they are naturally grateful for your assistance in the war, and the question in India is not one of religion.'　The Bashi-Bozuks were never wanting in military courage.　The crimes, by which they had earned a bad name, were the necessary consequences of ill-usage on

the part of their commanders, who cheated them of their pay
and let them loose for subsistence upon the countries which
they passed through or occupied. Habits of pillage led them
by easy transition to murder, rape, and other acts of violence
and cruelty. I have always thought that except in cases of
latent insanity, or inveterate depravity of nature, the human
heart is to be reached by good treatment under any kind of
clothes or adverse condition.'

In recording the progress of Lord Stratford's plan for
reinforcing the British army in the Crimea we have anticipated
the order of events. Several months before the Contingent
received its marching orders, a great assault upon Sevastopol
had been attempted, and had failed ; and this disaster had
been followed on 28 June by the death of Lord Raglan. Not
long after this the Elchi again visited the Crimea. It was
the month of August, and the visitor little suspected how near
was the final triumph for which all were so eagerly longing.
The account of this second excursion is given in the last frag-
ment of autobiography which will be quoted.

" The object of my second visit to the Crimea was to invest
several of our officers with the Order of the Bath. Little
more than three months had passed since the first. Lord
Raglan had died in the interval, and the chief command had
devolved upon General Simpson. No action of decided consequence had taken place in the field since the days of Balaklava and Inkerman. The siege operations were still going   .
on against the outward forts, but the town and arsenal of
Sevastopol were not yet bombarded, and the attack on the
defences of the harbour under the special command of Sir E.
Lyons had been more distinguished by the habitual bravery
of our seamen than by any decisive result. The *Caradoc* did
not return to its former anchorage at Balaklava, but took up
a position nearer to Sevastopol and the Allied squadrons.
There was some inconvenience in this, the distance from headquarters being considerable and to be traversed only on horseback. Consequently I saw more of our naval than of our
military commanders, particularly Sir Edmund Lyons and

Admiral Houston Stewart, the former a man of active mind eager for distinction, and striving incessantly by thought and deed to carry out the object of the day, the latter an officer of merit, never lagging in the performance of duty, and a most agreeable companion. The Sardinians with judicious foresight were now taking part in the war. They had thrown in their lot with the belligerent Allies, and their contingent, commanded by General La Marmora, was encamped eastward beyond Sir Colin Campbell's position at and near Balaklava. The

Russians not long before had made an advance on that side with a certain display of force, but being effectively opposed, their plan, whatever it was, had ended in their retreat. The attempt had been followed by a state of inaction on that side of the lines, which was put to trial one day in my presence. I accompanied the French commander on a visit to the Sardinian quarters, and on our ride thither we halted on open ground in front of a steep declivity garnished half way up with a strong Russian battery. Our party was numerous. The officers composing it were in uniform, and Pélissier himself wore a white African burnous, which fluttered with every motion of his horse, and offered a tempting mark for gunners in the opposite fort. Not a shot however was fired, and after stopping some little while without the slightest molestation we went on to the Sardinian encampment, where we found an abundance of good cheer and a most enjoyable repose.

" The ceremony, for which I was sent to the Crimea, took place under canvas at the British headquarters. Such arrangements as a camp could afford to express the dignity of the occasion were carefully prepared. It was my business to sit in a sort of extemporized state-chair, to make three or four little speeches suggested severally by the merits of the intended knights, and finally to lay my sword upon the shoulders of each when invested with the star and ribband of the Order. The commanders-in-chief of both armies and their respective staffs assisted. We were all within hearing of the guns which almost continually announced the progress of the siege and suggested solemn thoughts. Sir Edmund Lyons was singular in receiving a second Grand Cross, the civil deco-ration having been already conferred upon him. Among his colleagues in honour was General Sir Harry Jones, an engineer officer of distinguished reputation. He was confined to his tent by illness, and I thought it my duty to convey the insignia to his bedside, a trial of patience for those who had to wait my return, which they all bore—Marshal Pélissier the foremost—with remarkable courtesy. To my great regret, and without my knowledge, the reporters of the press were refused admittance. Something on their side had occurred to irritate the officers ; but their exclusion was not the less resented by those to whom it was an occasion of disappointment and vexation."

Hardly had Lord Stratford left the Crimea when the south side of Sevastopol fell into the besiegers' hands (8 September). The ambassador's joy at the great news, however, was clouded by the fear that the Allies would be satisfied with this success, instead of following it up, and bringing Russia to her knees. He foresaw a temporary " shortcoming " peace, which would only leave the struggle to be fought over again. In this dread he wrote to Lord Clarendon :—

To judge from the first remarks or questions of my German colleagues, you will be earnestly solicited to make peace now that the great arsenal of the Black Sea has fallen. It may sound hard-hearted, and it is certainly against my private feelings and wishes, to express the thought, but nevertheless I do think that for our own national honour and European interest we have still more exertions to make before we can satisfactorily return the sword to its scabbard.

To Lord
Clarendon,
Therapia,
13 Sept.

In *justice* the Russians have no indulgence to expect from us. Having reduced the Russia of *accumulated power*, we have to guard against the Russia of *prospective growth*. This, I imagine, might be effected by interposing a barrier of independent neutrals along the whole frontier. The Principalities are already better than independent. The remaining part of the line seems to offer more difficulty as to the arrangement in peace than to acquisition in war.

This, on the side of Georgia, would open a noble field for British valour and energy *next year*, after the ground shall have been tried by Omar Pasha *this autumn*, and the results, if successful, would be in their character *compensatory* as to our military credit in Europe, and highly influential as to our political power in Asia.

It may be presumed that Russia is not yet quite prepared to

accept such terms of peace. But Russia must be losing her self-confidence from day to day, and in a nation of superstitious slaves, when devotion is puzzled, and fear of authority relaxed, to say nothing of pressure on trade and property, the spirit of resistance declines rapidly, and the moral preparation for peace on any terms makes progress in proportion. A bold advance from Eupatoria, or some other well-selected point, would probably be attended with success beyond our expectation ; but to produce its full effect the Russians ought not to be allowed time for looking about them and recovering their breath.

I abstain from pushing the speculation further, and I have already betrayed my conviction that enough is done or in progress even now to secure a *complete* satisfaction on the *Four Points* ; but surely our title to more solid guarantees and a more perfect settlement grows naturally out of a larger amount of hazard, sacrifice and success on our side. It can hardly be denied that in such matters a heavy responsibility attaches to unseasonable moderation. It may justly be said that the duty of Governments, who have required so much of their subjects, is to take care that the profits of the sickle shall be equal to the labours of the plough.

Sir Edmund Lyons was as impatient as the Elchi for some forward movement which should prove that we were not content with the successes we had gained, but were resolved to beat Russia back to a safe frontier both in Europe and Asia. Something of this appears in a letter written a week after the entry of the Allies :—

From Sir E. Lyons, Royal Albert, off Sevastopol, 15 Sept.

I thank you for your hearty congratulations on the fall of Sevastopol. I wish that we were doing something to follow up the blow which, physically as well as morally, has been tremendous for the Russians ; but, alas ! *Marshal* Pélissier is reposing upon his laurels and receiving compliments, and less likely to do anything than he was when the tempting bâton was glittering before his eyes.

The question of moving Omar's troops from the Crimea [to relieve Kars] was summarily settled by Pélissier producing an order from the Emperor not to sanction any reduction of the forces, or the departure of any of Omar Pasha's army unless replaced by equal numbers of equal value. Since that, General Simpson has been directed to place the Contingent at Eupatoria instead of Balaklava.

We believe that the Russians lost 15,000 men, killed and wounded, on the 8th, but we have no idea where the remainder now are, and it is melancholy to think that on this, the eighth day since the capture of the place, we are doing nothing, absolutely nothing, to follow up the blow. Seldom have I been more astonished than in seeing the devastation produced by the fire of the Boxer guns. It confirms the opinion I have always expressed that we ought not to have opened our fire in the spring until we were prepared to keep it up until the place surrendered ; for it would have been impossible for the enemy to have strengthened their weaker points or to have repaired damages if we had maintained a continuous fire.

Oh, what a place is this Sebastopol ! such a harbour, such docks, such resources even now after the protracted siege, all shewing what a depôt it was at the threshold of the Bosphorus.

The opinions of those on the spot, however, went for little in the Peace negotiations. Just when our army was in splendid health and spirits, when the defects of transport and commissariat had been overcome, when 20,000 sturdy Turks had been enrolled and disciplined by Englishmen to swell the muster roll of our forces, when Russia was all but on her knees ; just then the golden opportunity was let slip, the armies were suffered to lie inactive, while diplomatists were gulled into negotiations for a false peace, which left Russia almost untouched, instead of making any further encroachments, not only in Europe, but above all in Asia, impossible so long as treaties have force. But the peace had not yet been signed, and in the autumn of 1855 there was still hope that England might prevent such a disaster as a surrender of all that she had striven for.

CHAPTER XXXI.

THE SURRENDER OF KARS.

1855.

1855
——
ÆT. 68

From D.
B. Morier,
22 Oct.

As Lord Stratford de Redcliffe, one day towards the close of the eventful year 1855, sat before his desk, strewn with despatches, reports, orders, requisitions, and all the other material of an immense official correspondence during a great war, a letter was brought to him which carried back his thoughts to the very beginning of his career at Constantinople. It was signed "Your ancien sécrétaire perpétuel, D. B. Morier," and it announced the death of the old ambassador, Sir Robert Adair, under whose benevolent sway they had both won their first experiences of diplomatic work in Turkey nearly half a century before. "My dear Canning," wrote Morier, "you must let me still address you by that old familiar name, while, like Pharaoh's chief butler, 'I do remember my faults this day,' and no longer delay to fulfil the promise I made some months ago to our dear old Chief of times past, now in his grave. He was very very aged, and well he might be at ninety-two,—but although failing both in sight and hearing, and in the memory of recent trifles, his *heart's memory* was as retentive as ever, and of you he never spoke without the most warm expressions of affection and sincerest regard, making me promise that whenever I wrote to you I would not fail to convey them to you with the special assurance of these his unaltered sentiments." The younger man,—and he was but one year short of seventy,—was deeply moved by this message from the old master who had taught him diplomacy in 1809. "It has touched my heart," he said "and brought tears into my eyes."

As he read the words, his mind wandered back to those 1855
early days at Stambol, when life was in its morning glow,
and the world lay before him like a country to be explored. ÆT. 68
He had seen much of that world in the forty-seven years
which had passed since then.　To use, as he would have
done, the words of his favourite author, *multum ille et terris
jactatus et alto.*　On the very spot where he and Adair had
held converse together he could now stand and contemplate
the work of a life already long.　He remembered the Treaty of
Bucharest, his first, and in his own eyes always his greatest,
triumph.　He thought of the brilliant throng at Vienna, and
the sudden shock, like the boom of a distant gun, when the
news came that the " Enemy of Europe " was again at large.
His thoughts quickly sped from the tidings of Waterloo,
which blazed forth like a beacon fire in the midst of " rustic
diplomacy " in Switzerland, to that lonely island in the
Atlantic where the mighty Enemy had breathed his last,
while the man who had successfully opposed him in the East
was enduring the rude experiences of a mission in the Western
world.　Then memories of the Greek struggle for liberty
crowded upon his mind ; he fought his battles o'er again with
the Porte, recalled the tragedy of Navarino, and the final
founding of the State of Greece ; and there was sadness in
the thought, for the kingdom had not realized his hopes.　He
had laboured to create a nation, but so far neither he nor any
one else had been able to teach it how to live.

With the recollection of the War of Independence came
memories of the first step in its aid,—his mission to Petersburg ;—and then his rejection by that second " Enemy of
Europe " whose armies had but lately been worsted in open
field and stubborn forts by the men of the West.　Nicholas
Paulovich, Emperor of All the Russias, had fought his long
duel with the Elchi, and was dead ; and there on the littered Feb. 1855
table lay one of his last letters—a despatch to Lord Stratford
himself, thanking him for his kindness to the Russian
prisoners.　So the old rivalry ended in a gracious act.　There
was no hardness in his mind as the memory of Nicholas
arose.　The Czar he had detested ; for the man he had no
feeling but pity.　Besides, the Czar had lived to see his armies

1855
—
ÆT. 68
thrice hurled back by the very English who had so long
excited his jealousy and hatred ; and it was no part of the
Elchi's nature to triumph over the fallen. In his hour of
crowning glory, moreover, there was much to make him grave.
It was true that he had met and faced the great Eastern Question, that he had upheld the right when all others flinched,
and with a clear conscience had seen our soldiers go forth to
maintain the cause of justice. But much remained. Turkey
had been sustained for awhile in her corner of Europe, but if
she was to keep her place as Warden of the Marches over
against Russia, she must look to herself. It was of no
avail to pour forth English blood and treasure for people who
would not help themselves, but who, by oppression and bad
government, almost made their protectors ashamed to shield
them. The one great aim of his later years in the East had
been to raise up a new Turkey, a State worthy to be defended,
a moral as well as a material barrier to the encroachments of
Russia. His consistent plan had been to remove all disabilities of race and creed, to make the Christian subjects of the
Sultan in every way the equals of their Mohammedan neighbours, and to infuse into every department of the administration such a proportion of Christian and educated influence
that the old corrupt system of government should become
impossible. The task was Herculean, well-nigh hopeless ;
yet more had been accomplished than those acquainted with
the East could have expected. Reform after reform had been

See pp.
100 ff.,
144 ff.,
206 ff.
enacted, and the main difficulty that remained was to insist
that they should be rigidly enforced. The Turks as a body
were not to be trusted to do this : there was always a party
of reaction and bigotry which was sure to check the moderate
efforts of the reformers. Effective supervision could only be
exerted by the personal influence of a European ; and as
the Great Elchi meditated on the long years of his work in
Turkey he could not but see reason to distrust the future.

There were grounds for these misgivings. Several circumstances had combined to diminish the prestige of England
and the popularity of her representative. The first and most
important of these was the position which France had attained
in Turkey and at Downing Street. Ever since 1840, when

England rescued the Ottoman Empire from the hands of
Mohammed Ali, in direct opposition to the policy of France,
British counsels had been almost supreme at the Porte.
Turkey was convinced that England was her truest friend,
and with this conviction, and such a man as the Elchi to enforce it, the task of asserting English influence at Constantinople had been comparatively easy.   Lord Stratford had
enjoyed a scarcely interrupted reign for many years, not
indeed unopposed by the Turks and uncontested by the other
embassies, but on the whole the opposition had been unavailing and the contest had left him unshaken in his power.

The Crimean War brought about a change in this position.
The immense numerical preponderance of the French army,
their taking of the Malakov and the consequent withdrawal
of the Russians from the south side of Sevastopol, and the insidious skill of their latest representative at the Porte, had
materially strengthened the ascendancy of France in Turkey.
The Ottoman ministers were now almost disposed to think
that, after all, France might be their best ally ; or if they
did not go so far as this, they were at least fully alive to
the advantages which must accrue to Turkey by playing
upon the jealousies of the rival allies.   Lord Stratford could
easily have held his own, had he been adequately supported by the Government at home ; but unfortunately
Ministers had not yet sounded the depths of Louis Napoléon,
and were just then more disposed to take the part of the
French than of the Elchi.   Deserted by the Foreign Secretary, Lord Stratford found himself contending at the odds
of one against three instead of even numbers.   From the
beginning of the war the unequal duel never ceased.
Publicly indeed, the forms of courtesy were observed, and
in private there was even a good-humoured cordiality
between the two embassies ; but officially there was undying
suspicion beneath the polished surface.   As an instance
of the intrigues which were carried on in 1855 we may
revert to Lord Stratford's first visit to the Crimea.   Hardly
had his back been turned, when the French representative
succeeded in inducing the ever-complaisant Sultan to recall
from exile his brother-in-law Mohammed Ali.   This man, as

we have related, had murdered one of his Christian concubines, and had consequently been denied admission to the
British embassy on the ground, as the Elchi expressed it,
that "the Queen's ambassador cannot receive a cowardly
assassin." Mohammed Ali had further embellished his
career by other crimes. He had engaged "in dangerous, not
to say treasonable practices," he had been "publicly convicted
of frauds on the Imperial revenue," and the Sultan had himself admitted the truth of these accusations and had banished
the culprit. This was the man whom the French smuggled
back to Constantinople during Lord Stratford's brief absence
in the Crimea. On his return the news was immediately
brought to him on board the *Caradoc* by Mr. Odo Russell,
and before Lord Stratford landed he was aware of the success
of the intrigue and the consequent resignation of Reshid.
In reply to his indignant remonstrance, the frightened Sultan
gave his word that Mohammed Ali should not be reinstated
in office. Nevertheless, on the ambassador's return from
his second visit to the Crimea in August he found the
delinquent, at the instigation of the French, comfortably installed in the office of Kapudan Pasha, or High Admiral.
This was too much; and Lord Stratford forthwith approached the Sultan with a memorandum couched in words
such as no sovereign, one would think, had ever before been
forced to hear. Indeed Abdu-l-Mejid would not listen to it,
and something of the nature of a "scene" ensued,—the angry
Sultan calling for his secretary, and the Elchi pausing in the
recital of the terrible indictment in his hand. It was clear
that matters could not be pressed to extremes without the risk
of throwing the Sultan completely into the arms of France,
and the ambassador succeeded in pacifying him at the cost of
sacrificing the rest of the memorandum. How much of it was
read we do not know, but the concluding paragraph will give
the tone and tenor of the rest :—

Your Majesty is master of your own decisions. Your will is the
law of this Empire. Setting aside treaties and international rights, I
have nothing to offer but counsel, nothing to appeal to but truth, and
that which is its seat, your Majesty's conscience. At the same time I

can neither surrender my opinions nor change the nature of facts. For your Majesty's own service I have principles to uphold, a character to maintain, and duties to perform. Even if I were to witness in silence the progress of evil counsels, neither my Government nor the world at large could be kept in ignorance. The facts would speak for themselves and their effects would follow in confirmation. Divested of all colouring the case stands thus. The presence of Mohammed Ali in the Council and ministry is an open contradiction to your Majesty's laws against venality, to your Majesty's previous commands and course of government, to the declarations which accompanied them, to the efficiency of your Majesty's administration, to the hopes of your Majesty's subjects, and to the just expectations of your Majesty's allies. The result of such contradiction between an act of favour and so many stringent public considerations, must necessarily be a false position pregnant with evil to the State and with trouble to your Majesty.

It is instructive to observe that both these intrigues took place at a time when Lord Stratford's absence freed the Turkish ministers for the moment from the dominating influence of his will. As we have seen, while recognizing the truth and loyalty of their British adviser, the Ottoman statesmen could never bring themselves to relish the high hand with which he compelled their adhesion to his views. Even Reshid had been known to entreat him not to assume so ostensible an air of authority, but to give the ministry a freer hand, while when Fuad and A'li, both French partisans, came into power, they desired to reform their country in their own way, and they resented the autocracy of a man who would not submit, they pretended, even to "*corregner*" with the Sultan. The truth was that, as true Turks, they disliked being worried about such trifles as wrongs and abuses, and, as half-bred Parisians, they were pledged to the Emperor of the French.

The jealousy of the French and the disaffection of some of the Turkish ministers were not the only blows aimed at the Elchi's sway. The people of England themselves were now turning against one who had not long before been their idol. There was no more popular man in Europe than Sir Stratford Canning in 1849, when he made the Sultan protect the Hungarian refugees ; and his triumph over Menshikov had sustained and renewed his reputation. But a change had now come over the popular sentiment. There was a considerable section of the Radicals who disapproved of the war, and could not rid themselves of the false impression that the ambassador was its cause. During the troubles of the winter of 1854–5 England had become frantic against everyone in authority, and the Elchi, as we have seen, was not spared. The attack soon collapsed, but there is an old saying about the adhesive property of mud, and the imperfect recollection of even false charges is apt to tinge so unstable an element as public opinion. Towards the close of 1855, a fresh charge was preferred, which gathered to itself all the rancour that had remained over from previous assaults, and swelled to such monstrous proportions that one wonders it did not instantly burst like an overblown bladder. In November the fortress of Kars in Armenia, which had been gallantly defended by the Turks for about four months, under the direction of European officers, among whom General Kmety, General Williams, Baron Schwarzenberg, Major Lake, and Lieutenant (now Sir Christopher) Teesdale were the most active, was starved into surrender : and the good people at home, prompted by malicious journalists, jumped to the conclusion that Kars fell because Lord Stratford would not try to relieve it.

The story of Kars is soon told. On 15 August, 1854, Colonel Williams arrived at Constantinople on his way to his post as Commissioner to the Turkish Army of Asia. The office was analogous to that of Colonel Simmons in the Turkish Army of Europe : he was to advise and report, but he held no command. There had been nothing but pleasant relations between him and the ambassador during the dozen years of their official connexion. Lord Stratford had himself selected Williams for the Persian Boundary Commission in 1842, and had employed him in that work ever since. Writing from Constantinople, 25 January, 1853, Williams said " I have the gratification to receive your lordship's kind private letter of 28 December ; the Gazette had preceded it, and revealed to me the honour [the C. B.] which your lordship had procured for me ; . . . I beg your lordship to believe that I shall ever grate-

fully remember this act of more than kindness, and when a
trip to England shall have quite re-established my strength,
there is no country I would hesitate to go to, nor no danger
which I would not cheerfully confront, to fulfil instructions
emanating from your lordship's hand. . . . After all your
lordship's toils for them [the Turks] if I *dared* express a wish
for a further sacrifice of your life, I would say ' God send
your excellency speedily here.' "   On the Colonel's return
to Constantinople on his way to Erzerum, nothing occurred
to alter these grateful sentiments.   The ambassador wrote
to him, 15 August, that he was happy to hear of his arrival
and would be glad to see him at Therapia.   On the 23rd
he wrote to Lord Raglan in friendly terms about Williams,
and urged both the British Commander-in-Chief and the
Turkish ministers to take vigorous measures for the
strengthening and reorganizing of the Army of Asia.   On 23
September he wrote to Williams, who was then on his way
to Erzerum, " It gave me much pleasure to find that you had
got so far on your journey with so much success. . . . I
am anxious to receive your first reports from the army."   On
26 September he wrote again, informing him of the detention
of a Pasha who had been appointed to take command at
Kars.   On 1 October Williams's reports came in, and Lord
Stratford immediately urged his various requisitions upon
the Grand Vezir, upon Reshid, and upon the Seraskier or
War Minister.   In reply, these officials enumerated a large
quantity of supplies which had, they said, been ordered and
partly sent to Erzerum.   More reports arrived from Williams
on 14 October, and concerning these the Elchi wrote to
Lord Raglan on the same day, " I rejoice that a sensible
and dispassionate professional man should be on the spot
to report the exact state of things.   I propose to act vigorously on all his recommendations."   Williams was so volu-
minous a correspondent that it was not always easy to get
at the gist of his requirements without prolonged study.
Sometimes his despatches came in batches of seventeen or
more at a time.   Lord Raglan, with all his patience, found
it no trifle to wade through the Commissioner's papers, and
feelingly wrote to Lord Stratford (30 October) " Williams

is a good man, but he is prolixity itself." In the overwhelming pressure of business at the Embassy it might have been excusable if the Elchi had overlooked some of the requirements buried in reams of despatches, but this was not the case On 14 October he again strongly addressed the Turkish Government on the subject of supplies for Asia, and he told Lord Raglan later that he had made a comprehensive *précis* (as the Commander-in-Chief had advised) of all Williams's requests :—

To Lord
Raglan,
15 Nov.

I have done what you wished for Williams. The Turkish ministers are in possession of all his wants, enumerated distinctly and amply explained. It cost me five or six hours to put the despatches into a comprehensive shape. I hope the supplies will be sent without much delay. Meanwhile the Colonel is to be raised to the dignity of a Turkish *Ferik*, or a General of Division, and the new Commander-in-Chief of Kars is to be instructed to follow his advice. I have demanded the recall of two Polish officers, who, under Turkish names, are doing their best, if they be not grossly calumniated, to counteract our influence and views of amendment.

There are official records of other earnest remonstrances addressed to the Porte, and correspondence relating to the Asiatic army and its wants, on 2, 16, and 29 November ; 1, 6, 9, 13, and 16 December. The newly-appointed Commander-in-Chief in Asia, Vasif Pasha, was made to understand that an essential condition of his appointment was that he shall pay attention to Colonel Williams's advice, reform the army, and punish the officers who had been guilty of corruption, drunkenness, and peculation.

So far two things are clear. There was nothing but friendly feeling towards Williams on the part of Lord Stratford ; and every effort had been made to compel the Turks to send the supplies recommended in that officer's despatches. The Porte manifested no opposition to these recommendations ; everything was promised ; supplies were ordered ; corrupt officers were recalled and put under arrest. How far these promises and orders were genuine is another matter ; but it was not easy to pursue a consignment of goods through Asia Minor, and the ambassador naturally could not be expected to trace the course and fate of every load or case that was supposed to have arrived at Kars or Erzerum. So far as he knew, everything was in course of preparation ; the progress was slow, as progress is wont to be in Turkey, and the Turks were really at their wits' end to provide the necessary supplies and transport ; but there was nothing to cause suspicion of foul play, and as the winter was setting in, when the Russians would be compelled to postpone all military operations, there was every hope that the provisions and stores would arrive at their destination in ample time for the necessities of the army.

We have brought affairs at Constantinople up to 16 December. We must now turn to Erzerum and Kars. Williams was apparently as well pleased with the ambassador as the latter was with him. Writing on 7 October, the Commissioner referred to his lordship's " most welcome letter " and agreed with the opinions therein expressed. In this strain he continued to correspond throughout October and November. He made no complaints about the manner in which he was treated by the Embassy. His letters are full of reports of the bad state of the army, and he apparently entertained, and certainly expressed, no doubt that Lord Stratford was taking all possible steps to have the evils remedied. The aspect of these letters, scored along the margins with the ambassador's pencil, shews that each separate suggestion or complaint was carefully noted for immediate reference to the Porte.

On 27 November,—the date is important,—Williams wrote as follows to Lord Stratford :—

Private letters have just reached me from Kars, giving me the welcome news of the arrival of considerable supplies of provision at that city and intrenched garrison. The weather here is *too* fine, for it allows the Russians to operate in the direction of Toprakalé and to consume the harvest of that line of country as far as Bayezid. I am extremely anxious for the forthcoming of Ismail Pasha : but as soon as this post is despatched I will work on the fears of Old Ismail (the Wali) and try to get a few redoubts built here ; the very fact of their being constructed will turn the attention of the Russian generals from any plans they may have formed for possessing themselves of as great a prize as Erzerum. I see with hope and pleasure that the more recent military crimes of Pashas have been met by dismissal and exile, and I am therefore led to hope that to those just punishments may be added *confiscation* as regards the greatest of culprits, Zarif Mustafa Pasha.

It will be noted that in this letter he records with satisfaction the arrival of provisions at Kars and the punishment of military Pashas, both of which must, as he knew, be the consequences of the steps taken by Lord Stratford, acting on his own reports.

On 28 November, one day after this amicable communication, Williams wrote to Lord Clarendon to complain of the total neglect with which he had been treated by her Majesty's ambassador at the Porte. So sudden a *volte-face* requires explanation. It is also strange that having informed Lord Clarendon at that date of his charge against the ambassador, he did not see fit to address his complaint to Lord Stratford himself till 8 December, ten days later. To one who possessed so fluent a pen the fatigue of composing a despatch could not have been great, yet it was not till 17 December that Lord Stratford was put in possession of the accusations which had apparently been growing in the Commissioner's mind ever since the beginning of October.

Lord Stratford received the communication with amazement. He was conscious of having spared no pains, of having neglected no method, opportunity, or argument, to goad the Turkish Government into action in the sense of Colonel Williams's recommendations, and this sudden assault from one for whom he entertained nothing but friendly feelings, and for whom he had been working hard, was to him simply incomprehensible. The gravamen of the charge was that he had not written often enough to the Commissioner. He had in fact only written twice since the latter's departure from Constantinople. Lord Stratford had no leisure for writing about nothing, and up to December there was little that he could communicate bearing upon Williams's recommendations. The Porte was considering them; the Porte was gradually pushing forward preparations for sending

supplies; the Porte was thinking about making Williams a 1854
Ferik, &c.: such would have been the sum of his despatches, Æт. 68
had he written them. There was so much other work to be
done for the army in the Crimea, for the hospitals, and other
pressing affairs, in the winter of 1854, that the ambassador
necessarily found himself unable to spare time for merely
formal communications. Had there been anything worth
telling he would have told it. So he wrote to Lord Raglan,
on the day on which he received Williams's denunciatory
despatch. "He has misunderstood my silence," he said, To Lord
Raglan,
17 Dec.
"which was simply this: I was unwilling to write long histories
until I could state distinctly that all my recommendations
were either executed or in course of being so. You know
what people I have to deal with, and will understand the
rest."

This was the true explanation, and Lord Stratford's
silence had nothing to do with personal feeling of any kind.
In view of the storm that was afterwards raised about this
really insignificant incident, it is to be regretted that the
ambassador did not commission one of his attachés to write
formal acknowledgments of Williams's despatches and assure
him that their contents had been emphatically pressed upon
the Turkish authorities. But he was one of those men who
prefer to do everything themselves; he seldom entrusted the
drafting of a political despatch to an attaché, and the consequence was that merely formal business sometimes, as in
this case, got into arrears. He admitted as much in his *Affairs in
Asiatic
Turkey,*
No. 83
explanatory despatch to Lord Clarendon; but that he should
have been seriously censured for so trifling an omission never
entered his mind. Nevertheless, Lord Clarendon's despatch
of 11 January amounted to a severe condemnation of the *Ibid.* 86
ambassador's silence, and elevated Colonel (or as he then
became Brigadier-General) Williams into the position of a
forlorn martyr deprived of the support of his "natural protector" the ambassador at the Porte.

Here the incident appeared to have terminated. There
has never, I believe, been any pretence that, after the correspondence which took place in November and December 1854,
Lord Stratford neglected in any way the interests of General

Williams and the armies at Erzerum and Kars. The Blue-Book on *Military Affairs in Asiatic Turkey*, with its 400 des-patches and numerous enclosures, contains abundant evidence of the zeal and perseverance with which the Elchi pressed the Turkish Government to reinforce and provision its army in Asia, and, from the papers of the Embassy now before me, I could add a mass of supplementary evidence of his untiring activity in its cause. He wrote thirty-two official despatches to Williams between January and November 1855. He communicated weekly, sometimes daily, with the Ottoman ministers in support of the Commissioner's requisitions. He never ceased to impress upon them, and upon the authorities appointed to command in Asia, the necessity of complete reliance upon Williams's advice. If little was accomplished, it was partly due to the exhausted resources of the Porte, and partly the result of the evil influence of the Seraskier, who was the same Riza Pasha who had made a point of opposing Lord Stratford throughout his career. Fortunately in June Riza was dismissed, and his successor, Mohammed Rushdi, was a decided improvement. The Elchi's first communica-tion with the new Seraskier related to the urgent necessity of succouring Kars, whither General Williams had at length repaired from Erzerum. One of his instructions to the inter-preter at this time is here quoted :—

I learn from Brigadier-General Williams that the Russians ap-peared when he wrote to be meditating an attack on the army at Kars, and I fear we shall have to deplore the little or tardy attention paid to my earnest and repeated requisitions for supplies and rein-forcements. Even now at the eleventh hour it is most desirable that all which it is in the power of the Government to do in these respects should be done without a moment's delay. According to my last advices from General Williams money was greatly wanted, and he presses the demand most earnestly upon me. See Fuad Pasha and the Seraskier without delay, and urge them to send off as large a sum as they can possibly spare while they are preparing whatever may yet be forwarded in point of men and supplies. The case does really seem to be very urgent. . . .

Now that Circassia is cleared of the Russians, why should not the old idea of uniting the army of Batum with that of Kars be acted upon in the presen emergency? Suggest this impressively. I am assured that Batum may be held with a very small force, supposing it to have works sufficient to be relied on ; but of this I am no judge.

As the reports of the advance of the Russians upon Kars gained strength, the Turks began at last to take serious measures. On 27 June they proposed that the Turkish Contingent, then mustering under General Vivian, and part of Beatson's Horse, should be ordered to relieve Kars by making a diversion from Redoutkalé and Kutais, so as to take the Russians in the rear. In a few days the details of this scheme were fully arranged. General Mansfield, who had lately been attached to the embassy as Lord Stratford's military adviser, spent many hours in consultation with the Turkish ministers on every branch of the subject, and sanguine hopes of success were entertained by all who were professionally able to estimate the chances of the proposed expedition. The British Government, however, interposed, and positively prohibited the transfer of the Turkish Contingent to Asia. It was fully determined in Downing Street and Pall Mall that Kars should be relieved by way of Trebizond, and that the relief should be executed by Turkish troops alone. The grounds alleged for this decision by the War Office were such as, in Lord Stratford's words, to " shock the British military people " at Constantinople. Lord Panmure seemed to be afraid lest a possible failure should be detrimental to British prestige, and to Vivian's reputation : he forgot that forlorn hopes are seldom attempted in a spirit of caution. The preference for the Trebizond route, which was known to be extremely difficult in autumn, was not shared by anyone out of London. Williams himself proposed a diversion by way of Redoutkalé. Colonel Olpherts at Erzerum said that at that season this would be the best route. Nevertheless the home authorities were unconvinced, and their decision lost a month of precious time.

What was to be done next ? There was a talk of detaching some of the English from before Sevastopol, but their numbers hardly admitted of diminution, and it was thought that if they were further reduced they would be really little better than a brigade of the French army. The French, who did not care about Kars, would not dream of leaving the scene of their coming glory. The only alternative was to send Omar Pasha with Turkish troops from the Crimea. Omar himself, as soon as he learnt the critical condition of Kars, strongly urged this measure, but he was met with decided opposition from the English and French Commanders-in-Chief, and the latter especially would not hear of any reduction of the forces in the Crimea. Louis Napoleon still shewed himself " insensible to the consequences of any serious disaster in Asia," and his opinion had more than its due weight in the camps before Sevastopol. The difficulty was at last met by proposing to supply the place of the troops under Omar Pasha by the now completed Turkish Contingent. Then came a further obstacle. Were Omar's men to be taken from the Turks before Sevastopol or from those at Eupatoria? And so the negotiation wore on, to the disgust both of the Elchi and the Turks themselves, who were at last thoroughly in earnest. Finally Omar managed to satisfy the Home governments and the Commanders-in Chief, and set off for the Circassian coast with the object of operating upon the rear of the Russians. This was not arranged till September, and the time was then running very short if anything was to be done for Kars. There were delays in land transport, and other obstacles, and Omar had not advanced far on his road through Mingrelia when General Williams suddenly surrendered on 23 November, 1855, and, with most of the other officers, became a prisoner of war.

This is not the place to discuss the various causes which contributed to the fall of Kars, the apathy and cowardice of Selim Pasha, the commander at Erzerum, and the possibility of provisioning the town from the stores which were known to exist, not only at Erzerum, but at a day's march from the beleaguered fortress itself.[1] What concerns us is merely how

---

[1] A few lines may be quoted from a letter addressed 17 March, 1856, by Lord Stratford to a very staunch supporter—the Duke of Newcastle:—" Kars did not fall from want of men, of artillery, of clothing, medicine, or ammunition; but simply, as the proximate cause, from want of provisions ; and it is well known that a large depôt of provisions, at a day's march from the town, was left to the mercy of the Russians. When I asked Dr. Sandwith how it had so happened, he said that General Williams had urged the Turks to convey it into Kars, and that they had promised to do so from day to day without redeeming their pledge.

far the relief of Kars was hindered or promoted at Constantinople ; and enough has been said to shew, and a perusal of the Blue Book will confirm the statement, that not only was Lord Stratford perseveringly zealous in his endeavours to get provisions and reinforcements sent out, but even the Turkish Government itself, as soon as Riza had been replaced by a new Seraskier, was honestly active in the same direction, and was foiled to a large extent by the objections of the British Government to the first plan of relief, and by the obstacles thrown in the way of the second plan by the commanders in the Crimea and by the French Government. So far as Lord Stratford was concerned, there never had been a time, from the day Williams set out to that on which Kars fell, when he had not done his utmost for the Commissioner and the Army of Asia.

The news of the surrender of Kars caused immense excitement in England. The people, naturally moved by a story of brave resistance to privations and more than one stirring feat of arms, could not shew enough sympathy for the defenders of Kars. Sympathy for the distressed is seldom complete without indignation against the cause of distress, and popular indignation is not choice in the selection of a victim. So, after a year had elapsed, the old tale of the unanswered despatches was dragged to light ; dates were forgotten ; 1854 was confounded with 1855, and Kars with Erzerum ; and in the excitement of the moment the remarkable theory was advanced, in effect, that because Lord Stratford neglected to reply to certain letters of Colonel Williams at Erzerum in October and November 1854, he was responsible for the fall of Kars in November 1855.[1] What happened between those two dates did not interest them.

Stated thus plainly the charge appears in its naked

If such neglect could take place under the Commissioner's own eyes, why should he marvel that I could not always succeed in flogging the Turkish ministers up to his mark ? "

[1] It must be repeated that no one ever attempted to argue that Lord Stratford neglected Kars in 1855 ; indeed one of the defenders of Kars, and certainly no admirer of the Elchi, when I asked him to enlighten me on the story of Lord Stratford's neglect of that fortress, interrupted me by saying, " It had nothing to do with Kars : that happened at Erzerum. "

absurdity : but it was far from seeming absurd to the excited populace in the early months of 1856. As soon as he heard the first rumour of the attack, Lord Stratford telegraphed to Lord Clarendon to beg that every word he had written on the subject might be laid before Parliament : " I have no fear of my countrymen," he wrote, " when they have the means of judging fairly before them," and the Blue Book on the *Military Affairs in Asiatic Turkey* was the result. As soon as the documents had been published, sane men regretted the temporary infatuation which had possessed them. But meanwhile the hero and the victim had received their respective meed. Williams returned triumphant and a pensioned baronet ; while Whiteside gave notice of a motion in the House of Commons. The Blue Book was out before the motion came on for debate (1 May), and the result was a triumph for the Government. Whiteside's vituperation of Lord Stratford was forgotten when Palmerston, with all his manly straightforward vigour, dwelt upon the long and honourable career of the Great Elchi, his many services to his country, and his fair unspotted fame, and demonstrated in unanswerable terms the absurdity of the charge brought against him. He fairly carried the House with him ; they turned away from the petty detail of unanswered despatches to the great facts of Lord Stratford's career, and the motion was triumphantly defeated by a majority of 127. Lord Malmesbury, who had a corresponding motion in the House Lords, hastily withdrew it, to the disappointment of the Duke of Newcastle, the Earl of Harrowby, Lord Glenelg, and others, who had looked forward to a field-day in defence of their friend. The Elchi's name was safe.

CHAPTER XXXII.

THE CHARTER OF REFORM.

1856-58.

In the preceding chapters the centre of interest has been seen to shift itself from Constantinople to the seat of war, and the work of diplomacy has been overshadowed by the stern business of battle. We are now to witness another and much more violent change of scene : the crisis was no longer to be met by steady firmness at the Porte or by gallant deeds of arms in the Crimea ; Lord Stratford's great influence and the zeal and courage of the armies were alike superseded, from no defect of their own, but in consequence of treachery in high places. For the fall of the south side of Sevastopol was followed by an event perhaps unparalleled in history. In 1854 two great nations bound themselves together by a solemn treaty to withstand by force of arms the encroachments of Russia ; in 1855, one of those great nations betrayed the other in presence of the enemy. To treat separately for peace was expressly prohibited by the treaty of alliance : yet at the close of 1855 the Emperor of the French was in secret communications with the son-in-law of the Russian Chancellor, and their purport was treasonable to England. Satisfied with the half-successes of the siege, Louis Napoleon was now as anxious for peace as he had formerly been eager for military glory. All the plans for the coming campaign were thrown over, and after a while, the secret negotiations bore fruit in Russia's acceptance of an Ultimatum. Plenipotentiaries were summoned to Paris, where Lord Clarendon soon discovered that England stood alone, and that peace was not so much offered as, in the words of Brunov, thrust down the jaws of Russia.

1856

ÆT. 69

Jan. 1856

Some extracts from his letters to Lord Stratford, who had no part whatever in the negotiations at Paris, describe the position of affairs with what might well seem perfect frankness, if the Foreign Secretary was still ignorant of the Seebach intrigue and the Emperor's defection :—

From Lord Clarendon, 18 Jan.

I suppose we must now consider ourselves to be on the eve of peace, as Russia has knocked under. She has managed her affairs ill, as she has exposed herself to unnecessary humiliation by first refusing the essential parts of the Ultimatum, and then accepting them under threat from Austria. If the terms are really and *bona fide* adopted and carried out, we cannot say that such a peace will be a bad one or that the country upon the whole has a right to be dissatisfied with it ; but in my inmost heart I cannot feel satisfaction, for we shall not leave off well for the honour of England. I should have liked another campaign, and in conjunction with France to have made a great effort which would have enabled us to impose more effective conditions, and thus to have rendered peace more lasting. But France flags and fears, and the only man in France who is true to the Alliance and is not swayed by some ignoble sentiment or other is obliged to think of his own position if he sets himself too doggedly against the wishes, not alone of the *tripotiers*, but of the commercial and producing classes *and of the army.* Then again we cannot feel sure that another campaign *would* have restored our military prestige —on the contrary, we have turned experience to such small account and there is still so much that is radically defective in our military administration that the chance of failure would be quite as great as that of success. So upon the whole I look at the peace prospect with very mixed feelings, even supposing that everything turned out as well as we could wish ; but I am convinced that Russia has accepted the terms with the firm intention of evading them when she gets round the green table, in which she will be stoutly aided by France and feebly resisted by Austria ; so that the whole battle of negotiation will have to be fought by us.

21 Jan.

Things are in a state of great embarrassment and complication, and it is impossible to foretell what will be the solution of the present difficulty. France—i.e. the Government, the people, and the *army* of France— are bent on peace *at any price.* We have no such feeling, and are determined not to have peace unless it be a safe and honourable one. The Emperor inclines towards us, but his position is becoming daily more embarrassing, and in one way or another the Alliance is being sorely tried.

The French people seem to be gone mad, kissing each other upon the *restoration of peace*, and giving ovations to Hübner, whom they treat like a demi-god! It is not the people alone, however, who are for peace: it is the *army*, which is quite as strongly pronounced for it, and there is the Emperor's great difficulty; for upon the army first and a certain amount of public opinion next rests his throne, and as there is already a notion (of course actively promoted by the Government and the *tripotiers*) that we are making difficulties about the *form* in which negotiations shall be commenced, the English alliance is going at a discount.

1856
——
ÆT. 69

The French have really in the most reckless and wilful manner destroyed our chances of a good peace by their open and avowed determination not to continue the war. The Emperor of Russia must be overflowing with generosity and self-abnegation if he offers good terms to people so ready to take bad ones as the French. The Emperor, however, is still our hope, and he is now in good earnest, giving orders for the recommencement of hostilities if negotiations fail. He has agreed with us that the armistice shall only last till 31 March, and that it shall only include operations *by land*; he agrees with us that the Russians must be driven out of the Crimea, and that if proper means are actively taken the operation ought not to last a month, and that then we shall be able to do what we want in Georgia and Asia Minor.

8 Feb.

The Emperor wishes to make *le généreux* and *le gentleman* with the Russians, and Walewski takes his cue from that and regularly sides with the Russians. France has therefore no plenipotentiary in the Conference, and Russia has three, and Cowley and I, as I always anticipated, stand alone, though I must in justice add that the Austrians have stood by us firmly, and are much disgusted with Walewski. It was quite out of the question contending for Circassia and the adjacent countries, as well as other points of minor importance, for the Emperor said he could not conscientiously insist upon them and would not support us--in fact upon the Bessarabian frontier we had to choose between a concession to Russia or something very like a rupture with France—upon the separate convention between the Porte and Russia everything that Orlov wanted would have been conceded by France; and now that Orlov sees in what vein the Emperor is, he is making difficulties about everything, and we shall be lucky if the treaty is signed by the day that the armistice expires However I trust that the instructions sent out not to renew hostilities without fresh orders will prevent any mischief happening. The Russians wanted an article about the Christians that would have

22 March

given them more power of *ingérence* than the Menshikov note dreamed of ! and they have not yet agreed to the article that A'li has consented to.   In short, things are in a maze now, and I have asked for an audience of the Emperor to tell him that they will end ill unless he can Anglo-Gallicize his own Russian plenipotentiary.

25 April   I think as you do about the terms of the peace, but am not the least sorry that peace is made, because, notwithstanding our means of carrying on the war, I believe we should have run risks by so doing for which no possible success would have compensated.   We should have *been alone,* for although we should have had the Turks and the Sardinians, yet they would have weighed as nothing for us in Europe. If you could have seen (and it required to be seen and heard in order to be believed) all that was passing when I got to Paris—the bitterness of feeling against us, the kindly (I would almost say the enthusiastic) feeling towards Russia, and the determination if necessary to throw over the Vienna conditions in order to prevent the resumption of hostilities (money matters and Bourse speculations being the main cause)—you would have felt, as I did, that our position was not agreeable, and that Brunov was justified in saying that they did not come to make or to negotiate for peace, but to accept the peace which was to be crammed down their throats.

If the Russians had done again what they did at Vienna, and shewn that they did not want peace, we might perhaps have dragged France on with us; but she would have been furious at her disappointment, and would have given us a most reluctant support. Unluckily, too, just as negotiations began, the French army fell ill, and the Emperor himself admitted to me that with 22,000 men in hospital, and likely to be more, peace had almost become a military as well as a financial and political necessity for him.

If Lord Clarendon really felt as the ambassador did about the terms of peace his sentiments must have been very warm, for Lord Stratford's first words were " I would rather have cut off my right hand than have signed that treaty."   It was hard to see all the hard-won triumphs of his diplomacy of 1853 utterly abandoned in the Treaty of 1856.   His own notions as to what it should have comprised have already been outlined in former extracts from the correspondence, but the two following letters, one written before the negotiations at Paris, the other after their conclusion, will complete as far as it is needful the statement of his views :—

1856
———
ÆT. 69

To Lord
Clarendon
3 Feb.

I was glad to learn that you are to go to Paris. Your labours there will no doubt be attended with vexation and risk, but proportioned thereto will be the credit of success, or the consolation of failure. It gratified me to observe that your opinion and mine, let me add, of the peace agrees with the general impressions of the country. The attempt was a necessity under the circumstances, and a continuance of the war, if such be the will of Heaven, might atone for the loss of an occasion which, however advantageous in the main points, would leave much to desire. Nicholas's Russia is to all appearance on its knees. The Russia of nature is still in its growth, shorn of its most forward branches, but capable of shooting into greater luxuriance at no distant period. Against this latter Russia I should like to see due precautions taken, and I know nothing better than a barrier of neutral or independent States prolonged between the two empires in Europe and Asia.

As for the Crimea, I know not what could be done with it if severed from Russia. Restored without its fleet and fortifications, laid open to a free commercial intercourse, and placed under the surveillance of consular dragons, I conceive that it would offer the maximum of advantage to us and our allies.

I have already troubled you with my notions about the Dniester as a frontier, and the means of raising a title to it. My impression is, that you would be fully justified in demanding it in lieu of a pecuniary indemnity so justly due to the Allies, and more especially to the Porte itself.

I may be wrong, but it seems to me that without further success in the war, you would only do a high act of justice in reviving the Duchy of Warsaw, which was created by Europe, for European purposes, out of the spoils wrested from France by the alliance of that day, and in establishing the independence of Circassia, which the Porte had no more right to cede than Russia to receive.

A'li Pasha will try to make the fourth point of the treaty as loose as possible, and yet there is little prospect of keeping the Porte steady to the execution of the measures which are necessarily to be founded on the arrangement now in progress, unless some kind of supervision be retained, which surely may be done without violating any principles of justice, on the grounds of our assistance to the Empire, and the proposed guarantee of the Empire's integrity.

If the integrity of the Sultan's dominions be formally secured, there is but too much reason to fear that the Porte will give way to its natural indolence, and leave the firman of reform, now almost completed, a lifeless paper, valuable only as a record of sound principles.

It was kind of you to make a point of sending me the treaty so soon, and it may gratify you to know that I was enabled, by your promptitude in sending it, to share my early knowledge with Thouvenel and Prokesch. The present ministry, whatever A'li may tell you, is so French as to be contented with any treaty which pleased the Emperor. The Sultan, too, who was never enamoured of the war, is delighted at peace without reference to the terms of the treaty. Elsewhere, as would seem to be the case in England, another campaign would have been preferred, and when the terms of peace are known, it is not impossible that a feeling of positive dissatisfaction may be got up here, whatever may be the case in more polished parts of the world.

It does seem hard, I confess, that with all but 60,000 rank and file in the Crimea, nearly 400 sail ready for the Baltic, no lack of financial means, our commerce undistressed, the wishes of the nation steady, and our soldiers and sailors with few exceptions eager only for fresh trials of strength, we should have got under the harrow of a gratuitous necessity, and found ourselves inextricably committed to an act of voluntary abnegation. As you have done me the honour to sympathize with my *wishes*, I cannot doubt that you have done all which you thought practicable in reason and prudence to obtain a more complete settlement. Few men can do more than see things from their own point of view. Looking from mine, which officially, and perhaps naturally too, affords a more limited horizon, I fancy that the die was cast in the very commencement, and that if of the pipers concerned we are the least well paid, it is because we were then content, from necessity or indifference, to play second fiddle to our Imperial ally.

I perceive with surprize that the peace does not go comfortably down with my Austrian colleague, and I hear, moreover, that the Austrians in general are not much pleased with the result of their own contrivance.

Have they found out that Russia is weakened enough to have been more thoroughly clipped? or has their intimacy with France declined? or does their discomfort lie no deeper than a feeling of regret for the transfer of the seat of negotiation from Vienna to Paris?

But I am wrong to take up your time with idle speculations. Long before this can reach you, the measure of British opinion will have been shewn in all its length and breadth; nor should I be at all surprized if, after a good grumble, the press and the public were to resign themselves quietly to the blandishments of peace and reserve the dregs of their bile for audit-day.

Here the peace gives rise to many anxious thoughts. How are

the Sultan's reforms to be carried through—the Allied troops all gone, and no power of foreign interference reserved ?   How is the country to be kept quiet, if hopes and fears, equally excited in adverse quarters, have to find their own level ?   What means shall we possess of allaying the discordant elements, if our credit is to decline and our influence to be overlaid by the persevering artifices of a jealous and artful ally ? How can we hope to supply the usefulness derivable from our command of the Contingent and Irregulars if they are to be given up ?— In short, when I hear the politicians of the country remark that the troubles of Europe with respect to this Empire are only beginning, I know not how to reply.

If the Treaty of Paris was unsatisfactory in other respects, there was one special point in it which gave Lord Stratford deep concern.   In order to understand why, it is necessary to go back a little and trace the progress of the ambassador's schemes for Turkish reform.   As has been frequently repeated, this was his mission in Turkey, to reform her from within : and at the same time to provide such external surveillance that it should not be possible for the native indolence of the official classes to make the reforms of no effect.   A letter to Lord Clarendon pointedly refers to the necessity for such supervision and enforcement, if reforms were to have any real effect :—

What did Lord J. Russell write to me on leaving Vienna ?   I forget the words ; they amounted to this : All that can be done for the rayas in *principles* and *measures* may be said to be accomplished. Now for the *enforcement*—turn in that direction and complete your work.

I ask for nothing better, not only as regards the rayas, but the improvement of the Empire generally, if possible so as to restore it on sound principles of humane and civilized government.   How is it to be done ? there's " the question," aye, and " the rub."   Three levers are requisite ; where are they to be found ?   First, the provincial authorities to act in a right spirit ;   secondly, the power of the Government duly exerted for their appointment and direction ;   thirdly, *a force from without* to keep up a steady animating pressure on the Government.

The last, I am persuaded, can alone constitute,—if even *that* can,—a durable and efficient *principe moteur.*

What shall it be ?   England alone—the Alliance—or Europe ?   One of them it must be.   *Which,* is the question.   I should prefer the first,

To Lord Clarendon, Constantinople, 3 June, 1855

as more single-minded, steady and trusted. But France would insist upon having her moiety, and *she* often works by means and works for ends which would not suit us. While the war goes on, however, there is nothing better, as far as I know, and a thorough understanding between the Governments, expressed in common instructions, might perhaps give a uniform direction to the process.

So long as Lord Stratford was on the spot, there was no lack of *a force from without* to carry reforms into practice ; but it was necessary to look forward to the time when Turkey should be deprived of his counsels. To guard against future backslidings two things were vital. One was to confirm corroborate, and so to speak codify, all the reforms which had been wrung from the Porte since the decree of Gulhané in 1839 : the other was to provide an external engine for their enforcement. The Elchi was busy with the former of these two points before the opening of the negotiations at Paris. It was extremely important that the details should be settled by the Sultan himself before Russia had the opportunity of putting in her oar. To effect this the ambassador set to work with all his might, and the result was the crown of all his many efforts for the regeneration of Turkey, the famous *Hatti-Humayun* of 21 February, 1856. In this Imperial proclamation the Sultan announced his desire of renewing and enlarging the numerous improvements which had been introduced into his institutions with a view to making them worthy of the place which his empire held among civilized nations ; he was anxious, he said, to assure the happiness of his people, "who in my sight are all equal, and equally dear to me ;" and with this object he first confirmed the former guarantees of the Hatti-Sherif of Gulhané to all his subjects, without distinction of class or religion, for their security in person, property, and honour ; and at the same time renewed all the privileges and spiritual immunities granted *ab antiquo* and subsequently to Christian and other non-Musulman communities established in Turkey. The proclamation went on to enumerate various ecclesiastical privileges, guaranteed the free exercise of its religious rites and the control of its sacred and educational buildings to each and every sect ; and announced in bold terms that "Every distinction or designation tending to make any class whatever of the subjects of my Empire inferior to another class on account of their religion, language, or race, shall be for ever effaced. . . . As all forms of religion are and shall be freely professed in my dominions, no subject of my Empire shall be hindered in the exercise of the religion which he professes nor shall be in any way annoyed on that account. No one shall be compelled to change his religion." The eligibility of all Turkish subjects, without distinction, to public offices ; their admission to the civil and military schools ; the acceptance of sworn evidence according to the oaths of the several sects in courts of justice ; the reference of all inter-religious causes to Mixed Tribunals ; the reform of the penitentiary and disciplinary systems ; the absolute equality of taxation among the different classes of the population without distinction of creed ; the abolition of the system of farming the taxes ; and various other reforms tending to the repression of corruption, extortion, and mal-versation, and the equal encouragement of good citizenship without prejudice of class or creed, were all promised in this great charter. Lord Stratford's hand is traceable in every line ; these were his reforms, either already carried, or often pressed upon the Porte ; this was the culminating moment in his reforming career, and the seal to all his labours on behalf of just and equal government in Turkey.

It was a signal triumph to have extorted such a pro-gramme of reform from a Mohammedan sovereign, in face of the hostility of the vast majority of his Muslim subjects, despite the opposition of most of the men in office, and not-withstanding the indifference, if not contempt, manifested by the European Powers for all dreams of Turkish regeneration. The Ambassador himself was astonished : "Considering that of the five persons who joined me," he wrote, "in drawing up the Charter, two were Mohammedans, two Roman Catholics, and one a member of the Greek Church, its acceptance was little short of a miracle. I confess that I had no previous ex-pectation whatever of overcoming the prejudices of such col-leagues in negotiation, and particularly of those who professed the Musulman belief." No one but Lord Stratford could have won such a victory. But, like the Alma, like Inkerman, it was a victory that required to be followed up; and just at the crowning point, when the whole position of Turkish bigotry and exclusiveness and corruption had been carried by the Elchi's impetuous charge, the Powers of Europe combined to refuse him and his successors the means of securing for ever the advantages he had won. The Hatti-Humayun was indeed part of the Treaty of Paris: it was formally recognized in Art. IX. But it needed more than recognition—it needed enforcement. This was the point upon which Lord Stratford had never ceased to insist. In the midst of the Paris conferences he telegraphed thus to Lord Clarendon :—

19 March   There are able and experienced men in this country who view with alarm the supposed intention of the Conference at Paris to record the Sultan's late Firman of Privileges in the Treaty of Peace, and at the same time to declare that the Powers of Europe disclaim all right of interference between the Sultan and his subjects. They argue thus: The Imperial firman places the Christians and the Musulmans on an equal footing as to civil rights. It is believed that the Porte will never of its own accord carry the provisions of the firman seriously into effect. The treaty, in its supposed form, would therefore confirm the right and extinguish the hope of the Christians. Despair on their side and fear on that of the Turks would in that case engender the bitterest animosity between them, and not improbably bring on a deadly struggle before long. Some go so far as to see in this contingency enough to warrant a suspicion of evil purposes elsewhere, and danger in proportion to the Ottoman Empire. Might not this hazard be avoided by substituting for a disclaimer in the treaty a separate agreement among the Christian parties to the negotiation, regulating the work and occasions of interference, so that any such eventual act on their part should be concerted previously in common and strictly limited to the necessities of the case?

But the Treaty of Paris, while recognizing the importance of the measure, specially enacted that the recognition of the Hatt did not entitle any of the Powers, collectively or severally, to interfere in the internal affairs of the Ottoman Empire. The qualification abrogated whatever effect the recognition might have had.

The great Charter of Reform of 1856 was the climax of

Lord Stratford's career. In it he had at last accomplished what his friend Reshid had attempted at Gulhané in 1839. Reshid's effort was premature, and for many years the Elchi's life was one long struggle to overcome the reaction which had ensued. Then one by one the degrading distinctions of creed and nationality had been effaced from the Ottoman institutions; one by one the rights and privileges of the Christians had been secured; and finally the Hatti-Humayun had recapitulated, confirmed, and enlarged all that had gone before. Whatever might hinder the execution of its provisions, the Great Elchi could view with satisfaction the accomplishment of his desire.

His mission in the East was nearly ended. As soon as the Treaty of Paris was signed, he asked for leave of absence. After four years of incessant toil he felt the need of repose. He did not however immediately use his leave. The Government begged him to stay so long as the various details of the peace arrangements required his supervision, and one thing after another delayed him till the following year. He left at last in a depressed frame of mind, due partly to physical ill-health and partly to political considerations. The betrayal of England at Paris had naturally affected her prestige in the East. The French cared nothing for Turkish reform, and what weighed most heavily upon his mind was the fear that their influence might make the Hatti-Humayun a dead letter. He felt very keenly the pusillanimity of his own Government, who had made him a victim to their deference to France. But with all this to discourage, there was much to inspire hope and confidence. He was satisfied that the work he had accomplished was the right work for Turkey and for England, and he was not conscious of any material loss of his personal influence for carrying on that work. "To be the victim," he wrote to his brother, "of so much trickery and dupery and charlatanism is no small trial: but I have faith in principles, as working out their own justification, and fix my thoughts steadily on that coming day when the Peace of Paris will be felt in its miserable consequences."

If the years succeeding the war had seen his labours aggravated by intrigue at the Porte, by want of support at home, by

1856

ÆT. 69

Dec. 1857

23 July, 1856

1856
—
ÆT. 69

partisan writers, and by all the personal hostility that a strong
uncompromising character is apt to arouse ; on the other
hand they had witnessed such an approximation between
the East and West as few who knew Turkey in the earlier
decades of the century could have imagined possible. The
barriers between Muslim and Christian, Turk and Frank,
were breaking down. The year had opened with a sign of
the changes that were taking place : the Elchi had received a
congratulatory New Year's letter from " Abdu-l-Kadir, the
Champion of the Faith," in which the noble old chief said " We
have not forgotten the day on which we met your Excellency at
Therapia : that was a fête day for us." Two years before, a
Mohammedan General had been decorated with the Christian
Cross of the Bath. In 1856 a still more novel and imposing
ceremony took place at Constantinople. Sultan Abdu-l-Mejid
was invested by Lord Stratford, as the Queen's representative,
with the most exclusive order of knighthood in the world.
Assisted by the King of Arms, the Elchi made his Majesty a
Knight of the Garter. Did the Sultan know what the stately
ambassador was saying, as he placed the George and Riband
round his neck ? " *Tacniam hanc gestato, imagine Sancti
Georgii Martyris et Militis Christi insignitam, cujus aemula-
tione accensus, per adversos simul prosperosque casus feraris
invictus, donec tam animi quam corporis hostibus fractis, non
solum palmam pugnae terrestris, sed et aeternae victoriae coronam
reportes.*" When a Sultan submits to be enjoined to emulate
the career of a Martyr and Soldier of Christ, who shall say that
the fanaticism of Islam is inextinguishable ?

Other signs there were that the work of the Great Elchi
had not been vain ; that his efforts to draw East and West
together, so that perchance the East might be saved by the
West, had not been fruitless. Let us picture him (as he has
been described by one who witnessed the scene) as he stood,
bareheaded, surrounded by his staff, in full uniform, at the
gate of the embassy in Pera one evening in February, 1856.
Over his head coloured lamps traced the linked names of
" Victoria " and " Abdu-l-Mejid " in lines of fire across the
court, lighting up the arms of the Grenadiers, Highlanders,
and Horse and Foot Artillery, who formed the guard of

Mrs. E.
Hornby,
*In and
Around
Stamboul,*
i. 254 ff.

honour. In front, a troop of English Lancers clashed up to
the gate escorting a carriage in which was seated the Commander of the Faithful himself, "Sultan of Sultans, Lord of
the Two Seas and the Two Continents, Abdu-l-Mejid Khan,
son of Mahmud." As the Grand Turk alighted, an electric
wire communicated the fact to the British fleet, and the
Golden Horn forthwith rang out with salvos of cannon, while
the band in the court played "God save the Queen." For
the first time in the history of Turkey a Sultan was the guest
of a Christian ambassador. Lady Stratford was giving a *bal
costumé*, and the Sultan had honoured it with his presence.
Never at Pera was a more gorgeous sight witnessed. The
dress uniforms of the English, French, and Sardinian officers
were matched and outshone by the rich costumes and jewelled
arms of the Armenians, Persians, Kurds, Greeks, Turks, and
Albanians who crowded the rooms, by the robes of the
Greek Patriarch, the Armenian Archbishop, and the Jewish
High Priest. Abdu-l-Mejid took in the sight with the wonder-
ing enjoyment of a child; and as he redescended the staircase, which was lined with Lancers and Light Dragoons,
many of whom wore the Balaklava clasp, he might have
fancied that he had changed places with his predecessor,
Harun er-Rashid, and lost himself in the enchanted palaces of
the Thousand and One Nights. The Sultan was delighted with
his "first ball:" and it must have been a proud moment for
Lord Stratford, when, in the presence of all his colleagues, he
walked hand in hand with the Grand Signior through the files
of British soldiers, to the amazement of all beholders. Whose
was the triumph that day, when the bars which fenced about
the seclusion of the greatest Musulman sovereign were
loosed, and Christian and Turk met on equal terms? In the
midst of opposition and dejection, of despair of doing good,
of sad forebodings for the future, this hour of triumph shone
forth like the flash of a beacon at sea, telling the storm-tossed
mariner of firm ground and a haven near at hand. Whatever still remained to be done, the Great Elchi knew that this
was certain : the distinctions of class and race and creed had
been publicly done away with in Turkey, and it was he who
had worked the miracle.

1856

Æt. 69

As he approached the shores of England, Lord Stratford learnt that Reshid Pasha, whom he had left, to all appearance well, at Constantinople, had suddenly died almost immediately after his own departure. "Alas! poor Reshid!" he wrote to Alison 14 Jan. 1858, "the news of his death overtook me at Calais. I need not tell you it grieved me as much as it surprized me. Without overlooking his faults or exaggerating his merits, we must in fairness admit that in him, all things considered, the Sultan has lost his best man. As for my own share in the loss, whatever it may be politically, I feel it deeply as a friend, and the more so as I despair of meeting any Turk who can ever interest me in the same manner."

The Elchi arrived in London at a time when the popular sentiment about him had veered round again, and the papers were, as he said, "braying panegyrics." Lord Palmerston welcomed him cordially; Lord Clarendon was civil; and the past was not discussed. A very few weeks had elapsed since the Ambassador's return, however, when a circumstance occurred which altered all his plans. He had then no intention of resigning his embassy; on the contrary he had left Constantinople with the expressed intention of returning, and this expectation was alluded to in the Sultan's parting speech. But on 20 February Lord Palmerston's Government was turned out on Milner Gibson's amendment relating to the neglect of the Government to reply to Count Walewski's despatch complaining of the asylum given to conspirators like the then notorious Orsini in England. The Elchi could not conceal a certain sense of humour when he learnt the cause of the defeat: "I confess" he remarked to a friend, "that it interests me to hear of a government being dissolved on account of unanswered despatches;" for he remembered the Kars dispute and the censure passed upon him by the same Foreign Secretary who had now been dismissed for the same fault. But his prevailing feeling was that of sympathy for Palmerston, whose loyalty to the Elchi during the attacks of recent years had confirmed his old admiration for a manful English statesman, once connected, too, by political ties with the party of his illustrious kinsman, George Canning. In a generous impulse he resolved to shew his personal respect for the

defeated minister by declining to hold office under his successors, and accordingly as soon as Lord Derby's administration had taken possession of their posts, he sent in his
resignation to the Foreign Office. On 28 February Lord
Malmesbury informed him that he had sent the resignation
to the Queen, adding " I don't know how to replace you," and
by 3 March the Queen's acceptance was known. Writing to
Alison, who was still at Constantinople, where he now held
the post of First Secretary and Chargé d'affaires, Lord
Stratford thus announced his retirement :—

The curtain has at last dropped on my Eastern drama. I have To C.
resigned the embassy, and other hands than mine will in due time Alison,
receive the archives from you. I know not who is to be my successor, 4 March
but you may perhaps hear from the Office. I would have wished to
close my long connexion with Turkey more decorously, and would
not have shrunk from the trouble of going out again for a moment to
take leave and wind up. This however could not be. On my side
having made up my mind to give Lord Palmerston a mark of sympathy, I could only send in a simply unmistakable resignation.

How the news of the resignation was received among the
reformers at Constantinople may be judged from the letter of
a well-known American missionary. Mr. Goodell wrote :

I cannot let this opportunity pass without assuring your lordship Constanti-
of the deep regret we all feel at the little prospect we have of seeing nople,
you again at Constantinople. But certainly we should be very un- 1 July
grateful not to acknowledge the wise Providence that brought you
to this land, and that kept you here for so many years, and this, too, at
a time when in the changes called-for your influence was mighty, and
mighty for good. In these changes your name stands connected
with all that is worthy to rise and prosper, with all that is stable and
enduring. Connected as it is with the great cause of civil and religious liberty, it stands connected with that which shall never pass
away, for it is as eternal as the immutable purpose of Infinite Goodness can make it. And when this cause shall triumph in Turkey,
(and triumph it shall), and the future history of the country shall be
written, the influence and important agency of your lordship will not
fail of a public recognition and a due acknowledgment.

There can be little doubt that, in spite of a pleasant sense of unwonted freedom, Lord Stratford had no sooner resigned his post than he began to regret it. He had become so accustomed to diplomatic work that he did not quite know how to exist without it. Disliking Constantinople as he had done all his life, so many years had been passed there, so much both of happiness and trouble, of triumph and failure, had been experienced in those palaces on the shores of the Bosphorus, that all his chief interests and all the salient epochs of his life seemed to be indissolubly connected with Stambol. Lady Stratford moreover was warmly attached to the spot where she had spent so many years. It was not unnatural, too, that the Elchi should desire to end his connexion with the Sultan in a more ceremonious manner than his last parting. Lord Malmesbury's statement about the difficulty of replacing him offered an opening for some such suggestion, and it was speedily arranged that after an interval of rest Lord Stratford should go back to the Porte to take a formal leave of the Sultan, and "wind up" the affairs of his mission. He naturally considered that the expressed wish of the Government that he should return for a while to the Porte temporarily suspended his resignation; in his view he was practically ambassador until he had gone out and taken leave. Any business that might call for special attention during the interval would be, according to this view, entrusted to him; for by "winding up" he meant quite as much the conclusion of pending affairs of a political kind, as his own personal business. The Government, however, viewed the arrangement differently; they considered his embassy closed, his services no longer available, and his return to Constantinople purely a compliment to himself and to the Sultan. Accordingly, as the aspirations of Montenegro were just then assuming a critical aspect, they appointed a new ambassador who was to go out with all possible speed and undertake the question. Many people might say that it was a waste of public money to send out a second ambassador when Lord Stratford was in any case going, and had repeatedly given proofs of his readiness to start almost at a day's notice on important service without considering personal convenience ; and it must certainly have appeared odd that a difficult problem in Turkey should have been given to a comparatively new man when the old and trusted adviser of the Sultan was at hand ; but most amazing of all is it to read that the appointment was made without a hint to Lord Stratford, and that the diplomatist chosen to succeed him was one who was notorious for holding diametrically opposite views on almost every political, moral, and religious subject, and who had already had disagreements with him during the negotiations concerning the Principalities in the preceding year. The cause of reform in Turkey, the cause for which he had striven for so many years, began its downward course when the Turks began to understand the altered character of the British Embassy under Sir Henry Bulwer.

In spite of his wonder and indignation at the appointment, Lord Stratford did not relinquish the plan of returning to take leave of the Sultan. On 4 September, accompanied by his family and suite, he left London for Marseilles, where H.M.S. *Curaçoa* awaited him. The stately vessel, for she was a frigate, lent an additional dignity to this final leave-taking.

Once more the Elchi revisited the scene of so many toils and triumphs ; once again he paced the Palace at Pera ; but his time was short, and he came only to depart again, for ever. All the stately ceremony with which he was welcomed by Sultan and ministers, all the grateful devotion of the many whom he had rescued from oppression, all the hearty loyalty of the British subjects whose champion he had stood for half a century, could not reconcile him to the mournful nature of his task. For he knew that he was assisting at the obsequies of his hopes. His long struggle for reform in the Ottoman Empire was at an end, and in the character of his successor he believed he could trace the antithesis of all he had striven for, the abandonment of all that he had won. The very respect with which he was received had a melancholy side : it was the last time that he would witness that reverence which he had conquered by his own firm will and lofty purpose. With some such thoughts the ambassador entered his ten-

oar caïque at Tophana, and crossed the waters of the Golden
Horn to Yali Kapu on 22 September, 1858. The Ottoman carriages of state were awaiting him on the other
side ; a guard of honour presented arms as he alighted at the
official residence of the Grand Vezir ; and A'li Pasha himself,
attended by the Master of the Ceremonies, came forth to
receive him at the entrance of his saloon. A'li, despite his
French proclivities, was moved as he welcomed the old and
staunch friend of his country ; he told the Elchi how his departure was deplored, and how gratefully and unreservedly
his great services to the Ottoman State were recognized and
applauded. The interview was cordial ; but in the midst of
the Grand Vezir's courtesies, Lord Stratford remembered the
affection of his old friend Reshid, and felt that in his grave
lay buried whatever hope might have remained for the future
of Turkey.

Three days later the scene changed to the Sultan's palace,
and once more the Elchi stood before his imperial pupil. As
he delivered the letter addressed to " Sir, my Brother," and
signed *regiâ manu* " Victoria R.," the ambassador failed not
to dwell on the theme which was ever uppermost in his mind :
he spoke of the great measures that had illumined his
Majesty's reign, he touched on his own share in them, and he
begged for a firm assurance that the course of reform which
had begun so auspiciously should not be stayed when he was
no longer there to see and warn. The Sultan's reply was
brief : he was very glad, he said, to see again one who had so
largely contributed to drawing closer the links that bound
his Empire and Great Britain together ; reforms were being
attended to ;—he repeated, he was glad to see him. Abdu-l-
Mejid had begun to be but the shadow of his former self.
Intemperance was already too evidently undermining his
weakly constitution. Yet he was still capable of real emo-
tion, and his countenance evinced the deep feeling with which
he now took leave for ever of his old counsellor and friend.
Three years later he died.

The return of the great ambassador roused the warm
enthusiasm of the British colony. The merchants of Constantinople gathered together, and presented him with an address,

in which they testified their "heartfelt pleasure" at seeing him once more among them, though only for a little while, and assured him of their undying "personal regard and esteem," and the "lively remembrance we shall ever retain of the constant and efficient protection of our various interests during the long course of years in which they have been under your lordship's care and vigilance;" they prayed for his health and happiness; they spoke of how the poor would never cease to lament the loss of Lady Stratford's untiring benevolence; and they begged the Elchi not to forget the country which he had so greatly benefited. Other voices were then lifted up in praise and honour, and none came more sweetly to the ear of the departing statesman than the memorial of the American missionaries, in which they recited the many reforms which he had brought into Turkey, and especially the abolition of executions for apostasy, the recognition of the Protestant community, the open sale of the Bible in the Turkish bazars, and the building of the first Protestant church in Jerusalem; and added "we love to consider your lordship's influence as one of the important providential means by which God has been pleased to carry on His work. . . . You have been guided wisely by Him whose cause you have served." The Armenian Protestants were not behind their American brothers in their tribute to the ambassador's noble work in their behalf, and their memorial is touching in its humble thankfulness :—

It is with unfeigned regret that we have heard that your lordship is now taking leave of our country, probably for the last time. On an occasion to us so mournful we find it difficult to give utterance to the true feelings of our hearts.

Our minds go back to the past, and we see everywhere memorials of your lordship's humane and benevolent endeavours to ameliorate the condition of the downcast and suffering in this our land.

We can testify that your lordship's benevolent exertions have not been confined to the narrow limits of race or sect, but have been freely extended to all who stood in need of your aid, whether Mohammedan, Jew, or Christian. But especially, as Protestants, are we now forcibly reminded of all your lordship's kind offices in our behalf, when men bearing the Christian name, through ignorance of our real motives, became our persecutors. By your lordship's favourable representations of us before the Sultan's Government, we were recognized as loyal subjects, and the same civil rights conceded to us as are enjoyed by the other Christian communities in Turkey. Although few in number, and of little political influence, through your gracious interposition we are a fully recognized community in Turkey, having our own chosen representative at the Porte, and our members scattered over the whole country, enjoying for the most part freedom to worship God according to our own consciences and His most holy Word. . . .

In the name of the five or six thousand Protestants scattered over every part of Asiatic Turkey, we desire this day to render to your lordship our most sincere and hearty thanks. The prayers and best wishes of a grateful people will follow you from these shores wherever you go. The memory of what you have done will never be effaced from our hearts, and our children and our children's children, to the latest generation, shall mention your name with veneration, gratitude, and love.

On 19 October a great assembly of merchants and other British residents met together on the brow of the hill of Pera, where a noble site had been given by the Sultan at the Elchi's request for the foundation of a Memorial church—a monument at once of the brave Englishmen who had fallen in the late war, and of the progress of religious freedom which had made the erection of an Anglican church, hard by a mosque, a possibility in a Mohammedan country. And now the foundation-stone was to be laid; and who could worthily lay it but the white-haired statesman who had spent his life in the defence of liberty of conscience and the protection of oppressed Christianity? So Lord Stratford stood forth before the multitude, and, before he took the trowel in his hand, spoke solemn last words to the people. He dwelt on the wonderful achievements of the past; on the changes which had made such a ceremony possible in Turkey; on the character of the war which had called forth such energies and ended in such a crowning triumph as the Charter of Reform; and he bade them consider how henceforward every Christian who sailed to the Golden Horn would see the Memorial church commanding the slope of the hill, and would think of the victory of free religious worship, while he remembered the successes of the battle-field, and the deeds of

those who had fallen in the fight over there to the eastward
amid the Crimean hills.

The parting followed soon. The people whom he had
succoured and protected crowded down to the landing-place
to see the Great Elchi take his last farewell of the scene of his
many labours. He stood on the steamer's poop, calm and
collected, no sign of the mental strain upon his unruffled
features, stately and courteous as an English gentleman alone
knows how to be. Outwardly unmoved, he saw his sup-
planter take his seat in the well-known caïque that had so
often carried the great ambassador to his conquests at the
Porte, and so, in sadness, he took his last leave of the land which
had received the best fruits of his long life's work.

Delayed at the commercial capital of Asia Minor, he received a second and not less hearty ovation. The merchants
of Smyrna vied with each other, with the consular body, and
the Turkish Governor-General, to do him honour, and he was
led in triumph to open the railway line from Smyrna to Aydin
— the first railway ever laid in Turkey, and a fresh witness to
the civilizing influence of the Sultan's tried adviser.

At last the farewells were said, the ship of war moved off
with a stately grace, as though conscious of the honourable
burden she conveyed, and many eyes were strained to see the
last of that commanding presence which had been the centre
of their world for the greater part of the century. The Great
Elchi would never again stand guard over the Bosphorus.

WITH many men the end of work is the close of life; few really hard workers abandon their profession or business till it has begun to forsake them; and in most cases the loss of the familiar desk or well-known office has something of the sharpness of a mortal blow. A hale old man too often becomes an infirm invalid when there is nothing left to call forth the energy which kept him in health; and with the cessation of the necessity, the capability of effort often disappears. And so the Seventh Age is reached, which, if protracted beyond the common span, is apt to realize the word of the Psalmist, and is but labour and sorrow, till we pass away.

The old age of Lord Stratford de Redcliffe was very different: it was a shining example of what faith and hope in the best things, and a bright intellectual activity, may do to preserve the fire and energy of youth to a period long beyond the lives of most of the strongest men. In 1858 his diplomatic work was done, but he had not retired from his labours out of any feeling of impaired powers. Mentally and physically he was still as capable of conducting the affairs of any embassy as he had been twenty years before: yet he had passed the traditional limit, and had all but completed his seventy-second year when he bade his last farewell to Constantinople. So far from being "labour and sorrow," the last twenty years of his life were the happiest of all. The loss of the accustomed occupation brought with it no corresponding diminution in the capacity for work or in the interest in all that was going forward in the world. Compulsory routine gave place to voluntary work: for his mind was of that active sort to which idleness is impossible and vigorous exercise is recreation.

Not all at once, however, did he arrive at this sense of peace and contentment. The disappointments that had marred the closing years of his mission were scars too deep for aught but time to obliterate. The healing work began at Rome, where he wintered after his farewell journey to the East. There, in the midst of an intellectual circle, courted by the most distinguished members of foreign society, many of whom he had met in former days, surrounded by objects of the deepest interest to a mind well stored in the archives of classical antiquity, and a spectator of the beginning of that movement of " *Italia Irredenta* " which has since developed into such happy results, the vexations of the immediate past were gradually forgotten, and their real insignificance was measured.

There is a passage in the *Lives of the Lords Strangford* which fitly expresses the part that the Great Elchi was to play in public life after his retirement from an official career. Lord Strangford—the same Percy Smythe who had been an attaché at Constantinople during the Crimean War—wrote to his wife in 1862 : " I want Lord Stratford de Redcliffe to feel that his position in foreign politics is that which was held by the Great Duke in war, and by Lyndhurst in law, and that he is not only able, but bound, before it is too late, to survey the world from his height, and to speak of the future with impartial utterance, like Moses from Mount Pisgah." It is possible that want of oratorical powers affected him almost as much in the Lords as it had done thirty years before in the Commons : but he never neglected the duty of speaking, and few great foreign questions came before the House without drawing from him some of those wise and spirited counsels which, from their brevity and rare occurrence, and their unmistakeable stamp of profound experience, carried with them the weight which belonged to " the genuine and naturally selected Nestor of foreign politics." Disclaiming all party ties, Lord Stratford was able to speak impartially out of the depths of his long acquaintance with the springs of foreign policy, and to confront boldly the inevitable issues of varying combinations. There was, it is true, little in his delivery to persuade, and much in his policy to alarm the timid, but yet there was that in his words which commanded attention and respect from all parties in the House, carrying with them as they did a sense of right and reason. His voice was always raised in the cause of freedom against oppression and for the weak against the strong.

He had not long returned to England in 1859 when he rose to call the attention of the Peers to the state of Italian affairs, and protested against the cautious neutrality which had induced the calamities of the war. The speech contained an eloquent appeal for the maintenance and enforcement of the treaties of 1815 : "Notwithstanding the wounds inflicted on them as a body of international right," he said, " far from being cast aside as a whole or being extinguished in public estimation, they are still the title-deeds of many an extensive territory, securities for Sardinian unity, no less than for Austrian incumbency ; and, what is more than being barriers against encroachment and confusion, they are the living records and guards of those achievements in civilization which have made the abolition of slavery a part and parcel of the law of Europe, and have consecrated the world of waters, whether flowing through separated States or expanding in boundless ocean, to the uses of an unfettered and almost unquestioned navigation. My Lords, there is a vitality even in their amputated limbs ; there is something judicial even in their submission to violence. The stroke which blasted the independence of Cracow, that last refuge and monument of Polish nationality, invested its memory with a sacred character, and the feeble protest issued on its behalf in a whisper from London and Paris now comes back in peals of thunder on the alarmed conscience."

Other speeches were in his own special province : as when, in May 1861, he moved to get the French troops out of Syria, and maintained that the chief cause of the disturbances in the Lebanon was the general misgovernment of the Ottoman Empire, and especially the neglect to enforce the provisions of the Charter of Reform. In 1864 he spoke against the cession of the Ionian Islands, and in favour of Denmark ; in 1867 on the insurrection in Candia, and in 1870 on massacres by Greek brigands. The Poles always had his warm support. On home affairs he spoke rarely, yet his earnest protest against the exclusion of the Jews from the privileges of the Oaths Bill, is worth recording.

Outside the House of Lords his influence was felt in public affairs, especially in those connected with the East. Like Palmerston, he had always opposed the Suez Canal, which he set down as a French stratagem ; but he was a warm supporter of the Euphrates route to India, and its chief promoter, General Chesney, was in constant communication with him in every stage of that long-struggling but still unrealized enterprise. He was a vigorous leader in the cause of the unhappy Circassians when they were exiled by Russia in 1864 ; and at almost the same moment, he was adding his voice to the protests which were raised by the Evangelical Alliance against the neglect of the interests and even of the bare protection of the missionaries in Turkey.

In 1869 an honour, wholly unexpected and unsolicited, came to Lord Stratford. As years rolled on, his great services stood out from the shadows of past politics bright and conspicuous ; and it was remembered that of all who had served England in those years of trial he alone had been left without adequate reward. Mr. Gladstone's generous admiration for intellect and character, as apart from politics, was conspicuous in his offer of the Garter to a peer who had never been a partisan. "Two garters are now available," he wrote to Lord Nov. 1869 Stratford ; "after your long career of distinguished public service, allow me to place one of them at your disposal. . . . It is scarcely necessary I should add that much as the Government might feel the honour and advantage of your support, this note is written neither with the expectation nor with the desire to modify your position of perfect political independence." As Lord Ellenborough said, it was a valuable example of the " recognition of services rendered not to a party but to the State."

Of his private life it is difficult to give any adequate picture. When he returned to England it was to settle down in the old house in Grosvenor Square, which had been his ever since

1829, but which, owing to his constant absences on diplomatic service, he had seldom occupied. Though he had been so much abroad, his love for England had remained just as strong ; all other places, however lovely, were indifferent to him in comparison with his own country—the country he loved so well ; and this house in London was his *home*, to which he always came back with pleasure. Here he found himself, after a time, the centre of a large circle of friends. Many of the old faces had indeed passed away, yet the youthful buoyancy of his spirit, and the charm of his manner and conversation, drew to him a new generation, who soon loved him as well and appreciated him as much as those who had gone. Instead of commanding homage as a right, he seemed to be surprised that anyone should take the trouble to come and see him ; and he laid himself out to interest his visitors with a courteous grace that had its own peculiar fascination. It was said by one who knew him well, " I always entered his presence as that of a great man, I always left it loving the *man* more each time."

Released from the vexations and the contentions of his official post, his character lost those elements of austerity and peremptoriness which were no longer fostered by circumstances. In earlier years the idealist's visions of " the Good, the True, and the Beautiful," were too often marred by some passing disturbance which called up the fighting spirit of the man, and rudely startled the poet from his dream. In later years there was no such disturbing force. Outward events indeed would move him deeply : he would rise to passionate indignation at a tale of wrong, at a base or selfish or false action ; and the cowardice of governments, or the meanness of a policy, would ever arouse that fiery wrath which was among Lord Stratford's titles to our respect. But these were no longer personal causes ; he was not himself concerned, more than any other Englishman ; and his passion, being abstract and impersonal, was no interruption to the poetry of his nature. We must not forget that throughout his long life no pressure of work, no load of responsibility, could ever make him forego the poetry which was the delight of his leisure. Most men, worthy of the name, feel the need of some mode of expressing their inmost thoughts and emotions which shall not have the blunt directness of open speech. Some find utterance in music, some in the painter's art, or the wide expressiveness of sculpture. But to others the forms of verse are the natural exponents of their inward nature, and they can say in metre what nothing could induce them to reveal in prose. Lord Stratford's was one of these minds, and his poetry is no artificial product of the fancy, but the natural expression of himself.

In *Shadows of the Past* (1866) we see some of the best of his earlier verse, and amid much that is indifferent to modern criticism, we find many beautiful lines. His old age, however, was the flowering time of his poetry. The faculty of expression seemed to develop, and the old metres were cast away in favour of more fervid and dramatic forms. This is especially notable in *Jubilee in Fatherland*, an ode on the triumph of United Germany in 1871, which burns with a fire and a spirit that, in a more than octogenarian, is amazing. Carlyle wrote of it :—

" I received with great pleasure the vigorous and brilliant piece of verse in honour of the Germans, whom I also, as you know, much honour. There is a fine old tone of classicality in these stanzas, a sound withal as of ringing steel, and the sentiment throughout has the great merit of being at once cordial, emphatic, and just. . . . This is a very pretty way of defending oneself against the attacks of illness, and converting one's imprisonment into a higher kind of liberty ! I wish we were all of us that need it able to do the like."

Another, who possesses a German's share of the true poetic nature, expressed a strong desire that " it could be read in Germany, and that people should know that it was written by the same pen which curbed the pride of the greatest enemy of Germany, and made it possible for her statesmen to follow an independent policy." From F. Max Müller, Oxford, April, 1871

Mr. Max Müller wrote again to support the entreaty of Dr. Abeken that the Jubilee Ode should be published in Berlin :—" A last appeal from Dr. Abeken, Berlin. Would it not be possible to win the very beautiful poem of Lord Stratford for Berlin ? It would be marvellous, and produce a 12 June great impression, if a sympathetic greeting from such a man were to meet our returning army. But we want his name—another statesman might hesitate to express his sympathy so strongly even for a friendly country, but Lord Stratford is too great for such considerations ; he can dare when others might be afraid." Accordingly, the poem was translated into German by Fritz Krauss.

In singular contrast to the German ode stands *The Exile in Calauria, or the Last Days of Demosthenes* (1872). The idea of this poem had evidently been in its writer's mind ever since the days in 1828 when he had worked for the freedom of Greece at Poros—the ancient Calauria : but the remarkable part of the performance is, as Abraham Hayward, no lenient critic, remarked, that it is " cast in the genuine antique mould, and breathes the best spirit of Greek dramatic poetry." The old Eton training had not been lost in the lapse of years, and despite half a century of absorbing occupation, Lord Stratford was still essentially a classical scholar. To the very end he retained his delight in the favourite authors of his school days, his Homer, his Sophocles, and his Virgil ; and often, when crippled by gout and unable to move, he would lie in the early morning hours, waiting for his books, that he might put down and correct the lines he had composed in the wakeful night. A friend once found him busily engaged in turning a collection of nursery rhymes into Greek iambics, and he confessed that " Little Jack Horner " had nearly baffled him, from the pagan indifference of the Greeks to the merits of Christmas pie.

A theme which was frequently in his thoughts was suggested by Shakspere's line : " Reverence is the angel of the world." An essay on the ennobling influence of reverence upon mankind lay at the time of his death unfinished on his table ; he intended it for the *Princeton Review*. The subject was one on which he was well qualified to speak ; for of all his qualities, reverence was one of the most striking : reverence for established institutions, reverence for national engagements, for the sanctities of home and honour, and above all for the Source and Object of all reverence. Firm in his own faith, he was very tolerant of those who differed from him ; but as the growing rationalism of the age forced itself upon his thoughts, he desired to leave on record his own steadfast belief in the God of his fathers—that faith that had stood by him in his active public life and had never failed him either in youth or age. The record was to be the brief statement of his own practical thoughts on religion, a humble testimony which, whilst leaving no doubt as to his own views, might, perhaps, be helpful to others of less assured faith than himself. The titles of the two small volumes speak for themselves: *Why am I a Christian?* (1873) and *The Greatest of Miracles* (1876). " I am most struck," says Dean Stanley, after reading the former, " with the amount of matter which you have been able to place within so small a compass. I trust that the world may be better for seeing that the result of your long experience is so firm a faith, and that the Church may be the better also for seeing that so firm a faith can be combined with so large and deep an insight into the great truths which all Christians hold or ought to hold alike."

The testimony of one who belonged to a different order of mind from Dean Stanley may also be quoted :—

" My dear and long-known Friend,—How could you suppose that I should feel otherwise than honoured, and delighted, by such a mark of your esteem and affection ? I accept it with gratitude and joy. Right glad am I to see such a clear stout handwriting as yours, in an age that has passed the ' threescore years and ten '—but still more to learn that, though the body may wax infirm, the heart has not grown cold. Somehow or other the love of Christ keeps people very young and fresh, however old they may be. God be with you and yours, in time and in eternity.

24 Dec 1875

Yours ever truly,
SHAFTESBURY."

The last years of his life were spent on the borders of his favourite Kentish country. He had always loved the neighbourhood of Tunbridge Wells, where he had met and won his wife, and in 1873 he bought a house at Frant which was gradually enlarged to the present extent of Frant Court. Here he finally retired in 1878, never again to move. Hither

people came to see and consult him about the struggle then
going on in Turkey and the reopening of the Eastern Question. Few letters to the *Times* have produced a greater impression upon sensible people than the temperate survey of
the " Bulgarian Atrocity " question which the ex-Ambassador
contributed to its columns in 1876. Letters of congratulation
and applause arrived from all parts of England and all ranks
of society. From 1875 to 1880 the menacing aspect of the
Eastern Question drew forth repeated comments, criticisms,
precedents, and warnings from the pen of the veteran statesman who had himself steered the Turkish ship of state through
so many storms. There was an impression that in his old
age he had changed his views and deserted his old *protégé*;
but the impression was due to a misconception of his earlier
attitude towards the Ottoman Empire. He had never been a
Turcophil, as people supposed ; but had always looked forward
to the creation of a belt of practically autonomous Christian
states, under the suzerainty of the Sultan, as the surest barrier
against Russian aggression. He would have welcomed the
formation of a Christian empire in the place of Turkey if he could
have discovered any Eastern Christians fit to rule it. Failing
this, he believed that the supreme authority of the Sultan was
essential to counteract the influence of Russia in the Christian
provinces, and he hoped for a regenerate Turkey worthy to
take a place among civilized nations. To deny that he was
disappointed with the course of events in the later history of
Turkey would be untrue. The reckless extravagance of
Abdu-l-Aziz, and the consequent financial catastrophe ; the
failure of the European Powers to enforce those reforms which
he knew to be the only palliative for the increasing decay of
the Ottoman Empire ; the want of union and moral courage
in the Powers which permitted such an outrage as the Russian
war of 1877, all these were sore subjects of reflection. But
disappointment did not alter his long and firmly established
views on the duty of England in the East, and on the only
method of saving the Turks from themselves. These papers,
written at the age of ninety—indeed the last was composed
in the summer of 1880, when its author had passed the
meridian of his ninety-fourth year—only confirm, explain,

and amplify what he had frequently urged in his despatches, and laid impressively before the Sultan, forty years before.

Deep as was his interest in Eastern affairs during these latter years, they formed but one of the many subjects that occupied his ever-vigorous mind. It is seldom that men retain in extreme age so marvellous a receptive, one might say acquisitive, power. In whatsoever company he found himself, whether of statesman, scholar, or plain working man, he had always something to ask and something to learn.

To the last his enthusiasm for heroic deeds remained fresh and warm as a boy's. Tears would come to his eyes as he read the news of some gallant act or heroic rescue. So was it when he was told the story of how the colours of the Twenty-fourth were saved out of the carnage of Isandlana by the devotion of two young officers. It was a deed to rouse the envious admiration of every man, but in no one did it awake a more responsive chord of sympathy than in Lord Stratford. Many who had perhaps almost forgotten that the great Ambassador still survived, were startled one morning as they opened the *Times*, to hear what was well named " the sound of a trumpet, signed S. de R." It was the dismal story of Isandlana told in vigorous verse ;—and then came the deed which had called forth the poem :— 1879

Far, far away, at fearful risk, a nobler charge was moved,
And those in trust right well achieved what more than valour proved;
Both still were young, and firm in minds that ne'er from duty roved.

Quick, quick, they mount the bridled steeds ; while near each loyal
  breast,
The colours lie, from ill secured, as in a miser's chest.
What could in haste be done they did ; to faith they gave the rest.

In fast succession forth they passed, along the straggling host ;
On, gallant youths! ye may not heed the peril or the cost.
Oh! speed them, Heav'n ; direct their course ; what shame if such
  were lost !

A stare of silent brief surprise, and then a deafening yell,
As if the imprison'd souls below had burst the bonds of hell ;
On dashed the dauntless riders still ; who dared to cross them fell.

Soon clear of foemen, side by side, athwart the pathless wild
Conveyors of a precious charge, by capture ne'er defiled,
On, boldly on, they stretched with speed, by youthful hope beguiled.

Alike through pools of rotten marsh, o'er beds of flint they rode ;
They cross'd the dell, they scaled the hill, they shunned the lone
    abode,
Nor ceased to urge the foaming beasts their weary limbs bestrode.

At length the frontier stream appears ; hurrah ! what need of more ?
Oh, fate ! They plunge, the waters flash, the rushing waters roar.
Unseated, wounded, all but drown'd, they touch, they clasp the shore.

A few brief hours of calm succeed, they share the joy of those
Who, purpose gained and danger past, from anxious toil repose ;
But nature sinks—too great the strain, and wounds are slow to close.

One slept, nor woke again ; like him, too soon the other slept ;
And those who sought and found them dead, the colours near them
    kept,
In pity—doubt not—stoop'd awhile, and o'er the bodies wept.

Melvill and Coghill, honour'd names ; ye need no verse of mine
To fix the record of your worth on memory's faithful shrine ;
To you a wreath that may not fade shall England's praise assign.

Ye crown the list of glorious acts which form our country's boast,
Ye rescued from the brink of shame what soldiers prize the most,
And reached by duty's path a life beyond the lives ye lost.

Perhaps one of the greatest pleasures that Lord Stratford
experienced at this time was that afforded him by the appreciation of his long services by the Queen, conveyed to him in
touching terms. The assurance that Her Majesty felt "how true
and faithful" he had been "and how valuable" was, to a mind
like his, a higher reward than pensions, decorations, or titles.
Such rewards the Queen well knows how to bestow, and the consideration with which they are given causes them to be doubly
valued. "Well might your letter gratify me," said Lord Stratford
in writing to Lady Ely, "containing as it did so gracious a
message from Her Majesty the Queen. It was very kind,
very kind indeed, very gracefully kind, to notice my Nestorian
age, and to shew an interest in the degree of health which

Providence still allows me to enjoy. . . . I need not say how gladly Lady Stratford and myself will avail ourselves of the Queen's very considerate permission to wait upon Her Majesty at Buckingham Palace next spring."

This, however, was not to be ; he never left Frant again.

A fortnight before his death, the son of his ancient comrade David Morier, who had preceded him to the grave but a few years, came to see his father's old chief. Sir Robert Morier thus records his last visit : " His intellect was as clear, his speech as incisive, his interest in poetry and politics as keen, as when I last saw him, three years ago. It was a beautiful English summer afternoon ; a warm sun lit up his pale features which fully retained their splendid outlines, and were entirely wanting in the wrinkles or withered look of extreme old age. I could not help thinking of the line,—

> Slow sinks more lovely ere his race be run . . .

He seemed some grand old Titan majestically sinking to his rest in all his glory, as if he knew the Infinite was waiting to receive him with all due honour."

It was very shortly after this visit that Lord Stratford's strength began to fail. One last drive (the first that summer) he took, and with characteristic kindliness went to "shew himself" to the doctor who had attended him all through the winter ; a few days of weary restlessness, and then, in the early morning of Saturday, 14 August, beautiful in death as he had been in life, he passed, without pain or struggle, to where " beyond these voices there is peace."

" Even now his presence seems to fill the room where he lived and thought and wrote. Here, the trifles and vexations of everyday life did not come—it seemed to be another, better, higher life, that surrounded him, and glorified all he touched. Truer views of men and events, calmer judgments, higher appreciation for a noble aim, even though it seemed to fail, in the least as in the greatest ; with a scorn, or rather pity beyond all expression, for everything in a man or a nation that was mean, cruel, or self-seeking. Gathered round him in that room were the treasured relics of the past,

each with its own story : the books he was so fond of ; the
prints of the men he most admired, silent companions of his
exile for so many years ; the little picture of Nelson which
had never left him since his earliest days ; George Canning,
his honoured master in public life ; Pitt, Wellington, his
country's heroes—all cared for to the very last. The table at
which he wrote, and from which he could look out on the
broad stretch of woodland crowning the heights of Eridge—
look out, beyond, to the distant hills and to the sunset that
he loved to watch ; the sunset that always spoke to him—
spoke clearer as each year passed on—of the unseen home
above."

On the Saturday following, he was laid to rest in the
churchyard of Frant village, followed to the grave by many
friends and mourned by his countrymen as few men, perhaps,
have been mourned whose life survived so long the close of
their public career.

22 August,
1880
" Yesterday,"—so spoke Dean Stanley in his sermon,—" the
greatest ambassador of our time was, after a life prolonged
far beyond the natural limits of human existence, laid to rest
in a little churchyard in the county of Sussex. Many are
they who will be grateful to the end of their days that they
had known his majestic character. No one could enter into
his presence, either as he sat on what may truly be called his
throne at Constantinople or during the long years of his
dignified retirement, without feeling that they had seen a
king of men. No one could hear the name of Stratford
Canning named throughout the far East without feeling that,
so long as he retained his post, the honour of England was
safe in his incorruptible integrity, in his magnificent liberality,
in his unshaken firmness. No one could hear his influence
spoken of by Christian or Musulman, Protestant or Catholic,
Greek or Turk, without feeling that each man knew that he
was a terror to evildoers which none could confront with
impunity, a refuge for the desolate and oppressed which none
could seek in vain. No one who had ever witnessed it could
forget the boundless industry, the noble generosity, with
which through all the chaos of the Crimean war he laboured
for the sick and suffering soldiers, or defended those who went

out to succour them. No one could mistake that in his energy, in his remonstrances, in his purity, the tottering fabric of the Eastern Empire, which for years he held in his mighty grasp, had at once the best bulwark against its ruin, the best guarantee against its evil deeds.

" Such an example did indeed lift us up from the base and sordid atmosphere of party strife and bitterness. Such an old age, with the fire of youth subdued but not extinct, with the experience of years giving ever fresh life to the memory of the past, was worthy of remembrance to every toiling sufferer. He had chosen that better part which neither falling empires nor political rancour, nor worldly disappointment nor ungrateful obliviousness, could ever take from him."

Four years later, on 24 May, 1884, a statue was unveiled by Lord Granville in Westminster Abbey. The occasion was memorable ; for now, for the first time, was diplomacy honoured with a place among England's greatest sons, in the person of " one who had rendered the profession brilliant by his genius and invigorated it by the manliness of his character."

It was a national tribute, freely and publicly subscribed to the memory of a great Englishman who had signally upheld the honour of his country at the post of danger.

The Poet Laureate wrote the lines engraved upon the base :—

> Thou third great Canning, stand among our best
>   And noblest, now thy long day's work has ceased,
> Here silent in our Minster of the West
>   Who wert the voice of England in the East.

INDEX.

(Proper Names only : for Subjects see detailed Table of Contents.)

THE END

www.ingramcontent.com/pod-product-compliance
Lightning Source LLC
Chambersburg PA
CBHW032012110726
47901CB00004B/1052